WORLDS APART

WORLDS APART

John Cairney

MAINSTREAM
PUBLISHING

First published in Great Britain in 1991 by
MAINSTREAM PUBLISHING COMPANY (EDINBURGH) LTD
7 Albany Street
Edinburgh EH1 3UG

British Library Cataloguing in Publication Data
Cairney, John
  Worlds Apart
  I. Title

ISBN 1 85158 355 6

The characters and situations in this book are entirely
imaginary and bear no relation to any real persons or actual
happenings.

Typeset in 11/12pt Garamond by Falcon Typographic
Art Ltd, Edinburgh and London
Printed in Great Britain by Collins, Glasgow

For both our families

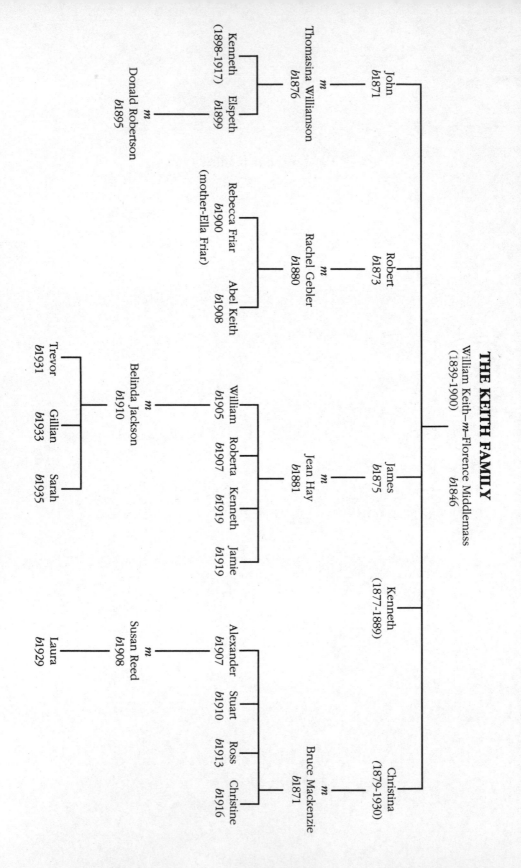

THE KEITH FAMILY

William Keith–*m*–Florence Middlemass
(1839-1900) *b*1846

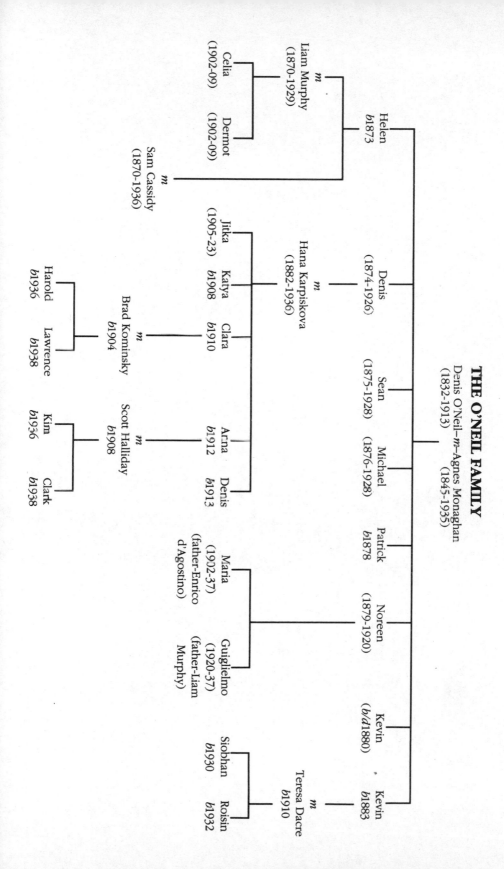

THE O'NEIL FAMILY

Denis O'Neil–*m*–Agnes Monaghan
(1832-1913)   (1845-1935)

ONE

On a fine May day in 1900, Glasgow was en fête. It wasn't a public holiday or anything, but quite spontaneously the citizens had decided to make it one. It was holiday time in the grey, grimy, sooty city and everybody wanted to join in. Glaswegians need no second bidding to enjoy themselves. Carts and carriages vied with hansom cabs, horse-trams and three-horse buses in the crowded streets where the tar was already melting around the granite setts and cobbles between the pavements and the tram-lines. It was to get hotter yet under the yellow-smoke sky and the press of people on every side added body heat to the urban temperature. George Square, heartland of the prosperous city centre, was a sea of bowler hats and bonnets and parasols as the citizens of the Second City of the Empire celebrated with the rest of Great Britain the news that had just come through – Mafeking had been relieved!

All that day, since a red-faced clerk had come running in his shirt-sleeves and waistcoat from the *Glasgow Herald*'s new offices in Buchanan St and broken the story to men at the corner of Gordon St, the news had spread like wildfire through the city – from the businessmen in Craig's Tea-Room in St Vincent Place, then down through the tailors in Argyle St along to the shoe shops of the Trongate and down by the hardware stores in the Saltmarket and into every one of the hundred pubs along the Broomielaw. Everyone came out into the street, pipers marched, drums were beaten and flute bands squealed. Some people thought it was a parade, others thought the old Queen had come to Glasgow even though everyone knew she hated the place. Others again thought it was Tommy Lipton, the grocer, up to his tricks again and putting on some stunt or other to bring people out, but everybody who could walk that day in Glasgow came out into the streets. Every class and kind of person, from the respectable well-to-do to the disreputable poor. There were young factory girls out for a laugh and young mechanics out for the young factory girls. People who'd never heard of General Roberts or Colonel Baden-Powell until that very day were singing their praises lustily with the rest. Minor clerks and shop assistants, who couldn't have told a Boer from a milk bottle, were fiercely discussing all the implications. Ladies out for high tea at Miss Cranston's in Sauchiehall Street had little idea where South Africa was, never mind Mafeking, but found themselves caught up in the general hysteria. Nothing is more contagious than singing and laughter and the epidemic of celebration swept through the city like a plague. Much of it was a purely reflex herd action, and such crowds could just as easily have been following the tumbrils. It is astonishing in any large city how soon a gathering becomes a crowd and the crowd becomes a mob.

Underlying the noise and all the bravos however, there was also the sense that a war was over and that British – more particularly, Scottish – soldiers would come home again. The South African War, or Boer War, as most people called it was a silly war, a companies war, a private affair almost. It was a project bungled and misdirected from the start by inept generals and where ironically, public sympathy had been on the side of the Dutch settlers to begin with. Whatever it was, and whatever the reasons, a bullet was still a bullet and a shell was still a shell no matter what kind of war it was. Whatever the rights and wrongs of it, people got killed and maimed just the same. Causes didn't matter much to the ordinary soldier, even when those soldiers were 'the soldiers of the Queen, my lads' and the sweethearts of 'Dolly Gray'. The goodbyes had been said only the year before as the boys in red had marched behind their bands to the docks. Now it was a welcome home for those who had survived – those suntanned silent men who wore the unfamiliar, practical khaki.

That's why Glasgow's citizens were out on the streets among the barrows and prams and the legs of the horses. And that's the stage Glasgow had reached about four o'clock in the afternoon. They were still singing and shouting and laughing. That's why the noise was deafening. And that's why young Christina Keith was a little apprehensive.

She stood on the parapet of St Enoch railway station looking down on the mass of people in St Enoch Square. She had never seen so many people together in one place. It was frightening, but it was also exciting. She could feel herself trembling under her new coat.

'Keep hold of my hand, Tina.'

Jim Keith found his sister's hand and she was only too happy to take it.

'You're hot,' he said.

She could only nod, but her eyes shone.

'Are you alright?'

She nodded again and he gave her hand a little squeeze. When she spoke at last she found she was shouting.

'Where's Bobby?'

'He's gone to find a cart for the luggage.'

It was his father who spoke from her other side. He didn't shout. William Keith rarely spoke but his soft, kind eyes spoke sufficiently for him. The boys, his big, grown sons were rather in awe of him but Tina, the youngest, adored him because she knew that she too was adored. The old man looked imposing in his deer-stalker hat and Inverness cape, although it must have been a bit warm for that late afternoon heat. His temperature was not improved by his rising indignation. All this fuss in the streets for a stupid, pointless war that had been begun impetuously and even now was being continued wastefully and inefficiently. So Mafeking had been relieved. A temporary siege of an unknown town in a faraway country had been lifted. What great victory was that? Now a whole city was out making a fool of itself. Of course, his son, Bobby, didn't agree with him, but then Bobby seldom agreed with anybody about anything. Where was he anyway? He had only gone to fetch a cart.

'I hope he'll no' get lost in a' these crowds,' said Mrs Keith from behind them. She hadn't been too well on the long train journey south from Forres and she still looked a bit pale under her broad-brimmed hat with its muslin veil, as she stood with her back against the luggage cart, now piled high with cabin trunks, suitcases, bags and parcels from the Keith household. She held tightly to the iron rail of the cart. Mrs Keith always needed something to hold on to.

'Bobby'll never get lost in a crowd, Mother,' said Mr Keith almost to himself. Mrs Keith smiled weakly. She had heard him. She was used to his tone. Florence Middlemass had married William Keith reluctantly but it had been better than she thought. William was a good man, almost a saintly man, and there could not have been a better husband for a girl who had been brought up by a grandmother, but he could not be crossed once he had made up his mind. And he had made up his mind to emigrate – at sixty years of age. What would Grannie Middlemass have said?

The little Victorian family group – father, mother, sister and brother – all dressed befittingly in their best for travelling in the gritty train since very early morning might have been standing on the parapet of the Colosseum in Rome during the Christian persecutions, or in the amphitheatre at Epidaurus in Greek times, or Paris during the Terror, or in Hogarth's London, so bewildered were they by the noise and confusion in the Glasgow square

11

below them. This shouting of men and screeching of women and neighing of horses and bursts of laughter and bouts of swearing and the sound of distant bands and not-so-distant bagpipes, and the random mix of dull colours in the mêlée, the greys and tans and blacks and browns of the smoky city, was something they had never seen in Forres, not even in Fraserburgh or Aberdeen, and they also knew it was something that they would never forget.

Old William, as befitted his years and intelligence, was phlegmatic, and drew rhythmically on his briar as he looked down on the hectic scene. Florence was totally bemused but reassured by her grasp of the iron bar.

'We'll never see him again,' she said.

But nobody heard her. She was trying to be calm but the flecks of white at the corners of her mouth indicated the panic she was just holding back. And who could blame her? She was out of her world. Jim, her youngest son, was quietly taking it all in, but then he was more his father's son and both carried their quietness about with them. Tina, on the other hand, was exhilarated. With her family beside her, her hand in her brother's, her strong father beside her and the wall of piled luggage like a barricade behind her she felt safe to enjoy the mayhem. She hardly gave a thought to her mother. She was her father's favourite, and her mother knew that. Bobby was her mother's boy. Daft, wild, generous Bobby. But where was he?

'Isn't it great?' she shouted in Jim's ear.

He nodded without speaking but his eyes were fixed on the crowds below.

'Look at that.' Tina pulled her brother's arm.

'What?' he answered, still keeping his eyes on the scene.

'That building there – BONANZA – it says. What's that?'

'It's a shop by the look of it.'

'It's a big shop.'

'Everything's big in Glasgow.'

'It means a heap of gold.'

It was her father speaking.

'What did you say, father?'

'Bonanza, it means a heap of gold.'

Mrs Keith sniffed, and muttered to nobody in particular, 'It looks an ordinar' kinda place to be a gold mine.'

'That's Glasgow,' quipped Jim.

He and his sister laughed. Mrs Keith didn't see what was funny. Then Tina gave a shout that made them all start. She was pointing to the street below.

'Look, there's our Bobby and he's got a horse and cart!'

Mr Keith smiled and drew the pipe from his mouth and looked for a place to spit. Seeing nowhere else, he leaned over the parapet.

'William!' shouted Florence, in horror.

'Father!' exclaimed Tina in amusement.

Both women shouted at once, but William only shrugged and put the pipe back in his mouth.

'They'll never notice in Glasgow,' he said, 'they'll think it was a bird!'

'They say it's lucky,' murmured Jim.

'BOBBY!'

Tina called out to her big brother as loudly as she could. He looked up and waved. He was standing on an empty dray cart with his hand on the carter's shoulder and pointing up to them. He was obviously trying to convince the Glasgow man he could persuade his old horse through the crowd and up the gradient to the terrace in front of the railway station where they waited. The man however had his eye on the mountain of luggage behind them. The bargaining went on with much shaking of the head and flailing of arms on Bobby's part, but conviction came with the exchange of coins. They saw them glint in the last of the sunlight. Bobby waved to them again, the carter gave his reins a shake and the carthorse obediently made its shuffling way through the crowds at the edge of the square and to the station entry away to their right.

'Bobby can talk anybody into anything,' said Jim.

'So can the coin of the realm,' added his father.

It was an hour or more before they had the cart up beside them and fully loaded up. The carter refused to assist in the loading.

'I have trouble enough with the horse. Anyway, it's the bad back I've had since I got rained on at the football excursion.'

'I hope your team got beat,' muttered Bobby, whose forehead glistened with perspiration. He'd been working hard since he got off the train.

'Don't worry, we'll manage.'

Mr Keith and Jim were already loading and even the women helped, but even so they needed two porters, at sixpence a man, to get it all up securely and arrange a place at the front behind the driver where the ladies could sit. One of them was heard to drawl huskily in his Glasgow way: 'Is a' this for wan faimily? Looks mair like a toon flittin' tae me!' 'An' a fair-dain' toon at that, by the look o' it a',' said his mate.

William Keith was pleased to hear this. It hadn't been easy to select what to take and what to leave behind from Craigend House, not to mention the shop contents and the two storehouses, so they decided to take everything that was movable. Anyway, he could afford it. The business had gone for a good price to John Robertson, the tailor, who had always had his eye on Keith and Sons, Drapers and Woollen Merchants in Main Street. Craigend itself went to Dr French who knew the house well from his visits and intended to use the dining-room as his surgery. He was glad the house had found a good home. John Keith and his wife Thomasina would move into the town flat which their old charge hand had. It was big enough and they could make it look good if they spent a bit of money on it. And he'd seen to it that they had a bit of money. John and Thomasina had decided to stay on in Scotland – 'for the sake of the children'. Wee Kenneth was just a toddler and Elspeth was still a baby. Thomasina was afraid to take a baby on such a long journey. William didn't really blame her, but he thought John could have made a better stand for keeping the family together on the great adventure. He worried about his first son. There was a weakness there. Not from his side of the family. 'Shears' Robertson had kept John as General Manager during the change-over. He knew the business, he'd been in it since school, but his heart was never in it. William never really understood why. But then he never really understood John.

'Right father, up you get.'

It was Bobby beside him. William was startled to see that his wife and daughter were already up in their position behind the driver, snugly inserted between two of the largest trunks, their legs just clear of the cartwheels. Florence was as unsmiling as ever but Tina was beaming.

'OK, Teenie?'

Tina's smile faded and she pouted with annoyance. She hated being called 'Teenie'. But it was only a small annoyance and soon passed. She wasn't all that happy about sitting on top of a pile of luggage like the fairy on the Christmas cake. She had wanted to walk with her brothers and enjoy the crowds in the streets. But her mother was afraid to sit on her own, and here she was, sitting up like a good girl.

So, this is emigration! she thought. It smells! She couldn't get over the smells in the streets. She didn't know what caused them – the buildings, the shops, the sewers, the people. All she knew was that Glasgow had a rotten smell. She also wished her brothers were a bit nearer. Some of the things shouted at her weren't very nice. At least, they were things she never heard in Forres. Is this what her beloved father had brought her to? From where she was sitting she couldn't see him for boxes and bags, but she knew he was there. Her father was always there. She could rely on that.

14

Bobby was now waiting to give his father a hand up to a top seat beside the carter in front of a screen of piled luggage.

'It's alright,' Bobby called to the carter, 'he won't annoy you. He used to be a referee.'

There was no response whatsoever from the said carter.

'Where are you going?' asked William of his second son.

'Jim and I'll walk behind,' he grinned. 'In case anything falls off!'

'Probably be me!' said his father as he climbed up to his place.

He sat up surveying the crowds below him, feeling a little foolish for a responsible Scottish businessman and very respectable citizen of Forres, but deep down, behind the sober façade, he was impishly delighted. For the first time in his life, William Keith had leisure, and the money to enjoy it. And if the freight costs were to be more than he bargained for, what of it? He could afford to spend a shilling or two and anyway, it would give them a better start in Otago. Besides, all their things would give them a wee touch of home in a far-away land. To be exact, it was rather a hefty slice of home once it was all gathered together like this. It had used up most of the guard's van on the train and doubtless it would serve as a very healthy ballast on the ship on the long voyage out to New Zealand. But any journey begins with a step. That step had been taken nearly six months ago.

'Let's be off then,' called out Bobby to the morose driver, who casually took up the reins again; just as casually, the weary old horse moved off dragging his over-laden cart and its passengers behind it.

'At least it's downhill to start with,' shouted Bobby to the carter.

'That's ay the haurdest part,' moaned that gentleman to Mr Keith, 'wi' a fu' loadin' like this the hoarse could get it a' up his erse!' Mr Keith only clenched his pipe in his teeth and pondered in that event where that would put him? This had all been his idea in the first place. He remembered the night he had told them . . .

He was looking out of the window at the wet, miserable night. It had been raining all day. Hard, relentless, unpitying, Scottish rain. He thought it was rain he was seeing before his eyes now, but with a gulp he realised he was crying! This was impossible. He hadn't cried since his own mother died – twenty years ago, and even then he had to walk out in the back garden so that nobody would see. Now this. He had been reading from the Book for the New Year and his text was from Genesis, Chapter 6, Verse 18:

'And I will establish my covenant with thee, and thou shall enter

into the ark, thou and thy sons, and thy wife and the wives of thy
sons with thee . . .' He had looked up and there indeed they were,
his wife, his sons, his son's wife – and Christina, his daughter. They
were all there on this Hogmanay for the usual family get-together.
As he looked, he had suddenly realised there was someone missing.
Another son. Young Kenneth. He hadn't thought of him since – he
was twelve at the time – and with a great welling, tears had started
to come. He had never shed a tear for Kenny, but he was crying
now. Or, at least, trying to stop himself.

'I'm sorry,' William Keith said at last, his voice sounding hoarse,
'I was suddenly thinking of Kenneth.'

Mrs Keith gasped slightly, and looked up at her husband sharply,
but he only put a firm hand on her shoulder, and she looked down
again. The silence in that small late-Victorian parlour, heavy with
ornaments, was as thick as the pile on the carpet, yet nobody dared
say a word. The china dogs on the mantlepiece stared fixedly at
each other as always but you felt even they were straining to listen
to what he had to say.

'It's not often that I have to speak to you all like this, especially
on such a night. But then maybe Hogmanay is not a bad night
to make a big decision. It's the time, they say, for resolutions,
for turning over a new leaf. Anyway, I have some news for
you. Whether it's good or bad it'll be for you to decide for
yourselves.'

There was an immediate murmur of reaction from the sons, but
the father went on, his voice gradually getting stronger. Florence
felt her husband's hand grip harder on her shoulder.

'Your mother and I have thought long about it, prayed much
about it and talked it over – between ourselves – since . . .'

His voice trailed away again, but he rallied quickly.

'Since events, both lately and recently, and in time past, have
forced us to consider how we are situated, not only here at
Craigend, but in the town and in the country generally.'

The young men were now very interested and sat up in their
chairs. This was more than a family matter, they suspected. Tina
moved over and sat on the floor at Jim's knee. What was going
on, she wondered. Her father suddenly seemed very austere,
remote even.

'As you know,' he said, 'things have not been good. Not
good at all.'

John and Bobby exchanged glances.

'And what is more important, they are not likely to get much
better. You know what it has been like in this town for me since
the outbreak of this South African War. I have spoken out against

16

it as a matter of conscience and as a result certain factions here made it clear that my views are not those of the country – well, certain people in the country. This war is wrong, any war is wrong, but it is doubly wrong when people are being killed on both sides to preserve business interests in London.'

'But, father –' interrupted Bobby.

'I am a businessman myself, and it's a good family we have built up between us, but now I find I am shunned and miscalled because I choose to speak out against the British government's intervention in a Dutch colony.'

'It's not Dutch –' protested Bobby. 'The Orange Free State is rightly named for the Prince of Orange, otherwise King Billy.'

'A King of England,' put in Jim.

'But a Dutchman,' said his father. 'Anyway, I don't want to go into the historical pros and cons of the business. I only know that Prime Minister Chamberlain has acted wrongly against Kruger and I have said so. This has been held to be unpatriotic in the present climate of opinion and as you know, we've had our shop windows broken on that account. This is not important, but what is, is my freedom to speak my mind on whatever issue and my right to hold my own opinion – however unpopular. Certain measures have already been taken by what we call the authorities to silence me, or at least to make my position in the town less secure, shall we say. I will not tolerate this kind of bullying, for that's what it is. No, not from anyone.' He checked himself. The family were unused to this side of William Keith. They rarely saw him impassioned and he would have regarded shouting out loud as a kind of violence. Any display of emotion was foreign to his natural restraint, but clearly he felt indignant about the wrong done to the Boers. Untypically, too, he had spoken out about it, and there were people in Forres who had been shocked at this, and a lot of trouble had been caused – behind closed doors. William paused for a moment, then continued calmly.

'I have therefore made up my mind on a course of action which you might think of as extreme but, in the circumstances, is the one I think gives us the best chance of not only keeping what we've all worked so hard to build up over these many years, but might even give us the chance to build up further, if in a different kind of way.' Bobby could contain himself no longer.

'What are you talking about, father?'

'I'll tell you what I'm talking about Bobby – I'm talking about emigration!' For a moment, the word hung in the air like a bat from one of the barn beams before the strange sound of it fell around each of their incredulous ears.

'Emigration?' shouted Bobby.

'Emigration?' repeated Jim in a whisper, as if it were a disease.

'That's what I said.' John said nothing. He was the only son privy to his father's thoughts on the matter over the past months. As the oldest son it was his privilege. He was totally against it, but he had stated his case and now he sat with his head bowed. Thomasina glanced at him wondering why he wasn't speaking. She had thought something was going on. Everybody then started to speak at once and Tina could be heard asking:

'What does it mean?'

'I'll tell you what it means, girl!' her father almost shouted.

They were all quiet again. Their father rarely raised his voice. He now spoke quietly and firmly. This was more like the man they knew. A gleam had now replaced the glint of tears in his eyes, his tone was even and he now seemed to stand taller before them.

'I have a letter here.'

They watched as he produced a paper from his waistcoat pocket and fumbled for his spectacles. William Keith had resented even the smallest impairment of his considerable physical powers and it had taken him a long time to admit that he needed glasses, and even longer to get used to wearing them. Now they were perched uncomfortably at the end of his long nose as he held his head back slightly to read:

'Dear Mr Keith – "dear" indeed,' he muttered dryly to himself. 'I thank you for your further communication of the 17th ult.'

He read stiffly and formally without any emphasis or stress, yet no soliloquy could have been delivered with more theatrical effect. He cleared his throat.

'I am advised by my company to inform you that passages have been reserved for you and your family as requested in your previous letter addressed to Mr Alexander MacKendrick dated 7th October 1899 and registered for Cabin accommodation on the steamship, Mataura, (Captain Richard Ellon) in the following names: Mr and Mrs William Keith, Robert Keith and James Keith (Over 21 years) and –' He cleared his throat again. 'And Miss Christina Keith (under 21). All of the above residing at Craigend, in the parish of Forres in the district of Morayshire, Scotland.' He paused and looked round.

'Is there more?' asked Tina.

'Oh ay.' The father looked down at his paper again.

'Where are we supposed to be going?' asked Jim.

'I'm coming to that,' said his father steadily.

Bobby's face was now pink with repressed excitement and even quiet Jim caught the tremor of excitement he felt rising from Tina at his knee. He gave her a little nudge. She looked up, smiling, but turned quickly back as he frowned and refused to catch her eye. William continued:

'Please confirm that these bookings are still in order. If there are any alterations or cancellations, the company must be advised of the same, one calendar month from the day of sailing, which is on the late tide, Monday, 21st May 1900.' He hesitated on the last number, being uncertain how to pronounce it.

'I have never seen the new century in print before,' he mused.

'Father –' It was Bobby again.

'Aye, Bobby, I hear ye. Now where was I? Oh yes, – late tide – right. Please note that embarkation may take place from noon on the sailing date and that all passengers must be aboard one hour before sailing. Signed. Edward Pomeroy, Manager.' He looked up, and taking off his spectacles, began to put them away.

'BUT WHERE ARE WE GOING?' Bobby was almost apoplectic, but his father seemed not at all put out and replied calmly, folding the letter.

'New Zealand, of course!'

'New Zealand?' This time it was Jim.

'That's right.'

There was another silence, broken at length by Tina's plaintive:

'But what about John?'

'I'm not going – I mean, we're not going.'

Thomasina looked keenly at her husband.

'I'm glad you told me,' she said.

It was a long time before a kind of order was restored in the Keith home that Old Year Night. It was a household unused to change or disorder, but then it had never had the experience before of having to consider uprooting itself and transplanting twelve thousand miles away on the other side of the earth. It was the longest journey one could take – from the north of Scotland to the south of New Zealand – and here the idea of it was sprung upon a family of grown sons and an adult daughter by an old man who should have been considering retirement, not emigration. But perhaps it was typical of William Keith to do the unexpected. Just like his father, people who knew him would have said. For hadn't the first John Keith left his father's farm near Elgin and set up as a weaver near Forres? His son George should have carried on the business, but things in the weaving went slack in the 1870s and he took himself and his family off to Lanark, near Glasgow, to try his luck in the new Co-operatives, where he could use his skill at the loom. William was the second son and looking every inch the northern farmer, but instead he went into a draper's shop of all

19

things. Before long he had built up a good business in the Main Street of Forres selling the woollen goods which his elder brother had once made from the wool that his father and younger brother had raised on the hills beyond Elgin. Now, just when everyone had imagined they were settled into the bourgeois life of provincial trade, they were suddenly to be pioneers in a very distant land. It was either mad or absolutely wonderful.

Robert Keith was impatient. Some people might even have said he was restless, like his mother. He preferred action. Not that he got much chance, as the middle son and with a father like his. He got on with his father well enough – everybody did – but William Keith liked everything his way. He expected it, but Robert had other ideas. New ideas. I mean, wasn't the new century just round the corner? Things were happening out in the world, and he wanted to be part of it before it was too late. If he didn't move now he would be left behind and would end up like his big brother John, like his father, trapped by Craigend, by Forres, by the business, by the Kirk, by the ever-tightening circle of friends. Like Ella Friar and her mother, who were determined to get him to the altar. Ella was alright, but not for a lifetime.

It seemed like a lifetime since his father had asked them all to come into the parlour. The parlour at Craigend was only used for special occasions – weddings, christenings, funerals. He remembered young Kenny. That was nearly ten years ago now. He could still see the thin legs sticking out from under the train wheels. He would have been twenty-two now. That's right, just younger than Jim was now. He glanced over at his young brother and wondered what he was thinking. Jim always seemed to be thinking, or reading. He lived in his own world, did Jim.

James Keith was in fact wondering what it was all about. He was always uncomfortable at family gatherings. Any kind of occasion bothered him. He was quiet like his father and never talked much. He preferred to read, when he had the books and the chance. Or make things with his hands, like the model train he was making when –.

He was with Kenny when they went to the junction that day. It was Jim's fault they were there. He had wanted to draw one of the big express engines from Inverness. He went over the fence to get nearer. He told Kenny to stay on the bank. It wasn't his fault . . .

But he didn't talk about that – then or since. When he needed to talk about anything, it was nearly always to his young sister, Tina. They had become very close since Kenny's – since the accident. She had only been nine at the time, and he had been about fifteen. They just came together somehow with the terrible shock it had been to everybody.

Now here she was, a grown woman – well almost – looking up at her father. She was shocked to see him cry. Men don't cry. She felt embarrassed and glanced at her mother who was sitting in her chair beside her husband, fingering the edge of her apron . . .

Florence Middlemass was uneasy. She did not enjoy sitting so long, there were things she could be doing. Floss, as her husband used to call her, liked to be busy. That way, she hadn't time to think. Some things couldn't bear thinking about. She left the thinking to her man. Now she was waiting for William Keith to speak again. She wished he would hurry. There was so much to do. She was glad at least the decision had been made. All the whispered debates in their bedroom had been a strain to her, trying to keep everything secret. It was like living a lie to her. She had wanted him to tell them right away what he had in mind that night he came back from his brother's. She had been afraid about how the boys would take it. She wasn't worried about Tina. She was a good girl, but sons could be awkward – especially Bobby. Jim was still young but John was now a married man with a family. She looked over at John as he sat with Thomasina. She had never liked Thomasina. It was said there had been trouble in her family but it had never been very clear what it was. Thomasina had had her eye on John from the start. Or was it the business she was after? She would have her nose put out now. But she wouldn't go short. William would see to that – for John's sake, and wee Kenneth's of course. He'd do anything for wee Kenneth. And now there she is with another one at the breast. A poor wee thing it is too. It came early of course. Elspeth. What a name. John was too soft with her. Not like her man at all. Poor John.

John Keith looked up at his father. He had never seen him so upset. Not even when young Kenny died. Lately, his father had been quieter than ever. He had put it down to the shock of Kenneth, but yet he seemed to carry on with the business as usual. He had been away to Glasgow a few weeks back. To see his brother George, he said. Some kind of business deal? He hadn't realised his father had been seeing old 'Shears' Robertson as well about selling everything up. Not that he minded. He'd be happy enough to stay on as manager. He knew Robertson would give him next to nothing to do. Not that he wanted it. John didn't know what he wanted. Maybe he should have stayed a bachelor. He certainly didn't want to live on at Craigend House. It had been in the family a long time, but he was glad the doctor got it. It was past its best, just like his father. John was immediately ashamed of the thought. He loved his father, respected him, admired him, maybe even feared him. But things must move on. After all, it was the last night of 1899 – almost the end of the century.

He himself was twenty-nine next birthday – nearly thirty – and if a break was going to be made, it had better be made soon. That's why, when his father told him about the emigration idea, he thought it might just be the right thing for all of them. All of them, that is, except him. He was now a married man with a son of his own, and a daughter too. He liked that, a wee girl. Wee Elspeth. Just like her mother – well, perhaps not. Not even like his own mother. Maybe a bit like Tina. He wondered if his son Kenneth was being alright at Mrs Beattie's. Thomasina's mother wasn't the best person to leave with wee ones, John thought. She liked her dram, so they said. Oh ay, she liked her wee tipple. And she had a notion to take her dram at the most unexpected times. Her Hogmanay celebrations started around the end of July and went on to the end of June! John suddenly caught Bobby's eye, and his brother winked. I know it is Hogmanay, thought John, but surely he could be serious for once.

Hogmanay, or New Year's Eve, is a serious business in Scotland. Whether this has anything to do with a deep Celtic twilight or a Calvinistic instinct to suppress any outward signs of emotion or pleasure is a question that only further prompts enquiry. There is a high pagan element in the rites of a Scottish New Year observance. Ancient gods were being propitiated and even for the staunchly Presbyterian Keiths there was a strong undertow of heathen awareness in the way the house was scrubbed from top to toe till brasses shone and glass gleamed, and not an atom of dust lived to tell the tale of a year that was dying while the infant year waited to be born upon the stroke of midnight. This was Scottish time, a Caledonian time to mark the end of the old and the beginning of the new. In a way it was reassurance too. An opportunity to wipe the slate clean, to confess as it were. Having denied himself the comforts of absolution by the Reformation of the Churches in the eighteenth century, Hogmanay was now the Scotsman's way of squaring his account with the Unknown before the hectic traffic of the working year re-converted him to his proper religion, which was making his way in the world! Not that any of the Keith family gave any thought to these philosophical matters as they each got themselves ready for the rite of the bells. For them it meant the passing of the quaich full of The Macallan and the singing of the world's family anthem – 'Auld Lang Syne' except that not even the very Scottish Keiths knew the words beyond the first chorus!

By five minutes to twelve the whole family was gathered round the big fireplace for the 'Bells', their traditional Hogmanay vigil on this special midnight that hangs like a magic spell between two years as well as two days. This time, however, it was also between two centuries! 1900 – the Year of the Rat, according to the Chinese. Was that why some people dreaded it? Others thought the twentieth century might mean the end of the world, and not just the end of another hundred years! Others were merely uncertain about how to pronounce it – were they to say nineteen hundred or one thousand nine hundred and nothing? However said, it would happen all the same – as inevitably, as relentlessly, as inexorably as time always happens – the seconds ticking away, the minutes mounting, the hours going in, the days passing, weeks flying by, months peeling away and the years rolling on. There was nothing anyone could do about time, except pass it. Either one stood in the centre of one's own time and watched events pass one by as if it were all a cosmic peep-show or one was carried along in one's own march of time, part and parcel of all that was happening around and within one. It was all either frightening or reassuring. It depended on how you looked at it. Whatever the way, one couldn't stop it. The least one could say was that the changing of 1899 to 1900 would be momentary and momentous.

It would be momentous too for the Keith family, for it might be the last in which they were all together in Scotland. For once, Hogmanay was a subdued affair. Everyone had been so stunned by the news of the day that the bells had come and almost gone before the family had raised the first dram to the New Year from the whisky quaich. While it was passed round the father read from I Corinthians 13 as he always did:

'Charity is patient, is kind; charity doth not envy, is not pretentious, is not puffed up, is not ambitious, is not self-seeking, does not rejoice over wickedness, but rejoices with the truth, bears with all things, believes in all things, hopes in all things, endureth all things –' His voice droned on through the familiar words like the bass line on a pipe tune, giving a sonority to the worn phrases that made them freshly meaningful on this very Scottish occasion as the cup was passed from lip to lip, between brother and sister and man and wife, father and sons, mother and daughter. Eye caught eye over the silver dish and there was an extraordinary sense of sharing the moment together. It was a bonding that was especially close this year. But then they had known this sense of family all their lives. 'When I was a child I spoke as a child, I felt as a child, but now I am become a man I have put away the things of childhood.'

In less than an hour, untypically, without any wait for their 'first-foot', who was always John the Postie, the whole family was abed. Or at least they were in their various bedrooms that Hogmanay although few were asleep. Each was pondering what it would bring for them. The father's voice echoed:

'We see now as through a glass darkly. Now we know in part but then I shall know as I have been known.'

Somewhere in the town the faint sounds of continuing celebration were heard in the night air and songs were still being sung – 'We're no' awa' tae bide awa, we're no' awa' to leave ye . . .'

But Johnny Scobie's lament went largely unheeded by the Keiths.

In the main bedroom, in her big, venerable bed, Mrs Keith was crying. For the first time in many years William turned from where he lay and took his wife in his arms, and kissed her gently on the brow.

'There, there, lass,' he murmured. 'We'll a' be fine. Why greet?'

'It's just –'

'It's just what?'

'I dinna want to leave my kitchen.'

William Keith sighed and turned back again to his usual side. 'Goodnight, wife.'

In Jim's bedroom, Tina was still sitting on his bed at two o'clock in the morning, and still looking as fresh as spring water.

'Tina, go to bed. I'm tired,' said Jim.

'You mean you just want to read your daft old books.'

'No, I don't, I just want to get to sleep.'

'Then just tell me again Jim – for the last time. Promise.'

Jim rose up on his pillow and pointed a finger at his young sister.

'Promise?'

'Promise.'

So, stifling a yawn, Jim went over the advertised route, in detail, for the fourth time that evening.

'First we take the cart and the two carriages to Inverness where we get the train to Glasgow and then we get on a boat called the Mataura at Pier 5 . . .'

In his bed, Bobby lay back with his arms clasped behind his head, gazing up to the gas-light still guttering feebly in the draught from the open window. He was feeling good, and smiled as his thoughts raced over what lay ahead.

'Glasgow,' he said aloud – 'then all aboard for Lisbon.' He laughed even as he said it.

'Colombo – Singapore.' My God, he thought, I'll go daft. And, still smiling, he reached up and put out the light. 'Whaur's your Ella Friar noo?' he said aloud.

And even in the dark, he was still laughing!

The whole lunch table was laughing – even Mrs Keith! She had never seen anything as funny as the three Keiths, their jackets flapping round their shoulders, trousers above their knees revealing suspenders and tartan socks over laced boots. They were all three, John, Bobby and Jim, trying to stand on their hands against the wall of the dining room at Craigend. Bobby was already there, pink-faced and smiling, and gazing with crinkled eyes at his brother's efforts to get up on either side of him. Jim, being the youngest, but the least physical, kept almost getting up but then rolling back; but it was John who was causing the most merriment as his ample posterior joined with an even more generous stomach to prevent his getting anywhere! This was further offset by young two-year-old Kenneth who kept tumbling over beside him. The fun and games were only stopped when Tina wanted to try, but a wagging finger from her father, his pipe in his hand, was sufficient warning and she took up little Kenneth and sat with him on her knee, but he wanted to go to his Grandpop. The brothers lifted John up and soon they were all sitting round the big table again.

'And I'm not even going to New Zealand!' puffed John.

'I'm telling you John, they walk on their heads down under so we'll just have to get used to it!'

'Enough of your kidding, Robert Keith,' said Mrs Beattie, who was an unexpected guest at the Ne'erday feast.

'You know that ladies wouldn't be able to do that.'

'Why not?' said Bobby teasingly.

'Because they've got soft heads,' murmured Jim, his breathing restored. The nonsense went on for some time before the men rose again to let the women clear the table.

'A woman's work is never done,' said Mrs Beattie, taking her time over the brandy. Thomasina took the glass fom her saying brightly,

'Come on, ma, there's a dish towel with your name on it!' But there was no denying the steel beneath the glitter. The men went into the parlour and left the ladies to it.

'I'll take Kenny up,' said Tina sweeping him up in her arms.

'Give Grandpops back his pipe, Kenny!'

'Thank you, Kenneth,' said his grandfather. 'Be a good boy for your Auntie Teenie!'

'Daddy!'

It was only late afternoon, but already getting dark. Mr Keith struck a match to re-light his pipe.

'James, will you light the lamps?'

'Yes, father.'

'I tell you Johnny boy,' said Bobby as he and his brother left the room, 'they'll just be having breakfast in Auckland now. French liver is the great delicacy you know.'

'Is it?'

'Oh ay! Liver of a Frenchman! They're all cannibals there, you know!'

Bobby's laughter could be heard in the kitchen.

'That Bobby o' yours is an awfy man, Mrs Keith,' said Mrs Beattie, a drying towel listless in her hand as she lightly skimmed one of the washed bowls from the sink drying-board.

'Ay, he's ay been daft,' said Florence working away at a stubborn pot. Mrs Keith was at her happiest working. She just never stopped cleaning things. If they were already clean, she made them cleaner.

'Ye'll be pleased to be goin' away on your journey then?'

'I can't do much about it, Mrs Beattie, can I?'

Like most women of her class and generation, Florence Keith was stoically accepting. Florence had no option and she knew it. The kitchen, the laundry and the bedroom would continue to mark the triangle of her life much as they had done since she had married William Keith thirty years before. What did it matter to her what house they were in. It was all the same routine to her.

'Is there room for a little one?'

Tina came in and picked up a dish towel to join Mrs Beattie in drying.

'Where's Kenny?' asked that worthy, always glad to chat.

'Thomasina took him. I think he was getting tired,' said Tina.

'No wonder,' said Mrs Keith. 'All that carry on with his uncles!'

'It was just fun, Mother,' said Tina.

'Just nonsense, you mean,' said Mrs Keith.

'A' men are just laddies at heart,' put in Mrs Beattie.

'As long as they're gettin' their way o' things, Mrs Beattie. Just cross them an' they can be devils.'

'And where's your young man, Tina? Ye'll be leavin' a lot o' hearts broke in Forres when ye go?'

Tina immediately thought of Mr Braid, the new young minister, and his bad breath. And there was Mr Thomson, the schoolmaster, and that awful sister of his. But she said nothing of either. She knew better than to tell Mrs Beattie anything.

'No, I'll be going away heart-whole and fancy-free as they say.'

Mrs Beattie smiled, putting the bowl down, having dried it at last. 'But no' for long, I'll wager!'

'I canna see how ye are a' so cheerful,' said her mother, her arms all soapsuds. 'We could a' be goin' to our deaths!'

'Mrs Keith!' said Mrs Beattie, sitting down at the table.

'It's just my way o' lookin' at it,' said Mrs Keith.

Her daughter was not quite of the same mind but had no real objections. The prospect of the journey terrified her and then excited her. The only city she had ever seen was Aberdeen, and that was only for the day, when her father took her with him to see about a big shipment of Belgian lace. She had never been as far as Inverness, never mind Glasgow, and names like London were only for story-books as far as she was concerned. She couldn't even begin to comprehend Lisbon, Colombo, Singapore and the rest. Best not to think about it yet, she thought, or she would be sick. But going away would get her away from Mr Braid's bad breath, not to mention Mr Thomson's snooty sister! There might be a lot to be said for emigration.

'Ay, it's dry work dryin',' sighed Mrs Beattie.

'Would ye like a cup o' tea, Mrs Beattie?'

'I was thinkin' o' a wee refreshment, Mrs Keith,' said Mrs Beattie, 'it being the time o' the year, ye ken.'

'I ken, Mrs Beattie, but a cup o' tea'll do ye fine. I'll just get the kettle.'

'I see it's goin' to be a right happy New Year,' muttered Mrs Beattie.

Tina hid her laugh in her dish towel, and she stopped laughing when she realised it was wet! Mrs Beattie leaned over to the girl confidentially.

'Can I ask ye somethin', Tina?'

'Of course, Mrs B.' The older woman looked round to see if Mrs Keith could hear, then said: 'Where is New Zealand?'

It was almost dawn and John was still trying to sleep. He had been awake most of the night tossing and turning in his bed, grunting and groaning and sighing till Thomasina sat up at her side.

'For heaven's sake, John Keith, you're worse than the weans. Can ye no' settle yoursel' like a decent man and let a' body sleep. You know I've got the doctor's in the mornin' wi' Elspeth.'

'Sorry.'

His arm was 'sleeping' where her ample weight had been lying on it and his neck was at an uncomfortable angle half-on and half-off his pillow. He made another attempt to get comfortable.

'What's the matter?' asked his wife unlovingly.

'I can't sleep.'

'I can see that. And neither can I with your goings-on.'

'I said I was sorry.'

'Oh ay,' sighed Thomasina.

There was a long pause, but being both long-practised, silent martyrs to marital expectancy they were used to tense silences in bed. John lay watching the reflections of the street lamps on the newly-papered bedroom wall of their town flat. There was a slight noise.

'Was that the wean?' whispered Thomasina.

'I don't think so,' said her husband.

He knew she'd had a difficult labour with their daughter at the back end of the year. There had been complications at the birth because she had been so premature. John remembered he had held the infant entirely in the palm of his hand. He couldn't believe that anyone that small was indeed a person with a full human entitlement and now here she was – wee Elspeth – in a cot in the next room – already a presence in their world. There was another sound. Like running water.

'Is that Kenny up?'

'No,' said John. 'It was the Robertson's side. Tam up to the chantie.'

They both giggled. Thomasina, like any mother of young children, was a light sleeper, and this made her expert on the nocturnal habits of her neighbours through the other wall! Especially big Tam whose capacity was not obviously equal to his appetite on some nights! There was another long pause. This time broken by John.

'They'll be gettin' on board about now.'

'Whit?'

'The family.'

'Oh ay.'

'On the Mataura. They sail the night.' There was another pause.

'The Mataura, eh!' muttered John.

'John?'

'Ay?'

'Do you wish you were goin' with them?' John didn't answer. The silence was suddenly broken by a baby's cry . . .

TWO

It was a very different kind of New Year in Ireland. There was only the rough strip of the Irish Sea between them, yet it might have been the whole of the Pacific Ocean, so great was the gulf between the Keiths in their Hogmanay in Forres and the O'Neil family in a cottage in County Down. For while the Scots were observing the tradition of the family quaich, the Irish were indulging in a very different rite. They were saying a family rosary.

'Hail Mary, full of grace, the Lord is with thee. Blessed art thou among women and blessed is the fruit of thy womb, Jesus.'

The voice of the women trailed in the fetid air of the cottage like a wisp of grey smoke, being answered by the men in a throaty grumble that hardly rose off the earthen floor.

'Holy Mary, Mother of God, pray for us sinners, now and at the hour of our death. Amen.'

A female voice announced, 'The second sorrowful Mystery, the Scourging of Jesus at the Pillar. Hail Mary, full of grace, the Lord is with thee . . .'

And away went the women again on the dolorous, mantra-like, prayerful repetition that Catholics all over the world called The Holy Rosary. But these particular Catholics on that Old Year night were a very poor branch of the illustrious O'Neils, and they were gathered round a smouldering peat fire in their tiny cottage near Rosstrevor in Down under the shadow of the mountains of Mourne. There could have been no more appropriate setting, for hadn't much of their life been in mourning – for their old ways, for the good soil now barren, for the large families now scattered and for the good life they once had now only remembered by the very old? The faces of the family reflected in the dying firelight told not only their own stories, but Ireland's. You could see it in all those very Irish eyes.

'Blessed art thou among women . . .'

Agnes Monaghan's eyes were bright blue like a child's. She was only fifty, but it seemed that every day had been etched in the lines of her face and dyed permanently into the weather-beaten cheeks that had known a rain of tears in their time. Only those blue eyes hinted, like the red strands in her grey hair, that she was a beauty once. She was thought the great catch for Denis O'Neil when he courted her at the Ballymullion dancing, twenty-seven years before. Now, as she led her family in their nightly devotion, like the good Irish mother she was, she tried to forget the young girl she had been. Red-headed Nessie Monaghan was always in demand at the socials, for wasn't she thought to be the great singer? There wasn't much to sing about for Nessie Monaghan now she was Mrs Denis O'Neil. Thank God for Nellie there to give me a hand with them all, she thought.

'Hail Mary, full of grace . . .'

Helen O'Neil, called Nellie by everyone except Canon Devlin and the schoolteacher, Mr Docherty, joined the response without thinking, but without worrying either. She did it because she had always done it and because it was expected of her, and Nellie always did what was expected of her. As the first child of the O'Neils she could do little else. Her mother needed all the help she could get as one babe followed another in the household, and Helen, with her Da's easy-going nature and her Ma's tireless capacity for work, was soon regarded as the perfect wee mother herself by the neighbours and the rest of the family. There were times when she would have liked a bit of nursing herself. Nobody noticed the times when she had a quiet wee cry to herself in the back room, or the fright she had that morning when she woke to find the blood on her nightie. But there had been little time to dwell on womanhood. There was too much to do to get the younger ones ready for the day. There was always something wanting or someone crying for her. It seemed to Nellie O'Neil that her own childhood had been forgotten in all the work that her brother and sisters were. Not that she was the only sister. Noreen was nearly seven years younger, but then again, Noreen was pretty. Red-headed like her mother, and could sing like her Da. And if you could sing in this house you could get away with anything. Sure, Noreen would do her bit, but it was only a very little bit and even then she had to be chased up to do it. Nellie often got angry with her, but not for long. There was a real skill in that, she thought wryly. She knew she was being taken advantage of, but she knew no other way and just got on with it. There wasn't a trace of self-pity in Nellie O'Neil, but there was much humour. 'Sure, if you can't laugh at it all, you might as well lie down and die!' she would always say. Not that anybody listened. It was only our Nellie. She wondered what it might have been like had she looked like her mother instead of her father – and if she had been able to sing like Noreen?

'The Lord is with Thee . . .'

Noreen O'Neil's thoughts were far from the Lord! In fact, they were singularly unholy. She was thinking about how much she liked Liam Murphy. She knew he was old, he was well into his twenties at least, and he had a bad reputation with girls. In fact, Annie McAteer told her he had put a girl from Milltown in the family way, but it was hard to know with Annie McAteer. She could be just jealous because Liam had once gone out with her. Just the once. And nothing happened or Annie would have told her. She told Noreen everything. All Noreen knew was that Liam Murphy kept looking at her at the St Anne's Parish Dance, and if he was really as bad as they all said then surely Canon Devlin wouldn't have let him through the door in case he scandalised the Legion of Mary. She would have loved to have danced with Liam, but Michael and Sean never left her side and Patrick wasn't any help either. She got the feeling that the boys didn't like Liam Murphy, and when they didn't like someone, a girl hadn't a chance. But Noreen couldn't get the girl from Milltown and her baby out of her mind. She didn't know about babies. She had been sent to her auntie's in Newry when the two Kevins were being born, so she missed out each time. She wished she could talk to someone. Someone who really knew. She couldn't ask Nellie. Even though she was much older than Noreen, she couldn't know about babies either – Nellie wasn't married, was she? And it was only married people who had babies, wasn't it? And it wasn't the sort of thing you could talk to your Mam about, was it? It would be embarrassing. I mean, her and Da –? And then she saw her mother was looking at her. God, she knows what I'm thinking! She felt herself blush. When she stole another glance her mother had her eyes closed. My poor Mam, she thought. She's had so many babies. Including me! But wasn't the first Kevin born dead? She shivered even as she thought about it and bowed her head and tried to concentrate. I swear to goodness the Rosary gets longer every night!

'– and blessed is the fruit of thy womb . . .'

There we are, babies again! Annie McAteer said they came out of your belly-button. When your belly swelled up, they just loosened the knot of your belly-button and out it popped. Annie McAteer should know right enough. She works in the chemist shop at Rosstrevor. But it's hard to know with Annie McAteer.

'Hail Mary . . .'

In Ireland it's the women who do the praying. As in Italy, Spain and Portugal, the other Catholic countries, prayers are not held to be men's work. Yet, ironically the Church itself is a completely male affair. In the O'Neil household, the pious initiative was undoubtedly matriarchal and the men of the house were happy to passively respond:

'Holy Mary, Mother of God, pray for us sinners . . .'

But like Claudius in the play, their 'words fly up, their thoughts remain below'.

On this particular night Denis O'Neil was thinking, as he did most nights at this time, that he could do with a drink. The smoke from the last of the fire got into the back of his throat and didn't it give him the helluva drouth? What he would give now for a black porter and a drop of the crater to go with it? Denis O'Neil recited the Rosary responses much as he had done for most of his life, getting the words out in time and in the right order, and with just the right pious tone in the voice, but with his mind, for the most part, on other things. Not that he had much of a mind to work with. Denis O'Neil was not a clever man (wasn't Nessie, his wife, clever enough for both of them?) but he was a man gifted, or was it cursed, with more than his share of charm. It has been a great undoer of many men, this indefinable attribute, and the handsome young Denis O'Neil that he used to be took no time at all in becoming the lazy easy-going rascal of a charmer that he was now at sixty-seven. However, he still had as great an appetite both for the food and the drink as he had had at one time for his sexual needs. He always had a high sensual appreciation, a fact that was well proved by their large family. Most of them were gathered about him now as he knelt by his chair on the only piece of carpet they had. As well as the two daughters, Denis and Nessie had five sons – six if you counted the first Kevin who – God rest his wee soul – was still-born. Yes, it was a sad time that, in the winter of 1880 when his wife carried to her full time and then had all the pain of delivering a corpse. He thought he had nearly lost her too. Holy God, that would have been bad had he lost Nessie. What would he have done then? It didn't bear thinking about. Listen to her now, he thought, leading the prayer like a Mother Superior. Ay, she was that, very superior and a good mother too. Denis O'Neil loved his wife dearly, but like all simple men took her many qualities entirely for granted. His one redeeming quality was his never-failing sense of humour. No matter how hard they had it, he and Nessie, and how hard it had been these last ten years, he could nearly always make her laugh. And when she wanted to be quiet, he would sing to her. Thanks be to God, he could still sing. Wasn't it that that had won her away from Dermot Kelly? The sweet tenor voice he had when they were both young in Burren. Sure wasn't he thought, at one time, to be an even better singer than she was?

Nessie Monaghan's only weakness was for a sad song.

'The third sorrowful Mystery, the Crowning of Jesus with Thorns. Hail Mary full of grace . . .'

And so on, and again the male voices of the father and sons responded: 'Blessed art thou among women, and blessed is the fruit of thy womb, Jesus.'

Denis O'Neil, the first son, was lucky. He had the best points of both his parents. The father's charm and voice, the mother's looks and efficiency and, caught as he was between two sisters, he had the best of all possible worlds to grow up in. Except that he was poor Irish, and there is nothing poorer. He was from a Catholic family in a Protestant region and he had no real education to speak of. But he was naturally smart and as the oldest son of five he was a born leader. There was no doubt he had latent quality but there didn't seem to be use for it around Rosstrevor. He was twenty-five years of age and still 'on the house', as they say. Not that he had any thought of moving. Not while he had a bed with Sean, a bowl of potatoes and eggs every night and a glass of beer after the hurling on a Saturday. He was a dab hand with the stick and the ball and there was talk that he was wanted by one of the flash teams in Newry. But Denis liked it fine where he was. While he didn't have his father's much practised indolence, there was a lazy streak in young Denis. So he was happy to take life as it came to him – only occasionally. Besides, what else did he know? God, his knees were feeling it tonight. That's where he got a knock against Bundoran last week, or else he must have a bad bit of the floor. With a grimace, he shifted the weight and grinned at Sean where he knelt at the table.

'Pray for us sinners . . .'

Sean O'Neil was tired and tried hard to keep from yawning. He had been up on the back hill with the horses all day. With two crop failures in succession the outlook was bleak for farming in this part of the world at least. He was thinking of joining the Constabulary. They might even give him a horse, and at least he would eat regularly. He would even get paid. The farm could just about keep his mother and father, the way it was, but not half-a-dozen hungry adults as well. Sean was the family worrier, but then, like every one else in Ireland, he had plenty to worry about in the first few months of 1900. Nearly fifty years ago the entire potato crop had failed and people had starved to death. It wasn't really as bad as that yet, but it was not far off it, the way prices were. Come to think of it, he was hungry. And look at Mick. Sean nearly burst out laughing as he gazed at his younger brother at the other side of the table, for, although

33

his lips moved and he was swaying slightly, he seemed to be fast asleep!

'Now and at the hour of our death. Amen.'

Michael O'Neil was by no means asleep, but he was not far from it. Mick, as he was called in the family, could not have been by any stretch of even an Irish imagination called a worrier. His was an enviable temperament and it saw him through all the typical circumstances that beset any healthy young man growing up on a farm. Certainly, he had his chores to do like everyone else, but a way with all things mechanical ensured that he was more often in or under some piece of farm machinery most of the day. At nights, he was more often down at Ingham's Bar, where, with all the skill of the poor man, he would make half-a-pint last all night, or at least till closing time when he would wander in, late as usual for the nightly supper of toast and tea. This was just as much a rite and ritual as the family rosary. Everyone was always hungry for supper. The rosary came right after it, so Nessie had them all trapped. If you had one, you got the other. Mick, as usual, just shrugged and got on with it. He said the rosary with his eyes closed and the tip of his tongue trying to get the last bit of toast from his teeth. Suddenly, he felt himself falling but a helping hand saved him. Startled, he opened his eyes to find Paddy holding his elbow with one hand and putting his fingers to his lips with the other.

'The fourth sorrowful Mystery, Jesus Carries His Cross. Hail Mary . . .'

Patrick Joseph, otherwise Paddy, leaned across to him.

'It's somethin' we all have to bear, Mick,' he whispered with a wink. Patrick O'Neil was probably the only one in the family, apart perhaps from his mother, who was really praying sincerely. Paddy liked prayers. He liked going to church. He even went on weekdays, when he got away from the farm, and it was noticed by all that he never missed devotions on a Sunday night either. People thought that Paddy should have been a priest, but he had always had a bad chest ever since he was a baby and the parish priest, Canon Devlin, had said his health would never stand up to the study. Yet his health had stood up to living off the scraps of a failing farm these past few years and Paddy even thought that his chest was clearing up. Going hungry might be good for it! Paddy was an optimist. He saw the bright side of most things. Even in being an O'Neil!

'– now, and at the hour of our death. Amen.'

The whole family then responded, 'Glory be to the Father and to the Son and to the Holy Ghost.'

Then the distaff side resumed. 'Hail Mary, full of grace . . .'

And while the women intoned, Kevin O'Neil, the second, and the youngest son, let out a great yawn and wished he was in bed. At seventeen he thought he was getting a bit old for this sort of thing, but he was in no great hurry to grow up. Looking around him, it must be admitted the boy had no great incentive. So Kevin kept a finger-hold on childhood. It was only a little finger, but he was a big lad for his age, and it allowed him to unashamedly dream big dreams about his heroes. His mind was full of heroes and they were all Irish – mythical giants and ancient warriors, wandering troubadours and soldier-poets. None of them real, but that's what was the most Irish thing about them. To Kevin, that was the best thing about heroes, they weren't real. If they had been real they couldn't be heroes. Real people are too busy making a living to be heroes. Real heroes could only belong in the imagination, so Kevin filled his mind with romantic versions of rebels and patriots fighting for Kathleen O'Houlihan or dear Mother Ireland, the Emerald Isle in the Silver Sea, Catholicised by the Scotsman, Patrick, and cleared for all time of snakes and any sense of normality. Kevin was fiercely proud of being Irish, but he didn't know why. He wished he was in his bed and dreaming his dreams.

'Hail, Holy Queen, Mother of Mercy, hail our Life, our Sweetness and our Hope. To thee do we cry, poor banished children of Eve. To thee do we send up our sighs, mourning and weeping in this Vale of Tears . . .'

Catholic prayers are hardly an exercise in exultation, but the O'Neils were always glad to get to the 'Hail, Holy Queen' because they knew that was the end of devotions for the night and they were minutes away from bed. Some families played cards of an evening before retiring, some played the piano or the squeeze-box, some played the fool and drank their own poteen, but the O'Neils played it safe – they said the rosary!

'Remember, O most gracious Virgin Mary, never was it known that anyone who fled to thy protection, implored thy help, or sought thy intercession, was left unaided . . .'

The O'Neils pressed hard on Heaven at this point, leaning heavily on this trusted Marist intercession for each particular need – there was no speaking right to God here – besides they wouldn't know what to say. They were even shy with Jesus, but with His mother, Our Lady, they could talk to her in their own voices, because they thought of this 2,000-year-old Jewish girl as being Irish like themselves. This is what having a strong faith means! So that Nessie, for instance, could quietly put in a word for a chance to get a bit of cash together at the end of each month, so that she could put a pound or two away in the back of the old cutlery box – just in case; and by the way, could she keep Noreen out of trouble? It's the age she's at, but being a woman Our Lady would understand. Such was Nessie's faith she believed she could indeed have moved the Mourne Mountains back an inch or two had she wanted, but that would have been asking a bit much. No, an extra couple of pounds would do.

Nellie, typically, never asked for anything for herself. If a bit of carpet fell from heaven she wouldn't object – and oh yes, would Our Lady ask Our Lord to keep Noreen out of trouble – you know what I mean? Noreen, quite unaware that she was the focus of such prayerful aims would have been quite happy for the chance of a walk along Warrenpoint front with Liam Murphy, but she daren't ask for that because she knew it would be a definite occasion of sin and she wasn't so sure she wouldn't give in!

Old Denis only wanted a bit of peace from the factor and maybe a winning number on the Irish sweepstake, or at least the spare cash to buy a ticket! If he'd the money he'd go and visit his brother Michael in New York, the one that was in the police there. In his romantic way Old Denis knew the truth of it. Their situation required the big gesture. Anything else was pointless. He'd written to his brother only a month since telling him the way things were in the Old Country, particularly on the farm. It would be a bad bargain to pass on to young Denis and his brothers. Young Denis, on the other hand, was certain of only one thing, that he didn't want to inherit Ballytreabhair Farm. Being son and heir to this bereft sprig of the O'Neil family tree had definite disadvantages, and running the barren Ballytreabhair was one of them. Young Denis spent his prayers going through some of the best goals he had scored at the hurling. The other brothers' wants were more direct – Patrick, for his own copy of the *Lives of the Saints*; Sean, for a chance to join the Ulster Constabulary, so that he could arrest Kevin and put him in a cell for the night! The same Kevin wanted an automatic pistol in a leather shoulder-belt holster and Michael only asked for a chance to get to his bed, but he hoped that one day, if God had the time, he could see his way to giving him the cash in his pocket to buy a pint one night at Ingham's, and even – hope beyond all hope – to stand a round! This then was the family wish-list, a nightly Christmas Stocking that was full of holes and empty promises. Never mind, the fantasising did them no harm. Indeed, the simple day-dreaming might have done them some good. However it all turns out, that's it for another day.

'In the Name of the Father and of the Son and of the Holy Ghost. Amen.' Then it was bed and a chance to dream in earnest.

Also, a chance to be on your own in the dark. It was a very small house in the middle of four fields under the back hill and they were a large family, even by Irish standards, so they had to squeeze up a bit. But what did that matter, they were all family weren't they? They were O'Neils and weren't they once Kings of all Ireland . . .?

They all slept soundly that night without the least fear that Mary, their much-loved Lady, would not provide for them. They justly slept the sleep of the righteous, until the dawn, when the old cockerel crowed, and naturally they denied it thrice! What they didn't quite realise was that prayers are answered sometimes by not being answered. God's ways are not only mysterious but downright misleading. Which is why a healthy dose of fatalism is a happy additive to any attempts to fathom His will.

It was at least a week before anything happened. It was a Tuesday, the day when Old Denis had to go marching up the drive to the big house in his best suit to see Colonel Mayhew, his English landlord, and pretend again that the year's rent was just around the corner. Colonel Mayhew was a gentleman and easily impressed, but Andrew Tait, his factor, was not a gentleman and not at all impressed.

'It's not good enough, O'Neil,' he rasped.

'Maybe no', said Denis, 'but you can't get blood from a stone and there's an awful lot of stones in that ground of mine.'

'It's only yours till the end of the next term,' said Tait.

'Perhaps Denis,' interpolated the Colonel, 'if you could make one last effort this season you and your sons might turn the position round.'

'I'm sure we could do that, sir. They're fine boys the lot o' them.'

'I'm sure they are. What do you say, Mr Tait?'

'I say that –'

'I was just going to say the very same thing Colonel!' interrupted Denis quickly. 'Even six months would do it.'

He was glad to get out with a three month extension. He noticed he wasn't offered a cup of tea this time, never mind a wee drop of the Jamieson's. Still, he had twelve weeks to think of something. He would discuss it with Nessie – and perhaps Paddy. He had a good head on him. It was no use talking to Denis or the others. They couldn't wait to get off the farm. It was typical of Denis that he should rack his little brains to think who he should turn to to help him in his difficulties. Such was his innocence that it never occurred to him to do anything himself. Nessie did most of the work on the place with the help of the boys. Denis was the family figurehead and like most figureheads was decorative more than functional. But Denis was disarming and could talk himself into and out of most situations, so he had his uses in the family. Going back down the long drive, he loosened his tie and the stiff white collar and felt immediately better.

He took a long route home by the road instead of over the four fields. He was in no hurry. He hesitated at Ingham's Bar and expertly counted the coppers in his right-hand trouser pocket without removing his hand to see if he would have enough for a half-pint and a wee Bush. He had a shilling and two pennies. Just a penny short, but if Tim was on the bar, he could toss him for it. He checked at the window. Good, it was Tim. He was just about to go in when Tommy Drennan, the postman, came out, still wiping the froth from his chin. He grinned broadly on seeing Denis.

'It's yourself, Dinis. I'm just on my way up to your place this very minute or sure you know I'd be glad to stand you one.'

'That's alright, Tommy,' said Denis, 'I know you'll be in a hurry.'

Denis knew that Tommy had never bought a drink in his life. He was always meaning to but he was either leaving for this reason or that. But people had got used to him and resignedly accepted the wish for the deed. He was just about to pass Denis in the doorway when he stopped.

'I have a letter for you out in the cart there, Denis. Will you be stepping over the road with me, or will I hand it in to ye here?'

'Just take it up to Nessie. I'm in no mind to read another Valentine from Andy Tait. I've just had an hour and a half with him.'

'Please yourself,' said Tommy affably, 'the top o' the mornin' to ye.'

'Right,' said Denis and went into the bar. There was no one else in the place and red-headed Tim was reading the paper on the counter.

'Quiet this mornin', Tim.'

'And I will be to the break time. It's not everyone can be a leisured gentleman like you Denis and come in carrying a collar an' tie!'

'I was up at the big house to see the Colonel.'

'An' did ye win?'

'I'm still here aren't I?'

'Well, Denis, what would ye like?'

'I know what I'd like, but I can't afford it.'

'A half pint o' stout then?'

'To be honest, I can't afford that either, Tim.'

'I see.' Tim folded his arms over his white apron and looked at Denis.

'Would you like a read o' my paper?'

By this time, Denis had his small change out on the counter, and to his horror he saw that what he thought was a shilling in his pocket was only a halfpenny. He couldn't even buy a cupful of anything with twopence halfpenny. Tim was enjoying the situation.

'It's not your lucky day, is it, Denis?' Just at that, Tommy Drennan came back into the pub waving a large bulky envelope covered in stamps. He put it on the counter.

'I realised that your letter Denis, was the only one taking me up over the four fields and I thought to meself why should I give me old bones the trouble of a hike like that when yourself is set here by the bar but two minutes walk from me own door?'

'I told you, Tommy,' said Denis, looking forlornly at his few coppers, 'I want to see no bills today.'

'And isn't it the funny bill with the head of George Washington all over it. Or is it with the Red Indians you've been tradin'?'

Tim had the envelope in his hands.

'It's addressed to you alright, Denis. And it's heavy too. Feel that.'

Denis took it and sure enough it was in his name but he couldn't recognise the writing. He pondered for a moment.

'Tommy, you said you were going to stand me a drink.'

Tommy looked discomfited for a moment, then his face brightened.

'Ah, you see I was off duty then Denis, but I'm on duty now you see and I can't be taken the Royal Mails an' me with the drink taken. You understand me, Denis?'

Denis shook his head, beginning to pick at the letter flap.

'Oh, I understand you alright, Tommy.'

'Yes. Right, well, I'll be going then,' said Tommy, making for the door. Neither Tim nor Denis answered as both were intent on the opening of the big envelope, so Tommy left, with a shrug of his shoulders.

He was in the street when he heard the shout. No, it wasn't a shout, it was a yell. Tommy was back at the bar in a bound and there on the counter was the envelope floating on a positive sea of American dollar bills and beside it, standing, aloof as a lighthouse, a full bottle of Bushmills Whiskey.

It was some time before the situation was clear. It took even longer to remove the prostrate bodies of Denis and Tommy Drennan, the postman, from the snug bar at Ingham's. It is understood that Mr Drennan was severely censured by the Postmaster for being drunk in charge of a post-bag! Sean and Michael called for their father in a farm cart. He was carried out into the street singing 'I'm A Yankee Doodle Dandy!' Tim, the barman, followed with the famous letter and a bundle of American banknotes wrapped in a copy of the local paper. Tim waved the cart and went back into his bar. He removed the empty bottle of whiskey and the two empty glasses from the counter without noticing the two pennies and the halfpenny still lying there!

Patrick O'Neil's face was almost hidden behind the large sheet of notepaper as he read it. The whole family was huddled round the bed in their parents' bedroom. Denis had been carried in there from the cart and was now lying on the old brass bed staring wide-eyed at the ceiling, one hand held in both of Nessie's. It had taken a time to collect everybody together, and the first lamps were already lit by the time they were all in the house and seated severally around their parents' bed waiting to have their Uncle Michael's letter read out to them. Denis moved up to his brother and tried to hurry him up.

'Here, come on, Paddy –'

'It's alright, Denis, I'm almost there.' He read on for a bit before he exclaimed: 'Glory be to God!'

'Has somebody died?' asked Nellie.

'No. No, Nellie girl. Will yez listen to this –' He began to read, slowly at first but gradually gaining in momentum. 'Dear Brother –'

'That's me!' called out Old Denis from the bed.

Paddy ignored his father and continued: 'So I had a word with a man I know and him owing me a favour, if you understand my meaning, and me knowing how you were all placed by your last letter, and him being in the shipping line on this side, and you being over there, I thought it would be just the thing to put the touch on him for bookings for as many of you as would like to join me here to see how you all get on.'

There was an immediate outburst at this and questions rained on all sides round Paddy's shoulder but he eventually got some order again. Old Denis was still staring catatonically at the ceiling. Nessie was crying happily. Nobody noticed the rosary beads in her hands.

'Sure, go on, Paddy.' 'What else does it say?' 'Read it out, Pat!' Noreen was almost squealing with excitement. Paddy went on: 'Knowing that I know what I know he was only too happy to oblige and so the form I am sending with this letter is to be filled in with all the names of them that wants to go and sent off to the office in Glasgow because that's where the ship sails some time near the end of May. You must take this boat as this is the only one where my friend has influence. His brother-in-law is the Captain. It is who you know in this world, not what you know. I hope you can all come and hope this finds you as it leaves me. Give my best to Nessie –'

'That's you, Mam!' squealed Noreen.

'And to all the girls and boys –'

A great cheer from the family.

'Your loving brother, Michael.'

There were more cheers at this, but Patrick held up his hand. 'P.S. I mind Denis how you sold our two best horses to send me out here and you just married yourself at the time. I am sending you some cash wrapped in tissue paper to pay back what I owe as I have been promoted to Captain. I hope a hundred and fifty dollars will help with the expenses of the trip – or pay that back rent you mentioned.' At that, old Denis raised his free hand from the bed and there in his grip was a fistful of Yankee dollars! The cheering and the crying and the laughing went on till the early hours of the morning. Old Denis cried for his brother. Nessie cried for Denis. Young Denis and Sean argued about the merits of New York and Dublin as the respective centres of the world. Kevin was asking Michael about getting a Winchester rifle, and the two girls discussed what they might wear on the voyage. Nobody said the rosary!

In the days that followed, once heads had cleared and senses had returned to normal, a lot of talking was done around the O'Neil peat fire. A lot of arguing too, but finally a kind of plan emerged. Old Denis and Nessie decided to stay on the farm after all, selling off the lease on the two back fields and paying two years' rent in advance to Mr Tait. They would also keep young Kevin by them – 'him being the youngest'. Kevin didn't mind. Not everyone wanted to go to America. Sean would rather have been a constable, but discovered that he hadn't the educational qualifications.

'It's professors they want, not policemen.'

'Well, you can ask Uncle Mick if you can join the force in Brooklyn,' he was told. Michael couldn't be bothered making the long journey. He was afraid he would be seasick. But he'd give it a go. Young Denis was for it one day and against it the next. Only Paddy was really keen, although he was his usual quiet self about it. Nobody thought to ask the girls whether they wanted to go or not, but Mrs O'Neil thought it would be the great chance for them. She thought the change would do Nellie good and, looking pointedly at Noreen, said it would be fine to put all that water between herself and the likes of Liam Murphy!

Paddy, as the bookish member of the family, took charge of all the arrangements, signing all the papers and writing all the letters between Rosstrevor and New York and Glasgow. Young Denis took what was left of the dollar bills and had them changed into British pounds through Canon Devlin's bank in Newry. During those first four months of the new century, Tommy Drennan of the Post was a busy man. He was never away from the door and he was a confirmed teetotaller now. Nessie and the girls cleaned and patched and mended till they had a kind of a wardrobe for everyone to take with them to America. Even just to say the word was excitement enough. The farm was tidied up by the five boys in record time. Ballytreabhair had never looked so good for years. Every piece of iron machinery was checked. Everything that could move was oiled by Michael and what couldn't was white-washed by Kevin. Sean and Denis brought the animals in, and Mr O'Donnel, the vet, came out from Newry – 'at a helluva cost' – moaned Old Denis, and checked them over. New curtains were run up for the house, and at last, window panes were put in the dairy windows where the women did the cheeses. Things were found that had been lost for years and other things thrown out that had been lying about for just as long. No farm is a tidy place; it is a working place but the O'Neil family, marshalled by Nessie, got Ballytreabhair as tidy as it had ever been. There was a banging and beating and a cleaning and a scouring of the place that would have made you think the Queen was coming and not that most of them were leaving.

Old Denis did his bit by keeping out of the way for the most part. He was in a great humour throughout and stood his round every Saturday at Ingham's like the fine man he was, and regaled the company with tall tales of the O'Neils and sang the sad songs his wife liked. Nessie herself kept busy – too busy. As if she were trying to distract herself by work from the thought she would soon be losing all her children – Kevin excepted, of course. She got very quiet and didn't sing around the house like she used to, but life went on more or less as usual. There was a tension however, a different air about the place and once the frantic work had eased it was almost as though everyone was holding their breath as they waited for the big day to come round. When word of the passage came through, it was found that Uncle Mick's 'friend' could only arrange a third class cabin for Noreen and Nellie to share with two other girls. The four boys would have to go steerage. They didn't mind. 'As long as there's no cattle!' said Sean. But certain events forced a last minute change in these travel plans. Something that no one in the family – except one perhaps – could possibly have foreseen. Liam Murphy came to call!

It was just after six in the evening and there he was on the front step, dressed in his best blue suit and wearing his brown bowler. Nessie opened the door to him. Luckily, the boys were all out. But it wasn't the brothers he had come to see.

'It's yourself, Mrs O'Neil.'

Such a smile was on him that Nessie was immediately on her guard.

'Yes.'

'A fine night?'

''Tis that sure. Is it Noreen –'

'Indeed 'tis not, Mrs O'Neil. I had an arrangement with Miss Helen –'

'Nellie?'

'That's right, mother!'

Nessie turned round and there was Nellie smiling under her best hat and squeezing past her to join Liam on the cobbles of the yard.

'I'm walking out with Liam. Didn't you know? Are ye right then, Liam?'

Liam raised his brown bowler,

'As ever I'll be, Nell!'

Nessie watched them saunter down to the road-end as bold as you like and still couldn't bring a word out. Our Nellie with Liam Murphy? 'Nell' he called her? What's the world coming to? And what about Noreen? Nessie rushed indoors to find her second daughter lying on top of her bed in her underclothes, quite unperturbed.

'Surprised ye, Mam?'

'I'm dum'foundered, I am. Never for a minute – but I thought –'

'Ach, sure he was too old for me. He'll be just right for our Nellie.'

Noreen laughed at her mother's incredulity and started to take off the rest of her clothes. She had to take the chance of the zinc bath in front of the fire while the boys were out. Her mother poured out the hot water and steam filled the little back kitchen of the farmhouse. Nessie shook her head and smiled to herself.

'That sly old Nellie!' she said, going out with the kettle. Noreen splashed in the tub, a soap-sudded nymph in the firelight, then she laughed out loud. 'It's a good job the boys were out!'

Her mother returned with a puzzled look on her face.

'But what about America?'

43

Noreen lifted a slim, shapely leg out of the water and raised it high.

'She's not going!'

The banns were cried for Nellie and Liam the very next Sunday and the parish was agog with the news of it. It was unusual for any couple walking out not to be noticed by someone in a country place like Rosstrevor, but Nellie and Liam had been very clever and were only seen together in groups of the younger people. Apparently, Noreen was in on it from the beginning. It seems that Nellie had caught Liam with Noreen down by Kelly's Brook one night and she had given him such a piece of her mind that Liam was highly impressed. He stopped trying to see Noreen as Nellie insisted but then started seeing Nellie instead! They were married by Canon Devlin on the Saturday before the boys and Noreen sailed for Glasgow. It was decided to combine the wedding reception with a farewell party and what a day and a night it was! The night of the O'Neils was talked about for years afterwards.

It began decorously enough at Mass in the morning and with young Denis as best man and Noreen as her maid of honour, Nellie O'Neil became Mrs Murphy. At the wedding breakfast there was the first skirmish between the Murphy brothers and the O'Neil brothers. It was said Noreen had started it. In the evening, a glorious brawl ensued that almost wrecked the church hall and had Canon Devlin swearing with vexation, but the company retired happily to Ingham's top room where Old Denis soothed the scars with sad songs and even Nessie sang again. It was well into the next morning when the party broke up and everyone went home in daylight. They had a whip round to pay for the damage to the hall and all agreed it was well worth it. The new Murphys left for their honeymoon at Moville and the young O'Neils packed their few things for the other side of the water and the great city of Glasgow. On the night before they left, Nessie did not sing. Neither did Old Denis. Instead they said a last rosary, had their toast and tea as usual and went quietly, but excitedly, to bed. Old Denis cried himself to sleep. He knew he wouldn't see them again.

It was a bedraggled straggle of poorly-clad, unkempt, unwashed and unwanted Irish who stepped hesitantly down the gang-plank of the Irish boat and on to the cobbles of the Broomielaw that bright May afternoon in 1900. Looking decidedly more cheerful were four young men in caps and plain dark country clothes and a pretty girl in a bonnet. Two of the young men struggled with a trunk, one more carried bed-rolls and the other carried two large bags in each hand. The girl carried an air about her.

The O'Neils had landed. Sean and Michael put down the trunk. Sean indicated Noreen, who was taking in the bustling scene on the dock.

'For Jesus' sake, Mick, we'll have to put a halter on that one, I'm thinkin', or we'll not get her out of Glasgow, never mind to Brooklyn.'

'Ach, sure, Sean, she's all show that one,' answered his brother. 'D'ye not see she's as feared as you are.'

'Whose feared?'

'Right then. Here we are.' It was Denis. He put down his two carpet bags beside the trunk, and pushed his cap to the back of his head.

'Will you be tellin' us, Paddy now, where we are in this heathen place? Noreen, there's a good girl. Come by an' sit down here.'

He indicated the trunk and Noreen obligingly sat as the brothers gathered round. Paddy on his two felt bags perusing his various papers. Mick looked around him.

'There's a helluva people in Glasgow, I'm thinkin'.'

'An' do ye's not hear the singin' boys, and the bands?'

Noreen's eyes were dancing with excitement. Sean nudged Mick.

'For a girl that's been dyin' since she put her toe on board, she's sprightly enough now.'

'I was just seasick, Sean O'Neil.'

'Ye're not sick now to be sure,' said Mick.

'I'm not on the sea now, am I?'

'Imagine the eedjit that would pay a good shillin' for the crossin' to be sick all the way,' laughed Sean.

'Quiet now,' interpolated Denis. 'Are ye right there, Pat?'

'I think I have it,' was the answer.

'Our ship is the SS Campania of the Cunard Shipping Line and they have their agent in Bothwell Street. Our tickets are there to be picked up before six o'clock tonight. We've to ask for a Mr Bradley. As soon as we have them in our hands we can get on to the – what is it now?'

'Campania,' put in Denis.

'That's right, Denis, the – we can get on at dusk.'

'And when would that be?' asked Mick.

'When it's neither night nor day,' said Sean.

'Sure that's a funny time,' added Noreen.

'She's at Pier 3.'

'Who?'

Paddy frowned at his young sister.

'The Campania, of course. But the first thing is to get the tickets. From a Mr Bradley it says. What d'ye think Denis?'

Denis thought for a minute, looking out at the busy quayside. 'Where did ye say that office was?' he asked his brother.

Paddy checked his papers again. 'Bothwell Street,' he said.

'Well,' said Denis, 'I've a good Irish tongue in me head. I can ask. Right. Let's me that has the money from our da find my way to that office and get the tickets. You can all make your way with the luggage to Pier 3, and get something to eat at that MacSorley's place they told us about in Jamaica Street. Just ask somebody where it is.'

'How can we get something to eat, an' you've got all the money?'

Denis grinned at his young brother. 'True Sean, true. I'll tell ye then.'

He reached into his shirt and pulled out a leather wallet. 'There's a ten shilling note. You take it Paddy, and mind for the change there. We'll need all we've got for the voyage. I'll see ye's all at the boat again afore six. You'll see to that Paddy?'

'I will that.'

'What about me?' asked Noreen.

'What about you?' said Denis.

'I don't want to stay here.'

'You're not staying here, girl. You'll go with your brothers and eat.'

'I don't want to.'

'Why not?'

'I'm not hungry.'

Denis sighed and looked down at her. 'Are we goin' to have trouble with you, Noreen Alannah?'

'Not at all,' answered the girl, looking up defiantly.

'I wouldn't bet on that!' said Sean.

Noreen wheeled on her brother, but Denis pulled her back again.

'OK. OK. What d'ye want to do then?'

Noreen didn't hesitate. 'I want to go with you, Denis.'

'But –.' He laughed. 'Alright. But you'll have to stay right by me.'

'Oh, I will, our Denis. I will.'

'She's just like all women,' said Mick with a grin. 'Alright as long as she gets her own way.'

The family then confirmed their plan. Denis and Noreen would go to see Mr Bradley as the letter had said. It was just after four by Paddy's watch. They'd have to hurry, and they didn't even know where to go yet. The boys would manage the trunks and the two bags along to the Customs Shed for embarkation and they would take turns with one looking after them while the other two looked around for MacSorley's.

'Get something for us,' chipped in Noreen.

'We'd better get going then, little sister,' said Denis buttoning his jacket. He turned to Paddy. 'You'll be alright, Patrick?'

'Sure.'

'Sean? Mick?'

'Fine.'

'Right. Come on Noreen. Let's see this Glasgow place.'

The three brothers watched their big brother and little sister walk briskly along the dockside towards the street. In no time, they were swallowed up in the crowd.

'Did ye ever see such a people?' said Mick in wonder.

As they walked they had ample opportunity of hearing what was being said all around them, but they had great difficulty in understanding it.

'Whatever language is that?' asked Mick of Paddy.

'Scotch, I suppose.'

'I thought they were drunk.'

'What a heathen tongue it is,' said Sean. 'Can't they speak the English like everyone else does?'

'You mean like us?' said Mick.

Paddy grinned at his brothers. 'Maybe they don't think they're like everyone else.'

'What are they so excited about?' asked Sean.

'Mafeking's relieved.'

'What did you say?'

'Mafeking. It's been relieved.'

'Why, what was wrong with it?'

'It's the South African War. Did ye's not hear on the boat?'

'No.'

'Sean, what world are ye livin' in?' cried Paddy. 'Did ye not hear about all the celebrations?'

'God save us, they're celebrating a war?'

'Or the end of it.'

There was a grunt from under the trunk and Paddy and Mick watched as the cabin trunk slid slowly down Sean's back and on to the cobbles. Just as slowly, Sean straightened up.

'Right our Michael, your turn.'

'Right our Patrick!' said Michael.

THREE

And so it was, on that late May afternoon, two very different families found themselves in Glasgow. Two very different backgrounds, two very different cultures, two very different houses in every way, but each with the common purpose of starting again and finding a new life in another land. Not only were these contrasting clans in the same city, they were in the same part of that city and virtually in the same street. For as the O'Neil boys made their way east towards Pier 3 on the Broomielaw, at that same moment, the overladen Keith horse and cart was turning from Dunlop Street and towards the Broomielaw and Pier 5 where the Mataura was berthed, waiting. It would have to wait a bit longer.

The Keiths' luggage cart had come to a complete halt at the corner of the Jamaica bridge where it joins the Broomielaw. Such was the crowd and the press of horse-drawn vehicles that it was impossible for anything to move. Neither right nor left nor forward, and not all the shouting, swearing, cursing or begging by drivers, passengers and on-lookers alike looked likely to ease the situation. The carter wanted to go straight ahead, but a horse tram was in his path, at least the horse was. It, in turn, was blocked by a hansom that wanted to turn into Clyde Street, so that an impasse was attained. Everybody was shouting advice to everybody else and not always in the politest terms either. All thoughts of celebration were momentarily forgotten as tempers frayed and tongues snapped. Bobby Keith made his way round to the driver.

'Can you not do something?' he shouted.

The sad old driver only shrugged. Bobby was beginning to get annoyed. They were now almost at Pier 3 on the Broomielaw – he could see all the different ships berthed at the dockside and somewhere in that long line was the Mataura. So near and yet . . .! He was also worried about the amount of luggage they had on the cart. Some of the smaller pieces had already fallen into the street and he could see them becoming a temptation to some of the more dubious passers-by in the crowd. He was sure a group was already

48

following them. The sooner they were all on board the better. He glanced back to Jim. He made a sign that he would check the ladies on the other side. Bobby nodded. Then he heard a quiet voice.

'Uncouple the tram horse.'

It was his father, sitting up on the cart.

'The driver would never do that!' said Bobby.

'No, but you could,' replied Mr Keith evenly, while calmly re-lighting his pipe. Traffic behind the Keiths was now building up heavily. Something had to be done. Bobby went forward to the horses. He beckoned Jim, who came forward with a puzzled look on his face. He was even more puzzled when Bobby started working at the traces of the tram horse in front of them.

'Here, wait a minute there –' shouted a Glasgow voice. It was the tram driver. Bobby paid no attention and worked all the faster.

'Jim!'

'Ay, Bobby?'

'When I let this one go, you run ours through.'

Jim wasn't so sure, but he replied at once that he would.

'GERRUP THERE!' It was Bobby slapping the tram horse hard and the free horse jerked away to the side leaving a gap through which Jim ran the cart-horse – as fast as a cart-horse runs at least. In minutes, the impasse was cleared. The swaying luggage cart was clear and was on its last stretch along the Broomiclaw towards their Pier, but Bobby, running after it, was still uneasy. The louts following them had grown into what was beginning to look like a mob. Unless they got there soon there could be trouble.

It was like swimming, Denis thought, as he pushed his way through the crowds, swimming through sticky porridge at that. He kept glancing back at Noreen, her bonnet slightly askew by now, whose little face was as red as her hair as she bobbed up and down behind him, one hand firmly caught in the back belt of his Norfolk jacket.

'Are y'alright?' he called to her.

'Great!' was the answer. 'Isn't it worse than Newry Fair?'

'Keep hold now.'

Denis pushed forward with one hand and with the other patted his chest, checking the tickets in one pocket and his money-wallet in the other. He knew the risk of being in such a crowd and he was taking no chances. He had little money enough as it was and had no wish to see it lost to a Scotch thief. Uncle Michael's dollar windfall had not lasted long at home and now he had the last of it to see him and his brothers – and sister – across the Atlantic. They found Mr Bradley's office by being taken there by the first person they'd asked in the Glasgow street. An uncommon courtesy, Denis thought, but the little toothless man who became their guide through the mêlée thought nothing of it.

'Nae borra,' he said cheerfully. 'A've naethin' tae dae onyweys!'

Denis wondered if he should give him something, but even as he was thinking about it the little fellow with a 'Cheeribye' had turned and was gone among the passers-by. So that was a Glaswegian. Denis turned and read on the wall-plate 'Agent for Cunard Shipping Line'. Taking Noreen by the arm, he went in.

Mr Bradley was round, bald and just as helpful. He must have had asthma, for he wheezed and whistled as he talked. After hearing their names he returned in a minute from a back room with papers in his hand and motioned them to come along to the end of the counter.

'Got everything here,' he gasped. 'The O'Neil party – arranged from New York – four male, steerage, two female, third class cabin, sharing.'

'Er – one female,' interjected Denis.

'Eh?'

'Nellie didn't come.'

'Wis she sick?'

'I was the one that was sick,' piped up Noreen.

'Quiet, Noreen. No sir, you see, Nellie got married.'

'To Liam Murphy would you believe?'

'Noreen! As I was sayin' sir, me sister got married an' she'll not be goin' ye see.'

'Ah see. Well, that's an extra ticket we've got then. Is there onybody else ye'd like tae take? Like your auntie, or your girl-freen or somebody?'

'Denis doesn't like girls,' offered Noreen.

'Not at all,' said Denis. 'I like them fine, but –'

'It seems a shame tae waste a paid-up passage.'

'It is, sir, but I don't know anyone in Glasgow, sir, and all me aunties are married to me uncles!'

'It's some uncle you've got in America onywey, that can send fares for the lot o' ye like this.'

'That's Uncle Mick, sir. He's in the Police Force, and he's got this friend –'

'Say no more,' said Mr Bradley. 'Here, take your sister's ticket. Ye could always sell it, ye know. There's always somebody wants tae gae to tae America.'

'Is that so, sir?'

'Ay,' wheezed Mr Bradley, 'and thank God for it, or we'd be oot o' business and I'd have nae job eh?' He attempted to laugh, but it ended in a fit of coughing. In no time, however, the paper-work was processed, the tickets collected, hands shaken, thanks expressed, good-byes made and they were back on the street again.

'What way is it to the boat, Denis?' wailed Noreen.

'The way we came, what else?'

'I'm starved sick, so I am.'

'We'll eat when we get there. Come on.'

'I don't like the look of those two.'

Bobby Keith turned to see where his brother indicated. 'What two?' he asked, and glanced to the side of the cart where two very rough-looking types were following alongside, pushing against the crowd on that side of the pavement, laughing and pointing to Tina and her mother. One of them called out coarsely, 'Can ah shove yer cairt, missus?'

The other laughed again showing all his broken teeth. 'Some flittin' that eh?' And he spat foully. Tina quickly turned her head away. She felt she was going to be sick. She jumped as she felt a hand on hers. It was Bobby.

'It's alright, Tina.' He squeezed her hand. 'We haven't far to go.'

It was now the early part of the evening and the first of the gas-lamps on the street were being lit. Noreen was thrilled. They had nothing like this in Rosstrevor. The crowds seemed even greater as they made their way through towards the docks and Noreen felt the beginnings of an inexplicable panic. Even Denis felt uneasy as they were swept along. He had a rough idea of his bearings, but he wasn't sure. He knew if he kept bearing right he must come to the river. Noreen's fingers were on his belt again, so he pressed on through the people and the traffic as fast as he was able. He checked his pockets again. Yes, they were still there – their tickets to America. And that extra one. What on earth was he going to do with it?

The O'Neil brothers had eaten. A bowl of soup, a bit of cheese and a beer each and they still had change left over. Ten shillings went a long way in Glasgow. Now they sat by their luggage on the quay waiting for Denis, Noreen and the tickets. Nobody said anything but they were each just beginning to get a bit worried.

'That's the lights on,' said Mick.

'It's getting darker,' said Sean.

'That'll be why they'll have the lights on.'

'I shouldn't wonder,' said Sean.

They sat in silence for a bit.

'A grand night for a sail,' said Paddy.

And he took out his fob watch and looked at the time. Seven o'clock.

The clock at St Enoch station sounded out the hour as Denis and Noreen passed below in the square. He had the feeling that he had been driven off course a bit by the crowds, so he was very relieved to find his bearings again as he turned into Clyde Street. When he did however, he wasn't sure whether he turned right or left to Pier 3. As Noreen wryly pointed out, it must be one or the other. Denis stood and looked both ways. Then he made up his mind.

'Come on,' he said.

Sean O'Neil turned to his brother. 'Shall you and me, Mick, take a little stroll to ourselves and find that brother and sister of ours?'

'Are you sure Sean?' wondered Paddy. 'Denis said –'

'Denis said one of us had to keep an eye on our things here. Sure you can do that fine, Paddy. Mick an' me will see the sights, eh Mick?'

'Whatever ye say, Sean.'

'Right then. See ye, Paddy.'

'Don't you get lost now,' called out Paddy as the two young Irishmen ambled off along the quayside.

'A fine night for a walk,' said Sean to Mick.

''Tis that,' said Mick.

'Look at that, Denis.'

Noreen was pointing to the other side of the road. A man was at the head of a horse, pulling at its rein and holding it back. The horse was rearing up and a crowd was gathering round. 'Have you ever seen such a stuff on a cart?' she went on.

Just at that moment a young boy made a grab at one of the smaller bags and a young man at the back of the cart tried to stop him. It was almost as if it were a signal for the crowd to close in with a baying noise like hounds round the fox. Denis and Noreen watched as the carter rose, jumped off his cart and ran off through the crowd. An old man with a pipe in his mouth stood at the front cracking a whip at the mob, although some in the crowd were trying to prevent any looting and scuffles developed between the two factions.

'Oh see, Denis. The girl.' Noreen was on her tip-toes pointing to the side of the cart nearest them. They watched as one man, an ugly-looking specimen, suddenly lunged at a young girl who was sitting there with an older woman who was kicking out at the encroaching would-be pillagers. The man grabbed her legs and pulled her down. She screamed. The horse reared again. The old man cracked his whip in their faces and a fight developed at the back. The girl was nowhere to be seen.

'She's fallen,' cried Noreen and rushed forward.

'Noreen!' Denis cried, and ran after his sister.

'A bit of a hooley goin' on there,' Sean said casually to Mick as they approached on the other side of the street to watch the fight going on around the cart.

'Ah, they're rough, these Glasgow fellas,' said Mick. They were about to move on when Mick spotted his sister's red hair bobbing in the thick of it. Her bonnet nowhere to be seen. 'My God Almighty, that's Noreen!' he suddenly cried.

'And Denis!' said his brother.

Denis and Noreen by now had a young girl between them and were dragging her clear. Sean and Mick stood either side and kept off the thugs as the three got through.

'Take her to the doorway there, and I'll –' At this point someone struck him on the back of the head with a bottle. Denis wheeled round and felled the fellow.

'It's a good job ye have a hard head on ye, Denis!' yelled Sean.

'My God!' gasped Denis. 'What the hell have we got into?'

'Don't ask, just enjoy it,' replied Sean as he was hit with a stone. 'Jesus Christ!' he exclaimed and dived on the thrower.

'It's just like Nellie's wedding!' thought Mick as he and Bobby Keith suddenly came face to face – or rather, nose to nose – in the fracas.

'Friend or foe?' growled Bobby, the sweat pouring from him.

'He's a friend!' called out Denis, who was busy with the scoundrel who had pulled down the girl.

'Good!' said Bobby and turned back to the fracas.

In the doorway to the shop, Noreen and an old Glasgow woman attended to Tina, who by now was standing up in Noreen's arm.

'Is it the time of the month?' asked the old body, in a rough kindliness. Noreen wiped Tina's brow.

'More like the time o' night, missus. We just pulled her through all them legs out there.'

'I'm fine,' answered Tina. 'I just got a bit of a fright when that man – oh, what's happening?' She tried to struggle free from Noreen, who held her back with some help from the old body who reeked of cheap drink.

53

'It's alright now, don't you fret yoursel',' said Noreen soothingly.

'But my mother – my brothers – daddy –'

William Keith was still flailing around him although by this time he had his pipe in his other hand. The surprise was Mrs Keith. She was by this time standing beside her husband at the front wielding her umbrella with great effect. Tina struggled even more to get free. 'I must go to my family!' She suddenly pointed. 'Look, that man –!' Denis was with her mother, warding off her umbrella and obviously trying to tell her something. He kept pointing back to them.

'That man is my brother,' said Noreen. 'Hey, Denis,' she called. Denis jumped down and came hurrying towards them. Noreen saw he'd a lovely black eye.

'I was just trying to tell the woman that – and – she hit me – with – her bloody umbrell –' The last part of his sentence faded away and remained unfinished as he got his first real look at Christina Keith. She also was aware of Denis. Suddenly, she swooned in a faint. Denis caught her in his arms. At this point the old Glasgow woman uncorked a bottle from her bag and took a hefty swig.

'Dinna upset yersel' hen, nae man's worth it.'

Denis found himself staring down at the girl he was holding. Seemingly from a distance he heard Noreen's voice. 'See's her here, Denis.'

But Denis for some strange reason was reluctant to let her go. He had never in his life seen a lovelier girl. She made him feel something that he had never felt before. It was at this moment, and for the very first time in his life, that Denis O'Neil fell in love. At the same moment, whistles were heard and the clatter of horses' hooves. Noreen's voice was now shouting even more urgently, 'Denis, will you give her over?'

It was then that Christina's eyes opened and she found herself looking into his eyes. There was a sound of running feet. 'It was that man,' she repeated faintly.

'It's alright,' said Denis hoarsely, his heart fluttering like a bird's.

'I can't thank you enough, Mr O'Neil. Mr O'Neil?'

William Keith gave Denis a nudge. Denis started. 'Eh?'

'I said I can't thank you and your brothers enough for coming to our help like that.'

'Sure, it was nothing sir, nothing at all.'

'Nonsense, we would have been in a sore pickle if you hadn't come on the scene the way you did. We are in your debt. If there's anything we can do –'

'There is something, sir.' Denis looked around. He was quite embarrassed. The two men were standing at the foot of the gangplank at Pier 5 and the hull of the Mataura loomed above their heads. On the deck, passengers looked down and he knew that Mrs Keith and Tina were standing by the lifeboat. Denis was sure Tina was looking down at him but he daren't look up.

'Well?'

He heard Mr Keith's voice but he couldn't answer. He didn't know how to say it. He could just hear his brothers and Noreen laughing with the Keith boys, one of whom, the younger one, had a bandage on his brow, but Denis felt just as far away from them too. He had to do something. There wasn't much time.

'Mr Keith?'

'Ay'.

'There is something.'

'Ay?'

'I'd like to have your permission to speak to your daughter for a minute.'

'Oh?'

'I won't keep her long.'

William Keith said nothing but there was a knowing look in his eye. He turned and looked up to the ship's rail. 'Christina! Ay you. Will ye come down here for a minute. There's a gentleman here would like to speak to you.'

Denis ignored his brother's jibes and the looks of the Keith brothers and the stares of Noreen as he faced Christina Keith. He was suddenly conscious of his black eye.

'Och, your eye,' said Tina softly.

'It'll be fine,' said Denis, and he found he was hoarse again.

'Sure, I have got another one.'

Tina didn't understand at first, then she laughed. The sound of it thrilled him but he didn't know what to say. He knew what he wanted to say but he daren't. He wanted to say 'I love you girl!' He wanted to shout it. He wanted to tell her to stay. 'Don't go! Stay! Stay with me!' The voices inside him were pounding in his ears. His legs were shaking but he managed to blurt out, still not looking at her, 'Listen –'

'Yes?' replied Tina, perhaps too eagerly.

'I wanted to ask you something?'

'Yes?' She wondered why her heart was racing, she could hardly breathe.

'Listen now – Oh God – Christina. We've only just met but –'

'Yes?'

'But I wondered – I wondered if ye'd like to go to Americkay with us?'

'What?'

'Ye see, I have this spare ticket on me –' He pulled it from his pocket and tried to press it into her hand. She pulled back slightly but he persisted and the words tumbled out: 'See, here it is – it was meant for me sister like and she got married back home and since I had the ticket anyway and it's paid for an' all, I thought that you'd like to have it rather than see it go to waste. It cost a lot of money a thing like that and I could have sold it easily enough but I wanted you to have it Christina, because you see – O God help me – I LOVE YOU!'

There! He had said it and he had said it exultantly and tumultuously, but she hadn't heard a word! For almost as soon as Denis had begun to speak, his words were drowned in the first blast of the ship's horn, which called the passengers aboard. He grabbed her elbows and shouted as loud as he could: 'Do ye hear me girl, I love ye!'

He saw her lips move as the hooter sounded again and bells clanged and people shouted and then Bobby and Jim began to pull their sister towards the gangplank. Denis saw she was crying and ran after her, but a sailor stopped him as the gangplank was being cleared away, and Denis realised that his brothers were holding his arms and that bells and sirens and shouts and calls were sounding all at once and he was crying too . . .

Later that night, Denis O'Neil stood on the deck of the Campania looking down on the oily waters of the Clyde as the last of the sun-set reddened the horizon. He was still thinking of Christina Keith. God, hadn't he made the clown of himself? Who cares? He meant it, every single word of it. He'd known the girl for no more than an hour or two, but he knew he loved her, and would love her for the rest of his life. And she knew. He knew she knew. He hadn't heard what she said but he knew what she meant. She loved him. He knew it. He knew it in his bones. In his blood. In his heart. He also knew he would never see her again. She had gone to the other side of the world. New Zealand. Bloody hell! She might as well have gone to the moon. He took the ticket out of his pocket again and looked at it. What if it had said – 'Christina Keith – spinster', or better still – 'Christina Keith – wife of –' NO! No, best not to think of it. Best to forget all about it. Pretend that it never really happened.

But it had happened. And in a cabin of the SS Mataura somewhere in the Clyde estuary with Scotland still faintly on the horizon at the stern, Christina Keith lay on the small bunk and cried her heart out. It was silly, it was strange, it was impossible but it was true. She loved the black-haired, black-eyed Irishman she'd met and lost in a day. Oh, why had I to leave Scotland? What was he saying in all the noise of the ship's hooters and the bells? He was saying he loves me. I know he was. I know because I love him and he knows it as well as I do. Oh Denis! There was a knock at the cabin door.

'Just a minute!'

She sat up, trying hard to dry her face on a stupid little hankie. 'Come in.'

It was her father. She rose and ran to him. 'Oh Daddy!' She threw her arms around him.

'You must love him very much,' he said softly. She pulled back from him, startled.

'How do you know?'

'Because I love YOU!'

'Oh Daddy!' Tina hugged into the comfortable, serge-suited, tobacco-smelling, familiar embrace and felt like a little girl again.

'Come on now, Christina,' he said gently over the top of her head, 'it's time to go up to the dining-room. You can't miss your dinner.'

'I'm not hungry.'

'I know but you can pick at something. It's just that your mother frets, you know how she is, and your brothers don't like to think of you down here moping. Will you come up with me?'

'Yes, daddy. But daddy –?'

'Yes?'

Tina felt a sudden surge of anxiety, or was it embarrassment? 'You won't say anything about – I mean – you know?'

'I know. Not a word. Anyway, do you think I'd get a word in with Bobby?' Despite herself, Tina laughed and in a few moments she followed her father out and along the narrow corridor and down to the second class dining saloon forward. The Keiths had a second sitting place and had a good table on the port side. On the Mataura, as was the custom on The New Zealand Shipping Line, passengers were often joined at the evening meal by one of the younger ship's officers.

On that first night, a smart Second Officer introduced himself as Martin Dickenson, from Newcastle, and asked permission to join them. Bobby made much play of the fact that their table was reserved for Scottish citizens only and that they would have to consider seriously whether to admit an Englishman! Martin affably maintained that he wasn't an Englishman, he was a Geordie, and promptly sat down between the two Keith brothers. Bobby kept him amused by recounting their Broomielaw adventure in great detail. None of the Keiths thought it was all that funny – especially Tina. When he was going on about the cart driver's running away and the fact that their luggage was brought to the ship's side and loaded by three young Irishmen, one of whom got a black eye for his trouble, Tina caught her father's eye across the table. He was looking at her and almost imperceptibly shook his head. Tina bent hers and picked lamely at some vegetables. Second Officer Dickenson laughed at all the right places in Bobby's recounting, but wondered why the attractive girl opposite said nothing throughout the entire meal. Not that she had much of a chance to get a word in!

Denis O'Neil took the steamship ticket in his hand and suddenly, almost viciously, tore it into pieces and threw them into the water. He closed his eyes tight shut and his knuckles whitened as he grasped hard at the ship's rail. Simultaneously, and quite inadvertently, his lips formed her name – TINA. He said it aloud but whether it was a curse or a prayer it was hard to tell, it was said so fervently. He felt a shiver of cold go through him and noticed that the sun had started to come up over the cranes now receding behind them as the SS Campania made its way out to the Atlantic. He was aware of the engine reverberation through the deck planks. God, he must have been standing here for hours.

'Denis!'

He turned and Paddy was coming towards him. 'What the hell are you playin' at? D'ye realise ye've been standin' out here all night? Do ye want to catch your death afore we start?'

'Sorry Paddy. I didn't realise –' He put his arm round Paddy's shoulder. 'Ach, to hell with it!' he said.

And as Denis hurried away below with his young brother, he never looked back. Nor did he look down. Had he done so, he would have seen the pieces of ticket in the water floating gently away on the lamp-lit, oil-skimmed, dawn-dappled water and out in the direction of the open sea.

FOUR

Steerage is not the way to travel at sea. What was designed for beasts is not the most salubrious accommodation for twentieth-century passengers even if that century was still in its first year. The sleeping area or dormitory, if one can call it that, was so far down in the ship's bowels that the next floor down was the sea-bed. A range of various mattresses was laid along the floor by the bulkhead, separated only by fixed wooden lockers which gave each mattress a small cupboard and an even smaller drawer. Neither of these was lockable. It was not thought that steerage passengers would have any possessions worthy of personal security. On the top of the cupboard was a linen towel containing a knife, a fork, a big spoon and a little one. There was also a large plate, small bowl and a tin mug. This little cache was contained by a narrow brass retaining frame around the top of the cupboard. Every receptacle was firmly marked as being the property of the Cunard Line Shipping Company. One wondered if the steerage passengers were similarly branded on embarkation. If they were there was no sign of it on either of the younger O'Neil brothers as they lay, arms flung wide, on their bed-rolls, on top of the company mattresses as blissfully asleep as if they were ensconced in palatial four-posters. Paddy and Denis stood looking down at them.

'Would you look at that,' said Paddy to Denis, 'that's been them since they come down here.'

'It's the clear conscience, ye see,' said Denis.

'It's the cheap beer, ye mean. We were hardly out of the harbour before they were at the little bar there for fourpence a pint. I should never have let Sean keep the change out o' that ten-shillin' note!'

'He'd've got it out of ye anyway. You know our Sean.'

Denis gave a big yawn. 'God, I'm bejaiskit, indeed I am,' he said, sitting on the mattress. 'It's been quite a day.'

'Serves you right,' said his brother, already with his boots and trousers off and getting under the two rough blankets. There were no sheets in steerage. 'Standing up there on the deck all hours and baying at the moon like a sick calf. Here Denis, see's over me coat there. I'll freeze here, I'm thinkin'. I'd advise you to do the same.'

Denis threw over the thick coat to Paddy who spread it over the blankets and put his head down quickly on the small round bolster. Denis did the same and in that growing early morning light he and Paddy were just two more inert, blanketed bodies heaped over with various coats and garments against the chill of their iron dormitory. Just then, Mick gave a mighty snore.

'Would ye listen to that?' said Paddy.

Denis wriggled about trying to get himself comfortable.

'Denis?'

'Yes?'

'Do you want to talk about it?'

'About what?'

'Fine and well you know. That girl. On the dockside.'

Denis didn't answer for a moment or two. When he did, it was quite definite. 'No,' he said.

'Fine,' said Paddy and turned over to face the other side. The one word had told him all he wanted to know, but in his heart the gentle Paddy said a silent prayer to God for his big brother's pain. At the same time, perhaps by religious telepathy, a not-so-silent prayer was being intoned by a bearded figure down at the very end of the mattress line. A man had already risen against the early morning light from the porthole and the sound of his soft intoning could be heard over the grunts, snores, moans and mumbles of forty-two sleeping men in that long narrow space. Denis looked up. 'What in the name o' God is that?' he whispered.

'The Talmud,' said Paddy.

'What?'

'Jewish.'

'Oh?'

'There's all kinds here, Denis.'

'I'm sure.'

Sean moved on the other side of him and Denis felt a kind of satisfaction in knowing they had made it – all of them. They were on board the big ship and Amerikay-bound! Just like all these other souls. There were sounds of stirrings now and the growl of a conversation in some foreign language was heard. Despite the spartan bedding, Denis begin to feel himself getting warm and drowsy. Yes, he was tired. He felt his right eye tenderly. It was still painful. That stupid umbrella. The thought brought back the other memories and they were painful too. He turned over and

tried not to think about them. Or her. She'd be miles away by now
. . . hundreds of miles away . . . miles away . . .

Clang-clang-clang-clang-clang-clang-clang-clang! The noise woke
Noreen with such a start that she sat up from sleep and thumped
her head on the bunk bed above her. The sound of laughter was
even louder than her own yelp of pain and as she lifted her head out
of her hands she found herself staring at two female faces gazing at
her from the other side of the room, each of them trying to hide
their smiles behind raised blankets. Then Noreen remembered –
she was on a ship, yes, the Campania – and it must be morning
and the two faces opposite belonged to the Fraser twins, Jenny and
Janey, with whom she was to share Third Class Cabin C198 all the
way to New York! They had all met last night in the ablutions room
at the end of their gangway. Oh yes, she remembered now, and she
rubbed her scalp dolefully.
  'Oh, did ye hurt your –' began Jenny, who was the elder by five
minutes.
  '– head?' finished Janey, who was the cleverer by a long way.
  Noreen was to learn the hard way about the twin sisters' habit
of halving the sentences. 'No,' said Noreen, 'I just forgot.'
  'She forgot,' echoed Janey.
  'She forgot her head!' added Jenny, and they both giggled again.
  There's going to a murder on board, a double murder – and
soon, thought Noreen as she put on her coat over her nightdress
and picked up her towel.
  'Are you going –'
  '– for your wash?'
  'Yes.'
  She couldn't help glancing at the empty top bunk as she opened
the cabin door, and it gave her a twinge. She suddenly wished
Nellie were there. Noreen had never really got on with her big
sister around the house, but she missed her now. She missed
her calm, good sense, whatever the situation. Nellie would have
sorted out the Fraser twins in quick time. As she walked along the
corridor, she remembered that Nellie hadn't even been nervous on
her wedding day. Liam Murphy will know all about it now. At the
thought, Noreen couldn't help smiling to herself. But the splash of
cold sea water in the primitive wash-room soon wiped the smile
from her face. However, Noreen's farm life had well prepared her
for cold comforts like this and it was a bright, shining, red-cheeked
young girl, the picture of youthful, glowing health, who eventually
escaped the duplicating Frasers and climbed all the stairs upwards
to find her brothers and breakfast.

Noreen, because of her cabin ticket, was allowed meals in the lower class dining saloon, but she preferred, this first morning at least, to take literal pot luck with her brothers. It was either that or the Fraser girls for another hour! So she hurried up on deck to look for the boys. They and all the other steerage passengers had to stand in a line for their meals, if one could call them meals. Porridge, toast and tea at eight in the morning, soup and potatoes, occasionally with a scrap of mutton at noon, tea again with hard biscuits at four in the afternoon, and tea with bread and butter at sundown, around six. And this was to be their unchangeable daily diet for the whole of the two-week voyage. No one was going to get fat on the Cunard Line Shipping Company! No wonder the steerage passengers made frequent recourse to the makeshift bar some crew members had set up near the bows underneath the foc's'le. Here, they sold cheap beer, tobacco and vicious spirits made up from various left-overs from First and Second Class. No attempt was made by the ship's company to make the lot of the steerage any better. They were still, in a sense, cattle to be transported. This was perhaps the reason why the rough and ready foc's'le bar became the social centre and ancillary canteen for all the steerage passengers during the voyage. It was also a kind of shop or bazaar and many of the passengers, short of spending cash for extra items, would stand with all kinds of goods, some of them valuable pieces of jewellery, or knitted garments, or even their best leather suitcase, and try to sell them to their fellow-passengers. A ruthless person with some ready cash, English or American, could have picked up a few bargains, especially as some of the sellers had a limited understanding of both the English language and its currency. Quite a few bargains were picked up in those few days at sea, for there is never a shortage of ruthless people in the world, and the complement of any ship at any time is a small world in itself.

On the first day out, however, people are still a bit shy with each other and things were rather quiet about the main decks. Which didn't prevent a certain rosy-cheeked colleen getting more than her share of approving glances from seamen and male passengers alike as she sought out her family. Her charms were especially noted by one deck-officer on the bridge, who, being on look-out duty, entirely accidently, caught her in the lens of his telescope. As he adjusted focus, Fourth Officer Teddy Bishop from Slough remarked: 'Ay, ay – female attraction by the starboard side and coming up fast. Flying a neat colour and showing the trimmest of lines. This voyage could be promising.' Luckily, no one heard him.

Noreen found Paddy first. He was sitting on a hatch, reading an old newspaper he had found. He hardly looked up as she called out to him.

'Noreen. Did you know that the World Amateur Championships were held in Paris?'

'Is that a fact?' she said without interest.

'May 14th, they started,' went on Paddy. 'They're going to call them The Olympic Games.'

'Fascinating,' said Noreen dully, looking around. 'Where's the boys?'

'They're still in the queue.'

She found the three of them looking very glum indeed, standing with their plates and cutlery, behind a group of black-hatted, voluble Jews.

'Good morning!' said Noreen brightly. There was a mumbled response from the brothers.

'Have you had your breakfast?' asked Denis.

'No, I came to join youse.'

'You're mad,' said Sean, 'when you can sit down to bacon and eggs in the saloon?'

'And to the Frasers?'

'What do you mean?'

She explained, but the young men were not impressed. 'Anything would be worth a good breakfast,' said Mick. And this was the kind of reasoning that led to Denis, Sean and Michael escorting their baby sister back to the lower saloon dining-room, where she ordered not one, not two, not three, but four cooked breakfasts from the galley which were hugely enjoyed by all concerned.

'You'll have me thrown overboard!' protested Noreen.

'Sure you can swim,' said Denis.

The highlight of the steerage day came to be the impromptu dance that was held each evening – weather permitting – on B Deck after the six o'clock bread and tea. Several of the Continental passengers brought out musical instruments. There was a violin, an accordion, a melodeon and a dulcimer, and in no time they were an orchestra! Their improvised arrangements of waltz tunes and simple one-steps hurdled all frontiers of language and nationality and Pole danced with Greek, German with Romanian, English with French and the Irish with whoever was left! Noreen O'Neil caused something of a sensation by being the cause of deck officers visiting steerage for the first time on the voyage. Led by Fourth Officer Bishop, a raiding party came most nights from the officers' mess with eyes only for the main prize – a red-headed colleen with fire in her eyes and laughter in her voice. She was protected however, on most occasions, by the company she kept – her two brothers, Sean and Mick, who were beginning to have their own problems with the Fraser twins! Paddy found a chess partner in a Scandinavian bookseller and Denis kept himself to himself. But on the second night out he found himself dancing with a charming little Bohemian girl called Hana Karpiskova. They made a striking couple, his lean, dark Irishness, her lithe, blonde, pert, Continental shapeliness. Watching them, people would nudge each other, nod and wink and make gestures, little realising that Denis and Hana had never even said a word to each other. And couldn't have, even if they wanted to, as she had no English at all. And Denis didn't have all that much either! Never mind, all the world loves a lover and the world was determined that since they looked so good together they must therefore be together. But only brother Paddy, watching from his similarly-silent chess game with Sven the Swede, knew the truth of the matter.

Most of the Keith family were good sailors. Only Mrs Keith showed any kind of stress as the Mataura rose and fell in its stormy voyage across the Bay of Biscay and down past Spain and Portugal towards Gibraltar. The sea was rough as it nearly always is in this part of the Atlantic Ocean and good, porridge-lined stomachs such as the Keiths possessed were certainly the best defence against the ups and downs of sea travel. Sea legs however, were another matter and Florence Keith had not so far found hers. The Mataura had now been three days at sea and just over the horizon on the port side was Lisbon, but Mrs Keith still preferred to remain in her cabin. Tina felt obliged to keep her company. She did not find this the most ideal way to spend the long sea days, but Mrs Keith had no desire to leave the snug security of her bunk and the reassurance of the next door toilet. Tina had little to say to her mother; she would much rather have been up on deck with her brothers, but she was quite happy to sit and read her book. At least, she was happy to look as if she were reading it. In reality she was glad of the excuse to let her thoughts wander to another ship . . .

Florence had her own thoughts and it would have surprised Tina to know just how much her mother thought about her, cared for her and worried for her, but like her generation of Scotswomen, Mrs Keith held that it wasn't a woman's place to question the whys and wherefores of any situation but to get on with it and see each day through to the next with as little fuss and bother as possible. The thing to do was to get on with the thing in hand.

For Florence Keith, on this particular May morning with the seas running quiet for once and the yellow sun bright at the porthole, it was her crochet patch. She had decided to make a bed cover. As her fingers worked on the wool, Florence too let her thoughts wander. She wondered about John and his wife – even in her thoughts, Mrs Keith could never think of Thomasina by name – John was far too soft with her. He should have been more like Bobby. Her Bobby. She smiled. Even the thought of Bobby could make her smile. She glanced up at her daughter, but Tina's head was buried deep in her book as usual. Florence sighed. Why had they never been close? But even as a little girl, Tina had never been affectionate. At least, never with her. Only with her father. Twenty years of age and still no husband. It was very different in my day, she thought, hardly out of the school and they had you running up the aisle to the altar! But then it was different for me, she mused, I wasn't pretty – well, not as pretty as Tina. At that very moment Tina glanced up at her mother, their eyes met for a second, and she smiled before bending back to her book. Yes, her mother thought softly, she's very pretty. There was another long silence before her mother spoke again.

'What was his name?'

'Who?' replied Tina, still reading.

'That young man in Glasgow? Mind, the one that was with his sister.'

Tina felt her heart jump, and the blush rising warmly on her cheeks. She kept her head down. 'Oh yes.' She tried to sound as non-committal as she could.

'He seemed very nice.'

'Yes.' Tina was sure her mother could hear the thudding of her heart.

'What was it he was saying to you that time?'

'When?'

'Mind – at the docks. Just afore we sailed.'

'Oh yes.' Her throat was dry.

'Well?'

'I can't remember – I mean – I couldn't hear.'

'You were standing next to him.'

'I know – but it was the noise. The bells – you know –' How could she tell her mother? How could she possibly explain to her mother that she had fallen in love with a man for the first time in her life – and only for an afternoon? A man she would probably never see in her life again?

'What's the matter?'

'I don't know. I think I need a drink of water.'

'There's a tumbler by the side of you there.'

Tina rose quickly, dropping her book on the floor. 'No, I think I need some fresh air.'

'Are you alright?'

'I'm fine.'

'You've dropped your book.'

'I'll be back in a minute.' Tina almost ran from the cabin. Her mother shook her head and went back to her crochet.

'I can never talk to that lassie,' she muttered to herself.

As Tina opened the door on to the upper deck and stepped over the high door frame, she almost knocked down one of the ship's officers who was passing. It was Martin Dickenson, dressed in grimy overalls with oil on his brow. He quickly drew himself together and gave her a playful salute. 'Permission to proceed, Ma'am?' he grinned. Tina was flustered.

'I'm so sorry,' she said.

'That's alright, Miss Keith,' said Martin, 'I was drifting too near the bulkhead.'

Tina smiled weakly. 'Yes' she said, and moved over to the rail. He followed her.

'You OK, Miss?'

'I'm fine, thank you – er –'

'This morning I'm unofficial Second Engineer. Just helping old Jock out.'

'Of course.'

'He's a bit under the weather – or so he says. I think he took another kind of cargo aboard when we took in water at Vigo.' He laughed and Tina couldn't help noticing his fine white teeth. 'Are you looking for your brothers?'

'Yes,' replied Tina quickly, 'Yes, I was.'

'They're generally up for'ard this time o'day. Sorry, I can't take you up there, but –' he indicated his overalls and grinned again – 'I'm not dressed for escort duty.'

'It's quite alright, Mr Dickenson –'

'Please call me Martin.'

'But not when you're on duty surely?'

He drew himself up again and gave her another salute. 'Ma'am. With your permission.' He was about to turn away, but stopped himself.

'Are you sure you're alright?' he said quietly.

'Of course I am.' She turned away and leaned on the ship's rail, looking out to sea. 'I was wondering where America was,' she said after a moment.

'About three thousand miles off starboard.'

'MR DICKENSON!' An authoritative voice called from somewhere above them.

'Ay-ay, sir!'

He was gone as she turned round. She was almost relieved and gladly turned back to the sea again – the vast, endless, unrelenting, unfathomable sea: green, grey, black and white all at once and darkly mysterious under a white sky. She leaned forward on her arms, feeling the warm, polished wood of the rail under her breasts. She was glad to be part of all this, even if it were only for a time of her life. There were no landmarks on the ocean, no fixed points, no limits, only unending water into which she could pour all her confusions and imaginings and lose them in the limbs of its natural and awesome immensity. For once, the sea's strangeness and enormous power didn't frighten her. In a way, she felt soothed, comforted even. He too was somewhere on this strange ocean. Perhaps he was leaning on a ship's rail, looking back the way he had come to where they had been only a few days before. Then again, perhaps he wasn't. She straightened up. This is silly, she thought. I must just forget all about it. There's no point. She felt herself starting to get angry. Why had it happened anyway? She hadn't asked to meet him. She hadn't meant to fall in love, had she? Had she? Oh God, this is terrible!

Christina Keith was a sensible, level-headed girl and she resented having her control shaken like this. She decided to take a brisk turn round the decks. They said if you walked round the deck six times it was the equivalent of a mile. Taking a deep breath, she turned and set off purposefully. She wondered for a moment which was starboard, but she quickly put the thought out of her head and strode on. She passed the Goanese sailors swabbing the already-pristine deckboards. They averted their eyes as she came towards them but she could feel the same dark, brown eyes boring into her back once she was safely past. Other passengers were on similar exercise, but none was applying him or herself as vigorously as Miss Keith, so perhaps it was not so surprising that she didn't hear the voice at first.

'Tina!'

When she glanced round to her left, she saw it was her father. Mr Keith, still in his Forres suit, but minus Inverness cape, was sitting smartly upright in a deck-chair while all about him were prone.

'Daddy! I never saw you.'

'Nor heard me neither. I saw you the first time round but you were past me before I could get the pipe out of my mouth.'

'Sorry.'

'Not at all. Glad to see you so active.'

'More than I can say for you.'

67

'When you get to my age, lass, it's the mind you have to keep active. Not an easy matter on board a ship, I can tell you.'

She sat down on the deck beside him. 'What are you reading?' He showed her.

'Walter Scott?' she exclaimed.

'The Waverley Novels,' said her father wryly, 'all twenty-five of them from *Guy Mannering* to *Castle Dangerous*. With a bit of luck we'll reach New Zealand before I'm half way through them. It was either that or Mr Dickens. I thought I'd better stick to what I know.'

'Oh Daddy. Where did you find them?'

'Mr Aitken, the Engineer. He has them all in his cabin. I called in to see him last night.'

'Was it you that got him drunk?'

'What?'

'He's been off this morning apparently?'

'How did you know that?'

'Martin told me.'

'Who?'

'Mr Dickenson.'

'Oh yes. Martin is it? He's the young officer at our table. They're supposed to rotate, you know.'

'What?'

'I mean they are supposed to change tables. I notice that our Mr Dickenson has been with us since Glasgow.'

Tina said nothing but adjusted her position so that her head lay back against his chair. She closed her eyes against the warmth of the sun and her ears against the background of mumbled conversation. She heard her father's voice as if from miles away.

'I also noticed that the Goanese sailors appreciated your passing.'

She smiled. 'I felt it. But they don't mean any harm. They're all Catholics anyway.'

'What is that supposed to mean?'

'I don't know. That's what Bobby said.' There was a pause. She felt herself getting quite drowsy. It was really quite pleasant and Tina could feel herself relaxing.

'I don't like Catholics.'

'What did you say, Daddy?'

'I said I don't like Catholics.'

Tina, for some reason, suddenly felt herself freeze. 'But you don't know any Catholics.'

'That doesn't matter. They are all the same. Ignorant, priest-ridden, superstitious idolators. They represent the Anti-Christ,

and from birth to death, they are, every one of them, in thrall
to the whore of Rome.'

'Who?'

'The Pope. The Italian Pope.'

Tina could hardly believe her ears. She noticed too, that the
'sleepers' either side of her father were rigid with closed-eyed
attentiveness. 'Daddy how can you talk like this?'

'Because I am a good Scotsman and an elder of the Kirk.'

'What's that got to do with it?'

Her father leaned forward. 'Lassie, don't ye know –' He himself
also realised they were the cynosure of all ears around them and
his innate good taste if not good sense stopped him abruptly. The
resulting silence was almost audible as a good dozen pairs of ears
around them strained to hear. He sat up.

'I'll go and see your mother. Do you want to come down
with me?'

'No, I don't!'

'Aye.' He reached down and kissed the top of her head and then
without a word she watched his legs cross her lowered eyes and
heard his steps, in those very Scottish boots, go tramping down the
wooden deck. As the quiet mumble of unintelligible conversation
resumed, she struggled to her feet, embarrassed and confused.
What was happening to her world all of a sudden? She almost ran
along the deck. Why had he turned so vehement so suddenly? And
about Catholics. What is so important about Catholics? Catholics
are not us, are they? They're foreign. They're Italian, Spanish,
French, Irish. She stopped suddenly. Irish? Oh God, was that
why her father was so angry? But how could he know? About
Denis? Even as the name came into her consciousness, she felt
dizzy. Goodness, was she going to faint?

'Seasick again, Teenie?'

There was no mistaking Bobby's voice. 'What's my little sister
doing running like a hare on the upper deck?'

She didn't answer.

'Do you want to be sick?'

'NO!'

William Keith found his wife supping from a bowl of soup on
a tray. 'I was coming to ask if you wanted anything,' he said.

'It was that nice black man brought me this just a minute ago.'

'It was the steward.'

'I don't know his name.' Florence supped away quite heartily.
For a self-created cabin invalid she certainly had a hearty
appreciation of her victuals.

'Aren't you hungry, William?'

69

'No,' answered her husband, removing his jacket and waistcoat, 'I had a good breakfast.' He took out a hanger from the narrow steel locker and hung them up. Oddly, he never thought to loosen his tie or remove his stiff collar.

'But that was hours ago, surely?' said his wife.

'Ay.'

Mrs Keith wiped her mouth with her napkin and said nothing. She recognised that her husband was in one of his quiet moods, and she knew from long practice that the best thing to do was to leave him in it. He would come out of it in his own time, he always did. She took a sip from the glass of iced water and put it on the tray again. William lifted the tray from her lap without a word.

'Thank you, William.' She settled herself back on the narrow bunk as best she could. 'My, I miss my big bed,' she sighed.

She heard the tray being put down rather hard on the dividing ledge between their bunks. 'Careful now, William.'

'What's this?'

'What?'

'This bottle here.'

She looked over. William was holding a small bottle in his hand.

'Oh ay. That was the black man. He thought I was sick.'

'What is it?'

'Holy water, he said. It'll cure anything, he said.'

'For God's sake!' William stared down at the bottle. The faint sign of a cross still visible. The Goanese steward. A Catholic! Without a word he turned and threw the bottle through the open port hole!

'William!'

Bobby and Tina eventually found Jim sitting alone in a line of empty deck chairs, obliviously reading a book.

'Don't tell me,' called Tina as they approached. 'It's *Oliver Twist*!'

Jim looked up startled. 'As a matter of fact, it's *A Christmas Carol*,' he said.

'It had to be Dickens.'

'How did you know?'

'Just call it woman's intuition,' answered his sister, taking one of the empty seats and desperately, almost hysterically, trying to be cheerful. Bobby gave Jim a glass of beer.

'See if your male instincts can tell a warm lager from a stale beer.'

'Thanks. All the best.'

'And so say all of us,' said Bobby, sitting back on the other chair.

'The Ghost of Christmas Present,' said Jim for no apparent reason.

'What are you talking about?' asked Bobby.

'Tina's dress,' said Jim. '"A simple green robe". That's what the Ghost wore in the story. In *A Christmas Carol*. The Ghost wore a green gown. Tina's wearing a green gown. That's all.'

'It's the Irish in her,' mumbled Bobby with closed eyes.

'DON'T SAY THAT!' Tina almost screamed the words before bursting loudly into tears and running off towards the cabin stairs. Bobby rose up open-mouthed:

'What did I say?'

Jim didn't answer but he looked thoughtful. After a moment he said, 'I think it might be something to do with that Irish fellow. Remember at the docks in Glasgow?'

'Oh yes,' said Bobby. 'The Irish family.'

'That's right. One of them took a fancy to Tina, I think.'

'That's right,' said Bobby, 'what was their name again?'

'O'Neil, I think.'

'So it was. A whole parcel of them. The fighting O'Neils.' Bobby grinned at the memory of it.

'I wonder if they got to America?' said Jim.

'I tell you this, wee brother,' said Bobby taking a hefty swig of his beer, 'they'll be there, settled and bringing up a family before we have our first sitting.' Almost in one movement, he rose, removed the hankie from his head and picked up his jacket from the deck. 'Come on.' Then Jim rose up, and followed his brother, already striding purposefully towards the Saloon deck and lunch.

FIVE

'QUIET!'

The veins stood out on the official's neck as he yelled out. 'For chrissake!'

Order among the O'Neils is not the easiest thing to achieve at the best of times and almost impossible in the Babel that was Ellis Island, New York Harbour, in the summer of 1900. As far as the eye could see, the lines of nondescript immigrants with their bulging suitcases, paper parcels and assorted bags stretched from the bare warehouses that served as United States Customs and Immigration to the harbour walls, and beyond them to the quays where the ships that had just disgorged them waited to see if they had to take them all back. Some indeed did go back, generally for medical and criminal reasons, but for the most part, for thousands of hopeful Europeans, the stone lamp of the massive Statue of Liberty on Bedloe's Island never ceased to shine as they waited for hours, days or weeks to see if they could cross the mile of water that separated them from statelessness and the new world promised by the Battery Park and Manhattan Island.

> 'Give me your tired, your poor
> Your huddled masses yearning to breathe free,
> The wretched refuse of your teeming shore . . .'

There was no doubt that these refugees from all kinds of ships, and from most of the countries in Europe, were tired. They were certainly poor, and as they huddled against the off-shore breezes, they undoubtedly felt wretched. Not so the O'Neils. For them the adventure had begun from the moment they set foot on the cattle-boat from Belfast, and anything from there on could only be an improvement. Their documentation was finally completed despite them and the Immigration Officer was perhaps the most relieved man on the island to see the voluble Hibernians re-board the Campania carrying them to the mainland and a new life. But even they were somewhat silenced by the sight of their

72

fellow-immigrants made mute by their lack of English. This hapless contingent sat or stood in their squares marked by their armbands – black, white, brown, or green – waiting for interpreters or death, many already accepting the new surnames indicated by their armbands. Their particular colour was for the most part the first English word they ever learned. The next being 'sir'. Similarly, mispronunciations, misunderstandings, official deafness, fatigue and just plain stupidity gave people new names, new ages and even the occasional change of sex, but, thanks to their own resilience, the O'Neils avoided all this and all five of them finally set foot in America. But not without a few final hiccoughs.

The problem for Denis for instance, was Hana Karpiskova. Not so much Hana as her mother. The Prague family, including brother Frantisek, was among the first of the Continental groups to be landed, thanks largely to Hana's very slender grasp of English. The credit for this linguistic advance was due in no small measure to the young lady's determination to communicate with Denis O'Neil. For most of the voyage she had unashamedly pursued the young Irishman, but his apathy was exactly equal to her enthusiasm and the romance did not prosper after the novelty of the first impromptu dances. Nor was Hana's case much helped by her mother. This wily Slav, unlike any other mother in the history of amours, was extremely keen to advance Hana's cause with Denis. No doubt she saw a strong, young, English-speaking husband for her daughter as a valuable asset to any settlement in the United States. Whatever the reason, her constant running commentary in Czech caused Denis to retreat more and more into an Irish boorishness, which did nothing to relieve Hana's growing frustration. There were many times on the voyage when the young couple might indeed have formed a liaison, but the remorseless presence of the Bohemian anti-duenna prevented this.

Frantisek, the brother, was of no help either as he was studying hard to be a drunk and was never far from the for'ard bar. When asked anything he only smiled and nodded like a lunatic, so he wasn't asked much. Hana herself showed remarkable resource in the face of an impossible position. By remaining poised and ostensibly at ease throughout, she inched her way slowly into Denis's liking and then into his affection, and had the voyage been across the Pacific rather than the Atlantic there is just a possibility that her charming determination might in fact have won the day. Or night rather, for meetings when they could be alone together were more nocturnal than diurnal. There was never any hope that the affair could be consummated emotionally still less physically, and by the time that the Campania pointed her nose into New York harbour, Denis was tense and Hana was drained, but Mrs Karpiskova was as indefatigable as ever in her daughter's cause. Now here, at the very last stage of their mutual journey, in all the Babel-confusion of so many languages, dialects and patois, among the orders and counter-orders, cries and calls, prayers and pleas, Denis could only stare impassively while Hana's large eyes implored his. He could not hear a word as her lips moved earnestly but soundlessly in the din. He could also see tears in her eyes and somewhere Frantisek could be heard laughing. This had happened before. Then he remembered where and for a moment Hana's face blurred, but then her arms were about his neck and her full lips were on his and pressing fiercely. His young brothers meantime were no less bemused by the Fraser twins. Janey stared up at Sean in just the same way that Jenny gazed up at Michael.

'Will you –' said Janey.

'Write to us?' said Jenny.

'I don't know,' said Sean.

'Your address!' finished Michael unexpectedly. The boys stared at each other in surprise but the Frasers went on quite unconcernedly.

'We'd like to come and see you,' they chorused.

'Both of you,' said Jenny.

'At the same time!' added Janey.

'Ah, well you see, that's difficult.'

'Why?' asked Janey.

'Because we don't know where we're goin',' answered Sean.

'But if we get there we'll let you know,' said Michael.

'But how will you know where we are?' wailed Jenny.

'Sure you can write to us!' Michael went on.

'But we don't know –' started Janey.

'Your address!' finished both girls together.

This circular conversation might have gone on indefinitely in that tightly-pressed multitude of all nations on the dockside. Sean made an attempt to change tack.

'Listen girls,' he said, 'it's Noreen you should be talking to –'

'Where is she?' said Michael looking around.

'She's kissing –' began Jenny.

'Mr Bishop!' continued Janey.

'Again!' concluded Jenny.

'I don't see them,' said Sean.

'Maybe we're not supposed to,' muttered Michael.

Not that Noreen would have cared if they had. At that very moment she was with Teddy Bishop only a few yards away in a narrow space between two large packing cases hidden by various bales and bundles. They were locked in a tight embrace,

as they had been on much of the voyage. This was as much to
their mutual frustration as satisfaction, for their frequent tactile
collisions on board were more a matter of fierce contact than
anything else for the truth was both young people were still
virgins! All Noreen's natural instincts made her flirtatious but the
same instincts preserved her intact, often to her own irritation, but
she knew she was young yet, although ripening rapidly. Fourth
Officer Bishop pretended to be annoyed by getting no further than
touching, but secretly he was quite relieved. He was also impeded
by the fact that he had genuinely fallen in love with this wild Irish
girl and this confused him. Now he drew back from yet another
bruising kiss, as much to get some air as anything.

'Oh Noreen!' he panted.

'Ay,' whispered Noreen, 'what is it?' she said right into his ear.

'Nothing really,' answered the young sailor.

'My brother Paddy says it's a terrible thing to be kissed by a
Bishop!'

Teddy looked puzzled. 'I don't understand,' he said.

Noreen tossed her hair back. 'Sure isn't your name Bishop,
silly?'

'Oh yes.'

She laughed and impulsively he held her close to him again.
They were both muffled in coats and scarves, but he could feel
her softness just as much as she was aware of his hardness. His
heart was in his mouth and hers was fluttering like a bird's.

'Noreen?'

'Yes?'

Their tones were urgent now.

'Can I?' asked Teddy.

'What?'

'Touch you again?'

'Where?'

'You know – there.' This time it was he who spoke into her ear.
She shook her head free.

'I meant where could we go, stupid?'

'Here.'

'Are you mad altogether? Aren't my own brothers but a step
behind that bale. Do you want us killed?'

'No, but –'

'Anyway, shouldn't you be on the boat?' The little altercation
was sufficient to kill all passion in both of them and perhaps they
were just as glad to welcome reality again.

'I suppose you –?'

'We'd better get out, in case they start looking for me again.'

'Of course.'

After some sartorial adjustment, they emerged hand in hand
from their hiding place to be confronted by the mate of the
Campania – a huge Liverpudlian called Mercer, who was pushing
his way through the crowds and now came face to face with his
startled young ship mate.

'Mr Bloody Bishop!' roared the First Officer.

'Sir?' stammered the Fourth, dropping Noreen's hand as if it
scalded.

'Now that you've finished your kissin' an' canoodlin',' Mercer
went on, glaring at Noreen, 'you might bloody well get back where
you belong at the bottom of the gangway aft. Move sailor.'

'Ay sir.' And with that he was off running. Running as fast as he
could considering the crowds and the congestion. Running back
to work and out of Noreen O'Neil's life. The burly mate looked
down at her with a grin. 'He's much too young for you, darlin'. I
think I'm more your size, don't you think, eh?'

With that, he lifted her bodily off the ground and was about to
carry her back into the shadowed space between the bales again,
but as she saw the huge sweaty face leer up to hers, Noreen drew
breath and spat right in his face. His eyes opened in astonishment,
and for a moment she watched in horrified fascination as her own
spittle ran down the side of his nose into his beard. Then he let out
a bellow and dropped her. As he did, she kicked his shin as hard
as she could in her new buttoned boots that Paddy had bought her
from a German girl on the ship, and ducking under his raised arm
she tried to escape into the crowd. But the other huge hand grabbed
her by the hair. She screamed as she saw a fist raised but then –
suddenly – he dropped like a tree at her feet. Looking up she saw
her brother Paddy standing over the bos'un, a heavy chessboard
in his hand. He was staring at the crack on it.

'He must have a helluva head!' he said in astonishment.

By this time, the crowds were pressing round and whistles were
blowing and the brawl-hardened Mercer was starting to sit up
again. Noreen pulled her brother's arm and as she did so the bulky
makeshift chessboard broke in two in Paddy's hands.

'Ach, dammit!' he said.

'Never mind, Paddy. We'll get you another one. Come now, or
he'll have both of us murdered.'

Paddy allowed himself to be pulled away but he was still
muttering about his beloved chessboard. It was Sven the Swede
who had made it and he had given it to Paddy as a memento of their
many games together. Now it was broken in two pieces over the
head of the brute who had been molesting his young sister. Paddy

had gone looking for her on the dockside and the thought was just dawning on him that he might have killed the man. For some reason, the thought cheered him up and he began to gather the bed-rolls as Noreen was trying to explain things to her brothers. It seemed that everybody was talking at once – Noreen, Sean and Michael, Denis, Hana and her mother, and the Fraser twins who were now joined by their father, a genial Highlander who had the Gaelic.

A further noise was added to the pandemonium with the arrival of a New York Police waggon drawn by two big greys. Two other policemen were on horseback forcing a passage through the press of people on the quayside. Men shouted and women screamed as they tried to get out of the way of the hooves. Some thumped on the side of the waggon as it passed, but on it came until it was almost on the O'Neils and their ship friends.

'Run Paddy. They're after you!' screamed Noreen.

'God,' thought Paddy, 'that fellow I hit must have died and they want me for murder!' He looked about him but was uncertain where to run. Almost as a reflex, the brothers moved together in a group round their sister.

'There they are!' yelled a voice above the din. It was the peak-capped police officer in charge of the waggon detachment and he was pointing with a white-gloved finger straight at the O'Neils.

'Get 'em!'

In minutes, they were surrounded by helmeted policemen and despite stout resistance by Sean and Michael especially, the whole O'Neil family found themselves, bruised and bewildered, in the back of the waggon along with all their various bits and bundles. The officer in charge turned to beam on them from the front cabin. He was holding a paper in his hand, which he held up as he roared out in a pronounced Irish accent:

'This is a warrant for your arrest – all of youse – for the crime of being related to a superintendent of the New York police force!'

And he laughed his head off. It was their Uncle Mick!

The waggon drove off in a hullabaloo of hugs and greetings and laughter. With the escort of the two police horsemen at the side and the full detachment falling into a trot at the rear, the waggonload of O'Neils made its way gradually through the crowds and into the streets that led to downtown New York City. Glancing through the back window, Denis could see Hana's tear-stained face running after them and waving her hand frantically to him. Steeling himself, he deliberately looked away. Hana stopped at once and she soon became a small figure in the crowd again. The Frasers left with their father in exactly the opposite direction, all of them talking at once. And at the aft gangway, Fourth Officer Bishop watched as the policewaggon disappeared round a corner of the quayside building and left him only with his thoughts of the bewitching Noreen.

'Prepare to cast off the gangway, Mr Bishop.'

Teddy looked up at the deck-rail to find Bos'un Mercer glaring down at him. And having done its work, and deposited its cargo, the Campania prepared to put to sea again.

SIX

Meanwhile, on another sea, the Keith family was still en voyage to faraway New Zealand. The blue waters of the Pacific were still weeks away but now the grey Atlantic had been exchanged for the tideless green of the Mediterranean, and for the comfortable, rosewood-familiarity of his bedroom at Craigend, Jim Keith now accepted the spartan solidity of the second-class cabin he shared with his brother Bobby. Jim was glad to escape to it during the day, if only for a break from the constant small conversations that the daily life on a passenger ship was. The more exuberant Bobby on the other hand, with his easy, gregarious manner had quickly won friends on board. They were fair-weather friends however, in the literal sense of the word, and at the first sign of white on the sea surface or the slightest rise in the wind, they retreated to their cabins to wait for the sun's return. Undeterred, Bobby would roam the deserted decks in search of a conversation. To him, talk was action and action was life. His younger brother could not have been more different. For Jim, conversation, except with Tina perhaps, was a strain and he was more than happy to keep his own company. Which was why he was quite happy to be in the cabin on this fine morning, writing a letter to his other brother, John. Not boasting a writing desk or suitable flat surface in the cabin for writing, Jim made do with a wooden tray on his knees, a pad of lined paper and a newly-sharpened pencil.

> . . . we got to Gibraltar by Thursday. It's just a huge rock sticking out of the sea between Spain on one side and Morocco on the other, but once you go ashore it's no more than a naval station full of sailors and wild apes and it seemed to have more pubs than Glasgow. Not that we saw inside one of them. You know Father. I don't know about Bobby. He disappeared for half the time we had ashore. Gibraltar is not at all foreign. In fact, it's more British than Britain. Yet here I am in the middle of the Mediterranean, with the shade down on the porthole to keep out the sun, sitting on my bunk writing this letter to you all at home in dear old Forres. Our mother still refuses to leave her cabin. She says she's staying there until we

reach New Zealand. I don't think she realises how far we have to go. Father is very patient and Tina spends a lot of time with her helping her with a bed-cover I think. Tina is quieter than usual.

I don't think she's unwell, but there's something bothering her. No doubt a few more weeks of sun will cheer her up and bring her back to her old self. I hope so. I don't like to see my wee sister so down. One of the young officers on board, an Englishman, already has his eye on her, but you know our Tina. Bobby is Bobby and working hard at being the life and soul of the party. He tries so hard at it you would think he would be exhausted, but no, he seems to thrive on it. We're the ones who are tired! The food is plain but there is plenty of it and we are getting quite fond of the wine. It's so cheap it seems a shame not to drink it. If they could see us in the Masons' Arms . . .!

In the Masons' Arms in Forres, John Keith took a long gulp of his heavy beer while he stared at the letter in his left hand. He could hardly believe it – Lisbon, Gibraltar! His family had actually been there. Now they were drinking wine! They were just like Continentals. John preferred his pint. And even though the wind was blowing hard outside, he still was glad to be in Forres. Not for him a gallivant around the world to a country he knew nothing about. He had said so at the time and he said so again. All that nonsense about the Boer War. His father needn't have been so pigheaded. What did a few Dutchmen in Africa matter when he had a solid business going here in Forres? But no, he had to throw it all up on a point of principle and risk the whole family in a madcap emigration. At his age? Well, it was no use going over all that old ground again. He might as well have another drink.

'Same again, Geordie.'

'As ye say, Mr Keith,' said the barman, sliding a small whisky along the shiny wood of the bar and begining to pull another pint. 'I thocht ye would have a mind to hae anither.'

John Keith's drinking habits were a well-known fact in the town. Since the family's departure he had become more than a regular at the Masons' Arms, and his managerial appearances at the shop in the High Street were becoming increasingly perfunctory. Not that it really mattered. Old 'Shears' turned a blind eye to John's long 'tea-breaks' and poor time-keeping. He knew the salesmen liked John and covered for him expertly. He also knew that the travellers trusted the amiable big manager and over the years the contacts John had built up in the trade had proved invaluable in the quiet spells in the season, so the new owner of William Keith and Sons was happy to let his manager enjoy a dram or two – or three. Which was why John was in his usual seat just after opening time reading a letter from Jim. It had come that morning just as he was leaving the house. The postman had given him the letter with the funny stamps on it as he was closing the door. He thought of going straight back in with it to Thomasina, but something made him decide against that. His wife was going through a tense phase, and the less that he bothered her the better. He'd read it right away in the back shop over a cup of tea and then again in the lavatory, now here he was reading it yet again in the pub. He quickly quaffed the dram and drew the fresh, frothy beer to him.

'. . . It was Malta this morning.'

'Incredible,' muttered John under his breath, already beginning to thicken with alcoholic fumes.
'Whit wis that?' called out Geordie.
'Nothin', Geordie man.'
'Oh aye.'
John continued reading.

Even more sailors, and hardly a Scotsman among them from what I could hear. Plenty of ships in the harbour and a white ensign on every one of them. Bobby and Father stayed down by the harbour. Tina and I walked into Valletta. It was very white and very poor and it seemed as if it had a church at every corner. Tina surprised me by asking if we could go inside of one. I wasn't all that keen as you might guess but she was determined, so in we went to the next one we came to. It was horrible. There was a mummified body of a Bishop or somebody lying under a glass case just as you went in the big door and the place was full of painted statues, with blood all over the place, and wearing oversize crowns on their heads and with real clothes on. And not a good worsted among them.

John chuckled again at that.

There was one of a woman with a real dagger stuck into her stone breast and there were candles everywhere, so that the walls that weren't painted were blackened by candlesmoke. There was a funny smell. A sweet smell like an undertaker's. Was it incense? And the noise was like Turriff Market. It was as busy as the High Street. People walking about the aisles, talking in groups, sitting in pews. Mostly women, old women all in black, and striding about the place as if they owned it, bald-headed priests, all with beards and black hats. There was some chanting going on at a side altar but thank goodness there was no service on, the Mass as they call it. I couldn't have taken that I don't think. I was glad to get out

81

of the place and into the fresh air again. I don't think Tina was too impressed either. 'Is that what Catholics are like?' was all she said when we were in the street again. I said it must be and she said she didn't think she would like to be a Catholic. I told her I should hope not. She was very quiet as we walked back through the narrow streets to the harbour again. I asked Tina why she'd wanted to go into the Papist church in the first place. She said she was curious, that was all, so we said nothing more about it. We didn't mention our visit to father. You know what he thinks of the Fenians . . .

St Patrick's Cathedral, on New York's Fifth Avenue was a very different kind of Catholic place – bright, clean, spare and high, it breathed the very confidence of the emerging Irish in America at the turn of the century. Like them it kept just enough of the Old Country about it, the picture of the Little Flower (St Theresa) and the statue of St Patrick in green and gold, to make them feel at home, but the vast size of the white edifice was in keeping with a new Irish optimism in a new country. Especially in New York. No other ethnic community, apart perhaps from the Italians, had taken such a firm hand and foothold on the workings, especially the inner workings, of this brash, burgeoning city. The Irish brogue is something worn very comfortably by the New Yorker, and never more so than when nearly five hundred of them, dressed in the dark blue of the City's Police Force, thundered out the familiar words of 'Hail Glorious St Patrick' in a plangent blend of tenors, baritones and basses:

> 'Hail Glorious St Patrick,
> Dear Saint of our Isle,
> On us thy poor children
> Bestow a sweet smile . . .'

The 'children' in this case were burly policemen, many inclined to an early plumpness under bulging belts, who were taking part in their Annual Mass at St Pat's. Row upon row of blue, silver badges gleaming; pink, scrubbed, Irish faces shining under centre-parted hair that was as uniform as their polished boots. And no face shone as brightly as that of newly-promoted Superintendent Michael O'Neil who belted out the hymn as if he were in the chorus of the Metropolitan Opera. His tenor wasn't as fine as his older brother Den's, but it was louder.

This fact wasn't lost on young Denis as he stood with Paddy, Sean and Michael in the side aisle seats. Noreen was with Auntie

Carmella, Uncle Mick's Italian wife, their son, Joey, and the rest of the police women folk and children at a special section of pews at the back. Denis glanced round quickly but he couldn't see his sister and aunt for the pillars in the way. Michael gave a loud yawn beside him and Denis gave him a sharp dig in the ribs.

'Will ye mind out!' Michael exclaimed.

'Shush!' whispered Denis as he faced the altar again.

They were all guests of their uncle's at the Police Mass, as it was called, and there was no doubt that Superintendent O'Neil was out to make his presence felt that morning. It was a presence that was difficult to ignore. Not that he was tall or commanding, or even imposing in his new uniform. No, it was rather that he exuded energy. It radiated from his sharp, blue eyes and was signalled in every thrusting move of his arms and hands and chin even when he sang a hymn in church. One had the feeling that Uncle Mick, as the boys soon called him, didn't have a full spiritual understanding or sympathy with the words he was singing so lustily, but he succeeded in giving an impression of mental and physical cohesion mainly because he was impressive. Mick O'Neil would have done well at whatever he chose to do and he couldn't have done better than choose the police, especially in New York, for there was no better place than the Force for a pugnacious Irishman with the gift of the blarney. As the hymn finished, Denis glanced across at his uncle who gave him a broad wink as he sat down for the sermon. It was no less then the Bishop himself who was to speak. Needless to say, another Irishman, Tom Monaghan from Cork. In his lovely lilting accent, he intoned, from the distant pulpit:

'"But now, brethren, if I come to you speaking in tongues, what shall it profit you, unless I speak to you either in revelations or in knowledge or in teaching." St Paul's first letter to the Corinthians, Chapter 14, Verse 6. In the Name of the Father and of the Son and of the Holy Ghost. Dear brethren in Jesus Christ . . .'

With the natural reflex of the born Catholic, Denis immediately switched off, and let his mind wander. They had been in New York for two weeks now, and already Sean and Michael had got themselves fixed up with jobs as bartenders and cellarmen in a downtown Bar and had found lodgings with a Scotswoman, Mrs Lennox, a cleaner at the pub, who lived nearby. Noreen, thanks to Carmella's cousin, Roberto, had found a job as a waitress in an Italian restaurant. It was only temporary, she insisted, until she found a job in the theatre. Some hope, thought Denis. I don't know where she got the theatre idea, but then he could never understand where Noreen got half her ideas from. She and Paddy were still with Uncle Mick and Denis thought it was about time

either he or Paddy moved. It was a bit of a tight squeeze for both
of them in the attic lumber room, even if Paddy was the easiest of
room mates. He was still very quiet, still kept himself to himself,
and as usual, spent a lot of time in the chapel. Denis looked along
the row, past the vacant stares of Michael and Sean to where Paddy
was listening to the Bishop, rapt. Sometimes, Paddy's piety gave
Denis the willies. Still he was a good lad, and he couldn't say
anything against his brother. Neither of them had been fixed up in
anything yet. Uncle Mick kept making hints about the Police, but
Denis thought that had been Sean's intention. However, after their
ship experience as a double act, Sean and Michael seemed quite
happy to work together at whatever came to hand, and Sean's old
police ambitions seemed to have evaporated.

'What about you then?' Uncle Mick had said one night after
supper.

'Me?' Denis had exclaimed. 'Don't make me laugh.'

'What's so funny, then?'

'Me – a policeman.'

'And why not?'

Why not indeed? They had talked jocularly at first, but over the
next few nights the idea had taken hold, and when Uncle Mick
brought it up again more seriously this time, Denis had said,

'They might not have me.'

'I'll see that they do,' Uncle Mick had replied.

Maybe that's why he was so keen they should all come to the
Police Mass. I suppose, Denis thought, a job in the Police is as good
as any, but who would have thought it – Denis O'Neil, sportsman
and farm labourer, a policeman – even in little old New York! He
glanced across the aisle at his Uncle, but Superintendent Michael
O'Neil was fast asleep.

In the Masons' Arms, John Keith slowly and deliberately folded
his brother's letter and put it back in the envelope. Geordie, the
barman, cleared the several glasses and beer mugs from before his
most assiduous customer.

'Ye'll be aff then, Mr Keith?'

'Aye, Geordie, I can't spend the whole night here. I've got a
home to go to.'

'So ye have, Mr Keith. Good night.'

'Good night, Geordie. I'll see you tomorrow.'

'Nae doot!' muttered Geordie.

John shivered slightly as the night air hit him. It was high
summer, but high summer in Forres can be a mildish winter
anywhere else! There was a chill in the wind that had a sobering

effect on John as he walked and he was glad to step out briskly, well, at least as briskly as he could after four pints and four 'wee halfs'. As he walked, the contents of the letter went through his head again in a jumbled fashion. Could he smell incense? Is this a dagger that I see before me? Was the Mediterranean really green? How would Tina look as a nun? Father would disown her. John wondered about his father.

'I really miss the auld devil so I do,' he said to himself thickly, as he staggered into the gutter for a moment. 'Whoops! Careful!' he called out to no one in particular. A woman passing at the time said 'Good evening, Mr Keith', but quickly turned her head away. John didn't hear or perhaps he didn't care. He was still thinking of his faraway family. He had worked out that they would be in Cairo by now. Good Heavens, they might even see the Pyramids! John suddenly remembered he hadn't been to a Lodge meeting for months. Not since before the New Year. And he'd never been on a camel either! But Bobby would have. Trust Bobby. John giggled to himself. He could just imagine Bobby wearing a fez – a red fez – and sitting on a camel.

'God would that no' gie ye the hump!' he said and laughed.

'What's so funny?'

The female voice was hard and penetrating and brought John Keith's fanciful musings to an abrupt halt. Thomasina was standing against the light of their own doorway. He couldn't see her face. Just as well for it wasn't a pretty sight. For Mrs John Keith was angry – very angry.

'You're late for your supper, John Keith!'

John hiccuped loudly.

'Am I too early for my breakfast?' he asked benignly.

'You're drunk!'

'You're right!'

She moved quickly away from the doorway and he stumbled in after her, blinking in the light, and went straight through to the privy in the small back garden. He felt a lot better and his head was much clearer after a long, relieving pee. Unfortunately, this was delivered against the wooden door of the privy and over his boots rather than in the aperture provided, but it was dark by now and nobody noticed. But Thomasina did as soon as he returned indoors via the kitchen. She was lying in wait for him. 'Get those boots off before ye come another step and button up your troosers. Man, you're a disgrace.'

'I want to see the weans.'

'They've no mind to see you the state you're in.'

'I've only had a few pints, woman.'

'Ay, but how often? Stand still!'

He was aware of her removing his boots and fiddling at his flies.

'Whit are ye daen' wife?' He could hear her muttering as she fussed around him.

'Whit are ye sayin'?'

'I'm sayin' that we've got visitors and ye're no' goin' ben lookin' like somethin' the cat brought in.'

'Visitors?'

'Ay.'

'At this time o' night?'

'An' whose fault is it it's this time o' night?'

'It's no' your mother again?'

'No, it's no' my mither. I wish it wis. Haud your heid steady.' With a shock John felt the cold wet flannel hit his face and the icy water drip down inside his collar.

'For God's sake woman!'

The next thing a hairbrush was attacking his scalp vigorously. John winced audibly. Thomasina persisted. She was taking every advantage she could, but it must be said that her husband looked a different man as he straightened up again and faced his wife.

'Who is it?' he whispered fiercely.

'Never mind, ye'll see soon enough. Open up.'

This was said in such a peremptory tone that he opened his mouth without thinking and Thomasina popped a hard, white ball into it. It was a Mint Imperial. A gob-stopper! 'That'll take the smell o' spirits aff ye. Come on.' She walked in front of him and held open the kitchen door.

'I'd like to see the weans,' he said with his mouth full.

'There's time enough for weans. First things first.'

She led the way along the short lobby to the parlour on the right. John could feel the pungent taste of the mint filling his mouth. He crushed it violently in his back teeth and could feel tears smart in his eyes. He was still chewing noisily when Mrs Keith opened the door and he saw his visitors. His jaw fell open revealing the broken white debris of a Mint Imperial on his tongue.

'It's yourself John Keith. An' aboot time tae.' It was Mrs Friar.

'Ye'll no' ken me sae weel, but ye'll ken my Ella here. At least your brother Bobby does. Or did.'

At this young Ella Friar burst into a loud wail that so startled John that he swallowed the remnants of the gob-stopper in a gulp.

'Quiet, oor Ella,' said Mrs Friar, staring steadily at John. He looked helplessly at his wife but Thomasina sat with a fixed, frigid face, her lips firmly pursed. Mrs Friar went on. 'I've come here to the hoose because you're the only Keiths left in Forres noo that the family has immigrated abroad somewheres. I've told your guid wife a' aboot it.'

'Aboot what?'

'Oor Ella, whit else?' There was another anguished cry.

'Quiet Ella!' snapped Thomasina. Ella was immediately quiet.

'What about Ella?' asked John weakly.

Mrs Friar glared at her daughter then at John.

'She's pregnant,' she said tersely.

Ella's hand flew to her mouth as if she thought the baby was going to emerge there and then. John's legs suddenly felt weak. He sat on the nearest chair staring at Ella, who turned her head away quickly. John turned vacantly to Mrs Friar.

'And by your Bobby.'

'Er – are ye sure –'

'Of course we're sure. She's missed twice.'

John was floundering. 'I mean are ye sure it was Bobby –'

'Whit's that?' Mrs Friar was on her feet in a fury but Ella was even quicker. She was now towering over John. She was a big girl.

'Of course I'm sure. Three times he did it to me. Twice in the park and once doon by the –'

'That'll dae, Ella! Spare us the details. The fact is he's bairned ye and noo he's no' here.' She advanced menacingly to John as he sat helplessly in the chair.

'So, whit are ye goin' to dae aboot it?'

'Me?'

'You're his brother, are ye' no'?'

'Ay.'

'Weel?'

John opened his mouth to speak – but nothing came out.

Bobby Keith was in full flow. Seated under an awning on the main stern deck he was holding forth after lunch to a semi-circle of the younger officers, among them Second Officer Dickenson. Jim was lying on a deck-chair nearby, his hands clasped behind his head, grinning at his elder brother's irrepressibility.

'I tell you –' he was saying, between swigs of lime and soda, 'it's the Oceanic syndrome you'll have to consider in the new century. Europe is tired; it needs a rest. The new world now is Australasia and the Orient.'

'I thought America was the new world,' said Martin.

'It was, but not now. The United States are anything but united.

87

As far as they're concerned the Civil War isn't over. There will always be a north and south divide there. They're two different countries in fact. They'll never agree about the negroes, and you mark my words, the negroes will turn one day and they'll have another revolution. Only this time, the slaves will win and they'll have a big black man as the President.' At this there was a burst of derisive laughter.

'I'm telling you,' went on Bobby quite unperturbed, 'it's comin' yet, as Rabbie Burns would say. You'll see.'

'If we live that long,' said someone.

'You will if you stay off the booze,' quipped Bobby.

'And the women!' added someone else.

'Wait a minute,' continued Bobby, 'you don't want to go too far!' There was more laughter, and then Jim rose up on one elbow.

'How far would you go, Bobby?'

'What do you mean?'

'With a woman?'

'Aye, that would be telling,' laughed Bobby.

'Tell us then,' went on his brother.

'Yes, tell us. Go on,' chorused some of the officers.

'Is there anything to tell?' added Martin.

For once, Bobby looked a little flustered. 'I thought we were talking about the world situation,' he said, a trifle pompously.

'Oh, this is much more interesting,' said Jim mischievously. The young men growled their agreement in various muttered comments. Jim was enjoying himself hugely.

'Yes, tell us about the women in your life, Bobby.'

'OK. First there was my mother. No, first was my Granny. Then there was my Aunty –'

There was a howl of catcalls and jeering from the little group, which was only halted by the clang of a ship's bell. This broke up the discussion and the young officers drifted away to their various afternoon tasks. It was time to prepare for the last lock on the canal. Then it would be Suez before dark. As soon as they were alone, Bobby turned on Jim.

'What were you up to, wee brother?'

'Nothing,' said Jim calmly.

'Why the interest in women all of a sudden?'

'It was your women we were talking about,' replied Jim, looking up steadily at Bobby from the deck-chair. Bobby went down on his knees and then lay flat out on the deck beside the chair and proceeded to do some press-ups.

'What do you mean by my women?' he panted.

'I think you know what I mean,' said Jim.

'No, I don't,' answered Bobby breathily.

There was a pause before Jim sat up on his elbow again and gazed down at his big brother.

'Ella Friar, for instance.'

Bobby collapsed immediately on the deck with a muffled exclamation.

'I thought that might get you,' said Jim lying flat on his back again. Bobby's head suddenly appeared at his shoulder. His face was flushed, even allowing for the tan, and his eyes were bright with curiosity.

'Do you know something I don't know?' Jim turned his head to meet his brother's eyes.

'Do you know something I should know?'

'What are you talking about?'

'A night you had in Grant Park. You couldn't wait to come and tell me about it. Woke me up, you did, remember?'

'I don't know what you're talking about.'

'Fine, you know what I'm talking about.' Mrs Friar's pointed nose was only inches from John's bulbous one. 'If the party concerned is not available, then the responsibility belongs to the next of kin and that's you.'

John made a brave attempt to show some dignity. 'I am not my brother's keeper.'

'Havers,' retorted Mrs Friar, 'it's a family matter is it no' and you're family. Ella is only a poor lassie and it'll no' dae for her to be disgraced by a man that's fled the country. If it gets aboot the toon that's she's expectin', her prospects'll be ruined an' I'll have her on my hauns for the rest o' my days.'

'Mammy!' yelled Ella tearfully, trying to look every inch the helpless victim which was not easy, considering her amply proportioned five feet ten inches. She had a pretty enough face, but in an Amazonian dimension, given her height and girth. No wonder the Forres bachelors had given her a wide berth. She was a formidable figure. Perhaps it had needed someone as big and assertive as Bobby Keith to scale the Everest that she presented to the average man. However he had managed it, the deed was now done, although the evidence had not yet begun to show. But it would not be long, and the thought of Ella at twice her size was a daunting thought for anyone. But for the moment, her mother was in charge, and Ella, as usual, was happy to let her get on with it. Mrs Friar was not a widow. It seems her very large, caber-tossing husband, Alec Friar, a star of many a Highland Games, could not compete at home with her tongue and had left quietly one morning to join the Merchant Navy. He had never been seen for years, so Robina Friar had taken her revenge on all men and for the moment, the genial and likeable John Keith was the target. Not that he was at his most genial at this time. He knew Mrs Friar's game well enough, and while he had every sympathy with her daughter's predicament, he wasn't ready to offer himself as a victim to their circumstances. He of course had a good idea of Bobby's ways, and was well aware why he was so eager to emigrate. The question was what was to be done now. Thomasina was of no help at all, and seemed almost relieved when there was a cry from the bedroom.

'That'll be Elspeth,' she said, 'I'll have to see to her.'

Mrs Friar had taken her seat beside Ella once more, and for a moment, a heavy uncomfortable silence filled the room. It was only broken by the entrance of young Kenneth, a sprightly dark-haired three-year-old, who was completely naked. He rushed to his daddy's knee calling, 'Me peed bed, Daddy. Els cry, no me.' He tried to climb up on his daddy's knee, happily revealing his damp boy's bottom, much to Ella's feigned embarrassment. Mrs Friar was not convinced.

'Ye'll have seen bigger than that, I'm thinkin', Ella Friar!' Ella only sobbed again. Thomasina hurried into the room in a flurry of maternal agitation and grabbed her son.

'Kenneth Keith, you wee besom, and you wi' yer breeks aff!' She carried him off under one arm, spanking his white bottom with the other. His yells only added to Ella's moans and John, lying back on his chair, put his hand to his forehead. This had not been a good night.

There was a knock at the front door. Thomasina's voice called out, 'You get that, John. It's my mother.'

It was John's turn to groan. Rising up, he trudged to the front door. Mrs Friar quickly wiped Ella's eyes with a hanky and told her to blow her nose. She did so – loudly – and it offered a trumpeting salute to Mrs Beattie as she entered in front of John. She was surprised to see Mrs Friar.

'It's yoursel'' Mrs Friar. And Ella, tae. My, it's quite the wee party.' She sat herself down in John's chair. 'There's nothin' I like better than a wee party. I hope I havenae missed much o' it,' she beamed on Mrs Friar, who scowled.

'It's nae party,' she said.

'But, Mammy,' put in Ella. 'You said I was a party to the –'

'Wheest you!' said her mother quickly.

'Oh,' said Mrs Beattie, her trained instinct rising immediately to the scent of scandal. 'It's that kind of party, then?'

'I think I'll go to my bed,' said John.

'You'll dae nae such thing,' said Mrs Friar rising.

Mrs Beattie's eyes widened. 'An' is it your hoose that ye can tell a man when he can go to his ain bed?' Mrs Friar sat down again, her lips tightly pursed. When she spoke again, it was with a great effort to be calm.

'Mr Keith and me has been having a conversation.'

'Mr Keith, is it?' said Mrs Beattie. 'I've never had a conversation with him in my life.'

'Ladies –' John began.

'An' I'm not goin' tae start now,' persisted Mrs Beattie. John sat wearily in his wife's chair. His mother-in-law continued. 'What I want to know is, why is it I come in to my ain daughter's hoose and I find a wifie mad wi' anger an' her daughter by wi' greetin', and my son-in-law like a big tumshie withoot a word tae say tae onybody?'

'I was just away up the stair,' tried John again, but this time it was his wife stopped him.

'No, John, away and put the kettle on. I'm sure Mrs Friar and Ella would like a cup of tea. And my mither tae.'

'Well,' said Mrs Beattie. 'It's late enough for tea, do ye no' think? Maybe a wee dram would be –'

'Mither!' said Thomasina hurriedly. 'We hae visitors.'

'I'm thinkin' they would be better for a dram an' a' by the look o' them.'

'I don't drink,' said Mrs Friar.

'Nor do I,' whimpered Ella.

'No,' said Mrs Beattie, 'I didnae think ye would!'

The ceremony of the tea-taking had all the formality of an Embassy gathering between hostile nations. Only John Keith and his mother-in-law seemed to have an *entente cordiale*, and this was mainly because he poured a generous whisky into each of their glasses. The company was astonished when Mrs Beattie raised hers in a toast.

'Shall we wet the baby's head?' she said.

There was a gasp of amazement from the Friars. Mrs Beattie continued serenely, 'Oh, aye.' She sipped her whisky daintily but with great relish. 'My neebour's man's brother, ye see, is a park keeper at the Grant, and he minds fine, so my neebor says, seein' Ella at the back end o' the summer wi' Bobby Keith. At least, I think it was Bobby Keith, so my neebor's man says. But he was sure fine it wis Ella. He has to shut the gates at night, ye see.' At this, Ella wailed like a banshee, despite her mother's commands to be quiet. Mrs Beattie took another sip. 'Mind you, we had a fine summer. An' the nights were long and warm, if ye remember, an' young lassies being what they are, and mair to the point, young laddies being what they are –'

'Mrs Beattie, are you insinuating –?' interjected Mrs Friar.

'No' a bit, Mrs Friar. No' a bit. I'm tellin' you. But mind, it's only whit my neebor says, and whit the whole toon says, and whit a'body knows but John here, it would seem – that your Ella's got herself bairned by Bobby Keith!' The Friars were stunned.

'Is that no' right?' Mrs Beattie added sweetly.

'It's quite right,' answered Mrs Friar in a steely voice. 'That's why we're here the night. Ella has tae get married.'

'Well, she canna marry John!'

'I dinna want tae marry Mr Keith,' cried Ella woefully.

'Nor can she marry Bobby. He's in Gib-a-raltar, or some place like that,' said Thomasina.

'No' he's no',' said John. 'He's in Egypt, by now.' Thomasina looked at her husband.

'Have you had another letter?' Her husband nodded.

'This mornin',' he said. Thomasina's eyes widened.

'You never mentioned.'

'I've never had the chance.'

Mrs Friar shifted her position in her chair and stated purposefully, 'She'll hae tae marry somebody, or –' she gave a little cough – 'er – "arrangements" will hae tae be made.'

'What do you mean, "arrangements"?' asked Thomasina.

'Ella has nae money,' answered her mother.

'You don't hae tae pey to hae a baby, ye know,' added Mrs Beattie.

'But there are things to be peyed a' the same,' insisted Mrs Friar, grimly.

'Like lip service?' muttered John downing the last of his whisky, but Mrs Friar had heard.

'We'll have none of your lip for a start,' she hissed.

Mrs Beattie put down her empty glass pointedly. John didn't take the hint. Mrs Beattie went on, addressing no one in particular. 'My neebour on the other side. Her man's a janitor at the school and he was tellin' her that Ella's been seein' a bit o' the schoolmaster. I canna mind his name . . .' Mrs Friar sat bolt upright, and put her hand over Ella's mouth.

'Aye,' continued Mrs Beattie. 'A fine big couple they make. Him being in the rugby team. You'll mind, Thomasina, he wis aye after Tina afore she went away. He should be the fine catch. I mean, a school teacher. It's a grand job, a school teacher.' Mrs Friar rose and walked over to stand at Mrs Beattie's chair. Her manner was altogether changed, and she spoke almost as if in confidence to the other woman, who looked up evenly at her with just the touch of a smile at the corners of her mouth.

'You seem to have your ear to the ground, Mrs Beattie.'

'That's where maist things start, Mrs Friar.'

'Aye. Well, you'll not be surprised to learn that Ella has a mind to mairry John Thomson.'

'Oh, is that his name?' queried Mrs Beattie.

'The schoolmaster. He has asked me if he can walk oot wi' oor Ella.'

'Oh my,' said Mrs Beattie. 'Isn't that nice.'

'Not quite,' said Mrs Friar. She hesitated and glanced back at her daughter. 'He – I mean – weel – a man likes tae think he's mairrying – er – ' She mouthed the word silently to Mrs Beattie but John caught and called out from his chair:

'A virgin, you mean?'

'John!' said Thomasina.

'Ay – weel, not to put too fine a point on it,' went on Mrs Friar, 'he'll no' marry Ella if he funds oot she's pregnant.' There was another bleat from Ella and Mrs Friar returned to her chair.

'So whit are we tae dae then?' asked Mrs Beattie of Mrs Friar.

'That's whit I came roon to discuss with Mr Keith here.'

'Oh, aye,' said Mrs Beattie. 'It'll be his money ye'll be wantin' for – the "arrangements"?' Mrs Friar looked solemn.

'Aye, that's right.'

'I see,' said Mrs Beattie quietly. 'John, I'll hae that ither dram, I think.' There was a silence as the women watched John pour his mother-in-law another drink. She drank it almost at a gulp, and put the glass down on the table with a thump that rattled the teacups. 'You'll be thinkin' o' that Mrs Campbell?' she said. 'The one that lives up by the new railway line.'

'That's right,' nodded Mrs Friar.

'Aye.' There was another silence. It was John who suddenly broke it. He spoke quietly, but very firmly.

'There'll be nae abortions here.' All the women started to speak at once, but John rose up to his full height so that he seemed to fill the room. John Keith was rarely assertive but now, without saying anything, he was. The women were quiet again. John turned and spoke directly to Mrs Friar.

'Let Ella come to her natural time then she can bring the wean here.'

'But John –!' cried Thomasina. John wheeled and almost shouted at his wife.

'It's my brother's blood in it, and it's mine tae!' He was immediately quiet again.

'I'll see it cared for till he can mind it for himsel'. Noo, I'm awa' tae my bed.' He turned at the door, and looked to Mrs Beattie. 'I'll leave you, mother-in-law, to make the "arrangements" as you say.' He looked pointedly at Mrs Friar. 'But no' in the way she had in mind.' He closed the door behind him. The women never raised their eyes as he went. Thomasina rose and went to the tray at the table.

'I'll just get these dishes.' She lifted the tray, but not before Mrs Beattie had retrieved her glass.

'Can ye manage Thomasina?'

'Fine, mither.' She seemed almost glad to get out of the room. There was a slight pause before Mrs Beattie spoke again.

'He has a sister, I understaun'?'

'Who?' asked Mrs Friar.

'Ella's intended. Mr Thomson.' Mrs Beattie was clearly enjoying herself. Mrs Friar seemed uncertain.

'Ay,' she said. 'She's no' been weel.'

'She'll no' feel much better when she hears her big brother's a faither afore he's a husband, I'm thinkin'. She's that fond o' him so I hear.'

Mrs Friar rose to her full five feet. 'An' I'm thinkin' you hear ower much, Mrs Beattie.'

'Ah weel, mebbe so Mrs Friar, but then –', she started to giggle, 'we're a' Jock Tamson's bairns, in a manner o' speakin', are we no'?' She started to laugh, and was still laughing as Mrs Friar grabbed Ella by the arm and dragged her out without a word.

SEVEN

Tina and her father leaned comfortably on the ship's rail and watched the sailors and the Egyptian dockers working below them. It was such a tangle of hawsers and ropes and winches and pulleys, and such a jangle of calls and commands in both English and Egyptian that it was a wonder to the Keiths that the Mataura had come through the many locks and got berthed in harbour at all. But now they were in Suez and the next stop was Aden. It was hard to believe, but here they were.

'You're not too warm?' asked her father.

'No, I'm fine thanks,' replied Tina. 'This big hat keeps me nice and cool. I thought it was daft when Jim bought it for me in Cairo, but it's certainly come in handy since.'

'Well,' said William Keith, 'it's a hat you wouldna find much use for in Forres, I'll tell you that.' Tina laughed.

'There wouldna be room for it an' me in the High Street!' William nodded and smiled and puffed away at his pipe. He was relaxed again with his daughter. This was the way they used to be. The way they'd been since she was a little girl.

'How was your mother this mornin', d'ye think?'

'Quite cheerful, I thought,' replied Tina. 'She's fairly gettin' on wi' that bedspread.'

'We'll have to hire another cabin to keep it in if she goes on at this rate.'

'Is she not even comin' out to see the canal before we leave it?'

'I don't think so. She said she can see out o' the windae, as she calls the port-hole.'

'Poor mother. Once she gets an idea in her head, that's it fixed.'

'Just so. She thinks she's in a railway carriage I think, not a ship's cabin, so she'll not budge till the journey's over.'

'When will that be now?'

'27th August in Dunedin. About twelve weeks away. If we live that long.'

'Don't say that, Daddy.'

'It was just in fun.'

'I know. But it gives me a funny feeling.'

'There have been many died in the emigration ships. Especially in the old sailing days.'

'It must have been terrible then.'

'It was. And it was only about twenty years ago. When it took nearly six months to come out from Britain. We're travelling in luxury compared with some of the old pioneers. Ay, they were a hardy lot then.'

'They must have been. Rather them than me, I think.'

'Ay.'

There was a pause as father and daughter continued to look down.

'Tell me, Christina –'

Tina tightened slightly. She was always slightly tense when her father called her Christina. It always meant a reprimand was coming, but she tried to keep her tone quite matter of fact. 'Yes?'

'Are you happy?'

'Of course I'm happy?'

'Are you though?'

'Daddy!' She might have said something else but just at that moment, Second Officer Dickenson came up to them at the rail.

'Good morning, Mr Dickenson.'

'Good morning, Miss Keith. Good morning, sir.'

'Good morning.'

'Nothing like watching other people work, is there?'

Dickenson looked smart in his white shore drills, and there was no doubt he knew he impressed Tina – as any young girl would be impressed by a smart-looking, sun-tanned, dark-eyed young officer. Some might even say he was too good to be true. As it was, he stood rather closer to Tina than she would have liked, but with her father comfortably on the other side, she felt safe enough. Mr Keith removed his pipe from his mouth and pointing with it, asked the ship's officer quietly, 'Is that the Red Sea?'

'Yes, sir, it is.'

'It's a pity it couldn't open up and let us right through to India.'

Dickenson laughed. 'We'd need Moses with us for that. But then we've just come a hundred miles down a canal that you might say was the parting of the sands. A hundred miles of it, and it's hardly seventy years old.'

'You ship people would have been glad of that,' said Mr Keith.

'You bet. The overland route saves a long haul round the Cape of Good Hope and cuts at least a month from the journey to the

East. You could say that this is where Africa joins Asia. Even Suez itself was reclaimed from the sea, you know.'

'You mean it was under water?' asked Tina.

'Exactly. Now there's enough room in the harbour to provide dry dock and basins for the whole of the fleet, if necessary, and it is also where the pilgrims halt on their way to Mecca. It's a kind of quarantine station.'

'I'd like to see that,' said Tina.

'I'd be glad to show you. I mean, both of you.'

'That's very kind of you,' said Mr Keith dryly, 'but I'm sure an old Scotsman would be unnecessary ballast in a voyage round the harbour. I'll stay on board, and keep Mrs Keith company.'

'She's got her bedspread,' laughed Tina.

'Well, that'll make three of us,' said her father. 'Off you go, and be sure and take care of her, young man.'

'You needn't worry, Mr Keith. It's not only a duty, it's a pleasure.' Tina thought again that Mr Dickenson was a lot more sure of himself than she had first thought.

'I'll just go and get ready, if you'll excuse me,' she said to the Second Officer.

'I'll wait for you at the main gangway,' he replied.

'Alright.' She hurried down the deck. Dickenson watched after her admiringly, then turned to Mr Keith.

'I'd better go and get myself ready if I'm going ashore.'

'What do you have to get ready?'

'Oh, a few things, you know. Just in case.'

'Such as?'

'A pistol – excuse me, sir.'

He was gone before William Keith could get the pipe out of his mouth again to say anything. A pistol? Had he heard right? His first instinct was to go after them to the main gangway and stop her going ashore. But at that, he heard the sound of laughter from the harbour side, and looking down saw a whole group of young people going off, and none of them seemed unduly worried. 'I suppose it must be normal practice for officers in these parts,' he thought to himself. 'I must be getting timid in my old age, or maybe it's just being fatherly.' He was musing like this when his two sons appeared at either side of him. Bobby, as usual, was his cheerful self.

'All ashore that's going ashore,' he said, slapping his father on the back, and nearly knocking the pipe out of his mouth. 'Sorry, dad, I should have known you'd be smoking. We've got four hours before sailing. Aren't you taking the chance to go ashore? See what it's like?'

'No thanks,' said Mr Keith. 'I can see it from here.'

'I must say it does look pretty drab,' muttered Jim from the other side. 'It's an isthmus.'

'I've never see an isthmus close up. Let's go and see. Oh, look, there's Tina.' Bobby pointed down to the main gangway. 'She's with that officer fellow, Martin.'

'That's right. He's taking her to look round,' said their father.

'Look round what?' asked Jim.

'The isthmus, I think you call it.'

'Let's join them,' said Bobby.

'Oh, let them be,' said Jim. But for some reason he couldn't explain, he wasn't too happy about it.

'Bless me Father, for I have sinned. It is one week since my last confession.'

A soft voice answered from the other side of the grille. 'The Lord be in thy heart and on thy lips that thou mayest rightly confess thy sins in the Name of the Father and of the Son and of the Holy Ghost. Amen.'

'I have offended against the First Commandment by being careless with my morning and night prayers, and against the fifth by losing my temper once with my sister.'

'And on that occasion with your sister, did you also offend against the Second Commandment?'

'Father?'

'I mean did you swear at her?'

'No, father.'

'And certainly nothing against the sixth or ninth?'

'Certainly not.'

'Good. Good. Anything else?'

'I don't think so.'

'You're quite sure now?'

'Yes, father.'

'Very good. Very good. For your penance, say three Hail Marys and now make a good Act of Contrition.'

'Oh, my God, I am very sorry that I have sinned against Thee. . . .'

At the same time, the priest's voice intoned: 'Domine noster Jesus Christus te absolvat; et auctorite ipsius te absolvo ab omni vinculo excommunicatsionis et interdicti in quantum possum et tu indiges. Deinde ego te absolvo a peccatis tuas in Nomine Patris et Filii et Spiritus Sancti. Amen.'

Paddy O'Neil loved the sound of the Latin, even in the incomprehensible mumble he heard every Friday night in the

dark of the Confessional. And Father Donnelly was the best of
the young curates at St Bride's in Brooklyn. Paddy liked going
to him when he could. Paddy was one of the few Catholics who
enjoyed going to Confession, even if most weeks he had to struggle
to invent a few sins. The truth was he had rarely done anything to
merit the awful enormity of the sacrament of Penance. Paddy just
loved going to Church. He responded genuinely to every aspect
of the Liturgy practised in the various services. He was a Daily
Communicant and went to both services on Sunday, just as he did
back in Ireland. He didn't see why he had to change just because
he was in America. Not that he was unduly pious. He wasn't a
saint or anything. He was just Paddy.

Outside, in the pews again, he cheerfully repeated his penance
in a low, warm, undertone: 'Hail Mary, full of grace, the Lord is
with thee. . . .' Even as he reiterated the child-familiar words, he felt
at home again, at one again with who he was, what he had come
from and with all that had gone into the making of him. He knew
this to be the Truth of all things – for Paddy O'Neil at least. Did
Jews feel this way about the Talmud, Muslims about the Koran,
Protestants about the King James Bible, Fundamentalists about
the Old Testament? Why were there so many books if they were
all saying the same thing? This sort of question only occasionally
troubled him. For him the Catholic religion served all his needs and
the faith it gave him secured him confidently against the World and
the Devil.

Not that there wasn't a bit of a devil in him. He wasn't an O'Neil
for nothing. But he'd never had the desire to compete that Denis
had, or to win like Sean, to cruise like Michael or dream like
Kevin. His brothers were his closest family, yet they might have
been Martians for all they resembled him. Paddy knew deep down
that he had only ever wanted one thing in this life and that was the
next life. He never understood this himself but even as a small boy
he had been haunted by those words he'd heard once in a sermon
at home – 'What doth it profit a man if he gain the whole world and
loseth his own soul?' He always thought that was so right. There
is nothing more dead than dead, and what does it matter then if
the corpse lies in a gold-lined coffin or on top of a dung-heap?
Paddy had always thought that. If this world doesn't count, why
were we all put here in the first place? 'To know Him, love Him,
serve Him in this world and to be faithful to Him in the next.'
That's what the Catechism says. That's what was drilled into him
by parents and priests since ever he could remember. God made us
just so we could all adore Him! How big-headed of God! Oh God,
is that blasphemy? Another sin against the First Commandment?

He must be careful of bad thoughts. Yet how can one prevent any thoughts – good or bad – coming into one's head? Thoughts were always there in everybody's head, all the time, weren't they? Paddy's prayerful musings were suddenly cut short by a gentle tapping on his shoulder. He jumped as if Lucifer had come to claim him, but it was only Father Donnelly.

'The church is about to be closed, Paddy,' he said.

'Oh, sorry Father,' mumbled Paddy, getting up numbly from his knees. He hadn't noticed that the lights in the church had gone out and only the candles at the Lady Altar and round the statues of the Sacred Heart and St Anthony gave any illumination. As a result huge, ghostly shadows were thrown around the pillars and up the walls. This gave the place an eerie, unreal atmosphere and Paddy was glad to run up the aisle after the retreating priest's back towards the side entrance and the reassurance of the electric lights in the vestibule. Father Donnelly was waiting for him.

'I'm sorry, Father –' began Paddy.

The young priest only waved his hand and smiled. 'Sure, you're full of contrition tonight, Patrick!'

'Sorry, Fa –' He broke off, and they both laughed and the young priest slapped him on the back. Yes, Paddy liked Father Donnelly, who, like most of the priests in New York at the time, was also Irish. It might even have been that Paddy was jealous of the priest and would like to have been like him. They stood easily together in the dimly lit vestibule.

'How are you getting on?' said the priest.

'Fine, thanks,' answered Paddy.

'And the family?'

'They're fine too. Denis is in the police now.'

'I heard that.'

'And Sean and Mick are in Rafferty's Bar.'

'A rough place.'

'They can manage.'

'And – er – what was your sister's name again?'

'Noreen.'

'That's right Noreen. How's she?' Paddy hesitated.

'She's alright,' he said.

'We don't see much of Noreen these days,' went on the priest. 'Well, at least, not as much as we see of you.'

Paddy laughed. 'Noreen always said I should have been a priest meself.'

'Why don't you?' The priest's tone was suddenly serious.

Paddy hesitated again. 'Ach, I don't know. Maybe I'm too late to think of such things.'

'Well, it's late tonight certainly, but I tell you what, Paddy boy, come round and have a talk one of these nights. Let me know when you can manage, and I'll lay on a drop of tea. But we'd better be going now, or the Canon will be wondering if I've skipped off to Rafferty's meself.'

'Oh, sorry, Father –'

'At it again, are you?' And smilingly, he opened the door to let Paddy out into the street.

He stood on the top step for a moment and heard the door being locked behind him, and had the strangest sensation of being locked out. Walking the four blocks back to his Uncle's flat, it suddenly occurred to him that he was the only O'Neil now without a job. But what kind of job? Perhaps he didn't want a job. Perhaps he was looking for a vocation. He felt a kind of shiver. He was having these thoughts again. He remembered as a young boy he had played at being a priest at his mother's old dressing table with a window curtain round his shoulders and a flower vase in his hands. And how Sean and Michael had laughed at him. Even old Canon Devlin had laughed when he heard about it. Nobody had ever taken him seriously. Well, maybe it was about time they did – weak chest or no'. It had taken him across the Atlantic, hadn't it? It could be that the sea air had done him good? Taking a deep breath, he started to stride out briskly.

Noreen O'Neil hated her job, or maybe it was more that she hated the customers, especially the men. They kept looking at her over their glasses as they drank, or talking to her in Italian with their mouths full of pasta, and taking every opportunity to touch her hand, her elbow, her shoulder, waist, but most of all her bottom, whenever the chance presented itself. Why are men all the same wherever they are, and whatever nationality, she thought. Why was she in an Italian restaurant in the first place? She couldn't speak Italian. If it weren't that she needed the money. . . .

She was sitting on a big wooden tray laid across the lavatory seat in the back kitchen of Ruffiano's restaurant in Queen's with her feet on the sink, and the tap running. She loved the feel of the cold water on her toes and after a particularly hectic lunch spell she was glad of the break, even if it were in a draughty, uncomfortable staff lavatory behind the kitchen. She had opened the small window, and could hear Luigi, one of the waiters, talking in low Italian to Francesca, another of the waitresses. Although Noreen didn't understand a word, she could tell by their respective tones what was going on, or rather what was coming off! But Luigi wasn't quite getting it all his own way, judging by his increased intensity, and Francesca's playfully outraged tones. Is that all they ever think about, thought Noreen. Is that all there is to think about? She remembered almost ruefully that was all she'd thought about in Ireland – boys. Now those boys had become men and were very much more dangerous. Did that make them more attractive? She wasn't sure. She kept waiting for this thing they called love to happen, but all she got at the moment was pestered and pawed by strangers, just because she was a waitress. Surely there was a better world than all this, where there was colour and warmth and comfort and best of all, money. She had only been a matter of weeks in America, but already she knew that money mattered. It was funny. Those who had it never thought about it, and those who hadn't, never thought about anything else. But how to get it, that was the problem. Not like Francesca, that's for sure. Peddling a feel of her body for pennies in a back alley.

Since the ship, Noreen's thoughts had moved in the direction of theatre. She had been surprised by how much the passengers had enjoyed her singing of popular Irish ballads. Even if it was only because they enjoyed watching her sing, rather than listening to her songs, she knew she had a pleasing voice and a natural gift for entertainment, and hoped there might be a chance to make something of both in New York. After all, her Uncle Mick had told her that Nora Bayliss had made a fortune as an Irish singer, when the immigrants first came over after the famine and she was actually a Jewish girl by the name of Goldberg! Noreen felt sure she could do the same, and make the money herself to buy the clothes she wanted and the apartment she wanted and the good life she wanted. But how? It was as if she were waiting for a sign, or a signal of some kind.

This came rudely in the form of a heavy fist on the flimsy wood of the toilet door, and in the angry voice of Roberto Ruffiano, the restaurant owner.

'You come outta there, eh, you Irish good-for-nobody. I don't pay you to sit and shit. You can do that in your own time. My time, you get out onna da floor, eh? We got tables out there, OK? Subito!' He gave a further thump at the door and added a kick just for good measure, by which time Noreen was already back into her shoes and tidying her hair in the half of a mirror which lay on top of the sink.

There was only one table occupied, but it was a large group and it was a very different type of customer from the kind she had served earlier in the day. These men had a certain style, class almost. They didn't shout or sing or call crudely to her. They talked together in what seemed like conspiratorial tones among themselves, not wishing to be overheard by anyone, least of all a twenty-year-old

Irish waitress who couldn't understand them anyway. But Noreen was smart. It had only taken her a week to learn the name of all the Italian dishes and she knew full well the value of a smile, so smilingly, she helped Francesca to take the table's orders, while Luigi did the wine. He did his best, but it was easy to see his mind was still on Francesca. Roberto had caught both of them in flagrante delicto, as it were, but had nevertheless lost no time in getting them both back on duty. It was at a time in the late afternoon, when even he stole a siesta – often with Francesca – but this party had suddenly arrived, and it was a case of all hands to the pump. Even Roberto.

He unctuously glided round the table talking confidentially with each of the men, but especially with a tall, commanding figure who headed the table. The stranger paid little attention to Roberto's professional courtesies. Instead his eyes were fixed on red-headed Noreen's attempt to take the order of another man at the opposite end of the table. He raised his hand and signed Roberto nearer. His eyes remained on Noreen and a long finger pointed to her, as he whispered with the owner, who in turn smiled in Noreen's direction and bent to the other man's ear. It was his turn to smile. Noreen was then aware that Roberto's arm was tugging at her while he pushed Francesca in her place.

'What are you doing? I was takin' this order!' exclaimed Noreen.

'You take orders from me. OK? And I say you take order from him.' He had pulled her up to the other end of the long table and stood beside the stranger with his hand still gripping Noreen's upper arm. His manner was very different to his usual.

'Mia cara Noreena. . . .' Noreen winced at the name. Roberto went on. 'I wanna you meet my cousin from Chicago. He is big man in the construction business, eh, Enrico?' The man only smiled. He was good looking by any standards, still young, no more than thirty, but his eyes were cold, his smile was icy. Noreen was immediately afraid of him, but fascinated despite herself. Roberto was burbling on. 'You take dis order, eh? You be nice. Be's nice you can be with my cousin from Chicago. OK? Signor Enrico d'Agostino. Him big man.'

'Not from where I'm standin'. They're all the same sittin' down.' Noreen had recovered something of her old poise. But she was unprepared for Enrico's retort.

'But tell me, Noreena, are they all the same lying down?'

She felt herself blush, but struggled to keep her composure. 'I wouldn't know, sir, bein' just off the boat meself. Are you for tellin' me what you'd like?' The suave Italian knew that he had scored, and gave an even broader smile. She noticed the gold in his teeth. She didn't know whether to be impressed or repelled. He had a nice voice, though, or was it the accent? Or was it the feeling of power he exuded?

'If I was to tell you what I like, little girl, we would be here for hours.'

'That's all right. I'm here till ten.' But she was aware her voice was husky and she had trouble finding her breath. What was wrong with her? He was just another customer, and weren't they all the same? Weren't they all after the same thing?

'I will 'ave the soup,' he said seductively.

Tina found she was holding Martin Dickenson's arm very tightly. The throng of white-robed pilgrims in the narrow street almost pinned them against the grimy walls. With the other hand, she held on to her hat, but this left her feeling rather exposed in such a proximity to many males, and not for the first time did she imagine that there was an uncomfortable pressure against her left breast as she and the Second Officer made their way towards the bazaar.

'You'll love it here,' he said. 'Bargains everywhere if you know what to look for and how to haggle.'

'I don't know how to haggle,' she said. 'My father believed in set prices in his shop.'

'That was in England.'

'No, it wasn't. It was in Scotland.'

'It's the same thing.'

'No, it isn't.'

He laughed. 'Sorry, I keep forgetting. You've got to remember I'm a Geordie myself.'

'I can hear that.'

By this time, they were on the edge of the market area and Dickenson stopped and looked about him. All this while, street traders and peddlers were constantly pestering Tina and touching her until she was beginning to get really frightened. She kept an even firmer hold on her handbag and wished she hadn't brought it. Martin kept pushing the sellers off roughly and muttering something to them.

'That sounds like swearing,' she said, trying to be cheerful.

'It is. It's the only thing they understand. That, and this.'

And he patted his pocket.

'You mean, money?'

'Yes, that too.' She frowned, but then he called out as he saw the person he had obviously been looking for. 'Atef, here! Atef!'

A thin man in a shabby white kaftan, wearing a red fez, waved from a few stalls away, then came towards them. He bowed to Tina and smiled at Martin. 'Ah, Sir Dickenson, you bring your mistress to visit us?'

'Not quite, Atef. Miss Keith is one of our passengers this trip from Scotland.'

'Ah, Scotland. Bagpipe, yes? You are much welcome, Mrs.' It was all so incongruous, Tina found it hard not to giggle. The thin man bowed again and beckoned with his finger. 'You will come to my place of commerce, please?' They followed him. She noticed that they weren't bothered or pestered now as they went after the Egyptian merchant. He must be something important, Tina thought. I hope he doesn't offer us anything to eat. The smell in the place was awful. She was sure she would be sick.

'You will have Indian tea, please?' He was seated behind a desk in a very dark little office with doors going off at either side behind him, or rather doorways, hung with beads. No one could come through there without his hearing them first. Perhaps that was the reason. There was a funny kind of smell in the place. Sweet, musky, aromatic. She couldn't quite place it. When the tea came, it was served in dainty little bowls, rather than cups, and it was delicious. As she sipped hers, Atef and Dickenson conversed in what she took to be Arabic. She pretended to be absorbed in her tea drinking, and hoped they could get out of the place soon. She had come to see all the pilgrims in their white robes, heading for Mecca. Instead she seemed to be eavesdropping on a business deal of some kind. Atef reached into a drawer, and produced a little wooden box, and holding his hand over it, suddenly glanced at Tina. So did Martin. He seemed embarrassed, and leaned over towards her.

'Look, Tina, he says he can't talk in front of a woman.'

'I don't know what he's talking about anyway.'

'I know, I know. But maybe if you'd be good enough to step out and look round a few of the stalls, I'll be through here in a couple of minutes and join you. We can then go and see your pilgrims. Alright?'

'Alright.' She didn't feel at all as confident as she tried to sound, but both men rose as she did, and Martin held open the door for her as she left.

'Shan't be a minute,' he said.

When the door closed, she felt the harsh reality of being a foreigner. These men and their faces were all so unreal to her, but the fact was it was she who was unreal to them. She tried to look unconcerned as she fingered some silks at the first stall and moved on to beautifully carved ornaments in the next. But all the time, she was aware that all these brown eyes were on her, examining her microscopically, devouring her with glances. It was a horrible feeling, and she wished Martin would hurry up. It was not very gentlemanly of him to leave her absolutely alone like this, but then maybe Martin Dickenson was not a gentleman. What was she doing in a market place anyway. She hadn't any money. Nevertheless, she pressed her handbag closer to her, but even as she did so, a brown arm grabbed at it. She screamed and pulled as another brown arm shot out and grabbed her, and then another and another, till she was pulled this way and that way by a weaving of brown arms that pulled at her bag, her blouse, her skirt, her legs, her hat. She screamed and laid about her as much as she could, until a shot rang out and then another and the hands left her body as suddenly as they had come upon her. She felt faint and steadied herself against the edge of the ornament stall, as Dickenson arrived beside her, a pistol in his hand. He put his arm around her. She could smell the cordite from the gun in his hand. This was unreal.

'God, I'm sorry. These damned Arabs! Bloody Gyps! Are you alright?' She could only nod. 'Come on, I'll get you back to the ship.' He tightened his arm about her and they moved towards the street again. As they went, she turned her head and caught a glimpse of Atef at his doorway. He slightly inclined his head to her before he closed his door. She felt sick.

'Do you want to go to the Hotel? You can get tidied up there.'

'I'd better.'

It was nearly an hour later when she emerged from the Ladies Room of the Marine Bar, the only European style resort on the Isthmus. But she had been very glad to make use of it. When Dickenson came forward to greet her, she could smell the whisky on his breath.

'You look charming, Miss Keith.'

'Thank you,' she said quietly.

'But then you always do.'

'Not always, Mr Dickenson. Shall we go?'

'I'm afraid the pilgrims are out today. They're confined in quarantine. That's one of their pilgrimage guides over at the bar.' She looked, and a jolly white-robed Friar Tuck kind of Arab gave her a cheery wave, as he sipped what looked like a glass of water. He raised it to her and smiled.

'It's actually neat gin,' said Martin.

'I thought they weren't supposed to drink.'

'They're not. They're also not supposed to talk to white women.'

'They don't!' said Tina wryly. 'Please can we go?'

'Of course.'

On the way back they were very quiet. He made the usual

attempt at small talk, but she didn't respond. She kept wondering about her luck in public situations. First, the Glasgow docks, then a Suez market place. Is it to be this way wherever I go, she wondered. She couldn't imagine a more distasteful predicament than the one she'd been in, especially for a girl from the North of Scotland, who had had little experience of the predatory male, but perhaps it was her Scottishness that gave her a kind of wild pleasure at lashing out with handbag, arms and legs and at least trying to give as good as she got. Her father would have been proud of her. Good Heavens, her father! Her brothers!

'By the way,' she said.

'Yes?'

'We'd better not say anything. When we get back to the ship, I mean.'

'Of course not. It'll be our secret,' he smiled. She did not smile, but wondered if her mother would notice the mark on her sunhat, which she now carried in her hand.

When they reached the harbour side, Martin Dickenson resumed his diffident manner and was no longer the presumptuous and slightly possessive man he had been offshore and in the market place. For the first time she noticed that he'd been carrying the little wooden box Mr Atef had given him in the market office. 'Just a few trinkets,' he said. 'Presents, you know. People at home.' She wondered why it sounded so much like an excuse. But then she looked up at the ship's rail and there was her old father just as she had left him. She gave him a wave. She'd never been so glad to see him. Suddenly she was grabbed by the arm again, and a man's voice said,

'You're under arrest!' Terrified, she glanced round, and it was Bobby.

'Oh, Bobby!' she cried, part in exasperation, but with a good part of relief. 'What a fright you gave me!'

'Why do you look so guilty?' said her brother. 'What have you done?'

'She's been with me, Bobby.'

'Then I'm sure she was in good hands.' It was Jim who had come up from the other side. Tina wondered if she heard an ironic tone in her brother's voice.

'Shall we get on board?' said Second Officer Dickenson genially.

It was almost eleven o'clock and they were beginning to get worried in the O'Neil household in Brooklyn. 'She mighta missed the street-car,' said Uncle Mick.

'She don't miss it other nights. Why she start now?' retorted

Carmella, his wife, who was playing a game of cards with her son, Joey. Carmella was small by Italian standards but she was the live-wire centre of the Michael O'Neil household and the brownstone apartment they lived in at Number 59, 57th Street in Brooklyn. It was a long narrow apartment with steps up from the street, there was a cellar below and two small attic rooms under the roof and two floors in the middle. A small army could be put up within these walls, but the American O'Neils hardly warranted a platoon, for they were a very small family indeed – only the three of them. Carmella had not had a good time with her first born. Joey had been affected by some kind of virus as an infant, and now at eighteen he was over six feet tall, curly-haired and very handsome in an Irish way, and was what people called 'a bit slow'. But he was the loveliest boy and during the day he worked casually with Paddy whenever they were required at Brady's Irish Deli. Joey didn't have to do very much, but Billy Brady was a pal of his Dad's, and anyway Paddy did most of what had to be done. It wasn't a proper job, but he was glad to help Joey out. Everybody loved Joey O'Neil. He, in turn, had made a hero of his big cousin, Denis, when he came to live with them. In addition, Paddy was trying to teach him to play draughts and dominoes, and he just worshipped pretty Noreen. Yes, Joey was the happiest young man on the block when his parents had decided to board the O'Neil immigrants. He was only sorry that Sean and Michael had moved out to their own place. There was plenty of room for everyone and Joey was delighted not to be the only one about the place. Not only were these wonderful people his cousins, they were pals as well, and they were beautiful to Joey. Especially Noreen. And it was Noreen that was causing the bother now.

'Why don't we call up the restaurant?' suggested Uncle Mick.

'Because we ain't got no phone,' replied Carmella.

'There's one at the drug store.'

'So a two-bit drug store gotta telephone an' we ain't got none an' you supposed to be a big-shot cop.'

Telephones were still a rare and luxury item in New York households at the turn of the century and Carmella had set her heart on being one of the first to have one, but Mick had always refused to have it installed. 'The damn thing would never stop ringing,' he had said, 'and if it ever did you would never be off the line to your sister in New Jersey.'

'Rosa's a doctor's wife. They gotta have the phone.'

'Then we'll wait till Joey goes to Medical School and maybe we can have one too!' His wife abruptly turned away. Uncle Mick suddenly realised what he'd said, and put his arm on his wife's shoulders. 'Hell

Carmella, you know what I mean. We have a phone, and I'll never get away from the Station. But maybe soon. OK?'

'OK.' She shrugged off her husband's hand and carried on her game. 'Your move, Joey.'

This then was the house that welcomed the Irish O'Neils to America, and for a moment there wasn't a sound in the room. Then there was the noise of feet on the front steps and the click of the lock on the front door.

'There she is now,' called out Joey from the card table. He jumped up and opened the door. But it was Paddy.

'I thought you was Noreen.'

'Isn't she home yet?'

'No,' called Carmella. 'And we're just getting a bit worried.'

'You wanna play dominoes, Paddy?' asked Joey plaintively.

'Hey,' said Carmella, 'jus' when I'm winning.'

'You play cards with your mother, Joey,' said Paddy, flopping into a cosy armchair. 'I'm beat.' He looked over to his Uncle Mick. 'Denis in bed, Uncle Mick?'

'Since nine-thirty. He's on the milk run in the morning.'

'An early start.'

'Yeh. At the station by six.'

'Joey, it's time you were in your bed.'

'But, mum – OK.' Joey shuffled off, but not before giving a kiss on the cheek to Paddy and a hug to his Dad. 'Good night all,' he called as he went.

'Where could she be, Paddy?' asked Carmella.

'Eh?'

'Noreen! She is more than an hour late. In New York. That's no good. Late night. Young girl.'

'She'll be alright,' interjected Uncle Mick. 'Whaddya think we got cops for?'

'Sometimes cops no good,' retorted Carmella.

'Not in my Precinct.'

'Queen's ain't your Precinct.'

'Do ye want me to go out and look for her?' said Paddy.

'No, I'll go,' said his uncle.

'Why don't you make the call from the drug store?' said Carmella.

'OK, OK, I will.' He rose from his chair and went to the window.

'Jeez, what a trouble is girls in a family, especially young girls. Well, I'll be –' He stopped suddenly and hurried to the door.

'Whassa matter?' called out Carmella. She could hear her husband running down the stairs outside.

Uncle Mick opened the front door and there was Noreen, standing with a broad grin on her face and a ten dollar bill in her hand, which she flourished triumphantly under her uncle's nose.

'How's that for a dumb waitress, Uncle Mick? Hey!' Uncle Mick had pulled her roughly inside and stepped out on to the steps just in time to see a horse cab drive off. He came back to her quickly.

'Who was that?'

'Just a customer, Uncle Mick. He gave me a lift home. It's alright. He was Roberto's cousin.'

'It ain't all right if you're an hour late.'

'It was a big table. They wanted a party. I gave them a couple of songs and got an extra ten dollars for it. Glory be, I thought you'd be pleased, Uncle Mick.'

'Are you alright, Noreen?' It was Carmella at the top of the stairs.

'Of course, I'm alright. What's everybody so worried about?' She ran up to her aunt. Paddy was also on the landing.

'You're late, Noreen.'

'Don't you start again,' snapped his sister. 'Here you are, Aunt Carmella, you can have this.' She proffered the ten dollar bill to her aunt.

'Noreen, you can't –'

'Sure, I can. Buy Joey something with it.'

'I wanna baseball bat.' It was Joey at the top of the inside stairs.

'Then you can have a baseball bat,' called out Noreen.

'Gee, thanks. That's means I can stop asking for it every night in my prayers.' They all laughed.

'Look Noreena, mia cara. Thissa too much.'

'Not at all, Aunty Carmella. Sure you deserve it for all you do for us.'

'You sure?'

'I'm sure.'

'You good girl, Noreena.' She kissed her niece on both cheeks and went upstairs towards Joey.

'Sure she is. She's an O'Neil, ain't she?' It was Uncle Mick. He'd come up the stairs behind them.

'Well, can we all get to bed now?'

'Not before time,' said Noreen. 'I'm done.'

'Good night, Noreen,' called out Joey as he was pulled away by Carmella.

'Good night, Joey.' She started to follow up the stair as Paddy said quietly from the sitting-room doorway,

'Good night, sister Noreen.' Noreen stopped and turned on the second step, then suddenly ran at Paddy and kissed him on both cheeks.

'Good night, brother Pat!' And she ran quickly upstairs. Paddy looked after her and found that he had a lump in his throat.

'Are ye right there, Patrick?' said Uncle Mick quietly.

'Oh, – sorry, Uncle Mick. Good night.' And he made his way to the stairs.

'Good night, son.' He switched off the hall lights, and the old grandfather clock in the hall sounded midnight at No. 59.

The same clock struck its shaky chimes for midday on the following Sunday, but it was hardly heard in the commotion at the front door as a whole concatenation of O'Neils assembled at the foot of the stairs to ascend for the usual weekly Sunday lunch. They had been in America for a month now and on each of the Sundays everyone had lunch at Uncle Mick's and Aunty Carmella's. Not only lunch, but drinks. That was the cause of all the excitement as the young men clattered up the stairs.

'Where's Noreen?' said Michael.

'Probably still in her bed,' said Denis.

'Why not?' said Sean. 'Sunday is her only chance of a long lie.'

'Not when she has to go to Mass,' added Michael, as they settled themselves in the various comfortable armchairs around the sitting room.

'Noreen doesn't go to Mass,' murmured Paddy quietly.

'Is that so now?' said Sean.

'Our little sister's a woman of the world now, you know,' explained Paddy with a smile.

'In three weeks?' asked Michael.

'Four,' said Denis.

'That makes all the difference!' said Michael. They all laughed.

'I don't know,' put in their uncle. 'I've known it take a night.'

'Ah, what do you know, Uncle?' bantered Sean.

'Tell us all about it,' continued Michael.

'Please don't,' said Denis. There was more laughter.

'What's so funny?' asked Joey.

'Nothing, Joey,' said Denis. 'They're talking about their sister.'

'Noreen?'

'Yea, that's right.'

'There's nothing funny about Noreen,' said Joey simply. That silenced the company for a bit, until Uncle Mick rose.

'Right, well, we'll have that beer now.'

It was a typical family occasion, the O'Neil Sunday. There was talk of work in the week, sport, the money made and lost, and all the great things they were going to do next week. As the beer went round, the conversation became louder and the laughter more frequent and all the time, the smell of a roast came up from the kitchen in a way that told everyone that Carmella had another Sunday treat in store. Her kitchen was hardly the size of a box, but it was a Pandora's box of culinary skills. It was amazing what came out of it. Not that it was a matter of money, far from it. She made every cent do the work of a dollar and squeezed every possible kitchen use from every ingredient used. No wonder Uncle Mick was getting fat. In fact, like most American policemen, he was dangerously overweight. If he weren't careful, he could have heart problems. 'Impossible,' he would protest, 'when my heart's in the right place.'

Denis told his brothers at length about being a police recruit in the City and probably made it all funnier than it really was. Sean and Michael had stories to tell of Rafferty's and probably only told the half of it. They were developing into quite a team and it was not at all certain what road they would take. They were at a funny kind of crossroads, caught as they were between the warring worlds of the booze and the cards.

'Youse'll watch yourselves, lads,' said Uncle Mick. 'They're a hard lot, these Irish, you know.'

'Don't worry, Uncle, we know who to go to if we get into trouble.' Paddy was even quieter than usual. It took a lot of fraternal teasing about his not having a real job to rouse him, until he eventually said,

'I've made up my mind what I want to do.'

'And what's that, Paddy?'

'I'd like to become a priest.'

This announcement caused an absolute silence of astonishment. It had always been known in the family that Paddy had wanted to be a priest, but he had never done anything about it until now.

'I saw Father Donnelly on Monday and he had me up with the Canon on Tuesday and he took me to Bishop Monaghan last night.'

'Was that where you were? I wondered about the suit,' said Denis.

'I thought it was my turn to wear it.'

'Sorry about that,' said Paddy.

'Not at all,' said Denis. 'Sure it'll be a blessed garment now.'

'Will that mean you'll get more when you hock it next time?' asked Michael.

'Them days are over now, Michael. I go on to half pay next week.'

'Then you can buy your own suit,' said Sean.

'Why does he need a suit when he's got a uniform?' asked Michael.

'Just to impress the girls,' said Sean.

'I thought that's why he had the uniform.'

'Where's Noreen?' interrupted Joey.

'Here I am.'

They all turned to the door and there was Noreen, looking ravishing in large hat and day dress and carrying a parasol. 'How do I look?' she said, whirling round. She knew she looked good, and so did they. But nobody said anything. They could only stare. Just at that moment, Carmella appeared behind her. What a contrast between the two women. One tall, young, gay, apparently poised, and radiant in the fashion of the time, and the other, small, aproned, red-faced from the kitchen, but each as proud of the other as they stared. 'Oh, you are so – molta bella. Si, una bella regazza.'

Noreen leaned forward and kissed her little aunty's glistening brow, 'Grazie tante, aunty!' She laughed at her silly rhyme, and turned to the men folk.

'What time is it?' Just then the clock in the hall sounded again. 'One o'clock. It should be here. Excuse me, aunty. See ye's all,' she called as she fluttered past her aunt and sailed downstairs.

The men rushed to the large bay windows and looked down into the street. There was a horse cab waiting at the lamp post and standing in front of it was a tall flashy-looking gentleman dressed in an expensive suit. They watched as he opened the door for Noreen as she came down the outside steps. She gave a little wave to them at the window and then lifted her skirts to try and mount the cab. She was playing the grand lady up to the hilt, but this effect was rather spoiled as she tripped on the step and disappeared into the interior of the cab in a flurry of underskirts and long white stockings. The boys upstairs laughed their heads off as they watched the expensive suit close the carriage door and hurry round to the other side. They were still laughing derisively as the horse-cab was driven off. But Uncle Mick wasn't laughing. He had recognised Enrico d'Agostino.

EIGHT

Old Den O'Neil was having difficulty reading the letter. 'It's the writing,' he said, squinting at it from arm's length.

'It's your eyes, sure,' retorted Tommy Drennan. 'Isn't that so, Tim?' Tim, the barman, went on polishing the glass in his hand. 'As ye say, Tommy.'

'How can it be me eyes,' persisted Den, trying the pages of the letter an inch from his nose, 'when I've had them man and boy these sixty-seven years – sixty-eight come November – and never a day's bother have they given me?'

'The only bother you've got is that you forgot your glasses. See me the thing here and I'll read it out to ye.' Tommy reached out his hand for the letter.

'Not a bit of it. I'll get it in a good light here, and I'll be fine. Just you wait now.' And he shifted himself round in his stool at the bar.

It was late morning at Ingham's and Den had just received the first letter from America. He had met Tommy, the postman, as usual just after opening time. Every morning he had asked him if there had been 'an American letter' and every morning Tommy had said no, so they always had one in Ingham's just to drown their disappointment. Now today, a letter had come and they were having one – or two – to celebrate.

'Man, Tim, it's thirsty work readin' a letter,' murmured Den.

'Set him the same again, Tim, or I'll never get to hear what it says. It's a terrible thing when a man comes into a pub with no money.' Den paid no attention and turned over another page and laid it face down on the counter, just missing a beer mug ring.

'And what about yourself, Tommy?' asked Tim, folding his newspaper.

'I'm fine,' replied Tommy absently, still trying to read the letter over Den's shoulder. Tim leaned into the old postman.

'Will you have another?' Tommy looked up, immediately alert. 'That's very kind of ye, Tim. I'll have the same again.' Tim shook his head and moved away, grinning, to the pumps. Den turned to his old friend.

'D'ye know Tommy –'

'Whassat Den?'

'They sent no money.'

'Eh?'

'No dollars this time.'

'Isn't that a shame, and you with nothin' on ye.' Den peered closely at another page of the letter then put it on the bar on top of the others. He held the last page up to his nose again, then tried at complete arm's length.

'What does it say, man?' pleaded Tommy desperately.

'Glory be!'

'What is it?' asked Tommy eagerly. Den relaxed his arm and turned to his friend.

'I can't see it,' he said simply.

'Let me read it then, that has the eyes in me head,' said Tommy, reaching out for it. Den was about to give it to him then changed his mind.

'No, you with the tongue in your head.' He picked up the pages from the counter, and checked to see that none was wet. 'I'll wait till I get me glasses.'

'Where are they?'

'I must have left them at home.'

'Ah, dammit! There's a good read missed.'

'Just so.' With great deliberation Den put the six-page letter back in its long envelope with all the fancy United States stamps on it.

'It costs money to send a letter from America,' commented Tommy.

'It does that. Even if they don't put money in it.'

'Better luck next time.'

'Aye so.'

At the end of the village, he saw that Sergeant Davidson was in his shirt sleeves digging his front garden. Den crossed the road and leaned on the Policeman's front gate. He watched him at work for a moment.

'A fine mornin', sergeant.'

''Tis that.'

'For the diggin', I mean.'

'Aye.' Sergeant Davidson straightened up, and putting his foot on his shovel wiped the sweat off his brow with the back of his hand.

'I had a letter from America this mornin', and there was an item I thought you'd like to know.'

'Oh, aye?' said the Sergeant, in a deadpan tone, but intrigued nevertheless. 'What's that?' Old Den then told the policeman about young Denis. Sergeant Davidson was quite surprised.

'I thought it was Sean was to be the Garda.'

'Not in New York at any road.'

'And Michael's doing well?'

'Grand. And Paddy too. Aye.' Den looked thoughtful.

'It's the fine boys you have, Mr O'Neil.'

'I have that.' The policeman slowly resumed his digging.

'And young Kevin there. He's getting to be a fine, big fellow.'

'He is that too.'

'But I wonder, you know.'

'What's that, Sergeant?'

'I do. I wonder sometimes at the company he keeps.'

'Oh, d'ye say now?'

'I do. There's grown men come out from Newry askin' for 'im.'

'Ah, he's a popular lad.'

'He is that. I would think he should be seein' more of boys of his own age.'

'Ah, well ye see, Sergeant, he was always old for his years. Bein' the youngest in the family, ye see.' The Sergeant stopped and looked at Den closely.

'I see.'

'Well, I'm glad ye do, Sergeant. I'll be on my way.'

'I hope you won't mind me mentioning the boy.'

'Not at all, Sergeant. It's something I'll be keepin' in mind.' He moved away. 'I'll not keep ye from your diggin'. Good day to ye, Sergeant.'

'Good day Denis.'

Walking on, Den reflected that the sergeant was a good man but Denis wondered why he had made such a thing of Kevin. And what was the company he was keeping? Den hardly saw his eighteen-year-old son these days. They might as well have lived in different worlds. Perhaps they did. He was nowhere to be seen as Den arrived back at the farm.

Nessie was busy in the dairy, separating the milk. She wasn't pleased to see her husband. 'Did ye forget ye were to go in to Rosstrevor this forenoon with Kevin and the cart?' Old Den had forgotten but he put on his usual leprechaun face and made a show of annoyance.

'Ye don't mean now he went without me?'

'He did and you know it. And the hardware store will not stay open all day while you get drunk with Tommy Drennan.'

'We did not get drunk woman. I had a pint.'

'Or two. Move out of the way.' She almost pushed him aside with the big bowl of cream she was carrying and laid it on the bench.

'I don't suppose there was a letter?'

'There was.' Nessie wheeled round from the basin.

'There was?' Den was enjoying the moment.

'There was I say.' He produced the letter from his pocket.

'From America?' gasped his wife. Old Den giggled at her open mouth.

'All the way. And here it is.' He held it up.

'Jesus, Mary and Joseph!' Nessie O'Neil sat on the dairy stool and wiped her flushed face with the end of her apron and held out her hand, still pink and damp.

'Give it to me then.' He did so. 'You've opened it.'

'I had to open it if I was to read it, hadn't I?'

'How could you read it when you left your glasses on the kitchen table?'

'Was that where they were?' Nessie suddenly looked up sharply.

'There was no money?'

'There was no money.'

'How did you pay for the drinks? You had nothing in your pocket?'

'How do you know?'

'I looked this mornin' before you were up to give Kevin some and you had only a shillin' and some coppers.'

'You've been through my pockets?'

'And why not?'

'And you gave it to Kevin?'

'Sure I did. He was to be all day in the town – where you should have been. Now let me read this.' She bent her head to the letter and Den moved to his wife and looked over her shoulder as she devoured every word of the first letter received from her children three thousand miles away. Naturally, Paddy was the writer and knowing what his mother would want to hear, he gave her all the news of every one of them in New York, including Uncle Mick and Aunty Carmella, but he kept his own news to the end.

'My God!'

'What is it?' asked Den. Nessie looked up and her face was streaming with tears. Den was startled.

'What's the matter, woman?'

'Oh, Denis,' she said, clutching him round the waist, 'I'm so happy!'

*

From the Gulf of Suez out into the Red Sea the Mataura had made its way into the Indian Ocean. Life on board ship had settled into such a routine for passengers and crew alike that it was hard to imagine either had known a life before the ship, or expected that there would be one after it. From waking in the morning till sleeping at night, life went by the beat of bells, and against the constant deep-throated throb of the steam engines far below. Occasionally a passenger might see an oil-spattered or coal-dirtied seaman, but for the most part, as far as non-crew were concerned, the ship propelled itself through the water by the particular kind of magic that cruising for a long time under the sun near the Equator induces. The nights were spectacular and star-filled, yet balmy and comfortable out on deck. In these hours it was possible to dream more dreams than in the stuffy confines of the cabins.

And Christina Keith was beginning to dream again, thanks mainly to the constant attention of Martin Dickenson, who now openly flaunted his infatuation with the young Scots girl. This left her wide open to the sarcastic jibes of brother Bobby and made her a cause for mild concern for brother Jim. He couldn't explain even to himself why he didn't trust the amiable Martin, but there was something just a bit flashy about the man that offended Jim Keith's native integrity. He decided, however, to say nothing to anyone, at least for now. William Keith knew what was going on, but didn't say anything either, except to comment at one time that Christina would be fine. 'What did she have two big brothers for?'

Tina, this afternoon, was lying in her shaded cabin, taking a siesta after the lunch on deck. She had sat with Martin Dickenson as usual, and he had been his usual attentive self. He seemed to manage to have all his off-duty times with her. Not only the family, but the other passengers were beginning to notice. It was funny, she had never paid much attention to the other passengers on the Mataura. Not that there were many, and, in the first weeks of the voyage, most people had kept themselves to themselves. But once the sun had begun to work on them in the Mediterranean, it was amazing how soon many of them thawed out. Since most were from Britain, they took a little longer to melt completely but now, in the common denominator of the sun tan they were all of one race – the human race. Even the crew were friendlier. Only the Goanese kept their distance, with the dignity and reserve of their people of course, but also because only a few of them could speak English. Samwar Ashib, or Sammy, as everyone called him had about three words of English, two of which were 'please', but he was such a friendly, caring, hard-working little man that people were more than willing to make linguistic allowances for him so that by smiles and signs, things got done in the cabin. Tina could see that her mother's Scottishness further confused Sammy, and the longer the voyage the more probable it would be that he would return to the beautiful island of Goa with a pronounced Forres accent!

It was Sammy who had pulled down the blinds in her cabin and laid out the sheet on her bunk for the siesta hour. The other bunk looked very empty indeed in the half-dark of the cabin. She could see the sunlight straining to pierce the canvas of the porthole blind and outside on the deck Tina knew it would be hot, very hot, sticking, sweating, burning hot. But here she was cool. Stretched out under the single, starched, white bedsheet, she was pleasantly aware of her very un-Scottish nudity. It was a state quite novel to her as the occasions to revel in a lack of clothes were not common at Craigend House. Draughts, brothers and her innate Calvinistic prudery saw to that. But now, secure behind her shaded porthole and locked cabin door, she could enjoy a rare and private freedom. She was supposed to sleep but she couldn't.

She wondered how many of the passengers actually did sleep in the middle of the day. It went so against their northern European ethos to steal sleep from the centre of the work span, but there was no doubt and despite herself, her class, her upbringing, her family inhibitions, Tina felt herself yielding to the drowsy, warm, easy sensuality of the cool bed in a hot room and she writhed for a second or two in sheer pleasure. Martin Dickenson came into her head. For the first time on the voyage, she started to think about him, or rather her developing relationship with him. Up till now she had tried to avoid thinking about it seriously, because she hadn't imagined that it was serious. But it was becoming more so, especially on his part, and she wasn't quite sure how she felt about it. When she was absolutely honest with herself, she had to admit that she didn't really like the English officer, but she was flattered by his attentions and enjoyed the fuss he made of her.

What was even more puzzling and intriguing, given the kind of girl she was, was that she enjoyed his kisses! From the first tentative peck in the corridor leading to her cabin on the first night out of Suez to the deep and passionate embraces they had shared only last night behind the lifeboat on the for'ard deck, her physical pleasure, and appetite, had grown unmistakably. From a vague stomach sensation the feeling had burgeoned to a lusty, tingling, leg-shaking sensation that had her head spinning and her heart pounding against her ribs. Yet what was it really but a labial collision, mere physical oscillation, but what it did to her! What it did in fact, was to awaken in Tina Keith, a latent and powerful sensual desire that had always been there within her. Certainly, it was something she had never known in Forres. The tentative peck there was the height of passion for the rugby-playing Mr Thomson and was undoubtedly a grievous sin against the flesh for Mr Braid, the minister! What scared Tina now was that if things went on as they were going with Martin it would lead to the inevitable conclusion, and what would happen then? They would have to get married, she thought in her Scottish way. I wonder if the Captain would conduct the wedding service? Or a funeral if her father were ever to find out. Her father? He was through the wall, in the very next cabin. With her mother. Despite herself, Tina felt a wave of guilt sweep over her. Yet what had she to feel guilty about? She had done nothing. She had only let a man kiss her.

But Tina knew she had returned his kisses. She knew she wanted what they promised, and now lying alone and vulnerable, she squirmed in frustration at the memory of his lips on hers, the pressure of his body, the hardness of that part of him against her thigh. Instinctively, she reached down and caressed that thigh and with her other hand she tried to cover the tell-tale hardening of the nipples on her breasts. Her hands moved all over her own body and she began to writhe again. Strange sensations were flooding through her – warm, cosy, sweet sensations. She knew she had a good body, a beautiful body, but now it was beautiful in another way. It was telling her that it was a living thing, from the curling in her toes to the tingling in her scalp, it shivered with aliveness and another kind of promise, a promise of rewards that were all its own. Her breathing was faster now and without realising what she was doing, her right hand sought that place between her legs and she held herself tight against the upheaval that was beginning there among the softer hair and even softer, yielding flesh. Her fingers found the centre of that storm and tighter and closer and harder they worked as her pelvis arched against the unspeakable, unstoppable, unbearable desire that engulfed her. She moaned in abandon, and then, in her climax, let out a cry that was primeval in its intensity.

The sheet was now on the floor and she lay, spreadeagled on the narrow bunk, panting with effort, spent with passion not knowing whether to laugh or cry with the unexpectedness of it all, rejoice in its terror and power, or wonder at the force that had taken possession of her. Tina Keith had never been more exposed to herself or to her innermost feelings in her life before and she wasn't sure how to react to the momentousness of it all. Like every girl she had always guessed that there was a whole underworld of her sex but for her it was a world forbidden her, and even in marriage there was no hint that any pleasure was to be sought in the body

120

matrimonial. For the Scottish wife, the sexual act was a necessary duty to be borne as seldom as possible. It was a means of making children and not an end in itself. To the woman her body was nothing more than a channel, a medium for the pleasure of the man, but Tina knew that now that pleasure could be hers too. She had just heard its first signal, felt its first powerful warnings. It was with such thoughts racing through her mind that she heard a noise at her cabin door. As she turned her head in alarm there was Martin Dickenson standing in the doorway. . .

'I don't understand Martin Dickenson.' The Chief Engineer made the statement with all the authority of his status on board and with the bluntness of the Dundonian that he was. Jock Aitken had been at sea since he was a boy. Not that he had seen much of it, having been incarcerated with the engines for all of his working hours and incapacitated in his cabin during his time off. For Jock was a prodigious drinker and was known in every harbour from Southampton to Sydney as Jock the Tanker because of the amount of liquid cargo he could carry across the oceans! But now he was relatively sober and playing a ponderous game of chess with Jim Keith in the cramped comfort of the Engineer's cabin.

'Aye,' Jock went on. 'I've never liked the man from the beginning. First of all, he doesn't take a drink, and that worries me. I don't trust a man that disna take a drink. Which reminds me, Jim boy, have another. The bottle's at your hand there.'

'No thanks.' Jim had already had plenty over the lunch. He was finding it hard enough to concentrate on the board as it was and listen to the gnarled old Scotsman's various opinions at the same time. He was especially interested in a fellow officer's opinion of Martin Dickenson. Jim had noticed that day at lunch how close the Second Officer had become with Tina, and this had bothered him even more. Perhaps Chief Aitken could throw some light on the situation.

'Have you known Martin long?' he asked the Engineer.

'This is our third voyage out on the cattle run.'

'Cattle run?'

'Aye, Down Under. Sailors' talk for the emigration ships, because for the most part they were shoved on board like cattle, poor souls, since the Captains got a pound a head per man and two pounds for the women. They packed them in like cattle, though they weren't treated as well once they pulled up anchor, I can tell ye. If you had seen some of the things I've seen in my time.'

'Through a glass darkly,' Jim murmured.

'Whit's that?'

'It's nothing. Sorry.'

'But then, them wis maistly sailin' days, ye have to understand. In the 1850s, and I wis just a boy before they sent me hame again tae learn the engines. But as I wis saying, young Dickenson was a puzzle from the start. I never heard tell what his home port was, although I think he's a Geordie, but he's no' like any Geordie I've met. For a start he's got money. He always had money, more than I have, yet he's on half o' what I get a month. And what's even worse, he disnae bother who knows it. You'll see him at every port, a box o' this, a parcel o' that. His cabin must be like a warehouse. What puzzles me is who is it all for? But here we mustna gossip like a couple o' fishwives. It's your move.'

'No it isn't. It's yours.'

'Dammit, man, why did ye no' tell me? Now, let me see. Bishop takes Knight. . . .'

Florence Keith looked up from her bedspread. What was that noise? A bump? Was that somebody crying? It seemed to be coming from Tina's cabin through the wall. It must have been her imagination, Florence thought. This was the quietest time of the day, when everybody took a rest, not that it made much difference to her. Her day was one big long rest, and yet it wasn't. Her bedspread was growing to such an extent that she wondered if she would have enough wool left to finish the six feet square cover she had in mind. But it was a lovely way to pass the time. And she was beginning to feel a bit better, although she wouldn't dream of telling anybody. She had no desire to find her sea legs, but she had to confess to herself that the journey was a lot longer than she thought it was going to be. Still the family came in to see her regularly, although she saw less of Tina these days. William was his usual quiet self. As was Jim. She never expected anything else from both of them. As long as they had their books to read, they were happiest in their own company.

It was Bobby's nightly visits before dinner that she looked forward to most. He always had stories to tell about what happened that day on the ship, who he had met, what they had talked about. And he was so funny, too, when he impersonated all the different people and put on their voices. Last night he was full of some of the new people who had come aboard at Aden, especially a young Jewish girl. He was an awful man for the lassies, Bobby. But there was no harm in him. He was a good boy, Bobby, and people could say what they liked. And what was the name o' the girl he was talking about last night? It was a kind of a foreign name, she thought.

*

122

'Gebler. G-E-B-L-E-R. It's a Prussian name, I think.'

'But you're not Prussian, are you?' The young, dark-haired girl laughed and Bobby was pleased to catch a glimpse of fine teeth. He was sitting with her in the empty dining saloon. They had come inside from the deck lunch, and somehow had just remained there when everyone else went off. Bobby, true to form, had made a point of getting to know the new arrivals, especially the young girl, who had come aboard with the Aden party. He had assumed this was her family, but she was on her own for the voyage, having travelled down from Palestine. True, she shared with the other three Jewish girls, but they were all going out to join families in Sydney. They were all from South Africa and had sailed on another ship from Durban shortly before the Mataura came down the Red Sea from Suez, and were part of a whole group of Jewish people who were anxious to start a new life in the Antipodes. Rachel on the other hand was going home. Bobby was curious about the whole thing, never having ever met a Jew before, not realising that Rachel Gebler had never met a Scot. Rachel was still laughing.

'No, I'm not Prussian.'

'Then you're South African?'

'Do I sound South African?'

'I don't know what South Africans sound like.'

Rachel smiled. 'I'm Jewish.'

'That's your religion. What does it say on your passport?'

'British. I was born in Poplar.'

'Poplar? Is that a place?'

'In London.'

'I thought it was a tree,' grinned Bobby.

'OK,' she said, 'I was born up a tree.' It was Bobby's turn to laugh. They were getting on very well, this twenty-six-year-old Scot and the twenty-year-old Jew. But then it was Bobby's style to get on well with everyone at first, and especially young girls.

In no time, he was in the full flight of his considerable imagination and she was listening wide-eyed, but with the safety catch of her natural scepticism still on. Rachel had come from too old a race, and had been to too many places in her young life thus far to be bowled over absolutely by the bravura of a talkative Scotsman. There was no doubt he was likeable, but to someone like Rachel, such garrulousness was highly suspect, though, for the moment, she was quite happy over yet another cup of strong coffee, to let him babble on. Anyway, he was good looking and had soft eyes and he could talk, so why shouldn't she let him? She had nothing else to do. What Rachel didn't realise however was that by doing so she was playing exactly to Bobby's greatest strength. Given this cataract of words, he let it play on her until she was helpless in the swimming sea of his verbal conceits. Women are especially susceptible to words, and Bobby had learned this early. As the afternoon drew on, they drew nearer, and it came as no surprise to either of them that at a certain point in his diatribe, he stopped suddenly, held her eyes, then bent towards her upturned face and kissed her.

'I'm sorry,' he said immediately. 'I couldn't help it. I was staring at your lips and I just wanted to touch them. I'm sorry.'

'That's alright,' she replied softly, as surprised as he was, but strangely enough, not at all insulted or perturbed. There was a silence until Bobby said eventually,

'What are you thinking?'

'I don't know if I should tell you,' she said solemnly.

'I can take it,' he said with a playful shrug. 'Tell me.'

'I was just thinking I wish he would kiss me again.'

And Bobby did.

It was the longest and most meaningful kiss Tina had ever known, and when Martin drew back, she let her head fall on his shoulder, glad to have the chance to get her breath back and try to get her thoughts in order. Had it really happened? Had they made love? Had she really been seduced, or had she seduced him? She was twenty years old and had hardly been kissed and now, after knowing this man, now holding her so tightly, after only knowing him for a few weeks, she had given herself to him gladly. Willingly. That was the amazing part. No, it wasn't. What was amazing was that it had been so good. She had been terrified, but he had been gentle. She had been willing, and he had been strong. What more could there have been? Yet she knew it wasn't love. At least not on her part. It was sex. Full-blooded, normal, happy, inevitable sex between consenting adults. And she had loved every breathless, palpitating, sweaty minute of it. She ought to feel ashamed, but she didn't. In the world's eyes, she was ruined. She was a fallen woman; her virtue and honour gone in a wonderful moment. But she didn't feel like that. She didn't know how she felt. But she wasn't sad.

'Are you alright?' he said.

'Yes,' she breathed.

'I'd better be getting back.'

'Yes.'

He gently released her and taking her hand pressed the cabin door key into it.

'How did you get this?' she asked.

'Love laughs at locksmiths, so the saying goes. No, seriously, I ordered Sammy to give me his. I told him I was making an inspection. I suppose it could be said I was doing that.'

'And do I pass?'

'With flying colours!' He gave her a grin from the door, then was gone. She stood in the middle of the cabin for a moment, then went and sat at the edge of the bed, then quite suddenly she burst into a flood of tears.

'What's the matter, my wee darling?' John Keith picked up little Elspeth as she sprawled face down in the rug at his feet. He enjoyed the feel and smell of his infant daughter as he held her closely into his neck and patted her back. He had been sitting at the table in the parlour about to write his first letter to the family on the ship. The shipping line had given him all the forwarding addresses en route, but many of them made little sense to someone sending a letter from Forres, so John thought it safe to send his first one to Sydney, where the Keiths could pick it up around 20th August, which was the date he had been given for the Mataura. At the same time he was keeping an eye on Elspeth while Thomasina was taking young Kenneth to the doctor for yet another couple of stitches. Their young son could be said to be injury-prone and was forever falling downstairs or putting his hand through window panes or pulling pans down on him from kitchen shelves. His three-year-old body was already a patchwork of scars and stitches. He was obviously being saved for something. Thomasina was constantly worried about him and the more she tried to repress him, the more he rebelled and consequently the more he was exposed to bumps and bruises. John was quite happy to let him be, knowing he had a healthy boy's instinct to survive.

Elspeth was the worry. She had been slow to put on weight and was a bad sleeper, but what she was good at was crying, and she was doing plenty of that now. John was always amazed that so much noise could come from such a little vessel. 'There, there, my wee pet. There, there.' He walked up and down doing his best to sing a nursery rhyme to her: 'Baa, baa, black sheep, have you any wool? Yes sir, yes sir, three bags full . . .'

As he paced up and down the thought came into his head of his father and his father before him and his before that: drapers, shepherds, farmers, and now going out to New Zealand to be wool merchants. That same thread, as it were, going through all the generations. So many lives all in the back of a sheep. 'Baa, baa, black sheep,' he 'sang' again. Was that Bobby? Or was he himself the real black sheep of the family? He knew people were talking about his drinking. What the hell? What else was there to do?

125

At least it got him out of the house. But this little thing in his arms was a good reason to stay about the hearth. She had stopped crying now. It couldn't have been his singing. She must have been tired, and maybe she liked to feel her big daddy's hands holding her tightly high in the air on his shoulder. Maybe babies know more than we think they know and like the innocents they are, know when they're loved and wanted.

Not like poor Ella's bairn. Poor Ella! She'd been sent to her aunty in Aberdeen to await events. Mrs Friar had told John Thomson she was on a special midwifery course at the Aberdeen Hospital, but big John's sister had her suspicions. Never mind, the child would be born, and John Keith knew he would have it up on his shoulders just like wee Elspeth here, pacing up and down just the same way to get it quiet and let it sleep. It would be just a bairn like every other bairn. No, it wouldn't. It would be half a Keith, and better a half of Keith than a whole nothing.

His cogitations were interrupted by the sound of the front door and in a minute young Kenneth had his arms round both his knees and was trying to tell his daddy that the doctor had given him a sweetie. Thomasina came in with the usual worried frown on her face.

'That laddie o' yours will be the death o' me yet,' she said.

'Why is he always my laddie when he's a trouble, and he's yours when he's good?' But his wife paid no attention and was already on her way to the kitchen with her laden grocery basket. Meantime, young Kenneth's chatter had wakened Elspeth again, but John just raised the level of his 'singing' and his bawling nursery rhyme drowned both children out. In the kitchen, Thomasina stood with a large cheese in her hand listening for a minute. She shook her head. 'Whit a noise!' she said. And continued unloading her basket.

It was very late that night before John was able to get out the pad of lined paper, the ink bottle and the pen and start his letter. He had been for his usual refreshment to the Masons' Arms and consequently neither his hand nor eye was steady as he began to write: 'Dear mother . . . .'

NINE

The rafters were ringing at Rafferty's. The singing had reached such heights of drunken enthusiasm and decibel strength that it was nearly impossible to hear the words of the song that tight-packed gathering of flat caps and bowlers were singing, but they were there alright. The tune was 'Skibbereen'. Not that it mattered. Any tune would do as long as the feeling was right.

'Oh, father dear, I often hear you speak of Erin's Isle,
Her lofty scenes and valleys green, her mountain rude and wild.
They say it is a lovely land wherein a prince might dwell,
Oh why did you abandon it? the reason to me tell.'

It was Saturday night and there was more than the usual tribe of Irish exiles gathered to celebrate the end of a long, hard-working week and the prospect of a lie-in tomorrow morning. The Irish constituency in New York had not completely won through from its lowest of the low position in post Civil War America. But at least it now vied with German sausage makers and leather workers as the foremost ethnic group in turn of the century America. Fortunately for the Irishmen, the Germans had elected to take the cheap trains to the middle west, and that other industrial capital of Chicago. Only the Italians now threatened the Hibernian element as resident immigrants in the main cities of the East Coast. But from Atlantic City up to Montreal in Canada, it was the Irish who had taken shamrock root, although, like the Germans and Italians, they were never allowed to forget their other roots, especially on a Saturday night.

'Oh, son I loved my native land with energy and pride,
Till a blight came o'er my crops – my sheep, my cattle died.
My rent and taxes were too high, I could not them redeem,
And that's the cruel reason that I left old Skibbereen.'

Jackie Rafferty, himself, was an Antrim man, and true to his

cautious background, learned hard in Glynn Village near Larne.
He still served behind his own bar. With his brown bowler firmly
fixed over beetle eyebrows and chomping on a cigar which never
seemed to be lit, he kept his thumbs in his waistcoat and an eye
on every pint of porter that was delivered over the busy counter
of his bar. Like most Irish publicans, he didn't only serve drinks.
He was the Postmaster-General for all the newly-landed families,
the Paymaster-General for those who hadn't yet found work and
the Adjutant-General for those who had managed to make a start,
and had aims to do better. Jackie could spot a lucky Mick as soon
as he crossed over his door. There was something about a way a
man carried himself, poor as he was, that Jackie could read at ten
paces. It was a set of the shoulders, a lift of the head, a look in
the eye, but he could always tell who was going to succeed, and
who was going to fail. He was also very wary of the story-tellers.
Everyone had their story to tell of the Old Country and none was
a happy one.

Sean and Michael O'Neil attracted the Rafferty eye almost from
the first night. They had all the requisites he looked for and in
addition a kind of swagger that was attractive, especially Sean. The
first night they had appeared with their Uncle Mick, who was in for
his usual look around and sealed envelope slipped surreptitiously
over the bar under a wiping cloth. This was Jackie's usual practice
with Mick O'Neil, but Sean had noticed, and remarked to his
brother,

'It's a late post they have in New York, Michael,' pulling the
cloth away from the fat white envelope. 'A special delivery, ye
might say.'

'There's no name on it,' said Michael.

'Ah, boys,' quickly put in Uncle Mick, 'youse can leave it to me.
I know the man it was intended for. Isn't that right, Jackie?'

'Right on, Superintendent. Ye know the very man.' Uncle Mick
already had it in his coat pocket and was beaming at his two young
nephews.

'What'll youse have, boys?'

From this incident, Jackie had kept an eye on the O'Neil boys
and when the chance came he offered them a job with him.

'Sure I've never worked in a bar,' said Sean.

'Nor have I,' added Michael.

'We're just two poor country lads,' continued Sean.

'I can see that,' said Jackie with some irony. 'But youse have got
an eye in your head and a tongue in your mouth, an' I'm thinkin'
ye wouldn't be shy in a barney.' A bargain was sealed that night
and both of them were hired to start in the morning.

There was a great shout from the crowd as the song ended. The babble of conversation and the calling out of orders resumed while they waited for the next song. Nobody knew who started it in the long room. It could only be the first words of the first line and before anyone knew it, it was taken up by everyone and became another anthem to their sentimental nationhood, and an idea of an Ireland that became greener each day they were away from it. This Saturday night was particularly busy. There must have been overtime on the construction sites for there was money to spend, and Sean, Michael, Denis and Paddy were being run off their feet. Sean brought his brothers in for each Saturday night. Denis couldn't always manage because of shifts, but Paddy was glad of the few dollars and the company. It was all a bit raucous for his tastes, but deep down he knew that individually they were good-hearted enough men and collectively they could be moved to tears by a song or roused to passion by rhetoric. But for the most part, they were quite content to drink and sing and drink and talk and drink and cry then drink and fight, until another Saturday night was over. By this time, the next song was underway:

'Oh! Paddy dear and did you hear the news that's going round,
The Shamrock is forbid by law to grow on Irish ground.
No more St Patrick's Day we'll keep, his colours can't be seen,
For there's a cruel law against the wearing of the green . . .'

The rowdy chorus continued among the men and the smoke as Paddy with a tray of empty glasses almost collided with Denis carrying a tray of full ones. 'Jeez, Paddy, will you look where you're goin'?' gasped Denis. 'Ye nearly had a week's wages on the floor.'

'I'm thinkin' they'd never notice,' yelled Paddy, 'with the stuff that's swimming round me feet already.' The brothers manoeuvred their way round each other and through the crowd during the next chorus.

'I met with Napper Tandy, and he took me by the hand,
And he said, "How's poor old Ireland and how does she stand?"
She's the most distressful country that ever yet was seen.
For they're hangin' men an' women for the wearin' o'
     the Green . . .'

Paddy managed to get his tray of empties to the end of the bar where Michael had another tray of full beers ready to go out again.

'Table Number 7 up in the corner. You get the money from the red-headed man with the sick on his trousers.'

'Not him again,' groaned Paddy.

'Never mind, Paddy, just pretend it's Lent and offer it up.' Paddy sighed and lifting up the heavy tray began to make his way to the far corner.

Sean stood beside Jackie Rafferty and it was all he could do to prevent himself putting his own thumbs in his waistcoat pocket. After all, he was chargehand now. Not bad after only a month on the job. He was enjoying the new responsibility, although he wasn't quite sure what it was. Jackie himself still handled the money and Michael was in charge of the cellar. Sean more or less moved between each, and made himself useful. He could see that Jackie liked him, but he'd wait and see how things worked out. Whatever the way of it, there was money here. A lot of it. And it didn't all come from pushing pints of watered beer across the counter at two bits a time. Sean decided to keep his eyes open. After all, his uncle was a cop.

'When the law can stop the blades of grass, from growing as
   they grow,
And when the leaves in summer-time their colour dare
   not show.
Then I will change the colour, too, I wear in my caubeen,
But 'till that day, please God, I'll stick to wearing of
   the Green.'

Another roar signalled the end of another song, and nearly the end of the night. Already some of the men were beginning to go. Those that lived out of the district – places like Long Island and Manhattan. The pace was easing off and the O'Neil brothers were glad of it. They were young healthy sturdy men, but being on the go without stop in that smoky atmosphere for hour after hour would sap anyone's strength. Paddy was particularly affected and now sat on a bench at the side of the bar with his head down and his elbows on his knees. His chest was feeling it badly and he was struggling to get his breath. He felt a hand on his shoulder. It was Rafferty himself.

'Are ye alright, Paddy?' Paddy managed to nod. 'You can give over now. I'll get Sean to finish your tables.' Paddy tried to rise.

'No, mister.'

'It's alright. Rest yourself. He's been doin' nothin' but act the boss all night. A bit of honest toil will do him no harm. No harm at all.' Paddy watched the pub boss go to Sean as he stood at the cash box. He saw them look over to him, then Sean gave a nod and came straight over.

'You OK, Paddy?'

'Sure I am. It's just my chest.'

'I know. And I thought you were past all that.'

'I am.' He lifted up his head and held it back, so that his neck arched, as he sucked in some air. 'Phew! It's the smoke. But I'm fine.'

'Sure you are. I'll get Denis to walk you home. Or would you rather stay over with Michael and me. I'll get Mrs Lennox –'

'Not at all, at all,' said his young brother. 'It'll be easier now the smoke's dyin' down.'

'Well, you just sit there. I'll take yer trays.'

He was taking the first one out as Denis and Michael came up from the cellar carrying a barrel between them. 'Don't be takin' that home now, Denis,' quipped Sean as he passed.

'I'll be lucky to get it to the bar,' gasped Denis.

'You're getting soft in that Police Force o' yours,' said Michael from the other side of the barrel. As they placed it behind the bar, Jackie pointed with his cigar how he wanted it to go. While the brothers were heaving it to and fro accordingly, the boss asked Denis if Paddy had always been a well man.

'Well enough,' replied Denis. 'A bit of bother with his chest now and again.'

'I think he's having a bit of bother now then,' he said, indicating Paddy who was now sitting with his head held back again. Denis looked a little perturbed.

'I haven't seen him like that for a while.'

'I think maybe he shouldn't be workin' here, eh Denis?'

'I think you're right, Mr Rafferty. Excuse me.' Denis went to his brother, and immediately put his arms round him. 'Don't say a word, Paddy. I think you and me'll be gettin' home.' At the bar, Rafferty took an envelope from his pocket.

'Will ye see this gets to yer Uncle Mick?' he said to Michael.

'Ah, no, Mr Rafferty,' said Michael. 'Ye'll have to see Sean about that sort of thing.'

'I see,' said Mr Rafferty, putting the envelope back in his pocket. 'Thank you, Michael.'

'Thank you, Mr Rafferty. I'll go to Paddy now.' Michael left as Sean put a tray of empties at the end of the bar and called to Jackie Rafferty.

'That's most of them away now, Mr Rafferty. Will I start clearin' up?'

'I think you'd better. I'll give you a hand. There's only me and you to do it.' Sean looked puzzled and glanced round for his

131

brothers. He was just in time to see Paddy fall to the floor. Denis was immediately beside him pounding his back. There would be no more singing tonight.

> 'I'll sing a hymn to Mary, the mother of my God,
> The virgin of all virgins, of David's royal blood.
> O, let me though so lowly, recite my mother's fame,
> When wicked men blaspheme thee, I'll love and bless
> thy name.'

Father Mooney, the young curate taking the service that night, was glad as always to hear the sound of Nessie O'Neil singing. Why was such a voice, he wondered, given to a woman who only put her nose out of the farm on a Sunday morning and occasionally, like now, on a Sunday night to come to the Church of Our Lady of the Sorrows? Father Mooney had plenty of opportunity to think such thoughts as he automatically conducted the prayers. His vocation was a very slight and slender thing, it being more his mother's idea than his, but he was stuck with it now, so he might as well get on with it. As he recited the set prayers from the pulpit, his mind wandered in a very unpriestly fashion to the two young girls immediately below him. . . .

Nessie was also preoccupied. She was giving thanks for the letter from America. She was grateful that her children had all made the crossing of the sea safely. She was glad that Mick was there to look out for them. She was relieved that they had all made a start, and that Paddy's chest wasn't bothering him. A mother's prayers are more often than not a catalogue of her children's particular circumstances and Nessie O'Neil was no different from any other mothers in that respect. The only slight worry was with Kevin. He never went near church now. And he was spending far too much time out of the house these days. She had asked Denis to talk to him, but he was useless. He needed a talking-to himself. As always, she sighed when she thought of her husband. There was annoyance and exasperation in the sigh, but there was a lot of love in it too. She understood her man and she let him get on with it. She knew that in his own way he loved her. Denis O'Neil loved everybody, especially when he had a drink in his hand. '– In the name of the Father and of the Son and of the Holy Ghost.' Father Mooney's voice brought her back to the present again and she rose automatically crossing herself as she did so.

To her surprise, a man suddenly came into the pew beside her.

'Hello, ma,' whispered Kevin. What was he doing here? She could smell the drink on him. She glanced up enquiringly. He grinned down at her and winked, joining heartily in the final responses. He genuflected properly at the end of the pew as they left and took his mother's arm as they came into the porch of the little church. She hurriedly pulled him out after her to avoid speaking to anyone, particularly Father Mooney. She didn't like Father Mooney. Canon Devlin was bad enough, but at least you knew where you were with him. Father Mooney was two-faced and she was sure he shouldn't have been a priest at all.

'What's the hurry, ma?'

'Your da'll be wantin' his tea.'

'Not after the skinful he's had up at Gallagher's Smiddy.'

'He hasn't gone there again?'

'I left him there more than an hour since.'

'To do what?'

'To come and see my own mother of course,' he said playfully. 'Didn't I know you were at Devotions?'

'I wonder they didn't have the flags out.'

'For what?'

'You stepping inside the Chapel again. After all this time.'

'Well, if they did put flags out, Mother, I can tell you it would be a green, white and gold one.'

'Now, we'll have none of that kind of talk, Kevin O'Neil. At least not in the public street.'

By this time they were well through the village, and passing the police house.

'You mean, not while we're passing Sergeant Davidson's.'

'He was asking about you the other day.'

'Was he now? And what did you tell the nosy man?'

'It wasn't to me he was speaking, it was your da.'

Kevin laughed. 'Well, he'll get nothin' out of me da.'

'And why not?'

'Because there's nothin' in me da.' His mother stopped suddenly. And when he looked down at her, her face was white with fury. Before he had time to say anything, she hit him a hefty smack across the face with her right hand.

'Don't you dare talk of your da like that in front of me,' she said, then marched on quickly ahead of him. She walked so quickly that he had to run to catch up with her.

'Ma!' he called. And he was a young boy again running after his mother.

The Keiths were subdued at their evening meal. They had put off that day from Colombo and were pointed now to the exotic waters of the Far East. However the wonders of the Orient did not engage

the family that evening. There had been a cursory walk about the
port area, but it had been really more a matter of stretching their
legs than seeking out any Oriental experience. There had been the
usual look at the local merchandise, but the Keiths were always
aware that they weren't tourists on a holiday adventure around the
world. They were necessary travellers going from one country to
another. They needed all the cash they had for the new life ahead,
just as they needed to reserve their strength and conserve their
energies, but it was difficult not to be caught up in this exotic,
not to say erotic, traverse from one unreal and fantastical setting
to another.

It was really all too much to take in, and the strain was beginning
to tell. Even Bobby was quieter tonight and was glad to leave the
talking to Second Officer Dickenson, who was regaling the table
with a complicated anecdote about a passenger who insisted on
keeping a parrot in her cabin. He thought it was terribly funny.
He was the only one who did. Tina could hardly look at him
now. Yet on the other hand, he was positively proprietorial with
her. Even her father noticed and had asked her about it one day
on the deck.

'We're just friends, daddy.'

'You don't seem to be so happy about it.'

'I just – I don't know – I'm not sure,' she had said.

'Well, take your time. You're a young girl yet.'

'I'm twenty-one in August.'

'Then you're old enough to know what you're doing,' he had
answered.

She looked across at him now at the table, and found that he was
looking at her. She blushed and busied herself with her napkin. Her
father looked down at his plate. Bobby was trying to get a glimpse
of Rachel behind Martin's head, just as Martin said, 'You know
what I mean, Bobby.' Bobby laughed.

'Ye-es.' But without an idea of what the Dickens-on he was
talking about! Jim found it hard not to yawn. This pompous
Englishman was a bore. Why had they never seen it before?
Probably because the fellow had been so ingratiating. They had
all been so strange and he seemed so at ease. Why shouldn't he?
This was his territory. A ship at sea. A new port every week.
What was strange to them was so familiar to him, but what was
even stranger was that Tina should seem to like him so much.
Dickenson was now laughing so much that Jim concluded that
it must be the end of this particular story. The Goanese waiter
came forward with fruit for Mr Keith and Jim noticed his father
wave it away. He noticed too that the plate in front of him was

untouched. He remembered that Mr Keith hadn't come ashore that day either.

'I hope he's alright,' thought Jim to himself. Suddenly Mr Keith rose.

'If you'll excuse me,' he said. He was already on his way before anyone could move.

'Daddy –' began Tina.

'Leave him alone, Teenie,' said Bobby. 'He'll be alright.'

'He's hardly eaten anything,' said Jim.

'It's the heat,' said Bobby.

'I hope he's alright,' added Tina.

'It could be the heat,' contributed Martin Dickenson. 'I remember once I had a very bad experience in Aden. It was about two years ago. . . .' The Keiths inwardly groaned and held their breaths.

In the cabin, William groaned loudly and let out a breath.

'What's the matter, William?' asked his wife.

'Oh, I don't know,' said her husband, sitting on the bunk and putting his two large hands on his knees. 'I just don't feel great.'

'Have you any pain?' asked his wife, busy with her dinner tray.

He put his right hand up to his chest and rubbed gently. 'Well – I've had a kind of sensation here,' he said.

'It'll be something you've eaten,' opined his wife with her mouth full. William glanced over at her, grimaced and lay back on his bunk. 'I suppose you're right. This damned fancy food. I suppose I'm missing my porridge.' He closed his eyes and tried to close his ears against the incessant drumming of the engines. For the first time on the voyage, William Keith let himself think of Scotland. True enough, he was sick – homesick.

TEN

Officer O'Neil couldn't believe his eyes. There, coming straight towards him, was a cart without a horse! At least, that's what it looked like. There was a man holding a wheel sitting at the front of it, and he was waving his arm at him as he came nearer and nearer. Denis could only stand and stare and had to be pulled out of the way by Sergeant Peters just as the horseless carriage went speeding past him with a noise like a factory engine. Wide-eyed, the trainee traffic policeman watched it rattle up Fifth Avenue in a cloud of smoke.

'You stupid Irish bastard, you'll get us both killed!'

Sergeant Peters was understandably aggrieved at being given such a fright so early in his shift, and for having his second-best uniform trousers completely bespattered by yellow mud from the tyres of the passing car, but he had to act quickly or Officer O'Neil would have been the first casualty of the day.

'Didn't you see it comin'?' yelled Peters.

'What was it?' asked Denis, still shocked.

'It's a motorised car, you idiot. Haven't you seen them on the streets?'

'No.'

'Where have you been, for God's sake?'

'Rosstrevor.'

'Where?'

'Northern Ireland.'

'That explains it. Come 'ere.'

Sergeant Peters was not a natural teacher, and he found it difficult to show the right degree of patience, objectivity and understanding in dealing with his Police Officer charges in the Traffic Department. Perhaps he had had too many frights in the two years he had been doing the job. This morning's incident had been the most recent of many. There had been too many near misses from cart wheels, horses' hooves, street car bumpers and now horseless carriages. Consequently, despite the fact that he was a native-born New Yorker, he was a very nervous instructor and his twitching manner did little to inspire confidence in his methods. Now he took his Irish pupil aside on the sidewalk and shouted raucously into his ear above all the street noises of the busy intersection at 47th Street and Fifth.

'You gotta be in charge, see. Least, you gotta look as if you're in charge. Dem drivers'll never stop for nobody unless you give dem a clear hand sign – like this!' He held up a right arm so imperiously that all the pedestrians hurrying towards him halted at once. He had quickly to wave them on again.

'See what I mean. People see signals, dey do somethin'. When dey don't see nothin', they still do somethin' – like keep on comin' at you! You see.'

'I see,' replied Denis in a tone that belied the words.

'Right. Let's see you do it,' continued the Police Sergeant aggressively. 'It couldn't be easier. Any kid could do it. You go to the centre there and you face one way. Street first, then the Avenue. De street goes up an' down see, de Avenue is from side to side. OK?'

'OK!' answered Denis. His mouth was getting dry.

'You start north, give dem ten, slow count see, den halt wid de right hand, turn right to de west, slow count again, den halt, turn on de right shoulder to de south, anodder count, turn anodder right an you face de east, count again an' you're back where you started from. Gottit?' Denis cleared his throat.

'Gottit!' he mimicked.

'Right, let's go.' With that the Sergeant stepped into the road and into the traffic flow. Moses never parted the Red Sea with more effect. Horses shied, street-cars clanged, the new-fangled cars screeched and swerved, but Sergeant Peters made it to the centre of the intersection and somehow Officer O'Neil made it too. It was only when they got there that Denis realised he'd been hanging on to the Sergeant's arm!

'What you doin'?'

'Nothin' Sarge.'

The sergeant stood in the middle of the road and solemnly put on his white gloves. Denis stood as near to him as he could and warily eyed the traffic churning past him on all sides. Sergeant Peters was shouting at him again.

'What you gotta remember is dat pedestrians – you know, street walkers – dey got rights too. You gotta make sure dey don't get killed see.'

Denis assured him that he would bear that in mind. The Sergeant then took control of the traffic. For all his nervousness he showed a remarkable bravura in controlling single-handedly that extraordinary press of traffic bearing down on him from both directions. Only occasionally had Denis to get behind his burly instructor as some recalcitrant driver or wayward horse tried to do things his own way. On such occasions, Peters would halt everything on all sides and slowly walk towards the offender and give him or it a long and pointed lecture. Denis could only watch in awe. Then, with a piercing blast of his whistle the sergeant would set the maelstrom in motion again. Denis wondered how he'd ever do it. He was soon to find out for the sergeant was peeling off his white gloves.

'OK O'Neil, you take over.' Denis waited to receive the white gloves but the sergeant put them in his pocket. 'Remember, you turn clockwise an' you gotta look confident. OK?'

'OK.' His voice was a whisper.

'I'll stay wid ye for de first spell. Right, take over.'

With that the sergeant moved behind him. Denis found himself staring ahead in absolute panic. Every kind of vehicle seemed to be rushing towards him. More in self-defence than anything, he held up his right hand – and everything stopped! It was amazing! He had never known such a feeling of power. A surge of euphoria swept through him. He turned to his right and held up his hand again. The same thing happened. This was fantastic. He turned again with his right hand up and found himself staring into the apoplectic face of Sergeant Peters.

'For Crissake,' yelled that alarmed officer, 'Get 'em movin'!' So saying he waved on the traffic facing him as Denis did the same but by now they were at right angles to each other! It was some time and a lot of whistle-blowing and bad language later before the resulting chaos was sorted out. Sergeant Peters was at his worst in a crisis and once things were moving again and a certain rhythm had been imposed on both vehicles and pedestrians, he removed his white gloves. He was obviously shaken. 'I gotta have a coffee. You can do what you like O'Neil. Only if you're gonna kill anybody, make sure you start with yourself. OK?'

'OK Sergeant.'

The sergeant stepped away from the centre of the road impervious to the panic and annoyance he caused in traffic moving both ways. By some miracle, he made it to the sidewalk and without a glance back to his trainee, deserted at the vortex of the storm, he disappeared into the passing mid-morning crowd. But fortunately, Denis O'Neil was at his best in a crisis. In no time, principally out of a sense of self-preservation and survival, he had all four routes under some kind of control and even pedestrians were able to cross from time to time. He was even beginning to enjoy it. Meantime, the heavy morning rain had stopped and a summer sun had come out. If his arms hadn't begun to feel the strain a bit, Denis would have felt on top of the world.

Nevertheless, he was starting to think that the sergeant had gone on leave, not taken a coffee break, when his eye was caught by one of the pedestrians now coming towards him from the Fifth Avenue side. She was a small, blonde girl and there was something familiar about her. He found himself staring at her as he waved her on. Then she caught his eye and her eyes almost popped out of her head. It was Hana Karpiskova from the ship. By this time she was past him and he had to wave the other traffic on hurriedly, and she was lost among the crowds on the other side of the road. Denis turned back to his duties but he was still thinking of Hana. Had she seen him? Did she recognise him? She had looked just the same, except that he'd forgotten how pretty she was. Suddenly, there were shouts and yells from his right and there was Hana threading her way through the traffic towards him!

'Denees!'

'Hana!' Before he knew it, she was beside him.

'It is you?' she cried.

'It is me!' Denis replied laughing, and still waving on traffic from the other side.

'You are police?' she shouted, her blonde hair blowing, her eyes shining.

'I am – and I'm supposed to be on traffic duty. Careful!' She jumped up beside him, standing on her tip toes, and laughing up to his face.

'But you are wonderful, Denees!' With that she reached up and put her arms about his neck and started to kiss him. Though taken by surprise, he was quick to relish the pleasure involved and responded to such an extent that his hat fell off and rolled under the wheels of a passing cart. Denis didn't even notice. Horns sounded, drivers yelled derisively, passengers shouted good-humouredly, but the petite blonde and her policeman continued their close embrace. Even as he struggled, his arms waved impotently under the tight, but determined onslaught of the little Slav. The snarling traffic gradually engulfed them and the street was a cacophony of noise from vehicles and pedestrians alike. It was exactly at this moment that Sergeant Peters turned the corner and, taking one look, turned on his heel and went back the way he way he had come!

It was a July day on the Indian Ocean. Everyone was on deck, either playing deck quoits or reading or sunbathing. Tina Keith was doing the latter, at least as far as her dress, sun-hat, parasol and conventional decorum would allow her. Here she was on the Indian Ocean and the best of the morning sun beating down on her and she was still dressed as if going in to her daddy's shop in Forres. Bobby and Jim were lucky they had stripped down to their vests and straw hats and were now arguing fiercely about the positions of the quoits on the rings on the white, scrubbed deck-planks. Tina half-opened her eyes to see her brothers but directly in her eye-line was that Jewish girl sitting in a chair watching the men play. 'Watching Bobby I bet,' thought Tina. She had noticed how close they had become recently. Still, she looked a nice girl. Not Bobby's usual kind of girl friend. Yet they say one should never trust a shipboard romance. Who was she to talk? Just at that, an English voice said quietly:

'Good morning, Miss Keith.' She opened her eyes with a start and there was Captain Ellon smiling down at her.

'I hope I didn't disturb you?' he said in his charming way.

'No, not at all.' Tina noticed that Martin Dickenson was with the Captain on his rounds and had his 'conscientious young officer' face on. He had so many faces, Tina thought. She found herself sitting up straighter.

'A lovely morning to sit on deck, don't you think?' said the Captain.

'Yes.' She couldn't think what else to say. She was uncomfortable with the Captain. He seemed such a removed figure, but he was pleasant enough. He smiled and moved on. Behind his back, Martin also smiled at her but it was a different kind of smile. The Captain now stood over the chair where Mr Keith sat reading, only a yard from his daughter.

'He seems to be asleep,' said the Captain. 'I think we'll leave him to it. Good morning, Miss Keith.'

'Good morning.' Martin gave her a little wave as the two officers made their way down the deck to where the boys were playing their game. Tina looked at her father. His cap had fallen over his eyes. He looked much smaller huddled up in the chair. The only concession he had made to the brilliant sunlight was to remove his hard, white collar and that old brown tie he always wore. She looked at the hunched figure and felt a warm glow for her old daddy. They had recovered much of their old closeness during recent weeks, especially as he had become aware of the Dickenson relationship.

There were many times when she thought she should tell him of her deep uncertainties in this regard, but her subconscious guilt still prevented her being really open about the matter with anyone, never mind her own father. Sometimes she thought she might

confide in Jim, but on the one occasion she tried, he had refused
to discuss Martin at all. In fact he was quite vehement about it. She
knew she was not in love with the man, yet why had she allowed
. . . no, she wouldn't even think about it. The feeling wasn't what
she thought it would be. Not as she remembered. But even that
was beginning to be a very vague memory indeed. It had only been
five weeks ago, and yet it seemed to belong to another age. So much
had happened since then. But deep down she knew that only one
event was really significant – she was a virgin no longer.

Involuntarily she turned towards her father and stretched her
hand out towards him, but couldn't quite reach.

'Daddy,' she said. He didn't stir. He must be in a really deep
sleep, she thought, and rose up so that she could reach him.

'Daddy,' she said again. This time her fingers touched his
shoulder. 'Daddy.' She reached even nearer him and prodded his
shoulder quite firmly. To her astonishment, he fell over.

'Daddy!' she shouted in fright. She stood up at once, but even
as she did, Bobby was already kneeling by his father. She found
she couldn't move. Jim's arm was round her.

'Is he –?' she started to say. Bobby looked up.

'He's dead.' Tina fainted in her brother's arms.

'Tina!' cried Jim, catching her before she fell.

People started crowding round, everybody speaking at once. The
Captain and Dickenson pushed their way to the front. The Captain
knelt by William Keith and Dickenson attempted to go to Tina in
the deck chair, but Jim looked up, his face deadly white, his eyes
brimming with tears and his voice was vehement and fierce.

'Get to hell out of here!'

It was half past three the next morning – the darkest hour before
the dawn – before eight bells had sounded, a huddle of shadowed
figures stood by the light of a lantern at the starboard bow. The
bos'un held the light while the Captain read in a soft, subdued
voice that seemed to feather the still, pre-dawn air, yet Bobby and
Jim, standing with him, beside the red ensign, heard every resonant
syllable.

'I am the Resurrection and the Life, sayeth the Lord: he that
believeth in me, though he were dead, yet shall he live: and
whosoever liveth and believeth in me shall never die.' The all-male
party were gathered round the plank which protruded through
the gunwhale out into the darkness of the night and the black
sea below. On the ship side of the plank, beneath the flag, was a
tarpaulin bag that held the mortal remains of William Keith. 'We
brought nothing into this world, and it is certain we carry nothing

out. The Lord gave and the Lord hath taken away; Blessed be the name of the Lord.'

It had been a heart attack. 'Angina' the ship's doctor had said. 'I could smell 'is throat. Must've bin that pipe of 'is.' He wasn't really the ship's doctor, he was the carpenter but he was the one with the medical books and with a rough and ready practical experience of thirty years at sea, he was generally recognised as the medical authority on board when no doctor was sailing. Applecross was his name and he had hacked off a few limbs in his time and had even removed an appendix. Now he stood beside Captain Ellon, ready to perform his part in the dead-of-night ritual as he had done so many times before. Captain Ellon went on: 'In the midst of life we are in death: of whom may we seek for succour but of Thee, O Lord, who for our sins art justly displeased? Thou knowest Lord, the secrets of our hearts. . . .'

Listening, out of sight, in the port side companion way to the cabin deck below, Tina jumped at the words. 'It was my fault,' she said to herself, 'I sinned. I killed him. I killed my own father.' She turned her head away and pressing her forehead against the cold metal of the bulkhead, she closed her eyes tight against the tears. She felt too ashamed to cry.

Martin Dickenson watched her from where he stood, a deck length away under the fo'c'sle entry hidden from everyone's view. He knew not to intrude. He bent his head again as the burial service went on. 'Forasmuch as it has pleased Almighty God of his great mercy to take unto himself the soul of our departed brother, William Keith, our brother –'

'WILLIAM!'

Suddenly there was a piercing repeat of the name in a woman's voice that was frightening in its manic intensity, and there, standing in the starboard companion way was Florence Keith. She was a ghostly figure, fantastic in the long white of her night-dress, her long hair streaming behind her, her eyes mad with grief and her voice crackling in her pain.

'He's my William, not yours. I have to see him. I must see him. How do I know he's dead? There's no doctor –' Her sons were at her side at once.

'Mother please!' cried Bobby.

'Oh Mother,' moaned Jim. In her place of watching, Tina let her body slide down so that she sat down on the top step of the stair way. She shivered in her dressing gown, but it wasn't with cold. The Captain had broken off his reading and stood with the book in his hand, looking down while the two young men struggled with their mother. Applecross and the bos'un went to help them, but only got in the way, and Florence, frantic in her demented state, broke free and pulled away the flag covering her husband's body. 'I must see him. I must see him,' she kept saying. Her sons had hold of her again, and Captain Ellon nodded to Applecross.

'Open the bag,' he said quietly.

'But, Captain!' said the carpenter.

'It's an order, Mr Applecross.'

'Aye, aye, sir.'

As Applecross worked at the ropes at the top of the tarpaulin bag, the group became silent, and all that could be heard was the hard breathing of Mrs Keith. When the bag was open, the head of William Keith was revealed under a white cloth. When this was pulled back, his face was seen, bright green in the light, and through his nose was pinned a heavy hook. Florence screamed.

'You've killed him. You've killed my William.' The voice of the Captain could be heard under her screaming.

'We therefore commit his body to the deep to be turned into corruption, looking for the resurrection of the body when the sea shall give up her dead.' At this, he nodded to Applecross, who by now had retied the bag. He stood aside. The bos'un lifted the plank, and the body of William Keith slid into the Indian Ocean. 'WILLIAM!' shrieked his widow, and the cry hung in the air, receiving no reply but the answering shriek of gulls, as they rose from the smoking black and red funnel above them to welcome the first streaks of another dawn.

ELEVEN

It had turned out a lovely summer morning in Rosstrevor.
Mrs Nellie Murphy, the former Nellie O'Neil, was visiting her
mother at Ballytreabhair and hearing all the news from America.
Nessie told her daughter all about Denis and the police, Sean and
Michael and the pub, Noreen in the restaurant but most of all,
about Paddy and the priest. Nellie was not impressed.

'I thought our Paddy was too clever to be a priest.'

'But are they not educated men, Nellie?'

'Sure wouldn't education not put the very idea out of their heads,
Mother? Maynooth's full of rich farmers' sons who had nothing
better to do than take up a vocation. You've heard the expression,
"a man's doin' well if he has a pump in the yard and a son at
Maynooth". It's more vacation than vocation for many o' them,
I'm thinkin'.'

'Hasn't our Paddy thought long about it since he was a boy?'

'Ay, about if his chest could take it you mean. They'd sooner
have a stigmatic than an asthmatic.'

'That's silly talk.' Nessie said it lightly but in her heart she
thought her daughter might be righter than she knew. The women
were sitting in the little front room at the farm, which was now
a lot neater than when four big sons and a wild young daughter
were running about it.

'I wonder how long before Noreen's wed.'

'Don't speak with your mouth full girl.'

'Sorry.'

'What makes you think she'll wed?'

'I know these Italians. And I know our Noreen.'

'Do ye now?'

'I like your new curtains, Mother.'

'Are you changing the subject, Nellie?'

'No, I like them, honest.'

The little parlour did look altogether different with curtains at
the windows and little rugs on the floor, although Nellie didn't
mention the same old festoon of Holy Pictures. But there was

some new furniture. Little things that Nessie had always wanted, but could never afford. One such item was a little tea-table, now standing between them at the window seat.

'Did ye never feel sorry that ye never went to Amerikay yourself?' Nessie asked her daughter.

'Not at all, Mother.' Nellie giggled. 'Hadn't I better things to do?' There was a cake stand on the tea-table, and on the three tiers of that cake stand was all the home baking Nellie had brought up for her mother. At least she said it was for her mother but the way she was tucking into the tasty little cakes, it appeared as if she had brought it for herself.

'You're maybe eating too much, Nellie O'Neil,' said her mother with mock reproof.

'Not at all, mother. Anyway, I'm not Nellie O'Neil now, you know. I'm Helen Murphy.'

'That sounds grander no doubt, but you're still Nellie O'Neil to me. And you're putting on weight.'

'I am not.'

'You are so.'

'I tell you I'm not, mother.' She took another bite of one of her own cakes. 'I'm pregnant!' Her mother nearly dropped the teapot.

'You don't say?'

'I do. Here let me.' She poured the tea. 'You'll have another cup?'

'You're quite sure?'

'Doctor Nolan confirmed it this mornin'.'

'Liam will be pleased?'

'He doesn't know yet. I'll tell him tonight.'

Nessie lifted her cup to her mouth, savouring the news as well as the tea. It would be a new sensation for her to be a grandmother. She knew how Den would react. It would be drinks all round for everyone at Ingham's once again, as if he had done the thing himself. But hadn't he, he would argue. If Nellie was his and the child was Nellie's, then it followed the child was his! Grandpoppy Den? God help us! There would be no living with him. Not that I see much of him anyway, Nessie thought. Nor Kevin either. A real grass-widow I've become in my old age!

'But there's another thing, mother.' Nellie cut in to Nessie's thoughts.

'What's that, alannah?'

'Doctor Flannagan told me to expect twins.' There was what in any other circumstances might have been called a pregnant pause.

145

'Twins, is it?'

'That's right.' Nellie was relishing her mother's consternation.

'But we've no twins on our side.'

'Liam has on his. His sister has two boys, and the aunt that is in England has a boy and a girl and they're all twins.'

'Merciful God! Don't tell your father, or it'll be twice the expense at Ingham's.' And rising from her seat, Nessie O'Neil gave her eldest daughter a kiss. Nellie blushed. It was the first time she could remember her mother's ever kissing her.

'Here, we'll have another cup of tea, I think,' said Nessie. 'I'll make another pot. See you and eat up now Mrs Helen Murphy.' Nessie laughed and moved off to the kitchen with the teapot. Nellie smiled and made herself more comfortable in the chair. Looking down to her tummy she gave it a little pat with her right hand. 'Be good now, the pair of you!' she whispered. There was one cake left on the cake-stand. Nellie stared at it, then with a sigh she reached forward . . .

It was the evening meal at the O'Neils' in Brooklyn and it was Noreen's day off. Once again the horse cab had come for her and once again she had sailed out under the eyes of most of the windows in the street. There was an Advent Calendar aspect given to the street when anything happened to interest the neighbours. By a kind of osmosis the word always got round and one by one the windows opened, as if by prearranged signal, and one by one curtains parted, windows opened and heads popped out to witness the goings-on. It wasn't often that a hired horse cab came down 57th street, and here was one that was becoming almost a regular occurrence. The neighbours weren't above making comments. The local Watch Committee consisted principally of Mrs Finklestein and Mrs Robovitch.

'It's dat Irish lodger again, Mrs Finkelstein, is it?'

'Yeah, it sure is, Mrs Robovitch. Nice to see some people get on.'

'Nice to see some people that's nice.'

'That's nice, Mrs Robovitch.'

'That's alright, Mrs Finkelstein.' Under such scrutiny, Noreen made sure not to trip on the step ever again, and in fact, took her time now in coming down the steps. She knew she was the centre of attention. She might as well enjoy it. She knew she looked good, and the actress in her told her to make the best of it. Enrico d'Agostino still didn't come to the door of the house for her. The only time people had seen him was that first Sunday when he had come round to open the door of the cab. Now he didn't even do that. Maybe he stayed inside to make sure she didn't fall again! At any rate, the driver always helped Noreen up now and he had again that day when they'd driven off.

'We only go round and round Central Park,' Noreen told the family.

'What does he talk about?' asked Uncle Mick.

'He hardly talks at all. I do all the talking.'

'There's a surprise,' said Denis.

'Shut up, you,' said his sister without rancour. 'It's not you that's bein' driven round like a duchess.'

'I'd be driven out of me mind sittin' with a fellow like that. I'll bet he stinks of garlic.'

'Garlic's good for you,' said Carmella, beginning to clear some of the dishes from the table.

'As a matter of fact, he does not,' said Noreen pertly.

'And how do you know that, sister mine?' Noreen couldn't help a slight blush, but replied without hesitation.

'Mind your own business.' Uncle Mick was looking thoughtful.

'What kind of man is he, do ye think, Noreen?' Just at that moment, Noreen was rising to help her aunt clear the table.

'Here, I'll give you a hand, Aunty.'

'No, I manage fine, Noreena. You sit. You been out all day. It's a hard work enjoying yourself when you're young.'

'Are you sure?'

'Sure, I'm sure.' Noreen sat again and beamed across at Uncle Mick. 'What were you saying, Uncle?' The Superintendent looked steadily across at his niece and replied in the same even tone.

'I was sayin',' he said, 'what kind of man is he?'

'Who?'

'Now quit stallin' me, child. I mean this Italian boyfriend of yours.'

'He's not my boyfriend,' answered Noreen a little too indignantly.

'Well, man friend, then.' Noreen didn't reply at once, but picked up the teaspoon and started to draw with it on the white tablecloth. Carmella lifted the loaded tray from the table and made for the kitchen door, but Denis rose at the same time. 'Here, let me, Aunty. Now, come on. You get the door.'

'Grazie, Denis.'

As they went on, Uncle Mick reached his hand across to Noreen. 'Agh, don't worry, child. I'm just your auld da's brother, and I'm sure he would be expectin' me to keep an eye out for you, you know what I mean.'

'Sure, Uncle Mick.' She looked down at his hand, and couldn't help noticing how large it was, large and red and Irish, just like its owner. As he withdrew his hand again, she got up.

'I think I'll go up and get out of these things. I've been in them all day,' she said.

'And very nice too,' said her Uncle, looking up appreciatively at the figure she made in her new yellow dress. 'Yellow suits ye.'

'It's nice in the sun.'

'Sure it's always nice in the sun. And expensive too, I'm thinkin'.' Noreen didn't answer at first. They looked at each other for a moment before she said calmly,

'I told you the tips were good.'

'Of course. The tips. I forgot.'

Noreen turned and went quickly to the door, almost colliding with Denis as he came back in.

'I'm sorry, Your Highness,' he said, giving way to her as he made a mock bow.

'I told ye to shut up,' she said curtly as she swept past. Denis watched her go then glanced back at his Uncle.

'What's the matter with her?'

Uncle Mick had now settled himself in his favourite armchair, and was in the act of lighting a cigar. It was quite an expensive cigar – courtesy of J. Rafferty, Publican. Denis settled himself in the other armchair and put his hands behind his head.

'You were quite nosey there about the boyfriend.'

'And wouldn't I be? Seein' that he's one of the biggest noises in the family business.'

'Family business?'

'I suppose you could call it debt collecting, Italian style.' He took a long pull as his cigar and the blue smoke hung like a pall about his head. 'But the same fella was run out of New York no more than two years ago for what might be called "irregularities" in the construction business.'

'Irregularities?'

'It was the way they mixed the cement.'

'Oh?'

'Like putting bodies in it.'

'You don't say!'

'Ah, but I do. The same Enrico had to run for it, as I remember, and I do think he got as far as Chicago. He had – er – connections there as ye might say. He just waited until things cooled down and now he's back in little old New York, as free an' easy as ye like, and still with dollars in his pocket from what I can find out. I dunno how the guy gets away with it. I'd like to get him.'

'You couldn't nail him then?'

'Not at the time. We couldn't prove it. You can't ask questions of dead men.'

'Jesus! And this is the fella with our Noreen?'

'That's just what I'm thinkin', Denis. So it'll do for us to keep our eyes on Signor d'Agostino.'

'And on Noreen.'

Noreen didn't go to her own room, but instead went upstairs to Paddy's. He was sitting up in bed with the domino games board on his lap. Joey had his chair drawn up to the bed and Noreen was standing on the other side of the bed with her back to the only window in the room. She moved to sit on the other bed, which was Denis's. It had not been made up since morning.

'Our Denis still doesn't make up his bed,' she said pulling up the covers and sitting down.

'It's his bed, so he must lie on it!' said her brother. 'Your turn, Joey.'

'Yeah, I know Paddy.' The young boy stared earnestly at the board. Paddy looked across at his sister.

'Did you have a good time?'

'Sure. I'm a good time girl, remember.'

'You're a good girl, Noreen,' said Joey looking up.

'So I am Joey,' answered Noreen, laughing. She did indeed look lovely. A cloudburst of yellow and white under her red hair, her green eyes dancing. Small wonder that Paddy was proud of his sister and no wonder Joey found it hard to concentrate on his game. He just sat gazing across at Noreen. Paddy noticed.

'Look Joey,' he said, 'let's say we leave the game for now, eh?'

'OK Paddy,' agreed Joey. 'I gotta go to the bathroom.'

'Poor Joey,' Noreen said to herself, as he left the room. She turned to Paddy. 'You're alright then?'

'I'm rarin' to go,' answered Paddy with a smile.

'You gave us all a fright.'

'I got a fright meself. But Denis was grand.'

'That's Denis.'

'Aye.' There was silence for a moment.

'Paddy.'

'Yes?'

'You're sure about this priest business?' Paddy's voice was calm.

'I've never been surer of anything. I go to Baltimore at the end of the week.'

'What? You mean you're going away?'

'I've to have another talk with the Archbishop.'

'Oh, Paddy, I don't want you to go.' She seemed suddenly alarmed.

'What's the matter, girl? You knew I'd have to go sometime.' She leaned forward and spoke urgently.

'Paddy, there was something I wanted to tell you.'

'Yes?' He had already assumed the easy manner of the confessor.

'It's about – oh, damn!' She had to break off hurriedly because Joey came back in. He went straight to the board on the chair and lifted it up.

'You gonna play a game with us, Noreen?' She rose quickly.

'I never play games, Joey.' She gave him a bright, forced smile and quickly left the little bedroom. Paddy looked after her, frowning. Joey placed the board on his cousin's lap again.

'You said it was my turn, Paddy.'

'Sure, Joey. It's your turn.'

On the Mataura in mid-ocean, Captain Ellon was in conference with his Chief Engineer. Jock Aitken was solemn, smart – and sober. He sat, ill-at-ease, on the other side of his Captain's desk and tried to hide his discomforture. The subject was not to his taste, and he was not enjoying the exchange.

'Well Jock, how does it look to you?' said Captain Ellon.

'I don't know, Cap'n, an' that's being quite frank wi' ye.'

'It was only Applecross with you?'

'Aye, sir.'

'Yes, I've sent for him.' There was a knock on the door.

'Ah, this'll be him now. Come in.'

'Ship's Carpenter reporting, sir.'

'Thank you, Applecross. Please sit down.'

'Thank you, sir.' He sat down on the other chair before the desk.

'Mr Aitken.' He nodded to the Chief, who nodded back.

'Chippy.' The Captain leaned forward.

'You'll understand why I asked you to come along.'

The carpenter quickly glanced at the engineer. 'I think so, sir.'

'Good.' The Captain glanced down at the little box in his hands. 'It's very awkward, but it can't be ignored, can it?' There was no reply from either of the other men. Captain Ellon went on quietly: 'When a crew member is acting suspiciously a watch is kept on him until he is caught in the act or reveals undisputed proof of his crime whatever it might happen to be. I see no reason why the same should not apply when a ship's officer is involved.' He paused slightly, then continued: 'If, on a routine ship's repair a senior officer and a responsible crew member find an article or articles stowed in such a way to suggest that they were contraband or at least illegally obtained then a full enquiry must be instituted. You agree?'

Both men nodded. He addressed Applecross. 'You say you found this' – he indicated the box in his hands – 'behind the panel of Mr Dickenson's bath while investigating an ordinary plumbing leak from the Third Officer's cabin next door?'

'Yes, sir.'

'And there were other packets and small boxes similarly stored as if hidden, you thought.'

'I didn't say that, Captain Ellon, sir. I said to the Chief Engineer 'ere, that I thought it looked as if the stuff was 'idden. A proper little treasure trove it were, sir.'

'Quite, and you sent for Mr Aitken right away?'

'No sir, not then.'

'Why not?' Applecross glanced uneasily at Aitken.

'I wasn't sure, sir. I didn't like to – know what I mean?'

'No, I do not.'

'Well, sir, I decided to play it safe – cautious-like – know what I mean?'

'Go on.'

'So I fixed the leak, but then I puts back the packets, so he wouldn't know. I waited then till after we docked at Colombo, sir, then when we puts up anchor again, I thought I'd take another peek, know what I mean? And blimey, sir, there was a 'ole lot more stuff. Lot's o' packets. 'E must 'ave 'ad a right 'aul with the ol' slant-eyes.'

'Quite. And then you sent for Mr Aitken?'

'I went for 'im meself, sir. I wasn't sure what to do by then, it bein' a bit out of my line, so to speak.'

'And you suggested, Chief, that you remove the goods, if we may call them that, and replace the panel again.'

'Well,' said Aitken, 'I thought it this way. If the beggar was up to somethin' he'd want to keep it quiet and even if he sees the stuff's missin' he's no' goin' to report it, is he, if it's hot.'

'Is that what you call it, Chief?' He opened the box. It was full of uncut diamonds. They gleamed and sparkled in the desklight. 'It looks quite cold stuff to me.'

'Not when it's worth thousands, sir. You couldn't 'ave 'otter!' The carpenter's eyes had their own diamond sparkle.

'You could have kept them for yourself, Chippy?'

'Not me, sir. I wouldn't know 'ow to get rid of 'em.'

'And you think our Second Officer does.'

'With the amount of stuff he'd got stashed away,' replied the carpenter, 'he's obviously got somethin' goin', sir.'

The Captain considered for a moment. 'I see,' he said pursing his lips. 'It's a rum thing, is it not? On every round-the-world trip, he links up with contacts ashore and acts as a courier of a sort. It's that sort of thing I suppose. As a ship's officer, he's unlikely to be scrutinised and so he more or less fetches and carries as he likes.'

'And is probably on a good commission,' added the engineer. 'No wonder he can afford the good life ashore.'

'What do we do now, sir?' asked Applecross.

'I think we'll do nothing.'

'Wot!' exclaimed the carpenter.

'Let him sweat, you mean?' said the chief.

'Exactly! We missed him at Colombo so we'll keep an eye on him at Singapore. We'll say nothing till then. As you say, Mr Applecross, if he has something going we ought to know all about it.'

'He's got somethin' goin' alright,' muttered the carpenter slyly.

'What do you mean?' asked Captain Ellon.

'Oh, it's nuffink, sir.' The Chief turned to him.

'You mean wi' that nice lassie wi' the Keith party.'

'Tina, isn't it?' added the Captain.

'Aye sir, a bonnie girl she is and certainly too good for the likes o' Dickenson, I'm thinkin'.'

'Perhaps so, but that's hardly relevant –'

'Excuse me, sir,' said Applecross hurriedly, 'but it might be revelant as you say, sir – 'scuse me for interruptin', sir.'

'Not at all. Go ahead,' said the Captain.

'Well, sir –,' the little Cockney hesitated. 'I don't rightly know if I should mention – I mean –'

'Go on, man,' said the Chief Engineer, 'an' dinna blether!'

'Aye-aye sir. Well, when I wanted to get into Mr Dickenson's cabin the first time, I couldn't find him to get his key.'

'You could've asked his steward,' suggested the Captain.

'I did, sir, but he said that Mr Dickenson wouldn't let him 'ave one. That's why I asked Mr Aitken here to let me in. Knowing as 'ow the Chief always 'as keys. Know what I mean?'

'Go on,' said the Captain.

'But then the other steward, Sammy, turns up. I'm on the passenger deck. An' 'e tells me that Dickie-bird, sorry Mr Dickenson, got a key from him for Miss Keith's cabin. C50, he said it was. An' that's where he was, sir. Most o' that afternoon.'

'What!' exclaimed the Captain.

'That's what I didn't want to tell you, Captain,' muttered the Chief.

'Sorry if I spoke out of turn, like,' mumbled Applecross.

'Not at all,' said the Captain. 'I think I need a drink.'

'I thought you'd never ask,' said Jock Aitken.

Officer Denis O'Neil pulled off his white gloves, and folding them neatly, put them in his pocket. Another traffic spell had been completed in the downtown oven that New York City was in the month of July. He raised his cap and ran his fingers through his hair as he walked from the intersection to the side-walk. His shirt was wet at the small of his back and he could only think that a very tall iced beer would be in order. Denis was two weeks on the job by now and was beginning to feel a little more relaxed about it all although Sergeant Peters was as hard to please as ever. Especially as he now had a broken foot! One of the new-fangled motor-cars had run over his toes one afternoon. Luckily it was a rubber tyre but nonetheless the Sergeant's language at the time of the incident or accident is reputed to have blistered the new paint finish on the vehicle. One side-effect was that the irascible traffic-tutor now required to use a cane, and he used this to telling effect on inattentive officers or lazy pedestrians! However, much to everyone's relief on this particular hazy afternoon, there was no sign of the limping sergeant.

But Hana was there as usual! Most days, she stood at the corner waiting for Denis to finish his shift, then, much to his embarrassment, she would take his arm and walk him to the station where she would wave him up the steps then run for her street-car to Greenwich Village. Her mother was cook-housekeeper to a European artist living there. He was supposed to be famous in the art world and his house was large enough to allow Hana and brother Frantisek to share a large attic. This much Denis had learned in his nightly perambulations along the side-walk with Hana. She held on so tightly to him on these occasions that he always had the feeling that he was under arrest and being taken to the station! Since their first kissing encounter, he had warned her to stay well away from the intersection and out of sight of Sergeant Peters, but each day she waited for him at the corner of the next block and here she was again today.

'She is hot, the day, yes?' she said as she bobbed along beside Denis.

'She certainly is,' he agreed, blowing the sweat from his upper lip. Glancing down at the girl by his side, he noticed that there was no sweat above her very kissable lips. But then girls don't

153

sweat, they perspire. Yet how did Hana manage to look so cool and attractive under that straw hat and with a long dress that trailed on the sidewalk? She worked in a dress-shop on 48th Street and seemed able to get away every day to meet him without any problem.

'The Madam she is kind, because I am good vorker with my finker.'

Denis had by this time cultivated an ear for Hana's very individual English and knew from this statement that her boss, who was Hungarian, appreciated the Prague girl's skill as a seamstress and allowed a certain flexibility in her working hours so that she could accommodate Denis's more erratic police shifts. There was no doubt that little Miss Karpiskova was as determined on Denis as she'd been on the SS Campania. The only differences were that he was slightly more accessible as a policeman than he was as a steerage passenger and that they had more room on the New York streets than they had on an immigrant ship's lower decks! And of course, there was now no sign of Mother. But that wasn't to last long. Hana had a plan.

'My mudder. Her man go to Vermont for hot days here, yes?'

'Lucky man,' answered Denis. He knew that by 'man' Hana meant her mother's artist-employer, and like most New Yorkers who could afford it he escaped to the cooler climes of Vermont, or upper State Albany, or even New England or Maine when the sweltering city became unbearable. Only the poor and the Police and Fire Departments were left to sweat it out till the Fall.

'My mudder make nice dinner. You come, yes?'

'Yes,' Denis answered automatically without thinking. Her yelp of excitement made him realise what he'd said. 'Wait a minute –' he began, but there was no stopping Hana.

'Is good. We will make time, yes?'

'Yes, OK,' replied Denis resignedly. They were at the station steps. Her eyes were shining. He had to agree she did look pretty. He had to smile. The die was cast.

Boredom had begun to set in for Bobby Keith and Bobby's threshold in that area was limited. He had done all that could be expected of a pleasant and gregarious young man who enjoyed being with people but even his extraordinary social energy began to wane. That is until Miss Rachel Gebler came on board. Since her arrival on the scene, Bobby had become a new man, or at least another man. Formerly, where two or more were gathered together, there was Bobby in the midst of them, but now there was a change, for Bobby Keith, for the first time in his life, was in love. From that first attraction to the young Jewish girl and especially from that first kiss, Bobby had grown increasingly interested in the introspective Australian and was often with her and her companions around the ship. Since their first meeting, her friends had made sure that he was never alone with her, but they had seriously underestimated the Keith ingenuity. He discovered Rachel had an interest in theatre, but because of her background had little practical knowledge or experience of things theatrical. Neither had Bobby, of course, but that didn't deter him from planning a means by which he could get near Rachel again and better still obtain another kiss. What better than a love scene in a play? But what play? There were no plays in the ship's library. There was no ship's library! Jim was the answer.

'What? Write a play? Me?' asked Jim in astonishment.

'Why not?' persisted Bobby. 'It doesn't have to be a real play. As long as it has a kiss in it. It doesn't even have to be long.'

'The kiss?'

'No, you idiot. The play.'

'Oh, I don't know . . .' Jim was very dubious, but Bobby was Keith-determined.

'Look,' he said, 'you can even set it on the ship. I can play an Officer. I can get the uniform from Martin. Rachel can play the girl. You can be the Captain if you like.' A faraway look came into Jim's eyes. He suddenly had an idea. It could be dangerous, but might be worth trying.

'Alright,' he said to his brother. 'I'll try to think of something.'

'Good,' said Bobby. 'As soon as you can, eh? I'll go and tell Rachel.' And off he went in search of his beloved. Jim shook his head as he watched him go. He had never seen his older brother like this before. At least never in Forres. Of course, there was Ella Friar, but she never made Bobby skip like an eight-year old. At least Jim never saw it. He remembered an old proverb he had read somewhere: 'In love there's always one who kisses and one who offers the cheek.' And if anyone had cheek, Bobby had! 'Well,' he said aloud, 'the play's the thing wherein we catch the conscience of the king.' But he wasn't thinking of his brother, Bobby.

TWELVE

'I love you, my dear. I have loved you from the first moment I saw you, and I will love you till I die.'

'Do you, George?'

'Yes, my dear. Till I die.'

'Oh, George!' There was a silence.

'It's you, Bobby,' called out Jim's voice impatiently. 'When will you marry me?'

'Oh, aye. When will you marry me?'

'Oh, George!'

'Oh, dammit,' said Bobby. 'I should have been kneeling here. Sorry, Jim.' Bobby, Jim and Rachel were in the Second Class dining saloon late in the afternoon rehearsing Jim's play, or rather his dramatic sketch. It was to be the first half of the proposed ship's concert and he had called it 'To Sea, Unseen'. Only Jim knew what he meant by that, but the piece provided Bobby with just what he wanted – a few laughs, a proposal scene, a chance to kiss Rachel again. The three of them had been rehearsing every day for the last week, often with Rachel's Jewish friends hovering in the background. Jim had finished the one-acter after a few days of hectic scribbling in an exercise book. Copies had been written out by each of the 'performers' and now they were trying to learn it. Bobby was so besotted with the opportunity of handling and fondling Rachel that he failed to see a distinct resemblance between the action of the playlet and the real life relationship of his sister with Second Officer Dickenson.

Jim, however, was enjoying all the allusions thoroughly but Rachel was oblivious to them. She was more concerned with Bobby's octopus tendencies. He had hands everywhere, even if one held the script. She soon learned to cope all the same and secretly was enjoying it nearly, but not quite as much as Bobby.

'Shall we carry on?' she asked Jim demurely.

'Oh, please!' said Bobby.

'Come on, Bobby,' said Jim in his best producer's voice. 'This is serious. You won't want to make a fool of yourself.'

'Why should he when nature has beaten him to it?' said Rachel, still in her demure voice as Charlotte. Bobby knelt again.

'OK. OK. Where was I?' he said.

'When will you marry me?' called Jim from his chair.

'Oh, aye.' He paused, looked up into Rachel's face and said the line as if he really meant it. 'When will you marry me?'

'Charlotte' paused as she looked down at George/Bobby, then replied very quietly as Rachel, 'Whenever you ask me, stupid!'

'That's not in the script,' yelled Jim. 'Hey, and neither is that!' For his brother had risen up taking the girl in his arms and was kissing her passionately.

The dining-room was in Greenwich Village, New York, but it might have been in Prague. The food, the drink, the songs played on the candle-lit piano, the loud conversation were all heavily Slavonic, and Denis O'Neil, uncomfortable in a new black suit and stiff, white collar sat in the middle of it all as perplexed and bewildered as he was on his first day of traffic duty nearly a month before. Hana, however, was in her element. Dressed in her national costume, she knew she looked good, and with Denis at last at her family table, she had him where she wanted him. He was not so certain. Sure, he liked the sense of occasion, the kindness he was being shown, the fuss that was made of him by Hana's mother – he could even tolerate her brother and his laugh – but it was the overwhelming difference of it all, the foreign-ness, that unnerved the young Irishman.

The house itself was so different from the careless, brownstone comfort of his Uncle's home in Brooklyn. Rather than a homely untidiness, here was a lofty, airy grandeur even if now a little seedy. There were paintings on every wall and no curtains on the tall windows. Instead of a fireplace in the large drawing-room there was a huge, tiled stove and where he had known mellow gas lighting in 57th Street, here it was only candles and oil lamps. It was this that may have given the dining-room its unusual smell. Or it may have been the flowers, an immense bowl of tulips as the centre-piece of the table. Or the strange dishes of meat served with cheese and so much beer. It was worse than Rafferty's! The copious jug by his right hand seemed to be filled constantly to the brim. It was a miracle of Cana-like proportions. Beer flowed all around him – into the bottomless mug of Frantisek, Hana's brother opposite him, and those of the other two men at the table, both bald and Bohemian. Their moustaches wore a white hem of beer froth for most of the evening but that didn't inhibit their lusty singing or even lustier laughs which showed the yellow teeth of one and the unashamed toothless gums of the other. Their wives were ample women, appropriate to the Balkan girth of their husbands. They too, like Hana and her mother, were dressed in brocades and embroideries layered under tight bodices and all wore incongruous little white caps trailing with ribbons. The ladies sipped becherovka from daintier receptacles than those provided for the men but this seemed to have no less effect on their jollity. They kept smiling over at Denis and nodding. He could only nod back and much of the evening was passed in this inane fashion, nodding and smiling across the table at each other.

Hana and her mother were constantly on the move, fetching and carrying and serving and pouring, all the time keeping up a stream of Czech to their friends and, from time to time, and only from Hana, smiling, staccato phrases to the principal guest.

'You are happy, yes?' 'Beer, no?' 'You try Becherovka, yes?' Denis kept smiling and nodding and holding his hand out. As a result he had to make many visits to the rear of the house where a primitive shower had been set up in an alcove off what looked like a laundry or scullery. Each visit became increasingly hazardous as his walk became less steady and his need the greater! Visibility too wasn't helped by the fact that the two moustaches used the same restricted area as a smoking room and two formidable briar pipes belched out enough grey smoke to screen any private or personal operations taking place. The ladies must have gone upstairs as Denis never saw them in that area. Not that he could see much as the night wore on. Hana's face seemed to be constantly before him and also to get nearer and nearer so that the pretty features became rather blurred as her English deteriorated.

At one time, he found himself sitting on the horsehair sofa, holding her hand, and staring at all the other faces nodding and smiling at both of them. Or were they laughing at them? He turned at one point to Hana to find that her face, and her lips, were only inches away. Inexorably, he was drawn to them and, hardly moving his head, he kissed them and she responded warmly in a mutual haze of alcohol. In the distance, he heard cheering and applause and yet another song was started up. During it, Hana pulled him up and helped him, with some difficulty, from the room and out through the French windows and on to the balcony. This was a feature of the house and was crammed with potted plants of all kinds, but over the cast iron balustrade the lights of New Jersey could be seen on the other side of the Hudson River.

Hana guided Denis to the rail and almost hung him upon it as he leaned over and gulped in the welcome, cool, night air. 'Is good, yes?' she said, snuggling close to his side.

'Is good, yes,' he replied, feeling his forehead. He was perspiring heavily. God, don't say he was going to be sick?

'You kissed Hana?'

'Yes.' Yes, he felt sick. It was all that bloody beer.

'You like?'

'Like what?' He tried to take a deep breath.

'Like kiss?'

'Er – Yes.' Or was it that becherovka? Hana snuggled even closer and slipped her hand through his arm.

'Good!' They stood like that for some moments staring down on to the oily surface of the water broken only by the occasional wash of a passing barge, a black outline in the moonlight, or by the oil drums themselves, and cans and broken pieces of wood thrown up against the lock wall below them. Random sea-rubbish, seeming to go nowhere, but still floating. Just like us, thought Denis, Hana and me, thrown together in the water, or on the water, by chance and accident but staying afloat, and even getting closer. He felt her hand tighten on his arm. She was a lovely girl, no doubt, but there were a lot of lovely girls in the world. She was kind and all that, but there were even a few kind girls about. And she was certainly persistent. Tonight was proof of that – oh, there was that wave of nausea again!

'Denis?'

'Yeah?'

'Why you kiss me before my mother?'

'Should I have kissed her first?'

Hana laughed. 'No, no!' she said, 'I mean – you kiss me – in front of my mother, my brother, my two uncles, my aunts. You know it is big thing this.'

'What is?'

'To kiss in the family.'

'Don't they kiss in Prague?' She laughed again. He loved her laugh. He thought he might be beginning to feel a little better. He took another deep breath.

'Look, Hana –'

'Yes?' Her face looked up eagerly.

'I kissed you because I wanted to.'

'Ah!' she exclaimed. 'You want me?'

'Er – yes – I – er – want you.'

'You want me!' she exclaimed even louder. He was slightly puzzled, but nodded and said hesitantly,

'Er – yes.'

'Ah, Denis!'

And with that she threw her arms about him and kissed him

159

violently on the lips. Not a clever thing to do in his condition. But before he could say or do anything, she was off into the house, calling, 'Mama! Mama!' following it with a whole stream of exuberant Czech.

'Oh, God,' said Denis, turning back to the railing and to the dark river below him. What was she on about? What had he done? What had he said? He could hear the noise of applause and excited chatter coming from through the French windows. 'Oh, God!' he said again and held his hand over his mouth as his stomach heaved. He bent over the railings and just as he did, Frantisek came out on to the balcony, a glass in his hand. With the other, he thumped Denis on the back, and almost in reflex, Denis retched and emptied the night's exotic dinner and what was left of the beer and becherovka into the canal below. This act only made Frantisek laugh all the more and when Denis looked back again after a second spasm, there were the two uncles still with glasses in their hands, still smiling their respective toothy and toothless smiles, and holding out their hands to him. Feeling very shaky indeed, Denis held out his and let it be pumped vigorously by each man in turn. He had no idea what they were saying, but a terrible suspicion dawned on him as he saw Hana's mother and the aunts framed in the French windows beaming at Hana, then at him. Hana pointed towards him and then the realisation came. He knew what he had done. Oh God! With yet another retch, he turned away from them all and heaved any reservations he had left into the flotsam and jetsam in the dank, scummy water beneath him.

Tina had never been seasick before, not even in the Irish Sea or the Bay of Biscay or at any part of the long sea journey that had taken them from the slate-grey Clyde to the blue of the Indian Ocean, but this morning she was feeling, if not sick, then decidedly ill. 'It's something I've eaten', she kept saying to herself. Or, 'it might be a touch of the sun'. She even hoped it might be appendicitis, but all the time she knew in her heart, or rather deep inside another part of her, the awful truth – she was pregnant. When she missed her period she blamed it on the upset of her father's death, but now this nausea had started. The dreaded morning sickness. What could she do? Who could she ask? Should she . . .? No, the very thought was horrible. Oh what a stupid fool she had been! That's what everybody says, I suppose. Yet how true. She felt no remorse as such, only anger. And not anger at Martin either, but at herself.

'Stupid fool!' she said aloud and rose up from the lavatory seat. She checked again the gusset of her white knickers. No welcome red spot. Nothing. How often she had cursed that redness on her garments. How often she had had to hide it from her growing brothers. Now she knew she would have flown them from the masthead today if only to tell the world – and more importantly herself – that she was safe, that she hadn't held, that she wasn't carrying. 'Oh mother!' Then she thought of her father. And she was glad he was dead. Quickly, she rose and adjusted her long skirt. She felt a sob rising in her throat, but averted it with a sigh and tugged violently on the chain above her head.

Getting dressed in the cabin she tried to compose herself and think clearly of what to do. There was no doctor on board. Only that snivelling little carpenter. The thought was so gruesome it buckled her at the knees and she sat quickly on the edge of her bunk, her shirt blouse still unbuttoned. She looked down at her stomach. Was there another life in there? Was it her life? It still seemed unreal. She looked up to the ceiling, her eyes closed, her long neck stretched. 'I wish I could pray,' she thought. And without knowing it she did. Ach, she would have to hurry. It was nearly time for the play.

'When will you marry me?'

'Oh, George!'

'But, Charlotte, I love you.'

'What will my mother say?'

'I do not love your mother.'

'Oh, George!'

'Of course, I do. But it's you I want to marry.'

'We can't.'

'Why not?'

'I cannot tell you.'

'Oh, Charlotte.'

'Oh, George!'

'Oh, hell!' a voice said from the audience. There was a huge laugh from the passengers and officers assembled in the first class lounge for the World Première of *To Sea – Unseen* by James Keith, and starring Robert Keith and Rachel Gebler. It had been a great success with lots of laughs, some of which were not intended. However, there were two in the audience who did not find it funny – Tina Keith and Martin Dickenson. From his seat, Jim had been watching them closely, almost like Hamlet in the play, but their reaction was not as he had expected. Tina was almost tearful and Dickenson looked grim. There was something going on here Jim didn't know about. The prank appeared to have misfired, as it was only intended as a rather barbed joke, but instead it seemed to genuinely upset Tina and that's the last thing he would have wanted in the world. He was also surprised by Dickenson's reaction. Jim had wanted to embarrass him and make him look foolish, but instead the officer looked preoccupied as if something else was on his mind. As soon as the playlet finished and while the audience was applauding, Tina, looking straight ahead and clapping her hands just as eagerly, said to Martin out of Jim's hearing,

'I must talk to you.'

'What? Where?'

'My cabin.'

'When?'

'Now.' She rose as the rest of the audience rose for the interval and, excusing herself to her brother, hurried out. Several of the passengers came forward to congratulate Jim.

'Jolly good show!'

'Jolly well done!'

'Jolly funny, what!' Since his attention was given to these bland remarks, Jim failed to notice Dickenson also leave and hurry after his sister.

'I don't believe it!' Martin Dickenson's face was incredulous. 'Are you sure?'

'Yes.' To her amazement, Tina found she was very much in control of herself. Admittedly, she had had nearly three weeks to think about it, but now that it was an inescapable fact she found she was able to deal with it. The same could not be said for Dickenson. He sat on the other bunk in her cabin, his white drill trousers at his knees, his shirt unbuttoned, staring at her. He had come to her cabin on a completely false assumption, assuming that their former relationship would be resumed. Perhaps she had been stimulated by the play. He had his tunic and tie off almost before she had closed the door behind him as he entered, and was in the very act of undressing when Tina had given him the news.

It was bad news as far as he was concerned judging by the look on his face. She had gone to the other bunk and now sat looking steadily at him. He felt uncomfortable under her unflinching gaze.

'Bloody silly, isn't it?' he snapped.

'Is it?'

'Course it is.' He stood and his trousers fell to his ankles. He pulled them up hurriedly allowing the braces to twang on his shoulders. Just as hurriedly he tried to do up the buttons on his shirt but in his haste he got them out of order.

'You're one out,' Tina said calmly.

'Bloody hell!' he muttered vehemently and started again. Tina watched him and marvelled at the change she now saw in him. Was

162

this the man she had allowed to seduce her? Was this the man who had professed such a love for her, who would take care of her for ever? And now couldn't do up his shirt buttons! She watched as he turned to her mirror fumbling with his tie. There was no poise here. She thought he seemed frightened.

'Well,' she said, 'what are we to do?'

'What do you mean?'

'I should think it was pretty obvious what I mean?' He didn't answer but picked up his tunic and started to put it on. It was her turn to feel a little frightened, but she kept her voice steady.

'Well?'

'I'll need time.'

'Time? For what?'

'To think, for God's sake!' he burst out. 'Oh hell,' he growled as he reached for his cap. 'I've got things on my mind just now.'

'Have you indeed?'

'YES I HAVE!' he shouted loudly. So loudly that it startled Tina. He stepped in to lean over her, his eyes wild. 'For instance, where is my box?'

'What?'

'A little wooden box. You saw it. You were the only one who did. In Suez. Well, it's gone – and so has everything else.'

'What on earth are you talking about?'

'I'm talking about –' He suddenly broke off, staring at her. She realised he was breathing hard but after a moment he controlled himself and, taking a breath, moved to the door. She rose at once.

'Where are you going?'

'I've got to get back. The old man will notice if I'm not –'

'Get back?'

'To the bloody concert!' She was across to him in two paces, her eyes blazing.

'To a concert? I tell you you are the father of my child and you have to go to a concert!'

'What else can I do?'

'You can show some guts, man. Some concern. Some kind of feeling. Some attempt at understanding.'

'I understand –'

'You understand nothing. Listen, Mr Second Officer Dickenson. I'm more than happy to take my share of the blame –'

'I'm not –

'But I'm not going to take all of it. You're in this as much

163

as I am and I want to know what you're going to do about
it.'

'What can I do?'

'You could marry me for instance.'

'I can't.'

'Why not?'

'Because I'm married already!' This was almost blurted out
before he realised it but it was sufficient to halt Tina in
full flood. He was red-faced with agitation. She was white
with fury.

'You're a bastard,' she whispered.

He said nothing but turned to open the door – and there was
Mrs Keith in her white nightdress, her long hair on her shoulders,
standing in the corridor. Tina gasped, but Dickenson was the first
to recover.

'Ma'am,' he said huskily and gave her a token salute. Without
another glance at Tina he quickly moved up the corridor. Mrs Keith
hadn't moved. She still stood staring at her daughter.

'Mother!' She stepped forward but Mrs Keith was already on her
way back to her cabin next door. 'Had she heard anything?' thought
Tina. 'My God!' She stood in the doorway, stunned.

'Tina!' It was Jim. He came up to her as she stood staring. 'I saw
you leave the concert, but then I noticed that you know who was
missing. I wondered –' He broke off as he saw her face. 'Here,
what's the matter?'

She turned and looked at her brother. She saw all the concern,
all the trust, all the love in him and, for the first time, she felt
ashamed. Here was all the understanding she needed. Should
she tell him? If anybody would forgive her, he would. All
she could say was, 'Nothing. Martin was helping me to find
something.'

Jim frowned. 'Did he find it?' She made herself smile and took
his arm.

'No. Come on. We'd better get back.' As they went, Tina glanced
back at her mother's cabin but the door was firmly closed. She
tightened her grip on Jim's arm.

Meantime, in the lounge, the second half of the concert was
proceeding. One of the passengers, Mr Faber, a short fat man,
was regaling the company with a ballad accompanied by one of
the young officers on the piano. As Tina and Jim re-entered to
their places in the row of chairs beside Bobby and Rachel, who
had joined the family after the interval, Dickenson was in his place
looking fixedly ahead as the perspiring little tenor took off in full
flight from his place at the upright piano. Tina sat and tried

not to look at anyone, but was aware of so many eyes. She also tried not to listen, but the words of William Bennet's sentimental song were more than coincidental. Besides, the tiny tenor was also very loud!

> 'There's music in a mother's voice,
> More sweet than breezes sighing;
> There's music in a mother's glance,
> Too pure for ever dying;
> There's love within a mother's breast,
> So deep, 'tis still o'erflowing.
> And care for those she calls her own,
> That's ever, ever growing.'

What Tina did not see was that Captain Ellon was watching Martin Dickenson closely, who was watching the singer. Chief Aitken was watching Tina but he kept an eye on Dickenson. He wondered . . .

> 'There's anguish in a mother's fear,
> When farewell fondly taking,
> That so the heart of pity moves,
> It scarcely keeps from breaking.
> And when a mother kneels to Heaven,
> And for her child is praying,
> Oh! who shall half the fervour tell
> That burns in all she's saying.'

And during all this Jim could not take his eyes off his sister and Bobby had eyes only for Rachel beside him.

> 'A mother! how her tender arts
> Can soothe the breast of sadness,
> And through the gloom of life once more
> Bid shine the sun of gladness.
> A mother! when, like evening's star,
> Her course has pass'd before us,
> From brighter worlds regards us still,
> And watches fondly o'er us.'

But what nobody could see, except her Maker, was that inside the locked door of Cabin C51, Mrs Keith sat rocking herself on the edge of her late husband's bunk, keening tunelessly while her eyes sought the cloudless blue beyond the porthole where she could still see the hirsel of the home farm above Elgin where she and young William Keith had walked once long ago, and both they and the sheep around them were heft to the green homeland that had sired them all. And while she watched the sky two big tears rolled down her pale, wrinkled face . . .

THIRTEEN

Rafferty's was going like a train, a particularly Irish train on a New York track, as it were. There was little regard for time but a whole lot of attention was given to arriving at the final destination – stupor, or at least a state of merry forgetfulness which allowed the customers to face the real world again in the morning. Getting there involved drinking at a rate that would have had the proverbial lords struggling, but it was a consumption that pleased Jackie Rafferty mightily and allowed him, on this particular Saturday night in July, to escape from the city to his bolt hole in New Rochelle and endless games of gin rummy with his pals. The pub he left in the firm hands of Sean O'Neil and his brother Michael. He did this more and more these days. His old charge-hand Emmet Ryan was happy enough to sit at one end of the long bar and sample the house wares on the sly. He imagined no one noticed, but his red nose and watery eyes gave some indication of his tastes and now his hands trembled so much he spilled more than he served. Nevertheless, old Emmet had been with Rafferty since they both came off the boat themselves in the early 1880s and Jackie was happy to let him drain a few dollars each night. What else had the old bachelor anyway?

Which was why Sean was now in charge. And he loved it. Sean had a way with people. He was a man's man to men yet women loved him. But there had never been any particular woman in his life. At least none that the family had ever seen or heard of. They'd only seen him with the horses or with Michael. They were more twins than brothers and each taller and more good-looking than the other. Sean, just like Noreen, had his mother's redness but his father's dark eyes. Michael, like Denis, was black Irish but his eyes were pale, hazel green like his mother's. Both in fact were striking young men – and that's just what both were doing – striking the stubbled chins of four navvies, who were not regulars. This was a group of Ulstermen by the sound of them, and they had broken up the usual singsong by shouting at the tops of their voices the notorious Belfast toast, banging their glasses as they did so on Table No 7 in the corner.

'Here's to the glorious, pious and immortal memory
Of Prince William of Orange.
King of England and Wales,
King of Scotland and Ireland,
Who freed us from knavery and slavery,
Pope and popery, brass money and wooden shoes,
And may there always be a Williamite,
To kick the arse of a Jacobite,
And a wife for the Bishop of Cork!'

They laughed and cheered as the regulars grew ominously silent. Sean and Michael exchanged looks, and Sean gave the signal for Michael to keep an eye on them. The last straw however was when one of the Orangemen, a particularly brutish specimen, started to urinate against the piano. Sean was over the counter in a clean vault, and the urinator, still in full flow, was felled by a single blow which sent him, conveniently, to the sawdust. An equally grimy companion was immediately on Sean's back and he joined the first in an almost continuous movement, headfirst on to the floor. By this time the table was overturned and Michael was dealing with the other two. This he did by simply yanking each by the throat and banging their heads together, a simple but effective manoeuvre, which meant that in the space of a few minutes there were four unconscious Irishmen on the premises. Thus reassured, Jock Lennox resumed at his jangle piano, but the other customers only took up the refrain half-heartedly, and soon fell into excited conversation. There was a time for singing, but this was a time for talking. Most of them had never seen such prompt, effective action taken in Rafferty's before. It was as good as a prize fight.

'Did you see Sean there?'

'Wasn't Michael your man?'

The two heroes, meantime, had dragged their awkward squad by their jackets out to the sidewalk and left them there. As they put the last one through, they collided with a group coming in. They were not Irish. They were too well dressed to be Irish. They were Italian and looked it. They pushed past the two boys as they threw the last body out into the curb, and walked into the pub with a swagger. There was an immediate silence as the regulars saw the new group appear. One of them, obviously the leader, asked quietly in his accented voice,

'Is Mr Rafferty here?' Nobody answered. They were overawed by the quiet menace of the voice and by the sharp cut of the suits. Sean returned. 'Is it Mr Rafferty you want?'

'Si. My friends and I would like a little talk with him.'

'I'm afraid you're out of luck, Mister. He's at home tonight.'

'He's always home on a Saturday,' added Michael. 'The cards, you know,' and he grinned at the Italian who remained unsmiling.

'I see.'

'If you care to leave your name –' began Sean.

'I never leave my name. My name is mine alone.'

'Sure, that's a funny name,' said Michael.

'But I give my name.' The stranger smiled icily. 'Tell him Rico called.' He started to go, but Sean put a hand on his shoulder, immediately alerting the other Italians.

'Haven't I seen you somewhere now?' Rico glanced at the hand on his shoulder. Sean withdrew it. Rico smiled for the first time.

'Who am I to say? Arrivederci!' He left, his three shadows following. Sean watched them go. Michael joined him.

'There was the queer customer,' he said.

'He's no customer,' said Sean. 'An' I'm not sure we could give him what he wanted, even if he were.'

'What would a man like that want here?'

'Jackie Rafferty,' he said. 'But I wonder. I know I've seen him someplace. Here, we'd better get back to work.'

The bar had never known a night of such contrasting incidents for a long time and the talk was intense, or as they said, 'the gas was good'. Which was not good for business. People either talk or they drink. It's difficult to do both, if one is doing either earnestly, and Irishmen are very earnest about their drink and their talk. Table 7 had been restored to its corner and nobody seemed keen to sit at it. Jock Lennox went home earlier that night, and even old Emmet gave up on his sampling at a more reasonable hour. He helped Sean make up the takings then shuffled off to put his old shiny black coat on.

'I'll bid ye good night,' he croaked.

'Good night to you, Emmet,' said Sean, 'an' mind how ye go.' With that, Emmet fell over the feet of one of the customers, but being well-used to him, he helped him up again and pointed him to the door. Watching, Sean shook his head and sighed. Michael came up with the last tray.

'They must all be going to first Mass. There's hardly a drink left in them. Never mind, I think I'll enjoy one meself tonight.'

'When you get home,' grinned Sean.

'That's right. When I get home,' replied Michael. 'And old Ma Lennox not letting a drop pass over the door.'

'No wonder with the amount Jock brings home with him.'

'Aye, but it's in him. That's her complaint.' The brothers laughed and carried on clearing up. Because of their rule never to

169

drink on the premises and Mrs Lennox, their landlady's domestic prohibitions, Sean and Michael did all their drinking at another Irish pub, Hogan's, two blocks west on 34th Street. That's where they both went when they closed up at 2.00 a.m.

And that's where they found Denis with their Uncle Mick, both out of uniform and both quite amiably drunk.

'What's the party?' asked Sean.

'We're celebrating,' beamed Uncle Mick.

'Can anybody join?' asked Michael.

'Certainly,' slurred Denis. The brothers joined the table and Uncle Mick called to the barman,

'Same again all round.'

'All round the clock, by the look o' things,' said Michael, eyeing the number of empty glasses on the table.

'We've only been here since nine o'clock,' explained Uncle Mick, blinking happily.

'This mornin'?' asked Sean. The barman brought the drinks. Four large glasses of Bushmills Whiskey and four foaming jugs of black porter. All four men looked down at them appreciatively.

'Black beer and the black bush from Ballycastle,' said Uncle Mick reverently as if intoning a prayer. 'Your good health, me boys!' The drink was drunk solemnly as befits the good stuff that it was.

'What are we celebrating?' asked Michael.

'The engagement of your brother here,' answered his uncle.

'Engagement?' queried Sean.

'To be married.'

'MARRIED?' expostulated both boys together.

'Indeed so!' laughed Uncle Mick, patting Denis heavily on the back, almost spilling his drink.

'Jesus Christ!' said Sean under his breath.

'He wasn't married!' muttered Michael.

'Nobody's perfect!' beamed Denis.

John Keith was sitting at the kitchen table reading a letter. Thomasina was trying to feed Elspeth, who was being difficult.

'Come on, John, read it out to us,' she said to him, pushing her hair out of her eye. 'Oh, will you be quiet, Elspeth.' She continued, turning to her daughter. 'You've had my heart roasted since you got up.' Then she called out, 'Kenneth Keith, where are you? Here's your porridge gettin' cold.' She returned to her daughter. 'Now see the mess you've made. Oh, who would be a mother?' She attempted to deal with the fractious infant while at the same time trying to have a bite of her own breakfast toast. A piece of it was in her mouth when she looked up to her husband again, who was staring straight ahead, the letter in his hand. She swallowed quickly. 'John, are you going to read it out, I'm sayin'.' He did not reply, but continued to stare. 'John, I'm sayin', your letter, are you –' She suddenly realised something must be wrong. 'Are you alright?' she went on quietly. 'Is it the letter? Was there something?' He was still silent. She rose, lifting the baby from the high chair. Elspeth started to cry, so Thomasina had to shout. 'John Keith, will you listen to me?'

'My father's dead,' he mumbled.

'What? I can't hear you.'

'MY FATHER'S DEAD!' he shouted. His shout stilled the child's crying and caused Thomasina to sit immediately. Elspeth began to whimper in her arms.

'Oh, my God!' said Thomasina. Just then young Kenneth came rushing in. 'Mummy. Mummy, Daddy. See what I've got. It's a sword. A real sword.' And he brandished a walking stick across the table. 'Me fight the big dragons. See, Daddy!'

'Leave your daddy alone, Kenneth.' The little boy turned to his mother with a puzzled look on his face. 'Want to show Daddy the dragons.'

'The dragons can wait! Your grandfather's deid.' The little boy didn't understand at all.

'Is he a dragon?'

'Never mind, son,' said his father, pulling him to him and hugging him close. 'We'll baith kill the dragons yet.' He smothered the little boy in kisses till Kenneth was impatient and then afraid of such intensity.

'Let him be, John,' said Thomasina. John let his son go, who immediately ran away.

'You forgot your sword,' called out the father, holding out the walking stick, but Kenneth had already gone.

'I'll take Elspeth up,' said Thomasina quietly. 'I'll be back in a minute.'

'Aye,' said John, looking down at the letter again.

When his wife had gone he sat there for what seemed a long time, the letter in one hand, the walking stick in the other, then suddenly rising, he smashed the stick on to the table with tremendous force, scattering dishes and plates in all directions. Bellowing in a mad rage, he continued to smash the table until the stick broke in half. He threw away the piece left in his hand and, putting both hands on the table, he bowed his head. Thomasina came running in and was appalled at the mess, but she knew better than to say anything, and without a word, came forward and picked up the letter from among the debris on the floor.

The Keith family lined the rail of the Mataura as it docked at the harbour in Singapore. Their sombre funereal garb contrasted with the gleaming white of the ship in the glare of the Oriental sunlight. Bobby and Jim stood either side of their sister. She looked smaller between the two men, and frailer. All three still wore mourning for their father and Tina, despite the sticky heat, shivered slightly. Her high-necked bombazine was not the ideal dress for the humid press of Singapore. She wore her net down on her face and both her brothers were hatted. They seemed to be waiting for something to happen.

'There he goes,' said Jim, almost in a whisper. Looking down, they saw Martin Dickenson walk down the gangway. When he reached the quay he looked up at them and smiled. Nobody reacted. Dickenson gave a wry salute and turned quickly away towards the dock shed.

'He's walking right into it,' said Bobby.

'Serve him right,' said Jim. Tina said nothing, but after a moment, she turned away from the rail.

'I'd better see to mother,' she said quietly as she went. Jim made as if to go with her, but Bobby restrained him.

'Leave her be.'

Jock Aitken joined them from one of the companion ways. 'Did ye see him?'

'Aye,' said Jim.

'He'll be watched all the way, and we'll grab him when he comes back.'

'Unless he sees you first,' said Bobby.

'No' me. It's wee Applecross on the job, and since he's half a villain himself, he'll make sure he keeps well out o' sight.'

'What do we do now?' said Jim.

'Just wait,' said the Chief. 'Unless you want to go into Raffles Hotel yourself. But there's nothing to see there but drunk tea planters and army wives – and a whean o' whores, o' course –' He tipped his cap to Tina – 'if you'll excuse me, miss.' But she didn't appear to hear.

By this time Bobby had spotted Rachel as she came up on deck. 'Excuse me,' he said, and went quickly to join her.

'Oh, I forgot,' said the Chief. 'The lovebirds.'

'Ay,' said Jim, smiling.

The Chief looked at his watch.

'The sun's still a mile and a half from the yard arm. Pity. Then again, there's no reason why we should wait, is there?'

'Ay, ay, sir,' said Jim. They walked down the deck towards the for'ard bar. As they went past Bobby and Rachel, they pretended not to notice them, but they needn't have bothered for Bobby and Rachel took no notice of them anyway!

In Cabin C51, mother and daughter sat silent. They never had much to say to each other, but nowadays they said nothing at all. After a few attempts at trying to make or rather force conversation, Tina gave up. She only had half a heart for the exercise in any case as she wasn't sure how much her mother knew and didn't know about her interesting condition. She had tried to raise the subject on several occasions, but her mother didn't rise to it and so Tina let it go. It was more important that she should at least keep her company, however tacit and mute. The older woman would come round in time. One could never tell about Mrs Keith these days. One day she would be talkative to the point of garrulousness, but then it would be all about Scotland. There were other days when she would never say a word, but sit in her cabin staring straight ahead of her. It wasn't that she was getting senile or anything. It was more like she had retreated within herself and would take her own time to come out again. She still refused to leave the cabin, and only on those two terrible occasions had Tina seen her outside it. She tried to read her book, but the light was failing rapidly. She was glad when Sammy came in to light the oil lamps. His smile flashed as brightly as the flame he created under the bowl, but his soft eyes gave her, so she thought, a look of sympathy and what was more appreciated, understanding. He then brought in tea and when she took the cup from him, in her thanks she tried to convey that appreciation for the second that their eyes met before he bowed and backed out as silently as he had come in.

Tina noticed that her mother sipped the hot tea readily enough, so she wasn't sick. 'A nice cup,' she said. Her mother merely nodded and took another sip, then laying her cup down on the bedside locker, she went to the porthole and looked out. Tina heard her give a sharp cry. More like an intake of breath. She jumped up and looked over her mother's shoulders. Second Officer Dickenson was in conversation with two other officers on the quayside. Mrs Keith turned round and looked at her daughter. There was a strange expression on her face. Tina realised she had to go. 'Excuse me, mother,' she said.

On deck she saw Rachel, Bobby, Jim and Chief Engineer Aitken clustered near the main gangway. She joined them, squeezing herself between Jim and Bobby.

'In at the kill, eh, Teenie?'

'Quiet, Bobby,' said Jim. They all watched as Applecross joined the discussion below. He seemed very animated and kept pointing to Dickenson, who suddenly lunged at the little ship's carpenter, but was held by Captain Ellon and the Shore Officer. Applecross ran for the gangway while other shore people came to grapple with the angry Dickenson. As he was being restrained, Tina was sure he had looked up to her, but she turned her head away. Inexplicably, she felt herself being engulfed by an ineffable sadness, which changed to a dizziness that swept up and over her till she swooned and would have fallen, except that Jim had noticed her reaction and held her round the waist.

'Hold on, Tina,' he whispered urgently. 'Don't let them see.' No, she wouldn't let them see. Martin, least of all. But Rachel had noticed. She was about to move to Tina, but there was more shouting and scurrying on the dock. Martin was dragged away. Captain Ellon and the other officers followed, and all was quiet on the quayside again.

'Well,' said Jock Aitken, 'the bait was swallowed.'

'Hook, line and sinker!' said Bobby.

'What had he done?' asked Rachel.

'Everybody!' said Jock Aitken with a chuckle.

'Will you excuse me?' said Tina in a faint voice.

'I'll help you down, Tina,' said Jim.

Just as they were going, Captain Ellon returned and made his way to the gangway. He was carrying a little wooden box.

'What's in the box, I wonder?' asked Bobby.

'Dickenson's ashes?' muttered Jim as he led his sister away.

Rico d'Agostino's cigar had at least half an inch of ash on it, which is said to be the sign of a good cigar. It was also an indication that Rico was doing quite well in the hard underworld of New York City. Like most men of his caste, if he had money he believed in showing it, hence the quality suit with its imperceptible gold thread inlay, the ring on each hand, the diamond in the tie-pin, even his tooth fillings were gold! This might have been considered an unnecessary gilding by some, as Enrico d'Agostino, formerly of Genoa, Chicago and now of New York was a handsome man by any standard, apart from Gold Standard. He was taller than the average Italian, lean and lithe from previous penal incarcerations, and there was a gleam in his eye that had as much to do with fanaticism as good health and vigour. These pale grey eyes narrowed now as he inhaled again on his cigar and stared at Noreen.

He was in one corner of the horse cab and she was in the other.

They were having what he called one of his little 'conversatione'. He enjoyed these intimate chats. Noreen was not so sure she did. This must be the umpteenth time he had taken her out like this after lunch and he had never as much as laid a finger on her, let alone make any improper advances. He merely stared at her all the time through the haze of the cigar smoke and encouraged her to talk. At the beginning, she had needed little encouragement. As her father said, Noreen could talk the hind leg on to a three-legged donkey. But her talk was forced now. She had exhausted both her repertoire and her nervous tension, and now she sat looking out of the window leaving him to talk if he liked. What she couldn't understand was that she still enjoyed being with him like this, just the two of them, with the world shut out behind the blinds of the cab. He was still the most fascinating man she had ever met, and yet she knew next to nothing about him. He had all the charm in the world, but there was also a menace. She would like to have known about that. Noreen O'Neil flirted with danger the way any other pretty young girl flirted with men.

Why didn't he tell her about himself? She was mad to know. She had told him all about herself. Ah, let him go for all she cared, and she turned her head to the side again to take in the passing trees of Central Park. What she didn't realise was that she looked even better in side profile and he was quite content to sit and admire. He had all the time in the world, and like a panther gazing down on an antelope, he knew he could strike when he liked. And he knew he could kill. So, she was a cop's niece, he was thinking. A Superintendent, no less? Could be useful. She's bella too. Multa bella. Una bella ragazza. He might even take her home someday. A casa mia. Meet his Mamma. Madre mia. Si. E fratelli e sorelli. La famiglia. Buona idea. What Rico didn't take into account was that a cousin of his cousin, Roberto, the owner of the restaurant in Queen's, was a certain Carmella Ruffiano, otherwise Mrs Michael O'Neil. His eyes narrowed to slits and his wide mouth opened only slightly as he brought the cigar once again to his lips.

'I hate the country,' Noreen suddenly said.

Rico nearly smiled.

In the Seminary at Baltimore the newest recruit, Paddy O'Neil, was at prayer, and trying to cope with the fifteen decade set of rosary beads. It had been given him by Jackie Rafferty at the pub. He had let it be known among the regulars that Paddy was going off to be a priest, and had been inundated with gifts, pictures, holy relics and rosary beads, handed in by the men over the next weeks. He didn't know whether this generosity was prompted

by the recognition of Paddy's sanctity, or a desire to get rid of
a whole heap of religious artefacts they had carted over from
the old country, some of them thirty years before. At any rate,
Paddy's little cupboard room in the Baltimore Seminary was a
very repository of holy effects. It came a near second to Lourdes
as a Catholic shrine and caused much amusement among the senior
priests who taught them and among the nuns who were the
domestics in the big house. Pride of place undoubtedly belonged
to these vast Marian prayer beads. He could have wrapped them
twice round his head and still had them dangling in front of him.
As it was he let the familiar shapes pass through his fingers, and the
thoughts pass through his mind as he had done all his life when he
prayed. It was perhaps not very prayerful, but it was comfortable,
and he was used to it, and he was sure the Lord and His Mother
understood. He'd been here for a month now and he knew he had
done the right thing. Not by anything specific or through any
wonderful sign, but just by that absolutely real and lucky feeling
of the round peg slipping easily into the round hole, he knew this
was the life for him. It was always what he was meant to do and
he thanked God every day for the chance.

The life-style may have been clerical, its intentions pious, but the
regime resembled more a celibate penitentiary. The student had no
real freedom. From the first pre-dawn prayers till the last rite after
sunset, every hour was allocated and every function prescribed.
But to minds like Paddy's this was the ultimate freedom. With no
real need to be worldly, he had no desire for it. With every basic
need provided, he was free to give himself to the life of the soul.
Liberated from material stress and pressure, he was better able to
cope with the spiritual stress and pressure caused by his adjustment
to this new life after the experiences of Ireland, the crossing and
Rafferty's bar. For the first time in his life, Paddy felt genuinely
at home, and was grateful. Not that it was easy. The day was long,
and nights short. The food was plain and scarce and the iron bed
uncomfortable. The rooms were draughty and the amenities crude.
The teachers were demanding, his fellow students were still shy of
him, but Paddy O'Neil was happy.

In his new contentment at his charity, he prayed for the souls
of those he loved – his parents, one worrying herself to death,
the other drinking himself the same way; Kevin, the dreamer, the
baby of the family, who always kept himself to himself; Denis,
the oldest, and his new foreign bride-to-be; Sean and Michael, the
terrible twins, and Noreen, dear Noreen, his favourite, if he had
to admit it, and his family spy. Only he knew the number of times
she had written to him from the back room of the restaurant, from

her own room at Uncle Mick's and even once on hotel paper he
didn't recognise. Noreen seemed to have her own life, but she kept
a corner of it for Father Paddy as she now called him, even though
he had seven years to do first.

The drone of the boy's responses to the priest leading the rosary
changed rhythm and tone now as they came to the final prayers.
Paddy was conscious of the noise and stir he made as he tried to
put away his gargantuan beads. It was time now for a mug of cocoa
and over-hearty exchanges of the day's trivia, before the silent hour
again in bed. The male voices rose up around him: 'In the name of
the Father, and of the Son and of the Holy Ghost. Amen.'

'Do you ever say prayers?'

'Sometimes. When I want something.' Tina laughed and Rachel
went on, 'Or when I've lost something.'

'I thought only Catholics did that.'

'I've never met a Catholic.'

'Neither have I.' Yet even as she said it, something stirred in Tina.
The boy on the Glasgow docks. He was Irish and they were all
Catholic, weren't they?

'Have you ever met any Irish people, Rachel?' she asked.

'Thousands of them. They're all over the place in Sydney.'

'I keep forgetting you're Australian.'

'What did you think I was?'

'I don't know,' said Tina. 'Jewish, I think.'

'Is it that obvious?'

'No, no – it's –'

'Like a hooked nose, for instance?' It was Tina's turn to laugh.

'Don't be silly.'

'Look,' said Rachel, sitting up on the bunk on one arm, 'I've had
this conversation with Bobby already. In fact I seem to have it with
everybody when I first meet them. I dunno what it is about us that
makes people want to ask questions.'

'It might be because you're supposed to have most of the
answers. The ancient tribe of Israel and all that.'

'Yoi! Yoi!'

The two girls were in Tina's cabin. Since the incident on the
docks at Singapore, Rachel had made a point of getting to know
Tina better, and she began to spend more and more time in her
company. There were even occasions when she stayed in the
other bunk in Tina's cabin, and this night somewhere off the
coast of New Guinea was one of them. The two girls were
having a long 'heart to heart', and it was by no means just
girls' talk and gossip. It was as wide-ranging and specific as

good talk is between two intelligent, well-read young people, who have the chance, the space and above all the time, to talk their hearts out.

'We have a legend, you know, in Scotland, that the lost tribe of Israel became the Irish and the Irish became the Scots and the Scots –'

'Became everybody else,' broke in Rachel.

'But we began as Jews!' insisted Tina.

'Like everybody else! So what's new?' Both girls laughed. It was a good time. Each was as relaxed as the other. They had a lot in common and a sense of fun was a good part of it.

'We'd better be quiet,' Tina giggled, 'or we'll have my mother up.'

'Sorry.'

'No, don't worry.' No one said anything for quite a time. It was the first lull in the conversation since they had come down to the cabin soon after dinner that evening. They had left the Keith brothers in the bar, but now the mention of Mrs Keith had put a sudden brake on things. Rachel was the first to break the silence.

'Tina?'

'Ay?'

'Can I ask you something?'

'You *may* ask me something?'

'Sorry, you old schoolma'am – may I ask you something?'

'Of course.'

'You won't be offended?'

'Not at all – well – I don't know yet, do I?'

'Yeah. Look, – why does your mother never come out of her room?' There was a long pause.

'I don't know.'

'Oh!' Another tense silence. 'I'm sorry, I –'

'Honestly, Rachel, I really don't know. She said she'll not come out till we get to New Zealand.'

'But that's ages yet.'

'Ay.'

'Wow! Funny isn't it?'

'Is it?' Silence once more, then it was Tina who spoke.

'Rachel?'

'Yeah?'

'May I ask you –'

'You may – and no, I won't be offended!'

'You might.'

'Try me.' There was a slight pause.

'Are you in love with my brother?'

'I'm offended!'

'Rachel, you said –' But Rachel was laughing again.

'I hardly know him!' Now it was Tina who sat up in her bunk.

'I don't mean –' but Rachel topped her protest and said in a loud whisper:

'I know what you mean alright, girl, and the answer is "yes".'

'What?'

Rachel leaned over and almost shouted, 'Yes, I love your Bobby!'

'SHSH!'

Both girls lay back breathless on their backs. Each throbbing with their own thoughts and excitement.

'Anyway he's not MY Bobby!' Tina said in a low voice. Silence.

'My turn now,' whispered Rachel.

'Oh Rachel, I'm tired.'

'I know but just one last thing.'

'Alright.'

'You won't –'

'No.'

'And you won't –'

'No!' Silence. The tension was unbearable for Tina.

'Go on then,' she said impatiently.

'Alright – are you pregnant?'

At the same time, in Cabin D27 the Keith brothers were also in debate with a full bottle of The Queen's Liqueur Whisky the only thing standing between them where they sat facing each other from their respective bunks.

'Bobby.'

'Yes?' Jim's tone was very tentative.

'You don't think there's any chance that she's –?'

'What? Teenie? Impossible?' Bobby's tone shocked Jim and it took a moment for him to realise what his brother meant. He then was terribly embarrassed, but after a breath, he continued,

'I was about to say – you don't think Tina really – you know – loves this Dickenson?' Bobby was contrite at once.

'Sorry, Jim. I don't know what I was thinking of.'

'That's alright. It's Tina we should be thinking of.'

'Ay.' Both young men were quiet for a moment. It was Jim who picked up the conversation again.

'Whatever it is, she's not well. She's not herself. Not since –'

'Dickenson, you mean?'

'Ay. I never did like that fella.'

'No. Here, have another.' Bobby reached for his brother's glass.

'That was a business right enough,' said Bobby eventually.

'Ay. Contraband, they said. Part of a world-wide network.'

'Who would have thought it?'

'There must have been money in it. There have been smugglers since we were all paddling canoes.'

'I don't mean that,' said Bobby, 'I mean her and Martin.'

'Oh that.'

'Ay, that. I thought by the look of them that there was something going on there.'

'People would think that looking at you and Rachel.'

'But there is!'

'Oh?'

'Oh, I don't mean –'

'You don't mean what?'

'You know.'

'No, I don't know.'

'Right enough, you wouldn't know. Would you, wee brother?'

'Oh, I don't know,' answered Jim, trying to be sly.

'Here, have you been hiding something from me?' said Bobby playfully, but Jim suddenly looked serious.

'Have you, Bobby?'

'What do you mean now?'

'I mean Ella Friar.' Bobby was about to reply, but changed his mind. He pushed the bottle across to his brother.

'Have another drink.'

'No thanks.' Bobby took the bottle back.

'Then I will.' He poured a generous measure while Jim watched.

'Steady on there, Bobby.'

'It's all right. I don't have far to walk home.' He took a good swig then lay back on his bunk, his glass still in his hand. 'I'll tell you about Ella Friar. . . .'

And Bobby talked as Jim had never heard him talk before, quietly, sincerely. Jim heard things that he had never guessed, and he suddenly realised that his voluble, over-assertive brother could also be a man of sensitivity, if not always restraint. He was just as often victim as well as predator and, as the time passed, Jim too lay back on his bunk and let his brother talk.

'. . . so you see, wee brother, things are not always what they look. The Friars had me where they wanted me, so when this chance came to run, I ran. But I wouldn't worry about Ella Friar. She's got her mother.'

'And what about Rachel?'

'Ah, that's a different matter altogether.'

'Why is it different? I can't see any difference between –' Bobby leaned up on one arm and looked directly across at his young brother.

'The difference is, Jim, that I'm going to marry Rachel Gebler. Good night.'

In the morning in his early tea round, Sammy, the Goanese steward, looked in as usual on Cabin C50. When he opened the blind over the porthole, the white sunlight spotlit the nearest bunk and there entwined like the babes in the wood, Tina and Rachel slept innocently in each other's arms. Sammy smiled and closed the blind again.

In D27, not having the benefit of a steward's attention, the porthole was still uncurtained from the night before and the early morning light discovered the Keith brothers sprawled in their bunks, still in their clothes, but with an empty bottle of whisky standing on the locker between them.

FOURTEEN

A row of bottles lay along the window ledge of the kitchen at 57th Street. Carmella O'Neil looked at them ruefully and shook her head, muttering all the time to herself in her peasant Italian. Since the announcement of Denis's marriage to Hana, every night seemed to be an excuse for a party. Everybody had come, except Paddy, of course. He wasn't allowed to leave the Seminary. What a shame, Carmella thought. He missed a good party and a good dinner. And a lot of booze, thanks to Sean and Michael. Denis had brought the girl here. That was nice. A little bit of a thing she was. Not like Italians at all. And without a word to say for herself. Not that she had much of a chance with all these Irishmen. Why couldn't Denis have married a nice Italian girl like his uncle did? Carmella laughed as she worked away among the soap suds. She now had all the bottles done and they were coming perilously near the edge of her draining board.

'Where is dat boy now?' she said to herself. 'He could come and take some of these away. Joey!' she called. She called again twice and there was still no reply. 'Mamma mia!' she muttered, drying her hands on her apron. 'Dove quello ragazzo? Joey!' She heard a door slam. 'Joey?' she called again. Going past his room she glanced in. She could see that his shirt and trousers were no longer lying on top of the unmade bed. He must still be with Noreena, she thought. She found him there. He was sitting on the edge of her single bed, holding a cup of coffee in his hand and he was crying.

'Joey?' cried his mother. 'What you do here? Whassamatter?' She put her arms round him.

'Noreen,' blubbered the young man.

'What about Noreena?' asked Carmella, crooningly, her arms tightly around him. 'Whassamatter with my boy?'

'She's gone away, mamma.' He lifted a tear-stained face to his mother. 'Mamma, she's gone.' Carmella glanced over to the old wardrobe. Sure enough the doors were wide open and the coat hangers were hanging empty on the rail.

'I call your poppa,' said Carmella.

*

In the Mount Vernon Hotel, Noreen was putting the last of her clothes away. She still wasn't sure it had all happened. But now here she was, emptying the contents of her dress basket into the wardrobe of an upstate hotel room, where Rico had taken her only a few hours before. She had been taken by surprise the previous week when he had asked her to go away with him. She still could hardly believe that she was here. It had all been on an impulse, and it had all happened since this morning.

When she had gone to bed after the party, she had made up her mind that she wouldn't go. The family would be horrified and she wanted it all to happen to her like it had happened to Denis and Hana. She liked Hana, even though she couldn't speak much English. Neither could I, thought Noreen, when I first arrived! She smiled wanly.

Everything had happened so suddenly. When Joey had come in as usual this morning to waken her, he was smiling too, she remembered. Joey was always smiling, and he always brought her a cup of coffee every morning and he would just stand there looking at her drink it, and smiling. She didn't like it. She didn't like coffee in the morning. She didn't like seeing him standing there while she tried to get her eyes open. She liked Joey. In fact, she loved him, and she knew that he certainly loved her. But there was nothing in it. She was a goddess as far as he was concerned. He was like a child to her, a big child, and he was getting to be a big guy. Indeed, you could say he was a man already, so that it was getting a little bit uncomfortable to see him standing there. She put her head against the wardrobe door even as she thought about it. . . .

Was it only this morning? He had come in as he'd always done, kind and smiling, holding out the coffee cup, still in his woollen combinations. In this stuffy weather he delayed as long as possible putting on his clothes and ran around the house till it was time to go to the Deli, as if he were a boy of ten. But he wasn't a boy of ten – he was a man – and his manhood showed as he stood at the end of her bed watching her. She saw it between his legs – in the aperture of his long johns. It was big and it rose. And all the time – poor Joey – he stood smiling at her. She closed her eyes and looked away.

'Your coffee get cold.' He came towards her. She froze as she felt his hand take the cup from her. 'I get you another one,' he said. Noreen struggled to make her voice sound normal as she called out after him,

'And put your clothes on, big boy.'

'Sure, Noreen,' he replied from the stairs. 'Then I bring you hot coffee, OK?'

'OK.' Her mouth was dry, but she was already up and moving to close the door. She stood with her back against it.

'Oh, Joey! My poor Joey!' She knew what she had to do and walked at once across the carpet and reached up to the top of her wardrobe for the dress basket Carmella had given her. . . .

She closed the wardrobe door and drifted across to the window. The view she saw was unfamiliar. Trees instead of houses. Carriages rather than street cars. This was Upstate New York, well above her normal line of street vision, not that she could see much. It was raining hard, and it beat against the window pane as if anxious to get in. The day's crying, she thought. She remembered that's what she thought when she was a little girl, huddled in bed with Nellie, watching the rain against the little window at Ballytreabhair. How long ago that seemed now. Yet it was hardly three months. Was that all it was? She was a little girl then, but she was a big girl now. The trouble was she still felt a little girl inside. She turned as the door opened, and Rico came in. Her heart was thudding against her chest. He gave her the slightest nod of his sleek, black head and went to light the gas lamp above the fireplace. A soft, yellow glow diffused the room as he turned up the gas light. She braced herself as he came towards her.

He put his hands on her shoulders and looked at her closely.

''Scuse!' he said and, moving her aside gently, he closed the curtains. She felt a little silly and moved quickly to sit on the couch by the fireside. It was a lovely room and it looked even better in the combined gas and firelight, although she still didn't like the smell of gas. She preferred the oil lamps they had at – she must stop thinking of the past. Home is where your heart is, they say. In that case, my home must be in my mouth, she thought! He sat beside her.

'You OK?'

'Sure,' she said as diffidently as she could.

'You want anything? A drink or something?'

'No thanks.'

'You wanna go to bed?'

'No thanks. I mean –'

'It's alright. It's OK.' He put his hand on hers as she held them clasped tight on her lap. 'Sento comprendere, mia cara,' he whispered. 'I understand.' He rose and started to take off his jacket. 'I go to bed,' he said. She watched him as he undressed, fascinated, despite herself. She was a little taken aback to see the pistol holster under his armpit. He noticed her reaction.

'Strictly business,' he said quietly. She noticed how very neat he was. Everything was folded slowly and precisely and laid in its exact place on the armchair nearby. When he reached his underclothing, she felt her face crimson with embarrassment, but she held her gaze steady as if trying to prove something. If anything, he seemed to be amused by her defiance. Not a word was said by either of them. It was an eerie kind of dumbshow, and only the slight pop now and then of the gaslight reminded them that they were in a hotel room in a street in a town and that people were walking up and down outside. At length he turned away and peeled off the white linen combinations, and when he turned back to her again, he was nude. As she stared, her lips parted slightly. For she saw too that Rico's manhood was large and that it too was rising before her eyes. The difference was that this time she thought that it was beautiful.

It was beautiful, so beautiful. She lay on the soft pillows of the bed, letting the early morning sun from the window warm her all over. She had been so afraid, so tense and he was so unexpectedly gentle. There was only one thing hard about him. Everything else was soft. His eyes, his voice, the gentle touch of his hand as he had caressed her body. Not only – there – but all over – her breasts, her stomach, her thighs. She could still feel the soft touch of his hand on her. He had taken time to rouse her, so that when he entered her, he didn't invade her as she would have been willing to let him do. But no, he entered as a guest and was made welcome. Made warmly welcome and he took his place within her as of a kind of right and not at all as a prize he had won or as the fruits of conquest. If this is what love is then I must love, she thought. There was only one little disappointment in the whole event. A minor flaw in the whole wonderful process. He did smell of garlic!

She couldn't remember falling asleep and when she woke he was gone. She glanced to the armchair at the side of the bed. His clothes were gone. Suddenly she panicked and sat up. Had he deserted her? Perhaps he hadn't liked it as much as she had. Oh God, what'll I do? What'll I tell Uncle Mick? And Denis'll kill me. Just then, she heard a noise at the door and scuttled under the sheet again, pulling it up to her chin. Rico entered carrying a tray. He was as smartly dressed as ever, shaved and coiffured, but on the tray he carried a bottle of wine and two glasses, with a bowl of grapes and a single red rose in a pencil vase. He put the tray down on the table in the centre of the room and, lifting up the flower, brought it to her.

'A tribute to the queen of the night from her subject.' He placed it on the bedside table and made a mock bow.

'And who are you when you're at home?'

'A king, for you have made me one.'

'Oh, Rico,' she said. She could smell the flower. It smelt just like a rose. He brushed her lips with the slightest of kisses. It might just as well have been a toothbrush, for he smelt this morning of toothpaste and hair lotion, and all other things Rico. He poured the wine and offered her the glass. It was red wine.

'Blood red for blood shed. Virgine non piu.'

'What?' He shrugged and sat on the bed beside her.

'Cheers, as they say.' They drank in each other as they drank the red wine. There is no closer bond than that of a man and a woman who have loved well and know it. There is total mutuality in the after glow and each is as proud of the other as they are of themselves. The rain of the night before was now exchanged for the sun of the morning after and, for the moment, Noreen O'Neil thought life was wonderful. She was glad to tell him so.

'Yes, wonderful,' she said. She put her glass down and pulled up her knees under her chin, gazing childlike upon him. 'And how do you feel, Rico?'

'I am wonderful, too,' he said.

'Sure, so you are.' He took another sip of the red wine.

'For now you are mine. Mine alone. I am your first man, little Noreena. And your last, OK?' The smile faded from her face and she felt a shiver run up her spine. Trying to cover up, she reached for her glass again, but knocked it over and she watched in horror as the red wine stained the white sheet of the bed.

Tina could hardly believe it. She must tell somebody and quickly. She thought of going next door immediately to her mother, but decided against that. The less her mother knew of anything at the moment, the less it would hurt her. She was all fingers and thumbs, trying to put in the buttons on her boots with the hook. There was a quiet knock on the door.

'Come in.' It was Sammy to do the room. When he saw that she was dressing, he immediately retreated, but she called, 'It's alright, Sammy. I'm just going.' He came back in, grinning all over his gentle brown face. As she passed him, she gave him a peck on the cheek. He watched her go in amazement, then touched his cheek gently with his fingertips and mumbled something in Goanese, which was not unappreciative. Tina flew up the gangway stairs, but in a quick whirl around the deck, she could see no sign of Rachel. She'll be in her own cabin, she thought. And turning, she went back downstairs to the D Level, not much above the waterline, where Rachel shared with the three other Jewish girls. She found it eventually, mainly because the door was open, and she could hear them all talking excitedly in a foreign language. It must be Hebrew, she thought, as she drew nearer. She stood in the doorway and took in the scene.

Two of the girls were standing on a cabin trunk; one was pressing down the lid from the front, and Rachel was kneeling trying to pull a leather strap through a buckle. All were talking at once, and it was some time before Tina made herself heard. When she did, Rachel was so taken aback that she let the strap go, knocked the girl off her balance beside her, so that the lid shot up and the two younger ones fell in a heap beside the bunk beds. More Hebrew confusion. Rachel came to the door pulling it behind her.

'Tina! What are you doing here?'

'I've got something to tell you.'

'Couldn't it wait till –'

'No, it couldn't. Rachel, I –'

'Just a minute,' said Rachel. She opened the door, said something rapidly in Hebrew, closed the door again and, taking Tina by the arm, said, 'Come on.'

She wouldn't let Tina say another word until they had got to their favourite place. This was as far forward as they could go on the prow behind a huge coil of thick rope, which was twined in such a way that it offered both girls a reclining hemp couch where they could be well out of sight of all the other passengers with only the rail a few feet away between them and the sea.

'OK? What is it?'

'I've bled.'

'No?'

'Yes. I woke in the night, and there it all was.'

'Wow!'

'Yes. That's what I thought.'

'That means you're not –'

'Maybe I never was.'

'You mean you could have missed?'

'Yes.'

'How do you feel?' Tina smiled broadly.

'Great!' Rachel gave her a big hug.

'Then I feel great too.' Both girls laughed again.

'You'd better get back to your packing,' said Tina.

'The packing can go blow,' said Rachel. 'Let's do something.'

'What?'

'I don't know.' She thought for a moment. 'I've got it.'

'Well?'

'Come with me, girl.' She rose up, taking Tina's hand.

'Where are we going?'

The two girls stood outside Cabin C51. 'Go on then. Knock

on the door.' Tina was very doubtful and Rachel made a face
and nodded for her to go ahead. Tina still hesitated, but perhaps,
she thought, with Rachel beside her, her mother would be more
forthcoming, or at least less off-putting. But it was curious that
Rachel had suggested they come down here.

'Go on,' Rachel whispered. Tina knocked. And then turned the
handle. Her mother could hardly be seen for bedspread. It impeded
the door as it opened inwards. It spread across the length of the
cabin floor and it was doubled in folds across the bunk bed.
Mrs Keith sat on the other bunk with the crochet hook still in
her hand. She didn't seem at all surprised to see her daughter,
and not at all put off by meeting a stranger. She was in her own
world and it was a question of whether she would allow them to
come over her frontier, as she certainly wouldn't make any effort
to cross theirs.

'Mother?' began Tina.

'Ay?'

'I'd like you to meet Rachel.'

'Ay.'

'She's my friend.'

'Oh, ay.'

'Rachel Gebler.' Mrs Keith looked up at her. Rachel was
surprised at how good looking she still was. The dark hair and
dark eyes were still those of a young woman, although the face
was wrinkled and from what she could see, the body was that of
an old woman, even though she could only be in her fifties.

'How do you do, Mrs Keith?'

'I dae awa' fine, considerin'.' Rachel was a little confused by the
unexpected Scottishness. That must be how Scots really sound, she
thought. None of the Keiths had that kind of brogue.

'Whit did ye say your name was?'

'Rachel, Mrs Keith.'

'Ay. Rachel. That was it.'

'What do you mean, mother?' asked Tina.

'Rachel. That was the name o' Bobby's lass.' The two girls
looked at each other in astonishment.

'We don't understand,' went on Tina.

'Oh, ay. Least that's what he told me. He comes in every day
to see his mother. An' this while back he's done nothin' but
talk about this Rachel.' Rachel giggled and looked at Tina, who
shrugged helplessly. Rachel moved as near to Mrs Keith as she
could without treading all over the crocheted bedspread.

'What did he say, Mrs Keith?'

'Oh, I canna mind. I canna mind. You know Bobby.'

'Oh, yes, Mrs Keith. I know Bobby.'

'An' here he is,' said Mrs Keith, pointing with her hook to the door.

Bobby stood framed in the doorway. 'What's all this? Is this a hen party? Or can anybody join?'

'Bobby,' said his mother. 'This is Rachel.'

'So it is,' replied Bobby in mock surprise.

'This is my son, Bobby.'

'How do you do, Bobby,' said Rachel in feigned politeness. Tina burst out laughing. She didn't know whether to go and leave them to it, or sit down and enjoy the fun. She was aware that her mother was looking at her, and stopped at once. She didn't know whether this would be one of her mother's good days or bad days.

'It's a while since I heard you laugh, Christina.' Tina didn't know what to say. As it happened she didn't need to. Bobby took his own initiative, and tramping all over the bedspread, without even noticing it, he sat down beside his mother and put his arm round her.

'Mother,' he said, 'since we've got everybody concerned here, there's something I would like to tell you.'

'Oh?' said his mother. Tina felt suddenly alarmed. She knew her brother. I must go for Jim, she thought to herself. She made a sign to Rachel who was about to come to her, but Bobby was also beckoning to her.

'Rachel, come and sit by me here. Come on.' As Rachel went to sit by him on the bunk, Tina fled. Bobby now had his arms round both women.

'Mother, you know I love you.'

'Oh, ay.'

'And, Rachel, you know I love you.'

'Bobby!' She had a dread of what might be coming.

'Well, it stands to reason, if you love me and she –' he nodded towards his mother – 'loves me, then you should love one another.'

'What are you trying to say?' asked Rachel.

'He's trying to tell me he wants to wed you, lass.'

'That's right,' said Bobby amiably. Rachel tried to free herself, but he held her firmly. 'Well, what do you say?'

'I don't know what to say.'

'It's the first time I've ever known you lost for words,' said Bobby.

'But it's – it's all so sudden.'

'Is it?'

'Just let him say on and you say nothing, my girl,' said the mother. 'Whit's for you will no' go by you.'

'What?' said Rachel. She was becoming quite bewildered.

'Alright. I'll give you time to think about it,' said Bobby.

'Till when?' asked Rachel, playing for time more than anything.

'Till we dock at Sydney.'

'But that's tomorrow.'

'That's right.' There was a pause. She shook herself free and rose, almost tripping on the patchwork of the bedspread.

'Well?' Bobby went on.

'I don't know. I'll have to ask my parents.'

Bobby rose. 'But why? You asked me yourself.'

'When?'

'In the play.'

'That was in a play.'

'But it wasn't in the script. I thought you meant it.'

'I did – at the time.'

'Well, what's the difference now?'

'This isn't a play.'

'It sounds like it to me,' said the mother. 'You're just a couple of play actors, if ye but knew it.' Bobby was about to retort when Jim entered with Tina.

'What's all this?' he said.

'Just in time, wee brother. And you, Teenie. I am happy to announce the engagement today between Robert Keith, formerly of Forres in the County of Moray, Scotland and –'

'SHUT UP, BOBBY!' cried Rachel, as she ran between Jim and Tina and out of the door. There was a shocked silence for a moment.

'Did I say something?' said Bobby.

'When do ye no'?' said the mother quietly, busy with her crochet.

Kevin O'Neil had the reins of the cart and let the old horse find its own way home from Warrenpoint Market. Hadn't Random done the journey more often than he had these last years? He's nearly as old as I am meself. Still, I'll be nineteen tomorrow. It's an old man I'm gettin', he thought. Nineteen, and never been kissed. Well, hardly ever. Not that he minded that very much. Kevin had other dreams, and there was no place in them yet for silly girls, still less for marriage, as his mother was always going on about.

'There's Hettie Nelson just adores you. You only have to say the word and her father's place'll be yours, and him the auld eedjit would be glad to be rid of it. Isn't he worse than your father for the time he never spends at his own place?' His mother's voice could be heard clearly as he rode along at the end of a late summer afternoon

through the leafy lanes of Down. It was a lovely countryside
and it was his. It was Ireland. And he was glad he had been left
behind at the emigration. He loved his country with a fervour
that edged on fanaticism but his elders put this enthusiasm down
to his age and stage, not realising that he meant every word of
it. Never mind, thought Kevin, they'll learn soon enough. I'll
have the chance yet to strike a blow, and by God, I'll take it.
Involuntarily he gave the reins a tug and Random responded by
coming out of her trot into a reasonable gallop, but then realising
that he didn't really mean it, she settled down to her comfortable
trot again.

In this easy manner, the young man and his horse and cart
arrived in Rosstrevor, just in time to see Old Den being carried
out of Ingham's Bar by Tim and Tommy Drennan. Kevin groaned.
Here we go again, he thought. It was a good job he had a reasonable
day at the market. He never knew how much his father would cost
him every Tuesday afternoon! Tim normally kept an eye open for
him as the cart came up by the Station Road, so that by the time
Random came to a halt at the Public Bar entrance, Tim generally
had Den ready for immediate transfer to the back of the cart, where
he lay as senseless as ever after yet another good day at the Bar.
This became something of an automatic occurrence whenever Sean
and Michael sent dollars over, and it always seemed to happen on
a Tuesday.

Tommy Drennan pushed the American letter and what was left
of its dollars into his pal's jacket pocket as he lay flat out on the
back of the cart.

'We was just havin' a jar on account of young Denis's
matrimonials,' he explained to Kevin.

'Oh, yeh,' remarked the young man casually. Just at that, he
noticed Tim at his other side, out of sight of Tommy Drennan.
He slipped Kevin a brown envelope.

'You've to let me know. But watch out for the Davie man.'

Kevin gave the slightest of nods but otherwise portrayed no sign
of acknowledgment. Tim quickly moved round to the rear again,
saying brightly, 'And isn't it the pity, Tommy, that a man doesn't
marry every day.'

'Sure, Tim,' said Tommy, 'don't ye know that in Amerikay they
can do anythin' they like. Isn't that so, Kevin?'

'I'll believe that,' said Kevin, and clicking his teeth sent Random
on his way with his extra cargo. As he went, he was aware of
the letter, now safely in his trouser pocket, and pondered on
what Tim meant about the Davie man. He must watch out
for Sergeant Davidson. You never knew about policemen. Even

191

country policemen. But then didn't he have an uncle and a brother in the police? But that was in America. That didn't count.

As Random and Kevin arrived home, Nessie came down to the gate to open it for him.

'By the Lord, is he dead?' she exclaimed on seeing her husband.

'Ay, dead drunk,' called out her son. They lay him down on the ground while they unloaded the cart. Being realists, the O'Neils had the right priorities. They had to get some of the foodstuffs indoors as quickly as possible, and Nessie had to finish the tasks she was at when she heard the horse at the gate.

'You'll have a cuppa tea, son?'

'I will that if you've done some baking.'

'I have that, and it's already on the table.' Kevin grinned. He loved his mother's home baking. It was better than Nellie's. Not that he got much of a chance with Nellie's. She nearly always ate it herself. He pulled off his jacket and threw his cap in the corner. After a brief visit to the outside latrine and his face splashed with cold water, he felt better again and came in to leave his market money on the table for his mother.

'You've had a good day then,' she said when she saw the amount of notes on the tablecloth.

'Not bad. I was lucky with that sow. There was two of them going for it. That new man up by the braehead. You know him. And some townie from Newry, I think.'

'That was grand. Luck for us, then.'

'It was.'

'And about time, too.' She poured the tea as Kevin was putting fresh butter on to the still warm scone. He could feel his mouth watering as he did so, and was just about to put it on his tongue, when his mother called out,

'Jasus, Kevin, we forgot your father!' Kevin almost choked on the scone with laughter, but followed his mother outside, still swallowing. They found the irrepressible Den sitting up with his back against the wheel of the cart reading the letter.

'It's a failin' light, wife, an' it's not just every word I can make out.'

'Ye daft old brute,' said Nessie, trying to pick him up. 'It's a wonder you can make out your own hand in front of you. Put your hand here, Kevin, and see your father indoors. Oh, would you look at that!' She pointed to several dollar bills lying on the ground where he'd been sitting. 'Would you look at that? Your da's laid a fortune!' She picked the money up and put it up in her apron pocket. 'And that's the last he'll see of it,' she said to herself.

Kevin got his father to the table and Old Den's eyes lit up at the sight of the scones and their delightful smell.

'Isn't it the great wife I have that makes her man welcome home and sees his feet under the table, so that he can enjoy the fruits of her labours?' He reached out his hand, but she smacked it with a spoon.

'Keep your filthy hands away from the table,' she snapped.

'They're not filthy,' he protested.

'They are so,' she said.

'Dirt,' he pontificated, 'is in the eyes of the beholder,' and so saying, he grabbed a scone and had it in his mouth before she could lift the spoon again.

It was late at night when Den was in his bed before Nessie got a chance to go through his pockets as usual, and retrieved the letter. She took it into the little parlour to read it by the good candle there and by the last of the fire. As she went in, she was surprised to see Kevin sitting in her chair and he too was reading a letter. He put it away hurriedly and rose up as she came in.

'Is that a letter you've got, Kevin?'

'Not really. It's – er –.'

'Ah, now, by the way you're blushing, it must be Hettie Nelson, is that so?' He looked down at his mother's smiling face in the candlelight.

'How did ye know?' he lied.

'A mother's intuition.' He turned away as she said that. He didn't like deceiving his mother, but orders were orders.

'Would ye like to hear the letter then?' He wheeled round.

'What letter?' he said abruptly.

'Sure, the letter from Americkay.'

'Oh, that,' said Kevin.

'It's Tuesday, is it not?'

'So it is.'

'I can't see a thing.'

'Take my hand.'

'Where is it?' A note of exasperation crept into Rachel's voice. It hadn't been her idea to come out on to the deck after everyone was asleep to meet Bobby, but he had been so insistent. Now they had emerged after much stumbling and bumping through the darkened ship and found their way forward to the secluded place where she and Tina often talked. Rachel was amazed that the night, or rather early morning, was so dark. She could hardly see a thing, but she could feel Bobby's big, strong hand covering hers and she was reassured by it. We're all children in the dark, she thought, and we all need a strong hand to hold on to.

'Is this the place?' Bobby whispered hoarsely.

'I don't know. Can you feel the rope?'

'Damn!' Bobby had just tripped over it.

'This is the place,' said Rachel, trying not to laugh.

They found the folded tarpaulin, more by touch than sight, and sat down on it with their backs against the circle of hemp. By this time, their eyes were becoming used to the darkness and they were both aware of the starlight – a canopy of tiny pin-pricks above their heads that just gave enough light and no more for them to see themselves as shadows.

'Are you alright?' asked Bobby.

'I think so.'

'Good.'

'Why did you want us to come here?'

'I didn't want anybody to see us.'

'I can hardly see you, never mind anybody see us!'

'Anyway, I wanted to talk to you.'

'What about?' There was a pause before Bobby answered.

'Well?' said Rachel.

'I'm thinking.'

'What about?'

'About what I want to say.'

'I see.'

'You're not cold?' he asked.

'No.' But she gave a little shiver just the same.

'Here, cuddle in.' She was glad to. It felt cosy, snuggled in like this, in the open air under the stars. The two of them, alone it seemed, in the Tropic of Capricorn.

It had been a long night. Bobby had asked her to join their table at dinner, but she wanted to stay with her own people for the last night. After the meal, some of the passengers had improvised a kind of party in the First Class lounge, and nearly everybody had gone, but she hadn't felt like that kind of silly fun, and went back to her cabin. Bobby had come for her there and when the other girls had returned, he had suggested that Rachel come up with him on deck and now, some hours later, they found themselves still on deck and still uncertain as to what to do. They had the rest of the hours of darkness until the morning and then it would be Sydney Harbour and the parting of the ways.

'Are you looking forward to going home?'
'A bit of me is.'
'And what about the rest of you?'
'Scared.'
'Scared? About going back to your own home?'
'Maybe I've been too long away.'
'Two years isn't long.'
'It is when you hated every minute of it. Palestine is not every Jew's idea of Paradise.'
'Why did you go?'
'It was my father's idea, but I wanted to see for myself. I have a journalist's nose, you know.'
Bobby laughed. 'I don't believe it,' he said.
'Please yourself.'
'No, I don't mean that. I mean, I'm here too because it was my father's idea.' He told her about leaving Forres.
'It's strange, isn't it?' she said. 'We're both here through no fault of our own.'
'Then we might as well make the best of it,' said Bobby softly. And he kissed her. And he kissed her again and again. They kissed often in the dark of that time until dawn came and they were still in each other's arms. In fact, at one point Rachel fell asleep. When she woke she found Bobby's face staring down at her. He seemed untypically solemn, but saved the moment by more typically sticking his tongue out at her. She laughed. She felt stiff all over.
'What have we been doing?' she said.
'We've been sleeping together,' he said. 'You'll have to make an honest man out of me.' He helped her up and held her tightly in his arms. 'You know what I want,' he said. She turned her head away, but said nothing. 'Come on,' he said. 'At least we'll be first for breakfast.'
The day ahead was a busy one for half the ship was disembarking at Sydney. But as far as Bobby Keith was concerned, it was the end of the voyage for him. Rachel was leaving and she had become, in the last few weeks, his whole world. Shipboard romances were not to be trusted, but any romance at all is suspect in the first instance, at least until love is proved and Bobby found no way of proving his other than letting the girl go. Rachel herself was quieter as she went about the final preparations for going ashore. Not even Tina was able to break through her reserve. Jim suggested they should leave both of them alone and just let them get on with it.
'Where are they now anyway?' asked Tina.

195

'Don't even ask,' said Jim. 'We've got enough excitement. Come on, let's get a place.' He pulled her to the rails, and they had to go someway along the deck before they found a space. Meantime, Bobby and Rachel shared a long kiss in her cabin.

'Rachel –' he said. But she put her forefinger up to his lips. Two sailors came in to get her big trunk. 'This one, miss, for Sydney?' said one.

'That's right,' nodded Rachel. She was all dressed for landing. 'You'd better go.'

'Ay,' sighed Bobby. He held both her hands for a moment, very tightly, so tightly that it hurt her, but nothing was said and he was gone.

There was indeed excitement on deck. Not only in the prospect of another port but, for most, the chance to stretch sea legs again on land, which for some, was the end of the journey. Sydney Harbour seemed to be hidden in sails as the steamer inched its way forward to the quayside. The passengers crowded the rails to see, and what a sight it was. Sydney was one of the most beautiful harbours in the world, and in the red morning light of that day it looked superb, despite mist on the hills beyond and a quayside black with people. There was even a band. As the Mataura drew nearer, they could hear it and the strains of 'The Wild Colonial Boy' enticed them like a siren strain towards Australia, which was not only a colony but a country, and not only a country but a continent.

Rachel took some time to find Tina and Jim at the rails.

'There you are,' said Tina. 'We were wondering –'

'Where's Bobby?' asked Jim.

'He's with your mother,' said Rachel. And moved in beside Tina. The two friends stood with their arms round each other's waists, watching the scenes on the dock below. Jim was also a spectator, but he couldn't help glancing first at Rachel. Had she been crying? With a great shout from all the people gathered on the quayside and with much waving of straw hats, the anchor was made fast and the band struck up with 'God Bless the Prince of Wales'. The conductor of the band on the quayside turned and conducted the ship, encouraging the passengers to sing along. They did, especially the little tenor from the ship's concert, Mr Faber, whose voice soared above all others including the three young people watching from the upper deck. Other interested spectators were Captain Ellon, standing with the pilot on the bridge, and Chief Engineer Aitken, standing with a glass in his hand. Ship's carpenter Applecross was with the bos'un and the purser at the upper gangway.

Bobby watched with his mother from the porthole of Cabin

C51. As the singing began, he turned to his mother who was also watching, and took her in his arms.

'Are ye sure, Bobby son?'

'I'm sure, mother.'

'Well then, on ye go.'

'Ay.' He gave his mother the tightest hug and without another word left the cabin. Nobody noticed as he picked up two large leather bags from the deck and made his way off the ship by a lower gangway.

FIFTEEN

Superintendent Michael O'Neil was on the telephone. 'Speaking,' he said. 'Go on then.' His grim face broke into a grin. 'Do ye say now? Good work, Phil, my boy. Good work. I'll not be forgettin' it. The Mount Vernon Hotel,' he said.

Denis O'Neil, in uniform, on the other side of the desk said, 'Do we go there?'

The Superintendent rose. 'I'd like to see who'd stop us.' Denis got up to follow, taking out his gloves. 'And you can put those away for a start. Kid gloves is a thing we'll not be needin' this trip.' Denis threw them down on the desk and followed him out.

At the Mount Vernon Hotel, there were two policemen at the door, two at the desk, two by the elevator and two at the door of Room 9 on the first floor. There were also two inside the room: Superintendent Mick and Police Officer Denis. The Super was in belligerent form as he faced a very calm Enrico d'Agostino.

'Then where is she?'

Rico pointed. 'In the bathroom.'

'What's she doin' there?' Rico shrugged and smiled. Uncle Mick blustered. 'Then get her out. We haven't all day to spend here.'

'Let me, Uncle Mick,' whispered Denis. And he went to the door, and knocked gently.

'Are ye there, Noreen?' The door immediately opened, and there stood his sister looking absolutely radiant.

'Sure I am. But it's not very polite you are.' And she swept past her brother to give the startled Uncle Mick a peck on the cheek. 'It's yourself, Uncle Mick.'

'It is and I'm here on duty.'

'Duty?' she asked, going to stand by Rico.

'It's my duty to take you home.'

'To Ireland?'

'Don't be silly, Noreen,' interjected Denis.

'I'm not silly at all. Perhaps I'm just coming to my senses.' She put her arm through Rico's.

'What are you doing, girl?' growled Uncle Mick.

'I'm staying here,' answered Noreen, lifting her chin defiantly.

'Like hell you are,' said Denis making a move.

'Please,' said Rico, lifting his hand. 'Your uncle here would tell you that if you use the force, it is assault.'

'I don't need the force. I'll bring her meself,' said Denis, still intending to go forward.

'Denis!' His uncle's voice had a new authority, and Denis was aware of it. He took a breath and stepped back, but his eyes glared at his sister, promising what he would do to her as soon as he got the chance. She seemed quite unperturbed, as she gazed confidently and nearly impudently at her uncle.

'Did you come here by your own free will?'

'I did.'

'Do you remain here by your own free will?'

'I do.'

'And is it your will that you remain here with this man?'

'It is.' It was almost like a marriage service, with Noreen and Rico as the happy couple and Uncle Mick as the disgruntled minister. Denis was the very unhappy witness of it all. But there was no doubt she had made up her mind, and the good Superintendent knew there was nothing he could do about it.

'Have you anything to say at all, girl?'

'No.'

'Noreen!' said Denis. 'Surely –'

'There is one thing.' She glanced at Rico, and then at her uncle again. 'Will you give my love to Aunty Carmella?' She bent her head and they heard her almost whisper, 'And to Joey.'

For a moment no one moved, then Uncle Mick turned on his heel,

'Let's get the hell out of here.' Denis moved in to Noreen, but she turned away.

'Whore!' he said fiercely. Noreen wheeled round, her eyes on fire, but Rico's grip on her shoulders tightened, and he smiled at Denis.

'Arrivederci, Signor O'Neil.'

'Ah, to hell wi' ye all!' He was white with anger and helplessness. Rico continued to smile. When Denis had gone, Noreen rushed back to the bathroom and slammed the door behind her.

Most of the passengers and the friends who waited for them had left the quayside at Sydney. Even the band had long stopped playing and marched off. Rachel had disappeared into the long shed in the company of her Jewish group and a hurried wave was the last that Tina and Jim had seen of her.

'Where did Bobby get to?' asked Tina.

In the cabin, Mrs Keith was standing looking out of the porthole. Most of the famous bedspread had been folded away, and a photo album was lying open on the bunk. Tina went to look at it as Jim went to his mother.

'Are you alright?' he said. She never answered. Just turned round and went to sit on the bunk.

'These are our photographs,' Tina said.

'That's right,' said her mother.

'What are they doing out here?'

'I was looking at them,' said her mother, taking up the album and closing it.

'What for?' asked Tina. The mother only shrugged.

'We were looking for Bobby,' Jim said.

'You'll no' find him here.'

'Then where is he?' went on Jim. 'He wasn't with Rachel.'

'How do you know that?' said the mother.

'We saw her when she left with her friends,' replied Tina. 'Bobby didn't even come to say Cheerio.'

'There wis nae need.'

'What do you mean, mother?'

'You'll find out.' Tina and Jim exchanged puzzled glances. Was their mother in one of her strange moods again?

Jim was about to pursue the matter when Applecross knocked at the open door.

'Sorry to disturb the family party, but the purser asked me to give you this.' He handed Jim a letter. 'It came through the agent. OK?' And he was gone as suddenly as he came.

'OK,' answered Jim automatically, and looked at the letter. It had a British stamp. 'I think it's from our John,' he said. 'It's addressed to father.'

He handed it to his mother. The mother made no attempt to take it. 'Read it out then,' she said breathlessly, convinced it was bad news.

' "Dear Father –" '

'You can leave that bit,' said the mother.

'Ay,' said Jim, and taking another breath, he continued: ' "I hope this finds you as it leaves me –" ' He glanced up at Tina. 'It's John alright. Now, let me see. Thomasina seems to be as usual. Wee Kenny's a right scamp and Elspeth never seems to sleep nights. "Mrs Beattie calls regularly." ' Jim looked up. 'Ay, I bet she does! "And last night we had a visit from Mrs Friar and her –" ' He broke off, his expression immediately sombre. Then it became incredulous. Tina could hold back her curiosity no longer.

'What does it say, Jim?'

'Just a minute,' he said impatiently. 'Good Lord!'

'Oh, Jim,' cried Tina. He raised his hand, then looked up at his mother. 'Do you want me to read the rest of it?'

'I daur say, or we'll a' die o' nosiness.'

'Right-o,' said Jim. 'Let me see. Where can I start? Ah, yes. "So the upshot of the matter is that Ella will have Bobby's child –"'

'What?' cried Tina. The mother said nothing, but kept her head down. Jim continued, getting firmer and louder.

'"Bobby's child,"' he repeated, '"when her time comes and I have agreed to accept it and bring it up as one of our own since Bobby will be with you in New Zealand."' Jim put down the letter for a moment as if waiting for his mother's response.

'He'll no' be in New Zealand,' she said quietly.

'No,' said Jim, his head bowed.

'And neither will our Bobby. He's away to find that Rachel.' Tina gasped and Jim's head shot up. He told me. Bobby ay tells me everythin'.'

'Well, I wish he would've told us,' said Tina.

'You would only have tried to stop him.'

'But, mother –'

'Leave him be. He's his ain man noo.'

'What about Ella Friar's baby?' asked Tina.

'Bobby's baby,' added Jim.

'The bairn's in good hands,' said the mother. 'Better hands than Bobby's, I'm thinkin'. We'll leave it be tae.'

'But, mother, do you not think –'

'No. I never did, and I've lived this long. You can leave me be an' a'.'

'Mother, would you like –' began Tina.

'No, I wouldna. Just leave me be.'

'Come on, Tina,' said Jim. They were at the door when the mother called again.

'Oh, James?' Jim turned surprised at the use of his Sunday name.

'Yes, mother?'

'Was there any word of your father's insurance?'

Jackie Rafferty was a worried man. It wasn't that he was losing heavily at cards, although he hadn't been doing as well there as he used to. And it wasn't as if business in the pub was falling off. On the contrary, the O'Neil brothers had lifted it right back to what it had been like in good old bad old days, when work was plenty and you could have served up vinegar and they would have paid for it gladly. His worry now was money. Not the lack of it, but how to pay it out. Part of the normal rent of any premises in New

York was the kick-back paid to the cops, and he didn't grudge this a bit, especially when he had to pay it regularly to a regular guy like Mick O'Neil. The story was that he sent most of it on to Ireland anyway, so it was all in a good cause. Isn't that what brought Sean and Michael out to him? Now he had this other problem. A new business venture, you might say. The Italians had moved into it in a big way. Protection, they called it. Jackie thought he paid rates and taxes for protection, but he was learning that the reality of it was slightly different. He was now being asked to pay to be protected from the protectors. It was all very puzzling for an Ulsterman who left school at twelve.

Which is why he confided in Sean O'Neil the first chance he could get. Sean called in Michael, as he knew Michael would agree with everything he said anyway, and to make up the quorum they called in old Emmet for his point of view. Consequently, this was the Hibernian quartet meeting in the back office before opening time one morning on the last Saturday in August. The weather was just beginning to turn and people were coming back to the city, including some of the mobsters. One of them had made an appointment – official – to see Mr Rafferty that evening.

'God knows what I'll do,' wailed Jackie. 'He's a bad one, they tell me.'

'What do they call him when he's at home?' asked Sean.

'He's never at home, that's the trouble,' said Jackie, withdrawing a fistful of dollars from his pocket. From between the dollar bills he drew various bits of crumpled paper.

'God,' he mumbled, 'is that where that was? And I must mind to do that. Ah, here we are.' He held up a card and squinting up at it, said, 'Enrico d'Agostino – At Your Service.' Sean and Michael were immediately alert.

'Was that his name?' said Sean quickly.

'Well, it wasn't the date,' said Michael.

'Why, do ye know him, boys?'

'We don't, but our sister does,' said Sean.

'Whaddyamean?' asked Jackie.

'Never mind,' replied Sean. Emmet raised a hand tentatively.

'Without wishin' to interfere with your deliberations, would that be the fellow who came in the night we had the table over, and youse threw out the four navvies?'

'You're right there, Emmet,' said Michael.

'And wasn't I right, too?' said Sean. 'Didn't I think your dago fellow was the man at the Sunday horse-cab?'

'You did that, Sean.'

Sean leaned back in his chair. 'So that's the fella.'

'That's the man,' said Jackie dolefully, throwing the card down on the table.

'Well, Jackie,' said Sean, leaning forward, and taking it up. 'You have, as you might say, put your card on the table. We'll do the same with you. You leave Mr Agostino to us tonight.' He looked at his employer. 'Will ye do that?'

'I'll do that, and gladly, Sean.'

'And if we manage to put him off, shall we say, we'll come to that "arrangement" we discussed.'

'Oh, yes,' said Jackie. 'The thirty per cent.'

'No, forty, Jackie.'

'It was thirty when we talked.'

'Ah, but things keep goin' up. Isn't that right, Michael?'

'It is, Sean.'

'Am I right, Emmet?'

'I'm sure you are, Sean.'

'You see, Jackie. Wouldn't sixty per cent of somethin' be better than a hundred per cent of nothin'?'

'Well, puttin' it like that, Sean, I see your meanin'.'

'I'm glad you do, Mr Rafferty. I'm right glad. But we'll see about tonight first. I'll need a word with Michael here and maybe a few of the regulars.'

'Just as you say, Sean. Will you be needin' me then?'

'Not at all, Jackie. I'm sure they'll be needin' ye more at the cards.' Rafferty rose and went to pick up Rico's card from the table, but Sean already had his hand over it.

That night the pub was busier than ever, it seemed. Most of the regulars were in their usual places, and there were some others who had joined them. They were larger versions of the regular customers and they had not been stunted by the rigorous application to the bottle shown by their present companions. But there was an undoubted family resemblance at the various tables. Pat Kelly appeared to have several other Kellys with him tonight. Willie Docherty was the same, so were the Quinns, and the whole Coyle table was taken up by Coyle look-alikes. The only regular missing was old Emmet. Being one of nature's survivors, he knew that the best way to fight was to stay out of it. The spectator gets the best part of the game, he always said. It was a question of whether it was a game or not. Sean was extremely earnest about it, and was seen in low conversation with several of his regulars as they came in. Jock Lennox gave himself a more than usual fortification at the piano, and his resulting handiwork on the keys took on an unexpected resemblance to atonality and the work of other musical modernists.

Not that anybody noticed. They seemed to be suppressing their natural excitement, as if they were all lying in wait.

It was just after ten o'clock when things started to happen. The same suits appeared at the door and, after a moment, the dapper Rico made his entrance. He looked even more preening than last time and almost swaggered up to face Sean.

'Mr Rafferty?'

'He's – er – been called away.'

'Again?'

'He's a busy man, Mr d'Augustinny.' Rico immediately stiffened, but said nothing. 'Is it a drink you'll be wantin'?'

'I only drink wine.'

'Well, it's a hard thing to find in Ireland, a good bottle of wine, but we've done our best.' With that he indicated a nearby table. On it stood an ice bucket outside of which protruded the neck of a bottle of the best champagne. 'Be my guest,' said Sean.

'Grazie.'

'Prego,' said Sean. Rico's eyes opened wide at the rejoinder. 'Me auntie's Italian,' said Sean. 'Michael, make the gentlemen at home.' The four Italian henchmen were made immediately at home around the various tables. In fact, they had never been made more welcome since they last returned to their own villages in Italy. Given their natural warmth, they responded easily to the Irishmen's conviviality. Jock struck up the piano again and in no time, Rafferty's had a party going. Sean and Rico did not converse. It would have been pointless in the growing noise. But they kept a wary eye on each other, each smiling, Sean widely, but Rico was not so sure. However, he accepted the champagne being offered. Another bottle was called for. Rico noticed that Sean didn't drink.

'I'm on duty,' he explained.

'So am I,' said Rico, and raised his glass to the young Irishman. The call of duty didn't seem to concern the quartet overmuch, and by the time the fourth whiskey had done its work, they were almost inclined to be Irish themselves.

Michael suddenly clapped his hands, and called for a dance. Tables were pushed back and Jock struck up with a reel. In no time, the Latin four were intertwining happily with the Hibernian eight and then, at the height of the dance, the music suddenly broke off, and the Irishmen stopped immediately, each holding an Italian hand – firmly. Jock Lennox scuttled from the piano stool. At the same time, Sean smashed the champagne bottle on the table and held the jagged neck of it at Rico's throat. Michael grabbed both his hands and held them fast behind the gangleader's chair. Nobody made a move, and there wasn't a sound, except that one of the Italians was being sick and vomited all down his good suit.

'Right now, ye bastard. You've got my kid sister, but ye haven't got me, nor her brother there.' He nodded to Michael behind him. 'I just want to tell you that you'll not buy us as easy with your perfumes and your fancy clothes and your luxury hotel rooms.'

'She would have come for nothing,' Rico said quietly.

'More fool she. But that's her business. This,' he said waving round the room with his other hand, 'this is our business, and unless you keep your Italian nose out of it, I'll have this up your throat and out the back of your head. This is Ireland, mister, and you'll need a passport to get over that door next time you call.' He took the card from his pocket and pressed it between Rico's teeth. 'Meantime, you can eat your words, mister. We don't need your trade here. Comprende?'

'Si,' Rico answered with some difficulty. Sean touched the Italian's throat with the point of the broken bottle causing a pimple of blood to appear. It was no more than a shaving nick, but it drew blood and a spot fell on Rico's immaculate lavender shirt. Both men saw it and Rico reacted.

'Sure, Noreen will wash that off no bother,' said Sean icily. When he stood up he had Rico's pistol in his hand. 'I don't know how to use one o' these things,' he said, 'but it's amazing how quick ye can learn. The gentlemen will be goin' now, Michael, as no doubt he has hotel business to attend to.' Michael released d'Agostino and as the Italian stood up, he tapped him on the shoulder. As he turned, Michael hit him square on the chin. He went down like a tree. Michael stood over him.

'Give my regards to Noreen,' he said.

'You shouldn't have done that, Michael.'

'Why not?'

'I was goin' to do it meself,' said his brother. 'Right then, lads.' He turned to the Irishmen. 'Let them go now. They'll need to carry his Lordship here to the horse-cab.' The Italians came sheepishly forward. As they did a shot rang out, and they dived to the ground. But all they heard was laughter as a Kelly, a Coyle, a Docherty and a Quinn each brandished an unfamiliar pistol. It was Pat Kelly's that had gone off. The Italians carried Rico away like the dead hero in a tragedy, but it was no tragedy that night at Rafferty's.

'Drinks on the house,' yelled Sean. There was a mighty cheer from the company. Jock Lennox emerged from his hiding to rattle the piano keys and the real party began in earnest.

*

205

Noreen sat among the d'Agostino family in their apartment in Richmond. Her head swam in the waves of Tuscan Italian which swept over her coiffured, red head. It was after midnight and she had been in this room since the middle of the previous evening. Rico had brought her there for dinner with the family then had left her there, saying he had business to attend to. She had been left alone among all these Italians, who all seemed to be speaking at once and at the top of their voices. The old mother couldn't speak any English at all. Not that that worried her, for in her home, as far as she was concerned, she was still in Italy. Everything in that house was Italian, from the huge, imported dining table down to the smallest imported coffee spoon. The only thing American she would tolerate was the weather and that was only because she could do nothing about it. Mamma d'Agostino generally got her way for she was a large woman, and like many Italian woman gave the suggestion that inside was still the slim, dark, beautiful young girl she had been until her first children. Now the children swarmed about her as if she were the Queen Bee – which she was – in her Mediterranean hive. Her husband had died years before. He had been shot before her very eyes in their previous home in one of the regular 'family' killings and ever since that time Maria d'Agostino or Mamma as she was always known, had ruled the roost in his place. She dominated Rico, her oldest son and his four brothers and she terrified Noreen as she did most of the other women in the house whether they were daughters, wives, cousins or the cousins of cousins. It was into this last category that Carmella O'Neil came!

Noreen had nearly died when she saw her there among the women when she first arrived. Was Uncle Mick with her? There seemed to be no sign of him. Only Aunty Carmella, chattering away in Italian like a native – which she was of course. Noreen remembered that Carmella was connected with Roberto at the restaurant. Hadn't she herself got her job on that account? What was she doing here tonight? Had she known Noreen would be here? It was bad enough having to face the whole d'Agostino family, but in Carmella there was also the link to her own family as well and she dreaded how Carmella would react. Over the long dinner she hadn't dared to catch her eye, but afterwards when Rico and his brothers left the house, 'on business' as they said, and the older men went into another room – 'to talk', as one of the wives explained, Noreen had no alternative but to remain with Mamma and the other women, and ultimately, face to face with Carmella.

'Ciao, Carmella!'

'Hi,' was the clipped response. Noreen swallowed.

'I'd like to talk,' she whispered. Carmella's expression was impassive.

'Sure.' She led the way out of the room through the chattering women and Noreen was aware of Mamma d'Agostino's eye on her every step of the way. Carmella led her upstairs and into the bathroom.

'Locka door,' she said in a cold voice. Noreen did so then stood in the tiny tiled space staring at her aunt in the wall-sized mirror. She had never seen Carmella dressed up before. She had never seen Carmella out of the house before, except to go to the Deli or to church on Sunday. Now here she was, with her hair up and powder on her face and a pretty dress on her like a young girl. Suddenly, Noreen realised that Carmella Ruffiano O'Neil was in fact an attractive woman.

'You look nice, Aunty.' Carmella did not react at all.

'What you wanna talk about?' Impulsively, Noreen made a move to her. Carmella froze. 'Donna you touch me!' she hissed.

'Sorry Aunty.'

'Me no' your "Aunty".' She made the word sound even more incongruous and there was danger in the way it was said – quietly but venomously. The two women looked at each other in the large mirror. Appeal in one pair of eyes, hate in the other.

'How's Joey?' whispered Noreen eventually.

'He sent you message,' said Carmella, looking straight ahead.

'Oh?' responded Noreen, brightening immediately.

'Si,' said Carmella, turning to face her niece, 'Dis is from my Joey!' And she spat in her face! Noreen put her hands up instinctively. She could feel the warm spittle on her cheek. She felt sick and shut her eyes tight against the feeling but was aware of Carmella's going past her in a stream of vitriolic Italian and struggling with the lock of the door. When Noreen opened her eyes again she stopped with her hand on her face for behind her shoulder she could see the ample frame of Mamma d'Agostino filling the doorway. She was standing with her arms open wide. 'Vene Mamma, mia figlia,' Noreen said softly.

Coming into the South Taranaki Bight from the Tasman Sea, the Keiths had their first real view of New Zealand. The Mataura sailed into the Cook Strait to dock at the city of Wellington. They were glad to stretch their legs on the steep inclines around the port, but Mrs Keith still refused to disembark. Next day, the Mataura set out into the South Pacific Ocean and by nightfall was past Christchurch and the Banks Peninsula.

It was early morning on Monday, 27th August 1900, when they

docked at Port Chalmers. It was certainly no Sydney Harbour, but Jim Keith's first sight of it was not disappointing. Otago was beautiful. At first glimpse through the mist it had looked a bit like Scotland, only brighter, and lighter. The weather though was Scottish – wet and chilly. But this was it – landfall. The end of the journey. To his surprise he wasn't as eager to get off the ship as he thought he might have been. In a way, he was sad to leave. After all, the Mataura had been his home since May. Over three months, and what changes these months had brought. His father dead, his mother, to all intents and purposes, bed-ridden and Bobby missing, somewhere in Sydney. Tina, too, had had her troubles but these he could only guess at, and hope they were all past her now. He only knew she was no longer his little sister, but a grown woman and he was no longer the shy, bookish, wee brother but the tanned and vigorous new head of the family. He braced himself at the unexpected thought. Head of the family?

'Did you not have breakfast?' He turned. It was Tina. She looked smart in a hat and travelling suit, and he told her so.

'Thank you. So you were up early?'

'At first light. I couldn't sleep. Anyway, I wanted to see New Zealand. Tina peered out at the landscape which was getting nearer all the time.

'Is that it?'

'That's it.' There was a pause as she studied the view.

'It's not very much is it?'

'It'll have to do us, whatever it is. There's no going back now.'

'No.' The brother and sister stood for a moment in silence.

'Jim?'

'Ay?'

'Are you frightened?'

'No, I don't think so. Are you?'

'I don't think so. I'm excited though!'

'So am I!' And he gave her a brotherly hug. They each knew they were all they had in this new life in this new land.

'It's funny to think of Bobby not here to see it,' said Tina.

'Ay, and Father,' added Jim.

'Ay.'

'There's always Mother,' said Tina.

'There's always Mother!' said Jim.

'Good mornin'!'

And there was Mrs Keith, coming out of the companion way, supported by the grinning Sammy.

'Mother!' The young Keiths cried together.

'Ay, it's me.' They hurried to her. 'They tell me this is New

Zealand.' She turned to Sammy. 'Thank ye, son. I'll manage noo.'
Sammy glanced at Jim, who nodded.

'Alright Sammy, you can leave her to us.' Sammy grinned again
and left. Jim took his mother's arm, Tina took the other. 'You
should've waited Mother. We'd have come down for you.'

'I said I would come up at the end of the journey, so here I
am.'

'How do you feel?' asked Tina. Mrs Keith looked out to land.
'Fine,' she said.

'Good,' said Tina. She looked at her mother, who was also
dressed for landing in the same coat and hat she'd worn to
board the Mataura in Glasgow. 'You look fine.' Her mother
didn't answer. Tina looked at her brother.

'Have you had your breakfast, Mother?' asked Jim quickly.

'I had a cup o' tea.'

'We'll have a bit of a journey when we get off the ship,' said her
son. 'A train first and then goodness knows –'

'It was a good cup o' tea.'

Tina looked at her mother with amazement. Since the cabin
incident with Martin Dickenson, she hadn't been sure how to
deal with her mother, who had given no indication at all whether
she'd heard or seen or understood in any way what had gone on
between her daughter and the Second Officer. Till now at least, her
mother had given nothing away and Tina had said nothing. In both
their Scottish ways, the two women thought that if nothing was
said, then nothing had happened! Tina, however was not so sure.
The vague woman who was her mother was perhaps not so vague
after all.

Jim, on the other hand, was a little afraid of his mother. The
character she had shown in deliberately confining herself to her
cabin all these months was contradicted by the fact that she had
appeared unpredictably and with shocking effect at the unlikeliest
moments. He would never forget the sight of her at his father's
burial at sea; the phantom-like figure she presented, like a mad
witch. This wasn't the preoccupied domestic mother figure he
had known in Forres, nor was this the woman who stood with
them now, pale-faced and neatly dressed between her two bronzed
children. He realised that she was the kind of maternal despot who
ruled through her weaknesses, rather than through her strength.
Almost tacitly behind the strong image of their late father, was it
she who had really held the reins of power at Craigend House?
No, this was impossible, thought Jim. Father was the boss in every
sense. It was his idea they should come here so here they were,
without him, but with his wife, their mother.

'I never thought I should set foot in New Zealand at my time of life,' Mrs Keith was saying. 'It's hard to believe.'

'But that's just what you'll have, mother,' said Jim, a little over-heartedly, 'the time of your life.'

'Ay, we'll see,'said Mrs Keith. Jim looked at Tina, who shrugged. Just then, there was a blast on the ship's hooter which gave them all a fright. They laughed, but it was a little hysterical. The truth was the Keiths were nervous, but they daren't show it, least of all to each other.

'We'd better get to our places,' said Jim.

Passengers were now beginning to congregate on the decks at given positions according to their classes. First Class passengers were of course dealt with first, and seen off officially by Captain Ellon and Chief Engineer Aitken. A glass of sherry was available to those who required it, and after many handshakes and assurances of future esteem, passengers and crew parted never to see each other again. Even though the Keiths weren't strictly First Class they were treated as such, and given high preferential treatment in all the disembarkation preparations. There were papers to be seen to, forms to be filled in, declarations to be signed, luggage to be labelled and allocated. Jim was a very busy man. Tina sat with her mother during most of it in the First Class lounge and read a book while they waited for their names to be called. She was still struggling to get through *Nicholas Nickleby*. Eventually Jim came back for them. By this time Tina was in conversation with Mr Faber, the little, fat tenor, who was introducing his even smaller and fatter wife, who kept giggling all the time. He was going to teach music – 'singing and the piano, you know,' – in Dunedin, and his wife was to take boarders, 'aren't you, m'dear?' More giggles. Jim finally extricated his mother and sister, and in no time they were shaking hands with the Captain.

'I hope you were comfortable, Mrs Keith.'

'As much as could be expected, Captain.'

'Quite. And you, Miss Keith? I hope your voyage was pleasant?'

'It was eventful, Captain, thank you.'

'Of course. Goodbye, Mr Keith. May I say how sorry I was about Mr Keith. Your father, I mean.'

'Thank you, Captain. We appreciated your – er –' Jim glanced at his mother, 'understanding.' The Captain nodded and shook Jim's hand warmly.

'You have all our best wishes for your new life in New Zealand.'

'Thank you.'

The Chief Engineer was less smoothly eloquent than his Captain, but was nonetheless as sincere.

'I liked your company fine,' he said to Jim.

'And me, yours,' replied Jim grinning. 'I learned a lot.'

'From me?' asked the gruff engineer.

'Oh, ay,' said Jim. 'Remember? You told me that a man has two hands and he has to use them. One to hold his tongue and the other to hold his drink.'

'Did I say that?' replied Aitken.

'You did.'

'I must have been drunk.' Jim was genuinely sorry to say goodbye to the old Scot and was touched to see how warmly he held Tina's hand. It was he who helped them down to the lower gangway for all passengers ending their voyage at Port Chalmers.

There were quite a few and the Keiths were among the last. With the help of Applecross who had decided to become their best friend at the last moment, Jim had found a couple of carts in the dock area and an obliging pair of carters. Things were extremely casual in New Zealand by his first dealings with them. To his ear, they sounded reassuringly Scottish, but were very un-Scottish in their relaxed attitude to the job in hand. 'She'll be right,' was the sum of their reaction to most of his requests for help in conveying them from the side of the ship to the train in Dunedin. From there to Gore could be half a day's journey.

Meantime, what had been brought on the ship twelve thousand miles away in Glasgow must now be brought off and for a time that looked as if it might be a full day's work. But thanks to Mr Aitken, Applecross and a few reluctant sailors, it was accomplished in an hour and the two small cartloads lay ready and waiting. It was a trickier business taking Mrs Keith from the ship. Since the gangway was only wide enough to take one person at a time, it was thought wiser that Jim should go first, his mother next and Tina follow up behind. Mrs Keith started off rather gingerly, but threw off Tina's helping hand. She did not find any great security in the swaying ropes at either side and was just over half way down when she fell. The heel of her boot had caught in the ridged gangway and she tumbled inelegantly and untidily from the middle of the gangway onto the quayside, where Jim had been waiting, gaping in horror, helpless to do anything as his mother fell towards him. Tina had screamed, and all had watched. But nobody could do anything. People came running from all directions, and Applecross and Jim carried her back on to the ship. The little Cockney correctly diagnosed a broken leg. Jim groaned.

'What do we do now?' he said.

'Splint,' said Applecross. 'Nuffin' to it.' The Captain gave them a First Class cabin immediately and Tina and Jim settled themselves in again to wait while their mother was attended to. The extraordinary thing was that as she was carried on board again, she was laughing.

'Hysteria,' explained Applecross to Jim, but Jim wasn't so sure.

It was almost the end of the afternoon when she was pronounced fit enough to be carried off the ship. This was done in a very careful operation. Applecross must have given her something, because she seemed dopey and unconcerned as she was manhandled from the cabin, down the gangway, and on to the second cart where a space had been cleared for her to lie. With Captain Ellon's help, Jim had been able to arrange accommodation that evening at the Bluestone Chick's Hotel in Port Chalmers, where his mother could rest until she saw 'a proper doctor', as Applecross had suggested. They would then travel onwards once she had been cleared. So they laid her, apparently sleeping, in the back of the cart, and Tina got up beside her. Jim would sit up with the driver on the first cart.

'Are you alright?' he said to his sister.

'Yes. I think so.'

'Careful you don't fall off, and make sure mother doesn't.' He looked at her lying there. 'She said she didn't think she would set foot in New Zealand.'

The mother's eyes opened slightly. 'I didn't, did I.'

Jim grinned. 'No, mother.' And patting his sister's hand, he went round to his own place and the two loaded carts trundled along the quayside towards the straggle of little wooden houses and the Bluestone Chick's Hotel.

Tina sat facing towards the ship as the cart pulled her away from it. How momentous the voyage had been for her. She would never forget the Mataura. And with a little wave of her hand, she said farewell to her girlhood, to her Scottish past, to the memories of Martin Dickenson and, most of all, to her dear father. But best of all, perhaps, to her phantom pregnancy. She was still young and ready now to start all over again. She was glad to do so in a new, young country.

INTERLUDE ONE

The momentous divide that separated the nineteenth century from the twentieth went largely unnoticed in the actual calendar transition, being marked only by an influenza epidemic in London which killed fifty people a day and the outbreak of the Boer War in Africa which both the British and American Stock Exchanges thought was good for trade! No wonder William Keith had been appalled. He, for all his practical good sense and basic charity, had his pet hates and biases like any other man, and like him, would think his own story the centre of his world and the sole preoccupation of his time. But every man's story is only the microcosm of that macrocosm they call world events. On the other hand, some might hold the contrary to be true. After all, as Paddy O'Neil had deliberated as a youth, what does it gain a man if he wins the whole world and loses his own soul? A man of the world is not always a man in the world, but the world has a way of crowding in on him, no matter how he might try to ignore it. For instance . . .

In the time it took the Keiths to cross to the other side of the world, the cake-walk had become a dance craze, Asa Candler had introduced Coca-Cola to the world, sound pictures had been seen at the Great Paris Exhibition, the first Zeppelin airship had taken to the skies and it was estimated that 11,000 British soldiers had died in the Boer War. William Keith's objections had not been ill-founded. By the time the O'Neils had established their various tendril roots in the New World, the Deutschland had crossed the Atlantic in nearly half the time it took them in the Campania, the Paris Olympics had taken place, Oscar Wilde had died, Sigmund Freud had published his *Interpretation of Dreams* in Vienna and Max Planck had offered his Quantum Theory to the science of physics. In short, the world went on outwith the Keith family chronicles and beyond the saga of the miscellaneous O'Neils.

Queen Victoria died on 22nd January 1901 and this could be seen as the first crack in the hitherto impregnable façade of the ruling establishment, but Florence Keith continued to survive in her self-imposed invalidism. Although she could never hope to compete with the chronic lethargy of James Thomson of Clare, in Ireland who took to his bed in 1877 and only got up in 1907 when his eighty-year-old mother died! Jim and Tina found their farm near Gore, and with the help of their father's insurance money, their savings, some new New Zealand friends, and some very hard work had the prospect of a good place. Unlike Mrs Taylor, who went over the Niagara Falls in a barrel because she couldn't pay her mortgage! There was an eclipse of the sun in May of 1901 but it wasn't noticed in Ireland where a state of emergency was declared as the United Irish League sought closer ties with the United States, where President McKinley was shot and Theodore Roosevelt became President for the first time. All this made little difference to Paddy O'Neil as he prayerfully prospered at Baltimore, or to the brothers Sean and Michael who un-prayerfully but tunefully, prospered at Rafferty's Bar, paying Jackie Rafferty enough each week to make up for what he lost at the cards! Gottlieb Daimler built the first luxury motor car and called it 'Mercedes' after his client's young daughter. It was one of the first vehicles to feature the twin carburettor but this fact was lost on Liam Murphy in Down when his wife Nellie gave him twins, Celia and Dermot. Although he did buy one of the new Brownie box cameras from Eastman-Kodak to record the event. Marconi spanned the Atlantic with radio waves but they gave no news of Ella Friar's child by Bobby Keith, a daughter whom she called Rebecca, after nobody in particular. John Keith took the child in as his own and pondered whether or not to adopt it. Australia became the second Dominion in the British Empire after Canada. Bobby Keith found his Rachel in Sydney and a job with the Trade Union movement and he found he needed all his practised persuasive powers with her family and with his new Irish-Australian union colleagues.

In 1902, the United States bought the site of the Panama Canal. Edward VII was crowned King in London and barmaids were declared legal in Glasgow, but Noreen O'Neil had still not won back her good name with her own family even though she was the darling of the d'Agostinos and the adored paramour of the thriving Rico. It was mere co-incidence that a popular song of the time was 'I'm only a bird in a gilded cage'. Noreen pleased Rico, especially when she was pregnant with their first child but this did not please Mamma. They were not married. And when it was a girl, it still pleased Rico. Noreen called her Maria after Mamma. Joey O'Neil still pined for her and began to be troublesome to his parents, but Denis and Hana bloomed in matrimony despite her mother and brother and uncles and aunts. Old Denis was on his last shaky legs in Rosstrevor and young Kevin was just finding his place in covert politics despite the close attention of Sergeant Davidson. Nessie O'Neil would have liked to see her youngest at home more often. She was happy to let Old Den do his worst. It wouldn't last much longer.

The year 1903 saw Paddy O'Neil as a deacon and senior seminarian as well as the death of Pope Leo XIII and the election of Pius X. Henry Ford opened a factory for the mass assembly of motor car parts and the 'Tin Lizzie' was brought suddenly within the the reach of millions. You could have it in any colour you wanted – as long as it was black! 'Kit Carson' was the first Wild West moving picture and 'The Wizard of Oz' opened on Broadway. Madame Curie received the Nobel prize for discovering radium and in the last month of the year the Wright brothers flew the first aeroplane. The world was changing fast, and not only for the Keiths and the O'Neils.

In 1901 Enrico Caruso made his first recording and Enrico d'Agostino bought it for his infant Maria – she would be an opera singer, he insisted. Roller skates became all the rage and there was a postcard mania. The Olympic Games were held in St Louis and tube-trains started to run in London. Messrs Rolls and Royce joined forces to make a new type of car and James Jeffries was the heavyweight boxing champion of the world. Hana O'Neil had a miscarriage and lost her first child. Sergeant Peters was knocked down by a car in the street and Denis was made Sergeant in his place.

By 1905 – the first motor show at Olympia in London – Russian sailors mutinied on the battleship Potemkin and the first meeting of the International Workers of the World was held in Paris. It took a long time for its effects to reach Bobby Keith in Sydney, who was having troubles of his own in his courtship of Rachel. International Zionism was her problem. Albert Einstein published his *Theory of Relativity* from Boston and nobody understood it. Jim Keith, on his New Zealand farm was fascinated and Jitka O'Neil was born to Hana and Denis in New York. Denis would like to have called her Christina.

San Francisco was torn apart by an earthquake in 1906, Vesuvius erupted, and suffragettes died for the women's vote in London while the first typewriters appeared and gas fires were advertised for sale. The age of Gibson Girls had begun. Ibsen died.

In 1907 the Irish Bill for Home Rule was lost in the House of Commons, Florenz Ziegfeld produced his Follies on Broadway, the Mauretania won the Atlantic Blue Riband, Pablo Picasso shocked the art world with his cubist nudes and suddenly everybody was smoking cigarettes. New Zealand became a Dominion of the British Empire.

And so, in the first seven years of the new century, the status quo of peace and prosperity was generally maintained although under the surface, like the rumblings of an earthquake the artists and thinkers all over the world were raging against the old order. However, the smug money men, the secure property men and the over-privileged aristocracy, though they never dreamed the day would ever come, were soon to get a terrible fright.

But not yet. Kings and Queens would be shot in cupboards, Archdukes have bombs thrown in their laps, thousands in the slums of great cities would share mattresses with rats, but for most people the halcyon days endured, the sun continued to shine on the British Empire and the established world, as it had been known since the days of Napoleon, went on its blissful, peaceful way towards Armageddon. Inevitably, irrevocably, year followed year, season followed season, day followed night and night followed day and time, from moment to moment, went mercilessly, or mercifully, by.

Our story continues . . .

SIXTEEN

'Introibo ad altare Dei.' Paddy's voice was firm and resonant as he uttered the opening phrases of the Mass. It was his first celebration as a curate.

'Ad Deum que laetificat juventutem meam.' Denis's voice was less certain. It had been a few years since he had served Mass last as an altar-boy in Rosstrevor, and even the new authority of his police sergeant's stripes did little to compensate for his nervousness at being on the altar again.

'Confeteor Deo omnipotenti . . .' As the brand-new Father Patrick Joseph O'Neil bowed to make his confession, Denis looked at him with pride. His little, chesty brother had made it. A priest in the family. That was something surely. His pride was shared by the rest of the family who were there in the front pews behind them – Hana, with little Jitka in her arms, Uncle Mick, who looked so much older all of a sudden, Carmella, who was much the same, but Joey had lost a lot of his old sunny quality and slumped sullenly in his place. Sean and Michael were there too, but they stood at the back looking usher-smart in new suits, and keeping a professional eye on the collecting plate. Father Donnelly was also there, looking plumper these days, but still the same cheerful personality he had been in Brooklyn. He too, was proud and as he looked round the crowded pews of St Christopher's in Englefield, New Jersey, he thought of what a good turn-out it was considering that so many of them had come up from New York.

Unknown to the priest, but easily recognisable as such, were even some of the regulars from Rafferty's Bar – the Quinns, Kellys, Coyles and Dochertys, but no sign of Jackie himself. He hadn't been too well lately they said. The old man asleep in the middle of them all was Emmet Ryan. Two of the boys had to carry him in. Jock Lennox found the harmonium in the choir balcony right away and he had caused something of a furore even before the Mass had started that Sunday morning. Jock decided to play as the congregation assembled and before the proper organist arrived, but his hesitant, hymnal efforts had a spare, Protestant

217

ring about them and when, in despair, he broke into a decidedly rag-time syncopation with 'Wait Till the Sun Shines, Nelly' the proper organist, who was a very proper spinster-woman, rose and hurriedly pushed him off the stool before he had got through the chorus. There was a definite sigh of disappointment from the congregation below, some of whom had begun to join in, but then an apathetic silence resumed under the usual, dirge-like strains of 'Soul of My Saviour'.

Father Paddy moved up from the altar-steps to kiss the altar-stone, then turned to the congregation. 'Kyrie eleison,' he said.

'Christe eleison,' responded Denis. Paddy turned and continued: 'Gloria in excelsis Deo, et in terra pax hominibus . . .'

As the prayer went on he showed he had already mastered the priestly mumble. Denis glanced round again. Everybody was there in the front pew. Everybody except – little Jitka gave her daddy a wave. Denis found it hard not to wave back! He turned to the altar again and gazed up at Paddy's back and tried to concentrate. At the rear of the church, Sean glanced out at the porch and then at Michael on the other side of the main door who shrugged and gave an extra-loud 'Amen' which made Sean jump. Where was she? Surely she would have got his message? He trusted Roberto. She must come. If only for Paddy's sake. He was brought back abruptly from his anxiety by Paddy's voice from the altar as he quickly turned to face out again.

'Dominus vobiscum.'

'Et cum spiritu tuo,' answered Denis. Isn't our Denis doing well? Sean watched admiringly as Paddy went to the side to read the Gospel from the Mass Missal, making the sign of the cross on the book, his forehead, lips and heart, saying, 'Gloria tibi, Domine.' Denis did likewise, saying, 'Laus tibi, Christe.'

So did Sean and Michael and the family and most of the congregation, except old Emmet, who was still asleep and Jock, who sat in the choir balcony with his arms folded, looking down on the Latin mumbo-jumbo with Presbyterian disapproval. He was only here himself because he liked Paddy and he was glad the lad had got through all his studies and everything. Like all Scots, Jock had a very high regard for education.

The Gospel being read, it was time for the sermon. Normally a solemn and serious part of the Catholic liturgy of the Mass, on this occasion its solemnity and seriousness were somewhat dented by the sudden arrival of a very pretty little girl of about four or five, who ran down the centre aisle towards the priest, her pig-tails flying, calling, 'Zio Padee! Zio Paddee!' Uncle Mick stood up; so did Denis on the altar. Up in the balcony Jock Lennox applauded, and some of Rafferty's regulars laughed as Paddy gathered the little child up in his arms as easily as his heavy vestments would allow him. All eyes then turned on the mother of the child, who had followed her and at once, everything was silent again. Noreen was by now a very attractive young woman and richly dressed in the height of fashion, but even the light veil covering her face couldn't hide her obvious embarrassment.

She stood at the altar-steps, uncertain what to do as she watched her daughter try to put her arms round her priestly uncle, prattling all the while in infant Italian. Denis came forward to his sister, looking stern and said firmly, 'Sit yourself down, Noreen.'

'We were late,' she whispered urgently, 'I couldn't –'

Sean and Michael came up alongside her. Michael went to take Maria from Paddy and Sean took his sister by the arm. 'It's alright now. Just sit down here.' His voice was soft and tender for he saw the terror in her eyes. With a reassuring touch, he guided her gently towards a seat at the end of the front pew, motioning for everybody to squeeze up and make room. There was an audible gasp as Noreen was seen by everyone else in the church. Uncle Mick sat down quickly, glancing at his wife. Carmella stared stonily ahead. Joey was quick to see his cousin, but slow to react. When he did, he made a gurgling kind of noise then rose to his full height in the pew and bellowed like a bull-calf, 'NOREEN!'

Uncle Mick reached across his wife and gave him a heavy slap on the knee. It echoed through the pews.

'Hey, that was sore!' Denis glanced round from the altar. Carmella bowed her head. Sean quietly gave Noreen's knee a little squeeze. She clasped both gloved hands together. Sean glanced quickly at her.

'OK?' he whispered.

'OK!' she replied in a hushed voice. He patted her knee lightly.

'Sure you are,' he said. Father Paddy was in the pulpit.

'My dear brethren in Jesus Christ.' He spoke quietly but such was the tension in the church, his every word could be heard quite distinctly. There was only the hint of a similar tension in his husky tones as he laid his hands on the ledge of the pulpit. 'I had intended to speak to you this morning on the Holy Father's encyclical "Lamentabili". Some of you might have heard about it in the press. That is, those of you who read the Catholic papers. That is, those of you that can read at all!' There was a chuckle at this from people in the congregation. 'In this decree Pope Pius was taking a good swipe at those who would bring the church up to date, the modernists as they call themselves. These are people who are so obsessed with the first decade of this new century that they're inclined to forget for a moment the nineteen hundred or so years that went before it. There are many, priests too, who would wipe out in a day all the familiar things about Mother Church that endear her to us all, even the precepts and practices that are the reason she has survived for all these nineteen hundred years. Traditional values are being threatened by this rush to modernise and go "twentieth century" as they say today, and if we are not careful we'll throw out the baby with the bathwater! Not that I ever knew much about bathwater. I never even saw a bath till I got to America! Back home in Ireland – I come from Ulster, as if you didn't know – I didn't know anyone who had a bath!' He paused effectively.

'No wonder they call us the black Irish!' There was a laugh at this. Father Donnelly pursed his lips. 'Don't go too far now, Patrick,' he thought to himself. Paddy went on, folding his hands comfortably under his cope.

'Of course, everything benefits from having a fresh look at it now and again. You can't get to be nearly two thousand years old and not have few cobwebs on you. But it's a duster you take to it, not one of the latest hydraulic drills, and even as you dust, you must do it lovingly. That way you see what it was you liked in the first place, and you see it fresh and clean again – like new. But if we rush, bang and crash our way to change we'll lose everything – and we might never get it back. Just imagine now, my dear brethren, if the modernists had their way we'd be having a banjo up there for an organ – sorry Miss Baker! We'd have white tie and tails to say Mass instead of vestments and you'd all be answering "OK" instead of "Amen"! It's not as bad as that I know but you get my meaning. OK?' The congregation responded as if with one voice – 'OK!' And for the first time in the twenty-year history of St Christopher's, a priest laughed in the pulpit.

'Serves me right,' he said, 'I was getting carried away with meself. Here was I, not going to talk about the Pope's "Lamentabili" and haven't I spent ten minutes on it already. I think, since this is, after all, my first sermon as curate here – in fact, it's my first sermon ever – I'd better stop or the Bishop will be posting me back to Rosstrevor. And you know what that means.' There was another pause. 'I'd never get another bath.' Father Paddy waited while they enjoyed his banter. He enjoyed it too. He was obviously so happy and content in himself and his vocation that he had no real worry about being himself – even in the pulpit. It was not that he was obviously going to be a good priest. He was a good priest already. He was now serious again.

'Finally, my dear friends and brethren in Christ, I must explain. The little girl you saw a moment ago was my niece. Her name is Maria O'Neil – and as many of you will know, that's her mother there below, my little sister Noreen.' He smiled down at her. You could almost hear some of the women in the audience working it out in their heads – if the name's O'Neil like the good young Father – and that's her Mother – and she's his sister – then she's not married! Paddy was well aware of this and with an imperceptible shake of his head, continued sardonically –

'Let those that are without sin cast the first stone.' Carmella's head shot up. Her expression was angry. Paddy went on imperturbably, 'Jesus said – "Suffer the little ones to come unto me." Our Lord made that remark to some well-intentioned apostles – some of the apostles were thick you know, quite thick. But then, faith and goodness have never been a matter of intellect. Otherwise how many of us would be here? Anyway, they were trying to keep the children from bothering the Lord. But children didn't bother him. They don't bother anyone, except perhaps their parents at times. But that's because they have them twenty-four hours a day. For the most part everybody likes a child, and nearly every child likes everybody –' At this point, Joey's voice was heard to croon quietly.

'Noreen I can see you.' Paddy bowed his head and let it register, then lifting up his head, he said,

'For I say to you, unless you become as one of these you shall never enter the kingdom of Heaven. Innocence, real innocence isn't "not knowing" – that's ignorance. "Suffer little children" and God bless them, there are some do suffer, and their parents suffer because they love them, and all their family and friends who love them –'

Paddy looked down for a moment at Joey, who beamed up at him, 'We gonna play checkers, Paddy?' he called out suddenly and laughed. Carmella slapped his knee again. Uncle Mick put his hand over his face, but Paddy was quite unperturbed.

'Sure, Joey,' he said. There was a slight pause before he continued. 'Innocence is goodness in faith. It's trust in hope. And it's the action of charity. Faith, hope and charity. It's all we need. And it's available to all; there to be used in every second of our daily lives. The faith to believe in ourselves and our fellow human beings. The hope for the future life and charity towards all and everything. For there is none here who does not depend on someone. And there is no one here who doesn't need a God of some kind. We are all family. All of one blood. His blood, who died for us on a cross. Our Father Who Art in Heaven. Making us all brothers and sisters and children again with God. Children of the soul. OK?' This time there was no response from the congregation. Instead there was a silence.

'In the Name of the Father and of the Son and of the Holy Ghost. Amen.' He said this quite casually, then stepped down from the pulpit and made his way to the centre of the altar once more. When he turned to face the congregation, his voice was strong. 'Credo in unum Deum, Patrem omnipotentem . . .'

The church was a different place now. It was no longer a social occasion, or a family occasion – it was a holy occasion. Noreen's face was alight with loving pride in her brother. Then she was aware of someone staring at her and looking out of the corner of her eyes she saw it was Carmella. She turned to her. Carmella was crying. Noreen wanted to go to her but Hana and her child were between. Suddenly the child reached out to Carmella. She took the baby and hugged her. Hana turned to Noreen and smiled. Noreen turned away. Where was Maria? She couldn't turn round so she fixed her eyes on her two brothers on the altar. The priest was offering his fingers to the policeman who poured some water over them. 'Lavabo inter innocentes manus meus . . .' She remembered Paddy having to wash Denis after football.

'Orate fratres . . .'

'Pray brothers!' Sean knew what it meant alright and was remembering all the prayers at home. The rosary last thing at night. It's something he'd never try at Rafferty's anyway! Wouldn't that make Michael laugh? Michael himself was now in the choir balcony beside Jock Lennox letting Maria look down on all the heads below them. Suddenly her hand was pointing as she called, 'Mamma! Mamma!'

'That's right,' said Michael, 'That's my kid sister.'

'No, no,' insisted the child, turning a serious face up to him, 'Mamma!'

'That's right,' said Michael agreeably, lifting her on to his knee. The O'Neil double-act started up again at the other end of the church, Denis responding to Paddy. 'Listen now, there's a good little girl,' said Michael. Maria turned to face the front as Paddy intoned, 'Dominus vobiscum.'

'Et cum spiritu tuo.'

'Sursum corda.'

'Habemus ad Dominum'

'Gratias agimus Domino Deo nostro.'

'Dignum et justum est.'

'Vere dignum et justum est . . .' And off Paddy went once more into his professional mumble. Michael could easily have followed every word of it in his Mass Missal, but he didn't have one.

Anyway, he just liked the sound of it, and hadn't he heard it for most of his life – until now. A bell sounded.

'Campana!' shouted Maria.

'That's right,' said Michael, 'A bell it is.' It sounded again. And again.

'Sanctus, sanctus, sanctus,' said Father Paddy.

Uncle Mick found it difficult getting down to kneel for the Consecration. He was getting old, he thought, and him not even seventy. Three score and ten, that's the score, is it not? Retirement wasn't as good an idea as he thought it was going to be. For one thing he was down to half-pay and even more important, there were no little extras coming every week in brown envelopes. And Rafferty's Bar wasn't the same with the boys running it now. Old Jackie was more easy-going. They were a couple of sharp boys, his nephews, especially Sean. Good luck to them. They'll need all their sharpness. It's a hard world these days. Not like the old days at all. Ah, the old days, when he first came over – his reverie was cut short by the boom of the gong announcing the elevation of the host.

'Hoc est enim Corpus meum.' He heard Paddy's whisper from where he was kneeling in the front row and it had quite a chilling effect. Not so long ago Paddy was lying ill in the attic bedroom, now here he was changing bread into the body of Christ and wine into His blood.

'Christ!' thought ex-Superintendent Mick, awed in spite of himself.

'That's nice,' thought Joey as he watched his Uncle Paddy lift the host high above his head. It was like a game – like basket-ball. Now Paddy had a silver chalice in his hands. 'Hic est enim Calix Sanguinis mei . . .' And he held this above his head too, and knelt down before it.

Ain't he gonna drink it? thought Joey. I sure would.

'Oremus –'

Why is old Paddy talking all this funny stuff? thought Joey.

'Pater noster, qui es in caeli –'

There he goes again! – 'Ouch! Hey!' Joey exclaimed loudly. His mother had dug him hard in the ribs.

'You sit uppa straight. Attentione, eh?' Carmella glared at her son and he sat up straight. She was tired, she thought. This hasn't been good coming here – no, no good. Not with her here. And she stiffened at the thought of Noreen. Bringing a bad name on two families. A child got no father. Well, not real, properly married father, like all people got. He's my cousin – well, second cousin. And she's my niece by marriage. What does that make little Maria? A little bastard! Why don't Rico marry her instead of keep her in fancy apartment all these years? She say she going to be entertainer. Is that what they call it?

'Agnus Dei qui tollis peccata mundi: miserare nobis . . .' It was getting near time for communion.

'I hope she don't go!' thought Carmella. Little Jitka started playing around her feet. 'Cute baby. Least she's gotta father! Funny little mother though.' As she was thinking this, Carmella caught Hana's eye. Both women smiled.

'What a sad woman,' thought Hana. 'Shame too about her boy. He's so good-looking too, you'd never think –'

'Confiteor Deo Omnipotenti . . .' Father Paddy had now begun to say the Confiteor in preparation for Communion. Hana looked at her husband with pride but wished he had cleaned his boots better. She could see the soles as he knelt down. 'Sole' of my Saviour, she thought and started to giggle, but then she had to take up Jitka who had fallen by the kneeling board and was crying. People had begun to file out from the pews. Hana, with Jitka in her arms, was among the first, squeezing past Noreen and then Sean. This left a gap between Noreen and Carmella. Noreen looked to her but Carmella rose at once and followed out after Mick and Joey at the opposite side. Sean nudged his sister.

'Are you goin'?' Noreen bent her head.

'I can't,' she said.

'Course, you can. There's Michael goin'. If he can go, then anybody can. Come on.'

Paddy turned with the host held above the chalice in his hand, to see most of his family gathered along the altar-rail. For the first time, his voice faltered. 'Dom . . . Domine, non sum dignus . . .' He advanced to his Uncle Mick with the wafer of communion bread in his hand. The older man looked up, his eyes moist. Paddy offered it to him, with the slightest of smiles while Denis held the paten below his uncle's chin. 'Corpus Domini Nostri Jesu Christi . . .' Uncle Mick bowed his head. Joey grinned. Carmella was still red-eyed, and seemed glad to return to her seat again. Little Jitka tried to grab it from Paddy's hand. Denis smiled at Hana. Michael was blushing as he received Communion and left quickly. When he came to Noreen, Paddy stopped, and brother and sister stared at each other. She had lifted back the veil and looked stunningly beautiful. The brothers could almost hear her heart beating. Denis hesitated and looked from one to the other, then he put the paten under Noreen's chin. She closed her eyes as if awaiting a kiss. Her lips parted. Paddy still did not move. Everything seemed to stand still.

'Come on, Paddy,' whispered Sean in a hiss. Paddy immediately resumed his communion ritual. 'Corpus Domini Nostri Jesu Christi . . .' And proffered it to Noreen. For a moment her eyes opened and then she hurriedly bent her head. Denis withdrew the paten and was ready to move to Sean when a wild yell rang out. It was Carmella and she was screaming vituperatively in Italian. 'Basta! Basta! Communione per una puttana! Perche il sacramento per una peccatrice comme le? Eh, sacerdote? Dire!'

Sean was so astonished that he almost swallowed the paten as well as the host and Paddy, his face bright red as his hair, hurriedly passed on to the next communicant. Noreen still stood with bowed head. Her veil now covered her face, but her mortification was evident to all beside her and around her at the altar-rail. There were cries of shock and protest at Carmella's outburst but Sean grabbed his young sister's arm and, roughly pushing people aside, he dragged her up the centre aisle. Denis was trying to comfort Carmella as she was sobbing in the pew. Uncle Mick sat forward with his head in his hands. Joey seemed bewildered as he put one large hand on his mother's shoulder. 'Wassa matter, Mamma?' he asked plaintively.

Michael came hurrying towards Sean at the top of the aisle and took Noreen's other arm. Jock Lennox, standing at the back, had Maria in his arms. The little girl was frightened when she saw her mother being hustled up the aisle towards her. 'Mamma! Que causa?' she wailed. Noreen quickly took her from Jock and with her brothers beside her ran through the porch of the church into the daylight. At the altar, Father Paddy had solemnly completed the giving out of communion, and after much prayer and ceremony in the cleaning of the chalice and paten at the altar, the ordinary service of the Mass was resumed with the prayers after Communion and the Conclusion. Throughout it all, there was an undisguised murmur of conversation in the church and Denis felt slightly sick. Paddy, on the other hand was now quite composed and when he turned again to the congregation, his voice was calm although his face was deathly pale. 'Dominus vobiscum,' he said.

'Et cum spiritu tuo,' replied Denis with a dry voice.

'Ite, Missa est.'

'Deo gratias.' And he had never said it more thankfully. Paddy then turned to kiss the altar and when he turned back his hand was raised to give his first priestly blessing. This should have been a happy and holy occasion but the expressions on the faces looking up at him – Denis, Hana, Uncle Mick, Carmella, now pale and shaken, even poor Joey – told him more than any words how empty the action was.

'Benedicat vos omnipotens Deus, Pater et Filius et Spiritus

Sanctus.' But no one responded with 'Amen'. The celebratory breakfast was cancelled. 'We have to get back,' explained Denis lamely, with little Jitka in his arms. Uncle Mick had left at once with Carmella. They'd been seen boarding the street-car with Joey still asking – 'Where's Noreen?' Little knots of people still talked earnestly in the street outside the church for a long time afterwards. Such excitement hadn't been known in Englefield since the Lowrie's house had burned down. For a first Mass it had certainly been a tough baptism. Poor Father O'Neil. Somebody woke up Emmet Ryan and Jock Lennox shepherded the Rafferty 'regulars' in the direction of the nearest drink. In the sacristy, long after a sombre Father Donnelly had left him, Father Paddy O'Neil, still in his new vestments, sat in a chair by the window as the afternoon shadows lengthened. And Paddy wept.

'Friends!' Bobby Keith spread his arms wide as he shouted the word from the improvised stage set up outside the gates of Mason's Proprietry. Mason's was one of the largest machine-works in North Sydney and it had a large labour force. For the most part they were unskilled, underpaid and underfed and most of them were here during the thirty-minute refreshment break in the middle of the day because there was a good chance they could stretch that break into an hour at least. And they did. 'Brothers!' cried Bobby, but that only seemed to make matters worse. The babble of cat-calls and obscenities continued. He tried again – 'Comrades!' Worse still. Bobby sighed and turned to the chairman but he was in earnest conversation with a ponderous constable. I'll have to hurry, thought Bobby. His voice was sore. He had been shouting in the open air for more than ten minutes and to no great avail. The chairman, an unsympathetic Englishman, then mounted the rough platform which had been quickly tacked together that morning. He tried to help matters by calling through his cardboard megaphone for – 'the best of order there for the speaker'. Unfortunately, he followed this up with some unkind comments about – 'A lot of bleeding convicts!' – which was heard by enough of the men at the front to turn the yard into a snarling cockpit again. Bobby had to make his own presence felt. He was getting nowhere making an appeal to their sense of order so he had to do something. He suddenly had an idea, and taking the megaphone from the chairman, and wincing at the soggy mouthpiece, he summoned the last of his voice from his diaphragm and sang to the sea of caps and hats, a Harry Lauder music hall song:

'I love a lassie, a bonnie Hielan' lassie,
She's as sweet as the heather in the dell,
She's as sweet as the heather, the bonnie bloomin' heather,
Mary, my Scots bluebell!'

Nothing could have quicker distanced him from the Pommie chairman or won him their attention so soon. He was allowed to finish his song in comparative silence and when he did, they gave him a cheer. This time when he raised his hands they were quiet at once, no doubt expecting another ditty, but instead, Bobby took his chance. 'Do you realise,' he proclaimed, 'that the British Empire extends to one-fifth of the land mass in the world. It had a recorded population only last year of four hundred million and is fully recognised as the richest crown on earth – and yet – and yet, friends – Britain allows ten million working men to live in chronic destitution and lets match-girls sweat their labour in factories. A quarter of a million people live on work-house charity in England and child-beggars run free in the streets of London.' Bobby had long ago learned the working man's love of facts as opposed to theories and he always made sure to have a few up his sleeve before he spoke at a union meeting. He was new to the Trades Union Movement but the union movement was relatively new to Australia. There was still an ingrained suspicion of what used to be called 'combinations'. The working man was learning slowly how to organise himself, but Bobby Keith was learning fast.

'Why do I tell you this?' he was saying confidently. 'Why do I tell you all this, when you yourselves know what poverty is and what starvation is and what a lack of cash is about?' There were growls of approval here and there. He had them now. But he must tread carefully. Another constable now joined the first and the chairman was getting fidgety.

'I'll tell you why. I'll tell you why, my friends. Because we are the children of that Empire. We are all part of King Eddie's growing family. For six years now, we have been a dominion in a commonwealth of dominated countries –' Two more policemen appeared. Bobby noticed but pressed on. '– just as our neighbours in New Zealand –' There was a cheer from some in the crowd at the mention of the sister colony. 'Yes, New Zealand is now a dominion too, and has been since September. But friends, comrades – consider – if Britain treats its own like dirt, how will it treat its faraway cousins down under the Antipodes?'

'Give us a song,' yelled somebody.

'Yeah, what about "Lily of Laguna"?' shouted someone else.

'I'll sing you a song, mates,' yelled back Bobby hoarsely, 'I'll sing it from the roof-tops when we see an end not only of this strike but of every useless, time-wasting, pointless strike we've ever seen in this country in the last half-dozen years. I'm a union man. I'm your man, as you all know, but I have to tell you, my friends, that the bosses can't lose in the present situation. And why can't they lose? Well, I'll tell you lads, because they've got the power where they need it – at the top. They've got the vote you see. So have we. But do we use it? No, we do not. But if every man here used his vote as he should and put a Labour government not only in the State of New South Wales but throughout the dominion, not only throughout the dominion but the Commonwealth, not only in the Commonwealth but throughout the world –' Bobby was enjoying himself now and so were most of his audience, standing under the afternoon sun. '– then the working man will have his true voice and he will make it heard in the corridors of power, for we will be the new power then – and we will use it for the greater good of all. For we are the real power – we are people power and we must win in the end for we are indestructible –'

Unfortunately, at that precise second, the makeshift platform gave way and Bobby disappeared at the very height of his rhetoric with the chairman, the union secretary, the workers' deputy and the four constables who by now had infiltrated the platform party. It had never been intended that the flimsy structure should support such a weighty assembly, so with a creaking and a cracking and much shouting and swearing down it went in a flurry of legs and arms and broken planks and red Australian dust.

'Are you feeling better?'
   'I think so.'
   'Aren't you sure?'
   'No.'
   'Oh.'
Bobby was lying in bed in his room at the Gebler's house in the Bronte district of Sydney. He was their paying guest and had been since that afternoon seven years ago when he had tracked Rachel Gebler down to her home in this seaside suburb close to the famous swimming beaches. Not that Bobby had much time for sea-bathing. His work as a paid negotiator caused him to travel through most of New South Wales arbitrating in disputes, taking part in conciliations and talking, talking, talking as industries grew up in the prospering state and workers flooded in from Britain, mostly from Ireland, to claim their share of what were meagre wages. Fifty years before, gold had been discovered at Bathurst and wages had been spectacular, but those boom times were well

over and the rush now was for any job at all and to fight to keep it. It was a boss's world and everybody knew it. That's why the workers' weekly pennies went to pay men like Bobby to speak for them and that's just what Bobby Keith could do best. He didn't always win, and occasionally he came a cropper – just as he'd done at Masons' gates a few days before. Now he was in bed with severe bruising, a sore throat and a dislocated left knee and being tended by Rachel.

'Sure you're comfortable?' she asked.

'No,' he grumbled.

'What's wrong?'

'There's a draught from the door.'

'What can I do about it?'

'You could shut it.' Rachel rose from the bed and took up the tray from the bed-side table.

'You know father says that the door must always be open.'

'But he's not even here.'

'But mother is. It's alright, I'm just going.' She went out, flashing him a smile – and closing the door behind her. She immediately opened it again from the other side. 'That better?' she asked brightly, and was gone again.

Bobby groaned – and not only from the discomfort of his bumps and bruises, but from seven years of continuing dilemma. He had first come to this house in a blaze of romantic ardour and passion. He had expected to sweep Rachel off her feet and carry her off to New Zealand with him on the next sailing, but he had reckoned without her Jewish father and mother, the new Zionism and Rachel herself. She said she loved him, they said they loved him, but somehow nobody would fix a date for a marriage. If it were ever mentioned at all, something else would turn up. Either he had to go up to the Broken Hill Ironworks at Newcastle or she had to go down to Canberra to see some official about tariffs or quotas or immigration levels. Rachel was a journalist, and a good one. Bobby was a Socialist, and a good one. They each believed that what they were doing was vital for the betterment of the world as each saw it and neither would give way to the other, or defer in any way to the other's claimed priority in attention, preference or responsibility. As a result, the weeks passed, and the months and before they knew it, it was years.

Bobby must have drifted into sleep for he was wakened by a knock at the door. When he opened his eyes, Mr Enoch Gebler was standing blinking over his half-glasses and smiling.

'Guten afternoon, mein Robert. You are better, ja?'

'Ja, Papa. Not so bad,' answered Bobby sleepily. Mr Gebler came forward smiling with two large books under his arm. He sat on the chair by the side of the bed.

'This day have I been in the library and it has been very interesting. Very interesting. Ja. I have been reading of Mordechai Noah.'

'Oh?'

'Ja. You know, that in 1825 he bought an island on the Niagara River in America and offered it to all the Jews in the world to make a Jewish state called Ararat. Interesting, ja?'

'Ja.'

'I am thinking that if all the Jews in the world come to the island it would into the water sink, ja?' He cackled with silent mirth.

'It's the same with Scotland. If all the Scots went back to Scotland – it would serve them right.' Mr Gebler was puzzled.

'Bitte?'

'Nothing.' The old man frowned.

'Nothing is nothing, Robert.'

'Sorry Papa. You were saying?'

'Ja. You will have heard of Eretz Israel?'

'Was he a rabbi?' Gebler laughed again.

'Nein, nein, it is the idea of the homeland, the land of Israel, you know? That we Jews have our own country instead of being small part only of many countries. In Konigsberg, in Prussia, my homeland, OK? There was much talk when I was boy of Haskala – which is civic freedom, ja? And we sang Hatikwa and Mishmar Hajarden – which means watch on the Jordan – and so we begin to think of Zion – and a home in the land of Palestine. And my books here – see – this one tells of the Hovevei Zion, and how from the Russian pogroms they come to settle in Palestine with money they get from Baron de Rothschild.'

'Capitalist.' Bobby almost spat the word out.

'So? He is good Jewish boy, ja?'

'Nein,' mumbled Bobby while Enoch lifted his second book.

'Here is Theodor Herzl. He is dead you know. Ja, only forty-four years. Nicht gut. Forty-four is not old.' He looked keenly at Bobby over his spectacles. 'You are not forty-four?'

'No, I am not. I'll be thirty-four on my next birthday.'

'Ja? And you are not married.' Bobby closed his eyes.

'No, I am not.' Fine you know I'm not, you old goat, thought Bobby. He wondered if Gebler was playing a game with him.

'You need to make child soon, ja?'

'Ja.' So I would, thought Bobby, if you would just let me close the door now and then, but he only said, 'I've heard of Hertzl.'

'Ja. He makes "Die Welt" and in it he tells of Zangwill who goes

230

to make settlement in Uganda, but mostly he tells of your English government.'

'It's not my government,' muttered Bobby. Enoch never heard him.

'And how they give much land in Palestine but some Jews are not happy with this.'

'Like Rachel?'

'Nein, nein. Rachel is one of Poale Zion.'

'What's that?'

'The workers for Zion. So she go to Palestine to meet with them, and she then meet you with boat in Aden when she is coming home again, you remember, ja?'

'I remember.'

'And this year she is in Switzerland at Congress.' Bobby sighed.

'I remember.' That's just what I'd like with her right now – 'congress' thought Bobby wistfully, and adjusted his bandaged limbs more comfortably under the bedclothes. Where was she anyway?

'Where is she, Rachel?' Bobby laughed.

'Why you laugh?'

'It's just what I was thinking,' said Bobby. Mr Gebler rose.

'I go and find her.' He walked briskly to the door then halted. 'I close the door for you. The draughts, ja?' And he went. Bobby smiled and shook his head.

'Just as you say, Papa.' And he closed his eyes again . . .

'Bobby!'

It was only a whisper but Bobby heard it clearly and his eyes opened at once. The gaslight had been turned down low but he could make out Rachel standing at the foot of his bed in her dressing-gown. She put her finger to her lips and he watched in astonishment as she opened her dressing to reveal that she had nothing on. The gown slipped soundlessly from her shoulders and she tiptoed like a shadow towards him. He tried to ease his body to one side to let her come in but he was surprised once again as she got hold of his hand and began to pull him out of the bed.

'What the –' she exclaimed.

'Sh-sh!' she whispered, with just the hint of the Rachel giggle in it. 'Momma and Papa are still downstairs and the bed creaks.' So Bobby found himself on the carpet – on the silk dressing gown – and on Rachel! Over the years they had often made love like this, in his back bedroom when the parents were in the house – Rachel seemed to enjoy the danger – although never on the floor before!

231

He had to be careful for other, more practical reasons. She daren't become pregnant, so he had to make sure to come out in time. But first there was the pleasure of getting in!

Her body was smooth and firm and easy to enjoy. There was no strain. A rhythmic, riding, gliding mutual movement born of long practice and an unspoken understanding. There was no need for words. They gave themselves to each other naturally, confident that she would take and hold as he would thrust and that she would give to let him thrust again – long and deep, longer and deeper, longer and deeper still – till both their hearts were thudding and each was lost in the act. Neither had been virgins when they first loved in this very room but each had learned from the other how to make real love, how to prepare and gradually extend the intensity until the explosion. Sometimes she would climax first, sometimes he, and on good nights they would explode together so that they felt the same tingling in the very tips of their toes and even then he'd had to remember to withdraw – just in case. This night, while it was not one of their magical occasions, neither had any real complaints but in their natural preoccupation they both forgot that Bobby had a dislocated knee!

At the very height of the paroxysm, he made a movement with his knee which caused him to give a great cry which she, lost in the abandon of the moment, construed as passion, but was in fact a loud, animal yelp of pain. Instinctively, she reached up to put her hand over his mouth, reminded again of her parents below. He sank, like a punctured Zepellin on her breasts.

'Is it your knee?' she whispered.

'No,' he croaked, 'It was the other one.'

'Good,' she said, and her arms went round him again. Suddenly, he felt her stiffen below him.

'You didn't come out.' Her voice was flat and distant in his ear.

'Oh, God!' he groaned. There was a long silence and they lay absolutely still and grew cold together in the draught coming in under the closed door.

SEVENTEEN

'Ay. There's nothing like a good bed,' said Nessie O'Neil to her daughter Nellie as they made up the bed in the box bedroom at Ballytreabhair Farm. It was Sunday and Nellie was visiting with the twins. The two women were in Kevin's room, where Nellie had found her mother when she and Liam arrived in the cart after last Mass in Rosstrevor.

'How that boy sleeps in a cot like this beats me.' She was tucking in the sheets at the wall side, and blowing the hair out of her eyes as she reached over. Nellie was doing the same at the other side.

'First of all,' she said, 'he's not a boy, he's twenty-six. And for another thing, why is he in this silly wee box of a bedroom when there's a perfectly good bedroom on the other side, and even the back one where Noreen and I were?'

'Because he's been here since he was a lad. Dynamite wouldn't shift him now. Besides, he has all this things here.'

'So I can see.' She couldn't hide the deprecation in her voice as she straightened up and scanned her eyes scornfully round the little room. The walls were filled with battles. Prints of every size showing every kind of combat from medieval jousting to the latest newspaper cuttings of the Zulu War. There was an Irish League poster announcing a talk by Mr Richmond MP in Newry, illustrations of assassinations of crowned heads in what seemed every capital of Europe, and most unexpectedly on the mantel above the tiny coal fireplace, a framed photograph of Noreen. Nellie picked it up. 'Oh, an' what's this doin' here?'

'What's that?' Nellie held out the frame. Her mother came over. 'My lord! I threw that out years ago.'

'You couldn't have thrown it far then.'

Mrs O'Neil peered at it. 'The devil he is,' she said quietly.

Nellie took it back. 'You mean she is.' She put the frame face down on the mantel. 'Do you hear from her at all?' Her tone was light but tense.

'Devil a word,' replied her mother. But Paddy mentions her now and again when he's writin'. She sees him and Sean and

Michael sometimes I understand. But it's been a while now since I heard.'

'Is Sean still sendin' the dollars?'

'He is, but not regular like before. I had to write an' tell 'im it was killin' his da'.' Nellie gave a short laugh.

'Da wouldn't be pleased at that.'

'He wasn't, but I told him that Sean 'n' Michael was havin' hard times and had to draw in the reins a bit. Not that they had to mind. Sure didn't they buy yon man Rafferty – I think that was his name – ay – they bought him out.'

'Don't tell father that,' grinned Nellie, 'or he'll be out on the next boat!'

'He'd swim if he know'd his boys had a public house.'

'I've never seen 'im so glad to see Liam.'

'Right enough,' nodded her mother, 'where did they go?'

'Looking for a "bone fide". Liam said he would drive him over by the Newry Road, with Kevin bein' away with the cart.' She busied herself with some clothes. 'Where is Kevin anyway?'

'God knows, I never ask.'

'It's ages since I seen him,' said Nellie. The older woman gathered up some shirts and underwear.

'Would ye look at the state o' this stuff?' Nellie laughed again.

'Dear God, does he still wear them things?' Her mother threw the bundle on the floor by the door.

'Here, we'd better get on. There'll be blue murder if he comes back and we've been in here.'

'Won't he notice that the place has been cleaned up?'

'Well, the damage has been done then, if ye see my meanin'. I'll just tell him he left his door open, and when I went to shut it, I saw the mess.'

'Mother, ye're a devious woman.'

'Well, he never lets anyone over the door and he sees to himself for the most part. I can only get in when he forgets to lock the door. Sure I have to, Nellie, for if I didn't give it a redd up at least once in a while he'd have the place like a right midden.'

'Isn't it?' commented Nellie dryly. She noticed her mother had replaced Noreen's photograph on the mantel so that it faced out again, but she said nothing.

'I'm wonderin',' said her mother, 'if we should clear out them ashes from the grate there. She stood looking down at the tiny fireplace. Nellie bent to look out of the window, parting the curtain with one hand.

'I don't hear the twins. I'm always suspicious when they're quiet. I left them in the parlour. I might just give them a glance.' She started for the door. Her mother knelt down at the fireplace and lifted the iron grill from the front of the fireplace. 'Bring that auld bucket for the ashes back with ye,' she called.

'Right,' said Nellie. Nessie began to lift off the larger embers and was surprised that the heap of ashes was so high. She had lifted the larger pieces clear when she saw something buried in the grey ash. It was a parcel wrapped in oil cloth. She pulled it out. It felt strange to her touch. She blew the ashes clear and spat as the dust went into her mouth. When she opened the cloth, she discovered a revolver. 'Jesus, Mary and Joseph!' she exclaimed. Nessie rose up, her heart fluttering. What was she to do with such a thing? She was pondering this in a panic, when she heard the scream of the children and the sound of feet running.

Nessie quickly put the gun back in its wrapper and into the pocket of her apron before she turned round. She held it with one hand while the other went to her throat, as Nellie's face appeared at the door. She was carrying Celia and Dermot was clinging to her waist. Both children were crying loudly and their mother's face was scarlet with excitement.

'Ma, will you come and see?' she said.

'Nellie girl, what a fright you gave me!'

'An' it's the fright we've had I can tell you. Would you just look and see?' She crossed over to the window, still carrying the seven-year-old Celia and dragging Dermot, her twin. The two children were positively screaming by this time and shouted to their grandmother. 'Nana, don't want to see it 'gain,' yelled Celia through her tears.

Dermot ran to his grandmother. Only her hand was between the revolver and his childish face looking up at her, tears streaming on his plump cheeks. 'Nana, I'm feared of the monster. It'll eat us all up, Nana.'

Celia buried her little head in her mother's shoulder as Nessie joined Nellie. Dermot couldn't resist a sly peak out of the window too, as the women bent to look. And there, bumping and jolting its roaring way up the track towards the house was a motor car. A monster right enough! Belching fire and smoke and scattering hens and geese before it. The 1907 Stanley Steamer was the first motorised vehicle any of the O'Neils at Ballytreabhair had ever seen!

'In the name of God!' exclaimed Nessie. 'What would you call that?'

'It's a horseless carriage, I think. I've seen pictures of it.'

'Would ye listen to the noise of it?'

'Oh, look,' said Nellie. 'It's stopped in the yard.' Celia screamed again.

'Don't let it come in, Mam. Don't let it come in.'

'I'd better go out,' said Nessie, putting Dermot down. 'You stay here with the childer.' She hurried away, but halted at the doorway. 'Did ye bring the old bucket?' she asked Nellie.

'It was full of slops,' answered Nellie, still gazing out of the window. She was less agitated now and even Celia had turned to look. Dermot was standing on his toes, peering over the window-sill.

'An' I told himself to empty it this morning',' muttered Nessie as she made her way out.

They were strangers, the two men in the yard. They stood by the car, staring at the farm front door. Nessie acted fast. In two steps she had reached the slop bucket, dropped the packet in, watched it splash on the cobbles and turned round as a voice rang out in the yard.

'Mrs O'Neil?'

It was the taller of the two men and he spoke with an air of authority. Nessie found herself reacting as if to the parish priest or the headmaster of the school.

'Yes, sir?' she answered.

'We have your son here, ma'am.' His voice was calm and he had a definite southern accent.

'Kevin?'

'Yes, ma'am.'

All subservient reaction was forgotten at once as Nessie yielded to more primitive instincts and rushed to the car to see her youngest son. He was lying in the back seat with his leg raised on a cushion. His trousers were torn to reveal bloodstained bandages on the leg.

'Kevin!' She was beside him in a moment.

His face was deathly white. 'I had a bit of an accident, Ma,' he said in a very faint voice.

'What happened?'

'I can't right remember, Ma –'

'But Kevin –'

'I think your son needs to rest, Mrs O'Neil.' It was the tall man again. 'If you will allow us, my friend and I will carry him into the house. You could show us his room perhaps?'

It was funny I should have just tidied the room this day, thought Nessie as the two strangers laid Kevin on the new-made bed. It was as if I had been expecting visitors. Nellie watched from the window, holding a child tightly on either side of her.

'Is Kevin dead, Mam?' asked Dermot.

'Not yet, wee Dermot,' answered Kevin from the bed.

The two strangers left with all the stealthy tact of professional undertakers, but Nessie heard the tall one say to Kevin, 'Rest well, O'Neil. We'll need men like you.'

'Yes, Captain.'

'I wish you good day, ma'am.' The tall, grave man nodded to Nessie, and did the same to Nellie. 'And to you, ma'am.' And they left the room. Nessie went to sit by her son and Nellie turned again to the window. The other man had difficulty starting the machine and had to put a long handle in the front and turn it several times before the engine roared into life startling the children again. 'It's alright, childer, the monster's going away now,' said Nellie.

In the bed, Kevin chuckled. 'I never had no trouble startin' up old Random, God Bless Him,' he said, 'though this new mare, Dandy's trickier.'

'Where is Dandy, anyway?' asked his mother. Kevin hesitated.

'It's hard to say,' he said at last.

'Why so?

'Because I don't know.'

'You don't know?'

'No.'

'A horse and a cart that stands as high as a house and cost the best part of thirty pounds and you lost them both?'

'Ma, I don't –' Kevin's excuse was cut short as Nellie came forward with her children.

'Ma! Can't you see the boy's badly hurt. Let's see to his leg first and then we can hear about Dandy and the cart.'

Kevin grinned weakly. 'Did you think I'd kicked the bucket, Ma?'

At the mention of 'bucket' Nessie was immediately alert again and hurried to the door. 'I'll get some water,' she said. As she left, little Dermot climbed on to the bed with Kevin.

'Why is your leg all red, Uncle Kevin?'

Nessie had the pig bucket in her hand when she heard the noise of singing in the early evening air. She stopped and listened. The voice was familiar but she couldn't place it. Then the cart came into view. Liam Murphy was lying across the back, drunk as a newt and singing his head off:

> 'There's a neat, little still at the foot of the hill,
> Where the smoke curls up to the sky,
> By a whiff of the smell you can plainly tell
> That there's poitin boys, close by.
> For it fills the air with a perfume rare,
> And betwixt both me and you,
> As home we roll we can drink a bowl
> Or a bucketful of mountain dew.'

'A bucketful, indeed,' said Nessie to herself, as Old Den brought the cart to a halt in the yard. He, surprisingly enough, was comparatively sober, which means he was drunk by any ordinary standards, but by the very gauge he had set himself over the years, he might be called a pillar of sobriety – and grumpy with it.

'Here, woman,' he said. 'Will ye give me a hand with your man here? He's drunk enough to float the Mauretania, and left me to drive him home that's had so little over me lips you would think it was Lent.' By this time he had hold of Liam's feet and was pulling. 'Will ye shut yer singin'? You've been the very opery since we left Kilkeel.' He called to his wife, 'Will you give a hand, Nessie?' His shouts brought out Nellie and the children, and the young ones rushed to the back of the cart.

'Is Daddy dead, too?' asked Celia, staring round-eyed at the prostrate body of her daddy.

'Dead drunk by the look of him,' muttered Nellie. 'Here, Da, I'll give ye a hand.'

'I was askin' yer mother,' he said, 'but she's –'

'Never mind, we've got him now,' said Nellie. 'He'll have to come into the house and sober up before he's fit to take the cart home. Come away, you big lump,' she said to her husband, as he tried to embrace her. Between them all, they managed to get Liam to the house, the twins being much amused by all the palaver. Old Den turned the horse and looked about him in the yard.

'Where's that old bucket?' he mumbled. At that Nessie reappeared with the bucket in her hand.

'Where have you been?' asked Den.

'To the pigs with the slops, where you should have been this mornin',' replied his wife.

'See's that bucket,' said Den, holding out his hand.

'What bucket?' she asked.

'Sure, the one ye have in yer hand.' Nessie was alarmed. The pistol was still in the bucket, covered with muck and mess, and she was on her way to put it under the tap.

'What do ye want it for?' she said.

'What does it matter what I want it for? I want to give the horse some water, woman. It's the only one of us has not had a drink this hot day.'

'I'll get you some from the tap then,' she said.

'Be quick about it then.' Den was wiping the horse down with a cloth, and Nessie turned to the back of the yard and the standing pump. She wasn't enjoying the intrusion of this foreign weapon into her world, and wondered what to do with it next. She let the water run till the package was clean again.

'Come on, woman, I'm starved. And here's a mare that's dyin' o' thirst.' He was on her before she knew, and had the bucket full of water from her hand before she could stop him. He never even glanced at it, and put it under the horse's nose at once.

'Here, let me do that,' said Nessie urgently, taking it from him.

Den, ever willing to let Nessie do the work, let her take over, and lurched towards the house, saying, 'It's a terrible thing when a good son becomes a responsibility. Isn't it he should be taking care of us?'

It was some time before they had Liam fit to drive the cart home. He kept apologising to Nellie and swearing undying devotion to her. She paid no attention and by the time she carried the sleeping twins out into the yard, it was already getting dark. Liam was helped up on to the driving seat by an even grumpier Den and the two women and the reins put into his hand. He promptly keeled to the left and slumped in the driving seat with a smile on his face.

'Would ye look at that?' growled old Den. 'I can't abide a man that can't hold his drink.'

'Not the amount you've poured into him, Da,' said Nellie. 'I'll have to drive meself.'

'Sure you can't take a horse an' it's dark already,' said her mother.

'There's nothin' else for it, is there,' replied her daughter.

'Not at all,' said Nessie. 'Sure you can stay here –'

'But, mother –' Their discussion was interrupted by another noise on the track and the frantic arrival into the yard of Dandy and the O'Neil cart being driven by Tim, the barman, of all people. He jumped from the cart and came straight to Den.

'Have you got Kevin here?'

'We have,' answered Nessie at once.

'We'll have to get him away. Auld Davie – Sergeant Davidson – is on his way here with two Garda from Newry. He's waitin' for them now at the railway station. They're comin' by train. We only just got word and they better not find your Kevin.'

'In the name o' God,' said Nessie.

'Why, what's he done?' asked Den with a puzzled frown.

'That doesn't matter now,' said Tim. 'Let's have him on the cart.'

'Wait a minute,' said Nessie. 'If the Sergeant arrives and sees our cart gone, isn't that the first thing he'll think, that he's got word and bolted?'

'But he can't find him here,' said Tim, 'especially the state he's in.'

'How do you know about the state he's in?' said Nessie.

'What's goin' on here?' asked Den impatiently.

On top of the cart, Liam started to sing again, 'On the banks of the roses my love and I sat down . . .'

'Shut up, you,' yelled Nellie. 'Tell you what, mother, can't we take Kevin away in the back of the cart with the childer? The Sergeant will never think to stop us, and Kevin can stay over until his leg's better. He can go to Liam's people at Hilltown over the mountains. They'll never think of him there.'

It took them half the time to get Kevin out to the Murphy cart than it took to get Liam sobered up again and it was Nellie who finally drove the cart away with its very full load. At the very last minute Nessie handed the pig bucket to Tim, who was sitting at the back with Kevin and the children ready to jump off at the road end.

'Just in case he's sick,' she said, pointedly, indicating the package in the bottom of the bucket. Tim glanced in and understood at once.

'That's very kind of you, Mrs O'Neil. Sure, that might just come in very handy.' The cart drove off at once.

'God bless ye, girl,' called out Mrs O'Neil to Nellie, 'and thanks for callin'.'

'Sure it's a pleasure, Ma. There's never a dull moment at Ballytreabhair. Good night, Da.' Liam came to life again with ' 'Tis the last rose of summer . . .'

'Will ye shut up?' from Nellie was the last thing the old couple heard as they watched the cart disappear down the track.

'You go to your bed, Den. I'll see to Dandy.'

'You gave away our pig bucket,' queried Den.

'There was a hole in it,' lied Nessie.

'Ah.' Apparently satisfied, he shambled off towards his bed.

Nessie had only closed the stable door when Sergeant Davidson arrived with two uniformed policemen in the police cart. 'It's late you are,' he said, 'putting your animal away, Mrs O'Neil.'

'Den likes to see Dandy get the benefit of the cool night air,' answered Nessie.

'I see,' said the Sergeant. 'And Den would be the man who'd know about horses.'

'He knows about his own at any road.'

'I'm sure he does.' He then explained that he had authority to search all premises for weapons and any suspicious matter or persons in view of 'information received'.

'Oh, ay,' said Nessie.

'Would ye mind if we looked around?'

'Not at all,' said Nessie, folding her arms in front of her.

'Is your boy at home?' asked the policeman lightly.

'Which one?' countered Nessie with a smile.

'The one that's not making a fortune in Amerikay.'

'Ah, Kevin, you mean?'

'The same.'

'Sure I never know where that boy is. He's that late these nights, I'm sure there must be a girl in it.'

'I'm sure there's something in it.'

'Well, that's both of us sure, Sergeant,' she said going indoors ahead of him.

Sergeant Davidson and his colleagues made a thorough search of Ballytreabhair Farm, but all they found that night was the sleeping form of Old Den snoring contentedly in his own bed.

'It's yourself, Mrs Beattie?'

'Oh, it's you, Mrs Friar.'

'A fine day for the time o' year.'

'It is that. Snell but no' bitter.'

'Ay. Christmas is comin'.'

'So it is. Ay. We'll have the weather for it.'

'Ay. So we will.'

And that would normally be the end of it. A street exchange no different from any other that takes place in the course of a day in the High Streets and Main Streets of any town anywhere. The only truism appears to be that the smaller the town the greater the extent of the exchange. Forres, being a smallish town and by no means a city, the passing of street pleasantries is not quite the folk art it is in villages but people still enjoy passing the time of day with their neighbours. The qualifying condition, however, in this particular instance, was that Mrs Beattie and Mrs Friar could hardly be classed as neighbours and even the most cock-eyed optimist would never even hope that they might even begin to be pleasant to each other. On this morning however, they dallied somewhat so that each might have the off-chance of that little bit of news that other people call gossip, which the other might add to the jigsaw of seemingly useless information built up bit by bit in small minds. Especially Mrs Friar's. A mind like hers had never been trained to encompass a vast concept or to accommodate any larger vision than what she could see with half-closed eyes. To look openly and plainly on anything or anyone would, in her mind, leave her exposed. She might as well be naked. And Mrs Friar had never seen herself naked since she was three years old, and even then it was an accident.

Mrs Beattie, on the other hand was a free spirit by comparison but even she was conditioned by her class and her religion – she could give nothing away for nothing. Even a piece of her mind could cost you dearly if you got on on the wrong side of her. But this sunny morning, she was expansive.

'This is me since I got up,' she said.

'Ay.'

'If it's no' one thing it's another,' she went on.

'Oh ay.' Mrs Friar was playing it close.

'Ay,' rejoined Mrs Beattie, realising she had lost the first round, 'I was just on my wey up to see Thomasina.'

'Oh? Ye've a nice day for it.' This was not in the rules. It was supposed to be Mrs Friar's turn to proffer a tit-bit. Anything would do. Mrs Beattie wasn't fussy. She decided to help her along.

'And Ella's well?'

'Fine. Ay.' Mrs Beattie waited, but nothing happened. There was a pause and both women looked past each other up the busy street.

'An awfy fowk aboot the day,' added Mrs Friar.

'It's ay busy on a Friday,' said Mrs Beattie with a touch of acerbity. And then by one of those quirky coincidences that make life interesting both women spoke at once, and both said the same thing: 'Wee Becky's –' Mrs Beattie laughed and even Mrs Friar smirked.

'Great minds think alike,' she said as if she'd invented the aphorism. Mrs Beattie nodded,

'Ay,' she said, 'fools seldom differ!' The set had reached deuce when Mrs Beattie decided to go for the advantage point. 'Ay, I wis just goin' to say wee Becky's seven the day.'

'Ay, so she is. I mind the date by my husband that was, Mr Friar. He was ay the day before. December the fifth.'

'Ay, his birthday would ay be the same date every year!'

Mrs Friar failed to notice the sarcasm and went on, 'I wis just thinkin' o' droppin' in a wee present. I've got it here in my bag.'

'So have I. I just got mine frae Ferguson's the now.'

'I was there yesterday.'

'Isn't that funny?'

'I don't think it's funny at all. It's a book.' Mrs Beattie laughed. Mrs Friar looked offended but continued. 'For readin'. Wee Becky's the great wee reader.'

Mrs Beattie laughed again, so hard in fact she had to put her hand over her mouth. 'You're not goin' tae believe this.'

Mrs Friar pursed her lips into their accustomed position. 'You're not goin' to tell me you bought a book as well.'

'I did. And here it is. It's no' even wrapped yet. I have some nice paper in the drawer in the house I was goin' to use.' With that she brought out a shining copy of Charles Kingsley's *The Water Babies*.

Mrs Friar's jaw dropped. She gulped and said, 'You're right. I don't believe it.'

'What book did you get then?'

'That one!'

'This one?' said Mrs Beattie incredulously.

'Well, no' that exact one. The same one.'

'I don't believe it.'

'I did. Oh, it's annoying.'

'No, it's not. It's funny, that's what it is.'

'Is it?'

'Of course it is!' Mrs Friar wasn't so sure.

'Well, what are we goin' to do?' she said.

'I tell you what we'll do, Mrs Friar,' said Mrs Beattie taking her arm. 'We're goin' to go right back to that shop and we're goin' to give my book back.'

'Are we?'

'We are. And we're goin' to use the money to buy something else.'

'But what?'

'I don't know. But we'll think of something. Come on.'

And Mrs Beattie and Mrs Friar, to their own and everyone else's astonishment, went arm-in-arm up the street.

Rebecca Friar and Elspeth Keith were just like sisters although they weren't. They had grown up in the same house since they were babies and were virtually inseparable. They did everything together and people thought they were twins. Their common love was reading and their common hate was Kenny, Elspeth's big brother who was ten, but worse was a boy! At seven, this was a vital factor for the girls. This didn't bother Kenny at all as he more or less ignored them and they did the same to him. They didn't like boys. At school, they kept well away from them even though they were both popular and pretty girls. Elspeth was fair-haired, almost blonde, Rebecca was dark but there was something about the eyes they had in common, yet where Elspeth was grave and silent most of the time, Rebecca, or Becky as she was usually called, was lively and voluble. As Uncle John was often heard to remark, 'I wonder who she gets that from.'

That Friday afternoon, the girls were back from school and talking in Elspeth's bedroom.

'I know what you're going to get for your birthday,' said Elspeth conspiratorially. Becky affected to be unconcerned.

'So do I.'

'What is it then?'

'A book. It's always a book.'

'Ah, but what book?' said Elspeth. Becky didn't answer. Elspeth was triumphant. 'Ah, see you don't know.'

'I can't be expected to know everything,' replied Becky pertly. The two girls were changing from their second best school clothes to their third best play clothes. The first best clothes were only for Sunday and when visitors came. Elspeth was determined to be excited.

'Do you know who else is coming to the party tomorrow?'

'Of course, it's my party.'

'Kenny!'

Becky stopped buttoning up her blouse. She looked shocked. 'But he's a boy!'

'So he is,' said Elspeth.

'It's a girls' party. Uncle John wouldn't let him.'

'It was daddy said he could come. It was his tea-time anyway, and he's coming too, and he's a boy.'

'But he's old.'

'So is Kenny. He's ten. And anyway he came to my party when it was my birthday.'

'But he's your brother.'

'He's yours too.'

'No, he isn't. He's my cousin. That's what Uncle John says. He says that he's my daddy's brother. He showed me a photograph once.'

'Of his brother?'

'Ay, and he said that was my daddy.'

'That must feel funny to see your daddy in a photograph.'

'Ay.'

'Did he look nice?' Becky didn't answer at once, and when she did it was very quietly.

'Ay,' she said.

The party was not a great success. At least at the start of the Saturday afternoon. Kenny's taunting drove Elspeth to tears and Becky was made to sit with Mrs Friar whom she did not like. Becky was put out in any case because her mother had not appeared. Mrs Friar explained that she had had to go to Aberdeen again. Why did her mother have to go to Aberdeen? Elspeth whispered to her one night in their room that that's where you go to buy babies.

'She's not going to buy another baby,' Becky had said indignantly. 'She hasn't finished paying for me yet.' For all their high intelligence and exceptional reading ability, they were still two little girls and the world was often a puzzle to them. What they didn't know they read about. What they couldn't read about, they guessed, and very often they got it wrong.

Becky didn't get a book after all. She was very disappointed. For all her pretence, she loved books. She loved the feel of them, the smell of them, especially when they were new, and her biggest luxury was to cut the new pages of any book. She and Elspeth had the most books of any girls in the street. Thomasina had said often that they should play more with their dolls like any other girls, instead of spending most of their time in the 'library' as she called their shared bedroom. Thomasina at this time was fussing around the table. The tea and cakes had been cleared and everyone was sitting now in the big couch and the two fireside armchairs.

'What are we waiting for?' asked Becky a little sullenly.

'You'll see,' said Mrs Friar mysteriously.

'Where's Gran?' asked Elspeth.

'She's away with your daddy and Kenneth to bring in the present.'

At this Becky sat up. 'What present?'

'You'll see,' said her Aunt Thomasina. Becky looked across at Elspeth, whose big eyes told her she didn't know either. Becky was puzzled. She thought she'd had her presents. A handkerchief from Kenny, a box of colouring pencils from Uncle John and a penny colouring book which Thomasina, or 'Aunty Tom' as Becky called her, got from a magazine, *Woman's Realm*. They were not especially close, Becky and her aunt, but they got on well enough. It was different with Uncle John. He was as good as a real daddy. And in her heart, Becky wished he was.

There was a sudden noise in the corridor outside and then several bumps before the door opened wide and there was Gran Beattie with a big smile on her face, indicating with her own vocal fanfare, 'Tarra!' John and Kenny stood in the doorway holding a huge wooden doll's house. Becky's face fell.

EIGHTEEN

Christmas in New Zealand was not what Tina had expected. For one thing, it was hot and sunny and not at all the weather she had associated all her life with Yuletide. And yet in many respects it was just the same kind of Christmas that she and her family had always known back home in Scotland. Like most migrants, she still thought of Scotland as home and Britain as the homeland, although she knew she would never see her native country again. Unlike other exiles, however, she didn't live in the half hope that she might. And what a country this was, especially at this strange summer-time Christmas. It was a tuppence-coloured Scotland. It had all the greens and blues and purples of the old country but more so and the sun undoubtedly shone brighter below the Equator. She and Jim had settled well. Even old Florence had adjusted. At least, she was venturing out on to the verandah of the Mackenzie farm steading on most days and lay in the shade, making an endless succession of crocheted table covers and mats. While she was doing so, she was company for little Sandy, who was just six months old and still in his pram, the image of his daddy, Bruce Mackenzie. Tina and Bruce had met at a farm dance near Gore. She had gone with Jim when they were both on the Keith farm at East Gore on the Mataura River. When they'd heard that name, they knew they must take the place. It was the Mataura that had brought them from Scotland, and it had to be a good omen.

The farm dance was the only way that young people could get together in those parts, and a great deal of matchmaking went on. Jim and Tina had made up a foursome with Jean Hay and Bruce Mackenzie. They were an obvious foursome from the beginning, and it was just a matter of time until they paired off. There wasn't much choice in any case. Younger, unattached people were at a premium in Southland. Most people had come out as married couples, so it was inevitable that four young people living within pony and trap distance of each other would become more than good friends.

Bruce and Tina were best man and bridesmaid at Jim's wedding to Jean Hay at her parents' place in Gore. The Hays were also Scottish, but they were from Edinburgh and thought themselves a bit superior to most of their neighbours. Jean, however, was a good plain Scottish New Zealander, born in Southland and ideally fit to be a farmer's wife. Which was just as well, as Jim was not ideally cut out to be a farmer! However, he had bought land from the New Zealand and Australia Land Company on good terms and he thought he might as well take the chance of a place while he could. With the help of a couple of good men and with Jean's know-how, they could just about make it. There would be time to get back to his books later, so like many others, he rolled up his sleeves and before long, he was a cocky with the best of them, and the farm prospered.

But the farmhouse could hardly cope with two women, still less three. From her reclining position, Mrs Keith still took a controlling interest in the household, but with only Jim in the house and two farmhands in the hut, Tina had become used to being in charge. When Jean Hay had become Jean Keith, it was only natural that she assumed head girl status, so for a time, things were a little uncomfortable. Luckily, Jean and Tina were compatible and amenable and between them, they softened the worst effects of Florence Keith's interference.

This then was the situation when Bruce Mackenzie, after much prompting from Jim and Jean finally proposed to Tina. It was obvious to everyone, including Tina, how much he liked her. But he was in his thirties, and already much set in his ways, and perhaps reluctant to make too many changes too quickly. Tina, too, wasn't entirely sure. The Martin Dickenson episode was still with her, and there was a faint memory of that feeling on the docks with the young Irishman. She had to think to remember his name – Denis, that was it. She had imagined, in her ingenuous way that when she married it would be a combination of that quayside romance with the close sexual intensity she had known with Martin Dickenson in the cabin. Instead, there was only a warm friendliness for that good man, Bruce Mackenzie. Jim liked him, and Bruce seemed to be able to manage with her mother. They often sat together not saying a word, which is maybe the best way to get on with anybody. At any rate, in the spring of 1905 she had married Bruce in Gore and moved to his farm outside Edendale. Alexander Keith Mackenzie had followed in eighteen months. Mrs Keith had stayed at East Gore with Jim and Jean.

The Mackenzies had invited the Keiths and their children, two-year-old Billy, and Roberta Keith, born only a few months before and named after Robert in Sydney, to join them for the festive season.

This was to be a real family Christmas, and Tina was hard at work in the kitchen with Hilda van Meer. She and her husband, Jan, were on the next farm to Bruce, and they had looked on Bruce as a son. Now they accepted Tina as a daughter, and were constantly on hand with advice and assistance. They were a Dutch couple and had all the practical good sense and household standards of that nation. Unfortunately, they also had the same lack of humour, but Bruce and Tina had many occasions to be glad of their proximity.

Tina wiped the sweat from her forehead with the back of her hand, and shooed away the flies as they played round her face. She was making hard work of plucking the goose. It was a tough old bird. What a way to spend Christmas Eve, she thought. Hilda was making a Dutch Delft Cake at the oven. This was her speciality and she made it on every occasion.

Tina, Hilda and Jean worked happily on their particular task. They were a congenial trio, and already the sense of Christmas excitement was making itself felt in the house. The presents were already wrapped and round the tree in the front room. The cards were hung above the mantelpiece. There was one from John and Thomasina and the children, but nothing so far from Bobby. But then Bobby was always late. He had written telling them about his recent marriage to Rachel in Sydney, but he hadn't given any address or any details of the wedding. Tina had felt let down, but knowing Bobby, he would tell them in his own good time what had happened. He was still in his Union job and seemed to do a lot of travelling. She wished he could have been here for Christmas. So did Jim, although he said they'd never get a word in if he came. Tina knew that despite their great differences, the brothers loved each other.

He was out on the farm now with Bruce and young Billy Keith. Bruce was showing him how the new tree planting was coming on. It had been old Jan's idea. He was with them too. Old Jan always tagged along when Bruce went round his place. He was very proud of the new trees, you would think they were his. 'Only God can make a tree,' he said, 'but we can give him a hand now and then. Besides you need the wind shelter, the birds need the tree shelter, the pests need the birds and the soil needs the pests. We all need each other. Everything depends on something. Only thing we don't need is 'possums. Them's the devil's creatures. Tree rats, I call them.' The three men were walking over the top paddock. Bruce had wee Billy on his shoulders.

'Me hungry, Dad.' Jim looked up at him, and patted his knee.

'You'll be home soon. You alright up there with Uncle Bruce?'
Billy wasn't so sure. His face was grave. Bruce Mackenzie was six
feet four and that's a long way up for a two-year-old.

'Nice place you've got here, Bruce,' said Jim as they walked.
'You've done well.'

'Needs the work,' said Bruce.

'Needs the weather,' added Jan.

'Like any place. It's all a matter of luck, I suppose.' Bruce
laughed. 'But it's funny,' he said, 'how lucky you can get if you've
got good soil.'

'That's true for sure,' said Jan.

'When I first came up from Balclutha, Hilda said what I needed
first was a good wife but Jan here said what I needed first was a
couple of good horses.'

'True,' said Jan.

'So I got the horses and Hilda said –'

'You get wife now!' interjected Jan and he cackled with laughter.

'That's right,' said Bruce, 'So I got a wife. You'll know her
Jim.' And Jim laughed. 'But then do you know what this old
devil says?'

'No,' said Jim obligingly.

'You get milk machine!' Jan just beat Bruce to it and both men
laughed. Up on his high perch, wee Billy felt a bit out of it.

'Dad, apple!' he cried as they went under a fruit tree on the edge
of the old plantation near the house.

'Help yourself, Billy,' said his uncle, and Billy reached up and
pulled an apple from the tree. Actually, he didn't pull it. He merely
held on to it, while Bruce pulled him, and with a gurgle of laughter
the boy found the apple was in his hand.

'That's a Cox's Orange,' said Bruce to Jim.

''Tisn't,' said the little boy, 'it's an apple.'

'Don't speak with your mouth full,' said his father.

That night the adults sat round in the front room, among the
Christmas lilies and gladioli in the last of the evening sun and
talked after supper. Even old Florence had been brought in and
sat in the most comfortable armchair while they talked. They spoke
of the Europe they remembered, of Christmases in Scotland and
Holland, of their different childhood memories and all the things
that adults talk about on a sentimental occasion like Christmas Eve.
Everybody had something to say and it was amazing how people
had such different memories of the same event. Jim, being Jim of
course, wanted to discuss Rudyard Kipling's Nobel Prize, or the
surrender of Dini Zulu, king of the Zulus, or the fact that the
Mauretania had run aground at Liverpool, or the rage that Lili Elsie

had become in 'The Merry Widow'. Jim got all his news from *The Southland Times*, which he was sent once a week from Invercargill. He was always keen to discuss the world news, especially the news from Britain, but he found few takers that night. The supper had been too good, the weather was too pleasant and the company too friendly to worry about newspaper stories. Real life was full and interesting enough for all of them. They had little need of a newspaper, faraway, world.

It was only when everyone was thinking of bed and Jean and Tina had gone off to give their respective babies their last feeds and Hilda was in the kitchen clearing the last of the dishes, that Bruce said, 'Would anyone like a nightcap?'

Florence Keith was the first to reply from her chair. 'That would be very nice.' The men were slightly taken aback. 'It's a special occasion,' she explained. 'Christmas comes but once a year.'

'So it does, Gran,' said Bruce.

'And it would be nice,' she added slowly, 'if someone was to give us a bit reading.'

'What kind of reading, Gran?' asked Bruce with the whisky bottle.

'From the book, of course.'

'Book?' asked Jan with a frown.

'My mother means the Bible,' explained Jim.

'Ah, the Good Book,' said Jan. 'I understand.'

'Your department, Jim boy,' said Bruce. 'Your wee nip, as I think you call it, Gran.' He grinned, giving her a glass.

'Thank you, Bruce,' she said almost primly.

'Well,' said Bruce, 'do we have the toast first?'

'If I have to do the reading we do,' said Jim.

'OK then. Cheers!' said Bruce.

'Slainte!' said Mrs Keith, unexpectedly.

Bruce went to the book shelf and took down the Mackenzie Bible. 'There you are, old son, it's all yours. Mind, it's heavy.' Jim took the big book and opened it on his knees. After a moment, he cleared his throat and read:

'From the Gospel of St Luke, Chapter 2, Verses 6 to 11.' He cleared his throat again. Bruce whispered, 'Do you want another drink?' Jim shook his head and read on. 'And so it was, while they were there, the days were accomplished that she should be delivered. And she brought forth her first born son, and wrapped him in swaddling clothes, and laid him in a manger: because there was no room for them in the inn. And there were in the same country shepherds abiding in the field, keeping watch over their flock by night. And, lo, the angel of the Lord came upon them,

and the glory of the Lord shone round about them: and they were
sore afraid. And the angel said unto them, Fear not: for behold, I
bring you good tidings of great joy, which shall be to all people.
For unto you is born this day in the city of David a Saviour which
is Christ the Lord.'

The next morning belonged to young Billy. He had most of the
presents and all the adults to himself, and it only came to an end
for him when he was very sick late in the morning, but whether
from too much excitement or too many sweets, nobody could
tell. He was put down in the spare bedroom with the blinds
closed against the sun, and Jim sat with him telling him stories
until he fell asleep. At the lunchtime Christmas dinner Tina, Jean
and Hilda decided to wear their new bonnets with the flowers all
round. Mrs Keith stubbornly insisted on wearing her old cap at
the back of her head with a ribbon under her chin. Jim suggested
that the men should perhaps wear their hats but Bruce said it
was too hot. The Christmas goose was well and truly cooked
and a good time was had by all. The van Meers brought some
wine which they said was Australian and the Keiths enjoyed the
reminder it gave them of meals on the Mataura. Florence stayed
with the whisky. It was medicinal, she said. She considered all
strong spirits as medicine. Florence Keith was a great authority
on medicines and even on the ship she had brought all her
favourites from home: 'Milne' Ointment for Eczema, Clarke's
Blood Mixture, Nervetonine, Dr J. Collis Browne's Chlorodyne,
Keatings Lozenges and for special emergencies, 'Roderick Dhu'
Old Highland Whisky. Unfortunately, that was finished now and
she had to make do with what was to hand, 'Johnnie Walker',
which was very nice indeed thank you.

After the lunch, they all sat on the verandah and looked at the
grass and listened to the wood pigeons and warblers. There was
not much else to do. The ladies had removed their hats but were
still constricted by their fashionable jackets and long skirts. The
men had taken off their stiff collars, but were still uncomfortable
in waistcoats and tight trousers and big boots. The thing to do was
move as little as possible.

'So that was Christmas,' said Bruce sleepily.

'It's not over yet. There's still Boxing Day,' said Tina, dangling
baby Sandy on her knee. Jean had Roberta up at her shoulder and
was patting her back and Billy was lying beside his dad in the long
chair. Bruce was in the hammock and Mr and Mrs van Meer were
sitting side-by-side on the steps.

'Boxing Day's not for me,' said Bruce. 'Can't afford it. Work to
do.'

'And we'll have to be travelling back,' said Jim. 'Two days of a holiday's enough. Even at Christmas.'

'Too much of a holiday is bad for you,' said Hilda.

'How do you know?' said Jan, adjusting the cushion below him. 'You never take holiday.'

'Women can't take holiday.'

'That's right,' said Jean. 'A woman's work is never done.'

'And a man's is never paid for,' said Bruce putting his hands behind his head.

'It's not so much the work we're never paid for,' said Jim. 'It's the worry.'

'You should worry,' said Hilda. 'With a good wife and a good place and a son already to take over –'

'Wait a minute,' said Jim, sitting up.

Hilda waved her hand, 'You know what I mean.'

And so the talk drifted nebulously into the haze of a farmhouse afternoon under a lazy New Zealand sun. They were well fed and well disposed to each other and they could hardly be blamed if they felt just a little smug. On that particular Christmas Day, their's was the nearest thing to an idyll to be found in the southern hemisphere.

'Dad?'

'Yes, Billy?' said Jim.

'Me want apple again.'

'Oh, Billy,' said his father. But the little boy's request was unusually apt, for, unknown to them all, they were not in Edendale, Southland, New Zealand, but the Garden of Eden by Gore.

Noreen's face was contorted in anger. 'You do that again and I'll kill you,' she whispered. And Rico did it again. He slapped her hard. Very hard. She kicked out at him at once. He winced with pain and made to grab at her. She ducked under his arm and made for the door but he caught her arm. She screamed and pulled hard. It hurt her all the more and she slumped to her knee. He hit her hard across the head and she fell to the ground crying loudly. He stood over her shouting just as loudly in Italian. He prodded her with his foot.

'Get up! Get up!' he hissed. She turned and lay on her back and looked up at him, her hair dishevelled, the tears staining her cheeks.

'You Italian bastard!' He drew back his leg as if to kick her, but she quickly turned and pulled the other one and brought him down. Scrambling, she got to her feet and made a grab at the kitchen knife at the sink. He was on top of her, but she pushed the knife right under his face.

252

'Leave me alone!' she screamed. He hesitated, then grabbed her wrist and twisted it so that she screamed again and the knife dropped. He pushed her away so that she fell hard against the door. Then he lifted the knife. This time he was calm and ashen-faced.

'You want to play with knives, little girl, you learn how to use them, eh?' He advanced on her. She covered her face with both her hands and screamed. The door behind her suddenly opened and she was pushed against Rico, who staggered back. Noreen felt a sharp little pain on her right arm and looking down, she saw the blood. Furiously, she sprang at Rico and pummelled him.

'Basta!' yelled a voice behind her. Rico threw her off, and she turned to see Mamma d'Agostino standing in the doorway. There was an Italian exchange between mother and son which Noreen couldn't follow, it was so fast and vehement. Noreen looked down at her arm. It was only a small cut, but it was bleeding and she put her hand over it to try and stop it. Rico was pointing to her, but his mother advanced into the room and, pushing him aside, went to Noreen and looked at her arm. She held Noreen's hand, then glared round at her son.

'Benda! Pronto! Rapido!' He left the kitchen. Mamma put her ample arm round Noreen's shaking shoulders and brought her to the kitchen table and made her sit down. Rico came in with a couple of white towels, which he threw on the table.

'Niente benda,' he growled. The mother motioned him to go with a shake of her head. He shrugged and went. Mamma d'Agostino took one of the towels to the sink and then came back and lifting Noreen's arm began to daub it. It stung hard and Noreen reacted.

''Scuse,' said Mamma softly.

''S alright,' whispered Noreen. Mamma then wrapped the larger towel round the arm.

'Tene!'

'It's a big bandage for a wee cut.' She tried to smile, but instead bit her lip.

'You tell Mamma what happen?' And Noreen told her, catching her breath between sobs.

'I took Maria over to Mrs Lennox in Queen's. You remember she had the apartment where Sean and Michael stayed before they took the house at –'

Mamma nodded, 'Si, si.'

'Well, Maria likes going to Mrs Lennox and Jock plays the piano for her. She likes to sing, you know.'

'Si.'

'Well, I left her there. She's OK with Mrs Lennox and it's good for her to get away from me for a bit just now and again. You know.'

'Si.'

'Well, I came back here to the apartment and Rico's not home. I hoped we could go someplace. Have a meal, you know. See some friends. Like you, for instance.' Mamma smiled and nodded and patted the girl on the shoulder.

'But he's not home and I wait all night. So I go to bed. I think I should call you, but then I changed my mind. I mean, why worry you? Normally when he's gonna be late, he says. Some job, you know.' Mamma nodded again. 'Naturally I can't phone the police.'

'Naturally!'

'And I don't want to ring Sean or Michael. They might be mad I should leave Maria in Queen's. Anyway, so I go to bed. He comes in about six o'clock this mornin' and he's in an awful mess. He won't say what he was up to, but his clothes are all dirty and a great big tear on his sleeve. So I ask him what gives? He wouldn't tell me and went straight into the bathroom there and it was ages before he came out. But instead of getting into bed, he gets into another suit, God save us, and says he's going out again. I ask him if he'll take me over to the Lennox's in his car. You know he's got one of these Ford cars now. And he says he's too busy. And I say, "Too busy for your own daughter?" And do you know what he tells me, Mamma? Do you know what he tells me? "She's your daughter, not mine." I couldn't believe it. "She's your daughter," I said. "I know because I was there at the time." And then he gets up on his high horse and he says, "Rico has no daughters, Rico only has sons. Why don't you make me sons?" he says. As if I had anything to do with it.' Mamma made sympathetic sounds and patted Noreen on the shoulder again. 'I don't really know what went on from there. One thing just seemed to lead to another, and maybe I said more than I should have done. I know he certainly did. Then when I told him that it takes a man to make a man, he hit me right across the face. Well, not even my own father did that. Nor did any of my brothers. So I kicked out at him, as any right-minded girl would do. And he hit me again and again. Oh, Mamma, it was terrible. And then when I fell and was trying to get up, he came at me with a knife and that's when you opened the door and – Oh, Mamma!' She broke down again and put her head on the older woman's shoulder.

'Mamma come just in time. But everything gonna be OK.

Everything OK. I speak to Enrico. He's my boy. I know how to tell him. You leave it to Mamma.' Noreen suddenly looked up at the Italian woman.

'Why did he never want to marry me?' Mamma looked away. 'Was he married before?' asked Noreen. Mamma looked down and shook her head.

'Yes an' no.'

'What do ya mean yes or no. Either he was married or he wasn't.'

Mamma d'Agostino sighed a sigh that shook her generous frame, then stood up and walked to the kitchen door and opened it slightly, then said in a low voice, 'Enrico. Resta la!' She closed the door and returned to sit with Noreen. 'My Enrico is a good boy though sometimes he not do good things. But he always beautiful. Very, what you call, 'ansome. Si?'

'Si,' said Noreen with a little sigh.

'He was young man, he wanted to be architecto. Comprende?'

'Si – er – yes.'

'An' he study hard at the scuola to make paper for architecto. But, at the scuola, also studente ragazza – bella ragazza.'

'A woman, you mean?'

'Si, a young girl. She fall in love, he fall in love. They wanna –' she waves her hand, 'sposarsi. Comprende?'

'Get married.'

'Si.'

'So, Cattolica. Matrimonio. Chiesa. OK?'

'I understand.' Mamma hesitated. Noreen didn't know whether the older woman didn't want to continue, or didn't know how to.

'Go on, Mamma.'

'La luna di miele,' said Mamma. 'On their honeymoon they go to Genoa, and –', she looked away again, 'when they make the love, Lisa, she make the blood. And the blood. And the blood and more blood, till everything is blood. And she die.'

'Oh, my God.'

'My Enrico, he is covered with blood looking down on pretty Lisa, lying on her bed of blood. It is – orribile, no?'

'Terrible. Poor girl.'

'Poor Enrico.'

'Of course.'

'He leava the hotel, he leava Genoa, he leava Italia. He leava his Mamma and he come to Amerigo, and he make big noise in New York, Chicago, Detroit. All the places with Italia famiglia. He make big noise, big bangs, you know.' She made a gun gesture. 'But he make big money. He send for one brother, then two brother, then

255

four brother, then for his Mamma to make house for him in New York. He lives for his Mamma, his famiglia, his money. Then he meet you. And he love you, mia piccola.' Noreen bowed her head. She felt herself beginning to cry again.

'But does he love me still, Mamma?' Mrs d'Agostino did not answer. 'Oh, yes, he loves his money, his life, his brothers, but does he love Maria and me? Would he have loved her more if she had been a son?'

'He is Italian,' was all the mother said.

'Is that what it is?' said Noreen.

'I dunno. I dunno anything. I am Italian too, see? But now you know why you hurt him and he angry. He no marry you because of Lisa, because he think he kill Lisa in matrimonio and no wisha kill you in matrimonio. Capisto?'

'I think so,' said Noreen. 'So you talk to him, eh?' Noreen made to get up, then sat down again.

'I don't know what to say.'

'You don't have to say anything!' Both women turned and there was Rico standing at the kitchen door.

'Rico!' said his mother. But he raised his hand.

'OK, mother, I speak to Noreen.'

Noreen rose. 'I know,' she tried to say.

He nodded. 'Yes, you know too much. You please dress. I take you to Mrs Lennox.'

Noreen rose. 'Yes, we'll get Maria and we'll –'

He raised his hand again. 'No. We don't get Maria. I leave you there.'

'What?'

'We leave you there with Maria. I give you money. You stay with Mrs Lennox.'

'But, Rico –'

'I LEAVE YOU! Mamma, you tell her.' He turned on his heel and left the doorway. Mamma rose to Noreen at once.

'Noreena –' she started to say.

'You don't need to tell me anything, Mamma,' said Noreen, surprised by her own coldness. 'I understand.' She shook her head in disbelief. 'I understand everything.' She felt the Italian mother press her arm and she winced.

''Scuse, Noreena, I no mean to hurt you.'

'I know you don't, Mamma.' And turning into the big, soft breast, she threw her arms round the woman's shoulders and cried like a baby.

The infant, Abel Keith, lay in his cot and seemed to smile. It was probably wind but to Bobby Keith and to Rachel, his wife, it was a smile.

'Isn't he a lovely boy?' said Bobby.

'He's OK,' said Rachel.

'That's the Scottish part in him,' said her husband, nudging her.

'What's the Jewish part then?' she asked.

'You can't see that,' said Bobby. 'He's got his nappy on. Can I not pick him up?'

'No, I've just got him down. Leave well alone is my motto. Don't pick him up unless you have to.'

'There speaks the natural mother.'

'I'm not at all a natural mother,' said Rachel. 'The whole thing was pretty unnatural to me.'

'What else are women for?' said Bobby playfully.

'Don't even joke to me about it. A nightmare, the whole thing. Let's leave him then.' She was already moving away from the little cot and had her hand on the gas mantle and was turning it down. He reached her before it popped off and put his arm round her waist.

'Would you like to – um – go up to bed now, or shall we descend to the ground floor?'

She removed his arm, saying evenly, 'Nothing could be further from my mind. Ssh. Be quiet now.' She kept hold of his hand and guided him from the room.

In the sitting room-cum-bedroom of their Darlinghurst first floor flat, the table had already been set for dinner.

'That looks nice,' said Bobby. 'What are we eating?'

'Wait and see,' she said, going into the small scullery.

'Don't be too long,' he called.

'Quiet!' she said. And rattled through the bead curtain that separated the tiny kitchen from the living area.

'Be quiet yourself,' he said, stretching himself out on the uncomfortable horsehair sofa. He adjusted himself and stretched out. Well, it's turned out not so badly, he thought, although it's been a rough ride. He remembered it all too well. Poor Rachel. She'd had a terrible time at the birth. He had blamed the doctors. They were shouting at her to get on with it. I think they needed the bed for somebody else. Two days he was hanging around the place. He was due to go up to the Blue Mountains that morning and she started having pains, she said. Then there was water all over the stairs and she'd yelled 'Get me to the hospital'. God, he remembered how frightened he was. He'd never ever got used to Rachel's being pregnant. She didn't seem to suit the fat tummy and at the end, she just looked awful. She'd only been annoyed because it upset all her work plans. Instead of having to cancel a trip to the Blue Mountains, she'd had to put off a trip to the Blue Danube. There was another Zionist Congress in Vienna, and she'd had to pass it up, because she was passing it up quite often herself then. He hadn't realised pregnancy was such a dislocating experience, or even that getting married itself would cause such an upheaval.

When he first mentioned it to Mr Gebler he thought the old guy was going to have a fit. Even Mrs Gebler didn't seem too pleased. It was all something to do with their thinking he didn't have a proper job, so they said. But really he knew it was only because he wasn't Jewish. He wasn't Kosher. They had stalled him for long enough, but with a baby coming, he couldn't wait any longer and then when Rachel told them she had to get married, she was thrown out of the house. Bobby couldn't believe it. Old, harmless Enoch suddenly turned into a Shylock and demanded that Bobby remove his pound of flesh. They were hardly given time to pack their things. It didn't take him long, and all she wanted were her books and all the time the mother was crying and rocking backwards and forwards and the old father was ranting on in Yiddish. It was eerie and he was glad to get out. Now, here he was in downtown Sydney. The flat was tiny, but it was cheap. Now they were down to living on his salary alone, this was an important factor. She had had to take the time off, but they wouldn't pay her for it. And she lost her university part-time lectureship in Hebrew Studies, because she was pregnant. Maybe sex is a sin with the Jews, he thought. Or at least with Jewish academics!

'Come and get it.' Rachel entered with two plates.

'What have we got here? Sorry – I didn't mean to ask.' They sat down and as always, Rachel bowed her head in a silent moment before she picked up her fork and began to eat her Gefillte Fish.

'I knew I recognised it. Your mother used to make it hot with this sauce.'

'Egg and lemon.'

'That's it. I would recognise her breadcrumbs anywhere. It's as if she made it herself,' he said, munching happily on the fish ball.

'My mother did make it.'

'What?' He gulped.

'Yes, she was here this afternoon.'

'And you didn't tell me?'

'I didn't know she was coming. It was just after you left for your meeting. There she was at the door.'

'Was old Enoch with her?'

'No, my father was not with her.'

'Well, well.'

'She's been before.'

'Now she tells me.'

'She's my mother.'

'She's my mother-in-law. I have certain rights,' he insisted jocularly.

'She's not well, Bobby. She's got terribly thin. Suddenly.' He stopped eating and reached across and took his wife's hand.

'She threw you out, darling.' Bobby meant it lightly, but Rachel looked up, her eyes angry.

'No, she didn't. It was my father threw me out.' Just at that, there was a cry from Abel in the next room. Rachel rose at once.

'I'll get him.' She left Bobby picking at his Gefillte Fish. Suddenly he'd lost the taste for it.

NINETEEN

The Pittsburgh Pirates were leading Detroit 4–3 in the 1909 Baseball World Series and only minutes remained in the game. High in the bleachers, ex-Superintendent Mick O'Neil watched with his favourite nephew, Denis. Denis, in his nine years in the United States had never really taken to baseball. As an ex-hurler, he preferred football, but Uncle Mick had dragged him time and time again to see his own beloved New York Giants. The trouble was that Uncle Mick loved baseball even more than the Giants and he would travel any distance to see a good game; so here he was at Pittsburgh watching the final game of the year. The excitement had been intense and Denis watched in alarm as his uncle went every shade of red before going into purple and subsiding again to pink as the tension eased. This can't be good for him, thought Denis, and he remembered the story he had read of an old man in England, although younger than Uncle Mick was now, who lined up to receive the very first old age pension ever issued in England and dropped down dead as soon as his money was passed over the counter to him. The excitement of free cash was certainly not worth it on that occasion and what the ups and downs of a baseball game did to Uncle Mick's blood pressure and heart-beat count was not something a loving nephew dared to consider. It was only a game after all.

However, on this particular day, since his idolised Giants were not taking part there was some degree of restraint in Uncle Mick's spectatorial behaviour. Unfortunately, he decided to side with Detroit on the day, so that he might be as comfortably partisan as usual, but he did so among a group of Pittsburgh supporters, whom he referred to throughout the game as Pitts-buggers, which did nothing to improve inter-City relations. But Uncle Mick was still, even at seventy, a man to be reckoned with and he managed without any great effort to intimidate the group or at least deflect their more sinister intentions. That is until Pittsburgh scored a questionable run on a slide in. And while the Pitts-buggers went wild with delight, Uncle Mick went wild with frustration, and started to remonstrate with the biggest of the pack. This man's joy at his team's win greatly tempered his reaction at being jabbed in the chest by a vigorous old Irish American, but even he had to retaliate when Uncle Mick pulled his cap down over his eyes and shoved him back in his seat. Soon a scrum developed which bore a greater resemblance to that other American game than to the former game of Redcoat rounders being played below, and Denis had to pile in beside his uncle to the great detriment of his new coat and the loss of one trilby.

They found their way to the Railway Station and the train back to New York and all the while, Mick O'Neil was fulminating against the unfairness of the universe, particularly as it related to Detroit in the last five minutes of the game. Even in the compartment he was explaining to the other half dozen men who had no option but to listen, how the New York Giants would have taken both of them on, one after another, and still have had time to take on the Chicago White Soxs as well. One stranger in the carriage suggested that the Philadelphia Athletics were the finest team in the world due to Connie Mack.

'If you mean Cornelius McGillicuddy –' said Uncle Mick.

'I do, sir,' said the stranger.

'– then you're talking of the worst catcher ever not signed by the New York Giants.'

'What about Jock McGraw?' said somebody else.

'John J. McGraw was an even worse baseman than I was.' Denis could hardly hide his smiles, knowing that Uncle Mick had never stepped on a baseball pitch in his life. He felt too seriously about the watching of it ever to have played it. The train drew in to Penn Station with the arguments still raging round Uncle Mick's grizzled head, but that head was still unbowed and at one time Denis was sure he saw a wink in the wicked old eye as he took on about three arguments at once and lost all of them.

Since real action in the world was now denied him, Uncle Mick gave himself over thoroughly to debate. There was no issue on which he wouldn't take one side or other and preferably the minority, or losing side. There was more fun as an underdog – and since he had more bark than bite it was a casting that suited the irascible old gentleman ideally. He was simmering down, or more exactly, getting a little tired as they stood on the sidewalk waiting for a street-car. The overhead lighting didn't suit anyone but it certainly didn't flatter Mick O'Neil. His normally rubicond visage looked wan and strained and Denis thought he was breathing a little heavily.

'You OK, Uncle Mick?'

'Sure, I'm OK. Wassa matter?'

'Nothin'. I was just wonderin'.'

'It's been a long day.'

'Sure.'

Their car came, and they climbed on, just managing to find a place on top at the front among the smokers. Denis noticed that his uncle, sitting about three seats ahead of him was coughing more than usual, and glaring openly at the briars either side of him. Don't let him pick a fight now, prayed Denis, we're almost home. Another fit of coughing and the street-car lurched to a halt suddenly. This caused Uncle Mick to lean heavily on the passenger on his left causing the pipe to fall from his mouth. It fell on the floor and rolled towards Uncle Mick's feet – and he promptly stood on it with all his forty-year police authority and his size ten boots. The man couldn't believe it and could only stare as Uncle Mick got up and marched triumphantly up towards Denis and the exit stair. There was a smile on his face and it was still on his face when he stopped as if seized up and fell headlong in the passageway.

'UNCLE MICK!' cried Denis and jumped up.

'Requiem aeternam dona eis Domine . . .'

St Patrick's Cathedral was a sea of blue for the funeral. It was a Police Force out in force to recognise a man who was one of theirs. A policeman and a man's man and at the heart of it, a blunt Irish cop in New York. His was a species that would last, but Michael O'Neil was one of the original stock. The family was in the front row right as befits the relatives of the deceased, with Carmella appropriately in place of honour between Denis, in his best uniform with black gloves, and Joey, extremely smart, in unaccustomed black. Looking at him one was sure he was just the smartest, young man about town, but then when he spoke – Next to him sat Michael and Sean with a sombre Noreen between them. Carmella had not acknowledged her as she took her place, but an exchange of looks between Denis and his two younger brothers indicated that Noreen was going to be there no matter what. Carmella sensed this and remained remarkably calm. Joey didn't recognise his cousin at first, and kept peering along as if to make sure. Noreen was only older by a couple of years, but their mark was laid heavily on her, just as it was on the Rafferty regulars. Jackie, himself, was there this time, looking as old as the late Emmet Ryan was at Paddy's first Mass. The rest were there in a self-conscious group at the side. Like Sean and Michael, they weren't too happy about being in the midst of so many policemen, with all the exits covered. Every known criminal in New York was there, and those that were 'otherwise detained' had sent flowers to the man who'd sent them up. They filled the aisle around the coffin and spilled on to the altar itself.

On the main altar, Father Paddy and Father Donnelly were concelebrating mass with the Bishop. Bishop Monaghan was brief in his address. He was getting old now and didn't bother overmuch about impressing people. He was waiting to impress his Maker, and he would have the chance before long.

'Michael O'Neil,' he intoned thinly from the pulpit in his Cork lilt, 'was a terrible man altogether. But a loveable man with it and a smile on him to the last. He leaves a grieving wife and a –' Here he hesitated just enough for everyone to notice, '– a fine son. And a family of nephews –' another hesitation – 'and a niece –' Noreen looked up at this, and almost defied the Bishop with her stare, ' – that do him much credit in this world and I trust will be of some satisfaction to his account in the next. Michael O'Neil knows what the score is now better than any of us here, and if I know Michael, he'll be arguing with St Peter at the gate and be telling him in his best Superintendent manner that celestial security is not what it was – if they let people like him in!' The old Bishop waited for the little murmur of sympathetic approval that ran through the ranks, and they listened just as sympathetically as he rambled on into the usual pious platitudes that ended his eulogy. At the end, assisted by the two younger priests, he came through the altar rails and sprinkled the coffin with Holy Water. Some of it spilled inadvertently on the nearest congregation, particularly Carmella and Joey.

'Hey,' Joey said, wiping his arm and knee, 'that's wet.'

'Amen.'

The procession made its very slow progress to the rear of the church, and the organ blared out the 'Dies Irae'. Two senior police officers stepped forward to assist Denis, Sean, Michael and Joey in the removal of the coffin, under the direction of the undertakers. Denis patiently instructed Joey in what to do and he and Michael kept him from talking too loudly. Sean looked back to Noreen as he left the pew. She nodded to him. As the coffin was lifted up on the shoulders of the men, Carmella stood and reached out her hand to touch its wood at Joey's shoulder.

'OK, Mamma?' he said.

'Oh, Mick,' she called. 'Oh, Mick, ne partire mi.' Every head bowed, except Noreen's. She rose and went to her aunt and put her arms round her shoulders. Carmella didn't react at first but then she looked up and saw who it was. Noreen held her gaze and her arm round her then Carmella reached up and patted her hand and turned her head away again. Both women watched as the coffin moved slowly away up the aisle, and gently, still with her arm around her, Noreen followed with Carmella. As she moved up, Noreen lifted her eyes to the choir stalls, as if in a signal, and the organ segued to a softer introduction to the Recessional Hymn. Then came a moment that electrified the congregation. It made its impact because it was so unexpected. For it was not the Police Choir that sang but seven-year-old Maria O'Neil. She sang solo against the humming of the male voices behind her and against the organ counterpoint. What the words were didn't matter. It was the sound the little girl made. Her pure unforced natural soprano soared into the air above them all and showered that hard school of auditors with a sprinkling of lovely notes that they turned into tears.

The scene at the graveyard was more than usually touching. Autumn had given the trees that extra golden lustre and the leaves that had already fallen lay round about the mourners' feet like a russet carpet. Liam Murphy stood at one side of the grave with a tiny white casket in his arms, and on the other side, Kevin O'Neil carried the same sad load. Canon Devlin intoned the burial service in a creaky Latin and pulled his long cloak tighter around him against the wind that sifted through the cemetery on the outskirts of Milltown. On either side of him stood Eugene Murphy, Liam's father and the children's grandad, and Tim, the barman, in his best clothes. Nobody noticed Sergeant Davidson standing by a tree nearby. Old Den stood at the opposite side of the grave with Tommy Drennan, each with a cord ready to help lay Celia and Dermot Murphy to rest.

An outbreak of scarlet fever had taken the nine-year-old twins in little more than a week. They were not the only children to die in the district and the Milltown cemetery was only one of several busy around that time in an awful traffic with children's white coffins. Celia, the younger by ten minutes, had always been the weaker, but it was Dermot who'd come home from school first, complaining of a sore throat. Nellie had put him to bed thinking it was a cold, then hearing of the scarlet fever in Newry through Tommy Drennan, she sent for Dr Nolan at once. He didn't come till the next day, he had so many calls, and all the same – sick children. By this time, Celia had the same throat and both were in the same bed for company. Nellie was convinced it would pass, even though she could feel that both children had high temperatures. Then next morning, both children had the rash, and Nellie sent Liam to fetch Dr Nolan from wherever he was. Liam complained that he had plenty to do with the new shop opening for him to be running around after doctors – 'just because a couple of kiddies are sick'. However, Nellie's nagging won the day and he agreed to go in his new Austin car and look for Dr Nolan.

Liam had joined his father, Eugene Murphy, in a series of newsagents' shops, which served as a cover for a very thriving bookmaking and betting business run from the back of each. Old Eugene had never worked in his life due to what he said was a bad heart, but he never lacked in daring and was never afraid to take a gamble. Fortunately, he had the luck and nearly always won, so he bought McLaughlin's old newsagents' in Hilltown as a front for his 'line'. In no time, he'd bought a second one for Liam in Milltown, and then a third in Warrenpoint and now Liam was just about to clinch a site in Newry. It would be Belfast and Dublin next, then Rosstrevor and the world.

Nellie would have liked Liam to have opened his next branch in New York, just to give her a chance of seeing her brothers and Noreen, but Liam had been adamant. 'Sure, we've got a fine life going here. What need have we of America? Aren't they all daft there?' There was no way she was going to get her husband to America, and Nellie would like to have gone. Just once. To see for herself. Letters from the States had been few and far between of late, although money from Sean still came from time to time. Only Paddy wrote to their mother and father on any kind of regular basis, but even he was busy with his new parish. Anyway it was not always easy for Nellie to get up to Rosstrevor as often as she'd like to catch up on any news. She understood from her mother on her last visit that Carmella had moved to New Jersey after Uncle Mick's death to be near her sister, and that Noreen was helping Sean and Michael in their new business. There was always a rumour that Noreen had had a baby to an Italian, but they had never heard the truth of it in Ireland. That's the way things go in families. Everybody gets on with their own lives and old links get used less and less till they're forgotten, and before you know it, people are dead and gone and it's too late. Nellie had hoped it would not be too late for her, and now this had to happen.

Liam had found Dr Nolan at Annie McAteer's house, Annie Fitzpatrick that she now was. She had always been the great friend of Noreen's and of Liam too in his young days. At that time, every girl was. Now she was a mother of five and the three young ones were all down with the fever. Fatally, as it turned out. Dr Nolan looked deadbeat as he came into the little bedroom at Milltown.

'Put out your tongues,' he said brusquely to the wee ones, who were sitting in their best night clothes, with their hair newly brushed. You had to be nice to see the doctor. It made little difference if a dreadful rash despoiled both little faces. As soon as he saw the tongues, he knew. He put the back of his hand on each forehead and asked Nellie if they'd complained about pains in the ear.

'Not really.'

'Well, either they have or they haven't, woman.'

'They haven't,' said Nellie firmly.

'And what about bed wetting?' Nellie blushed. The children had had a bad spell with that, but she thought it was over now.

'No, they don't –'

'Dermot did the other night,' said Celia righteously.

'Right,' said the doctor. 'Separate beds it is to minimise the infection, as much liquids as they can take, except milk. No milk under any circumstances.'

'And what about food, doctor? Will I –'

'If they want to eat, let them, but keep everyone away from them. No little friends visiting.' He was hurriedly packing his case while Liam fetched his coat.

'Is there anything else, doctor?' Nellie asked at the front door.

'Prayer,' said Dr Nolan tersely. 'Will you give me a lift back in your fancy motor car, Liam?'

'I will that, doctor.'

But prayer wasn't enough and Celia and Dermot Murphy died. The funeral service was a hurried one because of their condition. The coffin had to have an extra lining and the lid was screwed down earlier than it might have been, so that nobody could look on them dead, except the undertaker who came to the house and wore a mask and Liam who insisted on being with them all the time. Nellie wouldn't go near the room. She refused to look upon her two children dead. Perhaps that was why she still thought they were alive. She never cried at all. Indeed, she smiled. She smiled all the time, but it was a smile that put a chill in your heart.

The Temperance Army was on the march in the United States. More and more states were adopting laws which banned the sale of alcohol. Other places closed down saloons altogether, especially in Ohio. And in New York State, 315 towns banned saloons altogether. This was all part of a movement to prohibit the use of alcohol and the propagators began to be known as the Prohibitionists. Sean and Michael O'Neil could not be considered as such. They were known as Wets, and the Wets claimed that Prohibition would result in drinkers switching from drink to drugs. This problem was one that was confronting the brothers as they sat one late night at Rafferty's after everyone had gone. Sean was pacing up and down.

'We'll have to do something, Michael.'

'As you say, Sean,' said Michael, sipping happily on a full beer. Now that they were the owners of Rafferty's, they adjusted the rules sufficiently to allow themselves a drink after hours. Not that either of them were drinkers; one now and then was enough. They had seen enough of their father drunk and there had been a terrible scene at Uncle Mick's funeral when Denis got drunk and started arguing with them about their business practices. He'd been hearing things, Denis had said, and he wanted to know what was going on at Rafferty's. Mind you, he had told Sean he was speaking as a brother, not as a policeman, you understand. Although from his truculent manner, it was hard to see him as brotherly, but then Denis had been nearest to Uncle Mick. Why shouldn't he get drunk?

But why is it that there are always fights at family funerals. Especially Irish funerals. You've got to be awake at a wake, if you're to survive. Even the songs they sang on such occasions had a defiance in them, always remembering of course they had a drink in them at the time.

'Look at the coffin with golden handles
Isn't it grand boys to be bloody well dead?

Let's not have a sniffle, let's all have a bloody good cry,
And always remember the longer you live,
The sooner you'll bloody well die.'

Sean always had his wits about him and had tried to placate him by saying there was nothing they were doing at Rafferty's Bar that would offend a brother, or would concern a policeman. For some reason, Denis took offence at this, and was even more determined to 'get to the bottom of it all' as he put it. His voice was raised to a shout, 'You don't make the money at Rafferty's Bar for youse to dress like lords and drive a car.'

'Hey, that's poetry, Denis,' Michael commented. This remark had made Denis so mad he'd swung a punch at his young brother, and Michael, being used to that sort of thing at Rafferty's, easily avoided it. As a result Denis hit old Jock Lennox by accident, who fell on top of Pat Kelly and spilled his drink. Pat was so incensed he got up at once and hit Jock, and Mrs Lennox screamed. Jock then tried to hit Denis, who was still swinging at Michael, who didn't want to hit his big brother, and stumbled back into Sean, who jumped to one side and collided with Pat Kelly, knocking his next drink out of his hand! Pat was a big man and grabbed Sean and bundled him over the couch and into the laps of Mrs Kelly and Mrs Quinn who screamed blue murder. Before they all knew it, Carmella's front room was a chaos of flailing bodies, and a sea of broken glass. Joey stood in the door laughing his head off and Noreen peered over his shoulder, her hands over her mouth. Carmella was the only calm one, and picking her way through the shambles, she called the Police to sort it out! The boys hadn't seen Denis since.

'We'll have to be giving them cocaine instead of whiskey.'

'Ah, they wouldn't like that,' replied Michael. 'I mean you take a mug of cocaine at night before you go to bed.'

'That's cocoa, you idiot.'

'Well, same thing, it puts you to sleep,' said Michael, completely unfussed.

'The thing is we'll have to do something or we'll find we'll have to work for a living and we don't want to do that.'

'Heaven forbid!' agreed Michael.

'Right,' said Sean, 'we can do two things. We can sell up here altogether, or we don't.'

'That's two things right enough,' said Michel, pouring himself another beer.

'If we don't sell, we can lease the cellars to the Italians as they wanted. You remember that?'

'I do,' said Michael. 'That was Noreen's man.'

'Rico.'

'That's right. Didn't they have some idea of using our cellars as storage?'

'They did, Michael, but they also liked the fact that our cellars connected with next door, which connected with next door to that, which I believe led out to the East River.'

'Would you believe that?' said Michael. 'Isn't it extraordinary what goes on under your feet and you never know about it. You mean to say you could go down our steps there and if you keep goin' you'd come out on the water?'

'I do.'

'Then I move that we sell the cellar.'

'Why do ye say that, Michael?'

'Well, if you're tellin' me that our cellar leads out to the East River, then it follows that the East River leads to our cellar, and it could just happen that somebody would leave a door open somewhere, and we'd have the whole of the East River down round our feet.'

'Don't be daft, Michael. I mean that they have what they call "access" to the water, which means to the docks which means to the port which means to the open sea which means to the world. Do ye follow me?'

'Ah, you're a devious man, Sean. You've got me all at sea indeed.'

'Contraband, Michael. That's what it is. Contraband and the dope. They're into it already, you see. This Pro-hib-ition, or whatever they call it, is comin', you mark my words, or the Tally boys wouldn't be into other "arrangements", as they say, and lookin' to buy cellars and hidey-holes and places behind walls, if ye follow me. Now, you see, in Rafferty's here we could be sittin' on a gold mine.'

'Or a swimmin' pool,' said Michael.

'Not at all. If we go the right way about it, we could set ourselves up nice with a good little earner still in Rafferty's.'

'But you won't get your hands dirty, will ye, Sean? I mean there's Denis –'

'Sure, there's always Denis. No, Michael, I won't get me hands dirty. Nor, will I tell you, get me feet wet.'

'But listen, Sean.'

'What's that, Michael?'

'If you go in with this Rico lad –'

'Ay?'

'What will you say to Noreen?' Sean thought for a minute, then smiled at his brother.

'Nothin'.'

'But if you're goin' in with Rico?'

'Who says anythin' about goin' in with Rico?' He looked at his brother. Then Michael grinned.

'Ah, I see. Well then, I suppose I'd better learn to swim!'

TWENTY

The picture of the Child of Prague looked down in all its red and gold splendour on the framed photograph of the late Superintendent Michael O'Neal who smiled widely on three little blonde heads who should have been in their beds. But Jitka, Katya and Clara O'Neil, aged seven, four and two respectively, were taking every advantage of their father Denis, referred to by them as Pops, because their mother Hana was in the big bedroom on the first floor awaiting the arrival of her fourth child at any minute. The Brooklyn brownstone at 59/57th was formerly the home of the still-lamented Superintendent, but when Carmella and Joey had moved out to New Jersey, Hana and Denis and their three girls had moved in, glad of the extra room the Brooklyn brownstone provided. Clara had just been born then, and now, more or less on schedule, Hana was in labour again. Denis O'Neil was determined to keep going until he got that son!

It was St Patrick's Night, 1912, and Sergeant O'Neil had had a long day, what with the parade and all. He was tired already yet he knew he was in for an even longer night once he was home. Carmella would hardly have recognised her house now. Instead of her florid and much-ornamented, multi-coloured, Italian disorder there was a stark, severe Slavonic black-and-whiteness in the decoration of the house. Plain drapes replaced the flounced curtains and white paint covered the old, ornately wallpapered walls. No wonder Uncle Mick grinned as he looked down on the nearly-elegant sitting-room. He knew Carmella would have had a fit had she seen it. Not that his nephew Denis was in any better a mood as he chased his little women around the room.

'Come on kids,' he whined, 'Pops is tired.'

The girls continued to giggle and scream and run and hide and generally have fun with their father, whom they adored and knew they could do as they liked with – especially, Katya, the middle one and the liveliest.

'Gotcha!' He caught her behind the sofa and whirled her up in his arms.

270

'Me too! Me too!' yelled Clara, the two-year-old, who always had to have what Katya had. Denis dutifully bent down and Clara climbed on his back putting her little arms round his neck. Thus laden, and with eyes popping and face red, he motioned Jitka to go ahead and open the doors, which she did, and together, they climbed the stairs to the children's room at the back where Noreen used to sleep. Jitka turned and put her fingers to her lips as they came to the main bedroom and they tiptoed passed.

Hana was lying-in with Mrs Finklestein and Mrs Robovitch, who were the neighbourhood delivery and despatch team. They were expert in basic birth techniques and in the laying out of corpses. Mrs Finklestein was the midwife and Mrs Robovitch was her helper. They swopped roles for deaths in the street. There wasn't much the urban pair didn't know about life and death. They were street-wise in every respect. They had helped Clara into the world only the day after the O'Neils had moved in two years before and Denis knew his wife was in good hands. Her own mother was now living with her son who had married a Polish girl from Hoboken. It was too far for the old lady to come over. Denis was relieved. He liked Hana's mother well enough but she had just refused to learn any English at all, and every visit was a strain.

Speaking of strains, he was finding it was just that to get three little bundles of blonde mischief settled. How did Hana manage all the time? It would be different with boys, Denis thought. He desperately wanted a son to continue the O'Neil line, a line of Irish kings after all! And to be company for him in his old age among this sorority of Slavonic women he seemed to be siring. Surely this time? 'Come on Jitka, give me a hand with these two.'

Jitka, being the oldest was already in her own single bed, and the other two made the most of the other single with one at each end. They kept tickling each other's toes and would not settle. Denis made threatening noises, but they knew better than to take him seriously. Denis was the kind of man who was rarely taken seriously, especially by his own family, but he had to get these three down to sleep before anything started in the other room. He sat at the end of Jitka's bed, while she tried to lead her sisters in their song about St Wenceslas. Dear Jitka, she was always so serious and Katya so impudent, Clara so dreamy. Denis wondered sometimes if they came from the same father and mother. That reminded him. He gave a glance over his shoulders, but no sounds yet coming from the bedroom, only the occasional snatch of Yiddish as Mrs Finklestein conferred with Mrs Robovitch. My dear Hana he thought. What a wonderful wife she has been. He didn't care when it happened, as long as it did and that Hana would be alright again. They say the fourth child is the most dangerous. Now how would I know that, he thought. Still, he hoped she'd be alright. A man felt so helpless at such a time. As long as it was a boy. If he was born before midnight, he would be called Patrick. After that, any name would do, as long as it was a boy's name. Denis, he supposed, keeping up the first son tradition. Denis, the third.

'Come on now, Pops, it's your turn now,' said Jitka.

'Yes, your turn, your turn,' chorused the other two shrilly, bobbing up and down in the bed.

'Quiet! OK. OK.' And taking a breath, he sang softly:

'Let him go, let him tarry, let him sink, or let him swim
He never cared for me nor I don't care for him.
He can go and love some other girl and wed her if he can
For I'm going to marry a far better man.'

They squealed with delight as though they hadn't heard it a hundred times before. Denis raised his hands.

'Quiet, girls, you'll waken your mother.'

'She's not asleep,' said Jitka.

'She's making our little sister,' said Katya.

'Who said?' asked Denis.

'Jitka,' replied Katya at once, and laughed, putting her head under the sheets.

'Bye-bye,' said Clara, doing the same.

'Come on now, girls,' said Denis, leaning over to them, 'it's getting late and Pops is tired.'

'You can sleep with me,' said Katya.

'No, me,' said Clara.

'No,' said Denis, 'Pops sleeps with Mama.'

'Not tonight,' said Jitka, gravely with all her seven-year-old wisdom. Denis found himself a little abashed, and rose to cover his embarrassment.

'No, Jitka, maybe not tonight.'

''nother song Pops please!' whimpered Katya.

'Yes, please!' echoed Clara in exactly the same intonation.

'Pops can't sing,' Denis pleaded.

'I know,' said Katya, 'but just one.'

'Just one,' added Clara. He looked at Jitka. She shrugged. He knew he would have to go through with the nightly ritual. So once again, in the same quiet voice. Denis was no singer.

'Hurrah, me boys, hurrah! No more I wish for to roam,
For the sun it will shine in harvest time
To welcome our Paddy home –'

272

Just then Mrs Robovitch appeared at the bedroom door. 'Mrs Finklestein says maybe you should the doctor get.' Denis was already on his way downstairs. . .

Anna Patricia O'Neil was born at a quarter after two the next morning, so Denis didn't get his Patrick after all, nor even his Denis, but he got his much-loved and hard-worked Hana back and for that he was grateful. It had been a hard labour. Anna had come into the world feet first and it took all the experience of Mrs Finklestein and the skill of the young Dr Arlen, who had come back at once with Denis, to turn the baby round without strangling the little thing with its own cord. Denis had sat downstairs in the sitting-room while it was going on, praying fervently to the Child of Prague, or was it to Uncle Mick, to protect his little European wife from all her pain and bring her safely through. Oddly enough, he never gave a thought to the child being born with such difficulty; he could only think of his wife. But now it was all over and he sat in the big armchair as dawn lightened the front windows and gave thanks, with a cup of coffee, to the Child of Prague high on the opposite wall. The Child Christ King with two fingers raised and an orb in his left hand and a circlet of stars around his crowned head. It was Hana's picture, and she had brought it from Prague herself. It was one of the first things she put on the wall when they re-decorated the house. She wasn't pleased when he put Uncle Mick's picture below it. He raised his coffee cup to both of them, and he could have sworn that Uncle Mick in the frame below grinned even wider.

Liam Murphy knew he had to do something about Nellie. She had been strange at the funeral, and even stranger in the two years that had passed. She insisted on putting out the clothes for the children each morning and preparing meals for them as usual. It was weird and it was getting Liam down. Dr Nolan said it was just shock and she would get over it in time, but it was hard to live with just the same. What was even more worrying was that she had never cried and even when he remonstrated with her and told her bluntly that their two children were dead and buried she just smiled and turned away. She was always smiling, that was the worst thing.

'You don't think she's mad, do you, Dr Nolan?'

'If you lost both your children, wouldn't you be mad?' the doctor had said.

'But they were my children, too.'

'You're not the mother.' He had taken her up to see her own mother, and Nessie, to his surprise, humoured her in her chatter about Celia and Dermot. When Liam managed to get a word with

her alone, she said the less fuss they made about it the sooner Nellie
would get over it.

'What she needs,' said Nessie, 'is a good cry.'

'I know what you mean,' said Liam.

It was his father gave him the idea. Old Eugene had taken to his
bed. The last heart attack had been a big one, and he wasn't able to
shrug it off this time. Dr Nolan had said he would wash his hands
of him if he didn't rest up properly.

'So who wants a doctor with dirty hands,' said Eugene and
agreed to rest up. When Liam had gone to see him, the old man
asked about Nellie.

'Has she broke yet?' he said.

'Not a sign of it, Da.'

'Ah, there's the pity. What she might need is a good fright. If it
was a shock that made her quiet, it'll be a shock'll bring her round
again.' What he suggested gave his son a shock. 'I think you should
take her to Amerikay.'

'What?'

'Give her a bit of a break. Yourself too. A holiday would do
it.'

'A holiday, is it? When would I have the time the way things are
and you on your back?'

'There's always time, Liam. That's the funny thing, and then you
find there isn't enough. That's even funnier.'

'And for another thing, where would I get the money?'

'I'll give you it.'

'But you don't have it. It's all tied up in the shops.'

'Not all of it. I used to keep what I called me tithe.'

'Oh, you did, did you?'

'Ay, it's where an ignorance of good book-keeping stands you
in good stead.'

'And where is this money then?'

'Ah, that would be tellin' now. But I'll not have to reach out too
far to put my hands on it.'

'Tell me, Da, an' I'll – '

'I'll tell ye nothin'. Jus' you go into Newry and make enquiries
about that fancy new boat that's all the talk of the papers. I was
readin' about it only yesterday. It's going to make a try for the
fastest Atlantic crossing.'

'The Titanic?'

'That's it. The Titanic.'

'See what it would cost for a couple of places on her?'

'But I don't like sailing,' said Liam.

'But do ye like Nellie?' said the old man.

So the arrangements were made with the White Star line and unbeknown to Nellie, Liam eventually did get two reservations on the new ship, which was brought down from Liverpool to Southampton, where most of the passengers got on, and then to Cherbourg to pick up some more and finally to Queenstown before crossing the Atlantic to New York. Liam thought it would be best to join the Irish passengers at the latter port of call. It would save time and a little bit of money. Not that money seemed to be a problem. He didn't know where his father got it from, but there was plenty of it. So who was Liam to worry? As the day of their embarkation drew closer, he had to confess to feeling just a little excited. What annoyed him though was that he had to make most of the preparations. Nellie seemed to drift through each day starting a lot of things and never finishing them, and doing an awful lot of washing. She was always washing. Especially the children's clothes. She even packed a bag for each for them. Liam just decided to ignore it all and hope for the best.

They were to take the car to Newry on the morning of 10th April. Someone from McLaughlin's old shop would come and pick it up. Then Liam and Nellie would take the bus to Belfast, then the train to Dublin, where they would stay overnight at the Gresham Hotel. That would be like a holiday in itself. In the morning, the shipping line said there would be a special connecting train that would bring them and the other 180 Irish passengers to the ship at Queenstown in time for the sailing.

He tried to get Nellie interested in all the arrangements. 'Do ye know,' he said, 'there are more than two thousand of us and that's not counting the crew.' But Nellie only smiled. When the morning came, he had a terrible job getting the Austin started with the handle.

'I hope this isn't an omen,' he muttered. Nellie had packed the two children's bags and left them at the door. He quietly took them to the back of the house before they left. Eventually they got away, but they had got hardly a hundred yards down the road when she suddenly screamed out, 'We've left them.'

'Left what?' he yelled over the noise of the engine and the wind.

'The bags. The children's bags.' She kept on and on about them until he had no option but to brake hard, and with a great deal of difficulty in that narrow lane, turn the vehicle around and go back. Sheepishly he collected them from the back door and they started out again.

'We'll miss that bus,' he muttered. They almost did, because they had difficulty finding a man in the shop who could drive the car. Luckily the bus itself was delayed, and so they got themselves on board. Liam wasn't sure, but he had the feeling Nellie was beginning to take an interest, and was even enjoying herself as they sat in the bus. He asked if she was looking forward to the sea voyage.

'Oh, I am,' she said, 'and the children will love it too.' He sighed and looked out of the window. When they got to the railway station in Belfast, things got even worse.

'Where are they?' she said.

'Who?'

'Celia and Dermot.'

'Oh, Nellie.'

'I'm sure I saw them.'

'We'll have to get on the train.'

'I'm not going without them.'

'But, Nellie –'

'Say what you like. I'll have to find them.' And off she went into the crowd waiting at the platform until she was lost to sight. 'Nellie!' he cried. He had just got most of their luggage on board and now was in a dilemma. Should he continue getting it on, then go for her. Or should he just take it off again and hope that she'd come back in time. He felt a tugging at the case he was holding, and it was the porter, trying to take it from him.

'You'll want it on, sir.'

'What?'

'The case, sir. You'll want it on the train.'

'Oh, I don't know.'

'Please yourself. Will that be it then, sir?'

'What?'

'Your luggage?'

'Yes. I mean, no. Damn! Get it all off!'

'What's that?'

'Get it all off! I'll give you yer shillin'.'

'As you say, sir.' And the six pieces of luggage, two large, two medium and two small, were taken off again and laid on the platform. The porter got his shilling and Liam waited. He waited as the rest of the passengers boarded. He waited as the final farewells were taken, and he was still waiting as the train pulled away. And when the platform emptied, he could see at the very end of it, a forlorn figure sitting all by herself.

'Oh, Nellie!' he said softly, and with a great well of pity in his voice. He sighed and started to walk towards her.

Nothing much was said. Nellie seemed to have forgotten everything, even her children, and Liam wondered whether he would get his money back. He had toyed with the idea of taking her to Dublin anyway, but they had had a rocky road enough already and perhaps she would be better at home. Instead of Queenstown, they stayed in the Queen's Hotel that night in Belfast, and it was lunchtime the next day before they got back to Newry. Liam wondered why there were such long faces to greet him at the shop. It was only when they found the man who had taken the car back that the shop manager told him.

'Mr Murphy?'

'Yes.'

'Mr Murphy's dead.'

Liam thought long afterwards of the strangeness of those few days, and how he was brought back from what was to be a trip to America, just in time to arrange his own father's funeral. If Nellie hadn't gone looking for the children. . . . If the children hadn't died . . . If his father hadn't suggested a holiday? So many ifs. Life is full of them, but they only make sense when you look back on them. Everyone can see clearly enough with hindsight.

It was a modest kind of a funeral at old Eugene's specific request. Liam found a letter, which the old man had written just after Liam's mother's own death the year before.

'I don't want all that palava,' he had written. 'And I would never rest easy, knowing all that good money was thrown away on show, and to get people drunk at my funeral who owed me money, when I was livin'. So I just want a plain box and a plain stone, and a plain speech from the priest, and you can do what you like with the business. By the way, if you have need of extra funds, you can look under my bed.' And under the bed, Liam found a leather box full of banknotes!

Liam Murphy was now what could be called in any circumstances a rich man. He was a wealthy man however with a sick wife, and in this, he thought he was unfortunate, but really he didn't know how lucky they both were. For at the very time he was sitting alone in the house, in the early hours of the morning of the funeral day, reading again his father's will, the most modern ship in the world, the SS Titanic, was going down stern first, with all its lights blazing into the icy waters of the North Atlantic. The unthinkable had happened. The unsinkable had sunk, and taken with it half of its passengers and crew. A loss of more then 1,500 lives. Of the 180 Irish passengers who boarded at Queenstown, only twenty were saved.

*

It was sink or swim for Noreen O'Neil – 'The Singing Sensation from Ireland' – or 'The Sweet Colleen wearin' the Green' – as the posters outside the South Broad Street Theatre in Philadelphia proclaimed. This was a Monday night and the early show of a week's run in a tour which would take her round the Eastern States, and hopefully into New York for the spring of 1913, that is if audiences took to her in this first week. This was to be her try-out. It was all Sean's idea. He remembered how she'd sung for the passengers on the ship and how they'd all liked her. He got her in to see an agent who was a friend of Jock Lennox, and he had arranged an appointment with a producer who was sending out a show with the American Ragtime Octette and Cissie Loftus the impressionist, as well as The Ramblers, a famous juggling act, and an Australian called Pansy Montague, who toured as La Milo, an exponent of the art of living statues. The Scholtz Twins, a brother and sister musical act, was also on the bill and Rose and Bernie shared the same theatrical lodgings with Noreen and Maria at the Benson Theatre Home from Home off Vine Street. The Scholtz act was on stage now, Rose on the saxophone and Bernie at the piano. It may also be mentioned that Rose was also on roller skates! They were building up to a strong finish with 'The Skater's Waltz' and Noreen knew her number would go up next. Her palms were sweating as she stood in the wings in her best green dress waiting for them to come off so that she could get on. Part of her was wishing they would hurry up and the other part was hoping they'd take forever! Hell, let's get it over with, she thought. I've only got two songs, and an encore – just in case. There was a flourish of the saxophone, a twirl and a curtsy from Rose, a rise and a bow from Bernie and a scatter of faint applause from what seemed a very distant audience, and then there were Rose and Bernie almost on top of her, snarling at each other about something, going off into the darkened wings arguing at the top of their voices. They always had an argument at the end of their act.

'Quiet please in the wings!' hissed the Stage Manager.

'Sorry!' yelled Bernie, disappearing through the pass door to the dressing rooms.

Meantime the band had struck with Noreen's entry music and, taking a deep breath, she stepped out into the lights. And almost immediately she wished she hadn't. The air was cold on stage, the little orchestra seemed to be down a mine and all she could see was a very small bald head and a very long baton. The audience too seemed miles away and only a few coughs could be heard. Noreen felt her feet were in lead boots and there was no feeling in her hands at all. As for her voice, it seemed to be down at her elbow somewhere, and it was only by a kind of automatic reflex that she was singing at all:

> 'I know my love by his way of walking
> And I know my love by his way of talking
> And I know my love dressed in jersey blue
> And if my love leaves me what will I do?'

What will I do indeed, she thought? Mammy, Daddy, I feel the right fool up here like this!

> 'And still she cried "I love him the best
> And a tiring mind can know no rest."
> And still she cried "Bonny boys are few
> And if my love leaves me what shall I do?"'

Her internal agitation was greater than the poised picture she presented. Noreen O'Neil looked good as she pranced across that stage to the catchy Irish tune. It was a song she had known since she was a child and she'd heard her mother sing it a thousand times. She repeated it now almost like a child, and for a woman of thirty-two with a child of her own, she looked astonishingly childlike herself. This sympathy may have explained the level of applause she got at the end of her opening song, so that she came more confidently to centre for her second. Noreen had a small voice and relied on people listening to it for its full effect. Thanks to her appealing appearance the Philadelphia audience gave her the benefit of the doubt and listened.

> 'I'm bidding farewell to the land of my youth,
> And the home I love so well.
> And the mountains so grand in my own native land,
> I'm bidding them all farewell.
> With an aching heart I'll bid them adieu
> For tomorrow I'll sail far away,
> O'er the raging foam for to seek a home
> On the shores of Amerikay.'

She came off to a reasonable round. Perhaps it was her choice of material, or the fact that it was a big theatre. She knew she hadn't won them completely.

'Gotta give it more second house,' said the Stage Manager, as she passed. 'It's a big space. Ya gotta belt it out, lady.'

'Sure, Fred,' she said and hurried past on her way to the dressing room. If she were quick, she could get back to Benson's place and check that Maria was alright with Mrs Benson. She paid an extra dollar a week for Mrs Benson to put Maria to bed and keep an eye on her, but somehow she didn't think that Mrs Benson was all that reliable as a child-watcher. She didn't know if there was a Mr Benson. At least she'd never seen one. Bernie Scholtz passed her on the iron stairs as she was hurrying out.

'You goin' back to the digs, Noreen?'

'Yea,' she said. 'I've got to see Maria.'

'I'll come with you. Could do with the air.'

'That's nice o' you, Bernie.'

'Don't mention it.'

Bernie Scholtz was a youngish, good-looking Jewish boy, but there was a weakness in his face. Noreen had noticed it right away, but couldn't put her finger on it. All the same he seemed popular backstage and the girls liked him, but he didn't seem to bother much about them. Nor about his sister, Rose, either. For a brother and sister act, there was certainly no love lost between them. The only time they spoke was to quarrel, and in the dressing room and round the dining-room at the Benson's Theatre Home from Home they rarely sat beside each other. However, he was obliging enough and she was glad of his company as she hurried through the Philadelphia streets towards the lodging house.

When they got there, Maria was sitting on the piano stool in the parlour, picking out a song on the keys and trying to sing along with her halting one finger accompaniment, 'Jol-ly Go-od Luck to the Gi-rl Who Lo-ves a Sol-dier'. This was one of the songs Cissie Loftus sang in her impersonation of Vesta Tilley. When Maria heard her mother come in, she jumped up with a squeal and ran to her. At ten years of age, she was a dark-haired miniature of her red-haired mother, a striking little girl in every respect, and promising to be something of a beauty.

'Ma, you wanna hear me sing my song?'

'Not now, darlin'. It's time for your bed.'

'Oh, let her sing her song, Noreen. She looks cute.' Bernie was standing still with his coat on, staring at the little girl. Maria moved at once to her mother. Maria didn't like Bernie.

'OK,' said Noreen. 'You sing for Uncle Bernie.'

'He's not my uncle.'

'Well, you can still sing for me,' said Bernie, 'if I give you a dime.' He proffered the coin. Maria hesitated. 'Could buy you a candy,' he said.

'Maybe she's tired,' said Noreen. But Maria was already back up to the piano stool. She was an instinctive professional. '"Jolly Good Luck to the Girl Who Loves a Soldier".' Whether it was the incentive of the dime or the desire to get it over, there was little hesitation this time, and her hand shot out imperiously at the end of it. Bernie dropped the coin into the podgy little palm, and leaning into her precocious face, said,

'Don't I get a little kiss?'

'No, you don't Bernie,' said Noreen, lifting the child up and carrying her out. Bernie shrugged and removed his coat.

The second house went a little better, but not much. She tried to belt it out as Fred, the Stage Manager, had advised, but Noreen wasn't a belter and the heavier second house didn't warm to her as much, nor did she to them. By the Thursday night, she was getting tired and it didn't look as if the try-out week was going to be a success. It was not really the money. Mamma d'Agostino made sure that something came from Rico every month, and Sean and Michael looked after most things anyway. But she needed to do something with her life. What she didn't want to admit was that she needed a man in it. But she liked being taken care of, without being smothered. She enjoyed the freedom, but she dreaded being lonely. Noreen, frankly, wanted her cake and to eat it as well. The theatre experiment was no more than that – an experiment. She would see out the contract if they would have her, and then consider how things were at the end of it. Even in three mediocre nights in Philadelphia, she won her admirers. Cards and flowers had already come to the stage door, and Bernie was making mocking remarks at every opportunity. Bernie himself was becoming quite fond of her and Noreen thought he saw more of her than of his sister. Rose, on the other hand, seemed to prefer the company of the dancing girls, especially a little Milwaukee German-speaking dancer called Gerda. Rose, you see, was a lesbian, although Noreen didn't know that. Few people did. Perhaps not even Rose did. But Gerda did.

Noreen was kept on after the try-out week, but she knew that was only on the strength of Fred, the Stage Manager's sympathetic report, and for the fact that she got on well with everyone in the company, especially Bernie. The next week they were in Trenton, New Jersey, before going up to Hartford in Connecticut. Noreen used these weeks to polish her act and 'sell' the songs as Bernie had said she should. She managed so well that on the Wednesday in Hartford she even got her encore, which she had rehearsed and never had the chance to perform, 'The Last Rose of Summer'. It was a little ambitious for her, but the audience knew it and she got by.

Maria kept asking to be taken to the theatre. But Noreen kept saying she was too young, and should be in her bed. She should also be at school, and Noreen threatened to send her back to Uncle Michael who would take her to school every day, if she didn't stop going on about coming to the theatre. So Maria remained at home, or rather at whatever lodgings Noreen found in the town they were playing. And Bernie came too. And Rose of course. And, after a time, Gerda. They made quite a little group at train call: the mother and daughter, the two women friends and the altogether too amiable Bernie. As the weeks went by, Noreen was thrown more and more together with him, but nothing happened, and even Maria was learning to like him a little bit. Not that the Scholtzs liked each other any better. If they were really brother and sister, they were a strange pair, but that was nobody's business but their own, and like all the other members of the company, Noreen just let them get on with it. Never mind, the dates were going in and the last few weeks of the tour in the Eastern states were coming up.

It was at Binghampton that the first incident occurred. It was Sunday and they had all found rooms in a commercial apartment house. For some reason, Noreen had a suite on the first floor. She couldn't afford it, and Bernie offered to pay his share. Noreen wasn't sure.

'You can always lock the door,' he said with a grin. So they took it. She had gone out to the drug store to get a bottle of milk for Maria's bedtime cocoa, and when she got back to the suite, Bernie was in her section taking off Maria's dress. The girl was standing in bloomers and liberty bodice.

'I was just getting her ready for bed, it being so late and all,' he said without turning a hair. Noreen felt alarm and anger, but she couldn't say anything. Maria wasn't complaining. All she did was hold out her hand and say, 'Look, Ma, Bernie gave me another dime.' Noreen kept a closer eye on Maria after that. But there were no incidents of any kind, although Bernie's familiarity with the little girl seemed to grow as each day passed.

On the next Monday they were at Easton and Noreen was last in the band call. Two new acts had come into the show and they needed all the orchestra time they could get before going into Scranton. So Noreen was later home than usual. This time Bernie was giving Maria a bath! Walking back to the theatre that night, Noreen was extremely tense and said little. She gave a very indifferent performance, and walking home, Bernie asked her, 'What's the matter, baby?' She suddenly stopped and rounded on him.

'I'll tell you what's the matter. Maria's the matter. I don't want

you dressing her. I don't want you undressing her. And I certainly
don't want you giving her a bath. You understand that?'

'Come on,' he said. 'She's a big girl now.'

'She's ten years old, for Chrissake!' This was shouted so loudly
that passers-by reacted and Bernie put his hand out to her.

'Say, baby –' She hit it away ferociously.

'Take your hand off me. And keep your hands off Maria. She's
my baby. And I don't want you to as much as speak to her from
now on. Get me?'

'But, Noreen –' But Noreen was already walking away as fast
as she could in the direction of the apartment house.

From then on, Noreen took Maria everywhere with her, even
to the theatre. This, of course, delighted the child and every night
she stood in the wings performing everybody's act with them, and
even at the end of two shows, she was as bright in the dressing
room as she'd been at the overture. Perhaps because of all this
extra strain, the tour did not go well for Noreen after this. In fact,
things went rather badly. So bad that Noreen was called in to the
Stage Manager's office one morning. Fred was very solemn.

'Noreen,' he began, 'we all just love ya, lady, but you ain't doin'
the business.' Sitting in the swivel stool at his little desk in the
theatre, Noreen could only bow her head. 'Look lady, I've given ya
all the rope I could and I guess you jus' plumb hung yourself. We
got two new acts in. We gotta get this show right before we go into
New York. And Scranton's our last chance. There'll be new acts
coming in yet and there'll be acts goin' before we hit 42nd Street.
By the way, the Scholtzs leave Saturday.' Noreen looked up.

'Oh?' For some reason she felt a little disappointed for them.

'I know you two don't get on now, so you won't break your
heart about that. But you're gonna be next if you don't pull
something out by second show Saturday yourself. I told the boss
I would report to him Monday. OK?'

'OK.'

'Ya got three days, lady.'

'Thank you, Fred.'

'And, lady –' His voice stopped her at the door. She turned.

'Yes?' She felt like crying, but she knew she wouldn't.

'There was once a hell of a lot of work done by someone we
know in three days.' And his finger was pointing up to the ceiling.
Yes, and she went, immediately feeling lighter.

During the show that night, she tried so hard in the second song,
which was now 'The Last Rose of Summer' that her voice cracked
on 'No rosebud is nigh'. The orchestra ground to an embarrassed
halt and the audience was completely silent, as if not believing

it. Noreen bowed her head blushing in shame and was about to walk off when the song was taken up by a voice in the wings and out stepped Maria in her best dress to finish the song, 'To reflect back her blushes or give sigh for sigh'. The ten-year-old continued with all the aplomb of a veteran diva. As the orchestra took up the refrain once more, she came to take her mother's hand at centre stage, and sang as if it was the most natural thing in the world.

'I'll not leave thee, thou lone one, to pine on the stem,
Since the lovely are sleeping, go sleep thou with them.
Thus kindly I scatter thy leaves o'er thy bed,
Where thy mates of the garden lie scentless and dead.'

The audience cheered. Noreen cried. Maria jumped up and down, and even Fred, standing in the prompt corner, applauded and threw his hat into the air. He indicated that Maria should take a bow. Noreen pushed her forward. Maria went gladly. Noreen stood back, biting her lip to watch, as the applause still rang out for Maria. Noreen turned to the prompt corner and caught the Stage Manager's eye. He was grinning from ear to ear and pointing his finger up to the flies.

TWENTY-ONE

The summer of 1913 was a good one – especially for the Keiths and the Mackenzies in New Zealand. Things had gone well for both families over the past few seasons and each farm was thriving. The boys of both houses, Billy Keith who was now seven and Sandy Mackenzie, five, and his young brother Stuart, or Stu, who was three, were growing up strong and healthy under the sun. The only girl, Roberta, or Berta, as the family called her, was the same age as her cousin Sandy and although 'chesty' as they said, she was certainly spirted enough, and more than kept up with all the boys. She kept wishing her mother would have a sister for her, but Jean Keith was in no great hurry to oblige.

Nevertheless, during the winter of 1909 she had become pregnant again at almost exactly the same time as Tina did with her second son, Stu. The sisters-in-law used to refer to themselves as Mary and Elizabeth, but they were never quite sure which was which, although big Bruce Mackenzie was quite sure – 'that there was nothing bloody immaculate about Tina's conception, I can tell you that!' Jim was more apt to consider that with both farms pretty much under control there really wasn't much else to do! Whatever the way of it, Tina was a month ahead of Jean and had Stu with little trouble in her own bedroom instead of going into the hospital at Gore as she'd done with Sandy. Mrs Keith, Senior, who had been staying with Jim and Jean during Tina's confinement, then came back in the trap with Bruce to take up her old room at the Mackenzie's again, and to help Hilda look after the house and wee Billy. Not that she did much of either. She said she was tired after the journey!

When Jean's turn came for her third, she fully expected it to be as straightforward as Billy and Berta, but in the last week she got a lot of bleeding. So much so, that the doctor, who was new to the district, thought that for safety's sake, Jim should take her into the hospital at Invercargill. The bleeding persisted and Jean was very weak when Jim left her at the maternity ward.

'Should I wait?' he asked the nurse.

285

'I'll have to ask the doctor,' she said, and left him standing in the bare corridor. It was a senior nurse who came out to him.

'Mr Keith?'

'Yes?'

'Mrs Keith is very sick.'

'I thought she was pregnant,' said Jim, trying to keep his voice steady. The nurse looked at him keenly, then indicated left.

'We have a waiting room, Mr Keith. Perhaps you'd like to –'

'I'd like to see my wife.'

'That would not be possible, I'm afraid. The doctor is with her now.'

'Then I'd like to see the doctor,' said Jim, meeting her eye. The burly nursing sister was just as firm.

'If you'd like to wait.' She pointed again to the left. Jim waited.

He waited a long time, and when the young doctor finally came out, it was almost dark. Jim could nonetheless tell by his anxious face that something was wrong. He stood up, and his heart was beating fast.

'I'm sorry Mr Keith. We've lost the baby.'

'And Jean?'

'She's fine – well, she's tired let's say. It was –'

'I'm not really interested, Doctor. I know you did your best.'

The doctor said nothing. Jim had to swallow hard. 'When can I take her home?'

'She'll need a bit of a rest. I've given her something –'

'Of course. I'll be back in the morning.' And Jim went out and got drunk in Invercargill with a man he'd met at the last A&P show, Bill McKirdy, and he stayed with Bill that night to sleep it off. It was actually two days before he was allowed to bring Jean home. They were a very sober pair as they set out again for Gore. Neither said much.

'Was it a girl?' Jim asked Jean eventually as they drove home in the cart.

'Yes.' There was a long pause before Jim spoke again.

'You going to tell Berta?' Another pause.

'No.' That night, Bruce came up to Gore and got Jim drunk again.

All that was three years ago, and Jean had soon got over it, but now Tina was pregnant again and showing it, much to the amusement of Sandy and Stu. Old Florence had left as usual for East Gore to stay with Jim and Jean and ostensibly to clear her verandah room for Tina and the new baby, but really everyone knew it was to get out of the way before all the excitement. 'Excitement is very tiring at my age,' she said.

Ross John Mackenzie was born without any complications, and took his place at the end of the Mackenzie line. A new generation was taking root, and certainly a more fortunate lot than their British counterparts whom Jim and Tina had left behind. Florence Keith still got the *Forres, Nairn and Elgin Gazette* from John regularly. And apart from football results and local scandals, most of the stories seemed to deal with dock riots, railway strikes, suffragettes throwing themselves under horses, derelicts in the London embankment and half a million children ill-fed and diseased. If anything was an inducement to emigration, reading the paper was. Life in New Zealand was hard for the original settlers, but not quite as hard for Bruce and Jim's generation, and it looked as if it might be a veritable paradise for the children's. Yes, the summer of 1913 was a sunny one in every sense of the word.

The big occasion for country folk was the A&P Show. Most people had their own Agricultural and Produce Show and the main one for the Mackenzies and the Keiths was the big Gore Show. Everybody came, because it was a great day out for the family. As well as a chance for the farmers and traders to do business, it was an opportunity to meet old friends and to make new ones. It was a mixture of agricultural show, horse show, trade exhibition, Highland Games and garden fête. It had a bit of all of these things rolled into one and best of all, on the last day it had the races. This was a chance not only to see some sport, but to make some extra money, and many a good profit made on a good deal on the Friday was lost on a poor horse on the Saturday. Similarly, if you hadn't been lucky in the market, one lucky bet could send you home the richer by a season's takings, if you could spot an outsider. Jim Keith was particularly adept at this, and everybody sought his advice. Naturally he didn't give everything away. He had to keep the prices up. Bruce was not so lucky, but in this particular year, he had a good week with his stock prices and could afford to lose a few shillings on the nags as he called them.

The children loved the hectic activity of the day, and it was difficult to keep track of where the boys were at any one time. Little Stu stayed with the women most of the time, and Ross was in the pram, but Billy and Sandy went wild. Berta, as usual, tried to keep up with them, and Jean noticed she was becoming breathless. 'You take care, Berta, girl.'

'I'll be jake, mum,' but Jean wasn't so sure, and kept an eye on her as the day progressed. There was a little merry-go-round and primitive swings for the children, but it was a wonderful playground for the Keith and Mackenzie offspring, and while the two fathers were winning and losing money at the races and the mothers were scrutinising the cakes and clothes stalls, Berta kept up with her brothers in and out the sideshows. Like most families the Keiths and Mackenzies had brought picnics, and they decided to have theirs in the paddock where the Highland Games were being held. They could listen to the pipe bands and Tina liked watching the Highland dancers on the raised platform. It reminded her nicely of home, and Mrs Keith particularly enjoyed the solo competitions. She had her own chair brought to that particular paddock right at the start of the day and never moved until it was time to go home.

It was while they were sitting on the grass *en famille* watching the Highland dancing that Jean first noticed Berta. The little girl was on her own a few yards from the rug where she had been sitting eating some moments before. Jean nudged Jim.

'Look,' she said. 'Berta thinks she's a Highland dancer.' Jim looked over and smiled as his daughter made rather ungainly attempts to emulate the lively young girls above her, but then as he watched he became slightly concerned, because her movements became even more ungainly and then spasmodic, and then jerky until her head was nodding, her legs shooting out in a frenzy, her arms twitching, and she fell, uttering a loud cry, which was so strong and unreal, that it stilled the noise of the bagpipes and everyone looked to see what was happening. Jim ran to her. She was no longer writhing, but lay on the ground, rigid, and seemed to be choking. Her face became blue, the veins in her neck swelled up and the pupils of her eyes were huge. Suddenly the convulsions started again, and her legs and arms moved in violent, jerking spasms.

'Get her tongue, her tongue!' Florence Keith cried out. Jim reached into her mouth and prised it open enough to pull the tongue forward. He was amazed at how difficult it was, but gradually it eased as she eased, and he noticed that she had wet her dress. He lifted her up and felt her nearly rigid in his arms.

'Take her to the cart,' whispered Jean.

'Poor wee Berta. She's had a fit,' said Tina.

'It's the falling sickness,' said Mrs Keith quietly. But Jim knew as he carried his daughter through the crowd that now circled them, that Berta was an epileptic.

Everyone turned up at the 42nd Street Theatre that night to see Noreen make her New York debut. The only thing was that it wasn't Noreen. It was Maria. News of the child's intervention on stage at Scranton had spread through show business and some of the vaudeville columns had picked it up. There was quite a run on the unfashionable theatre's box office but it didn't take old Fred by surprise.

'We gotta star,' he had said. Noreen's role had diminished to little more than a chaperone for Maria. The act was now billed as 'The Singing O'Neils – Noreen and Mary – a Colleen and a Colleenette!' Maria had become Mary because the management thought it sounded more Irish. Maria objected strongly but Noreen had said it would only be for a little while until she went back to school in New York, now that Noreen had money enough to get them their own place. She needn't rely any more on Rico – or her brothers, she could be entirely independent. But she reckoned without the impact her daughter was to make.

The act now took the form of a double act. Noreen would come on first as before with her song – and then be joined by 'Mary' who would take the melody while Noreen harmonised and then Maria would conclude with a solo – usually 'The Last Rose of Summer' – and they would finish together with 'Let Him Go Let Him Tarry', another of the O'Neil family songs which both knew backwards. It was noticeable to everyone that audiences much preferred the little girl on her own and as Fred said, she was the 'star'. There had even been a phone call the previous day from one of the new Moving Picture companies asking if 'Mary O'Neil' would like to come out to California? All Maria wanted was to get back to Mrs Lennox and old Jock again. She loved singing, and being on stage, but she hated the travelling. Six months had been too long and she wanted to be home. Noreen felt much the same so it was with great relief that for the New York engagement they could at least travel in from Queen's each day and sleep in their own beds at night. First, however, there was an opening to get through. The difference from six months before was that The O'Neils were near the end of the first half instead of being just after the opening. This also meant that they could get away earlier at night after the show, as they didn't need to wait for the curtain. Noreen was also worried about having Maria up so late – she was after all, just turned eleven.

The O'Neils occupied most of the first row of the circle. Denis was there with Hana, Jitka, Katya and Clara. Anna had been left with old Mrs Finklestein. Mr and Mrs Lennox were there in style and enjoying just being in the circle instead of up in the gallery where most of Rafferty's regulars were. Carmella was there with Joey and her sister Rosa and her husband Mario Malcase, in from New Jersey. They had also brought Father Paddy in from his parish, and he had brought Father Donnelly who had invited Bishop Monaghan, but he had declined, saying he was a bit too geriatric these days for modern vaudeville and ragtime singing. The old

Bishop didn't know what he missed. The O'Neils were anything but ragtime. Their infectious Irish rhythms and lilting harmonies captivated the house, but when the little pocket diva sang her solo this time, she 'wowed' them, she 'knocked them cold', she was 'sensational', or whatever other cliché theatre people use to describe a successful performance. For there was no doubt about her success that night, and for the encore this time, she came on alone. The audience went immediately silent as the little tiny diva stood centre-stage and 'belted out' in a voice much older than her years:

'Dear thoughts are in my mind and my soul soars enchanted
As I hear the sweet lark sing in the clear air of the day.
For a tender beaming smile to my hope has been granted,
And tomorrow she shall hear all my fond heart would say.'

Noreen appeared at the prompt side and little Maria turned to her and sang the next verse to her.

'I shall tell her all my love, all my soul's adoration,
And I think she will hear me and will not say me nay,
It is this that gives my soul all its joyous elation,
As I hear the sweet lark sing in the clear air of the day.

As the final chords swelled to the close, the 'star' revealed all of her eleven years by running from centre stage to her mother's arms while the audience stood on their feet and cheered. Except the O'Neil family in the first row of the circle, who sat in stupefied amazement, hardly believing what they had witnessed. It wasn't 'The Singing O'Neils' to them. It was Noreen and her little daughter. What they couldn't see though was that another interested spectator was Rico d'Agostino in the stalls.

In the dressing room afterwards, brightly lit by the new Tantallum electric lamps, the atmosphere was just as electric. Everyone crowded in and Maria had to sit up on the ledge of the window to be seen and heard. It was her hour and she knew it. There was something alarming in the way an eleven-year-old girl – or 'nearly twelve' as she kept saying – could so easily comport herself among a press of adults. Noreen stayed by her just in case and she clung especially to Michael whom she seemed to adore. Only Father Paddy seemed a little dubious.

'She has to consider her schooling you know,' he tried to tell Noreen above the noise of a roomful of O'Neils.

Noreen nodded over her drink, 'She never gives it a thought,' she said, 'but I do.'

'She'll be in these moving pictures next,' said Paddy.

'They've already asked,' said Noreen laughing.

'God save us,' gasped Paddy. 'Will she be with all those little midgets that play at being children?'

'They are children, Paddy.'

'They are never children,' he answered, 'that let themselves be photographed like that for all the world to see.'

In the other corner, Carmella had her hand in Joey's, who, as usual, couldn't keep his eyes off Noreen. They were with Sean who was telling his aunt how things were with him and Michael.

'You see, Carmella, we've had to move with the times, you understand. There's no bucks in moving beer these days. The public wants a bit more these days – some music, maybe a meal, girls – you know.'

'No, I dunno,' replied Carmella.

'But I do, Sean,' put in Joey grinning. His mother turned on him.

'Where you know from eh?' she flashed at him, 'Here, gimme that glass. Mamma mia!' It was half a tumbler of whisky. 'See that Rosa.' Rosa only laughed. So did Sean as he took it from Carmella.

'Here, I'll take that,' he said. Carmella glared up at Joey, but turned to Sean again. 'So you in the big money now, Sean?'

'Gettin' there, Carmella,' he grinned.

'Gettin' into what?' she persisted.

'Hell, Carmella, you're as bad as Uncle Mick!'

'Dad's dead you know,' said Joey simply. Carmella raised her eyes.

'I know, Joey,' Sean answered quickly, then turned to his aunt.

'You could say we were into real estate now.' Carmella still looked doubtful but she managed a smile.

'I hope you no' do anythin' Uncle Mick wouldn't do, eh?'

'Never!' answered Sean at once. And there he was speaking the truth.

Under the window, Hana was similarly quizzing Michael, despite the fact that Maria's arms were around his neck.

'How come you an' Sean no' marry yet?'

'We're not allowed to Hana, it's against the law!' It was a moment before Michael's quip got through to Hana. She wasn't used to his humour, but she quickly laughed and pummelled his chest with her free hand. The other held a very generous Bourbon.

'You know what I mean, you big stiff.'

'He's not a big stiff,' said Maria defensively.

'I mean,' Hana went on, 'if you were in Prague, two beautiful young men like you, you would have wives, yes?'

Michael grinned. 'Yes. If they looked like you, Hana.' Hana was pleased.

'When Mike grows up,' said Maria, squeezing his neck, 'he's gonna marry me, aren't you, Mike?'

Mike laughed. 'How could I refuse?' he said.

Jitka and Katya were playing with Noreen's make-up at the mirror and painting circles on their cheeks with lipstick. Denis, with Clara asleep on his shoulder, was in earnest conversation with Jock Lennox. 'I'm tellin' ye, Denis, yon's a voice, a real voice,' Jock was saying.

'You're tellin' me,' said Denis with some astonishment.

'I'm tellin' ye' alright,' said Jock, 'an' another thing,' he turned to his wife, '– isn't this right Margaret –' She nodded dutifully. 'I've always said that she'd be an opera singer, didn't I?'

'That's right,' said Mrs Lennox, 'so he did.'

'Ay. I can ay tell a voice when I hear one,' said Jock, quaffing his drink with a gulp.

'An opera singer, ye say?' said Denis. Jock nodded.

'Another Gall-Curci, if she wants.'

'Good lord, is that right?' He glanced over to the prodigy at the window. She was fast asleep on Michael's shoulder.

Daddy Den O'Neil died taking the high note in 'The Londonderry Air'. It was one of his favourite songs and he was showing them all in the lounge bar at Ingham's how it should be sung one Saturday night. It might be said truthfully he died at the high point of his fame! The truth was Denis O'Neil Senior could well have been a professional singer. When he was younger, he had the voice, he had the looks, the physique, the charm. All he lacked was the opportunity. And when he met and married Nessie Monaghan, he was immediately aware, like any true artist, that she had the better natural voice and he contented himself with being a better-than-ordinary pub tenor and a hit at every christening, wedding and funeral he attended. Now he was attending his own, but in a non-singing capacity! That must have hurt him. To have to lie there in his coffin on Ingham's counter and hear somebody like Tommy Drennan murder a good song like 'Slievenamon' and himself lying there and could do nothing about it! Even Sergeant Davidson making a try at 'The Bard of Armagh' sounded better. He looked strange out of uniform. People hardly knew him. Nessie didn't sing. She was very quiet. She sat with Nellie and Brigid Drennan, Tommy's wife, at the corner table and never said much the whole night. Which was unusual for her. Hardly a word out of her, even

292

when the curate, Father Mooney, insisted on making a speech to the company, and him hardly knowing Den at all. Trust him to be smart whenever he had the chance in public. He even had the cheek to sing himself. 'Mother Machree' and even if everyone hated to admit it to his face, Father Mooney sang it well, considering he was a man that had no formal training at Ingham's. Liam Murphy on the other hand, was a natural. He was one of the few who didn't give the company a song. Colonel Mayhew was another, and Canon Devlin, but then they could be excused as being respected elders, as it were, of the community. They had their dignity to consider and Mr Tait, the factor, didn't know any better, and had little dignity, but Liam should have sung. He had no dignity to speak of, only money, but he said he had a sore throat. Perhaps that's why Bushmills Whiskey is so often referred to as 'the gargle'. Whatever it was, Liam's throat must have been bothering him something terrible for he got through an awful lot of the stuff that night. And he was by no means the only one. Old Den would have liked that.

Liam was holding forth to one and all, and to Den in his box. 'He was a good one was auld Denis. Didn't he and I get drunk many a night together –'

'Once!' called out Nessie from the corner. Liam jumped.

'God woman, what a fright you gave me. I thought it was Denis!'

'How do you know it wasn't, Liam?' called out Tim from the side bar.

Everyone laughed. Liam wasn't sure. 'Youse can be at the codding, when youse like,' he mumbled thickly, 'but if this auld one in here –' he tapped the coffin with his glass – 'if this fella wants to, I tell ye, he'll be sittin' up as bright as ye like and be givin' us all the "Lark", just as he was doin' that night when –'

'Sit down, Murphy, ye're blootered.' This time it was Kevin.

'I am not,' said Liam, with some difficulty.

'Ye are so,' called out Tommy Drennan, 'but it's no' fair, you had a start on us all.'

'That's right,' agreed Tim. 'He's here before me sometimes.'

'Are ye tryin' to do Old Denis there – God rest him – out of a hard-won and well-deserved record of attendance?' enquired Tommy jovially.

'I wanna sing now,' said Liam. Groans all round. 'I wanna sing a song for my poor wife who's – who's gone off her head.' There was an immediate silence in that crowded lounge bar that morning. Those who had the nerve looked at Nellie. She was all smiles – as usual. Others looked at the drinks in front of them. Liam started to sing drunkenly.

'Poor old Dicey Riley, she has taken to the sup,
Poor old Dicey Riley, she will never give it up,
It's off each mornin' to the hock
An' she drops in for another little drop,
Ah, the heart of poor auld Dicey Riley!'

On the last line he slumped against the bar and his arm hit the coffin. It slewed alarmingly and everyone shouted. Kevin pounced on Liam and was going to hit him, but Sergeant Davidson was even quicker. 'Here Kevin,' he said breathlessly. 'Give me a hand with him. He needs some air.'

'He needs a punch in the mouth.'

'I know,' said the Sergeant quickly, 'but sure, he's drunk. Come on.'

Reluctantly, Kevin helped Sergeant Davidson to get the senseless Liam out of the door and into the morning air. They sat him down roughly on the outside bench, and his head hit the wall with a thud.

'Good job he can't feel it,' said the Sergeant.

'He will in the morning, thank God,' said Kevin. The two men stood in silence for a moment, glad to take in the freshness of the late morning after the stuffiness of the bar. They'd all come straight to Ingham's after the Requiem Mass and they were waiting now for John Burns, the undertaker, to come and tell them when the grave was ready at the cemetery and the men would walk the coffin there. The women would take Nessie back to the house and they'd all meet there again for something to eat and they'd start all over again where they left off. It was the best way with grieving – drown it.

'Talking about my sister like that,' muttered Kevin.

'He was drunk,' said Davidson.

'That's no excuse. Everybody else is.'

'Here, have a Gold Flake.' And he offered a cigarette. Kevin hesitated. 'Don't ye smoke?' Kevin chuckled as he took the cigarette.

'I don't know.'

'Try it. Everybody else is.' Kevin looked at the policeman as he leaned to accept the profferred match which he was shielding with his fingers. He was friendly enough, but Kevin was wary. He had to be.

'I'm sorry about your da.'

'Ay.'

'He was a fine auld man, was Denis O'Neil.'

'Ay.' He coughed on the smoke.

'Alright?'

'Sure,' spluttered Kevin.

'You'll soon get used to it.'

'Ay.' There was a slight pause. Inside they could hear Mr O'Donnell, the vet, playing his accordion but nobody was singing.

'I hear Liam's booked to go to America again,' said Davidson, looking out on the empty road. Kevin looked at him in surprise.

'How do you know that?'

'Oh we have our ways. It's in our line of business you might say.'

'Ay. It's funny my mother didn't mention it.'

'She doesn't know. Nobody knows.' They glanced round at Liam who by now was fast asleep with his mouth wide open, his head back against the wall. Kevin tried another drag at the cigarette. He quite liked the feeling it gave him, but he didn't know if it was it or the drink was making him feel rather dizzy.

'So he's goin' to have another try at takin' Nellie over then?'

'No.'

'But you just said –'

'I said he had booked a passage. One. And one-way.'

'What?'

'Ay. But remember, this is confidential. Between us. On the Lusitania I understand.'

'What about our Nellie?' asked Kevin. The Sergeant shrugged. 'The bastard.' And he glanced round at the still-insensible Liam and threw away the cigarette in disgust.

'What about yourself, Kevin?'

'What do you mean?'

'I mean, with all this Home Rule for Ireland agitation and Ulster fighting to stay loyal –'

'Loyal? Loyal to what?' interrupted Kevin.

'The Crown, of course. King and Country and all that.'

'Of course.'

'I would have thought with 50,000 men training already under General Richardson to fight for Northern Ireland there was a place for a fine young Ulsterman like you.'

'With guns made of wood and bought for one-and-six each?'

The Sergeant was startled. 'How do you know that?' he said. Kevin smiled.

'It's in our line of business as you said yourself.'

'Ay.'

'Anyway,' said Kevin slowly, 'I was thinkin of emigratin' myself.'

'Oh?' The Sergeant was immediately interested.

'That I am,' said Kevin, 'and soon too.'

'You'll be joinin' your brothers then, in New York is it?'
'No.'
'No?'
'No. I'm goin' to friends you might say.'
'Friends?'
'That's right. In Dublin. Excuse me now, me mam will be lookin' for me.' Davidson noticed that Kevin still limped slightly. The Sergeant was thoughtful as he carefully stubbed out his cigarette with his thumb and finger and put the stub back in the cigarette packet. Then, blowing on his fingers, he turned to follow Kevin. As he passed Liam, still asleep, he gave him a shove and sent him sprawling into the gravel. The fall seemed to bring Liam to his senses and he sat up on the road wondering where he was.

John Burns had arrived and Kevin and Tommy Drennan already had the front of the coffin on their shoulders. Tommy Drennan and Mr O'Donnell came next and they were looking for two to bring up the rear. Only the priests remained, and the Colonel and the Factor and none of them could really be asked. 'Just a minute,' said Sergeant Davidson, going out of the street door with a bucket of water in his hand. He returned in a few minutes with a very wet and chastened Liam and the cortège was complete. Thus Old Den left the scene of his many triumphs on the shoulders of his son and his friends, leaving behind him on the bar fond memories of countless great nights of debates, discussion and song, echoed now in the keening of the women from their seats in the corner. Behind the empty and desolate bar, stood the solitary figure of Tim, the barman, calmly tearing up at least half-a-dozen pages of unpaid drinks in the name of Denis O'Neil.

A circle of O'Neils sat in silence round the dining table in Sean and Michael's new service flat in Gramercy Park, New York City. Both men had moved up in the world recently and the evidence of their new wealth was all around them in the curtains, the carpets, the original paintings and the quality of the ornaments and effects. Not that Sean and Michael chose any of them. The decor was inclusive in the rent and all that can be said was that the decor was expensive. Few New York flats boasted an early Rousseau. Not that an animal picture on the wall meant anything to either of them that particular evening. Father Paddy had rung the previous day to give them the news from Rosstrevor. It was Kevin who had written. It was the first letter they had ever received from him. Its style had made Sean's terse epistles to his mother seem like florid prose:

'FATHER DIED LAST NIGHT. FUNERAL MONDAY. ALL WELL. KEVIN' They all knew, however, the well of love that was hidden beneath the bleak words of the cable, but nobody could talk much about it. Their careless, feckless, irresponsible father was gone and though he contributed little or nothing to their care or well-being while he lived, his going left an enormous gap in each of their lives. Just to know that he was there could bring a smile to the face and to know now that he wasn't brought an ineffable sadness to them all. He would be missed to a degree all out of proportion to his usefulness. Perhaps we need men like Denis O'Neil to give us the pointless perspective, to underline the fact we do not live by bread alone but by blarney and beauty and other indefinable things that don't always make money.

'You're the only Father we've got now, Paddy,' said Michael, breaking the long silence at last.

'Not to mention the Son and the Holy Ghost!' added Sean.

'I wonder how my mother is,' said Noreen softly.

'She's got Kevin there,' offered Denis.

'I doubt if that's much comfort,' said Sean.

'And Nellie and Liam Murphy,' added Noreen.

'That's even worse,' said Michael.

'Poor Nellie.' Nobody said anything after that for quite a long time.

'Well,' said Denis at last, 'we're not the children we were.' There was a muffled, vague sort of reaction to this.

'I would say that was very profound, Denis,' said Paddy.

'No, what I mean is we were still children when we arrived here in a sense.'

'We arrived here in a boat!' muttered Michael. Denis took no notice.

'We'd been sent out here on Uncle Mick's money. We hadn't tuppence between us and Irish accents you could cut steak with. And look at us now would youse – look at this place now – Sean and Michael live like kings – whatever they might say – and I'm not going to go into the whys and wherefores here.'

'Thank God for that,' muttered Sean.

'The point I'm tryin' to make is that we've done well – even you, Noreen. I know you've had your difficult times, but you've also had your easy times too.'

'Now then, Denis,' said Paddy quietly. Denis raised his hand in an appeasing gesture.

'Don't worry brother, I'm not going to preach.'

'Deo gratias,' said Michael.

'Where'd you pick that up, Michael?'

'I heard Denis say it somewhere.'

'The fact is we've all done for ourselves and in less than thirteen years. I think that's something.'

'When are you goin' to be Superintendent, Denis?' asked Sean. Denis grinned.

'Whenever I get some hard evidence on you two!' he said. 'Don't think I don't know what's been goin' on.'

'Tell us, Denis,' said Michael in his innocent voice. Denis was about to when Noreen interjected.

'It'll be time for me to go and collect Maria soon –'

'Where is she tonight?' asked Paddy.

'A Charity Night at the Harvard and Yale Club. Jock and Maggie are with her.'

'Who?' asked Paddy.

'The Lennoxes.'

'Oh yes.' Noreen turned to Denis, her face earnest.

'But what I wanted to ask Denis was, what did he mean by saying we weren't children any more?'

Her brother didn't answer at once. He sat with his arms folded, staring down at the fancy tablecloth and when he did speak again he was so quiet that they could hardly hear him, so they had to listen seriously – even Sean and Michael, who were never, or rarely serious.

'What I meant was,' said the oldest son, 'is that we are free at last. At least, as a son I feel that. As long as my father was alive I felt that I was not myself but his son, as I hope my son will feel for me – if I ever have a son, that is.'

'How is Hana?' asked Noreen.

'Oh yes, Hana.' He looked shy again. 'Sure she's fine. I think. She's standing by, shall we say?'

'That'll be five now Denis,' said Paddy.

'Please God.'

'Thanks be to God for another one,' said Paddy.

'Good old Denis!' said Sean.

'Good old Hana!' said Michael.

'God be with her any road,' said Paddy. 'Has she long to go?'

'I dunno,' said Denis, 'They're not sure –'

'Even Mrs Finklestein?' asked Noreen.

'Even Mrs Finklestein,' laughed Denis. 'It could be next month or next week or tomorrow. Who knows? But they know I'm here, in case anything happens.' He glanced at Sean. 'I left them your number.'

'Number?' queried Sean.

'The telephone number,' said Denis.

'Oh ay,' said Sean. 'D'ye know I forgot we had a telephone!'

'Well Denis, you'd better hurry up and say what you were going to say,' said Michael.

'Why so?' asked Denis.

'In case you've got to go and become a father again!'

'Go on Denis,' said Sean, 'never mind him.'

'Right,' said Denis, trying to get his thoughts together again, 'Well – what I was trying to say was – with Da gone, good old wonderful irritating undependable Da –'

'God rest his soul,' murmured Paddy.

'Ay,' continued Denis, 'well, with him away, I can be my own man now. I can be myself. I can begin to be a real father to my girls and prepare for the day when I'll be a grandfather to their children. What I mean is, you always think that you're tomorrow's man and yesterday's child and then suddenly you realise that today is the tomorrow you were always looking forward to, if you see what I mean, and quite soon you'll be yesterday's man yourself.' He looked up and round his brothers and sister. 'D'ye know what I mean?' Nobody answered, so Denis went on. 'Until we all got the news yesterday, we were all Den O'Neil's children. Well, we're not the children we were, ye see. We're not children no more. That's what I meant. That's all.'

There was a long silence again. Noreen was crying and trying hard to hide it. The brothers pretended not to notice. Suddenly, the telephone rang out. It was so loud that everybody jumped.

'Dear God, what's that?' cried Paddy.

'It's the telephone,' said Sean.

'So it is,' said Michael.

'You answer it, Mike,' suggested Sean. Michael rose.

'Sure,' he said. Then he hesitated. 'Where is it?' he said. All this time the phone was ringing out.

'I don't know,' said Sean. 'I've only been here a week.'

'So have I!' rejoined Michael.

'For Pete's sake!' cried Noreen, rising, 'I'll get it.' But she didn't know where it was either and soon the whole family was up on their feet looking for the source of the noise. It was Noreen who found the instrument. It was out in the hall. They all crowded round her to hear.

'It's Mrs Finklestein,' she said. 'She wants you, Denis.' Noreen handed the receiver to Denis. They watched as he took it, his face grey, his voice tight.

'Yes?' He listened gravely, then gradually his expression relaxed and he broke into a wide grin, then a laugh, then with a loud yell, he threw the telephone into the air.

'It's a boy!' he cried. Suddenly everybody was shouting and cheering and crying and on the carpet under their feet Mrs Finklestein's distorted voice was still telling nobody all about it. . .

INTERLUDE TWO

The seven years between 1912 and 1919 saw the changing of the world. From this time, nothing was ever to be the same again. Yet it all began so simply. Two pistol shots around ten-thirty on a summer morning in Bosnia and the Edwardian idyll was shattered forever. And while Hana and Denis O'Neil celebrated their first son and their tenth wedding anniversary, another European couple, also celebrating their wedding anniversary, met their deaths together in a carriage in a Sarajevo street. Admittedly, they were of the royal house of Hapsburg but they were no less dead for that. It was the repercussions of this relatively minor event in the Balkans that led to the Great War as it was called, the First World War. As early as the summer of 1912, the year of the Titanic and of the Suffragettes and of the first Variety Performance by Royal Command at the new Palladium Theatre, Europe was already building up its armies. The hit song of the year was 'It's A Long Way to Tipperaray' but old Ireland was singing an older song and building up a hidden army. Kevin O'Neil was just thirty years old and already a part of it in Dublin.

In 1913, Liam Murphy did sail for New York without Nellie, promising to send for her 'as soon as he was settled' but Nessie O'Neil wasn't sure and took her daughter home with her to the farm 'for company'. Liam wasn't made welcome by his in-laws in New York and after an awkward lodging, first with Denis and then with Sean and Michael, he took Noreen's room at the Lennox apartment when Noreen got her own place in Manhattan with Maria.

In England, Emily Davison died under the King's horse, Anmer, at Tottenham Corner during the Derby, but more people worried about the injury to the horse. At the same time, at Edendale in Gore, Bruce Mackenzie, with the help of old Jan, bought a couple of good horses for his sons Sandy and Stu – 'for when they grew up a bit'. The Kaiser banned the tango in Germany as 'immoral', but took delivery of a thousand new Maxim machine-guns. Lloyd

George called the build-up of arms in Europe – 'organised insanity'. But then . . .

On 28th June 1914, Gavrilo Princip, a nineteen-year old student, took advantage of a corner, and as the State carriage made its slow turn, dashed forward with a pistol. He was known to be linked with a Serbian secret society known as the Black Hand. It was the two shots fired from this hand on that summer morning in the Balkans that ignited the smouldering embers of war in Europe and led to the fire that caused the conflagration that created the holocaust. It was the First World War because it affected most of the people of the world. It was the Apocalypse. It was Armageddon. Yet at that moment in Forres, John Keith tried his best to stop it happening.

'Lloyd George is right!' he yelled from his cart at the corner of the Main Street. 'War is insane and we mustn't go mad with it.' It was Saturday afternoon and he was standing, as usual, on the cart he hired as his platform. Every weekend he gave Mossman the baker a shilling for his cart and every Saturday afternoon he pushed it from the bakery to the square in the High Street and harangued the passers-by about the stupidity of the forthcoming war. Everybody seemed to know it was coming. It was common talk and all the young men wanted to be in on it before it was all over. It was nothing more than ridiculous hysteria and totally unreal, but only a few people saw this and John Keith in Forres was one of them. Being his father's son, he was a man of strong principles and he was not afraid to speak up for them. Just as his late father was reviled in Forres for siding with the Boers fourteen years before, so John was mocked and jeered for speaking up for peace. He was even accused of being a German spy!

'The government,' he yelled to the crowd of mechanics and young men listening, 'try to tell you that it is your duty to fight. It is patriotic. You must play the game. But lads, it is not a game. This is for real. Patriotism is meaningless to the working man. It is not his duty to die at a general's whim.' John did not have his brother Bobby's ease on a platform but he had more integrity and honesty and he knew he had to do it. He had to do what he could. Thomasina was profoundly embarrassed and went to her mother's with Elspeth and Becky every Saturday afternoon to escape all the comments. But Becky often skipped away to listen at the back. The thirteen-year-old was proud of her Uncle John but his own son Kenny was ashamed. Like the rest of Britain's youth he was determined to go if war came, and John and he had some awful rows in the house about it.

'It's as bad as a war wi' you two,' Thomasina had said.

Kenny was eager, ardent and just as principled as his father and in his seventeenth year. When war did come on Bank Holiday Saturday – 4th August – young Kenny was nowhere to be seen, but John was in his same position, shouting loudly to the crowd as usual. This time the crowd was in a different mood, high on euphoria and drunk with patriotism. This time the men didn't tolerate John. This time they saw him as a public enemy. Pushing his cart and yelling like Dervishes, they jumped up and pinned him down. Becky screamed but couldn't reach him. Singing the national anthem they pushed John through the streets, finally dumping him in the Town Mill pond. Meantime Becky had run to Mrs Beattie and brought back Elspeth and both of them, with the help of a man who was passing, pulled John out and walked him, dripping and stinking of the pond, back to his house and to his bed.

Kenny didn't come home that night. It was three days before he appeared and when he did he was in uniform. He had been to Aberdeen and joined the Gordon Highlanders. His mother cried, Elspeth was so proud, Becky couldn't believe it, but John was very solemn and quietly ordered his son from the house. Kenny never said a word. He kissed his mother on the cheek, nodded to Becky and turning at the door, saluted his father in the chair, then was gone. John was never to see his son again. John himself was warned by the local Police Inspector not to speak at the square again or he would be arrested for speaking against the national interest.

'But it's a matter of conscience,' protested John.

'It's a matter of Crown regulations,' replied the Inspector. John did speak. He was arrested and after a trial before the Tribunal, all of whom he knew well, he was sentenced to a year in Peterhead Gaol.

Second Lieutenant Kenneth Keith of the Gordon Highlanders looked over the parapet of his trench on Christmas Eve and was astonished to see one of his soldiers talking to a German soldier in No Man's Land. The German soldier was holding out a box of cigars.

'What does he want, Thomson?' Keith shouted to his own man.

'Jam, sir.'

'Give him a cigarette.'

'Yes sir.' Then followed a most extraordinary scene. Despite Second Lieutenant Keith's orders to keep their positions, his soldiers swarmed over the trenches to meet their counterparts in No Man's Land. He could only watch helplessly. No officers were invited. It was strictly other ranks – a vast congregation

302

of privates. The ground between the trenches was milling with men singing and joking and laughing. A game of football was played – Scotland versus Germany – which ended in the dusk in a draw 2–2. Meantime, senior officers had gathered to watch from the rear observation and the order went out that all ranks must return to their posts. Some men protested, saying it was Christmas, others refused point blank to return to the trenches. One of the leading spokesmen was Private Thomson. A Major and a Captain hurriedly came on the scene, Lieutenant Keith bringing up the rear. The men began to drift back. Eventually only Thomson remained obdurate.

'Why dae we have tae kill each other?' he kept saying. Kenny couldn't help thinking of his father on the cart.

'Deal with this fellow, will you,' said the Major, walking back to the trenches, annoyed at getting his polished boots muddy. The Captain turned to Lieutenant Keith.

'You know what to do, Keith.' Kenny sprang to attention.

'No, sir.' He had only been commissioned a week.

The officer looked at him scornfully, but there was pity in his voice as he said quickly, 'Shoot him, man! And that's an order!' He also left.

'Ye widnae dae that, sir?' said Thomson in his gruff voice.

'Have a smoke, Thomson.'

'Thank ye, sir.' And as the soldier lit up there in the open ground, and twilight faded around them, someone started playing 'Roses of Picardy' on a mouth organ. Second Lieutenant Kenneth Keith slowly, and with heavy fingers undid the button of his holster and, like Garvilo Princip, fired two shots between Thomson's startled, incredulous eyes. That night both sides sang Christmas carols to each other, but Second Lieutenant Kenneth Keith sat alone and apart, staring straight ahead, his back against the wet, trench wall, thinking of his father.

> 'Stille nacht, heilige Nacht!
> Die der Welt Heil gebracht . . .'

And a star-shell lit up the winter night sky. . .

In the New Year, Field Marshall Kitchener sternly pointed his finger at half-a-million more men who reluctantly answered the call. No cheering this time. A hundred thousand were already dead. Zeppelins appeared over the south coast and the first civilian war casualties were a little boy and his sister killed when a bomb destroyed their cottage at King's Lynn.

At that same time in New Zealand, Billy Keith and his sister

Roberta were playing war games in the back paddock and nine-year-old Billy was shooting her with a walking stick, but seven-year-old Berta would not lie down. She was getting her dress all dirty, and it made her cough.

'And anyway, why do I always have to be the German?'

'Because you're a girl!' Berta had no answer to that kind of logic. From the rear verandah, Gran Keith called them for lunch, still with her knitting in her hand. She had found her vocation. At the express wish of Queen Mary herself, Florence, like thousands of women throughout the Empire, was knitting socks for soldiers at the front. Women in Britain enrolled at the Labour Exchanges for war work in the factories. The battle for Hill 60 at Ypres had begun. Nearly 70,000 men died for a quarter-mile of wood. Americans rejoiced in white heavyweight boxer, Jess Willard's victory over black Jack Johnson in Havana, but raged over the sinking of the Lusitania by a German submarine. It was the very ship that had brought Liam Murphy out the year before. When he heard, Liam couldn't help thinking he was lucky. That was the second time he had been saved from drowning. 'I must be spared for a reason,' said Liam and began to chance his luck on the Stock Exchange on Wall Street. And he was lucky.

So was English comedian, Charlie Chaplin, who made a hit as the little tramp. D.W. Griffiths made 'The Birth of a Nation' and the O'Neil brothers made a down-town night-club out of Rafferty's Bar. The regulars retired to the Shamrock Club in Brooklyn. Sean asked Noreen to act as hostess now that Maria, at Canon Paddy's insistence, was at school in a convent at Baltimore. She would get special singing lessons – from an Italian nun. Rico d'Agostino started up the same kind of place in what used to be Hogan's Bar only a few blocks away. He asked Noreen to join him there. She refused. He offered Joey a job, but Carmella nearly had a fit. Joey was disappointed not to be able to wear a 'monkey suit' as he called it, but Carmella was adamant. Then Sean asked her if she would let Joey come to their place. Carmella wasn't so sure. She needed a lot of persuading, but Sean was persuasive. 'He's a big, good-looking guy,' he said. 'He'll be OK,' added Mike.

Italy meanwhile, prompted by a young radical called Benito Mussolini, negotiated to come into the war on the side of the Allies. Nurse Edith Cavell was shot as a spy. Rupert Brooke died of blood poisoning *en route* to the Dardanelles where 25,000 Australian and New Zealand troops were killed, 76,000 were wounded and 13,000 reported missing in a bungled and mismanaged expedition against the Turks.

In Sydney, Bobby Keith, now an important figure in Australian trade union affairs, and beginning to consider a political career, railed against the war at every meeting. 'It was England's bugles that sounded and it was our young men who answered. And look what they do with them. Throw their young lives away in a stupid, ill-considered and bloody botch of an idea to come in through Europe's back door. Did they they think the bloody Turks would leave it open for them? And where was Churchill when the bullets were flying? Crying his eyes out about that bloody poof, Rupert Brooke? There is a corner of a foreign field alright. It's Turkish and its thick with ANZAC dead and the guilty party therefrom is forever England!' And the Aussies cheered, daring the policemen to make a move.

In 1916, conscription was introduced in Britain. The Old Contemptibles had become a compulsory and unwilling army. On Easter Monday rebels in Dublin led by James Connolly and Padraig Pearse proclaimed an Irish Republic. All seven leaders were later executed. Connolly was allowed to recover from his wounds in hospital and was then taken from Kilmainham Gaol to Dublin Castle and shot by firing squad sitting in a chair. Kevin O'Neil suddenly arrived back at Ballytreabhair – 'for a wee holiday' he explained to his mother. He played cards with Nellie. She told him about Liam in America. He was there looking for a place for her – 'and he had the children with him'. Kevin glanced questioningly at his mother. Nessie put her finger to her lips. 'And they're growing up to be quite American,' Nellie went on. It was better to leave her with her dreams, Nessie later told Kevin.

'Aren't we all better off with our illusions?' she said.

'Who said dreams are an illusion, Ma?' replied Kevin. He left soon after for the south again with a stranger. Sergeant Davidson came asking about him.

'He's away again,' said Nessie.

'Ay. I waited,' said the old Sergeant. It wasn't long after that Sir Roger Casement was hanged for smuggling German arms into Ireland. Armoured 'tanks' were introduced. An epidemic of venereal disease in London was blamed on soldiers. The price of a loaf rose to tenpence. In a bleak mid-winter Lloyd George became Prime Minister.

Some joy, however, came to the Keith family. At least to that branch of it that had rooted at Edendale in Southland, NZ, where it was now summer. For Christmas that year Tina Keith gave her husband Bruce the present of a baby girl! Her pregnancy had been uncomfortable and she feared she might not carry, but here it was – a girl for Bruce. He insisted on calling the child Christina, but of course she became Chris at once to everybody.

January 1917 – Sergeant Denis O'Neil was promoted to Captain, Buffalo Bill died but the USA knew a boom year – so did the other O'Neil brothers even if Rico d'Agostino was proving a bit of a nuisance in trying to buy them out. Or was he trying to buy back Noreen? Wilson armed his ships against submarines. Noreen wondered if it would be safe to go home again for a visit? The United States entered the war – 'to save democracy'. Aeroplanes bombed London. Mata Hari, Malay wife of a Scotsman called MacLeod, was sentenced to death in Paris as a spy. The Virgin Mary appeared to three children at Fatima in Portugal. The Pope sued for peace. Canon Paddy was promoted to Monsignor and transferred to Boston. British troops were bogged down in the Flanders quagmire.

Captain Kenny Keith succeeded in making a break-out with his platoon and for his bravery was awarded the Military Cross. 'He was a mad bastard,' said his Sergeant, 'just didnae care.' The next day he rescued one of his men from a shell crater and was shot in the back by a sniper. He died that night in a forward hospital, choking on a cigarette. He was buried in a war grave and the little boy who ran through the house in Forres waving a wooden sword now had a wooden cross with his name on it in Belgium. When his effects were sent back to Forres, John Keith said little but took the medals his son had won in battle and late at night, after his session at the Mason's Arms, walked to the Mill pond and threw all four of them in, ribbons and all. He said later that he'd lost them.

Arthur Balfour, the British Foreign Secretary declared Palestine a homeland for the Jews. Rachel Keith would like to have gone there but her mother died and instead she went to see her father to try and effect a reconciliation, but her old father wouldn't let her over the door. Abel was now nine and his grandfather had never seen him. Bobby took the boy to his house. Enoch Gebler would not open the door. Bobby pounded on the door with his fists, but Enoch only responded with a Jewish incantation. Abel suddenly bent down to the letterbox and called through, 'Grandfather Gebler, it's me – Abel.' He stood back and waited. Inside, the incantation stopped and then the door slowly inched open. Enoch Gebler embraced his grandson, then took the boy inside, closing the door against Bobby, who gave the door a good kick and grinning, walked away.

'The old bugger,' he chortled. Soon afterwards General Allenby captured Jerusalem and Lawrence of Arabia galloped into Damascus and into uncomfortable legend. Mary Pickford was proclaimed the world's sweetheart and Maria O'Neil in Baltimore, now fifteen years of age was jealous!

The year 1918 began with meat rationing in Britain, then the Russian Bolsheviks sued for a separate peace with Germany. Von Ludendorff smashed through the Allied lines at Arras in the hope of rolling the British back to the Channel before the fresh American troops arrived and Paris was shelled by 'Big Bertha', a huge gun named after Mrs Krupp. The French, under Marshall Petain retreated to attack again and drove the German offensive back over the Marne. The British tanks pushed them further back to the Hindenberg Line. After Cambrai, the corner had been turned and now there was no going back. The Americans came 'over there' for the last act and the curtain came down in Belgium where it had all begun four horrific years before. Shortly after dawn a party of Germans entered a railway carriage at Compiègne and by the eleventh hour of the eleventh day of the eleventh month, the Armistice was signed and the war was over.

Germany was not only humbled but humiliated, yet the Kaiser was swept off to exile in a train twenty carriages long followed by a cavalcade of twelve motor cars. He had refused to shoot himself. But ten million people had died in a campaign that had begun as a summer frolic in 1914 and now ended in a shower of November rain. What a price to pay for an Imperial whim. It was a debt that was never to be repaid by the politicians or the generals of both sides, no matter how many red poppies were later bought or how many 'Last Posts' were sounded on dismal anniversaries.

Nearly as many women died too, in a sense, as spinsters and widows of the lost generation in the decades that were to follow. How many wives waited and how many more waited to be wives? The brave heroes returned to an epidemic of influenza which all but carried off those who had survived a living hell. Other victims it carried off were the acid Mrs Friar in Forres and old Jan van Meers in New Zealand. A virus is as impersonal as a bullet or a shell. They say if it has your name on it . . . But who can write on a virus? Except perhaps, another New Zealander, Professor Ernest Rutherford, who, at Manchester University, succeeded in splitting the atom and in the process started off a chain of events that would be even more shattering than that set off by two shots.

But in 1919 disenchantment set in around the globe. The world was never to be the same again, but when everything has been changed, nothing is changed. Nevertheless, life went on as it always does. By the accidents of distance and dates of birth both the Kiwi Keith and the Mackenzie houses had been spared the effects of war and neither knew the pain of loss or the sadness of wounds in young bodies. Indeed, it could be said that they had prospered. Only in Forres had the family known the universal sorrow of war in the death of Kenneth, but then in 1919, coincidental with the Versailles Peace Conference, Jean Hay Keith surprised her husband with twin boys, Jamie and Kenneth. Another Kenny Keith! 'The Lord giveth and the Lord taketh away.' Our story continues. . .

TWENTY-TWO

It was a time of speeches and parades, platitudes and prayer. All over the English-speaking world, the language was twisted and tortured to accommodate the lies, half-truths, inaccuracies and apologies that passed for truth in the year following the end of the First World War. Political rhetoric now seemed even more of a sham in the face of blinded, maimed and gassed young men who stood as a living reminder of the crass incapacity and cretinous apathy shown by most of the ruling classes during the watershed years 1914–18. Too many lives had been lost, ruined and perverted by the squalor of waste and the obdurate idiocy of the hitherto privileged. There were now men in their twenties who had already been to Hell and come back. They wanted no truck with the gilt of medals or the guilt of those who would label them 'hero'.

They only wanted to come back to the lives they had known, the loves they had known and from whom they had been wrenched so cruelly. The question was, having survived the horrors of war, could they survive the realities of the peace? The young bloods who had gone hurrahing into war in 1914 were mostly dead now in any case. The few who were still alive had no desire to give any credence at all to prating padres who had once blessed guns and now said the hosannahs for victory, or for blimpish officers who hardly wished them a curt 'good morning' before sending them over the top while they went back to the château in time for cocktails. The number of generals who died in the four years of combat could be counted on the fingers of one hand, whereas the number of 'hands' who were lost in battle was uncountable. As was the sea of white crosses that spread from under the marching feet to far beyond the horizon of anybody's consciousness. The number who died was unthinkable, therefore few dared to think about it. This didn't prevent people trying.

One such was Jim Keith, flushed in the pride of twin sons, who pondered on why he had been spared his older brother's pain. John had lost an only son and never even mentioned it in his letters.

309

Now in 1919, at the age of forty-four, reclining on a comfortable verandah with a beer in his hand, Jim pondered on why he had been given the double gift of sons when so many had been denied or been deprived of the only son they had. He could so easily have been called up himself. He was thirty-nine then and they were taking men up to forty-six. More than 100,000 New Zealanders up to his age had been called up under the Military Service Act and most of them went overseas, some even back to British Units. For some reason his name hadn't come up for embarkation, and he'd spent the war at home with the Defence Force. Not that they had to do much – a few drills and a summer camp. But of those who went over, one in ten didn't come back. What was the point of all this life waste? No one in their senses would wish the death of another, yet there were men standing now on platforms who knew they sent thousands, even hundreds of thousands to their death. Jim took another long sup of cool beer. In his New Zealand apartness, he was extra-aware of this. His war happened in weekly instalments via a newspaper. His was a conflict at several removes from its reality and he felt a little twitch of guilt about this. That was why he gave so readily to war charities and war bonds and any other vicarious, purchasable substitute for actual involvement. He knew that many people in New Zealand felt like him. Big Brucie had mentioned it as well. Men who had actually been born and raised in the Old Country, or Home as they still called it and had yet to commit themselves totally to Oceania or the Antipodes or Down Under or whatever else people in Britain liked to call this other Britain under the southern sun.

What the hell! He could do nothing about it. It wasn't his war. And anyway, it didn't matter now. The milk had been spilled, or did he mean the blood? It didn't bear thinking about. He rose up from the wicker chair and drained his glass. It was time for the parade.

'Aren't ye ready yet, Jim?' It was his mother. She had come up from Edendale the previous day by the new bus and had never stopped complaining.about it. Now she had on her best bonnet and black coat and was leaning on a stick watching him.

'I was just coming, Mother.'

'Ye'll have to hurry. Three o'clock, they said. Jean's getting the twins.'

'Right.' He wiped his mouth with the back of his hand.

'And take that glass to the kitchen.'

'Yes, mother.'

The victory parade at Mataura didn't amount to much. There weren't a hundred returned servicemen from the farms round about, so they filled up with scouts and two policemen, and a couple of men from the Post Office and the railway porter because he had a uniform. They all sort of straggled along by the railway station, but there was a pride in it. They had done their bit for the Old Country, and there was also the faintest swagger in the knowledge that they had been the lucky ones. They had survived. The schoolteacher raised the Union Jack and said a few words about Geoff Tait and Joe Robertson who had been killed at Gallipoli. Then the minister, Reverend Dawson, said a prayer, and that was that. The marchers and the watchers went into the schoolhouse for tea and buns, but Jean said they should go home. The twins were crying, Gran said her knees were sore standing and now Billy was moaning because he couldn't go to the schoolhouse and Berta wasn't feeling well because of the heat. Who would have kids, God bless 'em, Jim thought. He would be glad to get home. Get another beer. He looked up at the flagpole. Nobody could find a New Zealand flag but somehow that Union Jack didn't look right. It even seemed ashamed of itself the way it hung limply round the flagpole.

'Left-right, left-right, left-right, left-right . . .'
The boyish voices brought Bruce Mackenzie on to his shaded verandah at Edendale just in time to see his three sons march past in the garden below. Sandy, Stu and Ross. Sandy at twelve, was just a little bit self-conscious as he carried his 'rifle' which was a garden broom. The other two however were in their element, strutting it out in good style, especially little Ross who was running to keep up.
'Left-right, left-right, left-right . . .'
Round the gooseberry patch they went and past the vegetables and now they were heading up towards the house again.
'Tina! Come and see!' Bruce called his wife and she came out carrying little Chris just as the boys passed for the second time. She smiled at the sight of her three sons marching, but then on the second turn by the gooseberry bush little Ross fell flat on his face and lay on the grass bawling.
'Get up Ross,' shouted Stu, 'you're supposed to be a soldier!' By this time, Sandy had 'marched' on ahead.
'Hey,' shouted Stu again, then he turned back to Ross, 'come on, stupid.' But Ross would not be comforted and lay with his face in the grass, kicking his legs behind him. Stu left him lying.
'Wait for me, Sandy!' Sandy had now become bored with the parade and was running across the paddock towards the horses.

'I'd better get the little fella,' said Bruce moving to the verandah steps.

'Yes,' said Tina, 'somebody always gets hurt in a war.'

'But why has it to be one of ours?' called Bruce as he strode towards his youngest son. He couldn't help thinking as he walked the few paces over the lawn how much he had wanted to go. Flat feet they said. How embarrassed he was to have to tell everybody. Flat feet. The shame of it. And as he bent to pick up his son, he couldn't help looking at his feet again, and was very relieved.

'Alright, Rossie boy, what's the trouble?' The baby in Tina's arms began to snuffle. Tina put her face to hers.

'Why is it, wee Chris, that all boys' games nearly always end in tears?'

At the beginning of that Victory year, Abel Keith and old Enoch Gebler were in the crowd of waiting relatives and sightseers at the Sydney dockside watching wounded soldiers being disembarked from a hospital-ship. Abel and his grandfather had become the best of friends since Mrs Gebler had died and although the old Jew kept up a pretence of being angry with his daughter and her husband he no longer denied them his house and he even came to their apartment for Abel's tenth birthday party. Bobby considered himself to be in a state of unarmed truce with his father-in-law, but there were times when he wasn't sure of the unarmed aspect. Old Enoch never failed to get a barb in when he could. Rachel didn't mind the sparring between the two men she loved. They both loved her son and he adored them, so she let them get on with it. Besides, she had her new interests at the university. More Australian Jews were becoming interested in modern Zionism and she was in correspondence with Dr Chaim Weizmann, the leading British Zionist, who was behind the campaign for a Jewish Palestine.

That was the one thing that had caused another big row between Bobby and her father only yesterday, when the three Keiths had gone to see him for their customary Sunday tea. The two men were waiting at table. Abel was reading.

'I'll tell you one thing though,' said Bobby in the course of the 'discussion', 'if our boys went off to Egypt and Souvla Bay as Colonials they came back as Australians, I can tell you that.'

'They are men whatever. Or names on a stone.'

'I wonder,' mused Bobby, 'when they come to build the ANZAC memorials if we'll find many Jewish names on them.'

'We need not names on stones to remember our dead,' countered Enoch angrily.

'What I want to know,' continued Bobby leaning in, 'is whether you're a Jew or an Australian?'

'And what I want to know,' retorted his father-in-law, also leaning in, 'is whether you're an Australian or a Scotchman?'

'Tea's ready!' said Rachel, entering with a tray.

'Good – I'm bloody starving,' added Abel, rising from the couch.

'ABEL!' cried all three adults at once.

'Well, I am.'

Now Abel and Enoch were at the harbour docks. They had been there since after lunchtime. It was one of their 'expeditions'. Every now and again Abel and Enoch would decide to go somewhere for the day and the old man would buy the boy a good lunch. Abel was always hungry. And when they were out they would talk. About anything and everything, especially religion and politics.

'I gotta do somethink to make up for that father you got, Abel!' Enoch would say munching on his chicken and dill sandwich. Abel would just grin with his mouth full. When he had finished his sandwich he threw the crust over the barrier and into the water of the harbour.

'What a waste,' said Enoch.

'It's only an old crust,' said Abel.

'No, no,' went on the old man, 'I mean them.' He pointed to yet another line of men stringing down the gangplank to be helped into the ambulances waiting at the dockside.

'What a waste of good lives.' Enoch was appalled, but Abel was fascinated. All those different men and everyone it seemed with a different injury. Some had bandages round their heads, others round their arms or their legs and some, on stretchers, that were just all bandage. Some men didn't seem to have anything wrong with them, but they just stared straight in front of them. They were the blinded soldiers, his grandfather had said. Other staring men weren't blind, but they looked it.

'What's wrong with them, Grandad?' asked Abel.

'Shell shock.'

'What's that?'

'It's hard to explain.'

'That's never bothered you before.' The old man considered.

'It's what happens to a man when fear and noise and mud and cold and smells and lice and rats and hopelessness all get to him.'

'Sounds awful.'

'It is awful, my dear Abel.'

'Do they die from it – the soldiers?'

'No. That is the pity. They have to live with it and sometimes they can never forget.'

'Have you ever had it Grandad – this "Shell-thing"?'

'Never. But you forget one thing.'

'What's that, Grandad?'

'I was born a German.' At this, a man standing just in front of
Enoch, a squat, red-faced man with no collar on, but wearing a
hat, turned round and glared into his face.

'What was that you said, mate?' Enoch was surprised and said
nothing. The man turned right round and put his face into Enoch's.

'You said you was German. I heard ya.' He turned to the crowd.
'Hear that, cobbers! This 'ere's a bloody Kraut, a 'un would ya
believe. He says it hisself.'

'I am a Jew,' said Enoch with a quiet dignity. The man turned
back to him.

'Christ, that's even worse! Hey mates, we've got a Yid! A Tin
lid! An' is this another one in the make, eh?' He sneered down at
Abel, who looked up at him with eyes wide.

'Come along, Abel.' Enoch took the boy's hand firmly and
pulled him away through the crowds and away from the dockside
barrier. The rough man's taunts still continued, and his jeers and
taunts were taken up by some of the crowd. 'Kraut! Hun! Swine! Yid!
Jew!' Abel was more bewildered than frightened and even though
his grandfather didn't run, he walked as fast as he could along the
dockside. For a moment, it looked as if they would get clear, but
some of the mob had picked up stones and pieces of wood and
were throwing them.

'Run Grandad!' shouted Abel, pulling at his grandfather's hand.

'No Abel. I will not run from a mob,' he said, but his face was
very pale. A police whistle sounded and some soldiers ran out
from the docksheds. Abel could hear the sounds of their boots
on the wood of the jetty. There were more shouts.

'Don't look back, boy,' ordered Enoch and just then, something
hit him on the head and knocked his black hat off.

'GRANDAD!' screamed Abel.

Enoch was taken into one of the Army ambulances to have his
head treated. There was a huge cut in the back of his bald head
and he needed two stitches, which a young Army doctor gave him.
Abel watched, fascinated. As the doctor was putting the stitches
in Enoch's skull, without any anaesthetic, he said to him, 'What
happened to you then?'

'Shell-shock,' said Abel proudly.

In Forres, there was the open-air peace parade and service at the
Cross. A military band played hymns while the soldiers of the
Argyll and Sutherland Highlanders and the Black Watch stood

314

with the Gordons at strict attention, their kilts and plaids slightly swaying in the breeze. The pipe bands did not play at the service. Their war-like sounds were perhaps not thought ideal for kirk monody. The minister, who was in army uniform beneath his robes, fortunately said only a few words. As the wind began to get up and blew at his whites he was more concerned about how it also lifted the long strands of back hair he had arranged so carefully across the top of his bald pate. His right hand kept moving from the fluttering pages of his hymn book to the few fluttering strands of hair on his head. Someone shouted up from the crowd: 'Let it blaw meenister, it'll no' blaw awa!'

'I wadna be sae sure,' said another voice.

'Shove a lum hat ower it, man!' called another. A few laughed. Forres had never seen so many top hats on one platform before. The Provost doffed his to announce that a children's street tea-party would be held in the square that afternoon to celebrate the Versailles Peace Treaty. 'A peace and jam, ye might say!' Nobody laughed at his wee joke, but he did. Everybody was to bring out a chair and a cup or a plate and a cake. The Council would provide the tea. He then put on his lum hat again and led the Town Council and the army officers, as well as the bedraggled minister, from the platform.

The man who supplied most of those tile hats to the Council watched the scene from the front of a close at the other end of the square. John Keith had no wish to join in any celebrations of victory or peace. For him the war had been lost the moment it had been started and he didn't want to waste another word on the whole dreadful enterprise. He had paid dearly enough with his son's life and a year of his own. But his life was fast approaching its winter. Kenny's had never reached its summer. The anger had long left John Keith. Only sorrow filled him now and it was a thirsty emotion. It constantly called for drink and John tried his best to keep it watered. He was now known in Forres as the town drunk and he cared not. Approaching fifty now, he cared little for public opinion on any score. He worked at the shop occasionally, but less and less these days. He still received his full wages from old 'Shears', but only out of respect for the Keith name in the town and for the fact that, because of John's previous good work in the business, the place virtually ran itself now. Mr Robertson however was getting impatient.

'You must realise, John Keith, that you have a position in the town and that it's not always in the lounge bar of the Masons' Arms! You have responsibilities too in your home with two fine girls growing up and you'll not want to see them go in need, will you?'

The girls were John's only solace. Especially Becky. It was wrong of him, he knew, to prefer his niece to his daughter, but he did. Elspeth was like her mother. Nice enough, but dull. She was the kind of girl who lived by what other people thought, just like Thomasina, who judged her existence by her standing with the neighbours. Becky, on the other hand, lived by her own standards. She was tall like her mother, dark and voluble like her father and full of charm and mischief – like herself. From the very beginning she and Uncle John had had a bond which neither could define, nor did they wish to. It was an easy, natural uncomplicated trust and both of them sat easily in it. Thomasina had her reservations, naturally, and mentioned them to her mother. Mrs Beattie was sanguine.

'If the lassie's bad she'll go to bad, but if she's good, she'll ay come to good. And your man, Thomasina, for a' his wee weaknessness, or his one big one I could say, is a good man. You should see that for yoursel'.'

But Thomasina only listened to what other people said and they said unkind things about John and his being seen so much with his own brother's lass.

'And him away in Africa – or is it America?' one would say.

'Australia,' would correct another.

'Is that it? Weel, they're a' the same tae me,' would say the first. And they would go on their ways again.

The parade was over and the crowd began to disperse. John straightened up from his leaning position at the close and found that his legs were a bit unsteady. He cursed himself for having come out at all. He steadied himself with his hand and turned to go back the way he had come. He wanted to avoid the square. Too many people he knew. He wished his legs felt stronger. He took the first faltering steps just as a girl's voice sounded far away in his head.

'Uncle John!'

He turned vaguely and there was Becky running towards him waving her arm. What a lovely young woman she was growing into.

'Wait for me!'

He waited. Behind her he could make out Thomasina with Elspeth, both still in black for Kenny, but Becky was in blue.

'Uncle John. Why did ye no' come to the parade?'

'I – er –'

'Are ye' comin' to see the street tea?'

'No lass – I – er –'

'Uncle John! Ye havena' been –?'

'Just to keep oot the cold, Becky.'

316

'It's not cold,' replied the girl.

He indicated his temple. 'Inside it is.'

She laughed. 'Oh, Uncle John!'

'But I'm alright.'

'No, you're not. Here let me give you a hand.' She tried to reach out for his arm as he turned again, but he was trying to reach the wall with the other and as a result he lost his balance altogether and fell in a heap on the cobbles of the close. The girl gasped as her uncle spreadeagled beneath her feet. Her hands were still covering her cheeks as he smiled benignly and looked up at her concerned face.

'As the man said, Becky, let us remember those who have fallen!'

They read the Riot Act against striking workers in Glasgow and tanks patrolled the City streets, but in Dublin, Eamon de Valera sought a place for Sinn Fein at the conference tables of Europe, but the Mother Parliament in London declared the Dail Eireann illegal. Police and soldiers surrounded the Mansion House to arrest Michael Collins, the provisional Minister of Finance, but he escaped through a skylight and got over the roofs to freedom. Captain Kevin O'Neil of the new Irish Republican Army cut his arm in assisting the portly politician through the narrow aperture, but he was delighted. He had spilled his blood for auld Ireland at last! He couldn't count the leg injury he had at the incident in Down, because that had been more of an accident than anything. But here he was in action. Here he was doing something. He was last to come down from the roof and when he did, the streets were empty.

He kept quiet as winter came and his arm mended, but he was glad the scar could still be seen. Lloyd George said – 'No party in Ireland is prepared to accept anything except the impossible.' Kevin O'Neil puzzled his southern colleagues with his northern accent but he in turn was also puzzled. Why was a United Ireland impossible? 'Money' he was told. 'Land' – 'Religion'. The big three. The Unblessed Trinity of Vested Interest. Go home to Ulster, Kevin O'Neil. But Kevin was determined to cling to his dream. The Council of Ireland was a start at least. There would be a United Irish Parliament one day with equal representation North and South, Catholic and Protestant and he would be member for Rosstrevor!

Meantime, there was work to do. It was a Saturday night meeting in November and most of Dublin seemed to be rain-swept streets. The police raided the hall and Kevin made his escape into an alley.

His limp prevented him keeping up with the others so that once again he was last. Then turning the corner, he found himself face to face with a policeman who drew his whistle from his pocket at the same time as Kevin drew his pistol . . . He had no alternative, he told himself later. The policeman was dead. Kevin O'Neil had shed his first blood – someone else's this time – for a United Ireland. Why did he feel sick?

Captain Denis O'Neil stood on the steps of St Patrick's Cathedral on Fifth Avenue and watched the parade go by. It was a chilly day with the raw kind of cold only big cities provide near the end of the year. Denis stamped his feet to keep warm, but he didn't need to. He positively glowed inside, as he looked down on the street a few steps below him. The lines of soldiers were almost hidden by the rain of ticker tape that came down from the windows of the skyscraper offices on either side. Denis glanced up but he could not possibly see Liam Murphy as he looked down from his Fifth Avenue office window high on the 28th floor.

Liam had prospered. He lit an expensive cigar and did not object when two of his young stenographers, Maxine and Joan, came either side of him and took an arm each.

'Gee, isn't it great, Mr Murphy?'

'Great, Joan.'

'We've won the war, Mr Murphy.'

'We sure have, Maxine.'

'Whose side were you on, Mr Murphy?'

'Why Joan, you know I'm on everybody's side.'

'You're cute, Mr Murphy.'

'Why, thank you Maxine.' There was a cry from one of the other windows where others of the staff were gathered looking out. The two girls ran off squealing. Liam took another puff of his cigar. Nice girl that Maxine. Pity she's a Negress.

Denis saluted with pride. This was his country now and he had to let people see it. The soldiers marched into peace time, having won the war for Britain as they thought. The band played 'I'm Forever Blowing Bubbles' and the United States was now United Artists. World leadership now passed from the British Empire to Hollywood and the Big Parade of 1919 was drawing to a close. It had been another long day for Denis O'Neil and his downtown traffic department. In an hour he would be at home with his feet up and Hana would be telling him all about this new place called Czechoslovakia they'd made out of some bits and pieces around Prague. Europe seemed a long way now from St Pat's. He must take Hana on a trip some day. But there's the children. Denny's

318

only started at school and Anna's still in First Grade. Clara and Katya were still in Junior School and Jitka had only just begun at Senior School. The nuns thought –

Jitka? Yes it was! The Captain started as he saw his own daughter among a group of young girls running alongside the marching soldiers! What was she doing so far downtown? These girls were a hazard to traffic. And what's more – it was his daughter! He ran down the steps as fast as his boots and Captain's dignity would let him.

'Jitka! Jitka! Hey! You come back here! Hey!'

The crowds laughed to see the Police Captain chase a group of young girls as they ran by, not just parading soldiers, but the relentless March of Time into a new decade.

TWENTY-THREE

In the United States it was quite a New Year Party. It wasn't so much that they were welcoming in the new year of 1920 but that they were having possibly the last few drinks before national closing time. It was a country-wide 'Last orders please!' With the coming into force of the Eighteenth Amendment to the Constitution on 16th January, prohibiting the manufacture or sale of alcohol, it meant that liquor could not be shipped into dry areas and that all persons were forbidden to drink alcohol under the full penalty of the law. Put simply, drink was banned. Prohibition was in order, but before it came into force, the country embarked on the biggest binge since Cana. Drinking parties begun at Christmas were still going strong at Twelfth Night and none more so that January evening than at the Two by Two, the new downtown club on 36th Street which formerly traded as Rafferty's Bar.

The old regulars would never have recognised the place. Gone was the old bar with its brass and cash drawer, and in its place a dance band and the Dixieland Quartet playing the new ragtime. Gone was old Emmet Ryan and in his place Claude, the French head waiter, who was actually from Liverpool, but had picked up a bit of French on the Mauretania. He had brought François the chef, who was a real Frenchman, but was never allowed out of the kitchen. He and Vince Gorman, otherwise 'Claude', obviously had a 'relationship', but neither Sean nor Michael enquired too closely into this. Their business was to put a good meal on the tables, or at least an expensive one. What they did in their time off was their own business. What it was, one can be sure, was quite unknown at Rafferty's! Gone from that time too was the sawdust and instead there was a dance floor – at present tight-packed with smart dancers. Gone from the floor were the Kellys, the Quinns, the Coyles and the Dochertys, and in their place came the smart set and their escorts, who went in and out two by two – hence the name. No single women allowed. This was a rule laid down by the owners, Sean and Michael O'Neil.

Their staff now amounted to Noreen as Hostess and Club Singer

320

with old Jock Lennox on piano. He was fumbling a bit for the right notes these days, but he had a good understanding with Noreen, both personally and musically, and this made them a good combination in the intervals between the Quartet led by Puff Hardie's saxophone. Clancy Hogan, formerly of Hogan's Bar, had come to work at the Two by Two on a part-time basis and he was at the door checking out for unlikely customers. He was a square kind of Irishman, Clancy, about five feet by five feet, and he was a handy class of man to have around, as they say. He had been given a good price by the d'Agostino family for his place and he was solidly drunk for a month thereafter. He went home to Cork for a visit and to dry out but was back in New York after a month to check out on any other business possibilities. He had met Michael O'Neil one Sunday at the Shamrock Club and Michael had asked him to come in with him and Sean on the Two by Two deal. Michael explained that Jackie Rafferty was a sleeping partner. 'We all do what we're best at,' he said. On that basis, Clancy agreed to hang around. Now he was having a few nights on the door meantime to see what he thought. This was not a thing Clancy Hogan was expert at so he was taking his time. Anyway, he was enjoying himself.

He was meeting all kinds of new people. People who would never come near Hogan's Bar or Rafferty's. Like the genuine, native-born Americans, for instance, real New Yorkers whom Clancy had rarely met. They were new to Sean and Michael too, this clientèle. They talked in funny accents and they wore bow ties and dinner jackets and their women spoke even funnier and hardly wore anything at all. They had their hair cut like boys, and their busts bound so tightly they might have been boys, but they were women alright – as they regularly proved. They were wild. Whether it was the end of the war, or the impending prohibition or what, the place was even wilder. The louder and faster the band played the better they liked it. Cigarette holders got longer as cocktails grew more lethal by the glass. Michael had to help out Clancy on the door to control the crowds and even Sean had to go back to serving and Claude forgot his French accent enough to tell one particularly arrogant party to 'Go and get fooking stoofed!'

Only Noreen kept her cool. She had already built up a kind of cult following among the bright young things, and many of the young men particularly were 'Noreenites', as they called themselves. Life at forty was beginning again for Noreen O'Neil. Her red hair may have lost its fire but it had gained, along with some attractive grey hairs, an auburn glow. From being a strikingly pretty girl, she had become in the last few years a beautiful woman.

Another beautiful person was Joey O'Neil. Unexpectedly, he had fitted in well to life at the Two by Two. All he had to do was lead people to their table and hand them a menu, which he did very well in his monkey suit, looking like a film star but with the manner of an engaging young boy. Joey was nearly forty himself but looked half that age. He was made a great fuss of by the girl customers and appeared to enjoy it. He was now much more relaxed in his attitude to Noreen and, as a result, she was able to keep a big-sisterly eye on him. This close watch was needed, for Joey was easily led and when the wild ones came in at the weekends, anything could happen. As for instance, on the night of the dreaded 16th January. It was a Thursday night, and what should have been the quiet before the storm of yet another hectic weekend was instead a veritable tornado in itself. The Anti-Saloon League may have had their way, but the drinkers were making sure of one last gulp before the dreaded drought came into effect. Orders for drink had never piled so high on Joey's tray – with some disastrous results. Whiskey Macs got mixed with gin and bitters, beer slurped high in the champagne buckets and bourbon and rye exploded on the palates of those who had ordered dry Martinis. Yet nobody complained. They were hardly in a state to do so. The noise of the band, of singing and laughter and shouts drowned the retching of those who were sick as they sat at their tables. Others were already asleep, some even as they danced and others again would have fallen in a stupor had they not been supported by the tight mass of dancers on the tiny floor.

The heat was equatorial, the cigarette smoke choked, the din was deafening, yet everyone thought they were having a wonderful time. Had the lobbyists for Prohibition looked in they would have found their case totally proved! More heat than light had been engendered by energies spent on both sides of the national debate that had been growing over the previous twenty years, but now the die had been cast. The 'Noes' had won and their time was coming, but there was still an hour to go.

'What'll we do?' asked Michael.

'God knows,' answered Sean.

'I wish he'd hurry up and tell us,' shouted Michael through the din.

'We'll think of something.'

'You always do, Seannie boy. Would ye look at that Joey!' And Michael pushed his way through the mêlée. He didn't see his brother's face. For once, Sean was serious and grave and beads of sweat could be seen clearly on his upper lip.

What the hell do we do? he was thinking to himself. He checked the tables, the two bars, the cloakrooms, the lobby. It was half an hour to go till midnight – and Prohibition. Perhaps Noreen could do a couple of songs – just to quieten things down a bit.

'No way!' was his sister's terse response. She was sitting at a table full of young men all in varying stages of drunkenness. He found Jocy similarly ensconced in a circle of girls. He pulled his cousin clear to the chorus of their squeal of disappointment.

'Do your tie up, Joey.'

'I can't, Sean.' And there and then, in the middle of that mayhem, Sean re-tied his cousin's bow-tie.

'Isn't that cute?' said one shingle-haired beauty to another.

'Are they lovers?' was the blasé reply. The first one laughed and leaned back showing the garter on her thigh.

'Hell, no darling, they're family!'

'Does that make a difference?' drawled the first.

A quarter of an hour to go.

'Where's Jock?' asked Michael pushing his way through to Sean who was now helping behind the bar. Sean jerked his head, indicating the slumped figure of the old Scotsman at the end of the bar. Michael hurried round to him.

'Jock –' he began, lifting up his old friend's head.

'If ye can't beat them –' Jock began in heavy, slurred tones.

'Jock,' shouted Michael into his ear, 'ye'll have to play. Puff's passed out and the band won't play without him.' The dancers on the floor hadn't noticed yet that there was no band. The banjoist and the bass player were dragging their leader out. He was still feebly attempting to play his saxophone. The drummer, a cigarette in the corner of his mouth, was mechanically beating out a jazz rhythm, but he looked as if he were asleep. He was asleep!

'Jock! For God's sake!' yelled Mike, even louder.

'Sure, Mike boy,' slurred Jock, 'be right with ye.' And he fell forward on the bar – out to the world. Michael left him there, and rushing on to the tiny stage he roused the drummer, whose renewed efforts wakened some of the dancers. Ten minutes to go.

Clancy didn't like the look of things at all. The night had been too wild altogether and there hadn't been the usual wastage. Few carried out, fewer still thrown out and crowds seemed to be gathering in the street outside to see what was going to happen at midnight. Some of them carried bottles in their hands and were drinking from them. Some had started up parties on their own and were dancing to the sounds of the different bands that came from the various jazz spots on either side of the street.

'This is not right at all, at all,' said Clancy to himself. 'There's just enough out there gettin' drunk as there is in here.' He turned from the door as Joey passed near with a tray full of drinks. 'Hey Joey!' called Clancy.

'Yes, Mr Hogan?'

'Come 'ere, son.'

'Sure, Mr Hogan.' And when Joey came up to him, Clancy reached to the 'boy's' tray at his shoulder and helped himself to a Scotch.

'Thank ye, Joey.'

'Pleasure, Mr Hogan,' said Joey who hadn't noticed.

'Better get about your business, son. You got thirsty customers.'

'Yeah, Mr Hogan,' replied Joey amiably and went on his way.

'A nice lad that,' said Clancy, as he thoughtfully sipped his drink. Five minutes to go. Michael found Sean at the kitchen door.

'François has gone mad,' he said. 'Claude's tryin' to calm him down.'

'What's up now?'

'Three soup bowls returned full of sick.'

'God save us.'

'But there was worse.'

'D'ye say now?'

'I do.'

'I'm not goin' to ask.'

'I'll tell ye just the same. There was a note on the tray and it said – "Our compliments to the chef!"'

'Sounds like the Noreenites,' said Mike.

'The same.'

'I'll sort them out.' Michael made as if to go but his brother stopped him.

'No, Michael. Ask Noreen to deal with them. They'll do anything for her. Then meet me at the fire door. I've got an idea. Get Clancy and Jock into the kitchen.' Two minutes to go.

Noreen hurried to the kitchen with a couple of bottles of champagne. Clancy followed soon after, dragging Jock, and Michael joined Sean at the fire door just as midnight sounded on bells and sirens, horns and hooters. For a moment the room stilled, uncertain what to do. Someone started to sing 'Auld Lang Syne' but was quickly shut up. There was the sound of a glass breaking, then another and another. A bottle smashed and a big cheer went up. It was as if it were a signal and the front doors burst open and a mob surged in agog for plunder and a free drink. Outside in the street, whistles blew and there were sounds of shouts and feet running. Inside the Two by Two the mob met the social set face to face over the littered dance floor.

'Get 'em!' someone shouted. There was a roar from the mob and they rushed the bow-tie brigade, but instead they were met with a gale-force blast of cold water from a hose now being held by Sean and Michael at the fire door. Both were laughing their heads off as the would-be looters slipped and slithered under the power of the water jet. Most of the dancers got soaked as well, but it did most of them the world of good and sobered them up miraculously. In what seemed minutes the place was cleared and Sean yelled to Michael to 'Shut the goddam water off!' And as it receded to a drip at the end of the nozzle, sitting there in the middle of the debris on the dance floor was Joey O'Neil, soaked to the skin, laughing his head off and trying with fumbling fingers to re-tie his bow-tie. And that's how Prohibition came to the Two by Two.

It was appropriate that the Two by Two should have been flooded out, for the scene next day on the premises resembled nothing more than the building of Noah's Ark. Ladders and benches and trestles and steps abounded and instead of Noah and his sons, there was Clancy Hogan come into his own with the Kellys, the Coyles, the Quinns and the Dochertys. Rafferty's Regulars had been remobilised in the form of building casuals and under Clancy's strong arm were reconverting the Two by Two nightclub into the Four Corners Dance Salon and Coffee House! Sean had been unable to get round the Volstead Act and claim an exemption for wines on the grounds that his clientèle was mainly Catholic and therefore he could offer them sacramental wine – 'for the good of their eternal souls'! Michael had suggested that they should put the licence in Paddy's name now that he was a Monsignor. 'We could sell it as Holy Water!' Even an attempt to get light beers on a medical subscription foundered on the grounds that the condition named was cirrhosis of the liver! So it had to be a dry house from now on. Jock Lennox, who had agreed to hold a bucket, while Pat Kelly painted, had suggested it should be tea instead of coffee, as the Tea Dance was the coming thing, but he was shouted down by the others because tea, they thought, was un-American. 'Anyway,' Michael had said, 'they couldn't have liked it. Wasn't it the tea they threw overboard in the harbour at Boston?' Jock was mollified by the thought that he had to provide the musical accompaniment, and suggested a more continental group than the Dixieland Quartet. Besides, Puff Hardie would be out of action for quite a time. His Coca Cola had been laced with something stronger than tea. Sean moved from one group to another, marvelling at the expertise shown by working men whom he had rarely seen completely sober. It dawned on him that he had never seen them during the day. Of course they were good workmen. They had spent years in the construction game when they first landed. It was only recently the Italians had moved into that area, as the Irish moved up and on into other things. However, it could still be seen that Pat Kelly was indeed a plasterer. Joe Docherty was no mean joiner. Phil Quinn knew about the electric lights, and the Coyles knew about nothing, but they were willing to put their hands to anything, and therefore were ideal labourers on the site. Besides, old Stephen Coyle was a dab hand with the billy can and could brew up exactly the kind of tea the boys remembered from the building sites.

'Will you get out from under there, Sean boy?' Pat's voice called out from the top of a ladder. 'The sight of you in that suit makes me think of bosses, and I could never work when the boss was around.'

'You could never work, you mean,' shouted Joe Docherty from a bench at the far end.

The general ribaldry continued until Clancy raised an arm and bellowed, 'You're hired to work, not to run off at the mouth. Get on with it now, or you'll answer to me.' The menace implied was not at all allayed by the melliflous tones of his Cork accent.

'I'll leave you to get on then, Clancy,' said Sean and backed out gladly from the scene of operations. He was well satisfied. Things were going according to plan. That had been one of the best moves they had made, he and Michael. To buy up the cellar below, and the others that led off from it all the way to the river. It hadn't been easy, but bit by bit, with the help of Jackie Rafferty's winnings, a few lies here and there, and some downright skulduggery, of which they were not in the least ashamed, they were now the legal owners of all the cellars to the sea. This route took every advantage of the New York sewage system, which had corridors and tunnels big enough for a man to walk through. The only snag there was that the d'Agostinos had similar access. But if each minded their own business, there was no reason why both houses shouldn't look to new business.

Sean picked his way towards what had been the old kitchen. There had been something of a scene this morning when he sacked Claude, whose French once again totally deserted him, and he left, thoroughly abusing Sean in Scouse.

He looked at his watch. Where was Michael? He should have been back by now. As if on cue, Michael appeared at the back door.

'There you are,' said Sean.

'So I am,' said Michael. 'I knew it was me the minute I opened the door.'

'What did you find out?' said Sean, always serious and matter of fact.

'Not a mark, not a trace,' said Michael, helping himself to a cold leg of chicken from the icebox. 'It was as if they knew,' he said, chewing hungrily on the chicken.

'I can't hear a word you're sayin'.'

'I'm starved. I was tellin' you, d'Agostino's was locked, barred and bolted and not a windowpane out. I'm sayin', it was as if they knew.'

'Well, is that not the interesting thing now? Throw us over a chicken leg, Mike. We'll have to chew on this.' Michael threw his brother a chicken leg and looked around.

'Is there not a beer?'

'Haven't you heard of Prohibition?' said Sean with his mouth full.

'I can't hear a word you're sayin'!' answered Michael, and bending down took out a bottle of beer from the oven.

'Same again,' called Sean. And the brothers sat down at the kitchen table to have their lunch.

Clancy Hogan put his head round the door. 'It's a visitor you have.'

'Friend or foe?' said Michael.

'Neither. He says he's family.'

'Then he's neither, you mean,' said Sean.

'Will ye make up yer mind? I've got work to do,' said Clancy. 'Are you comin' out or is he comin' in?'

'I'm comin' in,' said a voice. And there was Liam Murphy standing in a door as bold as you like, as smart as any paint Pat Kelly was using in the big room, and in the latest kind of suit that far outsmarted Sean's. He came forward to the table.

'Looks like youse are all goin' to do great things with the old Two by Two.'

'What d'ye want Liam Murphy?' Sean's tone wasn't friendly.

'Is that the way to greet family when they come callin'?'

'There's family and family,' said Sean warily.

'I'm family,' said Liam confidently, bringing over a stool to the table.

'I wonder now would our Nellie agree with ye?' said Michael.

'She'd be the first to say so, Michael,' answered Liam, settling himself comfortably. Sean regarded his brother-in-law steadily before he spoke next.

'I wonder,' he said, 'what she'd say about your black woman?' There was not quite a tension, but an edginess developing in the room. Liam Murphy seemed quite unperturbed.

'You were always ready to jump to conclusions, Sean.'

'You get finished quicker if ye jump,' said Sean. Liam calmly smiled.

'Ah now, not if ye jump in the wrong direction. Maxine is a good girl in the office.' Sean however was not to be put off.

'It wasn't in the office I was –' Michael stepped in.

'Sean – I think we better hear what the man has to say.'

'Thank ye, Michael, good man that ye are.' Michael winced but said nothing. Liam for a moment regarded both brothers benignly.

'Would it be right to say that youse were business partners?'

'You could say that. You could be wrong, but you could say that.'

'I'll tell youse why I called round. Here, are ye goin' to offer me a drink?'

'Sorry,' said Sean, taking a swig of his beer, 'it's against the law.'

'That's right,' said Michael, doing likewise. 'Prohibition they call it.'

'Ah, youse are an awful pair.'

'You were going to tell us why you called,' said Sean.

And Liam did, at great length, dwelling on every detail, but all it really amounted to was the fact that he heard from a friend he had in the police – not Captain O'Neil, he was quick to mention – that there had been street trouble and what they called 'incidents' all over New York on the night the Prohibition came in and that the Mayor had called for a quarter-million extra policemen to deal with the trouble they were expecting yet.

'And that's an awful lot of cops, is it not?' said Liam. 'Here Sean,' he broke off suddenly, 'wasn't it you was goin' to be the policeman in the family and not Denis?'

'Go on,' said Sean stonily.

'Well, as I was sayin' . . .' And on he went about this place and that place and how some places had no damage done to them at all – like the d'Agostino place, for instance.

'Yes,' said Liam, 'he had the door barred and the windows shuttered a full hour before anything started – as if he knew somethin' was doin' – know what I mean?' Sean and Michael exchanged glances. Liam noticed.

'Ye know the man then?' he asked.

'We know him,' replied Sean evenly.

'Ay so,' said Liam, 'it's a small world, New York.'

'Too small mebbe,' muttered Michael.

'Not at all, Michael,' said Liam generously. 'There's room for all of us, so there is. Oh it's a great place New York. It's a great place America.'

'Is that right?' asked Sean ironically. It was lost on Liam.

'Oh ay. You plant a dollar here and it grows into two. You take a cutting from each of them and you grow four. You do the same with them and before you know it, you have a forest of dollars right at your hand.'

'You must have green fingers,' said Michael.

'Itchy fingers, more like,' said Liam. 'But it's not the fingers that count, if you follow my meanin'. The thing is not to be caught red-handed,' and he laughed loudly. Liam liked his little joke. 'Anyways, I've not starved, and that's all I'll say.'

'Ye'll be goin' then?' said Michael brightly.

'What d'ye mean, Michael?' asked Liam.

'If ye've nothing to say, it's a shame to keep ye.'

'Oh, but I have somethin' to say, Michael O'Neil, and it concerns you and your brother here. Well, it has to be said that I seemed to have inherited my father's – God rest him – head for figures. Auld Eugene, as ye know boys, could keep a fortune at his finger-ends and know to a farthing the odds that would bring him a return. Thanks to this family gift, shall we call it, I can say too that I have more than a dollar, thanks be to God, and I want to see every one of them put to good use. And what better use is there than by keeping it in the family.' He glanced at the two brothers waiting for them to speak, but neither of them said anything. Liam's face suddenly hardened and took on another look. The look of a man who means business. He put his fingers together and glanced slowly to each of them in turn. It was odd. When he spoke again, there was no trace of Ulster in his voice. Instead, this was eighteen carat Wall Street.

'What I have to offer gentlemen, is a strictly business proposition.' He leaned forward on the table. 'Let me explain,' he said. 'There isn't a law in the world that'll change human nature, and bein' what it is, there's no way that they're goin' to stop people drinkin'. I mean, they can't stop in a night what they've been doin' for thousands of years, now can they? So I think that there exists in this country now, because of the present legal situation as we find it, an opportunity for us all to plant, not one dollar tree, but a whole damned plantation. And we'll do that friends, by giving people what they want – drink. And this is how we'll do it . . . .'

Despite themselves, Sean and Michael found themselves also leaning forward. Liam went on, 'I know that as a pair of bright Ulster boys you will have done your homework and prepared for the rainy day that came to us all last night.' Liam was not an Irishman for nothing. 'But it's more than a question of laying up some bottles in a corner, you know, and there's more to it than having the premises. Oh, I know about your cellar plan and the fine access it offers and all that to the boats. But the thing is, do you have the contacts?' Sean was beginning to look interested despite himself. 'You see, lads, it's what to do after the present stock runs out. Where's the new stuff to be comin' from? Well, this is why we have to be all united Irishmen, if you see what I mean. There are ways and means of getting stuff from the old country to Montreal and Canada via the Moran and Malone outfits in Chicago, and young Kennedy's in on this run too, though that needn't concern us here. But you can take it from me, this is the real McCoy. It's big stuff in the big time for big bucks.' Sean straightened up.

'Michael, give our brother-in-law a beer.'

'Thank you, Noreen. You're nice.'

'You're nice too, Joey.'

Joey was all tucked up in Maria's bed in Noreen's Manhattan flat. He had been taken there by Noreen and Michael after his soaking at the Two by Two and now Noreen was insisting he stay there for a couple of days just to make sure he didn't catch pneumonia.

'We'll let you up tomorrow, if you're a good boy,' said Noreen from the bedroom door. 'OK?'

'OK, Noreen.'

'You can go back to New Jersey for a bit –'

'I don't wanna go back to New Jersey,' he wailed.

'OK. OK. We'll talk about it in the morning.'

'There's that noise again.'

'What noise?' She listened. Sure enough there was a tremendous gurgling sound coming from the radiator.

'It's just the radiator,' she said. 'It's alright.'

'I'm too hot,' he moaned.

'It'll go off soon,' she said.

'Open the window,' he called. She was getting impatient and almost snapped at him.

'Look, Joey, it's late, and I'm tired. Just be quiet now and go to sleep. There's a good boy.'

'Good boy. Good boy,' he said like a parrot. She switched off the light.

'Good night, Joey.' He didn't answer. She shook her head and closed the door.

On the other side of the door, she sighed and leaned against it. Phew! Cousin or no, Joey was hard work. Yet he was right, it was very hot, but it was still January. She moved away from the door, and did not hear Joey get up as soon as she'd put off the corridor light. He opened the window almost half way, and then took a deep breath.

'Gee, that's good,' he said to himself, then went back to his bed, leaving the window wide open against the night air. He fell asleep to the gurgling of the radiator. Noreen meantime was in the sitting room about to close the piano lid. She changed her mind and sat down at the stool, and idly began to finger the keys. She could hardly be called a pianist, but she managed a few pleasant chords and found she was playing something that resembled, 'Oh, You Beautiful Doll'.

Her thoughts turned to her daughter. Maria now was seventeen and in her final year at the Baltimore Convent. She was now a black-haired version of what her mother had been in Ireland, the only other difference being that Maria O'Neil was an even more assertive and self-confident young lady. She hadn't let the nuns influence her overmuch and was only waiting for her eighteenth birthday in order to break clear. She was more of a real worry to Noreen than Rico. Luckily Paddy was keeping an avuncular and clerical eye on her. Noreen didn't like what had happened to Maria. The success she had had as a child performer made her more performer than child and the mother-daughter relationship suffered. She was glad Paddy had prevailed and made sure she'd gone to the convent. Just in time perhaps, or she would have been lost to Hollywood by now. Almost five years ago. She hoped Maria would be a different girl now. Almost a woman. She stopped playing suddenly. I'm too young to have a girl of eighteen, she thought.

She rose from the piano, closed the curtains, checked the windows and put out the light. In the hallway, she stopped. There was that noise again from Joey's room. That radiator had never been right since it had been put in before Christmas. Maria had complained that it kept her awake when she was home for the holidays. I must remember to speak to the man about that. She was always forgetting. But she never forgot to double lock the door and put on the chain. Rico had made a habit of coming to her door in the early hours of the morning when she had first come to live here and had not taken kindly to being locked out. She should never have let him come in in the first place, but he was very persistent, and she was only human. Anyway, he was her own daughter's father.

This was something that he was never to let her forget, but his very insistence on this point was the very thing that began to turn her feelings away from him. She had been attracted at the beginning by his European charm and restraint. There was no pawing or mawling from Rico then. He was very cool, almost distant, and that drew her to him. When he took her to the hotel, she was more than happy to surrender to him and was convinced she was in love with him. She was hurt and astonished when she found they couldn't marry, but then when Mamma d'Agostino had explained, she was ready to understand. But it was Rico who rejected her and Maria, and it was only when the little girl became a celebrity for a time that he appeared on the scene again. She was still attracted to him, but she wondered whether she was still in love with him. What did it matter anyway? Both of them were getting on, and might just be too old for affairs. Recently, however, his demands had become more and more possessive and she was beginning to be afraid of him. This was why the Lennoxes had come over for a while and lived in. But Margaret Lennox missed her own flat, and her neighbours and her little dog, her own shops and she and Jock had gone back last weekend. On Sean's advice Noreen had new locks put on the front door. She still felt good as she turned the two locks. It was good to feel secure and safe and private.

When she got to her own room the new radiator was still on from the morning. She was glad and guilty at the same time of the comfortable warmth that filled the room. She was also tired after that terrible night at the Two by Two, and getting Joey here afterwards. Sean and Michael hadn't been going home for a while so they'd asked Jock Lennox to take Joey meantime, but Joey didn't want to go back with Jock. He didn't like dogs. Since he couldn't go all the way back to Carmella, and was still feeling the effects of his soaking, Noreen had had no option but to take Joey in herself. After only a day of it, she found that looking after Joey O'Neil was tiring. Coping with his open admiration was tiring. She was aware of his devotion at every moment of the day and she was surprised how ennervating it was – a heavy pall of affection hanging over every ordinary event of the day. She was glad of the respite she had when he had to go to the bathroom. How is it that any weight of love can be borne when it is mutual and that the lightest love is unbearable when it is unilateral? She liked Joey well enough, he was after all a blood relation, but she certainly didn't love him. And his love for her was like that of a puppy for its mistress rather than any full-blooded, lusty feeling a young man of his appearance and physique should have had for a woman. What a waste – the little boy's mind in the grown man's body.

By this time she was almost undressed and caught sight of herself in the long mirror. She stopped, as if taken by surprise, then slowly she straightened up again, all the time regarding herself in the cheval glass. She wasn't bad. Not bad at all for forty – OK, forty-one! Hardly knowing what she was doing, she lifted her silk slip over her head and enjoyed the feeling as it smoothed past her breasts. She threw the garment on the bed and put her thumbs into the elastic of her knickers at her waist and slowly drew them down to let them fall at her feet. Yes, not at all bad. She took a deep breath and straightened up, holding her head high. Her right hand lightly held her left breast and her left hand explored the faint line of stretch-marks left from Maria – seventeen years! It was hard to believe. Noreen remembered herself at seventeen. She was the beauty then alright. She tossed her lovely hair back, as if in defiance of age and the passing of time. What did age matter? What did time matter? She was still herself, wasn't she? She was still a beauty. She turned and looked at herself from the side. Unconsciously she drew her tummy in, and pushed her breasts forward. They weren't big but they were still well-shaped. When she was 'growing them', as she and Annie McAteer used to say, she used to envy Annie's big bosom. Boys seemed to prefer big ones and hers were so small compared with Annie's and Annie's were always pointing out. Well, I wonder how Annie's are looking now, thought Noreen? Probably dropping to the floor. She'd probably need a horse's harness to keep them up! She cupped her own pert breasts in each hand. And here am I, with a good shape yet, and me a grown woman with a girl-child as big as meself.

Noreen felt young again as she admired herself. She also felt slightly uneasy, but sure that was part of the fun of it. From her early childhood she had been told that it was a mortal sin for her to look at herself in a mirror – this way. She looked down at her pubic hair marvelling at the blackness of it considering how red her head hair was. Her hand moved down across her belly – and how soft it was to the touch. Made softer by the firm mount beneath it. She closed her eyes and let her head fall back. 'Noreen!'

She let out a sound which was part-scream, part-sob, part-gasp, and her hands flew to cover her parts, her shoulders hunching. She stared, wide-eyed and frightened into the mirror at her own, startled expression, and heard the voice again.

'Noreen!'

It seemed to be coming from outside in the street, but she didn't recognise it. She hurriedly grabbed for her dressing gown, just as Joey's tousled head appeared round the door. He stood staring at her. His mouth opened but he couldn't utter a sound.

'Joey,' she snapped, 'you should be asleep.' She sat on the bed and was putting on her slippers, when she realised he was staring at her knickers on the carpet at the mirror.

'Joey, for heaven's sake!' She thought it best just to ignore them.

'Who's that down on the street?'

'It's a man, Noreen.'

'I know it's a man,' said Noreen, quickly gathering up her clothes, including the undergarment.

'I think it's that man, Murphy.' Noreen stopped in her tracks.

'Who?'

'That man who came from Ireland.'

'Noreen, for the love of God!'

'I think he's drunk,' mumbled Joey.

'Murphy? My God, it's Liam.'

'Noreen, here I am!' The voice was growing more querulous and insistent. The neighbours'll be out, she thought. That Mrs Kershaw misses nothing. Noreen hurried to Joey and bundled him out of the room.

'Bed now, Joey. There's a good boy. I'll see who it is, or we'll get no sleep this night.' She hurried him across the landing and into his room where the radiator still burbled and the window was wide open. That's why they had heard the voice so clearly.

'For God's sake, will you look at that window?' and hurried to close it. And there was Liam Murphy down on the sidewalk, under a lamp post, jacket wide open, tie undone, looking up to her like an Italian serenader.

'There ye are, girl,' he sang up. She leaned out.

'Quiet now, Liam Murphy, or you'll have the whole street awake.' She was surprised at how Irish she sounded, even to herself. Perhaps Liam Murphy brought out the girl in her. She closed the window and quickly resettled Joey, who was beside himself with excitement.

'Ain't it somethin', Noreen?' pulling the bedclothes round him.

'No, it's not, Joey O'Neil. And you just go to sleep and mind yourself. You shouldn't have left the window wide to the world.'

The doorbell then rang. 'Jesus, Mary and Joseph!' Noreen led Liam Murphy into the sitting-room and closed the door behind her. He swayed a little as he looked round the room, but he wasn't as drunk as she thought he was. Or at least he didn't look it. They looked at each other.

'It's an awful time to be calling, Liam Murphy.'

'Didn't you used to say that when I came to Ballytreabhair?'

'I can't remember that far.'

'I'll never forget. Do ye mind Kelly's Brook?'

Noreen was taken aback and thrown a little offguard by the reference, but she replied, 'I'll never forget.'

'Will you be offering a man a drink?'

'Have you not had enough?'

'One can never have enough, Noreen O'Neil, of a good thing.'

'Still the same smooth old Liam.'

'There's some of us never change.'

'My sister has.' Liam didn't reply, but turned away and went to the window and pulling back the curtain, looked out.

'It was your brothers told me you were here.' She sat on the arm of the settee.

'You saw Sean?'

He turned. 'And Michael. They send their best regards.'

'Very nice of them, I'm sure.' He came towards her, and stood for a moment looking down on her.

'Jaysus, you're still beautiful,' he said huskily.

'Am I?' Her voice came out in an unexpected low register.

'You always were.' She felt herself begin to tremble all over.

'I always fancied you, you know. Even before Nellie.' She rose quickly, and found that she had risen right into his arms. He held her immediately, yet not so hard as to frighten her, but firm enough as to keep her there. She wondered why she didn't resist. She shivered.

'You're cold, Noreen?' Almost in a reflex, he tightened his arms round her shoulders. Noreen found herself relaxing.

'No, Liam,' she tried to say, but her voice was no more than a whisper.

'You're alright now?' he whispered. They both knew something had suddenly happened between them, and were both mutually taken aback by the total surprise of it all. She looked up at the face looking down at her. She saw the face of Liam Murphy past. She was young again in Ireland by Kelly's Brook. Lovely memories came flooding back in a moment of being young and innocent and in love and yearning for the impossible. Now here was the impossible within inches of her mouth. Impulsively, she reached up and kissed his full lips. It was a firm, warm, even contact and the suddenness of it slightly parted his lips and gave the gesture an even greater erotic thrust. He held her even closer and pressed her against himself till she could do nothing else other than respond.

'You're a woman now, Noreen,' he said at last, 'and a girl no more.' He could feel her tight breasts below the flimsy dressing gown.

'Am I, Liam?'

'You sure are. And you kiss like a film star.'

'Do I?' She gave a low laugh.

'Indeed you do.'

'Can we do it again?' he said, and she could see the beads of sweat on his brow before she closed her eyes and proffered her mouth to him.

'Sure you can.' They kissed again. And again. And again. Till their passion drove them both into an uncontrollable frenzy to which they both submitted as helpless victims. In a moment, they were on the carpet between the couch and the piano. And everything was forgotten in the abandon that followed. Gently and easily, and with something like real love, the female drew the male down on top of her. It was strange that something begun so long ago as twenty years and somewhere so green and lovely as Kelly's Brook in County Down, should have its consummation in a rented apartment by the light of a New York street lamp.

Rico d'Agostino's face was white with thin-lipped fury. 'Aparta-mento lei?' he hissed from behind what seemed like clenched teeth.

'Si, Enrico.' Roberto Ruffiano was not enjoying this conversation with his cousin and wished he hadn't told him that his other cousin Carmella's boy was living with Noreen O'Neil and had been there for the last few weeks.

'He's justa boy, Enrico.' He pointed a finger to his temple. 'In his head you know. A sciocco, si?'

'No!' Rico spat the word out. 'He's no boy where I worry about.'

'But they're cousins.'

'So?'

'Flesh and blood – famiglia.'

'So?' Roberto could only shrug and say nothing. When Rico gets in this mood, best to let him get it off his chest.

'Same house. Same thing. I know. Soon same bed. To me, to Enrico d'Agostino, he does this, this "boy" you call him?'

Roberto wanted to say he's not doing anything to you. He's a poor sick boy staying with his cousin while he gets better. Anyway, she's not your wife, legally at least, and yet you act as if you have rights. You didn't treat Noreena so good. But Roberto knew better than to try and tell his cousin any of this and continued to stare out of the window of his office above the restaurant. He looked down on the lane – and there was Francesca at it again! She was even smoking as the new waiter had her against the wall of the alley screened by the refuse bins and trash cans. Roberto shouted – there were still lunchtime customers in. If any of them should see – he knocked violently on the window but they didn't seem to hear him. He turned angrily to see Rico putting his coat on.

336

'Eh, Enrico, che–'

'I see this – "boy" – you call him – faccia a faccia.'

'Enrico –' But he was already gone.

Roberto sighed and shrugged. It was hard sometimes being Italian. He was glad he was not a jealous man. How could he be with a wife like his? Then he remembered Francesca and dashed to the grimy window again. She was smoothing down the front of her short black dress and adjusting her white apron. Then she threw down her cigarette and trod on it with a dainty black shoe. There was no sign of the new waiter. Satisfied that she looked alright again, she sallied down the alley again towards the rear of the restaurant and when she got under the window, and before she disappeared from view, she looked up and gave Roberto a cheeky little wave.

Rico rang the door bell and kicked the bottom of the door at the same time. He also shouted for Noreen to open the door. When there was no reply he bent and shouted through the letter-box. 'Noreena! Noreena! Open this door.'

He made such a racket in the late afternoon stillness, that the janitor came up from below wondering what all the row was about. 'Miss O'Neil ain't in,' he said. 'She gone out with a fella this mornin' an' dey ain't back, so you quit that hollerin' and don't be gettin' folks –' The negro's manner soon changed as he felt Rico's gun pressed into his stomach. The whites of his eyes made his teeth look yellow as he gazed in terror at the manic Italian.

'You will let me in. You will take me up. And you will let me into her apartment and you will say nothing to nobody. OK?' He prodded the revolver into the black man's belly and felt it go deep into the quivering fat. 'OK?'

'OK man!' Rico stepped back and the terrified man searched among the keys he had on a ring from his belt. They reached Noreen's flat on the second floor, by which time Rico could smell the fear coming from the janitor like an eye-watering odour. He opened the door and stepped well back to let Rico enter.

'Remember amico – not a word.'

Joey carried in the three large grocery bags through the main door of the apartment block. He couldn't see where he was going and trusted entirely to her directions. In this 'blind' way he had followed her all the way from the drugstore and she could hardly speak from laughing at what looked like three large paper bags with legs. Now they were inside, and somehow she got him upstairs. She guided him to the door of the apartment and stood him there while she opened the door.

'Straight ahead. Steady as she goes.' Joey, by now thoroughly enjoying the game, walked in grinning from ear to ear. As he did so, four shots rang out, three paper bags burst and Joey fell to the floor among the packets, bottles, cartons, tins and assorted vegetables. Noreen stood transfixed, then let out a scream which was immediately muffled by a gloved hand and she heard a voice shout in her ear as an arm seized her by the waist.

'You come with me now. No more big boy for my Noreena!' Wide-eyed she fought to free herself but Rico tightened his grip until she could hardly breathe. She couldn't shift the hand from her mouth and felt herself going faint, then suddenly – like a blind being drawn on a window – everything became black.

'Yessa – four shots I heard – den a noise like somebody falls – I dunno man – I ain't bin up dere. – Nossa – ain't nobody – a dude speakin' some foreign lingo – yessa – he had a gun – a big one too – just some neighbours – I ain't goin' up to tell 'em. You come do dat. Yessa.' He put down the receiver and lifted the whites of his eyes to the ceiling. 'Dis ain't dis baby's business,' he said.

Upstairs, the neighbours were gathered in a knot around the open door of the flat peering in to where Joey lay among the groceries. Like all crowds at any accident they were fascinated and repelled at the same time. None would go in yet none would go away. They just stared in silence. Then one woman said fearfully, 'Is he dead?'

'Looks like it,' answered an old man.

'That's blood anyway,' said another.

There was another pause. All the doors were open to the street and they could hear the police siren wailing to a silence as their car drew up squealing at the front door. One of the women, Mrs Kershaw, who lived in the next apartment, leaned forward and after looking closely at the body among the mess of broken bottles, said in a very matter-of-fact tone, 'Looks like ketchup to me.'

The group round the hospital bed was trying hard to be serious, but a ripple of a giggle was just under the surface as each bent their head to hide shaking shoulders. The subject of their mirth lay back in the bed, his head and arms swathed in bandages, a broad smile on his face.

'I'm telling you,' he was saying, 'it was ketchup. Well, most of it anyway.' Carmella patted one of his bandaged hands.

'Sure it was, Joey, but you losta lotta blood jus' the same. The doctor says you gotta rest up.'

'I'm OK, Ma. I just gotta bit of a headache, you know.'

'I know son,' said Carmella. She glanced at Denis who was at the other side of the bed in his Police Captain's uniform.

'You got a near miss, Joey,' he said. 'A couple of those shots

338

needed only half an inch of a difference and it would have needed more than a few tins of baked beans to save you.'

'I don't even like baked beans.' Everyone laughed again. Louder than they needed, louder than the comment deserved, but they needed to laugh to help them forget that they could just as easily have been sitting around Joey's coffin instead of round his bed in a casualty ward. A nurse passed smiling, but put her finger to her mouth.

'Sorry,' said Sean. He and Michael were on chairs at the foot of the bed and they had been there since they brought Joey back from surgery. The doctor told them what a lucky young man Joey was, and couldn't believe he was thirty-eight years old.

'The body of a twenty-year old,' he had said. 'Guess that was what saved him.'

From what they could deduce, it seemed that of the four shots fired from Rico's gun, one struck Joey on the forearm but ricocheted from a tin or bottle in the paper bag to graze his left temple. It was hard enough nonetheless to knock him out. Another bullet hit him in the chest but bounced off another tin and went through his right shoulder. The third went in at the ribs but was deflected to hit his left upper arm and the last one, which might have killed him, was embedded in a large tin of baked beans.

'I knew Rico couldn't shoot through a paper bag!' Michael had said, and that's what caused them all to laugh in the first place.

'Joey's life's worth no more than a can o' beans!' quipped Sean. And they laughed again.

'How long you goin' to be in, Joey?' asked Michael.

'Dunno.'

'The doctor says I can take him home to New Jersey –' said Carmella to the others confidentially but Joey heard.

'I don't wanna go to New Jersey.'

'Sure you do,' said his mother, patting his bandages again. 'Your Uncle Frederick take good care of you.' She turned to the others again and resumed her confidential voice, 'He's my sister Rosa's husband and he's a doctor. He's a good doctor. They got a nice house in Englefield.'

'How do you like it out in New Jersey, Auntie Carmella?' asked Michael.

'Sure, I like it just fine. Quiet, you know, after Brooklyn –'

'Anything's quiet after Brooklyn,' said Denis.

'Thassa true,' said his aunt, 'but you know, I missa the bustle, the talk, you know. Even missa the fights.' She paused slightly. 'I sure miss your Uncle Mick, boys.'

'So do I,' said Denis simply.

'Yeah,' said Michael.

Carmella looked at Joey. 'He's sleepin'.' She continued in a whisper to Denis, 'Say Mr Big Important Policeman Now, when are you gonna get the guy who done this to my boy, eh?'

'We'll get him, Carmella. One of these days. He's not in town, we know that.'

'How you know that?'

'It's our business to know. We're sure he's out of town.'

'Chicago?' asked Sean.

'Could be,' replied Denis. 'He has family there.'

'Italians have family everywhere,' said Carmella.

'And here we are,' grinned Michael. Joey stirred in the bed. They all looked at him. His eyes were still closed.

'Noreen?' he said.

'He's dreamin',' said Carmella.

Nobody said anything.

TWENTY-FOUR

It was autumn in New Zealand. From his seat at the end of the fourth pew of the Presbyterian Church of St Andrew and St Michael in Gore, Jim Keith could see the red and gold of the rata and kowhai trees tipping the long window and colouring the austere black and white squares. If he sat up straight and craned his neck he might just get a glimpse of the Hokonui Hills where the bootleggers ran their moonshine liquor in the old days, as the present day Whisky Creek and Whisky Falls testified. The old days? It was still in his own father's lifetime. How he would have loved it here in Southland, Jim thought. He himself had certainly settled well. Twenty years now and he'd never been back to Scotland. Never really thought about it. Yet when the Prince of Wales had come over on that visit to New Zealand in the summer he had felt a funny twinge for the old country. Not that he owed it anything now but something stirred when he saw the pageantry and the processions that day in Dunedin. He had taken the family. I mean when would they ever get a chance again of seeing a real royal prince? They weren't very impressed.

'So what?' said Billy.

'He's old,' said Berta. The twins were similarly less than agog about processions, but at one year old what else would you expect?

They were squirming about under everybody's feet even now. Jean's frequent glances at him meant he should do something about it, like picking one or both up, but he pretended to be engrossed in the sermon. And that wasn't an easy thing to do. The Reverend Murdo Farquharson, BA, DD (Edinburgh) was not the most charismatic preacher in the South Island –

'– I am reminded of the occasion, my dear brethren, when an old friend of the family, a delightful old chap, who often visited my old aunt in Helensburgh, a lovely wee spot back in Scotland, some of you will know it, or your parents will know it, or your grandparents certainly. Anyway, as I was saying, this old friend was with my aunt – a remarkable woman she was, oh

341

a remarkable woman, and said to her, in that way he had, he said . . . .'

Mention of the Reverend's aunt caused Jim to remember he had left his mother at home. Or rather she had elected to stay at home. It was odd how she was always sicker on a Sunday morning. Come to think of it, his mother had been playing the part-time invalid ever since she arrived in New Zealand. Good Lord, he thought, that's almost twenty years ago now. He started to think what a big slice of anybody's life twenty years was. He also realised he had spent it all in this country on the other side of the world. Wait a minute, if he was here, it was Britain that was on the other side of the world, not New Zealand. He'd never thought of it like that before. That's what education does for you. All that reading he had done in his life. And what had it taught him that helping a cow to calve hadn't, or seeing a bird rise in the morning sky hadn't, or the black branch of a tree shaking in the wind? Experiences are what life is about. He glanced up at the window again. Yes, the tree was still there, and the minister was still there . . .

'– for it behoves us all to think of just such examples in our own lives. The ordinary lives that all of us lead in our ordinary way as we trudge down Life's rough way with our shoulders bowed in our heavy-laden boots,' – Jim heard a smothered giggle and looking across the aisle saw Matt Cowie stuff a white hankie in his mouth – 'weighed down by the cares of every day' old Murdo went on, 'we wait for God to come and lift us up to His bosom and cradle us with the angels for all eternity.' He made one of his polite little coughs. 'I am reminded friends, of the man who was struck down by a terrible illness. He was a friend of mine. A relation, well, a near relation you might say. His uncle and my aunt, the one I was telling you about, were related by marriage on my father's side. Well, one day, this poor chap was . . .'

There was almost an audible groan in the church as another hoary anecdote was dragged out, its every syllable made contemptible by an ancient familiarity. Jim looked across again at Matt Cowie. He was trying to ease out his fob watch in order to have a peek at the time. Matt was the local banker and a great golfer. No doubt he had a date on the first tee after the kirk. Matt glanced across and caught Jim's eye and he raised his eyes skywards. Jim grinned and looked down. He was a good lad, old Matt. Many a good night they'd had at his place.

There were a lot of Cowies in New Zealand. They had been here a lot longer than the Keiths. Matt told him once that old William Cowie, his grandfather, had been an 'economic emigrant' from Aberdeenshire in the 1870s. In those days it was a twelve-week non-stop voyage in the Timaru – Glasgow to Port Chalmers, just as the Keiths had done in the Mataura thirty years later.

'May God Bless to us this reading from His Holy Word, and to His name be praise for ever more,' intoned the Reverend creakily. The congregation almost shouted a grateful 'Amen' as the service was concluded and everyone rose for the final hymn:

> 'My God and Father while I stray
> Far from my home on Life's rough way . . . .'

Jim Keith was suddenly aware of Jean's glare. His wife was struggling with Kenny while Jamie was asleep in Berta's arms. She couldn't rise because of the dead-weight of the toddler.

'Lift Jamie will you!' The imperative in Jean's voice was unanswerable and Jim quickly reached down to take his son from his daughter. The oldest son, Billy, was standing on the other side of his mother, staring up to the outside door through which the congregation was slowly moving, their conversation drowning the recessional hymn being pounded out by Charlie Livingstone.

'Where were you?' said Jean, all red-faced and indignant.

'What d'you mean?' responded a puzzled Jim.

'Kenny's been down around everybody's feet and you're sitting there in a doze.'

'Sorry love, I was day-dreaming.'

'You don't have to tell me. You alright, Berta?' Berta rose without a word. 'Come on, Billy.' He turned and followed his mother, and the family made their way slowly up the aisle.

'He looks happy enough.' It was Mrs Cowie, Matt's wife, and she was indicating the sleeping Jamie on Jim's shoulder. She was pulling at one of her own young sons. 'Wish Matt could do the same with this rascal.'

'Off to the golf then?'

'Who, Matt? Oh yeah, nothing gets in the way of his golf.'

Jim nodded and smiled at the easy-going Mrs Cowie, who was now engaged with Jean in mutual commiserations about children in church.

By this time, they were in the porch and the bright afternoon sun flooded the wooden interior bringing a warm glow to the faces of the sober-suited congregation who all seemed to be talking at once. Jim was glad of the chance to hug young Jamie closer to him as he pushed his way through the throng, nodding to this one, smiling to that, checking that Berta was still coming up behind him. When he got to the front door and outside at last, he nearly dropped Jamie when he saw that the Reverend Farquharson had Matt Cowie by the shoulder and appeared to be telling him a particularly earnest story. Matt was writhing with impatience and was caught between his own good manners and a basic respect for the minister's cloth. Jim could see it was getting to be a near thing though. He decided to come to his friend's help. He was his bank manager after all.

'Good morning, Mr Farquharson,' he said, loudly advancing to the minister, 'Thank you very much for a most interesting sermon.'

'Ah, – er – Mr Keith, isn't it?' Jim realised that Jamie was hiding most of his face. He tried to adjust the warm, little body while extending his right hand. 'And is this wee Kenny?'

'No, this is Jamie.'

'So it is. I hope the sermon didn't send him to sleep?' Before Jim could think of a reply, the ancient Reverend was already looking beyond him to Jean and the others coming up behind. Jean was still in conversation with Mrs Cowie and they had now been joined by Mrs Livingstone, the organist's wife. Berta stood with them listening as all three women talked at once. Billy stood aloof at the side, a picture of fifteen-year-old indifference.

'You have the whole family I see.'

'That's right, Mr Farquharson, I never leave the house without them!' His little sally was quite lost on the minister who was still nodding his way to his next platitude.

'A great comfort and joy, a family.'

'Indeed, Minister,' answered Jim dutifully.

'I don't know what we'd do on a Sunday without the Keiths and the Cowies. I was just telling Matt here –' He turned with a wave of his hand, but Matt Cowie was nowhere to be seen.

'Och, where has he gone?'

Jim didn't have the heart to tell him.

Big Bruce Mackenzie didn't go to church on Sunday. He didn't go at any time. He was happy to observe the Lord's Day as a day of rest and to sit listening to a sermon was too much like hard work for him. Tina took the boys off in the trap each week. They tried to find excuses to stay at home with him but he ordered them to go – 'to please your mother and keep her company'. She wanted to take four-year-old Chris with her, but Bruce found as many excuses to have the little girl with him every Sunday – 'for company'. There was no doubt that it pleased him too. Pleased him mightily. His only daughter was not only big Bruce's pride and joy, she was his favourite toy. He would take her out and play with her at every opportunity, even strapping her on to one of the huge working horses and taking her round the farm with him. But Sundays were the best. Especially now that old Grannie Keith was at Jim's homestead for a spell. Bruce liked the old stick well enough, but while she was about he couldn't relax around the place as much as he liked and have a couple of beers on the verandah of an evening. And she hated his pipe. He didn't know why when by all accounts her own husband had been a pipe man. However, to keep the peace, and please Tina, he had his pipe and a bottle of beer in the big shed. Except on a Sunday morning. Then he would lie full length on the old sofa, which served as a verandah recliner, and light up his briar with a bottle of beer already opened on the table beside him. Best of all, wee Chris would sit on his legs, watching with glee as he 'put the fire in his mouth' as she called it. When he got the bowl nice and warm, he would let her feel it with her little chubby fingers.

'Hot,' he would say.

'Hot,' she would reply. Then, ' 'moke' she would go on. And the doting father would make smoke signals from his mouth with occasional rings for her extra delight, and the little girl would scream with pleasure.

This Sunday morning he was preparing to go through the same routine. He had his pipe and his matches to hand, but no Chris. He looked back to the house, and called, 'Chris! Where are you, my wee pet? Come to Dad, come on.' He struck the match and sucked on the first draw. 'Come on, Chris.' What's she doing? he thought. He took another long contented draw, and as he was doing so, the little girl emerged from the front door, hurrying towards him.

''Moke 'moke,' she was calling.

'I know, I know. Dad made the 'moke now.' And he drew again.

''Moke 'moke,' she said.

He nodded. 'I know. I know. Give me time.'

''Moke,' he heard her say again. Women, he thought, no patience, any of them. And he drew one last big breath. The briar was now bright red in the bowl and drawing well. Bruce then went through his repertoire of puffs and rings, and little Chris seemed as fascinated as ever, although her insistence on ''moke, 'moke' seemed to go on much longer than usual. He took the pipe from his mouth and looked at her steadily.

'Dad's made all the 'moke he can, Chrissie. Let him have his beer now, and you go play on the hammock. There's a good little girl.'

''Moke, 'moke!'

'No, I've done the 'moke.' She kept on.

''Moke, 'moke!' But this time, she pointed behind him. He turned his head where he lay, and sure enough, billows of grey smoke could be seen coming from the open front door.

'Jesus Christ!' exclaimed Bruce. He jumped up so suddenly that he knocked his little daughter on to the wooden steps of the verandah, dropped his pipe and knocked over the beer on the table. For one instant, he didn't know which disaster was the greatest, but sense prevailed and he picked up Chris. Running with her, he took her down the lawn to where the hammock swung between the two big rimu trees. He sat her down as she was still calling, ''moke, 'moke.' Bruce looked back quickly. The smoke seemed to be getting worse. 'Hell's teeth,' he muttered. 'It has to be a bloody Sunday.'

There was no one to run to at the Jacksons on the next farm. Even old Hilda was with the Lutherans. He ran back to the verandah steps in about three paces and in a futile gesture picked up his overturned glass and threw what remained of the beer in the direction of the door, then taking a handkerchief from his pocket and with a backward glance to his child rocking happily in the hammock, he pushed open the door. The hall was filled with smoke. Crouching, bent double, his eyes already streaming, he stumbled along the hall, closing the sitting room and dining room doors as he went, coughing his way towards the kitchen where most of the smoke seemed to be coming from. He pushed the kitchen door open and the blast of heat almost knocked him over. He could hardly breathe. He took one of the kitchen stools and threw it through the window. There was a crash of glass, but the consequent draught drew out much of the smoke and he could see where the source of the fire was. The oven door was open and he could see the roast in there for the Sunday lunch. He kicked away the wood beside the stove, but the washing hanging on the pulley above his head was completely alight. Most of the smoke was coming from the armchair, where a bit of the washing had fallen. The horsehair was a mass of flame. His eyes were streaming badly, and his hand was scorched by sparks from the wood, but he found his way to the water bucket and emptied most of it over the chair. Taking a couple of washing-up towels which were hanging under the table, he wrapped one round each hand, and dragged the chair towards the back door. As he did he saw little Chris come in through the smoke, coughing and crying.

'Chris!' he yelled, leaving the chair and making a grab for her.

He got her under one arm and with difficulty, because of the burning towels on his hands, got her under his armpit. The child was now screaming with real fear and he knew he must get her away from the flames and especially from the smoke. He gave the chair a hefty kick through the back door, and bending low with Chris, ran for the outside. By this time, the whole place was in danger of going up since everything but the tin roof was of wood. But his daughter was his only real concern. He kicked over the chair with his feet again, so that it rolled over several times on the gravel at the back, smothering most of its flames. Then still with Chris under his arm, he hurried into the stable and seizing a harness from the wall, tied her up in it as quickly as his fumbling fingers would allow. She was now screaming with annoyance and frustration, and as he struggled with her, found that she had wet herself.

'Well, that won't do you any harm, at least!' he muttered, and left her on the earth floor, well out of reach of both smoke and flame. 'Let Dad go and see about the bloody 'moke, will ya?'

The chair was now smouldering in the yard. With its removal, most of the smoke had cleared, and going into the kitchen again, he found that the washing had now almost burned itself out on the pulley, and only the charred remains of the pulley itself, the kitchen tablecloth and the bit of old carpet that Tina had kept by the door for their muddy feet were evidence that a fire had raged in the kitchen confines only minutes before.

'God help us!' said Bruce, standing in the middle of it all, looking round him. The only thing that seemed at all ordinary in the scene was the sight of the roast in the oven, now brought earlier to cooked condition than on a normal Sunday. The smell of it was even stronger than the smell of smoke and charred wood.

'Bloody beautiful!' said Bruce, wryly. 'Talk about roast!' Then, looking down at his hands, he saw they were burned to the knuckle. Only then did he feel the excruciating pain. Going to the water bucket, he saw that it was empty. 'Jesus Christ!' and this time, it was more prayer than oath.

Outside in the stable, Chris was still crying loudly, but this time they were the tears of a frightened child. Her cries had upset the two workhorses, who were kicking in their stalls. Their noise had started off the cows in the near paddock. The hens of course were running round in their typical circles and even the pigs grunted in curiosity at this Sabbath cacophony on the farm. Bruce joined in with a hysterical laugh, as he stood with his burned hands over the empty water bucket, looking at the blackened waste all around him. ''Moke, 'moke, bloody 'moke!' he bellowed at the top of his voice.

He was lying in the hammock with Chris asleep on his chest, when Tina and the boys arrived home in the trap. His hands were covered by two wet pillowcases, and his eyes were still streaming red from the smoke. Tina screamed when she saw them both, and imagined that something had happened to Chris. The little girl was wakened by the noise her mother made and started crying again, which made Tina cry, this time with relief, while the boys, thrilled with the new excitement, ran shouting to each other to come and see this and come and see that. They were especially agog at the sight of the broken kitchen window. Sandy was dispatched at once to fetch the Jacksons on the farm to the north and Stu to get the Cargills from the other side. Hilda van Meer arrived on the scene, still in her best hat and coat, ready to help serve up the Sunday lunch as usual and burst into tears as soon as she saw the mess of the kitchen, but cheered up immensely as soon as she realised how nicely done the roast was! Being Hilda, however, she had her hat and coat off at once and was already into rescuing what was left of the washing. Seven-year-old Ross was persuaded to take his sister with him while he fetched more water from the well. Little Chris seemed not at all affected by her experience, neither from flames nor smoke, and was already back to form after her sleep. Tina, meanwhile, gave all her attention to her husband's charred hands.

'Anything I can get you, Bruce?'

'Bring us a beer, girl!'

'Thank you,' said Enoch Gebler, 'you're a good boy, Abel.' His grandson had brought him a glass of milk and two slices of brown bread and butter on a tray. Enoch was more and more troubled by his feet swelling up and so he spent most of his days in bed now. For most of the time, Abel was his live-in companion in the Bronte apartment, coming out on the bus from Sydney for every weekend and school holiday. His own parents were always busy in any case, his father with the Union, his mother at the university and Abel had no real, close friends of his own age. His best pal was his grandfather and there was no one else Abel would rather spend the time with than the old Jew who talked to him as if he were three-score and ten, too. Enoch, when he was on form, liked to talk, and Abel liked to listen, so they were a good combination. They were also great readers and the old man was always on to the boy about the importance of books – good books that is. 'What are you reading?' was almost the first question Abel was asked whenever he arrived from Potts Point, and if he was able to come up with an author approved by his grandfather, preferably Jewish, then the questions would begin, just to check that he was taking the subject matter in. Abel loved these sessions, even though he had to endure the usual diatribe against his father. If old Enoch's first hobby was reading and debate, his second was abusing his son-in-law. Abel had got used to it and knew that in a way his grandfather really rather admired Bobby Keith and the way that he had forged a position for himself in the Australian Trade Union movement. Enoch purported to scorn him for not going into active politics, but Bobby insisted he was doing a better job for the workers where he was, and so the debate went on. Rachel kept well out of it all. In any case, she had her own university and Zionist interests to pursue. Abel Keith was proud of his mother and father and admired each of them for their cleverness, but he truly loved his old Jewish grandfather. Especially on Saturdays.

Enoch kept a strict Jewish Sabbath and liked Abel to join him in the rabbinic ritual and practices of the Holy Day.

'It is written,' Enoch would say, 'you shall keep the Sabbath because it is given to you. You are not given to the Sabbath. The laws were given that man might live by them. They are not ends in themselves but are meant to enhance life here on earth while we consider the beforehand and the hereafter.' No work was allowed on the Sabbath, of course, but the teaching of a child was permitted and Enoch took full advantage.

'You see, my dear Abel, you don't have to go crazy you know. If I'm sick or don't feel well, I don't keep the Sabbath so good. Better to profane one Sabbath than to miss many eh? But most times I like to keep it. I like to recite the prayers, I enjoy the blessing of the Kiddush before we eat and the chanting of the Haftarah after we read from the Torah. And best of all, when we recite the Habdallah at the end of the day, before we return to the ordinary world again. Friday night to Saturday night is not so long to keep out of the whole week is it? Then you got Sunday too since you are half-Christian.' Abel made a face, but Enoch went on. 'It is good you hear these things. You have best of both worlds, ja? You are half-Jewish and half-Scottish.'

'I'm Australian,' Abel would protest.

And Enoch would spread his hands. 'Oy, what is Australian?' he would say. So, the better half of Abel, in Enoch's eyes at least, was well-tutored in Hebrew lore – and in many other things beside. Because of his remarkable and wide reading, Enoch knew all kinds of interesting facts and Abel was fascinated by the things he would suddenly come out with. He would pepper the day with unexpected and unrelated bits of general knowledge like – 'Did you know that there are no turkeys in Turkey?' Or, 'Shoes worn on the right foot wear out faster than shoes worn on the left foot.' And 'The word "bride" is German for "cook" ', also 'That the English language has more words in it than any other'. Etc, etc. Abel found all this sort of thing fascinating and never knew when or why his grandfather would come out with such factual gems.

This particular weekend he was going on about humility and

service, prompted perhaps by being served with something to eat in bed. Anyway, he was sitting up, with the tray in bed, quoting from his beloved Martin Buber, who in turn was quoting from Rabbi Nahman of Bratslav, who said – 'God does not do the same thing twice.' He looked at Abel over his glasses. 'Good ja? Worth thinking about?' He read again. 'Listen,' he said, 'That which is, is single and for once.'

'That doesn't sound humble to me,' said Abel.

'You got to think about it, mein liebling, like Bubar does. The happening-but-once is the eternity of the individual. This uniqueness is the essential property of man, but it is only given to him so that he may unfold it, see what I mean?' Abel didn't quite but nodded, trying to look as intelligent as he could. Enoch continued:

'Everyone who has ever lived, and that means you and me, Abel, knows that there has never been in the world anyone who is exactly the same as he was or as you and I are. If there had been there would have been no need for us to exist, see. Each person is a new thing in the world. By the way, did you know that on average, a newborn baby cries for more than two hours a day?'

'Did you, grandfather?'

'Ja, bestint. You too. We all cry to make the statistic, ja?'

'Ja, grandfather.'

'But back to Buber.' He looked at his book again, 'Where was I? Ah yes, "It is not he who knows himself who is proud, but only he who compares himself with others." That's true, eh? You see Abel, if we are truly humble, we can live happily inside ourselves because for us, there are no "others" – see what I mean? You've got to believe that every man's got what you got inside him and you've got to honour that. That's real socialism. Not like your father's communism by numbers. See here –' he pointed to the page '– No man exists who does not have his hour. Each soul stands in the splendour of its own existence, and every man should be honoured for that which is within him, and only he possesses.' He looked up at the boy with a smile, 'What you got inside you, Abel?' The boy shrugged, feeling slightly embarrassed.

'Your mother, my Rachel, has departed from our God. She is full of her politics and her dreams of a Jewish homeland, so what do I do? I love her all the more. The Hasidim tells us to do this. To love more. Love lives in the truth that is between us all and we must bear witness to that truth by loving each other, as you and I love each other Abel.' The boy blushed. 'No, we must not be too proud to admit to love, especially when it is true. Even if we cannot sing ourselves, we can all join in the songs, ja?'

'Ja,' replied Abel tentatively, hoping his grandfather wouldn't ask him to sing.

The old man cackled with laughter. 'Not to worry, my boy. Your grandfather is no cantor neither.'

They were both very easy with each other, this old man and young boy, and each learned from the other for they each had a different wisdom and they helped each other generously. This was more than family duty and affection. It was love and they knew it.

'All is in God,' Enoch read out, 'and knowing that we fear not the before or the after, nor what is above or beneath, neither this world or the world to come. The humble man is a just man and wherever he is, he is at home and can never be exiled. The earth is his cradle, and heaven his mirror and his echo.'

Enoch put down the book, and made a sighing sound and stared as if into space. Abel waited for him to speak again.

'Abel,' he said at last, 'give me your hand.' Abel did so and his grandfather's bony fingers felt hard and cold around his own.

'Abel?'

'Yes, Grandad?'

'I want to tell you something.' There was a pause. A long pause. Abel felt uneasy as Enoch continued to stare ahead. Then he closed his eyes and grimaced, muttering under his breath in Yiddish. Suddenly, he started as if in pain, and gripped Abel's hand so hard that the boy cried out. The old man now threshed his shoulders about the bed, his hand still gripping Abel's like a vice, and saliva appeared at the corners of his mouth. The stream of Hebrew, if that's what it was, grew in pitch and intensity interspersed with German and occasional English phrases like – 'it's not right' and 'my legs are cold' and 'what is happening?' Abel was terrified and mesmerised at the same time. Eventually his grandfather slumped and was quiet again, but he looked funny as he lay back on his pillows – sort of crooked and twisted, and the water running out of his mouth, like a baby's dribble. He was still staring and his mouth was half open as if he were about to speak. Abel waited but nothing happened. He was still waiting a long time later. He didn't want to speak. He was afraid that his grandfather wouldn't reply. That his grandfather couldn't reply. So he sat there at the bedside through that long Saturday afternoon with his hand in his grandfather's, which was getting colder all the time. And as the light grew darker in the room and he stopped hearing people in the street outside and an awful silence fell, he could hear nothing except his own heart thudding in his chest under his thin shirt. There was a terrible smell as if his grandfather had done the lavatory in the bed and Abel realised he was getting very cold himself. He was now very frightened and gradually he tried to ease his hand away from Enoch's. But he couldn't move it! It was absolutely caught as if glued to the old man's hand. Abel panicked but the harder he pulled the more it seemed to be held in that frozen grasp and he began to whimper. The whimper became a cry and the cry a howl of anguish as the afternoon gave way to night and Abel Keith became aware that Enoch Gebler had died! Bewildered by the suddenness of it all, Abel sat in a daze before he found voice at last to call out, as any child would, for his mother and father.

Bobby and Rachel found their son still at the bedside late the next evening when he didn't come home. He was sitting on a chair at the bedside with his head on the bed and his right hand in the dead hand of his grandfather. In the boy's left hand was a half-eaten slice of brown bread and on the tray on the bed was a drained tumbler of milk. Bobby sent his wife out into the kitchen, while he broke the old man's fingers to release his son. Abel immediately vomited all over his father, and out in the kitchen Rachel set up a wailing chant for her father which sent its mournful reverberations over the full moonlit Bronte Bay. Her words were from Isaiah – 'From new moon to new moon, and from sabbath to sabbath, all flesh shall come to worship before me.' Bobby Keith carried his son home in his arms and Rachel's voice carried the soul of Enoch Gebler towards the arms of Abraham.

The Keith household in Forres was sombre, despite the autumn sunlight, for it had just received unexpected visitors. John Keith and Thomasina sat at the parlour table opposite an unlikely couple, two very tall people, Ella Friar and her father, Alec. The former outrageously rouged and lipsticked, with all the connotations that they shamelessly represented, the latter a dark, lowering figure, but with the light, blue eyes of a sailor. At the top of the table sat Mrs Beattie, now a little frailer but still with a spark in her, and between her and John stood Becky Friar, now a most attractive, tall young woman of nineteen. Her stepsister, Elspeth, watched the scene from a chair beside her mother. John's head was on his chin. Becky's hand was on his shoulder. She stared defiantly at her gaudy mother.

'I don't care what you say,' she said, with a tremble in her voice, 'I still think of Uncle John as my father and Tommy –er– Auntie Thomasina, my mother, and I don't need, I don't want anything, or anybody else.' This was more or less blurted out in a rush without much thought or consideration. Becky was too distracted to be objective and too upset to be properly calm. She couldn't believe that this harridan of under forty was in fact the tall lady she remembered, or fancied she remembered as her mother, more than twelve years before. Had she dreamed her previous mother? If not, what nightmare had turned her into this? Becky didn't know it, but the nightmare had been Ella's, not hers.

'But I'm tellin' ye lassie, I am your mither,' cried Ella in a raucous, street voice. 'I'm your mither an' I can prove it.' She pointed at John. 'And it's his brither Bobby's your faither.'

'So you've said,' shouted Becky, 'ower and ower again.' The tears were in her voice but she was fighting to keep them back. 'But I'm tellin' you, I don't care.' John reached up and mutely patted the hand on his shoulder.

Ella was now in full flow. 'And this here –' She indicated Alec '– is my faither and your grandfaither. Whit d'ye think o' that?' Mrs Beattie then spoke before Becky could answer.

'It's a' right, Becky lass.' She then turned to Ella and her tone changed. 'I'm that happy the poor lassie aye kenned her ain situation. Kenned fine, Ella Friar, that she wasna John's natural dochter, and was ay his brother's lass, him that's in Australia. But ye hiv tae understaun' wumman, that the bairn, an' she's ay a bairn yet for a' her woman's look, the bairn's hardly set e'en on you for years till an hour since and that must be an awfy shock for onybody, still less a quiet-livin' lass that's never been oot o' Forres.'

'Whit dae ye mean by that?' asked Ella belligerently.

'Weel noo, onybody but Blin' Harry wad see that ye havena been workin' for the Band o' Hope since ye were last in the toon, and ye can see yersel, can ye no', the fright ye'd gie ordnar folk when they see ye in the daylight the wey ye are.'

'The wey I am?'

'Woman, ye're a' paint an' pouther, and whit's ablow your reds and greens is scarlet, and whit's under that's as black as the deil's erse!'

'Whit's that?'

'We a' ken whit ye are and if the lassies werena here I'd spell it oot for ye.'

Elspeth's eyes were out on stalks as she drank in the scene greedily, her eyes going from one to the other as they spoke, as if she were watching a play. Becky stood proudly beside John with her head turned away to the window but not seeing anything. Thomasina's head was averted to her husband, who still did not look up. Ella Friar was now on her feet, glaring at the diminutive Mrs Beattie who gazed up at her, unperturbed. Alec Friar pulled his daughter down beside him. He was a big, rough man and he had a big, rough manner as well as a big, rough voice, but there was the hint of a latent quality in him that suggested something good gone wrong, or having been forced wrong. He had said little since the first momentous introductions and had done little but gaze on Becky with open admiration. He and Ella had suddenly arrived at the Keiths while they were at table and the remnants of the midday meal were still on the table. Needless to say, they had not been invited to join the family and Elspeth had been sent to fetch John from the Mason's Arms. Mrs Beattie had met the girl running and had come at once to the house herself – to see what was happening. She had taken a position of arbitrator in the matter, although making no secret of where her bias lay. Thomasina had flustered between the calls of basic good manners and revulsion at the appearance and manner of the gross woman and the bulky man and had brought them in only to get them off the doorstep and out of the neighbours' eye-line. Now they sat opposite, looking incongruous in the semi-genteel pretensions of Thomasina's parlour, and it was big Alec's turn to speak. His accent and vocabulary was as much-travelled as he was.

'I see fine,' he said, 'that it must have been a bit o' a shock for the like o' us to blow into your snug wee harbour here like this, full sail up and wi' a good wind ahint us, but ye'll understaun' I've had tae take in quite a bit of new cargo since landin' – ay.' He glanced meaningfully at Ella. 'Ella here is as ye see, and it doesna break my heart efter whit I've seen in the world like. A' the same, I have to say that she wasna always as she is noo, and I'm led to understaun' that it was a son o' this hoose set her on the road. Him an' a certain schoolmaster, I hear, who also had his wey, as they say, then changed his mind, or had it changed for him by a sister who soon spread the wrong word about my poor fatherless bairn here. For she was fatherless, and that was my fault –'

'Or her mither's,' put in Mrs Beattie firmly.

'Or her mother's, as ye say, Mrs Beattie,' repeated Big Alec, not the least perturbed by this frank discussion of his daughter and late wife. 'After a' these years, who can tell eh? All I can tell ye, friends –' At this, John quickly glanced up, but Alec continued in the same even, unhurried tone, 'all I can say is, that before she fell, as they say, she was as straight and bonny as this young lady here – Rebecca, you called her – ay, bonny indeed.' His voice dropped as he looked at Becky again. Ella was crying noisily but no one paid any attention. 'What I mean is, like, that the daughter I once had could well ha' been the mother o' this lass here just as obviously as the woman berthed beside me at this minute could never be. Do I make my meanin' clear?'

'Ye dae that, Alec Friar,' said Mrs Beattie, 'an' it does ye credit for a fair man. I hope then ye'll see fair done by Becky.'

'We can only dae what's right and natural,' replied Alec quietly.

'And whit's mair right and natural than a mither should want to see her ain daughter?'

'But is she your daughter, Ella Friar?' shouted Thomasina suddenly.

'Oh, ay, that she is, and well you know it.'

'I don't mean that. I mean –'

'We a' ken what you mean, Thomasina,' said her mother, 'and so does she. Ay, kens fine. Comin' in here withoot as much as yer leave, and gi'en us, never mind the lassie, bother and upset wi' a' her nonsense.'

'Nonsense!' yelled Ella.

'Aye, nonsense!' retorted Mrs Beattie, now well and truly wound up. 'An' if it was my hoose, I wid have ye oot o' it, just as soon as I could say Jock Thomson.' The barb struck home and Ella rose.

'But it's no' your hoose.'

'No, it's mine.' John's voice came as such a shock, not only to Ella but to the room, that there was an immediate silence. 'An' I'm tellin' you to be about yer business, an' leave us in peace.'

'You canna keep me from seein' my ain flesh and blood. Is that no' right, faither?' But her father only bowed his head as if deep in thought.

'If I were you, Ella Friar,' said John, rising to his full height, 'I would hesitate to talk o' the flesh. And if there's to be blood in this house, by God, it'll be yours if you're not out o' my sight this minute.'

'It's no' fair,' snivelled Ella.

'No', it's no' fair,' said Mrs Beattie, 'that a bonnie lassie like Becky should hae a trollop like you as her natural mother.'

Alec Friar rose. 'I think we've had enough o' that Mrs Beattie. As you say, John Keith, it's your house and we'll leave it. Come on, Ella.' He pulled his daughter up. 'I think we a' need a spell in dry dock.' And in a minute they were both gone.

'Well, that was that,' said Mrs Beattie. There was an embarrassed silence. 'Well it would seem Ella never got faur wi' her midwifery!' Becky ran from the room.

'Becky!' cried John, but Elspeth was already following.

'Becky! Wait for me.' Thomasina was up at once.

'Elspeth. Leave Becky –' But Elspeth was already gone. Mrs Beattie rose and went to the window that looked out on to the street.

'Did ye ever see sicca pair?' She shook her head and turned to the table. 'Yet there's good in the man, I'm thinking'.' John strode to the door.

Thomasina called out at once, 'John!' But her mother put her hand on her arm, and said quietly, 'Leave him be.' Thomasina sighed.

'Whit do we dae noo, mither?' Mrs Beattie surveyed the table.

'I suppose we could clear the table.' she said.

In the bedroom that she shared with Elspeth, Becky Friar sat on the edge of her bed, her elbows on her knees, her head in her hands. Elspeth was kneeling up on the bed behind her. She could hardly contain her excitement.

'Oh Becky, wasna she awful? An' she says she's your mither.'

'Is she?' She said it in a very matter-of-fact tone.

'She said she was. Isna that awful?'

'It is.' Her voice was now distant.

'Whit are ye tae dae?'

'I don't know. Yet.' She rose and went to the window and put her brow against the cold, damp pane. It was all too much too suddenly. She couldn't take it in. The truth was she didn't want to take it in. She felt a lump in her throat again, but she fought it back. She would not cry.

'Never mind, Becks.' It was comforting somehow to hear Elspeth use her nursery name. 'You've still got us.'

True, thought Becky. An uncle who's an alcoholic, an aunt who's a snob, a cousin who clings, but as she says, they're all I've got. They've kept me for nearly twenty years, so I'll keep them. She turned to the bed, and lay down.

'Here,' said Elspeth. 'Weren't we supposed to be going out to Grant Park?'

'Not today, Els.'

'But you said –'

'Well, I've changed my mind.' She lay back stretching. 'You go if you like.'

'I couldn't go on my own. Not through the park.'

'Why not?'

'I'd get lost.' Becky said nothing, but in her heart, that's exactly what she wished well-meaning Elspeth would do.

In the Mason's Arms, John Keith sat hunched in his usual corner, but unusually he had a companion – Alec Friar. The two men sat regarding the drinks before them.

'It's a business,' said John.

'Ay, 'tis that,' said Alec. There was a pause before John spoke.

'I love her, ye know.'

'I know. She loves you.'

'Aye.' He gulped down his drink. 'As an uncle.'

'No,' said Alec, sipping his, 'as a father. Will ye have another?'

'Whit?'

'Another drink?'

'Why no'?' Alec returned in a few minutes with two more beers and whisky chasers.

'Cheers,' he said.

'Aye,' answered John. Both men drank in silence. They had been going steadily at it since tea-time, when Alec had seen his daughter back on the Aberdeen train. He explained to John that she'd been called back hurriedly – 'on business'. John understood.

'It's funny,' mused Alec, 'I'd almost forgotten I had a daughter. I came back to see if I had. It's something I'd often thought about when I was at sea. Coming into home port again. I don't think it's a great idea. Poor Ella. I don't think she'll be back in Forres for a while,' he added.

'Why'd she come back at a'?' murmured John.

'I think she had an idea of showing me off. And naturally she wanted to have a look at Rebecca. She is her mother after a'. And she's not getting any younger. She could be frightened.'

'We're a' frightened,' John muttered into his beer.

'But some more than others,' said the sailor.

'Ay,' said John. There was another pause.

'What about your brother?'

'Which one?'

'The father.'

'Bobby doesn't even know she exists.'

'I thought you wrote –'

'I did, but my father had died on the voyage, and Bobby left the ship at Sydney. My mother would have told Jim about Becky – he's the one in New Zealand – but I don't think he told Bobby.'

'He's bound to find out.' John made a scoffing sound.

'They'll never be back in Forres. Neither of them.'

'I wouldn't be too sure.'

'It's a long way and it's been a long time. I try to forget.'

'I see that.' He took another long sip and regarded John for a moment. 'You're her uncle,' he said. 'A blood relation.'

'You're her grandfather.'

'So I am.' The thought seemed to strike big Alec for the first time and he rather liked the idea. 'So I am,' he repeated.

Elspeth went to the park after all. Her mother went visiting a friend, and Mrs Beattie went mad, deciding for no reason at all to suddenly clean her little house from top to bottom. She was angry about something she couldn't explain, so she took it out on the furniture and the carpets, beating the latter over the clothes line in the back yard saying at the same time,

357

'The bitch! The bitch! The dirty bitch!
Lies in bed withoot a stitch,
And as a result she gets to be rich,
The bitch! The bitch! The dirty bitch!'

The neighbours all knew who she was talking about.

Mrs Beattie was thus happily engaged when Elspeth came rushing through from the back of the house.

'Gran! Gran!' she called. 'My mither says you have to come.'

'My God, whit's wrang, lassie.'

'It's Becky.'

'Whit's up? Has she –?'

'She's gone away.'

'Away?'

'On the train.'

'Whit?'

'I saw her from the bridge. She was carrying a case and had her good coat on.'

'Why didn't you stop her?'

'She was too far away, and then the train came in. Oh, come on, Gran, my mither says ye've to come to the hoose. My Dad's in an awful state. That Mr Friar brought him hame, and he's away to the station to see what train she got on.' Mrs Beattie shook her head, and wiped the dust from her forehead with her duster.

'Weel, if it's no' one thing, it's the other. Come on an' I'll get my coat.' She went inside, leaving the newly beaten carpets to get wet in the rain, which had just come on.

TWENTY-FIVE

Monsignor Patrick Joseph O'Neil was at his desk in Baltimore working on a Seminarian Report for his Bishop. Paddy had been His Lordship's secretary since the summer and he was anxious to make a good impression. Not that he need have worried. He had done that already or else he wouldn't have been lifted out of his St Christopher's parish in New Jersey and dropped into the secretary's chair in the Bishop's house in Baltimore.

'You're on your way now, Monsignor,' said his young curate at St Christopher's. 'It'll be Pope Paddy in no time.' It was true that in the Catholic priesthood not all roads lead to Rome, but in the case of those earmarked for promotion, invariably the path leads to the Vatican and the first step is generally to become secretary to a bishop. So here he was, at forty-two, virtually starting again – with a list of Maryland hopefuls – applications to enter, and begging letters to leave the seminary, reports on those in training and the numbers of those expected to be ordained at the end of the current session. To Paddy, it seemed no time at all since he was a seminarian, but that's how it is when you're happy in your work, and years had fairly flown for the Monsignor.

Suddenly, two hands covered his eyes. Two soft hands, two feminine hands. It wasn't the housekeeper, she wouldn't dare. It wasn't Sister Mary Rose, she wouldn't know how. It must be – yes, it could only be – Maria! He pulled the two hands down as he heard her laugh. Yes, it was his niece, Noreen's child and his favourite young woman – Maria O'Neil.

'Did I give you a fright, Uncle Paddy Monsignor?'

'You certainly did, and you made me make a blot.'

'What? Have you blotted your copybook, Uncle?' And she laughed again. Paddy swivelled round in his chair.

'Now look here, Maria girl, you can't really be coming in here at any time disturbing a man at his work. What would the Bishop say?'

'He'd ask me to sing a song for him, like he always does.'

'Well what would Sister Mary Rose say?'

Maria mimicked the nun, 'Mother o' God, and all the Blessed Saints in Heaven, girl, what are ye doin' here bein' a nuisance to the Monsignor, good man that he is, and you a single girl not out of the convent?'

It was Paddy's turn to laugh. He was really fond of this hoydenish girl whom he had come to love since Noreen, on his advice, had first brought her to the convent. He had come with them all those years ago – it must be five years now – and now here he was in Baltimore himself. It's funny the twists and turns of fate – or, as a good Monsignor, should he not say, God's will? Anyway, he was delighted at how it had all turned out and that he had the company of this charmer. She was eighteen years old, with her father's Italian black hair and good looks and her mother's green eyes and Irish spirit – or was it temper? She had her own waywardness which infuriated everyone at the convent but this was offset by a charm which let her get away with it nine times out of ten. Maria was her own worst enemy but she had a particular friend in her Monsignor uncle, and she wasn't ashamed to take advantage of it at every opportunity. She came to his chair.

'Uncle Paddy,' she said in her most coaxing voice, 'I want to ask you a big favour.'

'Oh no,' he said, 'I'm only just getting over the last one.'

'But this is a big favour, a really big one.'

'You frighten me to death.'

'Uncle Paddy!'

'Alright,' he said, putting down his pen, and sitting back, 'what is it?' She didn't answer at first, but walked round to the front of the desk and then wheeled round to face him.

'I want you to take me to the opera.'

'What?'

'I want you to take me to the opera.'

'Maria, I –' She ran round to his chair again.

'Listen, Uncle Paddy! The Fiske-Merton company are coming – and they're the best – and they come from Chicago – and listen – listen! They're doing "Martha" and that's the one has the song in it – you know.'

'Is it now?'

'It sure is. Remember? The song I did with Mummy on stage when I was a little girl.' At the involuntary mention of her mother, Paddy could see Maria start and bite her lip. She hadn't heard from Noreen since the Joey shooting, and her kidnapping by Rico. For all they knew, Noreen could be dead. Or in Chicago. Paddy reached out and chucked her under the chin.

'You're still a little girl.' She smiled and assumed her former, eager manner, as if she had just blanked out an unpleasant thought from her mind. She knelt by his chair.

'Who says! Listen, Uncle Paddy – it's an Irish song. You'd love to hear it again.'

'Would I?'

'Yeah. And funny thing – I was doing it with Sister Marcia in Music class, and now she says its part of this opera. We just got to hear it.' And she immediately began to sing:

'Tis the last rose of summer left blooming alone,
All her lovely companions are faded and gone
No flower of her kindred, no rosebud is nigh,
To reflect back her blushes or give sigh for sigh.'

It was almost unbelievable that this young girl should kneel there in the morning sunlight coming in from the french windows and sing with such simplicity and ease, but her voice was of such beauty and so unforced that it seemed the most natural thing in the world for her to do. Paddy was most moved but tried not to show it. Her face, looking up to him, was radiant.

'Ain't that just beautiful?' she said.

'Isn't that just beautiful?' corrected Paddy.

'That's what I said.' Just then the door burst open, and Sister Mary Rose burst in.

'What was that noise?' she demanded to know. Maria rose up indignantly.

'That wasn't no noise! I was singing to Uncle Paddy?'

'Is that what it was?' retorted the sister, unimpressed.

'It was opera, sister,' said Paddy, in a tone which suggested it must therefore be permissible in the office of the Bishop's secretary.

'Say you now, Monsignor? Ah, I'm sure you know best, good man that ye are. Will that be all then, Monsignor?' Paddy was taken slightly aback, but he kept a straight face.

'Er – yes – thank you, sister.'

'Thank you, your Reverence.' And she shut the door behind her. Maria burst out laughing and ran to the door to do an immediate take-off of the old nun, but Paddy held up is hand, saying,

'Now that's enough, Maria. You'd better be going back to the convent now. I've got work to do if you haven't.'

She came to the front of the desk.

'Then you'll take me?'

'What? Where?'

'To the opera, of course.'

'Oh? Well, we'll see.' She let out a cry and came round to his chair once more.

'Oh, thank you Uncle Paddy! It's Friday night!'

'Friday? Oh, I –'

'See you then. Byee!' And planting a big kiss full on his lips she was gone as suddenly as she had appeared, nipping through the french windows into the garden like Puck in the play. Monsignor Patrick Joseph swung back idly in his swivel chair but he couldn't keep the smile from his face.

They had a great night at the opera. The Fiske-Merton Company wasn't the New York Metropolitan and the leading singers were past their best but the musical experience was well worth it and even more so was Maria's obvious enthusiasm for it all. Unfortunately, this wasn't shared by Clare Connolly, Maria's room-mate at the Convent of the Sisters of Mercy. It was a house rule that a girl couldn't be taken to a public place by an adult person without the company of one or more fellow pupils – even if that adult person were a relative, a priest and a Monsignor to boot!

So Paddy had two eighteen-year-olds for company that Friday night. Clare found the whole opera thing very boring and laughed out loud at the fat, middle-aged hero and heroine trying to overcome his huge stomach and her huge bosom in the final embrace. It was meant to be a comic opera after all, but not for the reasons the two stout singers made it funny. They were built on the grand scale. Maybe that's why it's called 'Grand Opera', Paddy thought. They finally gave up pretending to be young and slim and turned and sang facing out front, which everyone, except young Clare of course, found perfectly adequate, for they still could sing. When the leading lady sang the Tom Moore song in it, Paddy knew it wasn't nearly as good as when Maria sang it for him in his study. He watched her now, her profile eagerly mouthing the words as the diva sang:

'I'll not leave thee thou lone one to pine on the stem,
Since the lovely are sleeping, go sleep thou with them!
Thus kindly I scatter thy leaves o'er the bed,
Where thy mates of the garden lie scentless and dead.'

Paddy was quite sure that Maria, given half a chance, would have been up on stage with them all. He was also sure that one day, and very soon too, she would be. So was she. She applauded so much at the end that other people in the upper circle turned and smiled.

On the way home, although it was against the rules, he took the girls to their favourite drug-store and they had huge ice-cream sundaes while he had a coffee. It was good to see their young faces bright with pleasure. Why not, Paddy thought, their young time is so short. As for the girls themselves, they couldn't wait to grow up and get out in the world. For a couple of Catholic convent girls they seemed to know more about it than he did.

'But Uncle Paddy, you surely have heard of Fatty Arbuckle?'

'He's fat,' added Clare, sucking her straw.

'He murdered an actress in Hollywood,' went on Maria.

'At an orgy,' said Clare, licking the end of her straw.

'Girls, please!' said Paddy, hurriedly glancing along the counter, but none of the other customers seemed to be at all bothered about them. Maria lifted her glass to drain it.

'It was in all the newspapers.'

'I don't read all the newspapers.' He tried to catch the old bus-boy's eye for a refill of coffee. 'And the newspapers I do read don't print stories about film actors.'

'What do they print, Father?' asked Clare as the attendant came along the counter with more coffee.

'Thank you,' said Paddy, proffering his cup. He thought of all the dull stuff he had to read, but he said, 'I don't know. Woodrow Wilson's stroke. Warren Harding running for president. Things like that.'

'Great,' said Clare, sarcastically.

'Will your daughters want another milk-shake, sir?' asked the bus-boy with the coffee jug still in his hand.

'They're not my daughters!' said Paddy quickly, but not quickly enough to stop the girls going into giggles.

'But she just called you "father",' said the coffee-server.

'I'm her uncle – well, not her uncle, but her uncle –' It was easier to go than to explain, so they went. He realised that his scarf had hidden his white collar. They laughed about that on the way home and Clare kept calling him uncle. On the street car, and on the street and at the convent doors, they talked and they even sang the latest hit song. Paddy surprised the girls by knowing the words:

'Margie, I'm always thinking of you, Margie,
I think the world about you . . . .'

In his own spare, little bedroom Paddy said his prayers for the end of the day but couldn't help pondering on their happy night at the opera and at the drug-store. A couple of nice girls, he thought, even if one of them were a relative. How they could talk. Everything and anything. The only thing they didn't talk about the whole night was Noreen – her mother. But he had noticed the pause she made. Did she not want to talk about her, he wondered?

In the girls' spare convent bedroom, the lights were already out when they got upstairs and both had to stumble around in the light from the street-lamp to get ready for bed. Sister Marcia came to their door and whispered at them to be quiet, but they only giggled again – after she'd gone.

'Monsignor O'Neil's nice,' said Clare from her pillow.

'He's my uncle,' said Maria from hers.

'He's still nice.'

'He sure is. 'Night Clare.'

' 'Night, Maria.' Maria stretched contentedly and relived her whole night again – the opera, the ice-cream sundaes, their laughter, all the talk. They had talked about everything except – her Uncle Paddy had never mentioned his sister. Was that deliberate on his part?

Then the song came back into her head –

'Tis the last Rose of Summer left blooming alone . . . .'

Noreen felt very alone in Chicago. She had liked it better in Cicero. At least she could get out and about then but since they moved up in the world, literally and metaphorically, she found that Rico preferred that she stay indoors, in his smart apartment twenty-three floors above Lake Shore Drive. She turned the comfortable sofa at an angle so that she could enjoy the view of the water. She took the bowl of grapes from the small table and lay back to eat them all. At least Rico saw she was well provided for. The wages of sin, she thought, as she spat another pip into her palm. Yes, Rico – it had all happened so quickly. It had been bad enough finding out she was pregnant after that time with Liam, but then right on top of that came the Joey shooting, and before she knew it, she was in Rico's car. At least the journey gave her time to think and she thought it best to keep quiet about her condition. She had to make a cold-blooded decision in the light of day about a hot-blooded act in the dark of night. Meantime, she would let nature take its course and Rico take full advantage. After all, he did love her so he said. But did she love him? She still wasn't sure.

She got the feeling that Rico didn't want anyone, particularly other men, to see her at this extreme stage. Not for any concern about her but purely for vanity – his. She remembered he'd been just the same with Maria. Pregnancy for him was seeing his woman fat and ugly and the less he saw her like that the better. He had never actually said as much but that's what she felt he felt and that was why he left her alone so much. Of course at the beginning there were sensible reasons to keep her hidden away from the family, but now she might as well be dead as far as they were concerned. She missed her family. She would have given anything to have joked with Sean and laughed with Michael. Better still to have talked with Paddy. And best of all, to take Maria in her arms again, if Maria would ever come to her arms again. She was almost a woman herself now. At the thought of her child, her heart ached. She sighed and had another grape.

Now that her time was drawing near, she was getting frightened. She didn't want to be alone. She wanted to be with a woman. Her mother? Too old and too far away. Twenty years too far away. Mamma d'Agostino kept writing asking in her half-English if Noreen would come to her in her new place in Scarsdale. Now that Sean and Liam had made her a deal she couldn't refuse for her New York restaurant – they just moved in and took over – Mamma thought it best to 'retire'. Rico was still furious about the business, but what could he do about it from Chicago? Noreen sometimes wondered if Sean and Michael were biting off a bit more than they could chew. And where did they get the money for all their operations? She knew Liam Murphy was in with them in some way and that it was all linked with liquor. She never asked them about their business. It was just the same with Rico. The less she knew the better. All she knew was that he was self-employed! She got the idea that Rico had set himself up as a kind of go-between between the Irish and Italian communities in Chicago. It was all very vague to Noreen, and there were Canadian connections now. She had heard him on the telephone to Montreal and once she even heard him call Dublin and her heart leapt. Rico called himself 'a technical advisor'.

One time, Carmella's cousin, Roberto Ruffiano, had come to Chicago. He was bringing Rico all the news from New York and some of her things from her apartment. Every time he came he brought something of hers. She liked her own things round her. The last time Roberto visited, she asked about Francesca. He told her she was pregnant too! Noreen was delighted but Roberto wasn't so pleased. 'The best waitress I ever had,' he said. When Noreen asked who the father was, Roberto shrugged and said that Francesca couldn't make up her mind, but they took ten dollars from every man in the Italian community just to make sure. She made so much money, Roberto said, she's going to open a restaurant herself when she's had the baby. She's going to call the child 'Lucky' she said, for getting caught out was sure a lucky break for Francesca! 'Yes,' Roberto had repeated morosely, 'best waitress I ever had!' Good old Francesca, thought Noreen. She still laughed when she thought about it.

She thought too about Carmella. Bustling Auntie Carmella. She hadn't really been the same since Uncle Mick died. None of us had. No, she couldn't go back to Carmella. Especially after the Joey incident. What a time that was. The relief when she heard he was alright. Even Rico smiled when he heard about the tins of beans. Poor innocent Joey. I wonder how he's doing in New Jersey, she thought. Thinking of Joey led her to thinking of Nellie. Poor Nellie and her lost children. Then thinking of Nellie made her think of Liam. A grape stuck in her throat and she had to cough. Rising uncomfortably, she quickly filled a glass from the cabinet with her favourite soda water and drank greedily. With the glass in her hand, she moved to the big window and looked out. Yes, Liam. Listen girl, she told herself, you still feel so guilty about that night, you choke on a black grape! What makes it worse is that Rico thinks it's his. She shivered slightly and went back to the sofa.

They had had to run from New York. They drove actually – in Rico's new Oldsmobile. The police had questioned the porter at the apartment but he, wise man, couldn't remember a thing. They gave up asking Joey. He thought it was all very funny and kept talking about ketchup. Everybody knew it had been Rico but they couldn't prove anything. It was more than a month before the two detectives arrived from New York to 'continue their enquiries' and talk to him about the shooting in the apartment. There was a charge against him of attempted murder, or at the least, assault and battery. Neither Joey nor Carmella wished to press charges, but the police were interested because it had been a shooting. Rico then produced the names of at least fifteen people who swore he was in Yonkers that night. Of course they were all Italian. The cops, though, warned him he would be watched. Rico said that in that case he would make sure he was well dressed! They then told him that their colleague, Captain O'Neil of the Traffic Division, was very interested in his sister's welfare, and they stressed that no alibi, however watertight, would save someone from a charge of kidnapping, that is, holding another person against their will. Rico's answer was to open the bedroom door and ask her to come through. When she did, they asked if she was Noreen O'Neil. When she said that she was, they asked if she wanted to return to New York with them. She remembered she had glanced at Rico, but he was pointedly looking out of the window. She declined their offer with thanks, stating that she wished to remain with Mr d'Agostino, as she was pregnant! She was aware of Rico's whirling round from the window and of the detectives' bumbling apologies as they went. She realised immediately that the admission would cut her off completely from her family, but she had made her bed in Chicago. She might as well lie on it. Then Rico had her in his arms, covering her with kisses.

He found a whole new energy in Chicago. He had quickly re-built his old connections and 'work' soon started to come in. Now here they were on top of the pile again. As for herself, the cage was no longer gilded, it was real gold. But still a cage. She got up again and started to pace up and down the expensive grey carpet. God almighty, she was so bored. Where was he this time? Oak Lawn or Oak Park? Evanston or Lombard? Hammond or Arlington Heights? Even back in Cicero? He could be anywhere.

Then she had the most awful pain in her stomach. It was so severe that it buckled her knees and she found herself kneeling on the thick pile, holding on to the armchair with her right hand. What was this? Was it those damn grapes? It must be. She should have washed them – there was another stab in her lower abdomen. It was like a knife. It was too early for any contractions. Or was it? Oh my dear God! She was frightened again. What was she to do? She didn't know a single person on the block. She couldn't call Rico. He could be anywhere. There was another pain. It was so bad she cried out – 'Mother o' God!' and fell forward on her face. Her nose drew up the dust from the carpet as her brain reeled from the options rattling through her mind – Chicago or New York? Rico or Mamma? Carmella? Sean? Paddy? Francesca? Francesca! She knew what she must do. Slowly she got herself up and going into her bedroom she found her notebook in her bag. She found Roberto Ruffiano's number and lifted the telephone at the bedside.

'Operator,' she said, finding that she was breathing hard, 'Op– what? Sure I'm OK. Yeah, you can help me. I wanna call New York . . .'

'Hullo Francesca!'

'Hullo little Noreena! And the two women hugged each other long and warmly. 'Boy, is it good to see you, kiddo. Come on in, you must be beat,' said Francesca taking her hand.

'Oh Fran!' Noreen gasped as she looked into the tiny room, for there facing her was a huge baby cot and looking out over the end of it were two little heads.

'Meet Lucky and Forty!' exclaimed Francesca gleefully. 'My twins. Boy and girl – what you think, eh? Their names are supposed to be Luciano and Fortunata, but they're Lucky and Forty to me. And they sure have been I can tell ya. Hey!' Noreen was crying and embracing her again. 'Come on now, it's your old pal Fran from way back when. You'll have me goin' if you start that, and then we'd have trouble. I look a mess when I cry. Don't you just hate those women who can cry beautifully?' Noreen let herself be carried along by Francesca's 'gioia di vita', and after the mandatory hello to Lucky and Forty, found herself seated at the kitchen table with a cup of coffee while Francesca wrestled the twins into separate high stools nearby. When she got them both installed safely, with some help from Noreen, she sat her down again at the table and said, 'Now you sing one of your little songs for them while I go get a surprise for you. They like being sung to, as long as it's Italian.'

'But I don't know any Italian,' protested Noreen.

'That don't matter,' answered Francesca airily. 'They don't know no different. 'Scuse.' She left Noreen staring at the two infants, and one of them, Forty she thought, started to whimper. Noreen rose to her, at which Lucky started too and Noreen was dithering between both when Francesca came back into the kitchen, leading a man by the hand. It was Roberto Ruffiano. He was smiling sheepishly as Francesca pulled him forward.

'Well, here he is. This is the guy who's gonna marry me!'

'Roberto?'

'As soon as he gets a divorce that is,' added Fran.

'I told you she was the best waitress I ever had,' said Roberto. And they all laughed, even the twins.

And when the babies were asleep, and Roberto had gone home to his plain wife, the two female friends talked in the kitchen until the early hours of the morning. The apartment in Queens was a small one and the only bed for Noreen was a pull-out from the sofa, but it lay untended as the hours flew by and they caught up with all the years. Fran had always been an easy-going, happy-go-lucky girl and she was no different now that she was a mother and potential wife. Noreen's experiences had changed her but not completely hardened her and she was glad to pour out all her worries to someone who was not family. Francesca understood completely.

'You love Rico, si?' she asked Noreen.

'Yes.'

'And he loves you?'

'I think so.'

'Think so? And you are full of his child?' Noreen didn't answer but bowed her head. 'Why doesn't the guy marry you?' Noreen shrugged. Francesca went on, 'I mean you ain't gettin' any younger and childbirth at forty ain't no birthday party, I can tell ya.' Noreen gave a little shiver. Fran noticed. 'You OK, kiddo?'

'OK.'

'No more of them pains?'

'Not for a while now.'

'Good. You don't want nothin' goin' on – birth-wise? You get me?'

'No. I think I'm just a bit tired.'

'Sure you are. Nobody comes all the way from Chicago and don't feel tired. Them trains is so noisy. Not that I've ever been on one, but I can hear them, especially at nights. Wonder how Rico liked reading the note you left him. He can read, can't he?'

'He can read alright. Probably rang his mamma right away. Or Roberto.'

'Funny, he never mentioned it,' said Francesca.

'He knows not to mention any business he had with Rico.'

'Rico sounds an important guy.'

'He is. To Rico.'

'I get it. But he knows you're coming back once you have a break. He'll understand.'

'I wonder. But I do need a break. I need to talk.'

'Then you came to the right place. Here, look at the time. We better get you to bed. You'll be needin' all the sleep you can get. It's a long way to Baltimore. Anyways it is in your condition. Come on, let's get you on that sofa, and if the twins don't wake you I will first thing, and you can get over to your brothers and one of them will take you to Maria, I'm sure. You'd like that eh?'

'Oh, I would.'

'Sure, you would. She's a swell girl. And ain't you got a priest too somewhere?'

'Paddy, yes. He's in Baltimore now. And he's a Monsignor.'

'My, there's class. Come on, you've a lot to do before you get back to Chicago and have that boy.'

'How do you know it's a boy?'

'I know. I know all about boys all my life.'

And the two women laughed as they went through to the sitting-room with their arms around each other.

In no time, Francesca had Noreen settled and she put out the light. The room was suddenly very dark.

'That too dark for you, Noreena?'

'A bit.'

'I'll open the curtains. If I can find them.' She did, and the night light of the city streamed in.

'That better?'

'Thanks.'

'Good night then. I think I got half-an-hour before one of them wakes up. Who would be a mother? Hey, what am I sayin'? Buona notte.'

'Buone notte e grazie tante.'

'Prego. Hey, you speak pretty good Italian. Ciao.'

And Noreen heard the sound of the door closing as she stared over the roofs at all the stars in the night sky.

'You're frightening me.'

'How am I frightening you?'

'You frighten me when you look at me like that.'

'I have to look at you if I'm going to help you.'

'Why do you want to help me?'

'Because I think you're sick.'

'I'm not sick.'

'Well, I think you are.'

'If the doctor says you're sick, Nellie, then you're sick. That's why he's a doctor.'

'Maybe I'm just sick o' doctors.' Nellie Murphy laughed loudly at her witticism, but neither her mother nor Dr Nolan laughed.

'I'm sorry, Dr Nolan,' said Nessie.

'Not at all, Mrs O'Neil, not at all. It's God's blessing. The sick don't know how sick they are, and the mentally sick least of all. I'm no psychiatrist, as you know, but even a general practitioner like me gets to know how complicated the mind of a patient is, and that some are more complicated than others.' He consulted his notes. 'I see, I see.' Nessie had brought Nellie to see Dr Nolan because she was getting more worried about her daughter. She tried to explain to the old doctor in his old, well-worn surgery.

'Truth to God, Doctor, she's getting worse.' And went on to explain in her own words why she thought so. According to Nessie, Nellie seemed outwardly perfectly well, but seemed to be living in a dream world a thousand miles away, so that she alarmed her mother from time to time with the things she would say. For instance, the conversations she kept having with her two dead children were getting the older woman down. It was funny but she never ever mentioned Liam. Everyone else in the district merely dismissed Nellie as being 'not quite right in the head' and strangers who hadn't known her just thought she was a bit 'slow'. But Nessie remembered better than most what a smart girl Nellie had been, and might have been a schoolteacher if she hadn't married Liam Murphy. Now there was hardly a word from him and he married to her for twenty years. A regular bank order came for her, it must be said, and Nessie was very glad of it at times. The farm was now too much for her with no man in the house. Nellie did the house and cooked the meals, but Nessie was getting tired with the farmwork, even with the help she got from the hired men. Though in her seventies she was fine and healthy yet, but knew she had to slow down. It couldn't do with two of them being slow. So Nessie had decided to see Dr Nolan and find out if anything could be done for Nellie. In case anything happened to her. Why was it, she thought, that people always use that phrase – 'in case anything happened' – when the surest thing in the world was that she would eventually die. Perhaps people didn't want to face up to the fact of death? Nessie O'Neil didn't mind facing up to hard facts. She had done so with a poor farm, a drunken husband, a rebellious son and a whole family that had left her for America. She could just as well face the fact of Nellie's insanity, if that's what it was. But, even after eleven years of it, Nessie didn't believe her daughter to be insane.

'What could it be, do you think, Doctor?'

'Dementia Praecox.'

'What's that?' asked Nessie. Nellie laughed at the name. The doctor went on, 'You could call it, I suppose, a kind of advanced absent-mindedness. It was when you mentioned her being a thousand miles away. People in this condition seem to live in their own dream world, as if the world of reality had frustrated them in some way and they preferred a world of their own making. Anything can bring it on. An accident, a bad failure, a severe shock, like the loss of a loved one – and she lost her children, did she not?'

'Ay, she did.' Nessie felt uncomfortable talking about Nellie with her sitting beside her, but Nellie didn't seem to mind. She just sat and smiled and nodded.

'I know they're dead,' she said suddenly. Her mother glanced sharply to her. The doctor looked up urgently.

'What was that you said?' he asked.

'I know my children are dead,' said Nellie. She looked at her mother, 'because you told me –' then she turned to the doctor, '– and because you said they had scarlet fever.'

'In that case,' said Dr Nolan, 'why –?'

'But I don't believe you,' said Nellie, stonily. She wasn't smiling now. 'My Dermot and my Celia are still alive.' Nessie's heart fell. But Dr Nolan leaned forward.

'Of course they're alive. In you. In your thoughts of them. In your memory of them. That's the real Nellie Murphy. But there's another Nellie Murphy who thinks they're still alive in

371

the flesh. That's the pretend Nellie Murphy. That's part of your schizophrenia. Do you understand me?' Nellie smiled again. It was frightening.

'Oh, yes, I understand you, Doctor. I told you I wasn't sick. And I'm not mad either.' The doctor sat back with a heavy sigh.

'Tell the doctor why you keep washing your hands then,' said Nessie suddenly. Nellie looked discomforted.

'Because of the dirt,' she said sullenly.

'What dirt?' asked the doctor.

'The dirt,' said Nellie again. Dr Nolan looked at Nessie.

'Sure there's not a speck o' dirt in the house, Doctor. She has it that clean. She's forever cleaning and scrubbing and running away good water.' Dr Nolan nodded.

'Another symptom of the same thing,' said the doctor. 'And if it gets worse, then we can look to her becoming genuinely insane.'

'What the hell do we do then – sorry, Doctor.'

'It hardly befits me as a medical man, Mrs O'Neil, but I should think a few Hail Marys might be in order.'

Nessie sighed. 'She's had plenty of them.' At this, Nellie started to repeat the prayer childishly, as if it were a trigger reaction to its mention. As if she were a little girl again back on the farm, telling her nightly beads.

'Hail Mary, full of Grace, the Lord is with thee. Blessed art thou amongst women, and blessed is the fruit of thy womb–' Both her mother and the doctor tried to talk over her at the same time, but she only got louder and louder, until she reached the word, 'womb', when the doctor rose up and banged his desk violently as she uttered the word, shouting it with her – viciously aloud.

'WOMB! That's it, Nellie Murphy!' and pointing his forefinger straight between her eyes, he brought his face near to hers and continued in the same ascending intensity. 'But that's it, woman. That's where it started – in your mind – and that's where it'll end. Where we'll finish it – in your blessed mind! You're forty-seven years old. Your womb is as dead as your children are, d'ye hear me? DEAD! Dead to the world. But you're alive and living and well and happy and strong, so Hail Mary for that, say I. And rejoice with her that your little boy and little girl are with her in heaven this day.'

'In Heaven!' Nellie gasped, bewildered by this sudden turn.

'As sure as they were born,' continued the good doctor, the sweat running from him. Nessie made a hurried sign of the Cross and bowed her head. Nellie stared straight at the doctor. Her expression had changed totally. She was shaking visibly, and tears were running down her cheeks. Dr Nolan hurried round and took her shoulders between his arms, and pressed hard, saying all the time into her ear, softly and tenderly, 'They're gone, Nellie. The little ones are away. They're in their own innocence now and there's nothing you can do to prevent that. They're away, as you say, but they won't be coming back because they don't want to come back. And you know that you wouldn't want them back either. You wouldn't have them alive now, and back in this dirty world, now would you? Isn't that why you're cleaning it all the time. It's a dirty world, ours. Theirs is a clean world, leave them there. Leave them where they are, woman. And let them pray for you now. As you've prayed for them. But have you ever heard now of anybody praying for angels? What do you say?' The last phrase was whispered. The doctor turned Nellie's face to his. Nessie could be heard sobbing quietly. 'What do you say?' the doctor repeated.

There was a long pause as Nellie gradually grew calmer. In the silence of the tiny surgery, Nessie could hear the doctor's heavy breathing and her own heart thumping, but Nellie seemed very composed now. They both watched her intently as they waited for her to speak.

'I want to see Liam,' she said at last.

Liam Murphy was on the carpet when his private phone rang on the desk just above his head. This annoyed him very much as he had given orders that he wasn't to be disturbed on any account. He was even more annoyed when he thumped the back of his head as he jerked up when it rang. He had just reached an interesting stage in the sexual intercourse he was having just at that time with Maxine, his coloured private secretary. They had regular 'private dictation' after work but the only thing Maxine had taken down were her cami-knickers. She lay on her back looking up at him now as he struggled to get upright at her feet. Of the two, he was certainly the more coloured as he shouted into the mouthpiece. He was a bright puce colour, which gave every indication of his recent strenuous efforts.

'I told you I wasn't to be disturbed, dammit. I don't care who –' He hardly looked a Valentino, Maxine thought, as Liam stood at the telephone, his smart trousers down about his ankles hiding the two-tone shoes. But he pays good, she thought – and come to think of it – she licked her broad lips creamily, he fucks good too.

'Hell's teeth!' Liam smashed the phone down hard.

'Get yourself out of here,' he said without looking at her.

'But Boss –' she began. He wheeled round on her.

'Goddam! Didn't ye hear me, girl? Get your arse out of it. And double quick too. I've got visitors.' He started pulling up his trousers, as she started pulling up her very shapely body, its dusky effectiveness set off by the bright red dress.

'Why don't we go to a hotel like everybody else does?' she moaned.

'Because I don't like hotels,' he said. Liam Murphy, like many sensual men, had unexpected pleasure in making love in the most unexpected places. He seemed to require an element of danger in his coital activities. This leant a greater urgency to his exertions and therefore a greater pleasure to his partner. Maxine could take it or leave it. Mostly she took it. She was now making her way to the side door.

'Don't forget your pad and pencil!' yelled Liam, indicating the notebook on his desk.

'There's nothing on it,' she said.

'Well, put something on it.'

'Like what?'

'Like "I must do as the boss says"', and picking up the pad and pencil he threw them at her. 'Now, get the hell outta here,' he added, putting on his jacket.

'You're the boss,' shrugged Maxine and, picking up the pad and pencil, wriggled her posterior out of the side door. Liam sat hurriedly at his desk. He was just in time, for the main door opened, and Sean walked in, holding the door open behind him. Liam's jaw dropped as he saw Noreen being helped in by Michael.

'Hope we're not disturbing you,' said Sean.

'No, not at all,' answered Liam automatically, feeling very disturbed indeed, as he noted Noreen's condition.

'You being the busy man,' continued Sean.

'I was just examining some figures.'

'I bet you were,' said Michael, nodding towards the ladies' shoes that were lying behind the desk. Liam had the grace to blush.

'My secretary. She has trouble with her feet.'

'Aren't you going to offer the lady a seat?' suggested Sean meaningfully, indicating Noreen.

'Of course – I'm sorry – I should have –' Liam was blustering and feeling very bad indeed about this visit. Noreen, however, was apparently very cool.

'There's no need, Sean,' she said. 'I won't be staying.' She went forward to the side of the desk and looked down at the shoes. 'And they're not cheap, either,' she said. And kicked one towards the wastepaper basket with her toe.

The three men watched her closely, as she regarded Liam again, and with a hardly perceptible shake of her head and a small smile playing on her lips, she turned and walked out, as proudly and gracefully as her shape and weight would allow. Sean looked at Liam. Liam looked taken aback. Michael looked at Sean.

'Let's go,' he said curtly. At the door, Sean turned.

'Don't forget we have a directors' meeting tomorrow night. You'll be there.' Liam could only nod. When the door shut he slumped down in his chair again, as the side door opened and Maxine appeared.

'GET OUT!' Liam yelled in a voice she had never heard before. She got out – fast.

In the elevator going down, Noreen held firmly on to her two brothers as she stood between them. The downward motion of the car was hardly pleasant, but rather that than walking down twenty-eight sets of stairs. Michael patted her hand.

'Won't be long now, sis.'

'Another month,' she said.

'I was meaning,' said Michael, 'till we get to the ground floor.' She couldn't help laughing, despite her queasiness. 'That was a short visit, our Noreen,' said Sean. 'Did you just want to have a look at Liam for old time's sake?'

'No,' said Noreen, 'I just wanted him to have a look at me.' The boys looked at each other over their sister's head.

'What time's the train?' asked Michael.

'We'll make it alright.' The elevator doors opened, and taking an elbow each, the two big brothers lifted their pregnant little sister out of the door high in the air, much to her terror and delight.

In the train Noreen was glad the boys were unable to take her to Baltimore. Apparently they had some big meeting the next night – something to do with their clubs – she thought there was some kind of trouble between them and Liam, but she wasn't sure. They would have gladly driven her down on the Sunday, especially as Sean now had a Cadillac, but she didn't want to wait that long.

Sister Mary Rose put her head round Paddy's study door.

'Monsignor,' she said, 'there's a Mrs O'Neil to see you.'

'Who?' said Paddy, looking up from a Diocesan Register.

'She says her name's O'Neil.'

'God Almighty!' Paddy muttered. 'It's my mother.' He rose quickly and went round his desk. As he did so, Noreen appeared.

'Noreen!' he said.

'Hello, Paddy. Have you a seat for a woman that's travelled far?'

He gave her as much of a hug as he could, much to Sister Mary Rose's high astonishment. 'Thank you, sister,' said Paddy. 'This is my sister, Noreen.' Noreen smiled wanly at the old nun, who clucked her concern at Noreen's condition.

'You look near your time,' she said. Noreen shook her head.

'No, not really,' wondering how a nun knew such things.

'The head's low and it's almost engaged,' said the sister. 'I was in the hospital before coming to work for the Monsignor here. And an easy job it was too,' she added, closing the door. Paddy led his sister to the couch by the window.

'Noreen, this is a real surprise. Not a word from you.'

'I wanted it to be a surprise,' she said, 'but instead it's you are the surprise to me. Indeed you are.' She was amazed at how easily she lapsed back into the Irish lilt as soon as she was with any of her family.

'What do you mean?' he said.

'I mean you looking the fine clergyman, now. A Monsignor no less, and the nice red braid round your black.' Paddy looked a little abashed, and was glad to reach back in order to pull up a chair.

'Sure, I'm still your brother first,' he said.

'But am I your sister?' she replied. He said nothing at first.

'It's been a long time.'

'Almost nine months.'

'Of course.' They sat silently regarding each other for a minute and when they spoke again, they each spoke at once.

'Paddy!'

'Noreen!' They laughed.

'Go ahead,' he said. 'Ladies first.'

'I came to see Maria.'

'Of course.'

'And I want to make my confession.'

'I can arrange that.'

'No, I want you to hear me.'

'Are you sure?'

'I am. Can you arrange that?'

'Yes. If you'll just let me get my stole. There's no time like the present.' He rose and went to a drawer of the desk and pulled out a narrow purple stole, which he put round his neck. Then, taking up a daily missal from the window ledge, he came back to the chair, turned it sideways to her, and sat down to lend his ear, indicating with his hand that she should begin.

'Bless me, father, for I have sinned . . . .'

Sister Mary Rose was on the telephone. She was still awkward with the instrument and had a tendency to shout into it. She might as well have opened the window and called across the gardens from the cathedral house to where Sister Marcia had her room in the convent.

'A Mrs O'Neil, I'm telling you ... That's right ... His sister ... Indeed it was ... Such a hugging going on ... He did ... Her mother? ... Oh, that explains it ... She's with him now ... Just talking, I suppose ... Haven't they plenty to talk about? ... Do you think that would be wise? ... Should I not? ... Alright, then, fetch her from the music room ... I'll keep an eye for her at the door. She knows about ... ach ... I've cut myself off again. The thing's gone dead.' She put down the telephone in the hall, and tiptoed across to the Monsignor's study door. Making a tiny Sign of the cross on her forehead, she bent her head to listen. Yes, they were still talking. She nodded to herself and then went as quickly as she could – which was not quick – to open the back door. She just had it open when Maria hurtled through, her hair flying out behind her, as she ran.

'Save us, girl, you nearly had me over!' exclaimed the nun.

'Where is she? Where is she?' cried Maria, eagerly.

'She's with your uncle, the Monsignor, good man that he is, and you'll have to let me take you there, and announce you proper, like every soul that comes to visit.'

'Oh, come on, then, Sister. Let's go.' She took the old nun's hand and laughingly pulled her up the corridor towards the hall again.

When they got to the door, Mary Rose, with a gesture stepped in front, and quietly tapped. Maria took the opportunity to pat her hair and straighten her dress. She wished now she wasn't wearing the uniform. She heard her uncle's voice call out, 'Come in,' and pushing her head back, she waited while the old nun announced her.

'Excuse me, Your Reverence, it's your niece.' She opened the door wider and Maria rushed in – to come to an abrupt halt as soon as she saw her mother. She was lying back on the couch, and was crying. She tried to rise up, but was finding it a struggle. Paddy looked very grave indeed and was hurriedly rolling up the stole in his hands. He looked up and tried to smile.

'It's your mother, Maria.' Maria could only stare.

'Would you be wanting me to stay, Your Reverence?' It was Sister Mary Rose still at the door, and with her eyes too on Noreen, who was now leaning up on one elbow. Paddy shook his head, and the old nun slipped silently out.

'Aren't you going to give your mother a kiss?' asked Noreen. Maria was still standing, open mouthed.

'Oh, you look so ugly!' she said.

'Maria!' said Paddy.

'She does! She does!' cried the girl. Noreen forced herself to sit up.

'Maria! Don't you understand?'

'No, I don't.'

'Maria!'

'And I don't want to.'

Paddy helped his sister to her feet. 'Try and control yourself. Don't you realise your mother's –'

'She's ugly! She's awful!'

'Maria!' Noreen put her hands out towards her daughter.

'Don't touch me!' she screamed.

'Maria!' cried Paddy, peremptorily.

'Oh, my God!' said Noreen and turned towards the couch. 'I feel sick.' Paddy stood between the two women, not sure who to go to first. His sister bent over, putting her hands on the couch. Maria stared in horror.

'Fetch the Sister!' commanded Paddy in a hard voice, as he moved towards Noreen, but Maria couldn't move. She was nailed to the ground. Her hands had come up to her mouth, as she watched, fascinated and horror stricken.

'Sister!' shouted Paddy.

Noreen turned, her face ghastly, 'Yes?'

'Oh, Noreen.' As Paddy went to hold her, she fell back on to the couch, clutching her stomach with a scream. Maria still stared, her eyes enormous. The door behind her opened, and the little nun bustled in, turned Maria by the waist, and said, 'Out you go, girl, and you, Monsignor.' She went to Noreen. 'Ring for the doctor, and tell the kitchen to make a bed up in the garden room.' Paddy almost ran into the hall, and as he went to the telephone, he had a glimpse of Maria running towards the back door.

It was dark in the hall, as Paddy sat there by the telephone. His arms were on his knees, and his hands were clasped against his brow. He had been there for hours it seemed. Sister Mary Rose had been correct. It was Noreen's time, and she was taken into labour from the couch in his study. Maria was in the care of Sister Marcia in the convent sick room, and Paddy was sitting by the phone with his address book on the ledge, waiting to ring the family as soon as he had news. While he waited, he said every prayer that he knew for his young sister and the child she was labouring to produce in the garden room. His mind was at war with his soul. The brother was in conflict with the priest. He knew whose child she was carrying, and the dilemma it put him in only heightened the tension he felt as he waited for events to take their natural course. Sometimes women came out of the kitchen and he would jump to his feet. But whoever it was would always avoid his eye. Then above the occasional yells and moans, there came a loud scream, which froze him as he heard it. Then it broke off abruptly, and – glory be – there was the cry of an infant. A brand new baby. Just born. He stood up, but he could have leapt for joy.

'Thank God,' he said. 'Oh, thank God that's over. And I'm only her brother!' He turned to face the garden room. It was a long time, he thought, before the door opened, and when it did, it was Sister Mary Rose who came out. She looked careworn and hot, as if she had been labouring too. She saw him standing there and came to him. He could smell the sweat from her, and was amazed at the soiled front of her apron. She came right up to him, and to his surprise, put her arms round him for a moment, and looked him in the eye.

'Good man that ye are,' she said softly, then turned and walked towards the kitchen. He could hear the baby cry still, and puzzled, moved towards the door, but as he reached it, Dr Carson came out and closed it behind him.

'A boy or a girl, Doctor?' said Paddy eagerly.

'A boy,' said the doctor. 'A fine boy.'

'And Noreen? Is she – '

'She's dead.'

The funeral was a private affair. With the Bishop's special permission it was held in the convent and Noreen O'Neil was buried among the nuns. As was the custom, only the men of the family came to the graveside – Denis, not in uniform, Sean, Michael and Monsignor Paddy, who conducted the brief service. A quartet of greying, middle-aged men in sombre black who stood with heads bowed, each with their own memory of their wayward sister – sister Noreen, now lain cold among the Sisters of Mercy, a small clump of red roses the only flowers on the grave's fresh earth. A flower from each brother – from Denis, for his sister's singing, from Sean for her spirit, from Michael for her beauty and from Paddy for her secret. He added a rose for Liam Murphy, her first love, and the love that only Paddy knew had killed her. Liam Murphy did not attend. His secretary said he was out of town, but Paddy still added a rose in his name. There was also one for Joey O'Neil who would always love her – alive or dead. Carmella was sick herself and could not bring him to Baltimore. The other man in her life was only three days old and slumbered now in the convent hospital – un-named as yet, but much cared for. His stepsister had refused to go and see him, but he got a flower too and thus Noreen O'Neil had seven red roses in her funeral posy. There was none for Enrico d'Agostino. Not that it mattered, for uninvited and unwanted, Rico came himself!

The last rite had been done and the O'Neil brothers turned away from the grave to let the gardener complete the final filling-in in the morning sunlight. As they turned, they saw Rico standing, almost obscured by a huge bouquet of white roses, among a group of women – his mother and two sisters. They were in mourning garb but Rico was in a light grey suit, so light it was almost white and in his lapel he wore his own red rose. Only a solitary bird could be heard in the hush of the little graveyard as the two groups faced each other over twenty feet of close-cropped, newly-cut lawn. Its fresh odour mixed with the perfume of the flowers and made a sweet-smelling canopy over the scene. Nobody said anything as Rico came forward with his bouquet to the grave. Paddy stepped aside to let him place it on the earth behind the red roses and before the wooden cross with its simple inscription –

'Noreen O'Neil – born in Ireland 1879 – died in Baltimore 1920. Beloved sister of Monsignor P.J. O'Neil, S.M.'

Rico gave a little gasp as he read it but everybody heard it. They also heard his whispered 'Noreena – addio mi'amore cara.' No one moved. Although Denis found it hard to resist a basic sense of duty which made him want to pounce on Rico then and there – and the 'Grievous Bodily Assault' this time would be his! The same thoughts engaged Sean and Michael but they were frustrated by the solemn occasion and the presence of the mother and sisters only yards away. Trust Rico to arrive with a bodyguard of women. He came now to Paddy's side.

'May we speak?' Paddy turned. 'In camera, per favore?'

Paddy nodded and led the way over the grass towards the gate. The brothers followed a few steps behind and the women fell in behind to make up the informal procession to the Bishop's House.

In the hallway outside Paddy's study the two groups sat facing each other from opposite benches. On one the three O'Neils and on the other Mamma d'Agostino and her two daughters. Not a word was said, either between them or to each other and the noise of the standing grandfather clock was made to sound like gunfire in the tense silence. Sister Mary Rose appeared from the kitchen, made a little bobbing curtsy to both sides and hurried into the study. It was odd to see her in the black habit, instead of her grey working apron. Sister Marcia appeared next from the garden door, also in black. She gave a little nod to both groups then hurried to the study door. Giving a little tap, she opened the door and went in. Michael suddenly stretched his legs. Everybody looked at him and he hurriedly sat up again. At length, after another long stretch of tick-tocking silence the study door opened and the two nuns hurried out and moved together to the garden exit. They were followed in a moment by Paddy and Rico, who emerged looking very solemn indeed. The waiting groups in the hall immediately rose and waited for one of the men to speak but nothing was said as Rico made a stiff bow to Paddy, who responded by a slight nod of the head. Rico turned and motioned towards his mother and turned to walk to the garden door. The women followed. Paddy watched them go then indicated to his brothers to come into his study. When they had done so he followed and closed the door behind him.

It was late that afternoon when Paddy and his brothers stood on the front steps of the convent and watched as Mamma d'Agostino carried out the infant, wrapped in white, to the waiting car, followed by the two sisters. The women guided her down the few steps and across the sidewalk where Rico stood holding open the door. The O'Neil brothers remembered his holding open a carriage door for Noreen long ago in Brooklyn. Michael felt a tear smart in his eye but he blinked it back. Rico closed the door, gave a quick glance up to them and quickly got into the front passenger seat. They watched as the car drove away to the north.

Paddy had christened the child in the convent chapel after lunch, after he had informed the brothers that Rico had claimed the boy as his own. No one objected as they considered he was. Paddy gave no opinion and the formalities were duly completed and the boy-child was baptised according to the rites of the Holy Roman Catholic Church. The O'Neil brothers had elected not to attend and spent the time with Maria in her room. She was still sedated. They discussed what they might do now that she was due to leave the convent.

'We'll leave it to Paddy,' said Denis. 'He knows best.'

'But does Maria?' muttered Sean.

Now they stood on the steps and watched the car disappear among the afternoon Baltimore traffic.

'Tell me, Paddy,' asked Michael.

'Yes?'

'What did they call the boy?'

'Guiglielmo.'

'What kinda name is that?'

'Italian,' said Denis.

'It means William,' added Paddy.

'Which is English for Liam,' said Sean. Paddy looked at his brother quickly, but Sean only shrugged and smiled.

'It's time we made for home,' said Denis.

The brothers left for New York soon after in Sean's car.

'Look after yourselves now, and may God Bless you,' said Paddy as he waved goodbye.

TWENTY-SIX

Becky Friar kept her eyes on the fly buzzing between the dusty window and the dirty net curtain of the tiny, rented room in Paddington. She sat on the bed with her knees pulled up to her chin, contemplating the little trapped insect, and pondering how long it takes a Sunday to pass in London. She thought she knew how the fly felt, caught between a vast outside world beyond the window pane, and the hampering net of circumstances. There was nothing she wanted more than to get out into the outside world, but somehow neither she nor the fly could seem to find a way of breaking clear of the small restraints that constantly hampered both of them. Money, for instance, or the shortage of it, some would consider a rather large restraint, but for Becky, it was something she was always able to earn, although unfortunately never in large enough amounts to enable her to do what she wanted. And what she wanted most to do in the world was to go to Australia. She was determined to find her real father. She only had that picture of him, which she'd taken from Uncle John's bureau. She reached down now and picked it from the pages of *Northanger Abbey* where it served as her bookmark. She put it there so that each evening she was able to take to sleep with her the handsome features of the young Bobby Keith in the family photo taken in Forres just before they emigrated.

Becky Friar was the kind of young woman who found comfort and reassurance in the fiction of Jane Austen, and a companionship in that author's pages, which she had not found as yet in life.

Becky's decision to run away from Forres had been an impulsive one – an emotional reflex following the visit of her mother and her new grandfather to the house. She hadn't had time to make any real preparations other than packing one case and drawing out her savings from the Post Office. She and Elspeth had been saving hard for an intended holiday that summer in Bath so that they could visit the scenes of their heroine's adventures. Both girls had always been bookish and during the quiet shop hours enjoyed many a quiet read. But perhaps the happiest reading of all was the statement in

383

her Post Office book which told her that, with interest, she had the tidy sum of £89/13/4! This allowed her to take the first train to come into the platform in Forres that afternoon. By chance this took her to Aberdeen, and unknown to Becky at the time, Ella, her mother, was in the carriage in front of her. Becky remembered hiding behind the shrubbery on the little platform, so that no one would see her get on the train. She didn't know that Elspeth Keith and her walking-out boyfriend could consequently see her easily from the bridge. It is difficult to know how Becky might have reacted had she seen the two Friars enter on to the tiny platform arguing loudly. When the Aberdeen train eventually steamed in, clanking and squealing and spreading its grey smoke, everyone on the platform getting off or getting on was too busy to notice one noisy couple shouting at each other at one carriage window and one young woman, carrying a parcel and a case, making her way into another compartment in the next carriage. When the train arrived in Aberdeen, Becky was so nervous that she was the last to get off, and stepped down from the train on to the virtually deserted platform. She wandered into the granite city uncertain what to do, and only hunger forced her back to the station, if only because it was already familiar. She was glad of a pie and a hot cup of tea. As she sat at the corner table watching the other travellers, she caught something of their excitement and when the woman at the next table smiled over at her and nodded, Becky could only smile back.

'Are you off to London too then?' said the woman, indicating her case. Becky gulped down the pie and nodded.

'Yes,' she found herself saying.

And so she had come to London. It was the longest journey she had ever known, and when she eventually arrived at King's Cross, she promised herself she would never travel again. If it took that long to get to London, how long would it take to get to Sydney? And the cost? Her purse was already a little bit thinner. How fat it had seemed when she crammed all those bank notes into it. However, she was a practical girl, and by the end of the first week, she had found more permanent accommodation with an Irish family in Kilburn. She'd never met any Irish people before, and found them very strange at first, but they had made her so welcome, especially the old Granny of the family, that she had stayed longer than she might have once she had found a job and began to earn more money again. Her first job had been in a bar, but she hadn't liked that. She hated the smell of beer and the tobacco smoke choked her. She next worked in a tea-room at Marble Arch, but the manager, a big, burly man with a moustache, was never away from her side. He kept touching her at every opportunity. First her elbow, then her shoulders, then the small of her back, holding his palm on her bottom, until she had to move away, and putting his hand under her armpit, so that his fingers reached her breast. It was unnerving and humiliating. But even worse than his irritating hands was his breath. He had the most awful halitosis. Anything within a six feet range of his least exhalation wilted on contact.

'I could take you up the West End, Becky. We could see Charlie Chaplin in "The Kid". They say it's luverly,' he drawled in his native Cockney. Which was more than could be said for the manager in Becky's opinion. She made yet another excuse to avoid his presence, and going to the back, put on her coat and left. She was finding that it wasn't always easy for a young girl alone. Walking in Hyde Park, she'd sometimes envy the couples she couldn't help noticing, not for any sexual implications – Becky was reticent to the point of coldness in that respect – no, it was their close togetherness she envied. She often wished Elspeth would come down for a visit, but she had never given anyone her address, and had only written to Elspeth to explain why she'd gone in the hope that she would explain to Uncle John. Now there had been a friend. Dear old Uncle John. Hardly ever really sober, but always considerate and kind, at least to her. She knew he loved her but he was five hundred miles away.

If there was no man in Becky Friar's life, there were certainly men. Sometimes they were every fifty yards in the park, in the next seat in the bus, and even in the street, some would brazenly walk alongside her, and even take her arm. This was why she found her safest refuge was in the National Gallery, or in the Reading Room of the British Museum. It was in the latter establishment that she had found her first London friend. She was a short, hunched woman with close-cropped hair and prominent teeth, who was poring over vast tomes with the help of the thickest spectacles Becky had ever seen. She found herself staring at these spectacles so much that one day the old lady took them off and said, 'Can I help you, my dear?' She had the most unexpected and beautiful, cultivated voice that Becky was taken by surprise.

'I'm sorry,' she said, 'I –' and she glanced without thinking at the spectacles.

'Oh, it's my glasses,' said the old lady softly. 'Yes, they are rather large, aren't they. But my eyes are getting worse, you know. Blind as a bat, really. If they get any worse, I shall need a telescope.' Becky couldn't help laughing, which caused a few heads to rise disapprovingly from around them. The old lady made a conspiratorial face, and nodding her head, put on her reinforced spectacles and resumed her reading. So did Becky, but she found it hard to concentrate on Mr Wells' *Outline of History* because she was so hungry. She had only her breakfast with the O'Learys and took pot luck with them when she got home. Sometimes this amounted to no more than an end of bread dipped into a cup of gravy. Frank O'Leary was on the building site, and when he didn't work, the O'Learys didn't eat. Becky's seven shillings a week sometimes saved their bacon – in more ways than one. Recently there had been days when Becky herself had been short on shillings, principally because she only worked afternoons in Covent Garden, clearing up after the morning market for a potato merchant. This gave her a shilling an hour for a few hours each day and five days a week with as many potatoes as she could take home in a bag. This was especially welcomed by the O'Learys. Old Granny O'Leary seemed to live entirely on potatoes – hot, cold, salted, roasted, boiled or mashed, with butter or not – every potato was a feast and a delight to the old lady. When the Covent Garden job had come to an end, she was down to her last few pounds, and pawned her best coat for five shillings. The one advantage in coming from a draper's family was that her wardrobe was of the best material, and the old Pawnbroker in the Tottenham Court Road was quick to spot this. 'Nice bit of material,' he muttered, but he still only gave her five shillings and a week to redeem it in. This was one of the reasons she escaped so often to the Reading Room. It was cold in London in February.

It had been only a few minutes to closing time. She finished at a suitable chapter end of Mr H.G. Wells and prepared to put him away. Pushing back her chair, she had reached for her leather handbag and it wasn't there. Startled, upturned faces greeted her reaction of dismay and disbelief. People called out. Attendants came running. The old lady opposite peered in bewildered concern through her three layers of glass, and Becky stamped her foot in rage and burst into loud tears.

'Have another cup, my dear. It will do you good.'

Becky sipped gratefully and gazed round the comfortable, if untidy, book-littered sitting room. She was in the Gower Street flat of her museum friend, Miss Elizabeth Garnet. Miss Garnet was a redoubtable relic of the old school, an old maid of disarming frankness, who lived in the real world of her books and her writing, while inhabiting the secondary world of everyday reality. Elizabeth found it a nuisance to eat, wash, buy shopping and remember to pay the occasional bill. She lived in a constant state of happy abstraction, but that may only have been due to the fact that she couldn't see her hand in front of her face. Of a gentle and genteel professional background, she had shared her childhood with many brothers who were inhibited by the same eye defect, but that didn't deflect all five of them from blindly following their own particular and eccentric paths towards their individual contentment. Miss Garnet was the happiest person Becky had ever met, and reminded her in some ways of Mrs Beattie in Forres. Both women were so uncomplicatedly themselves that they were at ease in whatever situation they found themselves.

In less time than it takes to prepare and clear a tea tray, Miss Garnet had found out all about Rebecca Friar and Becky knew as much about Miss Garnet as the old lady was prepared to tell her. But there was no doubting her kindness, despite her own limited financial circumstances.

'A fixed income, my dear, is a mixed blessing. I know it is very rude of me to talk about money, especially to strangers, but then I don't feel you're a stranger, having seen you so often in the Reading Room.' She pronounced the 't' in 'often', in a way that Becky had never heard before so that it sounded more like 'awften'. She also called herself 'gal' when she was talking of her days as a young girl, but Becky had the impression that Elizabeth had had a lovely Edwardian childhood. 'Was always reading, you see. We all were. As soon as we knew our eyes were going we tried to get as much reading as we could – while we could still see.' But it was when they got into Jane Austen that they were undeniably bonded. 'You see, my dear, everyone thinks Jane such a mousey little creature. Pale and loitering, you know, doing needlework and writing her little stories as a lady's hobby. But she was a rebel you know. Quite unconventional for her times really. She knew she had it good with an adoring sister and a loving family. Pity she had to get sick, though. Goodness knows what she might have done. She was only forty-one. Half her life again to go.'

Becky remembered wondering how old Miss Garnet was – anything from forty to eighty herself – ageless she was. A dynamo in violet and velvet. Becky stayed that night on the couch and the next night too, and then was persuaded by Miss Garnet to move from the O'Learys. She would give her accommodation in the box room in return for light housework, boring errands and companionship.

'You could be my "Fanny", my dear. Remember *Mansfield Park*?'

With just a hint of misgiving, Becky accepted. It was a novel situation in many ways, especially for a young woman of Scottish upbringing and attitudes. It was not the Forres norm to undertake a mode of living that carried with it no particular duties at no fixed reward. It was not in fact a job as such, but a way of living, and to Becky's relief and astonishment, it was a way of life she thoroughly enjoyed.

Old Miss Garnet toddled off every morning at ten o'clock, leaving Becky in charge. She came home at one o'clock for soup, again at four o'clock for banana sandwiches, which were her favourite, and again at six o'clock for a boiled egg. Occasionally she would go out to a concert with a friend and come back in the evening for a cup of chocolate and a biscuit. That was her life and Becky was happy to live in the very light shadow of it. She came to love the old woman for her style, her wit, her wisdom, her dogged ability to work and for the way she was able to make her ten guineas a month take care of both of them. Becky was determined to read every book in that sitting room, and even harboured thoughts that she might write something herself. Every condition in her life at that time was conducive to the literary effort. One day . . .

Then one day Miss Garnet hadn't come back at one, nor at four, nor even at six. Becky hadn't known what to do, but then put on her best coat, which was hers again, and hurried round to the British Museum. Yes, they remembered Miss Garnet, the researcher.

'Yes, she left as usual, Miss. Lovely old dear, ain't she?' Becky was puzzled and returned to Gower Street to find a policeman standing there.

'Do you know the whereabouts of Miss Elizabeth Garnet?' Becky nodded.

'Are you her maid?' Becky nodded again.

'Well, perhaps you'd like to come with me, Miss, and identify the body?' Becky remembered grasping the iron railings at the doorstep to steady herself. It was Miss Garnet, looking just like a 'gal' again in death, except for the great gash on her forehead.

'Knocked down by a 27 bus. Couldn't have seen it,' said the orderly. That night Becky slept in Miss Garnet's little bed and wept for her. She wept for her courage and kindness to her, but mostly she wept for herself. Next morning a very officious solicitor had come to the door and asked her to leave 'forthwith'. She remembered the malicious precision of his 'forthwith'.

'You will take only your own possessions, of course.' She had taken her best coat and a copy of *Northanger Abbey* – just to remind her.

She looked again at the volume in her hands and then at the fly, still buzzing at the window. Suddenly the noise stopped. Had it died, or escaped? She listened. Not a sound. She closed the book, and saw that she had left her father's photo on the bed. She replaced it in the book and pulled her coat more tightly round her.

It was a Monday night in Forres and it was Hallowe'en. Since early evening the 'guisers' had been going round the doors singing songs for a halfpenny or stabbing for apples in a basin with a fork in their mouths, and generally doing anything to prise a coin from household purses. They got very little response from the Keith household. Its door was firmly shut against Hallowe'en blandishments, and no amount of cavorting from 'witches' or chorusses from warlocks could persuade the Keith door to open that night. This led to the occasional rude noise on the doorstep and the inevitable scorn on anyone who didn't yield to the childpressure that was itself disguised as 'guising'. Like carol singing at Christmas, everyone recognised it as the blackmail it was and turned a blind eye to it – except John Keith. He had ordered Thomasina to keep the door tight shut.

It was mostly shut these days. It was almost exactly a year since Becky had left, and John Keith could still hardly take it in. He had never been a demonstrative man, but now he seemed even more withdrawn. His visits to the Mason's Arms were as regular as ever, but they seemed to be taken now more as a constitutional than as a pleasure, and even his attendance at the shop these days was even more perfunctory and random. Becky Friar had gone, and she had taken with her all the sunlight out of John Keith's life. He found Thomasina's pretensions tedious, and Elspeth's imitations of them irritating. It was as if mother and daughter had made up a team engaged in an ongoing contest with John as the head of the house. His position as such was acknowledged but never respected, and more and more he drifted into silence and introspection. He was prevented, however, from being an absolute recluse, by the ripening friendship which developed between him and big Alec Friar. They made a very unlikely team themselves. The exuberant, gregarious, ex-merchant mariner and the lugubrious shop manager – but perhaps it was because they were so very opposite that they fitted. Whether in long Sunday hedgerow walks, or long nightly sessions in the saloon bar, they made their comment on the world and the world's affairs without ever really mentioning the subject that essentially twinned them – Alec's daughter, Ella, and her child, Becky.

Only the silences that fell comfortably enough in the discussions spoke of their mutual preoccupation. John's anxiety was greater than Alec's. While Alec's was a rueful acceptance of a lost cause, John regretted the lost opportunity. He had seen in Becky the daughter he would have liked as opposed to the daughter he got. He never felt this was being disloyal to Elspeth. It was just that he preferred the personality of Becky so much more. She had made him laugh and she had made him think. Most of all, she had made him feel wanted. Thomasina and Elspeth in their domestic alliance only succeeded in making him feel redundant, so he kept out of their way and out of the house most of the time. Besides Elspeth had taken to bringing home that awful Donald Robertson. It was no assistance to liking him any better that he was the nephew of 'Shears' Robertson, now the sole proprietor of Keith & Sons of Forres. But this was a great inducement to Elspeth, bearing in mind her matrimonial ambitions, and no debarment in the socially ambitious Thomasina's eye. John, however, could not bear him, or his ridiculous stammer. Any conversation with him was protracted to dismaying lengths. It would have been worth the wait had he something to say, but, for the most part, it was only to utter something entirely fatuous, or to agree with what had just been said.

'I'm rather inclined to agree,' took the time of a paragraph. His entrance to the house firmly under Elspeth's arm and Thomasina's eye was invariably the signal for John to leave, much to his wife's annoyance.

'Have you no thought for your daughter's future? How can you be so impolite to a guest?' But John would make no reply, and reach for his hat.

He and Alec made a regular practice of calling on Mrs Beattie. She was bed-ridden now, because of her legs, she said. The two men were glad to take her word for it. She had had a bad fall on her back stairs and broken both heels.

'I should hae fell on ma heid. It would hae done less damage!' was her usual joke. She had two sticks by the side of her bed. 'That's ane for each o' ye,' she would warn John and Alec with a gleam in her eye. Mrs Beattie may have been down, but she was by no means out. Part of their routine was to share a dram with her on their visits – one round each was their limit, but it was noticed that the third was always larger than the first. It was undoubtedly a happy hour among the three of them, but some nights could be as full of laughs as others were quiet. But this Hallowe'en was to be full of surprises.

'I thought you were the "guisers",' said Mrs Beattie, opening the door to them, leaning on her two sticks.

'Do we look that bad?' said Alec.

'It's because ye look that guid – for guisers!' said Mrs Beattie. 'Come awa' in.'

'It's good to see you up and about, good-mother.'

'There were that many chaps at the door with the guisers, it was less work to get oot the sticks.' They settled themselves comfortably around her kitchen range and each brought out the familiar flasks.

'Jis reach out by yer hand there, Alec. Ye'll find my bottle ready.' Part of the regular ceremony was that Mrs Beattie would give out the first nip from her bottle, Alec would follow next with a round from his flask and John would be last from his. The first libations poured, they raised their glasses mutually to each other and drank contentedly.

'I take it, John,' said Mrs Beattie with the smallest smack of her lips, 'that since you're half an hour earlier than usual, you've had another visit from stuttering Donald.'

'True,' said John with a grimace. 'It's no' the lad's affliction that bothers me. I dare say he canna help that. It's what he has to say when he finally gets it out.'

'Ay,' said Mrs Beattie, 'a penny worth o' sense and a pound's worth o' words. He's no' like his uncle at any road. Old Shears was never short o' a word. Not unless it was gonna cost him.'

'He was always tight,' said Alec.

'But he's been a good friend to you, John Keith,' said Mrs Beattie.

'For my father's sake. No' mine.'

'Ay,' said Mrs Beattie. There was a pause, and once again a knock came to the door. 'Leave them be. I've nothin' left in my purse,' said Mrs Beattie. Alec stretched out a long leg to rifle in his trouser pocket.

'I've got a copper here.' He strode to the door, and stooping down, opened it. He gave the group of five to seven-year-olds such a fright as he loomed over them that they screamed and ran in terror of their lives. He came back into the room, slightly puzzled, but with his coppers intact.

'Man, Alec,' said Mrs Beattie, 'it must be the first time that guisers have ever been frightened awa' frae the door.'

'I never said a word,' said Alec.

'That was the trouble,' said Mrs Beattie, chuckling. 'And while you're on your feet –' she said, proffering her glass. Alex duly obliged from his other pocket and they resettled themselves again. There was another pause.

'I see John, the postie's awa'.'

'Oh?' said John.

'Ay,' said Mrs Beattie. 'Ay. The wife next door, her that gets my messages was telling me. Dropped dead in Cameron Street, his bag on his back.'

'Must have been heavy,' said Alec.

'He was a good age,' said John.

'He wis ages wi' me,' said Mrs Beattie.

'I didna know he was that old,' said Alec.

'Cheeky thing,' muttered Mrs Beattie. 'It's a funny thing though.' She paused as if uncertain how to go on.

'Aye,' said John encouragingly.

'He was at my door here only two or three days back.'

'Oh?' said John.

'Ay,' said Mrs Beattie.

'Had he a letter for you then?'

'Well, he wisna here wi' a bag o' coal,' said Mrs Beattie. 'Alec, jist at yer hand there, behind the tea caddy.' He looked. 'See it there. An envelope.'

'This ye mean,' he said, bringing it out.

'That's right. See it here. Give it tae John. I hivna got ma specs.' John took the envelope.

'You mean you want me to read it?'

'Ay.'

'Bit it's addressed to you.'

'I ken that. But ye'll want tae read this.'

'Why so?' said John.

'Because it's frae Becky,' said Mrs Beattie. John stiffened immediately in reaction. Even Alec sat up.

'Where is she now?' he asked.

'In London yet,' said Mrs Beattie with her eyes fixed on John. 'She wrote to me because she'd never heard back from Elspeth. Too ta'en up wi' stutterin' Donald, I suppose.' John continued to stare at the envelope in his hand.

'I canna read this,' he said in a low voice.

''Course you can,' said Mrs Beattie, reaching out, taking it from him and removing the three pages of tightly written script. John felt his heart jump as he saw the familiar writing again. He remembered Becky's school exercise books, her love of words, how she told him she would be a writer, and now he couldn't even read one of her letters.

'Here you are then,' said Mrs Beattie, handing back the folded pages. 'Start at the top there where it says, "Dear Gran,". It's nice that.' She repeated it again, 'Dear Gran.'

'Dear Gran,' echoed John in a voice that seemed to come from high above his head. He read in a flat, monotonous, unpractised voice that successfully cloaked the war of feelings that was going on inside him – the censure she deserved for running away versus the concern he had for her wellbeing. The forgotten hopes he once had for her future against the relief of knowing that she still survived, and underlying everything, of course, the continuing love he had for her – and always would. The letter told of the O'Learys and Miss Garnet and of her terrible time in Paddington, but now she had found a good position in the Strand Palace Hotel as a chambermaid and apprentice housekeeper. This meant she had free board and accommodation and a whole day off every week. She had even started to save again. But it would take a long time to make the fare to Sydney. At this point, John looked up sharply to Mrs Beattie.

'That's in Australia,' she said blandly. John resumed the letter. And when he got to the end, he stopped abruptly in the middle of one sentence and refused to go on. He handed the pages back to Mrs Beattie without another word. She took them saying at the same time to Alec, 'It jis goes on to say, you see, that when I next see her Uncle John here, I wis to give him a big hug and tell him "I'm sorry".' She then looked to John. 'Of course, I'll dae nae sic thing, an' I'm no' a bit sorry that I showed you her letter, I mean. The lassie's made her ain way for her ain reasons, but she's still the same lassie for a' that.'

'It can be a rough port, London, but it sounds as if she's found a good berth.'

'Australia,' John said, as if to himself.

'The lassie wants to see her father. Efter a', she's met her mother. Oh, and by the way,' she said, turning to Alec, 'how's Ella?'

'I never hear,' said Alec.

'I see,' said Mrs Beattie. 'Well, they say no news is good news.'

'Ay,' said Alec.

'But he doesn't know,' said John.

'What don't I know?' said Alec.

'Not you. I mean Bobby.'

'Bobby?' Alec repeated blankly.

'His brother, Bobby. Him that's in Australia,' said Mrs Beattie as if to a child.

'I see,' said Alec.

'He doesn't know Becky's his child.'

'All these years. Surely you've written?'

'At the beginning, regularly. But not so much these days. We've lost touch. All I know is that he's still in Sydney.'

'And that's all Becky knows,' said Mrs Beattie.

'Ay,' said John, 'maybe the less said, the better.'

393

'Ay,' said Mrs Beattie. 'No news is good news.' She held out her empty glass. 'It's your turn, John.' They raised their glasses again in a silent toast, but each made their different tacit salute – Alec to his lost Ella, Mrs Beattie to the good man who was her son-in-law, and John himself to his still-loved Becky.

Bobby and Rachel Keith brought in the New Year of 1922 by having one of their frequent quarrels. It was by now one of the regular features of their marriage, and hardly a week passed without an explosion of one or both temperaments. While neither would deny that they were still in love with the other, it was impossible for love to thrive without some time being given to it, and the main trouble was that neither of the Keiths had time. They were each busy on their own particular ends to such an extent that little time was left for their mutual home life, mutual love and even their mutual son, Abel. He was now a moody and sullen fourteen-year-old of striking appearance. His Celtic features were only accentuated by a Judaic cast in the nose and mouth, and these, assisted by a tall, loose-limbed 'Australian-ness', made him look much older than his years. But then he was much older than his years, and being free of the strictures of parental control, he was bringing himself up by trial and error along the Sydney harbour front and by its generous beaches. He was out of the house most of the time and it was just as well on this occasion, for there was a lot of noise going on in the Pott's Point flat. Not even the prattle of 'Dad and Dave' on the wireless, turned up to full volume to confuse the neighbours, could entirely hide the fact that the Keiths were having a go at each other.

It all began because each expected the other to have brought in the dinner provisions, and the last straw came when Bobby discovered he didn't even have enough grog in the house to bring in 1922 with the full Scottish appropriateness. Rachel had suggested that some good Barossa Valley wine would do just as well.

'Whoever heard of bringing in the New Year on bloody Barossa Valley wine?' yelled Bobby, banging down the empty whisky bottle on the table.

'It's only that your whole Christian religion is founded on the changing of wine.'

'Not my religion,' retorted Bobby, hotly. 'That's for Papists.'

'Aren't they Christians?'

'No, they're not,' said Bobby.

'Don't be so damned silly,' said Rachel, turning away to the cupboard to see what she could scrounge for their meal. 'Man has had wine since the ancients. The Greeks and the Romans –'

'We're not Greeks and Romans either.'

'Then why do you Scots always go on about "Roamin' in the Gloamin'"?' She laughed as she said this, but the bad joke had the effect of deflating the quarrel exchange, and Bobby turned away to the window, saying, 'Oh, for Pete's sake!' After a moment, he turned and came behind his wife, putting his arms around her waist. 'I'm sorry, love,' he muttered into the back of her hair. The radio at that moment was playing a dance band version of one of the latest hits and as the crooner sang its refrain, Bobby and Rachel did an impromptu dance around the empty table to a foxtrot rhythm:

'Dinah, is there anyone finer
In the State of Carolina,
If there is and you know her,
Show her to me.
Dinah, with your Dixie eyes blazin'
How I love to sit and gaze in
To the eyes of Dinah Lee.
Every night, why do I shake with fright,
Because my Dinah might
Change her mind about me . . .'

At this point, Bobby started chanting: 'The name of this song is Dinah; the name of this song is Dinah; the name of this song is Dinah . . .' Rachel joined in as they continued a kind of conga round the apartment, till one of them tripped and they both fell laughing on to the sofa.

'There's a track
Winding back
To an old fashioned shack . . .'

Rachel worked herself clear.
'That's enough of that.'
'What about "The Road to Gundagai"?'
'No, thanks.' She rose back to the cupboard. Bobby lay back.
'I've just remembered,' he said.
'What?' She called out with her back to him.
'I'm hungry.'
'So am I.'
'I've had a hard day.'
'So have I.'

'Don't let's start all that again.' Rachel was busy at the sink.

'No, let's don't,' she said. 'And turn that wireless down.'

He rose and went to the wireless on the corner table and turned it low. A voice was talking about 'thumping his bluey around the Nullarbor. Things were so dry the crows flew backwards to keep the dust out of their eyes.'

'Listen to this joker,' said Bobby as he sat in the rocker by the wireless set. The chair had been old Mr Gebler's and was everybody's favourite listening place.

'The Commonwealth of Australia rode to wealth on a sheep's back,' the wireless voice went on, 'but a million acres of desert scrub is no use to a soldier-settler, who has not only survived a war, but a 'flu epidemic, and life on the wood-heap beyond the black stump.'

'Fair go, mate,' cried Bobby. 'Here Rachel, this guy's a poet.' Rachel was peeling potatoes.

'We don't need another Banjo Paterson,' she said. 'Grab a knife and give me a hand here.'

'We started from nothing –' continued the wireless voice.

'So what's new?' said Bobby, turning the knob on the dial.

'Come on, Bobby,' called Rachel.

'Coming. Just trying to get some music from this thing. Ah, here we are.' The strains of yet another dance tune filled the room.

'Not so loud! You'll have the Coopers thumping the wall again.' Bobby obediently lowered the volume and joined his wife at the sink.

'Peel that onion there,' she said. 'I've got most of the potatoes done.'

'Peeling onions brings tears to my eyes,' said Bobby, holding up a large specimen.

'Stick a bit of bread in your mouth, then. It'll keep you quiet.'

'What are we having?' asked Bobby.

'Emergency pie,' answered Rachel, working away at grating some cheese. This was the meal the Keiths had when all else failed. Potatoes and onions with cheese and egg. Simple, cheap and highly nutritious.

'Once we get this over, I can give the place a clear up, and you can get down to the pub for your blessed bottle before midnight.' Bobby nodded agreement. He couldn't speak for the lump of bread in his mouth, and the tears streaming down his cheeks.

Rachel laughed. 'If your pals could see you now,' she said.

It was while they were eating, and he was pouring himself a second glass of beer, that Bobby suddenly said, 'Where's Abel?'

'I don't know,' said his mother. 'I've given up trying to keep track of that boy.'

'Don't you think you should? He's only fourteen.'

'Going on sixty-four,' answered Rachel dryly. 'He's your son too, you know. Anyway, man-management's more your line than mine.'

'He's not a man.'

'He thinks he is.'

'I'll scout around for him.' He rose wiping his lips with his fingers. 'If he gets into trouble again, I'll kick his arse for him.' At the door he turned and said, 'You know, Rachel, the way he's turning out, we should have called him Cain, not Abel!' Rachel sat for a moment with the teacup on her lips, then replaced it on the saucer. She went over to the wireless corner and turned the dance music off. Looking down at the rocker, she thought of her father and how good he had been with Abel. She fingered the cane of the rocker and set it in motion. As it rocked, she thought the old man might have been there. She wished he were. She sighed again and returned to the table and began to clean up.

Bobby's progress to the pub was impeded by the number of people he met on the way. His popularity and his status as a rising figure in local politics made his progress slow, so it was some time before he got to the corrugated iron shed that served as a pub for the working men in the area. A beer hall, Aussie style. Nothing more than a primitive enclosure to allow for the steady and relentless intake of beer by the local male population. Bobby had his jug with a few of the boys, while waiting for Eric, the big Swedish barman, to bring up his Scotch from the back.

'Seen anything of my boy, Abel?' Bobby asked diffidently. There was a vague kind of mumbled response. Bobby had the impression that they were embarrassed. Some of the men even looked away. He was about to comment on this, when Eric loomed up with the bottle of Johnnie Walker Red Label.

'Another bottle of Scotch for the Scotchman. OK?'

'OK, Eric. Put it on the tab for me. I'll raise a glass to you at the bells. See you, fellers.'

Bobby made his way out, nodding, smiling to everyone, but inside, he was just beginning to get a little bit uneasy about Abel. He made up his mind to give the boy a really good talking-to. He really had become a handful since his old grandad died. Was forever missing school, taking every advantage of his father's being away from home so much on trade union business, and his mother's involvement at the University. Trouble was he didn't seem to have any close friends. Poor kid, thought Bobby. Truth is, we've been neglecting him. We'd better make that a New Year resolution to give a bit more time to him.

It was getting quite dark as he approached his own street again, and as he got to the door, Rachel was on the balcony above him.

'Didn't you see him?' she said.

'No, I wasn't really looking.' Mrs Cooper appeared at the same level from the house next door.

'If it's your boy, Abel, I saw him down at the harbour a couple of hours ago. He didn't look too well to me.'

'What do you mean?' said Rachel, wheeling round to her.

'Oh, I dunno. See for yourself,' she said, disappearing into her own house again.

'What does she mean?' asked Rachel of her husband. She was now very anxious. 'You'd better go.'

'It's alright. I'll go. Come down and get this bottle here. Or shall I throw it up?'

'No, no, no. I'll come down.' When Bobby handed over the bottle to his wife, he noted her troubled face.

'Don't worry, love. The young scamp'll be alright. He's just a regular "Huckleberry Finn".' She smiled a little smile, and he patted her cheek and left her, but as he went back down the street again, he knew Rachel felt as guilty as he did.

As Bobby walked the familiar streets going down towards the harbour, he couldn't help thinking of how different the Hogmanay of his own boyhood had been back home. The lights were now on in the houses all around him. From some came the sound of a piano, from others, somebody singing. There was even an accordion playing. These were likely to be the houses of the Scots and Irish preparing to bring in 'the bells' in the traditional way. They were the old immigrants, the bone poor, as they were called. He wasn't far from being one of them himself even though people regarded him and Rachel as being part of the new professionals just emerging.

Where was the boy? Bobby wasn't even sure where to look. He could be anywhere. Then he noticed a crowd laughing and pointing at a figure that was lurching and swaying in the middle of the street, quite oblivious to the occasional cart or bicycle or motor car. Bobby paid no attention and was attempting to pass on the pavement when he suddenly realised that the focus of the crowd's ribaldry was in fact his own son, Abel – and he was drunk! Grim-faced, Bobby elbowed a few of the passers-by aside and moved forward to the centre of the road. Abel stood with his arms outstretched, beaming at the world. 'Happy New Year, Dad!' he called, as he saw his father approach. Bobby said nothing, but grabbed his son's wrist, and tugged him viciously behind him as he turned back in the direction of Pott's Point. Abel protested strongly and resisted as much as his condition and his father's strong grip allowed. It was a very different progress now that Bobby Keith made through the streets. This was not the 'Hail fellow, well met'. This was an angry father dragging a prodigal and drunken son behind him. How had it happened? Where did he get the money? Who gave him the grog? All these questions vexed Bobby as he dragged the boy behind him.

Suddenly Abel gave a cry and fell in a dead heap. The boy's face was bright green in the street lights. Bobby knelt down beside him and pulled open the boy's shirt. People gathered round and a voice said,

'Better get him home, mate, before he passes out altogether.'

'Before he conks out, you mean. That was a bottle of whisky he had.' Bobby looked up.

'What?

'Sure. Came into the pub. Said he had come for your whisky. Big Eric handed it over no problem.'

'Oh, hell!' Bobby looked down at his son whose eyes were now flickering open.

'I feel sick, Dad,' he said in a thin, breathy voice.

'Stupid, young bastard!' said Bobby.

'I just wanted to see what it was like,' whimpered Abel in the same reedy tone.

'Now you bloody well know!' And Bobby hauled him up. The boy's body hung from his hand like a broken puppet, which the father gathered unlovingly to him and humped over his shoulder. The boy's groans only added to the sound of the bells which now started.

'What a bloody Hogmanay!' Bobby Keith grumbled as he marched towards his house and his own unopened Ne'erday bottle. As he muttered these words, Abel was sick all down his back. Bobby was past all caring and marched stoically on.

There couldn't have been a prouder father than Jim Keith, as he watched his son, Billy, run on the wing for Gore High School in the first match of the new season against Invercargill Boys' High. He hugged the fourteen-year-old Berta beside him as Billy made another spectacular dive at the post for his second try. He hoped the excitement wouldn't be too much for both of them. His own heart was pounding, and he didn't want Berta to have another attack. They were also surrounded by other parents and friends, all of whom were just as caught up in the game, which was proving a real dingdong affair as the play moved from one end of the field to the other. It was only an ordinary schools rugby match on a Saturday afternoon, but it could have been the final of the Ranfurly Shield.

'Well played, Keithy!' a shout went up, and Jim Keith couldn't help beaming his pleasure as he heard it. He himself had never been a games player, and he was somewhat taken aback at the inordinate pride he took in his first son's sporting ability.

Billy Keith was obviously 'the boy most likely to succeed' in nearly every respect. He had the hay-coloured hair of his mother, Jean, and the quiet, likeable disposition of his father. He was good at school without being brilliant, was immensely popular with his classmates and already at sixteen was a responsible worker on the farm, but above all, was a rugby player of enormous ability and potential. He was already tipped to play Representative for Southland, and was even mentioned as a future All Black. He was glad to stay on at school because of the rugby and cricket, and Jim was happy to let him do so, even though he could have done with him on the farm. Sport in New Zealand was very much a way of life and although not at all professionally organised, was a means of introduction to many interesting connections that could later prove useful to the boy. Meantime, like the many other fathers, uncles and brothers ringed round the ground, Jim Keith was happy to bask in the reflected glory of his son's rugby prowess. No less proud was Berta. 'Come on, Billy' she yelled. She turned to her father, her eyes bright, her eyes flushed red. There was a final blast on the whistle and a roar from the crowd. Gore had carried the day 14–10, and Billy Keith was their hero.

'Ready! Steady! GO' And off they went down the big paddock like hares. Ross, being the youngest, was given a head start. Five yards behind came Stu, then at scratch, came Sandy, whose birthday the Mackenzie family were celebrating. After a normal Saturday's work they had had a lunch comprising all of Sandy's favourite foods, most of which seemed to be ice-cream. Then to counter the effects of a sharp winter's afternoon, Bruce had decided on the Mackenzie meet, in which the brothers were handicapped in a two-hundred-yard dash from one end of the long paddock to the other. Bruce himself was stationed at the official finishing line, complete with stop watch. Only Bruce knew that it didn't work, but he gave an approximate timing from his old fob watch, which gave the impression at least of Olympian timing. The starter for the afternoon was Gran Keith, who'd been brought out especially, despite her protest, to sit in a high-backed kitchen chair at the starting line near the gate.

Tina and old Hilda van Meer were interested spectators from the kitchen window as they washed and dried the lunchtime dishes. Little Chris was supposed to be in her Gran's charge, but she had a tendency to wander off, and at the start of the race was actually standing with one little arm round her big brother's thigh as he waited for Gran Keith's starting shout. Sandy was tense and excited and eager to be off, bending down to release his little sister's arm every few minutes. Stu, who was on the first mark, was already beginning to get bored, but little Ross, front runner, was imperceptibly edging his way slightly forward as they waited. He was so concentrating on stealing a few inches that he got off to a bad start and was already in tears halfway down the run. He was passed by Stu on the three-quarter mark, puffing hard, but immediately, both were easily passed by Sandy, who hardly seemed to have broken breath. As Bruce stood watching his three sons hurtling towards him, each with their own styles, he couldn't help marvelling at the grace, the ease and the style of his oldest as he glided effortlessly towards the finish. Bruce let Sandy rush past him to the fence behind him, Stu had already given up and Ross of course had fallen. Bruce went to pick him up. And as he did so, his eye was caught by another runner on the field. A little, fair-haired replica of her mother was running as fast as her chubby legs would carry her down towards them, her face like beetroot, eyes popping out of her head. The brothers gathered to watch with their father as Chris ran towards them, her hands held high, but with only twenty yards to go, her knickers fell down around her knees and she plunged headlong into the grass. It even made Ross laugh, and his father let him down to run with his brothers to where their little sister lay face down on the turf, kicking her legs in the air.

That night the family were initiated into the mysteries of the Euchre party. This was a Christmas time and 'special occasion get-together' enjoyed by most families in the country areas of New Zealand. It was a good excuse to meet up and catch up. Everybody brought something to eat and something to drink, and the farms took turns throughout the year at being host. On this occasion, it was the Mackenzies, seven of them including Hilda and Gran Keith. Little Chris, who was already in nightie and dressing gown, ran around among the feet. The company was seated at four tables, with four at each table, two sets of partners at each. The partnerships were distributed variously and indiscriminately, but generally with the experienced player helping the tyros. Thus the three Mackenzie children with the three Jackson children and the two Cargill children all had adult guides from the three families, at least until they got the hang of it all, then partners were

changed around just to add to the interest and confusion. It was
competitive without being grimly so, and the social aspect was
not at all forgotten. There was much laughter and ribaldry, and
underneath it all, the low monotone of gossip, especially among
the older players.

Five cards were dealt out to each, trumps decided and the game
begun. The idea was for the partners to prevent the opposition
taking three tricks, thus ensuring a Euchre. Points were awarded
for each Euchre and whoever had the highest points at the last hand
played won the game. Every player had a score card with them and
this card was marked, so that they were able to arrive at an overall
winner by the time supper was ready. The winner that night was
Gran Keith, a wily competitor. Most of the families knew better
than to pay any attention to her frequent enquiries of 'What do
I do now?' Hilda won the booby prize because she kept talking
all the time, and Tina ensured that most of the young children
won something for one reason or another. The tables were then
joined together, and while Messrs Jackson, Cargill and Mackenzie
had their beer and Gran Keith her medicinal whisky, the women
prepared the supper on the long table and the Mackenzie boys
stoked up the wood fire.

Mrs Jackson went to the piano, and played excerpts from the
operettas as background music. One fascinated listener who never
left her side was six-year-old Chris. After supper, they all danced.
It was a rough and ready affair, made all the more awkward
by the boys' reluctance to join in, but Tina matched them up
approximately with the two Jackson girls and the Cargill daughter,
and with Mrs Jackson still playing heroically, and Mr Jackson's
sometime assistance on a little melodian, a good time was had by
all. Except perhaps by the birthday boy himself, who was caught
between the unashamed attentions of the elder Miss Jackson and
the open admiration of the only Miss Cargill. His blushing
countenance between the two of them was a source of much
amusement to the fathers. If anything, he seemed to prefer the
younger Jackson girl, but she stood by the other side of her mother
to turn over the pages of the music while her mother played.

Young Chris was now half asleep in her Gran's arms, but she still
kept an ear open to the music. It was getting late and the younger ones
were becoming tired. Almost as if by a kind of family osmosis, the
room became quieter by itself, and only the plaintive sound of George
Jackson's melodian lulled the air. Archie Cargill sang his party piece
'Bless This House' and no song could have been more apt. It was
after midnight when the Jacksons went and the Mackenzies hurried
in from the cold night air to the embers of their log fire.

As they opened the door they heard piano music. For a moment Tina thought that someone had switched the wireless on. But then she saw little Chris, standing at the piano picking out with the fingers of her right hand a series of notes which sounded uncannily like 'Bless This House'. This was no thumping of a six-year-old hand indiscriminately along the keys. It was a deliberate and considered collection of notes on one hand. Perhaps slightly out of rhythm, but unmistakably the melody line of the song that Archie Cargill had sung:

> 'Bless this house O Lord we pray,
> Keep it safe by night and day . . .'

TWENTY-SEVEN

Ballytreabhair Farm looked as forlorn as Nessie O'Neil felt. The afternoon was bright, the harvest was in, the sale was complete, and everything was in order, yet Nessie felt a heaviness at her heart she couldn't quite explain. As she had said to Nellie the day before, 'It's hard to put fifty years in a chest and put a label on it.' All her children had been born here, her husband had died here, and Nellie herself had been married from the front parlour. When a house had become a home to so many people as this crumbling farmhouse had been to ten O'Neils, then the edifice itself became part of the family. The very walls had heard and seen so much that they almost spoke of the years they had stood. Nessie walked through the empty rooms, now looking better than they'd done for years, trying to keep back all the different emotions she felt welling up in her. At seventy-three, she felt she was too old to indulge in sentimental nostalgia. The long succession of days here had meant only work for her from first light to last. It was the associations that were brought to mind that hurt: the window that young Denis shattered with the hurling stick, the corner that Paddy had made for himself with his books, the fights that Sean and Michael had when they were young. Sean, who had wanted to be a policeman, always tying Michael up at the end of the bed. Michael always had to be the baddy. The box bedroom in the back where young Kevin dreamed his dreams for Ireland, and where the Kevin before – God rest his soul – had lain in a white coffin, hardly the size of a biscuit tin. God save us, Nessie thought. He would have been a grown man by now – more than forty years if he was a day. It was funny to see the kitchen emptied of everything. It looked a different place altogether, but she could still see where young Noreen had splashed her long legs in a bath, her red hair trailing on the one bit of carpet they had. Now, she's dead, and no pity in my heart for her, thought Nessie. The bad ways had taken her to a bad end, and only a girl and boy-child to show for it in America. Nessie found herself sighing and shaking her head as she came out into the yard again. For all her Catholic disapproval and condemnation, she couldn't stop loving her impetuous youngest daughter, even if she'd grown into an immoral woman in her forties. Never so much as a line had she had from her during more than twenty years. Noreen had cut herself off from her mother, even before she herself was cut off. Not even her father's death had brought her home, although Paddy, good soul that he was, had said in his letter that she had cried like the rest of them. Wasn't it strange that none of hers had come home to visit her, but Mrs Docherty's Brigid had been home these three or four times, but then her man was a schoolteacher and she was a nurse herself. They had the money.

Sean had the money – from the shop he had with Michael – and they were generous with it, but never a visit from either of them. They always said they were too busy. And not a word about a wedding for either of them. Two fine, big, good-looking boys like they were too. But likely they were too busy for that as well – and Irishmen are slow to bring to the altar. Only Paddy – God bless him – had kept in regular touch and his letters had been a saving to her.

One of the reasons Nessie had agreed to sell up was that she could meet with Kevin in Dublin. He was already there on his own business, which according to her information, had something to do with private hotels. Anyway, Nellie needed a change now that she was getting better and stronger, and living less and less in her imagination. She no longer wandered in her mind, and she was nearly like herself again, except that she was quieter. Only Dr Nolan still kept an eye on her and they seemed to have become the best of friends.

But the real reason Nessie O'Neil sold up was that she felt old and tired. The work of the farm was too much for her, even with the hired help – two men she had from the village, and whether they came or not depended on whether their horses came up at the Portadown races.

'There you are, mother. Where have you been?' It was Nellie's voice, and she was standing with a group of men in the yard, holding some papers in her hand.

'I was just checking,' said Nessie as she joined them.

'Ah, well, what's not on the cart, we'll have to leave for the mice.'

'A charitable instinct, Mrs O'Neil,' said Colonel Mayhew.

'Ay,' said Nessie. She still couldn't get used to seeing the Colonel in her own yard, even though strictly speaking it was his own yard. He hadn't set foot in the place till the auction that morning.

'With the prices she got, she can afford to be charitable,' muttered Andrew Tait, the factor, as grumpy as ever in his old age.

'I would think it's every penny my mother deserves,' put in Nellie testily. 'If you'd done the work she has, it's another shilling you'd be putting on the acre.'

'I must admit the improvements have been considerable,' said the Colonel. But the factor was quick to continue,

'The papers are signed, and in order, I think,' indicating the documents in Nellie's hand.

'I think so,' said Nellie, handing them over.

'Well, that would seem to be that,' said Tait, stomping towards his Austin Seven car. 'Ready when you are, Colonel.'

'Well, goodbye, Mrs O'Neil,' said Colonel Mayhew, offering his hand to Nessie. 'I wish you a very happy retirement in Dublin with your son.' Nessie glanced at Nellie quickly.

'I'm sure he'll be delighted to see us, sir.'

Kevin was anything but delighted to see his mother and sister in Dublin. Things were very tense in the Irish capital, with the death of Arthur Griffith only the week before. He had been elected President of the new Irish Free State only after Eamon de Valera had resigned. He was now committed to militant opposition, aimed towards a United Ireland with a Republican Government independent of Britain. This was the side that Kevin O'Neil was firmly on. To his mind, and many others in both north and south, Ireland was an unnaturally divided country, with the Irish Free State to the south and north-west, still a dominion within the British Commonwealth, and the six counties of Ulster to the north-east still a part of the United Kingdom. Even though he was an Ultsterman himself, Kevin was an unashamed republican and a United Ireland was still his dream to be attained by whatever means.

He was by now a leading member of the Independent Republican group, which wanted no part of the London treaty, and for the moment, it looked like Civil War as de Valera called for the Sinn Fein to declare for a Republican Government as the only legitimate government in all Ireland. This was Kevin's view – but it was not everyone's and as a result the political situation was volatile.

Nessie O'Neil arrived at Dublin station in the week after President Griffith's funeral and had some difficulty in finding Kevin. The address he had given them on the few postcards he had sent turned out to be a small commercial hotel near the cathedral. The man at the desk claimed no knowledge of him, but directed them to the pub at the corner. Nessie waited outside wondering how much the taxi was going to cost. The driver kept going on about 'the troubles'. Nessie had no real idea what he was talking about. Nellie came out eventually with an address in Rathmines.

'Would you credit the man wouldn't believe I was his sister?' she said huffily, settling back.

'How did you get him to believe you then?'

'I told him I changed Kevin's nappies when he was a baby, and that he had a pimple on his bum!' Both women laughed as the taxi made its way across the crowded bridge towards Rathmines.

'Do ye mean to say ye've not heard about the troubles?'

'Troubles!' snorted Nessie. 'I've had nothing but troubles all me life and I've no desire to hear another word of yours.'

'As ye wish, ma'am,' said the driver cheerfully enough, and was silent the rest of the way.

Kevin's lodgings turned out to be a terraced house, and number 28 seemed to be a dingier door than all the rest. While Nellie attended the driver and the three suitcases, Nessie looked up at the window. There was no sign of life at all. The driver obligingly lifted the cases up to the front door.

'For the pleasure of the conversational discourse,' he said sardonically, touching his cap. He was a Dublin taxi driver after all. He drove away, leaving them and the cases standing on the doorstep.

'Try the bell,' said Nessie.

'I did. It doesn't work.' said Nellie.

'Then knock with your hand.' Nellie did, and the door was eventually opened by a young girl of no more than twelve.

'Me Mammy's not in,' she said shyly, half hiding herself behind the door.

'It's not your Mammy we're wanting,' said Nessie. 'Is there a Mr O'Neil in the place?'

'Me Mammy says I was to say I don't know.'

'Will your Mammy be long?' asked Nellie.

'I don't know,' said the girl. Nessie's manner suddenly changed and she leaned down to the girl.

'Tell me, child,' she said softly. 'Is there a chance now that Kevin might be in?' The young girl's eyes brightened.

'He just went out now not a moment since. You've just missed him.'

'Well, now, isn't that the shame,' said Nessie. 'Here's his old mother now and his sister here come to visit him, and both of us dying for a sup of tea.'

'I don't know where the tea is,' said the girl.

'You just be showing us where the kitchen is,' said Nessie, gently pushing the door inwards, 'and we'll find it ourselves.'

Which was why Kevin found a tea-party going on in the kitchen when he returned sober-suited with the afternoon editions of the papers under his arm.

'Mother!' he gasped. 'What are you doing here?'

'Enjoying my second cup of tea.'

'And where were you, Kevin O'Neil,' said Nellie, 'and us arriving at the station and us having to take an eight-shilling taxi?' Kevin put his papers down and stared at the women. He seemed uncertain, and quite gauche despite his thirty-nine years.

'You surely were expecting us?' said his mother.

'I was, I was,' said Kevin quickly, 'but not today with the funeral and everything.'

'Sure I know you're a busy man, Kevin, but it's a funny son has no time for his mother when she comes to Dublin.'

'True, true,' said Kevin, his mind obviously elsewhere. Catching sight of the young girl, he said, 'Teresa, girl, will ye fetch yer mother from Feeney's?'

'I will that, Kevin,' said the young girl eagerly. Kevin was obviously her favourite.

'Will ye have a cup of tea, Kevin?'

'Thank you, mother, I will,' and he sat down with her.

There was no embrace between them, no sign of affection, but there was an immediate sense of family as the three sat together in that cluttered little kitchen. Kevin had always kept himself to himself, and his reserve was taken for granted. Nellie was spreading another slice of white bread and jam, and Nessie was waiting patiently for her son to speak in his own time.

'There's a war on, mother, don't you know?'

'A war? With guns, do you mean?'

'With guns and rifles and anything else we can lay our hands on.'

'And who are we?' asked Nellie, her mouth full of bread and jam.

'Us,' said Kevin, looking at his mother.

'Do you know what you're doin'?' she said, looking at him.

'We do, mother.'

'Well, that's one thing at least.'

No more needed to be said between mother and son. Yet a Civil War was happening outside on those very Dublin streets; the terrible time they called The Troubles had begun. It would set north against south, Catholic against Protestant, house against house, brother against brother, but not come between mother and son.

'Will you not show us your room then?' asked Nellie.

'No,' answered Kevin quickly. 'It's an awful mess, don't you know?'

'No, we don't,' said his mother, 'but we'll take your word for it. How's your leg?' she asked suddenly.

'Much the same,' replied Kevin.

'How do you manage?' she continued.

'Well enough,' he said. 'I've always got the other one.'

The trio had fallen into a silence when Sarah Dacre, Teresa's mother came in. It could be seen even from her present slatternly appearance that she once, and not so long ago, was an attractive woman. She brought a kind of energy into the room and also a strong smell of beer.

'You must be thinkin' me a terrible woman, Kevin's mother, and me not here to meet you in my own house. But it's to the messages I've been, you'll understand.'

Nessie nodded. 'I understand, Mrs –'

'It's a terrible name for the terrible man I married, and him an English man. Twelve years ago he's left me now and that's his child, Teresa, that you met. Is there a cup left in that pot? I'm dyin' of the thirst.' She lifted up the pot and busied herself around the kitchen as she talked. 'Ah, there you are now, girl,' and Teresa came in carrying two bags. She laid the one containing the vegetables on the table, and the other she laid down on the floor at the corner of the sink. There was a decided bottle clink as she did so. Mrs Dacre continued airily, 'It's an awful business keeping body and soul together, is it not? Will youse have a cup of tea, or will youse prefer something stronger?' The tea party became a bottle party as the afternoon wore on; although the O'Neil women both declined, Kevin had a glass and Mrs Dacre had several.

Gradually over the afternoon, a plan emerged. It was impossible for them to stay at the Dacres.

'I only have one lodging room and sure Kevin has that,' said the landlady. He would remain there – 'for personal reasons' – but he had fixed them up at Cassidy's Hotel, the place they first went to.

'I have contacts there,' explained Kevin. His mother and sister would be given accommodation and meals in return for Nessie's services for light housework, and Nellie's occasional duties as receptionist and telephonist.

'That is,' said Kevin hesitantly, 'if you think–' He broke off and looked at his mother whispering, 'If you think she can do the work an' all.' He seemed embarrassed.

'You know, her being – you know –' His voice drifted away, but Nellie had heard.

'I know alright, our Kevin,' she said. 'If it's my head you're worrying about, you need have no fear. It's still stuck on my shoulders.'

Kevin reddened and tried to laugh, but all he said was 'I'm sorry, Nellie.'

'That's alright,' said his sister crisply. Then it was time to take the suitcases to the door again. Mrs Dacre led the women volubly into the hallway.

Just before they left, Kevin called Teresa to him, and taking a spent bullet from his pocket, he said to her, 'Teresa, if you put those papers there up in my room while I'm gone, I'll give you this.' He held out the snubbed bullet in his fingers. 'Would you know that was the very bullet that was once in my leg?' and dropped it into her outstretched hand. As her fingers closed in on the souvenir, her upturned gaze of worship and admiration only told the more plainly of how much a hero Kevin O'Neil was to Teresa Dacre.

'Are you coming, Kevin?' cried Nellie's voice from the hallway. 'You can't be expecting us to carry these ourselves.'

Kevin winked at Teresa and left to help his sister and Mrs Dacre carry the cases to the car where Nessie O'Neil was already waiting.

Kevin got into the driving seat and they moved off. 'It's a grand big motor car,' said his mother. 'It's not yours, is it?'

'No, it belongs to friends of mine,' answered Kevin into the rear mirror. Nessie glanced at Nellie.

'It's fine to have friends who have fine motor cars.'

In response, Nellie said in an aside to her mother, 'An' it's fine to have friends like that Mrs Dacre. Did you ever see such a woman?' Nessie nodded.

'And the poor child-girl too.' The car sped through the suburbs until they were once again in O'Connell Street in the centre of the town.

Suddenly there were several big bangs. The women jumped in fright.

'God save us, what was that?' called out Nellie.

'It's not your tyres, is it?' cried Nessie.

'It's them guns I was telling youse about,' said Kevin, bending low over the wheel, glancing right and left as he speeded up among the traffic. They were now aware of people shouting and running in the streets, and of buses coming to a halt in front of them. They were near the Post Office and Kevin wound down the window. 'What's going on?' he shouted to a passer-by.

'They've murdered Michael Collins. Get yourself off the street before they start shooting here. Another shot rang out, and there was a noise of breaking glass.

'Jesus, Mary and Joseph!' said the man, and disappeared from the running board. Kevin swung the car out and pressed hard on the accelerator to turn round the first corner with brakes screaming, and as they sped towards Cassidy's Hotel, Nessie was amazed to see in the rear mirror that her son was laughing his head off.

'What are you laughing at? cried his mother.

'I've just remembered,' he shouted back to her, 'August the twenty-second. It's my birthday!' And he laughed again as the car raced on.

Sam Cassidy was an older man than he looked. His own hair and his own teeth, plus a good pair of eyes, gave the impression of a younger man than his sixty years. A bachelor, he had inherited the two houses that made up the hotel from his mother and aunt, and he had all the assurance of a man who lives comfortably from day to day without having to do a hand's turn. Some would say that this kind of service to the human condition was a helpful concomitant in a hurried world. For Sam seemed to have had all the time there was, and had plenty of it for everyone.

Behind that cosy sofa exterior, however, was an upright chair of the strongest steel, for Sam Cassidy, self-employed bachelor and Major in the Irish Independent Republican Army, was Kevin O'Neil's immediate superior. It was 'The Major', as Kevin called him, who first suggested that Kevin should bring his mother and sister to the hotel. A private commercial is a good cover, he said, with all the comings and goings, and a couple of northern voices wouldn't do any harm, especially when one is on the telephone. The West Britons, or Anglo-Irish of the establishment, associated Ulster voices with Protestantism and therefore Unionism, so they would be working for their keep in more senses than one if they were to come and live at Cassidy's.

All went according to plan. Nessie and Nellie settled into their respective light duties and their attic rooms. Nessie was still in her vigorous seventies, and anything she was asked to do at Cassidy's was feather duster stuff compared to what she had been doing at Ballytreabhair. She found the three flights of stairs hard going, but as long as she made a stop at each landing, she found she was able to cope. She discovered that if she said three Hail Marys at each landing, it was just time enough for her to get her breath back. She said one for Nellie, one for Kevin, and one to help her get to the top. Nellie, however, to everyone's surprise, settled in remarkably well at the switchboard. Her smile filled most of the small cubicle and her brisk, efficient manner was an immediate reassurance to first-time callers. What was totally surprising, however, was that Sam Cassidy fell hook, line and sinker for her. If Sam Cassidy looked younger than his sixty, Nellie Murphy showed every month of her forty-nine. But since coming to Dublin and the excitement of the street shooting, Nellie had shed at least ten years, and looked what she was – an attractive middle-aged matron.

From the first moment Sam saw her, he stared at her, and he kept staring at her at every opportunity. So much so that it caused Nessie to remark to her daughter, 'Is that man Cassidy a shillin' short?'

'Not at all, mother,' replied Nellie grandly, 'but what's more important is that he's not short of a shilling!'

Nellie revelled in the attention, and in the months that followed, she and Sam went to the cinema together and to the theatre and even to Bray on a Sunday for special dinners. Mrs O'Neil often wondered if it was the right way for Mrs Murphy to behave, but since everything in Dublin astonished her, she took her daughter's innocent affair with the same mixture of scepticism and incredulity.

'Sure what harm is there in them?' she told Kevin. 'They're both grown people.'

'They're not grown people,' said Kevin. 'They're old!' But neither Sam nor Nellie seemed to mind that.

Kevin worried, not so much about his sister, nor even about Sam Cassidy, genial Hotel Proprietor, but about Major Cassidy, his commander. At times both he and Sam had to be away from Dublin for quite long spells, and Kevin noticed that Sam never discussed Nellie, nor even mentioned her, while they were away. Kevin was anxious to hear the older man's feelings only because he was a younger brother, but when they were 'on duty', it was almost as if Nellie never existed. But she did, and was as happy as she'd been for years.

'What about Liam?' ventured Nessie one morning at breakfast.

'What *about* Liam?' answered Nellie, buttering her toast. The situation had begun to bother Nessie somewhat, and in her usual first Sunday letter to Paddy every month, she was tempted to mention it, but thought she'd better not in case it was a mortal sin – her telling, she meant, not Nellie's affair.

As if in answer to her dilemma, the next letter from Paddy told her that he was coming to Dublin and was bringing a surprise with him. What could that be, Nessie wondered. Had they made him a Bishop already?

His letter mentioned that since the death of Pope Benedict at the beginning of the year, and the election of Pius XI, things were being changed around in the church, and a series of Eucharistic Congresses were being considered, one of which was to be held at some future date in Dublin. He and his Baltimore bishop were coming over to represent the American clergy at the preliminary talks, and would have a week in Dublin before going on to London and then Rome.

'They get around, these Bishops,' said Nellie when she heard.

'Who pays for it all? That's what I wonder.'

'Sure, isn't that what Peter's Pence is for? A penny a week in the plate soon mounts up.'

It was that night that Sam came home with his hand bandaged.

'It's alright, it's my left,' he said breezily. 'It's not my drinking hand.'

'What happened?' asked Nellie.

'As you know, we went up to Belfast by road. We had a blowout on the road to Dundalk, and idiot that I am, when I was helping Kevin to change the wheel, the jack gave way and down came the wheel base on my hand.'

'Where's Kevin then?' asked Nessie.

'He stayed behind to wait for a new jack. I came on by train. I was eager to get back.'

'To me?' asked Nellie coquettishly.

'Oh, for Heaven's sake,' said Nessie, leaving the room.

Nellie made a great fuss of Sam that night, so much so that from her soothing caressing of first his poor hand and then his poor face and then his poor head, they moved from her tender inventory of his poverty-stricken parts to an engulfing embrace against the closed office door. She did not sleep in the attic that night, nor in fact ever again while Sam was at home. Nellie bloomed and Nessie was scandalised. For weeks, mother and daughter did not speak and Nessie was appalled that Sam and Nellie had the effrontery to go to midnight Mass at Christmas – and even go to Communion!

'Didn't we go to Confession?' protested Nellie.

'The priest must have been deaf,' said her mother.

'Did you promise not to do it again, that's the thing.'

'That's none of your business,' replied her daughter archly.

'I'm glad it's not,' muttered Nessie, 'but just remember you're a married woman.'

'I can never forget it,' answered Nellie. And nothing more was said on the subject. Because something happened that put their middle-aged 'amour' into its proper perspective. Monsignor Paddy arrived in Dublin, not only with his Bishop, but with his niece, Maria.

It was a Saturday afternoon in the middle of February, 1923, when the Baltimore party arrived in Dublin after a pleasant holiday voyage on the Mauretania, which landed them at Cherbourg, from whence they caught the steamship to Dun Laoghaire, and then the train to Dublin. Paddy called Cassidy's from Cathedral House, asking directions. Kevin insisted on coming to get him, and Paddy promised to be ready in an hour.

When Kevin called at Cathedral House, a thing he had not done in all his ten years in Dublin, he was nervous about seeing his brother again, whom he had not seen since 1900. Kevin had been seventeen when the boys had left with Noreen. Paddy himself had only been five years older then. A bookish, quiet asthmatic was all Kevin could remember of Paddy. His eyes were always in a book and he was never off the altar. Now here was Kevin standing in the vestibule of the Bishop of Dublin's house, waiting to meet one of the Monsignori of the Catholic Church who was Paddy O'Neil, his brother.

The Monsignor came in looking much taller than Kevin remembered. Perhaps that was because in his remembrance Paddy was always sitting down or kneeling down. 'Good Lord, Kevin boy, is that you?' Kevin was surprised at the degree of American accent and could say nothing as he offered his hand. Paddy in his turn was taken aback at the burly, filmstar good looks of his youngest brother, and the iron-hard grip of his handshake. After the formality of the hand clasp, they quite spontaneously gave each other a hug.

'What do I call you?' asked Kevin, blushing despite himself.

'I'm still Paddy to you, Kevin boy, but perhaps in public, it'd be better if you called me Monsignor.' Kevin felt a sudden awe at the realisation that his own brother was next door to a Bishop.

'How's my mother?' Paddy asked when they were seated opposite each other in the waiting room.

'She's just grand!' replied Kevin. 'Been like a little girl again since we had news of your coming.'

'Is that so?' said Paddy. 'She'd be a good age now.'

'Seventy-seven, I think, but she admits to fifty-eight.' The two brothers laughed.

'And Nellie's better again, I hear?'

Kevin had to look away as he thought of how much better Nellie was, but all he said was, 'She is.'

Paddy nodded. 'By the Grace of God.'

Is that what it was? Kevin thought. But he said nothing.

'Isn't it wonderful how things happen?'

'Ay,' agreed Kevin. A kind of embarrassed lull had come down after the first excesses of greeting, and it was Kevin who broke the silence eventually.

'My mother said something about a surprise you were bringing over.' Paddy brightened at once, and stood up.

'Forgive me, I was dreaming. I was thinking of the shy little boy you were once in Ballytreabhair when we were all young on the farm. You remember? When we all had to say the family rosary?'

Kevin nodded. 'I remember alright.'

'Tell me, Kevin,' he said, coming over to him, 'do you ever say the rosary these days?' Kevin stood up, not meeting his brother's gaze.

'Well, I don't have much time, Monsignor.' The brothers looked at each other for a moment.

'No,' said Paddy. 'Just wait there. I'll go and get her.' In a second, he was gone. Kevin pondered to himself. 'Her?' he said to himself. 'Her? Is it a dog he's brought over or what?'

It wasn't a dog. It was a very beautiful American girl, whose twenty-first birthday it was that day. 'Happy Birthday!' was all Kevin could say when Paddy introduced her.

'Gee, you're kind,' was all Maria's response. Paddy stood beaming between them, watching the obvious attraction the niece had for the uncle, and what was even more obvious, the uncle had for the niece. The effect that Nellie O'Neil had on Sam Cassidy was virtually replicated in the effect Kevin O'Neil had on Maria O'Neil, now calling herself d'Agostino. The Monsignor would have been less pleased had he known of the unashamed carnal nature of Maria's feelings for her uncle. Although she fully realised he was a brother to Sean and Michael and the good Monsignor, to her this dark commanding presence was a stranger and an attractive stranger at that. It was all rather much for Kevin, and he would like to have withdrawn for a moment to consider it all. Instead he had to help with Maria's luggage as she couldn't stay at the Bishop's House, and Paddy had presumed there would be room for her at Cassidy's. He had to remain as the Bishop's guest, of course, as he had work to do, but Maria was on vacation. She could really stay as long as she liked as she had completed her formal musical training at the Boston Conservatory, and was ready to begin work as a professional singer. If she couldn't find an opening in Dublin, she would try London and then perhaps Paris or Rome. If nothing happened, she would return to America. She was heart-whole and fancy free, and was ready to accept whatever fate had in store for her.

'Or God's will!' Paddy added, as they were both sitting in the back of the car.

'As you say, Uncle Paddy.' She agreed, but her eyes met Kevin's in the rear mirror.

It was nearly dark by the time they reached the hotel, and Nellie had the door open to them as they came up the steps.

'Oh, my God, you're Noreen!' she said, putting her hands to her cheeks. 'No, you're not. You've got black hair.'

'I'm sorry about that. You must be Aunt Helen?'

'That's who I am, though most people call me Nellie now.'

'Among other things,' added Kevin as he came up behind with two large suitcases. Nellie gave the girl a kind of awkward embrace then passed her on to Kevin in the hallway. Then she turned and screamed as she saw Paddy.

'Oh, Paddy!' she cried. 'My, you're beautiful!' and running down, nearly knocked him over with her embrace.

'God bless you, Nellie!' he tried to say as he was smothered by her. Sam, meantime, had come out of the office and into the hallway and had met Maria. He still kept his left hand behind his back, trying not to show the tips of the two fingers he had lost.

'Isn't this just the cutest place?' drawled Maria.

'We're quite happy,' beamed Sam.

'I'll go and get me mother,' said Kevin.

'No, wait, Kevin. Let me go and see her,' said Paddy with an air of surprising authority.

'As you like,' said Kevin. 'She's on the top floor. First on the left.'

The meeting between the Monsignor and his mother was a beautiful thing. When he knocked at the door, a voice said 'Come in.' He opened the door. She was sitting on the bed, her head bowed and rosary beads in her hand. She was putting these away as he stood looking at her.

'Has he come?' she said.

'He has, mother,' replied Paddy, standing at the door. Her head turned quickly. Paddy was appalled to see how old she was. He couldn't get over the whiteness of her hair or the crinkled lines of her face, but he gave only a momentary start. Controlling himself he moved forward to pick her up. She gazed up at him like a baby.

'My God, son. It's the great figure you are.'

'Mother!' Paddy held the bony little figure tightly to the red and black of his Monsignor's garb.

It was quite a time before mother and son came down, and when the door to the private sitting room opened, Kevin and Sam were in the two armchairs, with Nellie and Maria on the couch. Everyone rose as Paddy came in leading his mother saying, 'And here she is. The surprise I was telling you about. May I present to you Miss Maria O'Neil d'Agostino. Diva-to-be and only daughter of our dear sister, Noreen.' Nessie had been advancing towards the young girl with her hands held out, until the mention of Noreen's name, when she stopped, and put both hands to her mouth.

'Noreen, did you say?'

'That's right,' answered Maria, smiling. 'She was my Mom.'

'Was she now?' answered Nessie in the same low tone.

'Isn't she beautiful, mother?' said Paddy coming between them.

'She is that, I suppose,' said Nessie, lowering her hands and straightening up as much as she could. Suddenly there was a tension in the room. This was not turning out to be the happy family occasion everyone had thought it was going to be.

'Mother –' Paddy began. 'Mother –'

His mother stopped him with a look.

'Patrick, I'm proud of you and what you've done, but I am ashamed that you've brought to this house the child of a woman who was not married by the Church and in the eyes of God, and who stands now as living proof of the fruits of sin and wiles of the Devil. I would thank you to remove her from my sight now, or better still, I'll remove meself.' And with that she turned and walked out of the room. They were stunned and stood for a moment in absolute disbelief.

'Oh, my God!' Maria wailed. 'What have I said? What have I done?'

'It's not what you've done, Maria,' said Paddy. 'Excuse me, I'll go to her.' And he too turned and left the room.

'I think we should have a drink,' said Sam.

'Good idea,' said Kevin.

It was an hour before Paddy returned.

'It's no good,' he said with a sigh. 'She's made up her mind and nothing I can say or do can change it. She won't have Noreen's child under the same roof.'

'I guess I'll have to go somewhere else then,' said Maria, her spirits restored, not only by the sherry, but also by her own youth and optimistic vitality.

'Come on,' said Kevin rising, and putting down his drink. 'I'll take you to Mrs Dacre's.'

That larger-than-life lady was more than equal to the situation. In no time she had Teresa out of her tiny bedroom and in beside her. The best bits of everybody's room, including Kevin's, went in, a cushion here, a bedspread there, a bit of curtain and so on, until Maria had as good a room as she could have got in the Gresham or the Shelbourne. The only trouble with it was that it was small and Maria was tall. Teresa watched with mixed feelings as this extraordinary girl from America moved into her room and took over the whole house. Maria might have come from Mars as far as Teresa was concerned. She had never seen anyone remotely like Maria d'Agostino before and she found it hard to believe that this dazzling vision was actually related to her hero, Kevin. Right from the first, Teresa was determined to dislike her, especially as Maria put a long hand under her chin, and lifting it, cooed sweetly, 'Aren't you just a real little doll!'

'Dolls are toys,' was all she was able to say.

Teresa also noticed that her mother was quieter when the American girl was about and put on airs like a Dublin lady. Teresa didn't like her mother like that. She preferred the old beery, laughing mother she'd always known. Even Kevin was subdued and seemed to find every excuse for getting out of the house.

For the first few days, Maria stayed in her room, 'resting after the voyage'. Teresa used to have to take up a breakfast tray before she went off to school. She always left it at the door and knocked. She didn't like going into her own room now. It smelled differently and had all those funny dresses hanging up. It didn't look like her little bedroom at all. When Kevin was home from his trips, she was glad to take his tray in, because his room smelled of Kevin and she liked that. He would sit up and read out bits of the paper to her, and she would sit on the end of the bed waiting to take his tray down. She was always glad when her mother was away at Feeney's because that meant she could talk to Kevin longer, but now he was away too a lot, she might as well go to school. Anyway, she was glad to get away from all that screeching. 'Vocal exercises', Maria called them, but it sounded like screeching to Teresa. Even when she closed the front door and went out into the street, she could still hear it. Sometimes she would sing a real song and all the neighbours would listen at their windows. Mrs Delaney, who lived next door, called out to her one morning, 'Hey, Teresa, has your mother got a canary in?'

Occasionally Mrs Murphy, the woman Teresa remembered from that first day, came with a gentleman Teresa didn't know, and when the man went away with Kevin in the car, the woman who was Kevin's sister stayed on and talked with Maria. The last time they got into a bit of an argument. Then one day a priest came and he stayed a long time. When he came out, Teresa thought he'd been crying; at least his eyes were all red. Her mother made an awful fuss of him in the kitchen. He spoke the same way as Maria, and just for that reason, Teresa decided she didn't like him either. Then Kevin came back and everything was better again.

Until he started taking Maria out at nights. Teresa knew she was jealous, but she could do nothing about it. She just watched from the front window as they drove away, and she had to admit they did look like film stars. Mrs Dacre was in her element and her standing with the neighbours had risen enormously. As she told Mrs Delaney.

'She's an operatic class of a person. She has to have the best, don't you know. They've got to take real care of themselves. That's why she was sent to me. And her other brother, you know, the one they say that's going to be the Pope one day, didn't he have tea in the kitchen with me and tell me that Maria will be famous one day for her singing. And I'll be famous too, Mrs Delaney, for having the heart to give her a good Irish home when she needed it.'

'And take a good Irish rent for it, I'll be bound.'

'Not a penny for it. Not an old king's farthing.'

'Is that so?' said Mrs Delaney, in genuine surprise.

'Sure, isn't it Teresa's room she's in, but Kevin pays me a little extra for the inconvenience.'

'How convenient!'

'Well, being in the insurance, you see, he can afford it.'

Teresa was determined to stay awake until they got back. She put on her coat and sat by the window in the dark. She saw the car come back and heard Maria laugh that laugh of hers with Kevin trying to quieten her. He looked so handsome in his black coat and hat. They came in and she thought they made an awful lot of noise in the kitchen. It was a good job her mother was snoring. Then she heard the tinkle of glasses in the sitting room. Why do grown-ups have to drink so much? Her mug of cocoa did her all night. Then to her dismay, she found she needed to go to the lavatory. That meant she had to pass the parlour door, but she couldn't help it. She had to go. She opened the door of her mother's bedroom and tiptoed along the lobby, keeping to the edge so that the floor didn't creak. She thought she heard a mouse scurrying and stopped. But she didn't want to put on the light, and tiptoed on. She decided not to pull the chain, just in case, and came out just as the front door opened again and Kevin and Maria came out of the parlour and started making their way upstairs. She had to admit that Maria did look gorgeous in the shiny green dress and she noticed that Kevin had his hand round her waist. But then he could merely have been guiding her up the stairs. He was carrying his coat and his jacket and his shoes in his left hand, and his tie was pulled down from his collar. Were they drunk, thought Teresa. She stood there listening and she was sure she only heard one door shut. She tried not to think what she was thinking and began to tiptoe back to her mother's room, as quietly as she could. As quiet as a mouse. Why did people say that when a mouse always made a noise? You couldn't help hearing its little feet as they scraped on the linoleum. She didn't mind the mice as long as they didn't run over her bare feet.

As she got to the parlour door, she noticed they had left the gas light on. She decided to go in and turn down the gas mantle. As she did so, she noticed that Maria's cape was thrown across the sofa. On an impulse she took off her own coat and tried it on. She pretended that she too was going on the stage and was the fine Dublin lady. But then there was the sound of a door opening above her, and a snatch of angry voices, she thought. God help us, they'll waken my mother. Then everything was silent again. She came out into the hall again and was just crossing to her mother's door, when she heard the noise of a door knob turning on the floor above. She quickly stepped back into the shadow and saw the figure of Maria in her nightdress in the light of the skylight above her, crossing the landing and going into Kevin's room. Teresa felt her heart crack with disappointment. Oh, Lord save us, she thought. She's going into Kevin. Why's she doing that? Teresa didn't know why, but she knew it was wrong somehow. Wasn't Kevin Maria's uncle? She felt a shiver run right through her, and suddenly she wanted to be sick. She ran again to the bathroom, letting the cape fall from her shoulder. It lay in the front hallway gleaming in the light coming through the glass of the front door.

Next morning there were no breakfast trays at either door. Mrs Dacre explained to Kevin that Teresa was still in bed.

'She's come down poorly, the wee darling. Something came on her in the night. Sure, she'll be alright after a day in her bed.'

'Will she be alright?' said Kevin.

'Sure she will. Strong as an ox, our Teresa. Never a thing bothers her.' Kevin wanted to go and see her, but Mrs Dacre suggested that she be left alone.

'Let her sleep it off, whatever it is.'

Kevin then explained that Maria would be leaving that day 'to go to London'.

'She has ideas of taking some further lessons there, and has the address of some teacher or other. I'll take her to the station as soon as she's packed.'

'In that case, she'd better have this,' said Mrs Dacre. 'I found it this morning in the hallway when I was taking in the milk.' It was Maria's cape. Only Mrs Dacre waved the car off this time. Maria sat in the back alone, like a queen, with her cases beside her. Mrs Dacre waved loudly enough to make sure that the neighbours heard, but watching it all from the front window was a pale, twelve-year-old face, with just the ghost of a smile playing round its lips.

TWENTY-EIGHT

On Thursday 2nd August 1923, President Harding died of an embolism, or what was then called apoplexy. The next afternoon in a simple ceremony conducted by his father, a Justice of the Peace, Calvin Coolidge was sworn in as the thirteenth President of the United States.

Not that this historical event made much difference to a group of dancers in Hoboken, New Jersey. To them, the only thing was to keep going and going and going, till they and their partner were the last surviving couple on the floor, and so won the prize. This was marathon dancing and was all the rage in that year. Young people all over the country flocked to dance halls, and as the relays of bands changed over, the endless wail of saxophone and shout of trumpet and beat of drum sent millions of young people round in circles to the incessant sound of a band.

One such contestant was Jitka O'Neil, the oldest daughter of Hana Karpiskova and Denis O'Neil, who was eighteen years old, and crazy about dancing. Her harrassed police captain father thought that she was stupid to enter all these fool contests for a few dollars prize money. Even if she won she would only spend it on another damned marathon.

'What's it worth?' complained Denis. 'All that effort for a few measly dollars.'

'But it's fun, Pops,' said Jitka, pressing the iron on to yet another short dancing dress.

'The kind of fun that'll kill you.'

'It's only my feet that kill me, Pops.'

The doorbell rang. It was Brad Kominsky, Jitka's marathon dancing partner. He was a pleasant young man of Polish extraction, who had been to school with the O'Neil girls, and had been crazy about Jitka since Second Grade. The feeling was not mutual. Nevertheless, they made good dancing partners, and he was just glad of the chance to have his arms round her regularly. Brad was tall and strong. He worked as a smelter for the United States Steel Corporation. Jitka was small and slight. When the stress moment

came in the marathon contest and they had to break through the
fatigue barrier, it was nearly always the petite Jitka who carried the
muscular Brad, for the strain then was more psychological than
physical and it was Jitka who had the inner reserve. Once over
this hurdle Brad's own strength revived, and he carried her to the
finish. This was why they won so many local contests and were
tipped to win at Hoboken. They even had a chance of getting to
the All-American final at Washington when the President himself
would hand over the prize. So it was important they should keep
in practice.

'Sorry I'm late,' said Brad. 'Gee, I thought you'd be hopping
mad.'

'We got plenty of time,' said Jitka, putting the last touch to the
hem of the red dress. 'The train's not till seven.'

'No, it's six-thirty,' said Brad.

'What?'

'We just got time to get it,' he added.

Thereafter panic ensued. The dresses were flung in a bag after
being so carefully ironed, the shoes were thrown into another bag,
Pops offered to drive them to the railway station, and Brad said
he'd wait outside. Hana came bustling in from the kitchen.

'You ain't had no supper, Jitka.'

'Haven't time, Mama,' yelled Jitka. 'Where's my comb? If
Katya's got my comb again, I'll – I'll –' She disappeared again
in the direction of the bathroom.

'But you gotta have some supper, Jitka. You can't go out on no
empty stomach.'

'Don't fuss, Hana,' said her husband. 'She can do without
Stroganof for one night.'

'But she need to keep her strength up,' moaned Hana, wringing
her hands. 'For the dance.'

Denis was buttoning up his coat and going towards the door.
'Don't worry, Hana, there's enough Irish in her for that. Come
on, kid, we gotta get goin'.'

Jitka came hurtling out past her mother, stopping only to give her
a quick peck on the cheek. 'Bye, mama.' And then she was gone.

Hana sighed and turned back saying, 'Why do I bother about
the children?' As Jitka closed the front door, she could hear her
mother's voice from the kitchen, saying, 'Clara, you keep Anna
out of that Stroganof!'

Thanks to her Pops' immunity to speeding fines, Jitka and Brad
caught the train with seconds to spare.

The young couple got to the hall in Hoboken just in time to
collect their numbers and pay their two-dollar fee. One dollar

went to the promoter, the other went to make up the prize money. There must have been about forty couples Jitka worked out. That meant reasonable money tonight. Forty dollars could easily buy them each a new outfit and better shoes and still leave some over for the fares to Washington and at least one night in a hotel instead of the back of Brad's father's Lincoln saloon. Not that that had happened yet – and even if it did, they would both be too tired for there to be any danger in it. As the whistle started blowing to call the dancers on the floor, and the MC was bellowing through the megaphone, 'Take your partners for the Hoboken New Jersey Marathon', Jitka was hurriedly changing into her favourite red dancing dress and Brad was getting into the lucky white shoes he always wore. They gave each other a hug for luck at the edge of the carpeted area, then stepped on to the polished wood of the dance floor.

> 'I'll be loving you always,
> With a love that's true, always.
> When the things you've planned,
> Need a helping hand,
> I will understand, always, always . . . .'

Jitka let herself go in Brad's arms and he carried her effortlessly round as if she were a thistle down. His lucky white shoes swathed a path through the mêlée of forty couples also moving anti-clockwise on the sprung dancing arena. In the centre, the two umpires, an older man and woman, kept a casual eye on the press of dancers circling round them.

> 'Things may not be fair, always,
> That's when I'll be there, always . . . .'

Brad looked over Jitka's head taking in the opposition. There were a few stylish dancers on show, but marathons weren't won on style, they were won on stamina, and the thing to do was take it easy, reserve your strength and keep your partner close, cut back on the forward advances and minimise the reverse steps. The time for showing off was when you were the last couple on the floor.

> 'Not for just an hour,
> Not for just a day,
> Not for just a year,
> But always, always, always . . . .'

Back in Brooklyn, the same song was being played on the radio while Denis was trying to read his newspaper. Suddenly the door was thrown open and Hana pulled Katya, their second daughter, into the room.

'Pops, I want you look at this.' Denis sighed and lowered his paper, and let out a yell.

'Holy Moses!' Katya, or Kat, as they all called her, had cut all her beautiful blonde hair into a fifteen-year-old's approximation of the fashionable Eton crop.

'See what she done,' said Hana in exasperation. 'All her beautiful hair she had since she was a baby.'

'It's the fashion, Mama!'

'Fashion! Fashion!' said Hana derisively, then looked up at Denis. 'What you do about it eh?' Her accent was always more evident when she was angry.

'What can I do about it?' said Denis. 'I can't stick it on again, can I?'

'You can give her telling-off, that's what you can do.' Denis put down his paper with a sigh.

'What's the point, Mama? No use crying over spilt milk. It'll grow again.' But Hana had her blood up by this time.

'What do I care if the milk is spilled?' she explained. 'What you want we wait another fifteen years for her to grow from bald?'

'But, Mama, Malvina Jones got hers done just like this.'

'Who's Malvina Jones?' said Denis helplessly.

'She's my friend,' answered Katya.

'She no good friend for daughter of mine,' said Hana, turning on Katya.

'Why ain't she?' demanded Katya with some heat.

'Because I don't like her, that's why.' At this, Denis exploded with irritation.

'Goddamit, who would ever live in a house full o' dames?' And turning to the radio, he turned up the volume. It was playing,

> 'If you knew Susie, like I knew Susie,
> Oh, oh, oh, what a girl . . .'

> '. . . Tea for two, and two for tea,
> Me for you and you for me . . .'

An hour had passed and the tempo had changed, but the circling went relentlessly on. At one point, Jitka winced. There was a sharp pain in her tummy. Brad looked down. He was too good a dancer to have stood on her toe and he thought somebody might have clicked her heel. That went on a lot during the marathons. Of course, it was always excused politely as an accident, but some of the regular marathon dancers were never too sure.

'It's nothing,' whispered Jitka, 'hunger pains, I guess.' Brad hugged her just a little closer and sailed on into the quickstep.

'We will raise a family,
A boy for you, a girl for me,
Then you'll see how happy we will be.'

Bedtime in Brooklyn, and Denis was singing in the kitchen with his two younger daughters, Clara and Anna. As was sometimes their bedtime custom, the girls would sing in a delightful Bohemian harmony one of the many little songs their mother had taught them. Other nights it would be an Irish song their father had taught them. In this way, Denis had made his family 'musically ambidextrous' as he called it. Hana loved it when it was her night, and now she sat in her comfortable chair by the kitchen cooking stove knitting as the daughters sang.

'Dobru noc, ma' mila', dobru noc,
Nech je Jn sám P'au' Boh na pomoc.
Dobru noc, dobre spi,
Nech sa Jn sni'vaju
Sladke' sny.'

Meantime, things were jazzing up in Hoboken. They were just over the two-hour stage, and a vigorous Black Bottom session had got rid of the weakest challengers. The second band had opened with the Charleston and things were really going full swing.

'You're doing OK,' shouted Brad as he and Jitka crossed hands and knees together.

'I sure am,' replied Jitka, moving very smoothly, but she was just aware of a kind of heaviness in the pit of her stomach. What was it, she wondered.

Denis looked down at his son and heir. Young Denny was sleeping with his book of motor cars still open on the bed beside him and his light still on. All his little model cars were round about him on the pillow. Mad about cars was young Denny, including the police car the boys at the station had given him on his tenth birthday. There was a Ford from Uncle Sean, an Oldsmobile from Uncle

Michael. There was even a Cadillac from Uncle Liam. It had to be a Cadillac, of course. Denis gently gathered all the cars from round the bed and laid them in a line underneath the bed the way he knew that young Denny preferred. He leaned down and kissed the boy on the brow and Denny writhed in distaste. Denis grinned and put out the light. He found himself humming 'The Wyoming Lullaby' as he went down the stairs.

'Go to sleep, my baby,
Close your pretty eyes,
Angels up above you,
Wait to carry you to paradise.
Great big moon is shining,
Shining everywhere . . .'

There was a moon that night, but it took the form of a great big silver dome which sparkled in the artificial lighting of the Palace Ballroom. It shone down now on at least half the original dancers as midnight approached and the pace was hotting up. The perspiration was glistening on Brad's face, but he winked at Jitka, and she impishly winked back. The testing time was getting near, and both knew it.

Denis was now pacing the floor in Brooklyn. 'Where the hell does she get to? It's bad enough one girl being out all night. At least we know where she is, but darn it, she isn't sixteen years of age, and here she is out until midnight.'

'She's with her friends at a party.'

'But you don't like her friends. You said so.'

'But Katya likes parties. It's good for a young girl once in a while.'

'I'll give her what's good for her when she gets back.'

Footsteps were heard at the front door and there was Katya, breathless and bright-eyed and as pretty as a picture. It was hard for Denis to be angry with her, but he tried.

'What do you think you're doing –?'

'Look, Pops,' she interrupted, 'see what I got!' And she brandished a big cigar in its Havana wrapper.

'But I don't smoke!' he said.

'Then you can start now,' she said sweetly, gave it to him, and was gone. He stared at it as Hana watched.

'You were going to give her the piece of your mind?'

'It can wait till the morning,' Denis said, but he couldn't help smiling.

*

The strains of 'Charmaine' were filling the Palace now as the numbers had depleted alarmingly. There were only half a dozen couples left, and even the musicians seemed to be getting tired as they segued into 'Three O'Clock in the Morning'. For the first time Jitka faltered and Brad glanced at her in alarm.

'Sorry,' she said. They were now into their survival rhythm, virtually dancing on the spot.

'I wonder who's kissing her now . . .'
'After the ball is over . . .'
'Oh, oh, Antonio . . .'

Then suddenly,

'Pack up all your cares and woe,
Here I go, singin' low,
Bye, bye blackbird . . .'

This was the tester. The quickstep pace was deliberately intended to weed out the last. The lady umpire came close to Jitka.

'You OK, kid?' Jitka nodded, and looked up at Brad, who stepped up a gear or two and stepped forward. This had the effect of demoralising the couple next to them, because the girl burst out crying and her partner led her off. Jitka had another pain, but buried her head in Brad's chest. She could hear his heart thudding. Everything was beginning to be a blur around her.

'You awake?' Denis asked Mana.

'I can't sleep.'

'You never can when she's at one of these things,' said Denis sleepily. 'Do you realise it's nearly five in the morning? It's daylight the other side of these curtains.'

'I know, but I'm unhappy when she's doing these things. Not good food at these places. Not enough sleep when she work at the shop all day.'

'She's used to it,' mumbled Denis drowsily. 'Been doing it all summer. Anyways, Brad is a good kid. He'll look after her. You'd better get some good sleep before they come back for their breakfast.'

'They will be needing it.'

'So will I.' And he turned over on his other side, dragging the blankets with him. Hana didn't protest. She was lying staring straight ahead, and her lips started to form a prayer in her own language. She was worried and she didn't know why.

*

'Memories, Memories,
Days of long ago . . .'

There were only three couples left, and only a handful of spectators. Some press photographers now arrived to photograph the winners, and a smell of hamburgers started to pervade the hall as someone began to cook up breakfast. Jitka was literally being held up by Brad. She had already been sick on his suit, but he had held her so close the judges hadn't seen.

'You wanna finish now?' he croaked.

'I wanna finish first,' she answered, her face grotesquely rainbowed in the light. They were hardly moving now, moving back and forward like zombies. There was a thud as the man beside them fell, dragging the girl down with him.

'Oh, Chuck!' they could hear the girl whimper. Only two couples left now, as the melody changed.

'In her sweet little Alice Blue gown,
As she first wandered down into town,
She was both proud and shy
As she felt every eye . . .'

Every eye was indeed on the four young people as they struggled to keep going. The lady umpire then made a sudden move to the girl of the other partnership. The girl started to cry and explain, but everyone could see why she had to finish, as the blood ran down her silk stockings. The band immediately changed to

'All alone,
I'm so all alone,
There is no one here but me . . .'

It was 5.43a.m. Jitka and Brad had won their thirteenth marathon. As the newspaper men came forward, Jitka collapsed on to the floor, sliding down Brad's swaying body, till her head rested on his white shoes. She put both hands on her stomach and screamed out as she was hit by another excruciating pain.

This was the picture that appeared next morning in many of the New York papers, saying, 'Is this worth $40 to our kids?' But Jitka never saw it. She died in the Casualty ward of Hoboken Hospital of acute peritonitis.

Monsignor Paddy had returned from Rome to celebrate Requiem Mass for Jitka. Brad Kominsky did not attend. He hadn't been seen since they brought Jitka home from the hospital, but his parents had sent a huge bouquet of flowers to the house. Carmella came from Englefield with Joey. She was an old woman with white hair now and Joey was losing his. They sat together most of the time and didn't say much. Hana's mother came with her son Frantisek and his wife. The old lady was blind now and still couldn't speak a word of English. All through the Mass there was a dull drone of a male voice as her son explained everything that was happening in Czech. The three blond O'Neil daughters looked lovely in their matching long, black dresses and young Denny, quite the man in his first real suit. He was something of a hit with all the ladies present, especially the girls from Jitka's shop, but Denny preferred to stay close to his Pops.

Denis was bearing up well. He had coped with Hana when the hospital had first rung that awful morning, and with all the newspaper men when they kept coming to the house all that day. He had managed to deal with all the funeral arrangements and with contacting Paddy and also Canon Donnelly as he now was. But ringing Rome was easy compared to locating Sean and Michael. They were now ex-Directory and seemed to be of no fixed address these days. He had to ring Liam's office to get a message passed on and he didn't like that. He didn't like Liam Murphy, but that didn't stop Liam sitting with Sean and Michael on the O'Neil side. But Liam Murphy, for all his flamboyant show, wasn't important that day. Jitka was, or the dear memory of her, and Denis saw that everything was done to respect that memory.

Denis managed all of it, because he had to, because Hana couldn't. For all the good manager and housewife that she was, she couldn't cope when her daughter died and didn't even want to see her in the coffin. When Denis finally persuaded her, and held her close as she did do, she shrieked and yelled, 'They have put red lipstick on her!' The girls were more upset about their mother than they seemed about their sister, but that was because, like so many at the time, they hadn't really taken it in. Jitka had been so alive, so vibrant, that it seemed impossible she should be gone so quickly. She had never complained about her appendix. She had never complained about anything. Except about always being late. She was always late. She was never early for anything. Except her own death. Now Denis was trying to hold his family together while they dealt with that.

Only once did he let it get to him and that was when the three sisters sang 'Panis Angelicus' during the Mass. As their young voices soared in the unique Czech harmonies they learned from their mother, Denis thought his heart would break. He just let the floodgates open and he bawled like a baby. Only the tight grip of young Denny's hand in his helped him to recover himself. The tears also came to Denny's eyes but that was because his Pops was hurting his hand. The one solace throughout it all was Katya. Shorn hair or no, she was a God-send at that time, running between her mother and father, her father and the outside world, dealing with her young sisters and brother and organising the funeral supper with the help of the neighbours. Spoiled, selfish, self-centred, pretty Katya grew up in that traumatic week and no one could have been more proud of her than her Pops.

It was Katya who arranged that at the end of the long day the brothers should be left alone in the front room. Only young Denny was allowed to go in and only Katya brought their drinks, but at the start, she put a large bottle of Scotch in front of the three of them and left them to it. Liam had been taken aside by Monsignor Paddy and when last seen was looking very crest-fallen as he followed Paddy into the empty dining-room.

'Now talk your way out of that one, Liam me boy!' muttered Michael as he saw the stern-faced Paddy lead the way. Michael had little need of inclination to talk himself when he later found himself sitting on one side of Denis and Sean on the other, but he was glad to take the chance of a good sup at the whisky. Johnny Walker it was but it was no worse for that.

'Here's lookin' at ye,' he said. But nobody responded.

'I've been thinking,' Denis said at last. The brothers looked at him and waited, 'that it's time maybe that you moved on.' Sean and Michael looked across at each other, but still said nothing. Denis continued. 'You've had a good run with your operation I would say, and whether you call it moonshining, rum-running or hi-jacking for medicinal purposes, the fact is that a lot of wet stuff is getting to dry places, and strictly speaking, that's against the law.' Sean made to speak, but Denis raised his hand, 'Oh, I know all your arguments, Sean, about a legitimate public service and all that, but the Volstead Act is still in force, and somebody has to enforce it.'

'But not you,' said Michael.

'Not me, because I'm in the Traffic Division, but I hear terrible rumours that I might be made up to Super, and that could mean a move over into the speakeasy run.'

'Ah, Michael,' said Sean, 'wouldn't that be terrible?'

'An awful thing indeed,' agreed Michael.

'Indeed, it would be,' went on Denis, 'if a man were forced in the course of his normal duty like, to proceed against his own brothers.'

'Proceed against,' echoed Sean. 'Does that no' sound solemn, Michael?'

'It would put the fear of God into a man,' said Michael.

'It's really the fear of Denis, I'm thinking about,' said Denis. 'Look, boys, I am in no mood today – today of all days – to banter words in the old way with you. I'm just glad to get the chance to tell you now that they're on to you on all sides. New York State has repealed its Prohibition Enforcement Act, but that doesn't mean they'll stop going after the big boys. Now, I'm not talking about bath tub gin and cut liquor, or converted wood alcohol and stuff like that. I'm talking about the kind of operation Liam there's got you linked into. Hoover's fellows are on to that, and they'll get the big fellows in time, make no mistake about that. Now you're not big yet, but you're gettin' bigger and there's just a chance because of the outlets you've built up that you'll get in so far, I'll not be able to get you out.' Sean made a move to speak again.

'Now let me speak,' went on Denis. 'If you would take my advice, you would sell up your New York interests now. Liam will buy them, you know that. He can't resist the chance of an easy dollar. At the moment, you're tied into estate, and as I've pointed out to – shall we say, people of influence – you're on the scene in a renting capacity, not in actual participation.'

'There's clever you are, Denis,' said Michael. Denis suddenly turned on him.

'There's stupid you are, Michael,' he said fiercely, 'if you don't see now, I'm trying to give you warnin'.'

'It's alright, Denis,' said Sean, 'you know Michael and his teasing. What do you suggest?'

'You can move to one of two places,' he said, 'if you want to keep in your present line of business. Chicago, or Atlantic City. In Chicago, you might have to deal with the hard men. Dion O'Banion is on the north side there, but he's a killer. They say he was an altar boy at Notre Dame cathedral, and he keeps a flower shop, like Liam and his swanky office, or you with your coffee shops. You might be safer with the O'Donnell brothers on the west side, or Ragen on the south side. At least they're your own kind.'

'But I thought Chicago was an Italian matter,' said Sean.

'So it is; Johnny Torrio tries to keep the peace with the Genna gang and young Capone, but with people there like Hymie Weiss, "Schemer" Drucci, Bugs Moran and Frank McErlane, that's not an easy matter.'

'I hear Frank uses a Thomson sub-machine gun,' said Michael.

'You hear right,' said Denis.

'But wasn't there someone else in Chicago we wanted to keep an eye on? A certain Rico?' Denis took another sip of whisky.

'He went up with Big Jim Colosimo, and was working as a kind of link between the Italian and Irish.' Each of the three brothers immediately thought of Noreen, but nobody said anything, and Denis only lamely added, 'As far as my information goes, he works now out of a place called "The Four Deuces". He seems to have come up in the world as well, but he keeps himself clean.'

'Always a wise policy,' said Sean. 'It's a dirty world. And what's in Atlantic City then? for it would seem to me Chicago's pretty crowded out.'

'Gambling,' said Denis shortly. 'It's going to be big there and what's more it's legal, and people drink a lot of coffee while they're gambling. The brewery business is not what it was, and I have a feeling you should both look to other markets, unless of course you choose to marry and settle down like everyone else.'

'Well now, Michael, will you marry me and shall we settle down?'

'Sure now, Sean. I'll have to be asking my big brother, Denis, here for his consent.'

'But seriously now,' said Denis, 'what would you like to do?'

'I'd like to have another drink,' said Sean.

Young Denny came in to tell them that Anna and Clara were going to do a piano duet and they were to come in to the other room. His face told them what a treat he thought that was going to be! The whole company was assembled, and the brothers noted how glum Liam looked as he sat on the other side of Carmella. Katya was talking with Joey, who was gazing at her in the way that he had once looked on Noreen. Hana sat holding her mother's hand with her brother and his wife on the other side, and Paddy stood at the window with his friend Canon Donelly and the young curate from St Brides. Sean and Michael remained at the door while Denis took his seat and nodded for the young girls to play their piece. As they did so, haltingly, and out of time, a kind of calm descended on the O'Neil household for the first time in a week.

The same could not be said for the d'Agostino household in Chicago. Mamma d'Agostino had come to town and that meant the whole entourage of Italian sisters, aunts, cousins and their friends and friends of their friends had descended on the big new house that Rico had taken in Oak Park for his son and himself. Everyone said that Guiglielmo, or Tito as the family called him, was just like his daddy, although everyone knew he was not. For one thing, Tito's eyes were blue and Rico's brown. Tito's head was auburn, where Rico's was black, but should have been grey. Rico was thickset and Tito promised to be tall. These were minor discrepancies, however. As far as the 'famiglia d'Agostino' was concerned, Tito was another Rico and was being trained as such. Even at three, he strutted rather than walked and wasn't afraid to make his displeasure heard if he felt it. There was no doubt Rico spoiled the boy, but he was also concerned in the making of him. Rico's two married sisters had acted as wet nurses at the beginning, but now Tito relied solely on Francesca, the mother of Lucky and Forty. Francesca had never been able to marry Roberto Ruffiano after all, because his wife would not agree to a divorce, and threatened to kill him herself if he went ahead with it. Roberto would have liked to have killed her, but she had too many brothers, so he went back to a domestic situation even worse than it was before. And with no Francesca either, because Rico had summoned her to be a foster mother to Tito and occasional housekeeper to him. Her own two children were only a year older and served as company for Rico's boy, but there was no doubt who was the favoured among the three of them. It had been Francesca's idea to name him Tito. She was the only one who saw the resemblance to Noreen in the boy, but she knew better than to mention her misgivings as to who the father was. Like everyone else, she took a back seat when Mamma visited, and was quite content to revert to being the waitress again, knowing as Roberto had once said, she was the best waitress there was.

Most of them had been there for nearly the whole week, preparing for the big climax on Saturday 20th, Tito's birthday. Lots of great things had been planned for that day. The children's party was to be in the afternoon and they would all be there: all the little Torrios, Gennas, Colosimos and even Capone's boy. With Mamma in charge and in her element, preparations were well in hand. Rico himself was up on the north side through most of that week, arranging things. Something was obviously brewing – for many of the poorer Sicilian families were employed to make the bath tub gin in their own houses. Collections and deliveries had to be discreetly organised. There also had to be no straying into Irish territories. Rico didn't want a gang war to spoil his son's birthday. Everything was to be of the best. Even the birthday party itself was to be arranged as if it were a meeting of the Unions Italiane. The children would be seated round the big table with Tito in the godfather place at the top, with his back to the window. Rico himself would take the bottom place on this occasion, so that he could enjoy the scene. The six other places would be allocated according to status. Rico would decide that status. This meant there was no place for Lucky and Forty. Even Mamma's intercession was of no avail. Rico was adamant.

'Niente bastardi,' he pronounced loftily. At this, Francesca lost

all control, and in vituperative Italian wanted to know why her
children were bastards and his wasn't! Mamma joined by saying
that she shouldn't talk like that to Rico in his own house. Francesca
countered by saying it was more her house than his since he was
never in it, and she was never out of it, working for him in the
kitchen, in the dining room and in the bedroom – his bedroom.
This created an uproar, and as a result, after an hour or more of
further Italianate storms, tears and recriminations, Francesca was
ordered to leave the house. She was stunned. 'Where can I go?'

To Hell, as far as Rico was concerned. She asked to make a call
to some friends who might collect her and take her back to New
York. Rico laughed.

'I'm sure Roberto Ruffiano will be happy to come to you if his
wife lets him.' All this was on the Thursday before the birthday.

Francesca did make her call, and as a result on the Friday
evening, she had two callers, who were admitted by her into the
hall. They were Sean and Michael O'Neil. Mamma was surprised
to say the least, and showed it. Rico, when he came home, was
even more surprised, but didn't move a muscle. He offered them
a drink, which they refused, and the three men sat in icy silence as
Francesca went to prepare her children and her few belongings.
Mamma d'Agostino, true to her Italian instincts, left the room to
the three men. This was business and she wanted no part of it.
The cold triangle was maintained as the early evening gave way
to night. When Francesca was eventually ready, it was seen that
she was carrying Tito's three-year-old favourite teddy bear, which
always slept with him. Rico rose.

'You have Tito's toy!'

'I know,' said Francesca, 'I'm taking it with me.'

'You cannot take that. It is his. He cannot be parted from it.'

'I know,' said Francesca, icily calm, 'I'm taking Tito.' Rico
looked stunned, and gasped incredulously. He almost laughed as
he spoke,

'You cannot take my son!'

'But he's not your son,' said Sean.

'He's our sister's son,' said Michael.

'You didn't know that, did you, high and mighty Enrico?' said
Francesca with relish. Rico looked from one to the other of the
O'Neil's, then at Francesca.

'But I did! The padre told me.'

'You would take in another man's son?' she said.

'Yes!' he answered. 'If I loved the mother.'

'We loved her too,' said Michael, 'and we have orders to take
him back to New York.'

'Who gives such orders?' hissed Rico. He tensed at his most dangerous, and both Sean and Michael realised this.

'Whose orders, I say?' The clock could be heard ticking, it was so quiet. The door opened behind them and Mamma appeared, but no one moved. All eyes were on Rico.

'The real father,' said Sean.

At this, Rico reached into his coat pocket, but Michael was already on to his legs and Sean grabbed for the arm. Mamma moved forward as Francesca started back. Both women screamed as Rico went down, and the first shot killed Mamma d'Agostino immediately.

There was no birthday party for the children the next day at the d'Agostino house in Oak Park. Instead their mothers and fathers came to pay homage to the corpse of Mamma d'Agostino as she lay in state in the big dining-room, grieved by her whole family, led by her son, Enrico. The newspapers carried a full report of the tragedy which said that Mrs Maria d'Agostino had come to call her son to dinner as he was cleaning his pistols, and unfortunately a bullet was fired by accident. The report also stated that Guiglielmo, her grandson, had been taken to stay with relatives in New York during the period of mourning.

On the car trip back to New York in the early hours of Saturday morning, Michael had to deal with a toddler in his arms in the front, while Francesca dealt with her two in the back. No one said very much. Francesca was philosophical. Another chapter in her chequered career was over. What next? She would wait for the Good Lord to decide, or somebody lesser, she didn't mind. The only thing that bound all three was that they had once loved Noreen and this was Noreen's child they had stolen.

'But we're doing the right thing,' said Sean. 'After all, we're returning a child to its natural father.'

'Naturally,' said Michael. He couldn't help chuckling.

'Liam Murphy's going to be the surprised man this night.' He chuckled. 'No wonder he looked so long-faced after talking with Paddy. We'll see if our little birthday present here will cheer him up.'

They arrived at Liam Murphy's expensive East Side apartment late on Saturday morning. Liam was still asleep, and Maxine, nude under her diaphonous dressing gown, was too taken aback to do anything but let them in. They made quite a little group in the hallway, Sean yawning heavily after the long drive, Michael carrying the sleeping Tito, and Francesca, red-eyed and crumpled, trying to keep control of her two, now running wild around the room. They had slept most of the way and were in the best of form. Liam came out not looking his best in a dressing gown, and with only one slipper on, but even that support didn't help him when Sean told him the situation there and then, and Michael put Tito into his arms. Liam fell back on the plush settee with the sleeping child still in his arms, who awoke with a fright and started crying. The dusky Maxine, lighting her first cigarette of the day, almost choked with laughter. Lucky and Forty had run to their mother, who sat down wearily on the chair beside her, and Sean and Michael made their exit, leaving them all to get on with it. Going down in the lift, Michael turned to Sean.

'Touching, wasn't it.' And the elevator carried them down to the outside world and to breakfast.

TWENTY-NINE

'It was an accident, a pure accident, I tell you.' Billy Keith was almost in tears as he tried to explain to his father. 'I was coming from behind the big hedge. I didn't see her till I was almost on top of her! I swerved to the side, but she went the same way.'

'Idiot! You could have killed her! Coming round as fast as that.'

'I wasn't fast,' persisted the boy. 'When I braked, it skidded. I went straight into her. Couldn't do anything about it. Not with ice still on the road.'

'Poor old Gran. Broke her leg. Could just as easily have been her bloody back and then we'd all have been in trouble,' muttered his father, as he went down on his haunches to examine the buckled front wheel. 'You'll pay for this yourself, of course.'

'Oh, Dad!' Jim glanced up at his nineteen-year-old.

'You don't expect me to, do you? Brand new bike that cost me an arm and a leg in Dunedin, and you throw it about as if it was one of the farm wrecks. This is a speed bike, Billy. It was made for racing. You give it a bit of push and it'll take it. Coming down that hill by the bridge. No wonder you couldn't brake.'

'I'll need it mended for tomorrow night.'

'How's that?'

'Training for the Southland Reps, and with the Rail Strike, I've got to get to Invercargill somehow.'

'It's a long way for a training session,' said Jim, straightening up.

'It's the most convenient for most people, so they say. It's not my fault I live in the back of beyond.'

'Watch it!'

'Sorry.'

'Tell you what, you take it to the shed. I'll see what I can do with it in the morning. I can have one of the men take it to the garage in Gore if it's really bad. Listen –' He stopped as if he had an idea. 'Why don't you take the car?'

'I haven't got my licence yet.'

'But you were supposed to –'

438

'I don't see why I need a bit of paper to tell me I can drive when I've been driving since I was fourteen!'

'You'd better get one. We're all supposed to have one now. Just another bill for your old dad to pay.'

'Go on, you can afford it.' And with a smile, the boy picked up the bike, and hoisted it on to his shoulder, then strode easily to the shed. Jim stood watching him go, torn between annoyance at the boy's carelessness, relief that the accident hadn't been more serious, and pride in the figure the young man made as he walked away with the bike on his shoulder as if he'd been carrying a shovel. Not that he was a stranger to the shovel. Billy was a good worker and a fine lad. Jim turned towards the house. He was worried for his mother. The shock itself could have killed her. For a woman who was always pretending to be an invalid, she'd done pretty well. Despite her crusty selfishness, the boys adored her. Billy was genuinely upset, but Jim knew his mother would shake off this little setback as she'd shaken off all the others, but make sure she got every bit of attention and sympathy while doing so.

Florence Keith lay in her own bed with the damaged leg outside of the covers. It was an ungainly position for anyone, but for an old lady, it looked nothing more than incongruous, particularly as the affected right leg had two fence staves tied tightly with binding twine. For appearance's sake, Tina had put one of her silk shawls over it, which only succeeded in making it look even sillier. Florence herself was propped up on two cushions, and was giving a detailed account of the whole incident to Kenny and Jamie, who were leaning on the bed either side of her.

'And then what happened, Gran?'

'Gran fell on her backside, that's what happened.' And they laughed again, just as they had done before. Jean came in with a cup of tea.

'Come on you two, it's time you were in bed. Don't bother Gran when she's sick.'

'Gran's not sick. She's not got spots.'

'Away ye go,' cried Gran, 'or I'll be knocking spots off the pair of you.' They went reluctantly. Gran supped gratefully at the tea.

'Did Berta get through to Dr Rutherford?'

'Not yet. The line's still busy.'

'That's her up at the creek, she's never off the telephone,' muttered Gran into her tea leaves. 'I just hope the doctor arrives in time. I would hate to lose my leg at my age.'

'Don't be silly, Gran. It's a perfectly clean break. We heard the snap up here in the house. You shouldn't have been at the gate anyway.'

'I was seeing if there were any letters.'

'It's a morning delivery. You know that.'

'Second post then.'

'There isn't a second post.'

'Well, there should be.' You could never win with Gran Keith.

Just then Berta rushed in. She could hardly speak for her excitement. Her excitement made her asthmatic breathing all the worse, so she had to lean against the door.

'Berta, what is it?' said her mother a little frightened. At that point her father entered. The girl looked from one to the other of them and eventually gasped out.

'There's a man . . . he was trying to get through to us . . .'

'It's alright. Take your time,' said Jim.

'From Dunedin. He's a reporter.'

'Alright, Berta,' said her mother. And then it all came out from the girl in a rush.

'He said he had a phone call from Auckland to tell him that Billy is to be an All-Black and he's to go to London.' She then sagged with the effort, and was only caught by her mother. Jim was already on his way out to the shed, and Berta and her mother hugged each other, laughing or crying, or both. And then they too rushed out after Jim. This commotion roused the twins, who needed no excuse to jump out of their beds and scamper out on to the porch after their parents. Florence was left alone ruefully looking at her own big toe. 'Ha!' she snorted. 'Nobody gets any attention around here.'

The phone line between East Gore and Edendale that night was singing with the excitement. Big Brucie was just as thrilled as Jim Keith. To be an All-Black in New Zealand was to be brother to a prince and cousin to a king. There are some who might say that it is merely a game of rugby football but they do not know the importance of things. New Zealand itself was only about eighty-five years old as a nation in 1924 but already its athletes, especially the footballers, were being more and more recognised as its only aristocracy. To most New Zealanders, these fifteen strong young men, fit and fast and gleaming in bronzed good health, represented all that was best about this other Britain in the South Seas and there was hardly a household in the North and South Islands who did not aspire to have an All-Black in the family. And here were the Keiths with their first trialist. Official word had made it clear that Billy was being invited first to play in the Possibles versus Probables in Auckland in November, but the good news was that he was in the Probable side, and this meant that he had a good chance of the British tour during 1925. This last fact caused even more excitement in the two households for it meant a first visit back to the Old Country by a Keith in almost a quarter of a century.

But now here was a chance for one of them at least to be taken home – for New Zealanders still called Britain home – with all expenses paid and with the honour of wearing the famous white fern leaf on the black shirt to boot – a football boot! It was really something to think about and talk about and in the weeks that followed the Keiths could do nothing else. Billy himself was the least affected of them all. Being a natural games player, he took it for granted that he could play well and therefore it was only natural that he should eventually get representative honours. He was looking forward to playing with the best players in New Zealand, even though he knew many of them already from inter-school and inter-province matches, but the boy had mixed feelings about going 'home', as his parents called it, for Billy regarded New Zealand as his home and Britain, particularly Scotland, as a mythical homeland, which was real in the mind and existed more and more in the imagination of the exiled Scots, especially at the New Year time. Billy had often talked to his old Gran about this. While she still considered herself entirely Scottish in every way, and her son and his father partly New Zealand by adoption, she used to insist that Billy himself was a New Zealander and must regard himself as such. But she insisted, he remembered, that there was a good bit of Scotch in him, and as she would say with a smile, 'You can come to nae harm with a bit of Scotch in you.'

But in the Mackenzie homestead, the one who was affected most of all by Billy's news was, surprisingly, Tina, his aunt. When she heard at the end of the year that Billy had in fact won through the trials and had been placed among the names of those that were to travel to Britain during the close season, she was most unexpectedly moved, and for the first time in almost twenty-five years, she was homesick for Scotland. Of course, over the years she had pangs occasionally when they used to have more regular letters from John, or when she heard a song on the wireless, or Chris played something on the piano – then a shaft of Scottishness would run through her and she would feel a lump at her throat. The feeling came to her again when she put the phone down on Jean, for Jean had rung to tell her that Billy was in the touring party, and when Tina had picked up the phone, Jean had said, 'This is Jean Keith here.' Now Jean had probably said that a hundred times to Tina over the years since they had known each other, but for the first time Tina suddenly thought, But she's not a Keith. She's Jean Hay who married my brother. And I'm still

Tina Keith from Forres, even though I've married a man called Mackenzie. She stood by the telephone where it hung on the wall by the door for a good few minutes, pondering these obvious facts. Pull yourself together, woman, she found herself saying. Wasting good time mooning like a young girl. Here she was, she thought, rapidly approaching middle age, the change of life, and still hardly aware of the change in her own life she had known moving from one side of the world to the other. The feeling wouldn't leave her all day.

She spent that day mostly doing the farm accounts. Hilda had agreed to come in to do the men's lunches and to deal with Chris when she came home from school. Bruce had taken Sandy with him to a farm auction further up the Mataura, and Stu and Ross were going swimming with the Cargills after school. This left her time to get down to the year's returns in the lean-to addition to the kitchen which served as a farm office.

Instead she found her mind wandering back all the time to her own childhood and youth, particularly to her father. She'd almost forgotten him. It wasn't that she had stopped loving him or his memory, but as the wife of a farmer and the mother of three boys and a girl, she had little time for anything else other than keeping up with everything. She'd forgotten what his birthday was. Oh, yes, 5th May. Or the awful day she found him dead on the voyage. Gosh, that seemed a long time ago. She shivered as she remembered Martin Dickenson. Oh, but I was young then. I didn't know. It was all so hot, so strange, so exotic, so unreal, she didn't blame her young self overmuch. She realised now she had had a lucky escape, and how fortunate she was to have made it to New Zealand, and have found a good man like Bruce Mackenzie. He never said much, but she knew he was fond of her in his Kiwi way. He was almost as Scottish as she was, but he had been born in New Zealand, and was determined to be a New Zealander first and a Scot second. With the children emerging as people in their own right, he was just as determined to be father first and husband second, especially with young Chris. Not that Tina really minded. Her first marital passion had been long spent, and she had been happy enough to continue in this unruffled state of friendly co-habitation, secure in the comfortable life they were beginning to know at Edendale. The years of their marriage had been good to them, yet deep in her heart, Tina Keith or Mackenzie, knew that she had never really been heart-whole in the adventure of making a family. Heavens, she thought, I'd better get on, and she applied herself to the invoices before her with a steely determination.

But it wasn't long before her thoughts began to drift again.

Thinking of Scotland made her think of leaving it, and the leaving it she only associated with one event, the young man, whose face she never forgot. Could never forget. She couldn't even remember his name. She thought his first name was Denis. Not that it mattered. His face had been with her subconsciously in all that time, and often as she was drying a dish or folding some ironing, or hanging a curtain, his face would come before her, and she would find herself closing her eyes and remembering. The excitement and the bustle of getting away from Forres, the crowds in Glasgow, the fight at the quayside, all those men and then his face before her – that young, handsome face before her – the green eyes, the black curly hair, the smile. Was it only because she was young and carried away by the excitement of it all? Or was that what falling in love was? All she knew was that she had never felt that same headlong, engulfing, totally embracing, completely committed feeling to anyone else since that time. Certainly not to Martin Dickenson, and not even to Bruce. Yet she knew she wasn't being untrue to Bruce in remembering how she felt for that other young man in the halcyon days. Do we only get one chance of love, she thought, real love? And if it passes us by through no fault of our own, do we make the best of what we get? Certainly there was no resemblance at all between the reliable, if unimaginative Bruce, and the romantic image of her Irish Denis. But she knew even now as she sat at this desk, that it was this image she loved. All the more perhaps because it was only an image and therefore she could make it her ideal. I wonder if he ever married in America? Of course he would. There are so many pretty girls there. She was sure for some reason that he loved her. She could see even yet his face shouting at her through all the noise. What if – ?

She shook herself again. Ifs and buts will drive you nuts. There was little point in that, yet a tiny thought persisted all that afternoon. What was the point of all that love then if it came to nothing? What happens to that great surge of feeling? Does it just evaporate or does it hang in the air like a cloud waiting to descend like dew on another young couple in another place at another time . . . . The slam of a car door cut her musings short. There was the run of steps on the wooden verandah.

'Mum? It's me. I'm home!' There was a noise of a car driving away. 'Mrs Jackson gave me a lift.' Tina almost ran to meet her daughter and little Chris wondered why she got an extra tight hug that afternoon. Similarly, Bruce, when he got home later that night after the auction, wondered why the accounts hadn't been finished.

'I got held up,' she said quietly.

'She'll be right,' said Bruce, 'there's always tomorrow.' Yes, thought Tina, that's partly the trouble. There is always tomorrow. And she shut her eyes as Bruce went into a long description of the bargain he'd got at the auction.

By what is called chance, or what some people call coincidence, Denis O'Neil was at that very same moment thinking of the person he knew as Tina Keith. Ten thousand miles apart and twenty-five years later, he had no notion why she had suddenly come into his head – his bald head – for there were no curls now, and what hair he had was grey. Not that he minded that for he wore a police cap most of the time, a police cap that now boasted the badge of a Superintendent of the New York Police.

But underneath the uniform, inside the sagging breast and comfortable paunch, still lurked the embryo that was the essential Denis O'Neil, in as much as in all of us there is always a part that remains constant despite the natural and inevitable exterior changes. And inside the Superintendent remained the young Denis O'Neil. Sometimes it was hard to find him with the increasing responsibilities of his rank, not to mention the continued family problems. He had plenty to preoccupy himself with, so the luxury of personal introspection was not something in which he normally indulged. But it was when he was clearing out his old desk in the Traffic Department that he came across his Uncle Mick's letters about the travelling arrangements and his mind flashed back at once to that summer's day in Glasgow. He remembered it so clearly . . .

Arriving on the cattle boat, going through the crowds with Noreen to get the tickets from that office, getting lost, finding his way to the quayside, and then the fight. Then that girl. Tina, she was called. Her face loomed up at him as large as you would see it in the cinema. Like Norma Talmadge, only prettier. Blue-eyed and blonde, and with a skin that was – well, like a peach – that way it said in all the books. Not that Denis read many books, but he knew what he had seen, and he felt it again as he sat that late afternoon at the Police Station. Twenty-four years he'd been in Traffic. He'd seen it come and go in the streets from the horse and cart to Cadillac, and in all that time he'd hardly given a thought to the Scots girl. And yet he still knew, as he had known that day, that she was the love of his life, and there was damned all he could do about it. If he could have, he would have. He would have stopped her getting on that ship, or he would have got on himself. He would have done something. Instead he stood and watched her sail out of his life for ever. Since then she'd only been an occasional dream. She might have been even then. A mirage. An impossible hope. Beyond his reach. He'd never felt for anyone what he had felt for her then. It was just a simple fact. He wanted her and only her, and no one else would do. But he couldn't have her, so made do with Hana. Yet what a wonderful wife Hana had proved all those years. He knew he didn't deserve her. He hadn't wanted to marry her. He just let himself be carried along with it all until he found himself at the altar. He was long resigned to the fact that he had missed his one big heart chance and had shrugged it off years before. That's why he was so surprised it had come back today and hit him with the force it did. He must be getting soft in his old age. But it did seem a shame, he couldn't help thinking, that such a strong feeling as he had known then, and that somehow he knew she had known too, should just be thrown overboard on a quayside in Glasgow and be allowed to drift with the tide like that.

But who knows? he thought. Nothing is ever wasted. It might drift round and round and find its time again and wash itself up on another shore, where another young man won't find his words drowned, and another young girl might hear and respond. He sighed, but then shook his shoulders. It's the Irish in me, he thought. Don't I always get the same way when I hear a sad song? But the next thing he heard was the telephone as it jangled loudly on his desk and brought him rudely back to 1924.

'Hi Dad!' said a voice.

'Hi, Denny!' And he grinned and sat back in his swivel chair. It was almost a relief to be back in the present again.

They were just fooling about, Billy and the twins. The big brother was charging about the front lawn, and the little fellows were pretending to get the ball from him. Sometimes Billy would make it easy, sometimes he would make it hard, but he enjoyed it as he twisted and turned, ran, stopped suddenly, ran on again, with the little ones hardly able to follow for laughing and shouting. Their father kept calling for them to play a bit quieter, as he was trying to listen to the news from London, which was quite a new thing. Berta was helping her mother to get Gran's things ready again as she was going the next morning to Tina and Bruce at Edendale. She moved about four times a year at most, yet she fussed about it as if she were spending day and day about with each family.

'Nobody wants me, that's the trouble.' She grasped the handle of the stick she now carried since she broke her leg. 'I'd be better off dead.' Jean and Berta said nothing. Still Gran went on, 'I don't have that much time left to me now.'

'Oh, Gran,' said Berta laughing. There was a shout from outside.

'Listen to those boys,' said Tina. 'Billy should stop making the wee ones run like that. They'll get too tired.'

Suddenly Jim rushed in from the verandah shouting, 'What's the doctor's number?'

Jean straightened up. 'What for? Three-two-four.'

Jim was already muttering into the receiver. 'Come on! Come on! This damned woman!'

Jean put her hand to her throat, 'It's the twins! Oh, my God!' And rushed out into the garden.

But it wasn't the twins. It was Billy. He was lying on the grass in an almost comical position. His legs were splayed out on either side from the knees and he was lying with his hands behind his back, trying to rise. The twins were looking down at him, not knowing whether to laugh or cry.

'Billy!' said his mother, kneeling down beside him. The boy's face was ashen-white.

'Both ligaments!' he gasped. 'Might even be the cartilage. Sorry.'

'What are you sorry about?' she said, and made to lift him.

'No, don't,' he said. 'We'll have to take the legs first. Wait for Dad too. Ouch!'

Without thinking, Berta who had just joined her mother, pulled at one of the legs saying, 'Oh, Billy, you do look funny!' and was appalled as her brother let out a great cry of pain. The twins rushed to their mother's knee and had already begun to whimper. Berta started to cough.

'Oh, Berta,' said Billy, and reached up a hand to her. The figure of Gran appeared on the porch, leaning on the stick.

'What's wrong with Billy?' she called.

'Cartilage,' said Dr Rutherford, 'one worse than the other. The right will certainly need surgery. The rest we might get away with a bandage.'

'But what about the tour? Will he be able to play next month? He's going to London with the All-Blacks for heaven's sake,' said Jim.

'I'm not so sure,' said the doctor gravely.

'Not so sure about what?' said Jim.

'That this boy will ever play rugby again.'

Jim looked at his son. Billy was trying to keep back the tears and his clenched fist was thumping the side of the bed.

The Headmaster's face was solemn as he spoke. 'I regret that I have no option. Your son has shown increasingly disruptive tendencies over the past two sessions and his class reports are no better. This is all the more distressing, to us as much as to you, as there was a time when he looked to be one of our most promising pupils. Indeed, he was already marked as university material, but in view of recent events –' The Headmaster shifted in his seat uncomfortably. 'Well, you will both see what I mean – for the sake of the school –' He allowed the sentence to drift away and he raised his clasped finger tips to his lips and waited for either Rachel or Bobby to comment. They were sitting in the Headmaster's office in Abel's school and the interview had not been a happy one.

'What do you suggest, Headmaster?' It was Rachel who spoke first.

'It's hard to say, Mrs Keith. He's a bright boy, there's no doubt about that, but I'm afraid he shows no interest in school or school work. He is rarely here, and when he does attend I have complaints from one teacher after another. For instance –'

'That's alright, Mr Dorking,' broke in Bobby, 'we get the picture.'

'I'm sure you do, Mr Keith. All I can say, to answer your question Mrs Keith, is that if he were my son –'

'You'd tan the hide off the little bastard?'

The Headmaster smiled and folded his arms on his chest. 'You took the words right out of my mouth, Mr Keith.'

They found Abel kicking his heels in the outer office. As they were shown out of the Headmaster's study, the secretary, a plump, motherly person in cardigan and thick glasses, was jumping with indignation behind her typewriter.

'Mr Dorking, I just want to tell you what this pupil here has just –'

'It's alright, Miss Edwards,' interrupted the Headmaster calmly, 'I think we can both leave Master Keith to other hands than our own.' With that and a smiling nod to Mr and Mrs Keith, he quickly closed the door on them. Abel rose sullenly to greet his father and mother and was startled to be sent sprawling into the corridor following a hefty push from Bobby.

It was an uncomfortable family dinner that evening. Most of the talking had been done on the way home, and it had been straight indeed. Rachel had said little, and there was nothing they could say in the bus in any case. When they got back to the house, there was a pile of mail waiting for Bobby. He had taken the day away from the office in order to go to Abel's school. He wasn't too pleased that someone had dropped off this stuff on his doorstep.

'I'll leave it till after dinner' he said, throwing it on to the coffee table. 'And you,' he said, pointing to Abel, 'you get to your room and wait there till your mother calls you for dinner. Not that you should get any bloody dinner.' Abel looked at him coldly, nearly smiled, but thought better of it, then shrugged and walked towards his room.

'Christ, I need a beer! Care for one, love?' Bobby called to Rachel in the kitchen.

'No, I don't want a beer!' Rachel called back. He looked through the servery hatch.

'You alright?'

'No, I'm not. But there's not much you can do about it at the moment. Just let me get dinner.'

'Please yourself,' he said, and headed for the fridge in the hallway.

Little was said while they ate. Even indications along the line of 'Pass the salt' were done with grunts and points. Abel rose from the table, saying to no one in particular, 'Alright if I go out?'

'No, it isn't,' said his father.

'Oh, come on, Dad. There's nothing to do here,' groaned his son.

'There's plenty to do here. The dishes for a start. You can try to help your mother.'

'You don't help her much. I've never seen you do the dishes.'

'Less of your bloody lip!'

'Well, it's true.'

'Where were you going, Abel?' asked Rachel quietly.

'Around,' answered the boy with a shrug.

'Around the twist,' muttered Bobby.

'Well, can I go or not?'

'Abel,' asked his mother, 'would you do me a favour?' Bobby looked up. Abel was surprised.

'Depends,' he said. His mother was looking down at her plate.

'Would you –' She looked up. 'Would you go back to school for me.'

He laughed. 'Why, did you forget something?'

Bobby rose. 'You cheeky –' But Rachel continued.

'Please, Bobby.' Bobby sat again. 'Abel – the Headmaster told us you were one of his best pupils, and now suddenly you're one of the worst. He has asked your father and me to take you away. If we do you will never go to university. I would like you to go to university.'

'Oh, Mum!' The boy was uneasy.

'And to do so, you need to finish at school, and get your Matric.' The boy turned away to finger the edge of the sideboard. 'Would you do this for me?' his mother asked. He didn't answer, but bowed his head. 'Would you do it then for my father?' Abel wheeled round, red in the face, and then hurried to his room. Rachel looked at her husband, and she was smiling.

'I think our boy will go back to school. Would you like to help me with the dishes?' she said rising.

'Sorry, love, I've got these letters –' Then he realised what he'd said. 'Sorry.'

'It's alright. Go ahead with your silly letters.' She was still smiling as she carried the first of the dishes through. Bobby took his teacup to the coffee table and started on the letters. As he read through them, one in particular was of great interest. He read it, read it again, then leaned back on the sofa. 'I wonder!'

Rachel's voice came through from the kitchen. 'You still got your cup there?'

'Yeh.' He got up with the letter still in his hand and took the cup through to the kitchen. As he placed it on the sink, he said, 'I've got an idea.'

'Oh, dear, that's always a bad sign,' said Rachel.

'About our boy.' She was immediately alert.

'Oh?' she said, turning to him from the sink.

'How do you think he'd like a trip to London next year?' As her eyes opened, he said, 'Listen to this! "Dear Mr Keith . . ."'

'. . . I was glad to get your letter after such a long time, although it was sad to hear the news about young Billy's injury. Sorry he missed his first Kiwi jersey, but tell him he can always play for Scotland when his knee gets better.' Jim Keith grimaced as he read this. Both he and Billy now knew that the right knee might not get better. He returned to the letter from his brother. 'Remind him that he comes from good Keith stock and we're used to taking knocks. However, I'm writing now to find out how you might react to a plan I have had. Do you realise that you and I haven't met for twenty-five years? I know we've written and had photographs and all that and I know my mother keeps wondering why we don't come over and see her. She hasn't even seen her grandson and he's seventeen already would you believe? It's really because of him I'm writing now. He's been difficult to say the least since Rachel's father died. Abel was very close to his grandfather and since the old man went Abel's gone a bit wild. Recently we were asked to take him out of school just when he was getting ready to take his Matric. Rachel is dead keen that he goes to university next year. She is now a full-time lecturer there. After a lot of argument, he agreed to go back so we got him fixed up at another school. Rachel has the contacts. Anyway I made a bargain with him that if he got a university place I would give him a trip to London. You see, I got an official Government invitation a while back to become a delegate at a Conference in the Colonial Office in London to discuss the immigration of tradesmen to the countries of the Empire (that's us!) and Rachel insists that I take Abel instead of her. Well, it occurred to us that a young fellow might be bored hanging about London while his old man jawed all day about hourly rates and assisted passages, so what about letting your Billy join us? The reason he came to mind was that if he didn't get a London trip with the All-Blacks this year he could have one next year with his old Uncle Bobby and his cousin Abel. They're roughly about an age and it's about time they met. I could wangle him over with us as extra cabin baggage! (Joke!) Seriously, dear young brother mine, it's a Government trip with a block return booking on the ship and the London hotel paid. If you can get the boy to us in Sydney, I'm sure I can fix things from there. We'll be away three months in all. If you can spare the boy for that time, and he wants to come of course, we'd love to have him with us. Anyway, you and Jean have a think about it and let me know. Love to everybody and tell my mother I was asking for her. I can't work out whether she's with you or Tina but you know me . . .'

Jim needed little time to think about it. He even thought about going over himself but three months was a long time to be away from a farm. Billy was thrilled. He'd taken the injury set-back quite well. At least, he didn't say much, but then he never did. However, the disappointment had bitten deeply and made him more determined than ever to play again. Jokingly, he said he would never play with the twins again – they were too rough! The only one who did not like the idea of the London trip was Belinda Jackson, the youngest of the Jackson girls, and the prettiest. Billy and Belinda had what was called an understanding. It was an understanding more understood by them than by Mr and Mrs Jackson who thought Belinda was still too young. They would rather Billy's eye had fallen on their elder, plainer daughter, Annabel, but Billy was fixed on Belinda from the beginning and he was happy to wait. Now it was her turn to wait, but she and Billy had long walks out these nights and under their New Zealand stars the young couple made their own plans. Jean Keith was secretly delighted. She knew that Belinda would be just right for the quiet Billy, who was so much his father's son. They could wait. They had all their lives before them. Gran Keith's only reaction was to tell Billy to give his Uncle Bobby a piece of her mind for not visiting all these years and, if he got to London, he was to mind and take time to go up to Forres and see his Uncle John. And while he was there, he was to look up her old friend, Biddie Beattie and tell her that Florrie Keith was asking for her.

But at that time, in faraway Forres, Mrs Biddie Beattie was beyond trivial greetings from girlhood friends, for Mrs Beattie, the redoubtable, resilient, unquenchable Mrs Beattie was finally fading. She had taken a turn at the back end of the year and had been failing ever since. Thomasina was with her most of the day, trying to make her eat something and generally keeping her mother company and John and big Alec would come every night for their usual dram, but Mrs Beattie wasn't drinking these days. The doctor called in occasionally but he could do little. 'Just let nature take its course,' he said. This wasn't as callous as it sounded. The only thing wrong with Mrs Beattie was old age and she, more than anyone else, was quite happy to accept it as a fact of life. She had never been the same since her fall and had always resented the two sticks. She hated more and more being confined to bed. Above all she hated being an old woman. 'Oh, to be seventy again!' she said one night to John. No one was quite sure how old she really was – not even Thomasina was sure; she thought about eighty – but Biddie wasn't telling.

The only one not to visit was Elspeth, her own grand-daughter. She said quite bluntly that old people made her feel funny, especially when they were sick and she didn't want to see her Gran when she was 'like that' she said. Not all Thomasina's recriminations could make her daughter change her mind. Besides, Elspeth's head was full of her wedding. After much persuasion, Donald Robertson had finally agreed to marry her. Mrs Beattie had remarked when she heard the news of the engagement, 'He'll be that long stammerin' oot "I do", Elspeth'll be a pensioner afore she's a bride!' But Elspeth was in her element, and her mother too, to only a slightly lesser extent, in the bustle of wedding preparation – choice of hymns, bouquets, who was to be in the bridal party, where was the reception to be held – and all the minutiae every bride had to deal with on the eve of her wedding. Except that Elspeth's was months away yet! Little was seen of Donald.

One night, big Alec Friar had to go to Aberdeen. Ella had had 'a wee accident' whatever that meant, and her father had been asked by the local police to come through as soon as possible. So it was only John in the chair by the bedside the night Mrs Beattie actually died. John had been reading bits of the newspaper out to her when he was aware of the hand moving, trying to attract his attention.

'Did ye want somethin'?' he asked at once. She nodded.

451

'Leave the paper,' she whispered hoarsely, 'they're nothin' but rubbish. In a' my years, I never read anythin' in them I never knew a'ready. Just lies to make a fool o' folk so that other folk'll buy the thing. We've mair important things tae dae than read the paper.' She stopped to take a few breaths. John waited, watching her. He'd become very fond of his doughty old mother-in-law in recent years and he had her to thank for saving him from becoming a full-time alcoholic after Kenny's death. Kenny? It had been so long since he last thought of his soldier son.

'John. I'm talkin' tae ye.'

'Oh, I'm sorry, good-mother.'

'I should think so. Here's me on my death bed an' you miles away when I'm tryin' tae talk tae ye.'

'Sorry. What were ye sayin'?'

'I was sayin' that I'll miss ye when I'm awa' '

'I'll miss you, good-mother.'

'Ay. An' the crack we've had.'

'Ay.'

'Mony a time. Mony a time. An' the laughs tae.'

'Ay.' He could feel his chest tightening.

'But no' as mony laughs as we've deserved, I'm thinkin'.'

'No.'

'No, but then Scots folk like us are no' gi'en tae laughin' much I suppose.' John wasn't sure how to answer that, but it didn't matter for Mrs Beattie was in a mood for talking, even though talking was getting harder and harder for her by the minute. But she took her time and her breath, for both of them knew her last would not be long in coming. John could not keep his eyes off her old, lined, lovely yellow face.

'But there's somethin' I wanted to say tae ye, John.'

'Ay?'

'Ay. I have a wee bit in the Co-op insurance. It's no' much, but it's tidy. An' I want you tae have it.'

'Oh no, I –'

'I want you tae have it, I say. Thomasina's got you, and Elspeth'll hae this hoose here tae start wi'. That is if it's grand enough for stutterin' Donald.' At this she spluttered in a sort of wheezy laugh which nearly choked her. John rose forward and cradled the scraggy neck in his hand. It was like holding a chicken.

'Don't talk now,' he said. 'You're tired. You'll need to rest.' She shook her head.

'I've got eternity tae rest,' she said. 'But only a wheen o' minutes tae tell ye.' She stopped a minute and gathered her breath. 'I want ye tae take the money, John, and go to London for me.' He

452

started in surprise. 'An' I want ye tae find Becky for me.' His heart jumped. They hadn't spoken of Becky Friar for a long time, but he had never stopped thinking about her. 'I know that you love her, John Keith, and so do I. Always have. Lovely girl she was.' There was the touch of a tear welling at the rim of the old lady's red-veined eyes. 'There's no' that much love aboot, that we can waste any o' it, so you awa' down tae London, John. Gie her mine, and gie her yer ain. She might hae need o' baith, and while she hasnae, she'll aye hae need o' cash. You can bring her back here if ye like. Elspeth'll maybe hae moved on tae the big hoose by then. Happen no' ye'll dae what ye think best for the girl, John, for my sake.' She was now fighting hard for breath. 'And if no' for my sake, for Becky's.' And on the sibilant of that last word, Biddie Beattie passed away. John let go of her head and clasped his hands to say a prayer, but couldn't think of a word. Still holding his clasped hands, he leaned over the little body on the bed before him, and bent his head forward, being careful to be tender and not lean too heavily on the frail, dead bones under the blankets.

Becky Friar at twenty-five had developed into a very smart young woman. Her position as assistant housekeeper at the Strand Palace Hotel was a responsible one. Given that she had twenty chamber-maids, twelve daily cleaners, four back porters, four laundry maids, six page boys and three boot blacks, she was not without her daily problems, yet such was her poise and ease of manner, that she managed the hidden staff of the hotel well. So much so that the manager, the august Mr Trenchard, had mentioned quietly that when Mrs Blackstone left, Becky was very much in line to take over as housekeeper to the hotel, which would not only be promotion, but a considerable step up in salary as well. The 'Australia Fund' would be considerably boosted by an extra ten pounds a month. It hadn't taken Becky long to move up the backstairs ladder, as it were. She was so relieved to find a comfortable room, even though at the beginning she had to share with three other maids in the attic dormitory, and then two, until eventually she had her own when she was put in charge of a floor. She liked the other girls well enough, but kept herself to herself mostly, so that she was known as 'Toffy' by the other girls in the hotel, short for 'Toffy-nosed', but Becky didn't mind, because she knew she wasn't. She had her own ambitions in life and she was blinkered to everything else in her determination to attain her end. To this end, she kept clear of amorous porters and over-attentive waiters – even the spotty, shy young chamber-maids who sometimes had a crush on her. The cheeky pageboys were easier to control. She just answered back in their own coin and they would just grin and move on, and this was why Miss Friar, as she was called, got a name in the Strand Palace Hotel for being haughty and distant. She had every Wednesday off, and still spent much of her time in the British Museum. She could never quite forget Miss Garnet, and occasionally, as a treat, she would go to one of the many theatres on the Strand, or even as far as Piccadilly Circus or Shaftesbury Avenue. But such excursions cost money and she was loth to spend anything. She had learned that it wasn't safe to keep any money in her room, so she elected not to draw it each month, but to leave it on account with Mr Trenchard.

'Saving for your trousseau, Miss Friar?' She would draw herself up and answer firmly.

'Not at all, Mr Trenchard. I have no plans to marry.'

'Strange for a very attractive young gal like you.' The way Mr Trenchard pronounced 'girl' always reminded Becky that he had the same kind of Edwardian style that Miss Garnet had had. Theirs was a generation that had the security of status to indulge freely in affectation. 'Quite a little treasure we are accumulating, Miss Friar,' he would say, 'as indeed I have a treasure in you. Mrs Blackstone shows an increasing bias of attention towards her husband, who was badly wounded in the war. I fear she may yield to domestic pressure and an opening would thence occur within this establishment for a housekeeper of some experience, much tact and good appearance. What say you then, Miss Friar?'

'I would be very flattered, Mr Trenchard, but Mrs Blackstone told me herself she has no intention of leaving her job, and it might be a wee bit presumptuous of me to think I could do it as well as she does.'

'In time, Miss Friar, in time.' Looking at the girl as she stood before him in his office, erect in her black dress and piquant white cap, he wished time were on his side, and he were a little younger. But instead all he said was, 'Thank you, Miss Friar, that will be all.'

She had always an hour free after the morning rounds, and this was when Becky did her letters. She had ceased to write regularly to Elspeth and the last intimation she had had from her childhood sister-friend was an invitation to her forthcoming marriage to Donald Robertson. 'Mr & Mrs John Keith have the pleasure of inviting Miss Rebecca Friar . . .' It was hard to believe. She still couldn't understand how he had come into the picture, but perhaps Elspeth was getting desperate. That was all she had ever wanted – to get a man, to get a house, and start a family, and replicate her mother.

It was Thomasina who had written to tell her of the death of Mrs Beattie. She'd been sorry to hear that. She had been fond of old Mrs Beattie and liked her sense of humour, but then she was old. So was Uncle John. Well, at least he was getting on. He'd miss Gran Beattie more than anybody. She often thought of her Uncle John. She knew that he liked her, maybe even loved her, more than he loved Elspeth it would seem. That thought sometimes made her feel comfortable. He had a weakness for the drink, but then what man hadn't? She promised she would write a long letter to him soon. Now that Gran Beattie was gone, he might welcome a letter. But she wouldn't write today. This was the day she had to visit Australia House.

The man at the door recognised her now, and greeted her cheerfully in his Cockney way.

'Mornin' miss. This way to Australia,' he chortled. She smiled at him and made her way to the information table where the Australian newspapers and magazines were laid out. She always liked to read these, especially the *Sydney Herald*. Somehow it was able to bring her dream trip a little nearer, when she was able to assure herself that Australia really existed. Her reason for the odyssey – to find her lost father – had now become almost secondary in the desire to get there in itself. She had set herself to save £100. This was the magic figure that would allow her to pay her way over and start again on the other side. To date, she was hardly half way there, but she knew she would do it eventually, and meantime she contented herself with reading all about it.

This was how she learned about the Australian Government's intention to give assisted passages to tradesmen from Britain and other specially selected persons. She looked up and thought, how do I become a specially selected person? She glanced over to the door where the Australian Commissioner was and wondered if she should dare. Before she could think further about it, she was on her feet and asking at the Reception. She was never allowed near the Commissioner. 'You need to write in for an appointment, dear,' but another official, not an Australian, told her that, in any case, the scheme was not yet in force, and furthermore it only applied to men. For the first time in her life, Becky wished she were a man. It's so unfair, she thought, but there was nothing she could do about it. The doorman gave her his usual salute.

'Decided to stay on in dear old London?' he said.

'I'll be back,' she called, and started along towards the hotel. She came in through the back lane as usual, and one of the boys called to her as she went up the back corridor.

'Oi, Toffy! Sorry, Miss Friar – the Guv'ner was looking for ya.'

'What?' said Becky turning huffily. Little ginger George was the cheekiest of all the pageboys.

'Yes,' he said, 'Lord Pooh-bah Trenchard was asking for ya. Says if we saw ya we was to tell ya to get to his hoffice smartish.'

'Thank you, Ginger,' Becky said icily, and hurried to her room. She took off her daycoat and hat and quickly put on her dress apron and housekeeper's cap.

'Ah, Miss Friar, you were taking the air, I gather?'

'Just a little stroll, Mr Trenchard, in my lunch hour.'

'Of course, of course. It's just that you had a visitor.'

Becky was more curious than surprised. Who could it be? 'A visitor?' she asked.

'Yes. From a long way orf. From Scotland. A long way orf indeed.' From Scotland? She was immediately attentive. It could only be . . . And it was.

John Keith was sitting bolt upright in a massive arm chair in the inner foyer. He was still in his black overcoat and holding a bowler hat on his knees. Beside him was a medium-size carpet bag. He obviously did not intend to stay long. When Becky first saw him, she stopped, and all the old fondness for him welled up in her again. Dear Uncle John, he looked so much older, but yet he was still the same Uncle John. He sat as still as a rock among all that bustle. Uncle John in London. She could hardly believe it. But there he was only a matter of paces away from her. Taking a deep breath, she moved forward.

'Uncle John!'

He looked up. Their eyes met.

'Becky!' he said, 'I've brought you £100!'

THIRTY

Superintendent O'Neil's first public appearance in his new uniform was at Maria d'Agostino's debut recital at the Carnegie Hall. None of the family had heard much about her since she returned from Dublin, but apparently she had kept in touch with Paddy and he'd rung Denis to tell him of the recital. Denis wasn't sure. First of all, he wasn't sure about attending a recital. He didn't think that high-falutin' songs and bits of opera were really his idea of a good night out. Two hours of the high, female voice were really more than he would happily anticipate. However, Paddy thought they should all show some family solidarity – for Noreen's sake. And you never know, said Paddy, 'You might just enjoy it!' Another reason for doubt was Maria's decision to change her name. 'O'Neil' had been good enough for vaudeville but hardly for anyone with ambitions in Grand Opera. Though why not, thought Paddy, a good Irish name hadn't stopped John McCormick at the Met. or at La Scala, Milan. Notwithstanding, Maria was now d'Agostino and that was that. Carmella at least was pleased. She had family connections after all, and as she said, 'I became O'Neil so OK Maria become d'Agostino.'

It was the d'Agostino connection that worried Denis – in a professional capacity at least. Not much had been heard of Rico in Chicago recently according to Denis's contacts and it was said he was starting to build up a base in Miami. Rico was smart, he kept moving. You could never quite pin him down. But one day, yes, one day, thought Denis. The clinching reason for attending tonight, however, was Hana. The Czech part of her was starved of what was called 'good music' – there wasn't much call for it in Brooklyn – and she had no hesitation at all in insisting that they go when Denis mentioned the call from Paddy.

'But what about your headaches?' Denis had asked, 'You know you always get them when we go out.'

'I take a pill.' Hana O'Neil was increasingly bothered by migraine these days and it worried Denis. They had started

457

after the shock of Jitka. That was three years ago now, but the headaches still bothered her and she wouldn't see a doctor.

'Who wants to spend good dollars on doctors' guesses?' she said. Before coming out this evening, Denis had asked about the younger children. Denny was now thirteen and quite a handful. Luckily, Anna could always handle him. She was a real little mother. Anyway, Clara would be there. Although, since Brad Kominsky started coming around the house again, she had been inclined to be dreamy. Brad had taken a long time to get over Jitka and had become close to Hana but she hoped that he would get closer to Clara. So did Clara. But it would take time. She was only sixteen.

'What about Katya?' asked Denis. Katya was their problem child. Wild, impetuous, unthinking, self-centred, but strikingly vital and attractive, she was a flaxen re-incarnation of her Aunt Noreen. Denis and she had terrible rows about her hair, her way of dressing and her friends – especially her boy-friends . . . Katya had a string of them and they were of all types. The current specimen was a dancer and he was a black man. It wasn't this that bothered Denis so much, but that Jed Marshall was at least thirty, Katya was only eighteen. Admittedly eighteen going on thirty, but Denis still thought his daughter too young to be going about with a man who earned his living dancing in a theatre chorus. Katya insisted that he was a well-known dancer, but Denis had never heard of him. The trouble was Katya herself wanted to go on the stage, which was why she took dancing lessons at the down-town studio, where she had first met Jed. Meantime she worked in Art Bellof's flower shop in Brooklyn. It was he who had supplied Maria's bouquet for tonight. Sean had paid for it. He and Michael were here tonight from Atlantic City. Denis looked around to see if he could see them. He couldn't, but there was Paddy, looking every inch the cleric, with his old pal, Canon Donnelly beside him.

'A grand crowd, Paddy,' said the Canon, gazing around.

'What else would you expect for an O'Neil, Canon?' said Paddy.

'Or for an auxiliary Bishop?' said his friend with a grin. Paddy looked a little embarrassed.

'Now Jim,' he said, 'that's not for talking about. Besides,' he went on, 'she's a d'Agostino now, not an O'Neil.'

'That's right, so she is. At least that's what it says on the programme here.'

Yes, so she is, thought Paddy to himself. And what a business it was. She had come back from Dublin in a terrible state. All that wild talk about her Uncle Kevin, his mother and Nellie. It had taken Paddy a long time to sort it all out and even then he wasn't quite sure he had it right. There were things she'd told him he'd rather not have heard and things she'd hinted at he wanted to be told more about. Maria had not been completely happy during her brief stay in Dublin and Paddy might never know the reason why. He'd written to Kevin but never had any reply. The last letter had been returned marked 'gone away'. His mother didn't even mention Maria's ever being there so he assumed that something must have happened. Maria didn't even want to talk about it. She only wanted to get down to work on her singing. It was thanks to friends of Paddy's that she was fixed up with special coaching from Bryn Thomas, an eccentric, if effective vocal coach and singing teacher from Cardiff who now made a lucrative living in Boston persuading rich young ladies that they could sing. The fact that Maria could really sing forced the madcap Taffy to revise his tutorial methods somewhat, but he did and Maria made amazing strides under his guiding hand.

The fact that that guiding hand strayed over parts of Maria's anatomy not directly connected with voice production didn't prevent the intensive coaching going forward over that year until she was ready to make her first appearance in public. Now that time was come. 'Professor' Thomas was there in the centre of his usual entourage of gushing maidens and old aunts smiling all the while. He caught Paddy's eye at one time, and he bowed theatrically. Paddy could only manage a half-smile, hoping that the investment of several cheques in favour of Bryn Thomas, Esquire, would show a return greater than the exquisiteness of the Welsh wizard's wardrobe. If Maria got a career start from tonight, it would be well worth it. At this point, 'Professor' Thomas could be seen making a noisy, obvious, loud-voiced exit through the pass-door to backstage in the concert hall. It must soon be time to begin.

Carmella was there in the stalls with her sister Rosa. Both had noticed Bryn Thomas standing in his circle near the stage.

'Who's that?' asked Rosa.

'Dunno,' answered Carmella. 'Must be multo importante. He makes lotsa brio.' They had made the journey in from New Jersey because they'd had a call from Hana. Rosa's husband, the doctor, couldn't come because he was at a conference in Vancouver and Joey had preferred to stay at home as he 'didn't like to hear dames singing'. No amount of coaxing from Carmella could persuade him otherwise. Anyway, he wanted to play with his Meccano set, which was the latest craze with him. He was building an aeroplane just like Charles Lindbergh's 'Spirit of St Louis'. Joey was now forty-four years of age but had all the joy of a boy yet, and had no idea how lucky he was. But sometimes, he took everyone by surprise by suddenly remembering Noreen – 'who had gone away'. Now it was the night of Noreen's child and the buzz of excitement rose as the lights began to go down one by one and the curtains opened to reveal the grand piano on the stage.

Few noticed Sean's arrival at the back on the right hand side. He came as usual with Michael, but what was unusual was that he had Liam's long-time girlfriend, Maxine, with him. There was no sign of Liam. Liam had of late become a changed man. Francesca and the children not only domesticated him, but placated him. Francesca's complete womanliness was something Liam had never known before. Hitherto he had regarded the female as a toy and a plaything, and even his former wife, Nellie, had been mentally discarded, before she had been physically deserted, but such was the force of Francesca's natural ease that before he knew it he was settled happily in an unaccustomed role as Señor of an Irish Italian menage. Tito was so obviously his son that he was taken aback by the onrush of paternal fondness that overwhelmed him, and he spent more and more time with him and with the twins, Lucky and Forty, than he did at his office, which mattered little because the business now ran itself, even without Maxine. Maxine didn't like the new Liam at all, and was soon bored by the domestic rearrangements. Besides, Francesca made it clear that no house was big enough for two women, nor was she prepared to stretch it to accommodate a langorous negress, who never thought to lift a duster or boil a saucepan. Maxine had trained herself to live at home in disorder and eat out in style. This wasn't Francesca's way, so Maxine went.

She went straight into the arms, completely unexpectedly, of Sean O'Neil. The same handsome, icy, steel-eyed Sean, who had hitherto disdained women in favour of amassing dollars, was amused to accommodate the sensuous Maxine. They recognised each other as being of the same species, though, in Sean's eyes, by no means equals, so here she was, on Sean's arm, at Maria's debut. With them that night was Jock Lennox. They hadn't seen much of the old-timer since his wife had died, but both Sean and Michael knew that this was one evening he could not miss. He could hardly contain himself with the excitement of it all, and he kept telling the stranger on the other side of him, 'She'll be great, you know, just great!'

Michael sat on the other side of Maxine, with them, but not of them. His face wore the same impish impassivity that always characterised Michael, as if at any moment he would break into a grin. But if one had looked closely at him this evening, there might have been seen a concern in his eyes, not for Sean, certainly not for Maxine, hardly for himself, but only for the young woman whose imminent arrival was heralded by the hush that now fell across that famous performing place. Michael closed his eyes and for a moment uttered a silent prayer to whoever the patron saint of singing was. It didn't matter that he didn't know of St Cecilia, his sincerity was no less real. It was the first time Michael O'Neil had prayed since his kneeling farm days at Ballytreabhair. As if in answer to his prayer, Maria d'Agostino swept on stage, led by the portly and beaming Professor Bryn Thomas. They both bowed together at the centre of the stage to prolonged applause, and it could be seen that the Welsh professor was reluctant indeed to go up to his secondary place on the stool of the grand piano, while Maria glided easily to her singer's position at the bow.

And in the deep silence that awaited the first chords no one saw or heard the figure of Enrico d'Agostino accompanied by the shadow of Roberto Ruffiano as they took their places at the back where they stood just out of the light. Rico was seeing his natural daughter for the first time in more than twenty years. As she uttered her first note, he, at the same moment, whispered the one word – 'Noreena!'

'Visi d' Arte' . . .

From the very first note, Bryn Thomas knew that his protegée was on form. The audience could see no sign of nerves from her, and only the tell-tale beads of perspiration on her temple and upper lip indicated that the girl was feeling any tension at all. Such assurance. Never in a long and somewhat chequered career as a teacher and coach had Bryn Thomas known a maturity of singing technique so early. There was a danger of its being an over-confidence born of ignorance, but he knew it was rather the mark of a natural performer, who could be a great, given a little luck and the staying power. With each swell of the breasts, on every intake of breath, he noted the relaxed stillness of the shoulders, all the strain being taken at the back against the hooks and eyes of the ball gown, one hand resting lightly on the piano, the other hanging easily on the flare of her dress. He had been sceptical when the priest had brought her to him. She had seemed too tall, too assured and too impatient. Her vaudeville background was no great help either, but it only took three bars of her first song that morning to convince him that there was a voice there. The Irish priest had agreed to pay for as many sessions as would prepare her for a concert debut. Where he got the money from, Bryn didn't know. Priests were supposed to be paupers, he thought, but this one seemed to be high up, or at least rising high in Catholic circles, so perhaps he had access to funds. Actually only Paddy knew that it was Maria's own money which was paying for her tuition. It had been given to Paddy six years before when Noreen had visited him in Baltimore.

'See that she gets the chance that I never got,' were Noreen's own words, and Paddy had seen to it. From now on, it was up to Maria herself. Yes, she could make it, Bryn thought to himself, as he played. She was certainly bitch enough.

The applause at the end of the first song was more than encouraging. Although there was a considerable contingent of family and friends of family present, the audience was made up mainly of the regular concert-going public. Like most music lovers in any large city, they were a minority audience, but were highly knowledgeable of their own selected field of cultural entertainment and were not easily fooled by glamour, pre-publicity, or the charm of the performer. They had seen too many young singers high on personal appeal but low on musical talent make the wrong kind of exhibition of themselves when put under the spotlight/microscope of the solo concert recital. Carnegie Hall, after all, could be hired by anyone if they had the money. A concert could be given by anyone, if they could print a programme, so it was no big deal to make an appearance. Where the difficulty lay was in making that appearance effective from a musical point of view. Maria O'Neil, now d'Agostino, was doing just that.

She bowed again as the last of the applause died down, and when she was assured of absolute silence, she made the slightest turn, gave Bryn a dazzling smile, which only succeeded in flustering him, and indicated she was ready to begin the second item. The matter of waiting for that silence, and taking her own time in it, was the hallmark of an assured artist. It told the accompanist as well as the audience that she was in complete control of herself and of the evening.

'Caro nome . . .'

She felt 'on song' in every sense. She was, as some performers called it, 'right at her own centre'. The nerves she had felt in the dressing room that had caused her so many visits to the washroom were now well gone, and a kind of exultation had taken its place. All the hours of study over the past years now bore fruit. She felt like a little girl again, except that she wasn't singing in a child's blue dress but in a woman's white gown. Her mother wasn't standing upstage right, just out of the limelight, but, in a funny way, she felt Noreen's presence all around her. She had hardly given a thought to her mother recently. After that awful Dublin experience, she had in fact tried to forget her altogether. That was why she agreed to 'Professor' Thomas's suggestion that he should invite the music critics as well as people he knew from the Met. If she was going to make a go at all, she would have to forget family, and give herself entirely to her career. Music at the highest level was more than just a job. It was a vocation, a high calling, and she had to sacrifice everything to making herself worthy of it. She knew she had the natural equipment, but did she have the dedication? She knew she had the looks, but did she have the steel? She knew she had the will, but would she have the luck? Tonight would tell.

More applause, but this time it was much warmer, and she curtsied gratefully. No one applauded louder than Superintendent Denis. He was taken aback at how strong and forceful Maria's voice had become. He remembered her only as a little girl with Noreen, and now suddenly there was this diva in front of him, and to think she was a niece of his! Red with pleasure and the exertion of applauding, he turned left to Hana to say, 'Ain't she somethin'?' when he noticed that his wife wasn't clapping with the rest. Her right hand was at her forehead and her head was bowed.

'You OK?' he whispered urgently.

'Yes, I think so. I gotta bit of a headache.'

'I thought you said you had a pill.'

'I forgot to bring them.'

'Oh, Jees!' By this time, the applause was fading and a few coughs sounding to announce that the third song would be underway in a moment. As the silence descended, Hana gave an involuntary moan and bent her head still further.

'Hana,' said Denis, reaching his left hand out to her.

'Sh! Sh! Quiet please,' came from all round them.

'Oh, go to hell!' whispered Denis, as the silence was at its stillest.

He hardly heard Musetta's 'Waltz Song', as he was more concerned about his wife. He heard her whisper, as she half turned to him, 'I think I will be sick.' Damn, he thought, it's going to be another migraine. Suddenly she rose up. Instinctively, Denis did the same, and reaching for her hand, and with a series of abashed 'Excuse mes' and 'Sorries' and 'Thank yous', he led his abject and embarrassed wife past the protruding knees and hastily withdrawn feet to the end of the row and to the stairs that led to the exit. There was only a muttered resentment from the few, but a glare from the burly Superintendent stifled any direct protest. He put his arm round her waist as they headed for the door. As they reached it, with the applause for the third aria ringing in their ears, she vomited against her husband's brand new uniform. He held his wife even closer to him. 'Don't worry, baby, let's get you home!'

At home in Brooklyn, Anna was having her usual trouble persuading Denny to go to bed. He kept making excuse after excuse for remaining downstairs, and would not go up, despite threats, blandishments, coaxings or pleas, until Anna was beginning to lose her temper, which was not a commodity she normally displaced.

'I'll tell Pops,' she cried, 'and he'll turn your hide.'

'Mama won't let him,' answered Denny with a smirk.

'Mama won't know,' cried Anna, ''cos I'll tell Pops when she's not around.'

'There ain't no time when Mama ain't around,' retorted Denny. And so it went on around the sofa in the front room, in front of the wireless, round and round the kitchen table, out the back porch, on to the front steps. As he went through the sartorial stages from dungarees to pyjamas, she went through the different layers of coercion, until finally with the promise of candies, she got him up to the bath. With the promise of the 'funnies' to read, she got him into bed, and finally with the promise of a nickel for school, she got him to sleep. She put out his light with a sigh of relief, wondering not for the first time, how her mother did it every night. She came into the kitchen to make herself a cup of chocolate, looking forward to taking it into the front room so that she could enjoy the soap company's play which always came on the wireless about this time. But instead she found Clara and Brad Kominksy sitting on the sofa about two feet apart from each other, saying nothing. Clara made frantic dumb show signs to her sister to get out. Anna made the same dumb answers that she wanted to listen to the wireless. But the elder sister was adamant, and Anna retreated with her mouth full of chocolate to the kitchen again, and sat down disgruntled, bemoaning the fate of the youngest sister, who always had to give in to the sister just above her.

She just had the cup finished, and was supping the base of the drink out with a teaspoon, when she heard Katya at the front steps. Her head appeared at the kitchen door.

'Pops home yet?'

'No, they won't be back till it's gone ten. Eleven even,' said Anna, her lips smeared with chocolate.

'Good. What time is it now?'

'Quarter after nine. I just got Denny down.' Katya came in, her manner furtive, but her eyes bright.

'Good. Where's Clara?'

'In the front room. She's got Brad –'

'Brad Kominsky? That's swell.' Katya went to the window, then turned back to her young sister. 'Anna I want to tell you something.'

464

'What?' said Anna doubtfully.

'I got Jed here.'

'Jed?'

'Yeah. Jed Marshall. Our instructor at the dance class.'

'You got him here?'

'That's what I said.'

'Pops'll kill you.'

'Pops don't know. Jed brought me home in the street car, and I thought, seeing Pops and Mama are out at Maria's concert, I'd let Jed bring me home, see what kind of place I live in, meet my kid sister –' The last was said playfully, but Anna was not impressed.

'I don't want to meet no Jed Marshall,' she said darkly.

'Oh, come on, sis,' wheedled Katya. 'It's my only chance. I gotta impress Jed, so he'll give me a chance in the studio show. That way I get to be a broadway star.'

'Some broadway star,' muttered Anna, hunching over her empty chocolate mug.

'I'll go and bring him in.' Anna sat up with a squeal.

'Katya O'Neil, you'd better not.'

'Why not?'

'I don't know. It's not right, that's why not.'

'We ain't goin' to do anything,' whined Katya. Anna's eyes widened.

'You'd better not. Anyways, you can't go in the front room.'

'Why not?'

'Because Clara's there with Brad.'

'Then I'll bring him in here.'

'You can't.'

'Why not, for Pete's sake?'

'Because I'm here!'

Katya was becoming exasperated, and with a toss of her head, she left the kitchen and went back to the front door. She opened it, saying, 'I'm sorry, Jed –' But Jed wasn't there. 'Jed? JED?' she shouted, but there was no reply. 'For Pete's sake,' she said again, and going indoors, slammed the front door behind her. Anna was in the hall. So was Clara.

'What's all the noise?' she asked.

'It's Jed,' said Anna. 'He brought her home.'

'Jed Marshall?' said Clara. She looked at Katya with amazement.

'Katya O'Neil, that ain't right!'

'Now don't you start,' answered Katya, as she walked towards the stair.'

'Where are you going, Katya?' cried Anna.

'To my bed, where you should be.'

'I don't want to sleep in your bed,' answered Anna, going back into the kitchen. Clara followed her.

'Look here, Anna, you promised Mama you would be in bed by nine. It's more than a quarter after, so how about it?'

'OK, OK,' said Anna wearily. 'Gee, it's hard to be the youngest.' She came back to her sister, looking right into her face. 'But I tell you somethin', Clara O'Neil, I ain't always gonna be the youngest, so there!' And with that she stomped out of the kitchen and into the hallway. Brad was standing there.

'Goodnight, Anna,' he said, but Anna didn't even reply.

'Would you like a cup of coffee, Brad?' came Clara's voice from the kitchen. Brad shrugged.

'Sure,' he said, and went into the kitchen, closing the door behind him.

In her room, Katya had thrown herself on top of the bed in frustration. Where had he gone, she thought. It was a few minutes before she heard the noise. It was a breathy, whistling sound, as if somebody was trying to whistle through clenched teeth. Yes, there it was again. She looked round the room. There was no one there. Then the sound came again. It was coming from the window. She rose up and going to the window, pulled open the curtain, and there was Jed Marshall on the balcony of the iron fire escape, standing on his head, grinning at her.

Denis O'Neil was glad that his coat covered most of the soiled area of his new uniform. He and Hana were standing on the sidewalk outside Carnegie Hall, while Denis was trying to whistle down a cab.

'I'm sorry, Denis,' said his wife. She was quite pale under her hat, as she held tightly on to his arm.

'That's alright,' said Denis absently, looking from side to side, up and down the street.

'Maybe it was something I eat.'

'Well, you ain't got it now, that's for sure,' said Denis, not unkindly. He gave her hand a little pat. 'Where the hell are those cabs? You can't see the street for them when you don't want them.' Just then a police car passed on the other side. The driver gave Denis a salute with a long blast on the horn. Denis replied instinctively by raising his arm.

'It's No 634. That's Charlie McGuinness,' he said, and the car sped on. After five minutes there was still no taxi and from inside the hall, there came the faint sound of further applause and of doors opening for the first interval, and already some people were spilling on to the sidewalk, either side of them, feverishly lighting up cigarettes.

'Must be the interval,' said Denis. He squeezed his wife's hand. 'If you'd have waited ten minutes, we could have got out in style.'

'They would see all the mess I make,' whimpered Hana.

'Nah, the attendants woulda seen to that. Don't you worry.'

At that moment, a police car screeched to a halt on the roadway in front of them and a policeman sprang out. It was Charlie McGuinness. He pushed his way towards the Superintendent.

'You OK, Cap'n O'Neil? Sorry, I mean Super.'

'I'm OK, Charlie. It's the wife. She don't feel so well.'

Big Charlie put his arm round little Hana. 'Gee, I'm sorry to hear that, Mrs O'Neil.' Hana nodded weakly. 'Well, come on,' said the big cop. 'Let's get you guys home. Make way there.' He pushed the nearest concert-goer to one side and between them, he and Denis escorted Hana to the car.

'That's the woman who left in the first half,' said a voice.

'Was she the one who was sick?' said another.

'Must have been,' said the first.

'Shame she got arrested for it,' said the second voice, as the interval bells were sounded for the second half.

In her dressing room, Maria sipped the hot, sweet tea, and stared at herself in the mirror. Behind her, Bryn Thomas was ecstatic. He was bouncing up and down like a tennis ball behind her.

'For goodness' sake, sit down, Bryn. You're making me nervous.' He came behind her right shoulder, his face scarlet with delight.

'You nervous, girl? That'll be the day.' He put his hands on her bare shoulders. 'Like a diva, you were,' he purred in his lilting Welsh. Like most singers, his voice was 'produced', even in ordinary conversation, so that it sounded false. But whatever Bryn Thomas said usually was false, so this was no great handicap.

'Now we'll slow down second 'alf, and let 'em enjoy your legato.' By this time, his hands were under her armpits with the fingers inching towards her breast. Almost automatically, she pushed them away and rose up. Rattling the cup into the saucer, she noticed the champagne in the bucket.

'Where did that come from?' she said.

'The 'allkeeper said it was left by a man with an Irish brogue.'

'That could be anybody in New York,' said Maria, and disappeared into the washroom. Bryn moved to finger the top of the champagne in the ice bucket.

'I could do with some of that now, I could tell you. But, patience, Bryn boy, patience!' He read the card that was attached. It said, 'To Noreen's Maria. Good luck from Uncle Michael.' Maria hadn't even bothered to look.

'You shouldn't be in here!'
　'Well, I couldn't stay out there, could I?'
　'Pops would kill me!'
　'My, my!'
　'He'd kill you too.'
　'He'd have to catch me first, sugar.'
This conversation was being carried on in urgent whispers at the window of Katya's bedroom. She had let Jed Marshall in because she couldn't do anything else. She wanted him out of sight of the neighbours and quickly. He drew enough attention to himself as it was, and then for him to stand on his head . . . Now that he was in, what was she to do with him? Jed didn't seem at all anxious. In fact, he was enjoying the situation, and began to prowl around the room with all his dancer's panther grace.
　'So this is where li'l Miss O'Neil hides out? Little Katya. My li'l kitten.' He began to simulate the movements of a cat around the centre of the floor. At any other time, it would have been delightful to watch, but Katya was much too tense to enjoy it.
　'Jed, please!' said Katya, not knowing what else to say. Jed sprang to the door and proceeded to perform an elaborate mime as he spoke in a deeply melodious low voice.
　'Li'l Miss Kitten, she done come in, tired from the hard ol' world, to find her li'l nest here. And she so doggone tired, she curl up on the bed like li'l kittens do, and she purr and she purr, and she wait for the big daddy kitten to come along and lick all her tiredness away. First he lick her head, then he lick her neck, then he lick dis ear and den dat ear.'
　By this time, Katya was seated on the edge of her own bed, and Jed was prancing around her, occasionally touching her. Despite herself, Katya began to laugh. It was very funny. His crooning continued.
　'But best of all, he lick her lips, 'cos dats what all cats do when dey content. Dey lick der lips.'
　'Oh, Jed!' Katya laughed and pulled her head away from him. She knew there was no harm in the man.
　But Anna didn't. She stood outside the door, her ear against it, her eyes wide as she heard Jed's voice indistinctly going on and on, and Katya's occasional laughter. It sounded very like only one thing to her and she'd better not think about that. Even to

think about it was a mortal sin, so Canon Donnelly had told them. Not that she knew anything about it really. It was only a bit of a conversation here, or something overheard there, or listening to Katya and Clara sometimes, when they shared the bathroom. Sex to Anna was just a matter of talk. Perhaps it would get a bit clearer when she was fifteen. Meantime, the less she heard the better, and she walked across the landing to her own room and shut the door tightly against the noises coming from Katya's.

Hana tried to keep herself from laughing. It was such a ridiculous situation. Three cops and a police car and none of them could do anything. Denis's face was a picture, as he fumed in the back seat. Charlie McGuinness was pink with indignation as he fulminated against his driver.

'For Chrissake, ya dumb Polack. I mean you're supposed to be prepared for emergencies. That's what cops are for. And here you're in a department car and you ain't got no jack!'

The car was stranded along the Avenue of the Americas with a puncture and the Polish driver had just made the discovery that they were unable to do anything about it.

'Look, I'm sorry, Cap – Super – Cap. And you, Mrs O'Neil,' said Charlie turning to the back. 'Let me get one of the boys in another car and I'll – No –' His face suddenly brightened. 'No, no, I tell you what I'll do. I'll call you a cab!' And with that he got out of the car.

'Your call, Miss d'Agostino.'

'Thank you,' she answered in a matter of fact voice.

'You ready, Maria?' cooed Bryn Thomas.

'I've been ready for this, Mr Thomas, for the last eighteen months.'

'Of course,' said the accompanist soothingly. Yes, she is a bitch, he thought. 'Shall we go then?' he said. He opened the door and a man was standing there. He gave the rotund little Welshman such a fright that he started back. The man only had eyes for Maria.

'Parle Italiano, signorina?'

Maria caught the stranger's eyes, and felt a tremor go through her. There was something about that look. That authority he had. Something familiar, she thought. But all she said was, 'No, I don't.' He gave the least perceptible of shrugs and smiled.

'I only wanted to tell you how superbo I think your singing is.'

'Thank you,' she said. His eyes never left hers. Bryn Thomas was fidgeting uneasily.

'Miss d'Agostino has been called,' he chirped from her shoulder.

'I understand,' said Rico. 'I too am d'Agostino.' He gave a short nod of the head and left. Maria stood where she was, a frown on her face.

'He said he was d'Agostino?' she said, almost to herself.

'I don't care who 'e was,' blustered Bryn. ''E 'ad no right to be 'ere. Come on, your public will be waiting, Miss d'A-gos-ti-no.' The way he overly pronounced the four syllables of the name made Maria glare at him as she swept past. 'Oops, sorry, I'm sure,' and his Welsh 'sure' had two syllables.

At the O'Neil house, Brad Kominsky was on his third coffee.

'No thanks, Clara, I just couldn't take another. I guess I better go.' Clara rose from her chair opposite him at the kitchen table.

'But ain't you gonna stay for – I mean, you know Mama likes to – and Pops. They'll be back real soon.'

'I know, Clara. It was swell, but I gotta get home. I got an early shift.' It wasn't that Brad was uneasy or unrelaxed with Clara. He was more bored than anything. She opened the kitchen door and they came into the hall. As they did there was a noise from one of the upstairs rooms. They both looked up.

'I guess that'll be Denny. He's terrible for not sleepin'.'

'Yeah,' said Brad sheepishly. And he made towards the front door. There was another bump from upstairs and what sounded like a cry. 'He ain't having a nightmare, is he?'

'Oh, no,' said Clara with a laugh. 'He ain't like that.' But she glanced upstairs with a puzzled look. What was goin' on up there?

'Good night, Clara.' She felt Brad's lips touch her right cheek.

'Oh, Brad!' But when she turned, the front door was already closing behind him. She sighed, and went back into the kitchen to wash up the coffee cups.

Katya was frightened. Jed's 'dance' had become more and more energetic, till it was almost frantic. His 'cat' mime, based on her name, and all the feline associations it produced choreographically, had whipped him up into such a concentrated frenzy of movement, that he was lost in his own creation and beginning to frighten the girl. For the first time, she noticed the sweat under the armpits of his shirt, and she could sense the smell of him as he gyrated around her. She could see and feel he was aroused, and what was scaring her more was that she was becoming aroused as well. Was it true, she thought, that his 'thing' was white? It was certainly big by the bulge it made.

'And dis big daddy cat, he was a mean ol' tom cat, and he liked dem li'l kittens, but dis li'l kitten most of all.' His voice was low now – no longer mellifluous, but gravelly and gritty. The whites showed on the palms of his brown hands, as they played about all her external parts. She had fallen back on the bed, her mouth open, her blouse open, and now she felt her legs open. She felt all moist between them. His head seemed only inches above hers. She could see the red veins in the whites of his eyes. His fine nose glistened with sweat and she longed for his full lips to touch hers. They came nearer.

'You go right up, honey, I'll attend to this.' Denis helped his wife from the cab onto the sidewalk. Watching from her window, Anna saw her mother come up the steps, and then the cab drive away. Terrified, she rushed out of her room and downstairs. She must stop her father. Her mother was coming through the door as she reached the hall.

'Mama, you're early! You weren't due back till –'

'I know, Anna baby, Mama feels sick, so she comes home.' Hana was already feeling better for being in her own house again. 'I just go upstairs and –'

'No, Mama!' Anna almost shouted. 'You gotta have a cup of coffee in the kitchen. Clara made some for Brad.' She grabbed her mother's arm and started pulling her towards the kitchen as Denis himself came in.

'What's all this?' he said.

'Mama's gonna have a cup of coffee to make her feel better.' said Anna, still holding on. She almost collided with Clara at the kitchen door.

'Hey!' said Clara. 'Hi, Mama, Hi, Pops.' Denis had taken off his coat.

'I'd better get out of this uniform. It stinks.'

'What happened?' said Clara.

'Ask your Mama,' said Denis moving towards the stair.

'NO POPS!' Anna almost screamed and dived for her father.

'Say, what gives?' Denis turned round to her, puzzled by her insistence. Anna tried to be calm. She didn't know why she was so worried about them finding Katya and Jed, but she knew something terrible would happen if they did. Suddenly everybody was talking at once until a pyjama-clad figure appeared at the top of the stairs. It was young Denny.

'What's goin' on down there?' Everyone stopped and looked up.

'Say, Denny O'Neil,' said Denis, 'you should be in your bed.'

'I was in my bed,' said Denny, rubbing one eye.

'Asleep, I mean,' called his father from the bottom of the stairs.

'I was asleep, but you guys –'

'OK, OK.' Denis put Anna aside and mounted the stairs towards his son. Clara took her mother into the kitchen and Anna sat down on the bottom of the stairs and put her head in her hands. She didn't know why, but she wanted to cry.

On the top landing, Denis took his son in his arms. He smelled wonderfully of sleep, but Denis still smelled of sick.

'Phew!' said his son. 'You smell, Pops.'

'And you're gettin' too big for me to carry you to bed like a baby,' said Denis, still breathing heavily from the stairs. But he was glad to put his arms around his son and hold him tightly.

'Ouch!' said Denny. 'Your buttons are hurting me.' Denis laughed and let his son go.

Just then, there was a cry from Katya's room. Denis froze. 'What the –!' he said, then jumped forward. Unexpectedly, the door was locked. He shook the handle.

'Katya, you in there?' He heard noises from inside.

'You got somebody in there?' he called again.

'Pops!' wailed Anna from the foot of the stairs. Young Denny yawned.

'I'm gonna bed,' he said.

'KATYA!' roared Denis, really loud this time, but there was a hint of fear as well as anger in his tone. He stepped back, then aimed a standard issue police boot at the keyhole. The door flew open to show Katya standing by the bed, hurriedly buttoning her blouse, while at the window, Jed Marshall was in the act of putting his leg over the sill. Denis O'Neil stood in the doorway and couldn't believe his eyes.

'A fucking nigger!' he bellowed. And then it hit him, and he threw himself across the room at the window. He got hold of a leg. Katya screamed and threw herself face down on the bed. There was a noise of feet ascending the stairs. Jed was swearing mightily as Denis held on. But the shoe and the trousers came away in his hand. This momentarily took him off guard, and Jed took the chance to free himself, not only from Denis's grip, but from his own trousers. Denis fell back into the room, and by the time he had got himself up and through the window, the negro dancer was already down the fire escape and on to the landing below. Denis clanked along the iron balcony as fast as his big boots and his fifty-two years would allow.

By this time, windows were shooting up, people were calling, neighbours were shouting and Katya was still screaming. Denis's Irish dander was still up, and he leaned over at the next corner and shouted for someone to 'hold that black bastard there!' Perhaps it was his weight. Perhaps it was the force of his venom. Perhaps it was just the age and state of the old iron rail. Whatever it was, the corner section gave way under him and Superintendent Denis O'Neil fell two stories on to the concrete below.

At that very moment, on the other side of the world, Tina Mackenzie dropped the vase of roses she was filling at the kitchen sink. She had just lifted it clear and it left her two hands as if it had a will of its own and crashed in pieces on the red tiled floor of the kitchen.

'Goodness!' gasped Tina looking down on it. 'However did I do that? Oh, dear!' she said, and a cold feeling came over her. She shivered slightly. 'I feel as if someone's just walked over my grave!' She bent down to pick up the flowers.

They rose as one to applaud, hands raised above their heads, some shouting their approval. The concert debut of Maria d'Agostino had just concluded with the fireworks of Lakme's 'Bell Song'. The last note had hardly ceased reverberating when the applause began. They knew and Bryn knew, but most of all Maria knew, that another musical star had arrived, and nothing pleases an audience more than the knowledge that they were among the privileged at the first performance of a new career. There were repeated curtain calls, and Bryn Thomas enjoyed every one of them. Michael was on his feet applauding furiously. Jock Lennox was turning right and left as far as his rheumaticky old neck would allow him, thrilled by the reaction of this audience of swells. He kept shouting out, 'I told you so! I told you so!' to complete strangers around him. Paddy was showing a most unclerical enthusiasm. Even Sean was clapping moderately. Maxine didn't seem to know what all the fuss was about. Carmella was crying. So was Rosa because Carmella was. The only person in the hall not reacting was Rico. He stood with little Roberto at the back watching the scene impassively. But inside, Enrico d'Agostino was cheering more than any. He knew he was part of this triumph and to a degree only he knew. It had been his daughter up there – his flesh, his blood. In a way, he had been up there himself and now he was savouring the prolonged applause almost as his right.

There were calls now for an encore and finally Maria obliged. Typically, like all great artists at the height of their great moments, she did the unexpected. When she came on for her final bow, the gesticulating windmill Bryn was not with her. She was entirely alone and, as at the first moment of her recital, she stood centre-stage, waiting with head bowed, for absolute silence. It took longer than at the opening for the silence to come down, but when it did, it was complete and deafening. She could do no wrong now, and didn't. Just exactly at the right moment, she lifted her head and sang exquisitely,

"'Tis the last rose of summer,
Left blooming alone.
All her lovely companions are faded and gone . . . .'

By the time the ambulance came for Denis O'Neil, he was already dead. He had broken his neck.

'Would you look at the mess on his lovely uniform?' one of the neighbours was heard to remark.

The attendant at the Carnegie Hall delivered not one bouquet to Maria d'Agostino, but two. In addition to her uncle's via Art Bellof's Brooklyn flower shop, there was an immense floral creation which totally dwarfed it. It was in the shape of a harp, and had a card attached which read simply, 'From your father.' Alone in her dressing room, after the crowds had gone, Maria looked at the plain white card and the first time that evening felt a pang of real emotion.

THIRTY-ONE

Bobby Keith wondered how he would know him. He stood with Abel at the quayside waiting for the ship to dock. As they waited, Bobby scanned all the faces above him on the ship's rails, but he really had no idea what he was looking for. His brother, Jim, he supposed, although it had been so long since he'd seen him, he didn't know how he might look after twenty-five years. 'Look out for a big guy,' Jim had said in his letters. 'A typical All-Black.' Well, what did an All-Black look like? All Black? Abel hadn't wanted to come.

'Got things to do,' he said. He always had. But Bobby insisted. 'You guys are gonna be pals for a long time, so the least you can do is meet your big cousin off the boat.' Rachel had agreed, and since Abel would now do anything for his mother, here he was. It must be said for him, though, since he'd got his matric and his university place, Abel had seemed a little less restless than before, but he was still inclined to be moody and introverted, and very often this got the easy-going and extroverted Bobby on the raw. However, since father and son were both very much in love with the same woman they decided to agree to a state of armed truce for her sake. This was feasible while she was around but how was it going to work on the trip when she wasn't?

'We'll cross Waterloo Bridge when we come to it,' remarked Bobby somewhat cryptically.

Abel had decided that he disliked Billy Keith already. He had heard so much about his cousin and what a paragon he was that he decided before even meeting him that he must be a real prick and that he would have as little to do with him as possible. They could hardly have missed him. Billy Keith shouldered his way down the gangplank and on to the quay at least two feet above everyone else and carrying two large suitcases as if they were lunch-boxes. He saw them and grinned.

'Gidday, Uncle Robert!' he called. Blimey, he's enormous, thought Bobby. Billy was six feet three and looked every inch of it. Bobby went forward with hand outstretched.

475

'Hi, Billy. Hey, you're some guy.' Billy put down his cases and they shook hands. 'How did you know us?'

'I was just told to look for a bigger and better-looking version of my Dad,' Billy said amiably.

'You couldn't have picked a better man,' laughed Bobby, 'Oh, and by the way Billy, call me Bobby, everybody does. Except my boy here. He calls me everything under the sun. Abel, say hello to your cousin from New Zealand. Billy, this is my son, Abel.' Billy was first to offer his hand.

'Hi, Abel!'

'Hi.' Abel felt his hand engulfed in the elder youth's and had to struggle not to cry out as it was squeezed hard.

'Great!' he heard his father say. 'You two're gonna be pals, I can see that.'

'Why not?' grinned Billy.

Like hell we are, thought Abel, but he didn't say anything.

'And how're things in Kiwiland, Billy?' Bobby was in his genial mode. Billy didn't seem to mind.

'Fine, Uncle R– I mean, Bobby.'

'Bobby'll do, son.' Abel felt sick and went back to watching the other passengers come off. Bobby took Billy's arm.

'Family OK?'

'Sure.'

'That kid brother of mine behaving himself?' Billy laughed.

'I think so.'

'Good. And your mother?'

'She's fine.'

'Good. Well, let's get you home. You'll be glad to get your land legs again. Abel, you get the cases will you?'

'No, it's alright –' protested Billy, but Bobby insisted.

'Not at all, you're our guest. We can't have you carrying your own cases, can we Abel? He's a big, strong boy too, you know. He can manage. That right, Abe?'

His father only used that name when he was unrelaxed and showing off in company. He somehow thought it was less Jewish. Abel hated it and it always led to a fight, but this time he said nothing and bent his knees to take up the cases. Christ Almighty, he couldn't move them! What has he got in them for God's sake? He tried again and got them both an inch off the ground. Sod this for a lark, he thought, and looked around for a porter or some kind of wheels. Meantime he heard his father and Billy move away, Bobby as usual, doing all the talking. Billy gave a sympathetic look back to Abel, but he was in the relentless grip of Bobby's tongue.

'And how's my old mother then? Was she giving you orders to

get me over there? She's been saying that for twenty years. More. But you see, Billy lad, the way things are here . . .' The voices receded along the quayside but Abel still hadn't moved the two mammoth suitcases a yard. Just then a taxi passed. Abel stopped it and jumped in.

'Me and these two cases to Potts Point, mate.' With some satisfaction, he watched the driver struggling with Billy's cases, and even more, he watched his Dad's face as the cab swept passed him at the dock gates. It halted him in mid-sentence. Abel settled himself back in the back seat. 'Let the bastards walk,' he said contentedly. He had no money but he knew his mum would pay.

Becky Friar saw her Uncle John off on the overnight train to Inverness that night. Despite all her plans and the assurances that it wouldn't cost him anything, he wouldn't stay the night at the Strand Palace. He had done what he had come to London to do – hand over Gran Beattie's money, see for himself that Becky was alright and now that he had reassured himself on both points, he saw no reason to remain a minute longer in London.

'But why have you to go back so quickly?' asked Becky. 'You said yourself you've nothing to do in Forres.'

'That's right,' agreed her uncle, 'but I can do nothing better up there than I can here. I don't think I like London,' he muttered. 'It's too full of English folk and besides, it's dirty.'

'It's a big place.'

'Maybe I don't like big places.' She knew there had been no point in trying to persuade him further. She even had difficulty in coaxing him into the restaurant for lunch. Now here they were at the train, and in a few minutes, he would be on his way to sit bolt upright in a second class carriage all the way to the Highlands of Scotland from the bad lands of London. Suddenly he said to her out of the blue, 'Australia seems awful far away.'

'Not as far as Forres!' They looked at each other fondly, and he nodded. 'Will you get some sleep?' she asked.

'I'll try not to,' he answered. 'I've plenty thinking to do, and anyway, I can sleep for a week when I get home.'

'What will you think about?' Just then there was a whistle from the train that made her jump. He caught her in his arms and for a moment, held her, but just for a moment. He seemed very embarrassed all of a sudden, and ill at ease. She liked him all the better for it.

'I said what will you think about, Uncle John?'

'Oh, I don't know.'

'About Elspeth's wedding?'

He shook his head. 'Oh, no, I'll try not to. But I'll think about Bobby in Australia, and Jim in New Zealand, and Tina and all their families that I've never seen. And my old mother, of course. She must be gettin' on now.' He paused and looked at her. 'And then, of course, I'll think about –' The guard sounded his whistle only about a couple of feet from them. The train whistle answered and doors began to bang. Becky never heard the 'you', and he never heard her 'Take care of yourself, dear Uncle John'. But they didn't need to hear. Each knew how the other felt and they didn't have to put it into words. Ordinarily John Keith would never have said such a direct word of tenderness to a young relative, but he also knew he would probably never see her again and at the thought, the tears smarted in his eyes. She reached up and put her arms around his neck. 'Oh, Uncle John!' But he turned his head away towards the engine. There was a hiss of steam and a belch of black smoke.

'I think it's time I was in my seat,' he said. He looked around for the carpet bag. 'Where's my bag?'

'You put it on the rack,' she said.

By this time, carriage doors were shutting all around them. The guard's whistle was blowing again. 'All aboard that's going aboard for Inverness and points north!' Suddenly Becky reached up and kissed him full on the lips. He looked startled. Hurriedly releasing himself, he stumbled into the train and hardly had the doors shut when it started to move off.

Tina Mackenzie was settling her mother into her room again, and hearing all the news from the other Keiths.

'So Billy got away alright?' said Tina, as she made her mother comfortable in bed.

'Now, Christina, you know I take three pillows, not two.'

'Sorry, mother, I forgot. You've been away, you know.'

'That's hardly an excuse! Aye, he got away.'

'What?'

'You were asking, and I'm telling you, Billy got away fine. Although, my God, they gave the laddie so much tae take awa' wi' him, you would think he was gonna be away for a couple o' year and not a couple o' month.' Tina sat on the bed. 'Mind my bad leg!' said her mother, and Tina moved her position.

'Sorry! I was going to say do you remember the stuff we took away with us?'

'That's different,' said her mother. 'We were a family and we were going for a lifetime.' Tina suddenly had a vision of the cart piled high with luggage on the Glasgow quayside. No, she said to herself, I mustn't think about that again. She rose quickly.

'Well, you're alright then, mother?'

'No, I'm not alright. I've had a broken leg and a broken heart and a broken marriage and a broken family.'

'Fine, mother, fine. I see that you're normal,' she said in a low voice.

'What's that you said?' snapped the old woman.

'I said I hope you'll soon be back to normal,' said Tina in the loud voice one uses to deaf people. The only trouble was Florence Keith was by no means deaf, nor was she dumb.

'Just don't be too smart, Christina Keith, for I ken fine a' yer wee secrets. I'll say no more.' Tina found herself blushing.

'Was that someone calling me?' she said, and hurriedly left the room.

'There you are, old girl.' Bruce was standing in the sitting room with a big jug of beer in his hand. 'Here's your big brother all ready to leave and you're sitting in there jawing with that old mother of yours. You've got a couple of months of gossip ahead of you, so you don't have to start now. That right, Jim?'

Jim looked at Tina and saw that she was a little flustered, but only said, 'Strikes me women don't need a second invitation to chat, but I don't think either my mother or Tina here could be called a gossip. Isn't that so, Tina?'

Good old Jim, Tina thought. Stretching out a platitude, just to give her time to get her wits together. He always knew what she was feeling. Sometimes he knew too much, but never enough to stop him being a loving and understanding brother. Bruce Mackenzie was a different matter. There was no doubt he had a heart of gold, but there was a good part of him was cast iron. Pig iron, sometimes. He could be stubborn when he wanted, but now that he had a few beers in him, he was everybody's friend. Maybe Bruce needed a few beers to make him feel his real self.

Tina pushed her hair back and repositioned the clips. 'Yes, sorry you're rushing away so quickly, Jim. Sure you won't stay for tea?' Tea in the New Zealand sense meant possibly the largest dinner you could sit down to.

'That's what I was saying,' said Bruce, putting his arm around Jim's shoulder.

'No thanks, both. Gotta get back. Got an early start with two new men now that Billy's away.'

'You'll miss him, Jim.'

'You bet.'

*

Mr Trenchard was at his most florid yet there was no doubt he meant it all most sincerely. He was addressing the house staff at the Strand Palace Hotel on the occasion of Miss Rececca Friar's appointment as Chief Housekeeper and her resignation as such on the same day.

'It goes without saying,' said Mr Trenchard, but nevertheless he insisted on saying it, 'that Miss Friar's contribution to the smooth running of this establishment over the past most recent years has been exemplary and considerable. She embodies the qualities that all of us in the hotel service strive to attain. Efficiency with courtesy. Service with tact. Good manners allied with good appearance can only make for good results. And it is with this in mind that I was pleased to recommend to the company that they appoint her as Chief Housekeeper with effect from yesterday's date, Monday, 12th April, 1926, and regretfully accept her resignation with effect from today's date, Tuesday, 13th April, 1926. As well as a gesture of approval, this token of appointment also serves as a talisman towards new opportunities in Australasia. For even in the far Antipodes, they will recognise the qualities that go with the assignation, Chief Housekeeper of the Strand Palace Hotel, London.' He waited for some applause at this point, or even a reaction from the assembled staff, but none came. Undaunted, he took another breath and continued. 'For one so young to have attained such a responsible position is a fair indication of her character, qualities and merits. She has been like a good Scots lassie in doughtily applying herself to the task in hand –'

At that point, there was a loud yawn from Ginger, the page, and even Becky giggled. This set off the chamber-maids giggling, but Higgins the porter saved the day by clapping loudly and saying, ''Ear! 'Ear!' The pageboys joined in and Mr Trenchard beamed.

'Thank you, thank you, you are most kind. And now it is my privilege to present to dear Toffy – er – I mean – Miss Friar this token of appreciation and good will for her new life in far-off Van Diemen's land.'

'Where did he say?' said Ginger.

'It ain't Southend, that's all you need to know,' muttered Higgins, giving the lad a dig in the ribs.

'Thank you. Thank you,' said Mr Trenchard. 'And now if Miss Friar will please step forward.' Becky did so, feeling most uncomfortable, but was delighted to receive the cabin trunk the staff had collected to buy for her.

'Thank you very much,' she said. 'This is a big surprise.' There were a few catcalls at this as everybody knew about it up and down the corridors. Even some of the guests, the regulars, had subscribed. Becky smiled and looked at it.

'It's certainly big enough.'

'Why don't you jump in it and paddle all the way to Australia? We'll all give you a push off Land's End!'

'Shut up, Ginger,' said Higgins.

'I just hope I've got enough clothes to put in it.'

'Go on, Becky,' said Ginger, 'take me with you as a stowaway.'

Mr Trenchard realised that the presentation was getting out of hand and very quickly brought them to order. 'Staff will resume their normal duties. Thank you.' Being well trained, they obediently moved off in every direction, except Higgins, who said, indicating the large cabin trunk, 'I'll take it up to your room, Miss Friar.'

'Thank you very much, Bert,' she whispered.

'Everything is in order then, I take it, Miss Friar?'

'In complete order, Mr Trenchard.'

'Your money?'

'I took your advice and placed most of it in a banker's draft.'

'Most wise. There's nothing else I can do then?'

'Nothing, Mr Trenchard. You've been very kind.' He took her hand, and much to her surprise, he kissed it.

That night the cabin trunk was two-thirds filled, but locked and addressed care of the shipping line, and next morning, the hotel van delivered it to the quayside. Becky had nothing more to do than collect her handbag containing tickets and all her travel documents, put on her new gloves, pick up her umbrella and walk out. She had made all her farewells. She was now free to go.

She didn't know if what she felt was apprehension or excitement, but her knees were decidedly weak as she walked into the hall for the last time. She normally entered and left by the staff entrance at the side, but on this occasion she decided to walk out in style; comforted by Mr Trenchard's low bow and a smart salute from Bert Higgins, she made her way towards the front steps and the Strand, where a taxi was waiting to take her to Victoria Station, and from thence, who knows, to Victoria, Australia? She was so bound up in her own situation that she failed to see two young men enter with an older man as she was going out. The older man, in fact, held open the door for her, and gave her a smile, a most charming smile.

'Thank you,' she said, and she sailed down the steps. Miss Rebecca Friar was not aware that she had just passed her own father, whom she was going twelve thousand miles to find.

*

One day in the middle of April, John Keith came home for his tea. There was a much-delayed letter awaiting him from Bobby Keith, telling of the London visit with Abel and Billy, and hoping that John might be able to come up at the same time, as they might find it tight to get up to Forres since there were only five free days at the end of the conference and the boys might have other plans. At any rate, they would be staying at the Strand Palace –! John broke off at this point and laughed at the absolute irony of it all. This was a rare enough occurrence in the Keith household for Thomasina to stop ironing and ask,

'Are you alright?' John just shook his head, still chuckling.

'What's so funny?' Thomasina continued.

'It's just that Bobby's coming to London.'

'From Australia?' interrupted Thomasina in amazement.

'It's some kind of conference.'

'He's no' comin' here?' put in Thomasina, more as a statement than a question.

'They might not have time.'

'They?'

'He's bringing his son, Abel, and Jim's son, Billy.'

'Oh, my! They'll be grown men noo.'

'Very likely.' There was a silence as Thomasina resumed her ironing, pondering this titbit, and John grew pensive as he finished reading the letter. What about Becky, he was thinking. She might have met him . . .

'I think we'll send him an invitation anyway,' he said eventually.

'What for?'

'The wedding. What else?'

'You canna send invitations. That's Elspeth's business.'

'Is it? It says on that card, "Mr and Mrs John Keith have the pleasure of inviting . . .".'

'That disna mean anything.'

'It means I'm paying for it.'

'So does every father. But no' every father has to do with the invitations.'

John rose up, folding the letter and putting it in his pocket.

'Well, this one does, and you'll send one of those daft cards o' yours to Mr Robert Keith, c/o The Strand Palace Hotel, London.'

'Oh, but John!'

'And you can add, "and sons", too.'

'But ye canna dae that.'

'Oh, but I can. And if you don't, I'll refuse to give her away.'

'What does that mean?'

'I'll withdraw my consent.'

'Oh!'

'And that would mean the wedding's off.' This was too much for Thomasina. She was speechless. When she got her breath, she said,

'I'll have to talk to Elspeth about this. Oh, my! She's up in her room making out her list. She'll be fair flummoxed if I change the numbers noo.' Thomasina almost ran out of the room.

'No doubt,' said John, reaching for his coat again.

He was making for the door when he smelt a decided singeing. Something was burning. He looked over and saw that the iron had been left firmly on top of one of Elspeth's frilly blouses. 'Ach, let it burn,' said John, and closed the door behind him.

In their usual corner of the Mason's Arms, John brought his friend, Alec Friar, up to date on the situation. The two old pals hadn't seen much of each other, what with Alec's sudden call to go to Aberdeen and John's one day flier to London. But by the time of their third dram, Alec had got the picture completely.

'It's just as well she got a sailing date when she did. It would have been a hard thing for the lassie to meet her own father as a stranger like that.'

'Ay,' said John, sipping his dram. 'Many a father's a stranger to his own kin.'

'True,' said Alec, looking down at his own drink.

'Did you get your invitation?' said John.

'Me?' said Alec, looking up. 'Oh, no.'

'Why not? You're almost family.'

'Not quite, ship mate,' said Alec, taking a neat gulp.

'You're Becky's grandfather, and she's practically sister to Elspeth.'

'I think Thomasina has other views.'

'To hell wi' Thomasina,' muttered John. 'I'll see you get it. And to hell wi' her numbers too.' And with that, he took the last of his whisky. 'By the way,' he continued as he put his glass down on the table, and Alec signalled, 'Same again, George,' to the barman, 'how was your Aberdeen trip?' Alec didn't reply immediately.

'I wis sayin',' said John.

'It's alright. I heard you,' said Alec. 'I'm afraid, John, my visit to Aberdeen was not what you would call pleasant. I had to drop anchor there a bit longer than I thought.'

'Why was that? Was it Ella?'

'It was.'

'You said something about an accident.'

'It was a wee bit more than that, I'm afeared.' He looked John straight in the eyes. 'Ella was murdered. They think it was a sailor.' The barman brought the two whiskies and placed them on the table.

'There you are, gentlemen, same again.'

'Make them doubles,' said John.

In March 1926, a Royal Commission under Sir Herbert Samuel reported that British coal was being produced at a loss; the miners were being paid too much and the coal owners were taking too much of a profit. Nationalisation was recommended. Instead, Tory Prime Minister Stanley Baldwin cut the miners' wages and increased the working hours in the week. He did nothing about the mine-owners' profits even though the Duke of Northumberland earned, or rather drew, £82,000 a year from his mining interests, and the average wage of his miners in the Newcastle area was less than £3 a week! 'Not a minute on the day, nor a penny off the pay' was the slogan coined by the miners' leader, Arthur Cook. He demanded greater safety in the mines, accident compensation and decent living conditions for his men. These claims were also ignored by the Government and Cook prepared to pull out every man on strike. The TUC not only agreed with the miners' action but went further and prepared to call out not only the miners but every working man in the country, and all through April 1926, the country braced itself for the National Strike.

The Government too, however, had also been making preparations. Armoured cars appeared at the docks, tanks were stationed at all the railway stations and the first thing the three Keiths saw as they left their hotel one morning was a squad of soldiers marching toward Trafalgar Square. Soldiers in khaki uniforms, with puttees and cartridge pouches, rifles at the ready and bayonets drawn. Some of these men were survivors of Ypres and the Somme, yet the crowds watching that morning were silent and uneasy. This wasn't the Western Front, this was London, England, in peace-time. The only cheer that was heard was when one of the soldiers slipped on the cobble-stones and fell flat on his back. The officer's horse nearly trampled all over him as the poor fellow struggled to get up again. The passers-by jeered and cat-called. Yet this was one of their own soldiers whom not so long since they had welcomed home as heroes.

'Crikey,' exclaimed Abel, 'Is there a war on?'

'There certainly is,' answered his father grimly, 'and it's the worst kind.'

'What's that?' asked Billy.

'Between the classes,' replied his uncle. 'And there's nothing more bloody.'

'Why's that?' went on Billy, 'Oh look, they've got that poor guy running now.'

'He has to catch up,' explained Bobby. 'He'll catch it alright when they get him back.'

'You were saying, Bobby?' said Billy.

'Oh yes,' nodded the said uncle, 'about this class thing. Yes, there was a lot of money made in the war by the employers. Things couldn't have been better for them then and as for the working lads, well they had nothing to lose but their lives, had they? But in this do, if everybody comes out as they say, the work's not going to get done. Profits'll drop and you just listen to the nobs squeal. The miners are asking no more than their due, but the way this Government's going on, you'd think it was civil war. I suppose that's what it is in a way. Don't worry, the side that's got hold of the newspapers and the wireless can make it look the way they want it. They'll see that nobody gets into their pockets.'

'Are you a damned Red, sir?' asked a moustached city type standing ramrod straight behind them.

'No, mate, I'm an Australian,' answered Bobby chirpily. 'You know, one of your convict colonials. And it's time I got to the Colonial Office before they clap me in irons, whip me to the Tower and cut my bloody head off.' The city gent had no real answer to this and haughtily turned his head to where the line of soldiers had already disappeared into the distance.

'What about us then, Dad?' asked Abel.

'You two can do as you like,' replied his father. 'You're big boys now. With that, Bobby Keith sprinted across the road, chasing the bus that would take him up to the Colonial Office and the two young men were left standing on the pavement.

'Well, what's it to be then?' asked Abel, looking up and down.

'I dunno. What do you suggest?' answered Billy.

Abel looked exasperated. 'God Almighty, that's what you always say? Don't you ever have any ideas of your own?'

Billy was grinning. 'Not about how to pass the time in London.'

Abel was the younger by three years, but somehow, he was already established as the leader of the duo. Billy was quite happy to tag along as Abel suggested. The voyage over had started very uncomfortably, because Abel seemed deliberately to adopt an antagonistic, confrontational attitude to Billy. It was the case of the smart Sydney townsman versus the easy-going New Zealand countryman, and at first sight, it seemed that the former had the distinct advantage. Abel already had a street wisdom far beyond his years, and a slickness in any situation which could have been confused with sophistication. But his cousin Billy was the real thing. He required no pose or façade. He just was. He was by far the more intelligent of the two, but he never struggled to prove it. As a result he seemed slower, and his amiable good nature served to make him appear simpler than he was, but during the weeks of the long voyage, the waves made by Abel crashed pointlessly against the solid rock of Billy's integrity, and after a while, the overt enmity offered by Abel ebbed somewhat and the two became, at least for the purposes of this London visit, tacit friends. Billy was quite happy to leave the initiative to Abel and followed affably where the eighteen-year-old Australian led.

So far he had resisted Abel's campaign to introduce him to cigarettes.

'They make me sick,' he explained to Abel.

'Everybody's sick at the start,' retorted his cousin. That seemed poor logic to Billy and he laughed off all Abel's further efforts. On the first day they were free in London, Abel had persuaded Billy to have a different drink in every bar they could find from the hotel up to Leicester Square. The idea had been to find out which drink Billy liked best. Up till then, he had only taken beer, and even when he did, he could sip at a pint all night. Abel's was a more volatile alcoholic taste. The truth was that Abel had the lesser stomach of the two and it was he who couldn't take it. They had only got as far as the pub at the corner of Duncannon Street after a token whisky, gin, rum, brandy, vodka and sherry when Abel turned from the bar with his hand over his mouth, and staggered through the traffic looking neither left nor right in the direction of the Gentlemen's Toilets on Charing Cross Station. Billy laughed his head off. As he said to Abel, when the Aussie emerged again,

'It was the sherry that did it. Everybody's sick by the last drink!'

'Bloody woman's tipple!' grumbled Abel. After that, there were no further alcoholic experiments and Billy was left to sip on his beer.

Besides, they found they couldn't afford it. Bobby gave his son half a crown every morning, and if Abel had had his way that would have been gone by lunchtime. Billy had his own money and had carefully rationed himself to two shillings a day.

'Miser!' Abel had jeered, but Billy only shrugged. Now another day stretched before them and they had time to fill before they met up with Bobby again before first dinner sitting at the hotel at 6.30.

'Let's go up west,' said Abel turning right.

'Good,' answered Billy, and immediately fell in step. Abel was
tall, but he was small in comparison to his cousin, and they made
a formidable looking duo as they paced out their easy strides along
the Strand towards the West End and theatre land. This was what
Billy liked best. Taking in all the theatres. They had only been to
one show so far and that was a matinee of 'The Blackbirds' with
its all-negro cast. Florence Mills was the star. A beautiful black
girl with her own style of singing that they called crooning and
slinky sort of dancing that captivated both boys. Neither had seen
anything like her, and they were especially caught when the lights
dimmed, and the spot found Florence as she sang,

> 'I can't give you anything but love, baby,
> That's the only thing I've plenty of, baby . . . .'

It was an ordinary popular song, and had the usual syncopated
rhythm in it, but the coloured girl singing had a melancholy, a
quiet sadness that hushed the house, and affected the two young
colonials considerably. They even waited at the stage door to see if
she came out between shows, but all they saw were the comedians,
who were still wearing the check suits they wore on stage, and
whom neither Abel nor Billy found very funny, and the featured
dancer, Jed Marshall, whom they would take or leave. He seemed
to be very popular with the girls though. The hit of the show for
them was The Silver Rose herself, Florence Mills.

> 'Silver, silver, silver rose,
> How I wonder where she goes?
> God above knows how I love her,
> Silver, silver rose.'

'The Blackbirds' was still on at the Hippodrome and they stood for
a time, looking at the lovely stills of Miss Mills on display outside
the theatre.
  'It makes you think, doesn't it?' said Abel in a low voice.
  'Whaddya mean?' said Billy.
  'You know what I mean,' and he nudged his cousin.
  'No, I don't.'
  'Yes, you do.'
  'I don't!'
  'I mean look at those black tits.' Billy was a little startled
and glanced at Abel. 'I mean when did you ever see anything
like them?'

'We'd a Hereford cow with black udders,' said Billy with a grin.

'Oh, for goodness sake!' They moved on up Shaftesbury Avenue, stopping every now and then to look at the stars, and lunchtime found them wandering in Soho. Abel had all the mammary satisfaction he could ask for in what he saw all around him there. The trouble was it didn't satisfy him, and he was beginning to feel a little more sexually ambitious. But half a crown would hardly appease him in that direction.

'How much you got on you, Billy?'

'Why?'

'Just wondered.' They continued up Greek Street, with Abel stopping at every second doorway to look at the various invitations written on the cards.

'Listen to this, Billy boy!' And he would read out the most obvious of the calling cards, much to Billy's embarrassment and the amusement of the passers-by who could hear.

'"Maidie Brownlee",' read Abel loudly, '"will attend all your needs on a sound professional basis. No tricks or implements." Blimey!' He broke off. '"Strictly person to person. Ring top bell. Hourly consultation, five shillings." I've only got half a crown.'

'Maybe you could have a half-hourly consultation?' suggested Billy.

'Don't be silly, you couldn't do anything in half an hour.'

'How do you know?' Abel pretended to study the other notices.

'Everybody knows that.'

'Would you give it a go if you had the five bob?' Billy asked.

'Course I would. Who wouldn't?'

'Well, here you are,' said Billy. 'There's half a crown.'

'I thought you only had two bob a day!'

'That's my emergency fund. You can have it.'

'This isn't an emergency.'

'Isn't it?' asked Billy, a definite twinkle in his eye.

'Anyway, I've gone off it now,' mumbled Abel.

'You were never on it, mate. Come on,' said Billy and they moved on in the direction of Oxford Street.

At dinner that night, Bobby told them both all about his day at the conference and how things were going to be so much better for the working man in Australia, especially if they were able to bring out good people from the Old Country to help keep up standards. He also gave them a long commentary on the British situation.

'Bloody ludicrous. Toffs dressed up as special constables, undergrads driving buses, public schoolboys on the trains? You mark my words, the Government will employ the whole population of middle class and upper class blacklegs and student dilettantes to break the miners. The other workers won't show real sympathy either, whatever they say. They'll be too busy looking after their own jobs. You'll see. All I can tell you, it wouldn't happen in Australia.'

'Why not?' asked Billy, tucking into his Shepherd's Pie.

'We haven't this class thing,' said Bobby.

'That's us,' said Abel, 'we got no class.'

'What you boys do with your day then?' said Bobby with his mouth full. Abel glanced at Billy, who carried on eating.

'Well,' said Abel. And he proceeded to tell his father about their day in such a way that made it sound fascinating instead of the long, boring perambulation round the centre of London that both boys knew it was. Abel made their beer and sandwich lunch sound like an event and their long trawl round the zoo seem like a safari. Billy was amazed but impressed. Abel obviously had the gift of imagination. Bobby nodded.

'I knew you lads would make the most of London. Good for you. Oh by the way, we're going to a wedding.' Both boys looked up.

'Oh?' said Billy. 'Anybody we know?'

'Your cousin Elspeth in Forres.' Both lads looked blank. 'She's your Uncle John's girl.' See I got this at the desk when I got home tonight.' And he showed them the invitation.

'Forres? Scotland?' exclaimed Abel.

'Sure,' his father answered.

'Crikey. That's at the North Pole, isn't it?'

'Come on, Abel,' said Bobby. 'It'll be good for you to meet your Scottish cousins.'

'I bet,' said Abel sarcastically. Billy handed back the invitation.

'I know it'll be hard to drag you both away from the lights of the big city.' The boys exchanged glances. 'But it'll do you good to get up to Scotland and see how the other half live.'

The boys digested this with their apples and custard. By the time the tea was served, they had got more used to the idea.

'Right, then,' said Bobby, wiping his mouth with a napkin. 'That's settled then. We leave on Friday. That gives you another day to live it up, eh?' Abel looked at Billy, who refused to meet his eye.

'As the father of the bride it is my duty – they tell me – to welcome Donald here as a new member of the family and to accept him from now on as my son –' There was a murmur of approval and approbation from the assembled guests. John waited.

'I cannot do that,' he said. There was a shocked silence. 'Oh, I don't mean any offence to the lad by that.'

Donald smirked self-consciously and Elspeth twiddled her new wedding ring, staring at it as if she still couldn't believe it.

'He's got Elspeth now and he's welcome to her.' This time there was an audible reaction and mutters of 'Is he drunk?' could be clearly heard. It was hard to tell whether he was or not. Thomasina was openly glaring at her husband.

'I see my wife is looking at me,' said John, 'But I'm no' done yet. I have something to say and I'll stand here till I say it.' There was an uneasy silence. Bobby, watching from his table, wondered what his brother was up to. He had been appalled when he saw his brother at Forres station. He was fifty-five years of age but looked at least ten years older. He was thin on top and thick about the middle and in his eyes was a constant, faraway look as if his mind were always on something else. Or was it someone else?

'I had a son once and I lost him in the war. I've no wish for another. I had a daughter too and I lost her too.' Everyone looked at Elspeth as John went on. 'And she is away to Australia.' Elspeth jerked her head up. Donald leaned over and whispered something in her ear. The murmur of voices rose again. John spoke over it – 'Elspeth here was never my daughter. She was Thomasina's.' Thomasina rose, John pushed her down. 'It's the truth and you all know it.' His voice rose as he continued, 'And you all know too that Becky was never my daughter but my niece.' The guests fell silent again. John hesitated, then seemed to make up his mind. 'For Rebecca Friar was the natural daughter of my brother there –' and he pointed to Bobby as everybody started talking at once. 'And you all knew that too!' shouted John over the din.

Elspeth got up with Donald and they both left their places. Thomasina followed, crying, 'Elspeth, wait!' Donald tried to say something but couldn't get it out. 'Oh, never mind you,' said Thomasina brusquely and followed her daughter out of the side door. Not that anybody was bothering about the bride and groom, for all eyes were on Bobby Keith, who sat staring at his older brother. Abel sat staring at his father. Billy was looking around him hardly believing it all. Old Mr Robertson, Donald's uncle and still head of the firm of Keith and Sons, just puffed on his pipe and looked as if he were enjoying it all. Well, well, John Keith, he thought. John, for his part, seemed to have gained in confidence. He looked directly at his brother, and spoke very quietly.

'I know it was a shock Bobby but better a shock from your own brother in public than a lot of whispers from a lot of old women in private. At this, he looked pointedly in the direction of John Thomson, the schoolmaster, sitting with his spinster sister and the Reverend Braid, who was puce with excitement and pleasure at the scandal. 'Besides, you can be proud of your Becky,' went on John 'She was a bonnie lass to me and to all the friends she had here, and they were many even if some of them are no longer with us.' He made a slight pause, remembering Mrs Beattie. 'And others who were not invited. Where is Alec Friar for instance?' At this point the Reverend Braid rose in his place, raising his hands for order.

'Ladies and Gentlemen,' he began. 'Ladies and Gentlemen, please –'

'Why don't you sit down?' yelled a man's voice but no one was sure who he was meaning – John or the minister? John started to speak again. So did the minister and they both spoke at once:

'This may be Elspeth's wedding, but it's my reception –'

'I'm sure this would be an appropriate moment to adjourn –'

At the same time, Bobby rose and at that, Mr Braid and then John slowly sat. All eyes and ears turned to their former fellow-townsman, now an Australian. Bobby, like the practised orator he was, took his time and waited for his silence.

'Brother John. Reverend Braid. Ladies and gentlemen. Friends. And fellow guests.' His voice was soft and almost menacingly low but there was no doubt he could be heard clearly in the Victoria Hall that day. One voice could be heard asking: 'Is he American noo?' 'Sh!' said several others. Bobby continued.

'Some bloody wedding!' he said. There was no reaction. 'One thing I'm sure of and that is that my big brother is sober and I understand that that's something of a rare occurrence these days. I thank him then for his sobriety and for the nerve he has shown in standing up before you all and proclaiming his young brother as the father of a bastard. But as you might say, Reverend,' he nodded to Braid, 'the sins of his youth shall be visited on the father in his age.' The minister gave a weak smile. Bobby looked around him. 'But so many questions remain. For instance, the said daughter's mother –'

'Ella Friar,' said John evenly. For a moment, at the mention of her name, Bobby looked rattled, but he rallied quickly.

'I believe that was the name. Yes. And she is –?'

'Dead.' John's tone was curt. Bobby visibly gasped. 'In Aberdeen.'

'When?' Bobby's voice was weak as he addressed his brother.

'This year. She was murdered.' The guests gasped. It was Bobby's turn to sit. The wedding guests had never seen or heard anything like it. It was more like a court case than a reception. A play even. John rose.

'Are there any other questions?' he said. There wasn't a sound. When he next spoke, it was with a remarkable dignity.

'Then I formally declare this reception closed and invite you all, or as many of you as want to, to come to the house for a drink.' He sat down as everyone rose up in a buzz of excited chatter. Yes, it was exactly like the end of the play. Nobody spoke to John or Bobby, who still sat in their places. Abel sat with his head bowed. Billy leaned over to him.

'You alright, Abel? Abel raised his head, his face was deathly white.

'No, I'm bloody well not.'

'What is it?' In answer, Abel rose up quickly and hurried off in the direction of the lavatories. Billy watched him go then sat back in his seat as the hall gradually emptied. Mr Thomson and his sister hung back with Reverend Braid and old 'Shears' Robertson. The old man came forward leaning on his stick and solemnly shook hands first with John, then with Bobby, and slowly turned and left without a word. The minister then came forward to John.

'I must say, Mr Keith, this has been a most unseemly –' John looked up at the indignant clergyman as if looking through him. Braid turned for support to Bobby.

'I'm sure Mr Robert Keith would –' Bobby cut him off abruptly,

'Why don't you piss off, Vicar?'

'Oh!' Mr Braid had never been spoken to like that in his life. 'Really!' He rushed to the Thomsons, who clucked and tut-tutted with him all the way to the door. At length only the two Keith brothers and their nephew Billy remained in the hall. Nobody spoke. After a time, Billy rose.

'I'll see how Abel is,' he said and left. Neither of his uncles responded. At length, John spoke first.

'I never read the telegrams,' he said.

'And they never cut the cake!' added Bobby. Then he started to laugh. Quietly at first and then louder. John joined in with a kind of giggle until he got louder and then the two brothers laughed loudly and long, and rising from their places came together in that empty hall and laughed with their arms round each other till the tears ran down their cheeks.

In the lavatory, Billy couldn't see Abel.

'Abel!' he called. There was no reply. 'Where the hell is he?' He was just about to go when there was a noise from one of the cubicles and then the sound of a cistern running.

'That you, Abel?' After a moment, Abel came out. He looked
shaken. Billy went to him as he leaned on the hand-basin. 'What's
up, Abel? You crook?'

Abel nodded, looking down into the basin. 'I think I've got
something.'

'Whaddya mean?' asked Billy.

'What do you think I bloody well mean?' He bent over the basin
with a grimace of pain. 'My fucking dick's on fire!' he whispered.

'Christ!' said Billy, 'you'd better see about that.'

'Who the hell do I see in a godforsaken dump like this?'

It was Dr French who saw Abel that night. Billy had made
enquiries about a doctor, saying he had stomach pains, and Alec
Friar, who was the only one who came to the house that night
arranged for him to see Dr French at his surgery. Billy had said,
'Can I bring Abel too?'

'Why, do you need someone to hold your hand?' said the big
man jovially.

'Yes, I do,' said Billy with a straight face. So Abel's cover was
secure, and both boys now sat in Dr French's waiting room, with
four middle-aged women and a crying baby.

Back at the house, Alec Friar was more or less acting as a barman
for the two Keith brothers. They sat in two armchairs opposite
each other at the fireplace with a bottle of whisky each and were
quietly making their way through them. Alec had heard all about
the goings-on at the reception from some of the guests, who had
repaired immediately to the Mason's Arms. He decided to come to
the house to hear for himself, and found the two brothers well on
the way to being dead drunk. This was perhaps the best way for
Bobby to hear the rest of the story and of how he just missed Becky
at the Strand Palace Hotel. Alec soon saw that he was redundant
to their needs and rose up to go. Neither noticed as he closed the
door gently behind him.

'Gonorrhea,' snapped old Dr French. 'You're lucky.'

'Lucky?' echoed Abel.

'That's what I said. Could have been syphillis. Then you'd have
known all about it.' It had been a most embarrassing interview.
The doctor made him tell him exactly what happened. About
how he went back to Soho on that last night, alone, and how
he'd gone to Maidie Brownlee's flat, and hired an hour. No,
he'd never done it before, he told the doctor. 'Nor will you
do it again in a hurry,' the old doctor retorted. He made Abel
take his trousers off and his underpants. The smell was awful, and
the old doctor took Abel's penis in his hands and poked a long
thin rod right into it. Abel had to look away, but the result was

493

clear. The doctor gave him instructions on how to bathe it and keep it clean.

'You'll be fine in a month,' he said. Abel sighed with relief. In a month he'd be on the ship and he could see the doctor there, if need be. And he'd be alright by the time he got back to Sydney. He knew he couldn't face his mother if he had the pox.

'Off you go,' said the old man coldly, 'and behave yourself.' He showed Abel to the door. 'Next, please.' He saw Billy as he rose up. 'Are you the one with the sore stomach?'

'No thanks, doctor, it's better now.'

'Hmph!' the doctor said. 'Oh, it's you Mrs McCall? What's wrong with him now?'

'The usual, doctor,' said Mrs McCall, as she carried her crying baby into the surgery and the door closed behind them.

'Was it Miss Brownlee?' said Billy. Abel nodded. 'Bloody fool!' But he put his arm round his cousin as they both left the waiting room.

The next morning, Thomasina came down from her room to tell John she was leaving him. She had refused to let him into their bedroom the previous night, maintaining that he was too drunk to come near her. He had slept it off on the sitting room window seat. He was still lying there with his coat over him when she suddenly appeared in the sitting room, fully dressed and carrying a suitcase and a large bag.

'After yesterday's exhibition,' she told him, 'I've no wish to see you or your kind ever again. The shame and disgrace of it. I'll never live it down. Poor Elspeth! Her day absolutely ruined. They never even went off on their honeymoon to Balmoral, and that means a deposit lost. And how you can lie there in that state! Stop grinning at me, you fool. You'll see that the insurances are paid up?' John still didn't reply and when he heard the door slam, he merely turned over saying, 'Good riddance!'

Later that day, it was a very forlorn pair of brothers who made their farewell on a Forres station platform. They hugged each other without a word and both knew they would never see each other again. John solemnly shook hands with each of the young men, who were almost glad to escape into the carriage. Bobby followed next, closed the door and pulled down the window.

'You'll give my regards to Becky when you see her?' said John.

'I'll do that, John,' said Bobby. 'Are you sure you don't want to come with us?'

'Aye, I'm sure.' The whistle sounded and the train started to move off.

'You'll be alright, man?' said Bobby and his voice shook a little.

'I'll be alright,' called John above the noise of the engine, and he took a hip flask from his pocket for the first drink of the day. He waved it at the train as it disappeared, then turned away – a bachelor now. As he always should have been.

On 3rd May, a General Strike was declared, but Bobby and his nephews managed to sail safely out of Southampton just in time. Things had happened just as Bobby had said they would. They had gone down on the train, driven by two Oxford men with a Cambridge light blue as the guard. They had their luggage taken on the ship by a group of hearty sportsmen in plus fours, the angry dockers kept at bay by burly rugger players acting as special constables. Troops guarded the docks, and the trio saw their first tank at Waterloo Station. It offended every principle of Bobby's, but he had no option except to cross the picket line and shamefacedly he did so. But he went straight to his cabin. The two young men hurried to the rails to look down on the scene at the quayside, for a fight had broken out between the dockers and the rugger players, and the university men were not having it all their own way.

'And who said there wasn't a war on?'

'You're right, mate,' said Abel to his cousin. Just then shots rang out, and there was a rattle of machine-gun fire from somewhere.

'Blimey!' said Abel, 'let's get the hell out of here!' Almost on his word, the ship's hooter blew and it slid away from the dockside with increasing speed.

They were kept in touch with events through the ship's wireless. In nine days the General Strike was broken. The TUC weakly surrendered and the British working class deserted their miner comrades. The part-time bus drivers, train drivers and constables returned to their gin and tonics and rural pursuits, and the miners went back down the pits to less wages and more working hours. They had been literally starved into submission.

It's an interesting thought, mused Bobby in his deck chair one afternoon, that while there was a surplus of upper-class young men to fill every working class job in the country, not one volunteered to go down the mines. He smiled cynically and closed his eyes against the brilliant sun.

'Bloody Poms!' he said to himself.

Meantime, on the other side of the world, a young woman knocked at the door of the Keith household in Pott's Point, Sydney. She was smartly, if rather over-dressed for the heat, and looked weary as if she'd come a long way. She was carrying a small case and had a handbag over her shoulder.

'Yes?'

'Are you Mrs Keith?'

'I am.' The young woman smiled slightly.

'Mrs Cooper next door told me you'd be back at six.'

'Yes?' asked Rachel, a little frown on her face. 'I work at the university.'

'I know. She told me.' Rachel was intrigued by the Scottish accent. The girl looked suddenly embarrassed.

'Sorry, my name's Rebecca Friar, and I wonder if it's possible to see your husband?'

'My husband?'

'It's taken me a long time to find out . . .'

'Why do you want to see my husband?' The girl paused, then looked Rachel straight in the eye.

'I think he's my father.'

Bobby Keith was having difficulty finding a place at the ship's rail. After two months at sea, this was a very special landfall and everyone on board seemed to be trying to get to the rail as the big liner edged into the Sydney dockside. He hurried along the line of craning backs two and three deep along the main boat deck, occasionally stopping to stand on tiptoe to try to look over. Everyone was talking at once, faces flushed under sea-tans, arms raised, fingers pointing eagerly. It was not only the end of a voyage, it was a homecoming for most of them and excitement ran high through the entire passenger list. Even Bobby was feeling it and he strove to find a vantage point. Realising it was useless on the main deck, he decided to go up one and headed for the nearest companion way, threading his way through the procession of Goanese sailors laden with suitcases and struggling with cabin trunks. He hoped his own would get on to the dock in one piece. The two boys had carried all their luggage out to the foyer that morning and left it with the cabin steward. Bobby had tipped him the night before, which wasn't always the wisest manoeuvre. Never mind, too late now to worry about that. He was now on the deck above and it was almost as bad at the rails here. He had just begun to search for a space when a voice called him from one of the lifeboats.

'– Bobby!'

Bobby looked up to see Billy and Abel grinning down at him.

'Hi Dad!'

'What are you doing up there?'

'I heard we were sinking!' laughed Abel.

'Get out of that before the Purser sees you,' called up his father.

'Come on up. It's a great view,' answered Billy.

'Not on your life. What do you think I am?'

'You're a stiff old bugger. You couldn't make it anyway,' replied his son, and both young men laughed again.

The view from the lifeboat was spectacular. Bobby could see not only the whole of the docks but over most of Sydney as well. It was good to see it again, Bobby thought, and isn't it growing? There were buildings there he was sure he hadn't seen before. Yes, it was good to be home. Funny, that's where he just come from – home. But this was home now. He wasn't a Pommie or a Jock now – he was an Australian, and he was coming home again.

'There she is!' yelled Abel.

'Who?' asked Bobby and Billy in unison.

'Mum!'

They followed his arm and there was the tiny figure of Rachel standing a little apart from the main crowd. She waved as Bobby and Abel called to her and seemed to say something to the tall, young woman standing beside her, who then looked up to them, shielding her eyes against the sun.

'Who's the lovely Sheila with her?' queried Abel. Bobby was waving hard to his wife.

'Probably someone she's met on the docks,' he said. 'Waiting for one of the other passengers I suppose.'

'She's pretty, isn't she?' said Billy.

'That's what I was thinking,' murmured Abel.

'Not the girl, you idiot – your Mum.'

'She is too,' agreed Bobby fondly, then he glanced at the young woman beside her. But his heart jumped in his chest for he found himself looking at Ella Friar!

He almost crushed Rachel in his embrace. She laughed and drew herself free, using both hands to clutch at her hat.

'Hold it, Bobby you'll do us both damage. Let's get you home first.' Bobby didn't say anything. He was staring at the tall, young girl who was gazing at him steadily from under her straw hat. Now that he could see her close up she wasn't as like Ella as he had first thought, but there was something . . .

'Close your mouth, Bobby. It's not becoming,' said Rachel. 'I want you to meet –'

But Bobby knew already. He knew it in the girl's eyes, in the smile that was already at the corner of her mouth, in the attractive reddening of her cheek bones, in the way her body seemed already poised to move to him, the way her hands were clenched by her side. A lovely thought had just come to him and he blurted out –

'Bloody hell lassie – are you –?'

'Yes,' breathed the girl, nodding eagerly, her eyes sparkling. Holding his eyes, she extended her hand. 'How do you do – father?' Bobby took the hand and shook it mechanically, for once absolutely lost for words. Rachel looked on smiling.

'Yes, darling, this is Rebecca,' she said. Then she turned to her son.

'That's right, Abel – you've got a sister!'

'Christ!'

'And you've got another cousin, Billy.'

'How do you do, Rebecca,' said the young New Zealander, politely offering his hand. But Becky's arms were tight around her father, and he was crying like a baby, his chin on her shoulder, his eyes tight shut.

''Struth!' muttered Abel, and reaching down he lifted both of his suitcases and started to move away.

THIRTY-TWO

Throughout most of 1927, Kevin O'Neil was caught in the crossfire of two great loves. The first was his love for his mother. The redoubtable fortress that had once been Nessie O'Neil had been breached not from without, but from within. Senility had infiltrated, and she had reverted to a world of her own that was her own young time in Rosstrevor and all the people she'd known and loved then. She still lived in Cassidy's Hotel, but for the most part was confined to the room to which she'd gone on the afternoon she had rejected Noreen's Maria. She rarely left the room now, except to go to Mass every morning, where she insisted on putting notes instead of coppers in the collection plate. The ushers used to retrieve them and return them to Nellie on the odd occasions when she went to Mass. Nessie would sometimes get up at four in the morning and come down to the small dining-room to lay out tea for Denis, whom she was expecting to call at any time. She spent most of her time waiting for Denis to call. Sometimes, she would be found in the hallway with her hat and coat on, saying that she was going on an excursion with Denis to Warrenpoint. Nellie would have to be fetched from whatever she was doing in order to persuade her mother to go back to her room. Nellie had little sympathy for her mother. Perhaps it was because she had been ill herself for so long. She wanted no reminder of the frailty of the human condition and the inevitable end that comes to us all with the gradual disintegration of our faculties.

'Come on, Mother, pull yourself together!' But Nessie could no more do that than fly in the air. The skein of her life had unravelled. The jigsaw of a once powerful personality lay scattered about her person with no hope of ever joining up again. That one essential piece was missing.

All this broke her son Kevin's heart. Sam Cassidy tried to reassure him. He had seen his own mother go the same way.

'The pity of it is, 'tis a long dying,' said Sam. Kevin took to visiting Cassidy's more regularly in order to look in on his mother. He would find her in her room taking everything out of what she called her box: photographs, various trinkets, some crocheted item, a pair of baby shoes – 'they were the first Kevin's you know'. She had flashes of insight and awareness that suddenly made her frightened, when she would turn to Kevin like a small child instead of an old woman, and ask her son, 'What is it, d'ye think, that's happening to me?' Kevin could only shake his head and look down at his clasped hands.

The second love of his life was that given him totally and unreservedly and now openly by the seventeen-year-old Teresa Dacre, the waif-like only child of a voluptuous Dublin housewife and her English Black and Tan husband. She was filling out in the most attractive manner. With her ash blonde hair and dark eyebrows, she had more of an English look than Irish, and could easily have had the pick of the street as suitors, had she wanted. But she only had eyes for her mother's permanent lodger, Kevin O'Neil, the 'insurance man' who was old enough to be her father. It was common knowledge to everyone, this infatuation she had had since she was a small girl. Despite the fact that it was never encouraged by Kevin, it had ripened unilaterally into a deep love. This soon-to-be beautiful woman had never been diverted in the single-mindedness of her affection and no amount of gossip or stricture or alternative liaison could alter her feelings.

This did not please Kevin's sister, Nellie.

'You're a sound man, Kevin O'Neil,' she said, 'and you still have looks on you. Why waste your time dangling with a young girl's calf love when you could have a wife and children of your own and set up in a good job and prospects before you?'

'I've got a good job,' said Kevin, 'and if you must know, the prospects are limitless. I stay with the Dacres because I like it there, and I don't dangle, as you call it, with Teresa because I like her too.' The truth of the matter was that Teresa's relentless campaign was gradually bearing fruit. Kevin was a normal man with a normal man's feelings, and no one was more aware than he of how much Teresa might have to offer, but he had for so long looked on her as the child of the house to humour and joke with that he found it difficult to see her now as the lovely creature she undoubtedly was. This was also partly why he spent so much time at Cassidy's.

Occasionally, his leader and mentor, Sam, would quietly bring up the matter over their late night 'conferences' in the small bar.

'A man in your line of business, Kevin, has to watch how he uses dynamite, and a lovely girl's feelings are dynamite, I can tell you that. It can either knock you into the next world or blow you to pieces. And is it fair, think you, to offer a slip of a girl the sight of a home of her own and a man to match, and then take it from her as you would a toy from a child?' Kevin knew what Sam Cassidy meant. Already he had seen so many unhappy wives of men in 'his line of business'. It was a difficult thing to be a patriot husband. But it was getting even more difficult to refuse Teresa.

Mrs Dacre typically had a different view of the situation. And in her cups, fresh from Feeney's, she would tell her lodger frankly, whenever Teresa was out of the room.

'It's in the stars, Kevin, I can see it in the stars. You only have to look and there ye are, the two of yez, bound as tight together as the Siamese craturs that were joined head and foot. Bejasus, it's natural, is it not? Her turning into the fine woman, and you into the grand man that you are, and it's a mother's instinct tells me you've never laid a hand on her, and she almost burstin' out of her dresses for ye.' Kevin would squirm uneasily at the table, and wish she would stop, but Sarah Dacre was as determined as her daughter, and would lean in blearily to declare, 'It's not throwin' you together, I am Sure haven't you had plenty chances of that, but it's tellin' you that together you are and together you belong and together you will be, though I trust to God it's not this year and me behind with the rent and the water coming in through the roof at the back porch. And Mr Feeney himself, though he has been obliging, like the gentleman he is, is beginning to wonder if he has a slate big enough. So there can be no talk of a wedding in the meanwhile.'

'But I'm not talking about a wedding!' explained Kevin, who was beginning to get a very trapped feeling. 'I don't have the money either.'

'Sure, it's not money a man brings to a wedding, Kevin. It's his best suit and him in it. You leave the rest of it to the woman.'

She was on about it all again this evening, but this time Kevin wasn't in the mood for her garrulousness. He rose with his cup and saucer.

'I'll take my tea up with me,' he said.

'Take it, Kevin darlin', take it. It's all yours. Everythin' here is yours. The tay, the taycup,' she began to laugh, 'even the saucer.' Kevin laughed too and went out of the tiny kitchen, carrying the cup and saucer. As he closed the door, he didn't hear Mrs Dacre mutter in a totally different tone, 'Even me daughter!'

Teresa Dacre was in Kevin's room when he went up. 'I was making your bed up,' she said as Kevin came in.

'But you made it up this morning,' he said.

'I was making it up better then. I was rushed this morning, because I had to go and see about a job. See the nice flowers I got you.' She pointed to a vase.

'Very nice,' he said. Kevin sat in his easy chair, facing the window, and put the tea cup on the small table beside him. This was his favourite chair, with a view over the rooftops of Dublin and the table lamp by his side, where he had read and re-read all his books of Ireland's past, or where he sat and dreamed at times of all his hopes for Ireland's future. But for the moment, he eased himself back in the chair and looked at Teresa as she bent over his bed. God, she was shapely, there was no doubt about that. And to think she was such a scraggy, skinny little thing not so long since. It was all Kevin could do to stop himself reaching out and touching her. Instead he took up his cup and saucer.

'What was the job you were after?' he asked.

'It was in an office in Grafton Street. But I didn't get it. I didn't have the typewriting. Me mother was that disappointed. She thought it would be fine with me in an office and her getting the weekly money in. Well, that's that again.' She patted the pillow, then sat down, put her knees together, then clasped her hands around them and looked at him squarely. She felt easy and relaxed in the company of this older man, and even alone in his room, she felt no sexual tension, because she so palpably loved him. The print dress she wore now covered her knees, but delightfully defined her burgeoning breast. She was indeed as pretty as a picture and Kevin O'Neil was well aware of it. So was Teresa.

'And what sort of a day did you have yourself?' she asked pertly. Just then there was a bang on the outside door. Teresa raised her eyes. 'That's me mother off to Feeney's to see what else she can squeeze on the slate.' They were alone in the house. But then, they were often alone in the house. 'Are you dreaming, or what?' she went on.

'What?'

'I asked you what sort of day did you have?'

How could he begin to tell her, he thought. He'd been under orders to act as normally as possible. That's why he'd almost to break his neck to get home at the normal time and sit through that long supper with Mrs Dacre. How had he managed it? How had he managed it all from that first call from Sam the day before yesterday. Everything had happened so quickly. He'd been given the time, the place, where to collect the rifle and ammunition. He'd never carried a golf bag so heavy. In fact, he'd never carried a golf bag. He was glad it was November, and cold and blustery. People went about their business with their heads down, muffled up to the ears. Nobody had paid any attention to him as he went into the designated house, climbed the stairs and took up his position at the window. Everything had been laid out just as they said, and

there was the right hand pane missing just as he'd been told. He
remembered that he'd started to sweat and yet his fingers had been
cold. He'd blown on them, then rubbed them on the outside of
his coat. Two minutes from the scheduled time, he'd taken up his
rifle. When the actual moment arrived and the target moved into
his sights, he felt another kind of coldness, a calm coldness. He
felt his shoulders relax. His hands were steady on the trigger. He
was careful not to pull, but to squeeze. As he did so, he said, 'For
Ireland, in the name o' God!' Then he was out of that room like a
bat out of hell. The rifle was in the golf bag within seconds. The
golf bag was in the back of the van, which was at the door within
minutes, and he was in Sam's car going the opposite way not a
minute after that. Sam had said nothing. He only nodded. That
was information enough for Kevin and he had started shaking all
over. Sam dropped him at the door of the insurance office.

'Leave your coat!' barked Sam. Kevin looked puzzled.

'Cordite marks!' said Sam. Of course, thought Kevin, and there
on the pavement, he took off his coat and threw it in the car as it
sped away.

Luckily the telephone rang for him as soon as he walked into
the office. He had already arranged that Miss O'Riordan have her
afternoon off on that day to go to her mother's in Dundalk. So the
place was empty. He picked up the receiver.

'It's yourself, Phelim?' he said in a voice he hardly recognised.
Phelim was one of his regular customers. He ran a car showroom
for Austin cars and he had a good insurance turnover. Well
respected in the city, he was just the man to provide an alibi
for Kevin. 'I've been waiting in all afternoon for you to call about
that Ballsbridge collision . . .'

But now he looked up into Teresa's deep grey eyes. 'It was just
a day like any other, I suppose.' He could not believe he could lie
so easily.

'You'll be tired now?' He felt that shaking again.

'I am a bit.'

'So you'll want your bed?'

'I suppose so.' He had to put the cup and saucer down, it
was shaking so much. He was starting to breathe heavily, and
his chest felt congested. Her hands had gone to her sides and
he could see the knuckles white as she clenched the blankets.
Her lips were slightly parted, and the colour in her face had
heightened to an extent that made her irresistibly attractive. She
rose up.

'I'd better let you get on.' And he could see her bosom rising
slightly.

'Ay,' he said, holding her eyes. He was convinced they were turning blue in the twilight. He knew he could never rise up.

'That's a nice dress,' he whispered.

'Me mam got it for the interview. A waste o' money.' She tried to laugh, but only a little noise came, and she ran from the room.

He was in bed, lying staring up at the light in the ceiling. He'd left the curtains open, because he didn't want to lie in the dark tonight. The full enormity of what he had done was just settling in on him, and to add to all these strange new feelings, the power of emotion that he had felt with Teresa was also new. Was it only because he was particularly aware, his feelings heightened by the terrible events of the afternoon, or did he need today to tell him that he, in fact, loved this girl? He had to do something, say something, because he knew that at half past four in the morning, Sam was coming for him with the new papers and tickets for the American boat which was to leave on the first tide for New York. He was forbidden to say goodbye to anyone. He was merely to disappear from the scene, and Miss O'Riordan at the office would receive a letter at her home that morning, ostensibly from the London office, stating that her services were no longer required and enclosing a generous cash order in lieu of notice. She would have found the office locked in any case. Phelim's and other business had by now been diverted to another branch, and it was as if Kevin O'Neil no longer existed in Dublin. The only problem not resolved was Teresa. His mother was in her own hands, and in any case, Sam had promised that he and Nellie would look after her until she drifted away. Kevin had no wish to say goodbye to his mother. He wanted to remember her as she had been. Mrs Dacre could be trusted, because no one believed her anyway, but there still remained her daughter.

As he lay there in the semi-darkness, he made up his mind. Putting on his trousers over his nightshirt, and pulling his raincoat tight, he slipped on his shoes and went downstairs. He had to walk to the end of the street to find the telephone kiosk.

Sam Cassidy wasn't in bed when Kevin rang, but was very angry to be phoned up. He was also completely taken aback by Kevin's suggestion. It was more than a suggestion. It was a very urgent request.

'But that's impossible at this time of night. Do you realise it's after ten o'clock?'

'I know,' said Kevin, 'but there's no time to waste. I know you can do this for me, Sam. Look what I did for you.' He put the phone down and came out of the kiosk just as Sarah Dacre was meandering home in the company of two of her drinking companions. He happily joined their sing-song way and escorted Sarah to the kitchen. He then boiled the kettle. And prepared to make the strongest pot of tea he could.

Hurrying upstairs, he quickly changed into his best suit, the grey one with the stripes, over his best shirt and his best tie. His heart was racing like a young boy's. Pity about the shoes he thought, but they'll have to do. What is it they say? Something old, something new, something borrowed – he went to the vase of flowers Teresa had put in his room that day, took one, and put it in his buttonhole. The rest he drew from the vase, shaking the water onto the carpet. Looking around he picked up the small linen table cover and wrapped it round the flowers. Then taking a deep breath, he went across the landing to Teresa's room and knocked. She came to the door in her nightdress. She obviously hadn't been sleeping either. He presented his homemade bouquet to her and said, 'Teresa Dacre, will you marry me?'

Sam Cassidy arrived with a very cross-looking Nellie and a stranger, who turned out to be a Justice of the Peace, and Kevin and Teresa were married in the Dacre front room with Sam and Nellie as witnesses. Teresa wore the dress she had bought for the interview that day and no society bride could have looked lovelier than she did on the chimes of midnight when she married the love of her life. Mrs Dacre took it all in her stride and provided a large pot of tea for the reception. To her delight, Sam produced an even larger bottle of whiskey. Even Nellie relaxed to the occasion. Mrs Dacre and the unnamed Justice of the Peace got quietly drunk together after Sam had made sure the appropriate certificate had been signed and sealed. Kevin took Teresa upstairs and their two-hour honeymoon was spent gently and beautifully and wonderfully together in the marital bed she had made up twice that day.

As arranged, Kevin left on the ship for America just before dawn, but he left a married man. Teresa was ecstatic but resigned. He had promised to come back before long, and that was good enough for her. In their brief hours together, they had laid a solid foundation for a marriage, because it was based on the respect he had shown her in all the years she was growing up. As a settlement, Kevin also gave her fifty pounds, which was all Sam could raise in the time. 'That'll deal with the back porch and Feeney's slate,' Kevin had said with a grin. He also told her he had fixed a job at Cassidy's for her as receptionist/telephonist, now that Nellie ran the place. Sam would look after her as a father. 'And maybe you could keep a wee eye on my mother,' he added softly. Teresa did not go with them to the docks, but saw her mother to bed after they'd got rid of the Justice of the Peace, who by then was beginning to get amorous.

And it was a bright winter's morning before the newly married Mrs O'Neil thought of going back to bed. She was as happy as she had ever been in her life and looked down fondly on the ring Nellie had give her for the ceremony.

'I won't need it again,' her new sister-in-law had said.

'Won't you?' Sam had asked cryptically.

Teresa lay in Kevin's bed, her hands holding the little bouquet of flowers, like Ophelia. But Teresa O'Neil wasn't drowning. She was swimming in a sea of marital content. She slept all that day while Dubliners were reading in their newspapers – 'Cormac Browne, the well known pro-England politician, shot by unknown gunman!'

Francesca Capaldi opened the door to a stranger.

'Is this where Liam Murphy lives?' asked the man.

'Per que?' demanded Francesca in return. She now called herself Frankie Murphy, but her reactions were still Italian in any emergency. And a stranger calling at the door in Manhattan during the winter of 1928 was definitely an emergency. Besides, Liam had always told her to be careful about answering the door, but Frankie's natural curiosity always overcame her sense of caution. In the same way, she always pounced eagerly on the telephone. Frankie Capaldi or Murphy was a natural optimist, and she'd survived thus far because of that.

It was the stranger's turn to be puzzled by the Italian. 'I'm sorry,' he said. 'I was told that he lived here.'

'You speak like Lee.'

'Lee?'

'Lee Murphy. He's my man.' Then he realised that of course she meant Liam. 'Who told you Lee lived here?' The sound of children could be heard from indoors.

'His wife,' said Kevin O'Neil.

'Come in,' said Frankie quickly and she closed the door behind him.

Kevin entered an apartment which showed every sign of there being money in the house. But it also had that glimpse of welcome untidiness and domestic aberration which suggested children: a toy truck lying on its side on the expensive carpet, a paint mark on the superior wallpaper, shoes and jackets lying where they were dropped.

'Lee's still out on business,' said Frankie, ushering him into the sitting-room with its panoramic view of the city, 'but I guess he'll be back soon. He always likes a playtime with the kids.' The kids in question came running in as if on cue. At least two of them. Lucky and Tito. Two typically energetic seven-year-olds, each pulling strongly on a baseball bat.

'It's my turn!' cried one.

'No, it ain't. It's mine! cried the other. One of the boys, Lucky or Luciano, was typically Italianate with black curly hair and a tendency to be plump. But it was the other that made Kevin gasp when he saw him. He was much the leaner of the two, with auburn hair and striking blue eyes – the very image of Noreen! There was something else in him, but Kevin couldn't quite place it at first glance.

'Tell Tito, Mamma! It's my turn. I was pitcher last time.'

'Give me that,' said Frankie. 'It's none of your turns. I told you before not to play baseball in the bedroom. You break the window and I have to go down in the elevator to get the ball.'

It was some time before Frankie achieved order again, and it was only after threatening to use the bat on both of them.

'Sorry about that,' she said to Kevin. 'It's just the kids don't get out too much in winter time.' Kevin was further astonished when both Tito and Lucky ran out of the room again, the best of friends, talking loudly in voluble Italian.

'You want a coffee?' asked Frankie.

'No, thanks,' said Kevin, still shaken by the Noreen he could see in the boy.

'Forty. You there?' Frankie called out suddenly as she went round picking up the shoes and items of clothing. Fortunata, the daughter, came through, a very solemn girl with long straight black hair, and deep dark eyes. She held up a doll over most of her face as she stared up at Kevin. 'They're twins, but they're not identical. Know what I mean? Same father, though. Tito, the red head's not mine. He's Lee's, but one of the family just the same, know what I mean?' Kevin nodded, though he was not sure that he did.

When Liam, or Lee's latch key was heard in the lock, the three children were on to him before he could get properly in the door. This time they were just as voluble in English. The two boys virtually climbed up either side of him, and the little girl hugged him round the knees, effectively pinning him where he was. It was through this curtain of clambering children that Liam Murphy first saw Kevin. He was stunned, to say the least.

'Kevin O'Neil?' Kevin grinned.

'And didn't you used to be Liam Murphy?' The two men shook hands, the Murphy handshake being patently more enthusiastic than the O'Neil response. Once he had shaken the children clear and they had found the candies he had secreted in most of his pockets, he introduced Kevin to Frankie.

'Say, Frankie, this is a friend o' mine from old Ireland. A family friend you might say.' He glanced meaningfully at Kevin as he said this. 'Kevin O'Neil. Kev –' At this familiarity, Kevin's eyebrows raised somewhat. 'This is Frankie, an old friend o' mine.' He chortled as he gave her a hug. Frankie looked at Kevin and smiled, 'A family friend, you might say.'

'Sure,' said Kevin. Frankie shook herself clear.

'Why don't you two guys have a drink while I get dinner? You'll stay for dinner, Mr O'Neil?' Liam laughed.

'Call him Kev. Don't bother with this O'Neil stuff.'

'OK, Kev,' said Frankie easily. 'You want dinner?'

'OK,' said Kevin, prepared to go along with things.

'Great!' she said. 'Lee, you take Kev into the den and give him a drink.'

While Liam poured a very generous whisky, Kevin brought the letter from his pocket.

'What's this?' Liam asked as he handed over the drink.

'A letter from your wife.'

'Oh.' Liam's face was impassive as he took the envelope from his brother-in-law. 'You want I should read it now?' Kevin couldn't get over how American Liam had become. This 'Lee' business was no doubt part of the same transformation. He also saw how fat he had become. The tall, gangling Liam Murphy of Rosstrevor days was now a sleek, balding, spectacled Manhattan fat cat. He read the letter without a comment. At the end, he said, 'You know what it says of course.'

'No, I don't.'

'It was from Nellie, as you said, but it was signed "Helen Cassidy", as she now prefers to be known.' Kevin was genuinely quite surprised. 'It seems my former wife maintains that my desertion for more than a period of ten years constitutes a separation in moral law, if not in legal fact. She therefore wishes to have my written acquiescence to this status so that she can marry a Mr S. Cassidy.' Kevin's eyes widened even further, though he tried not to show it. 'You know this guy?' Liam asked.

Kevin nodded. 'Sure I know him.'

'Well, he's welcome to Nellie, if that's what he wants,' said Liam comfortably. 'New York's no sort o' place for a cookie dame.' At this Kevin felt the familiar chill come down on him, and he carefully put his glass down in front of him.

'You want another?' he said, reaching out his hand to Kevin's glass. Kevin's left hand came down hard on the other man's wrist.

'What the hell –' said Liam.

'Tell me,' asked Kevin icily, 'that kid, Tito. Who was the mother?' Liam went immediately white.

'It was some broad.' Kevin immediately swung Liam's left arm up into a half-Nelson behind his back and grabbed his collar with his right, lifting him up from his seat and running him against the wall. Liam's head hit the wall so hard, his glasses fell off and there was a crunch as Kevin's feet trod on them, but he never moved his eyes from the other's.

'It was some broad alright,' he whispered through clenched teeth. 'It was my sister.'

'No, Kev –' He now had a hold of the man's larynx and was pressing with his thumb and forefinger.

'It was Noreen's, wasn't it? I can see it in the little bastard's face.' Liam's face was going purple and his eyes stood out like pink and white marbles. 'Wasn't it Noreen?' Liam nodded and Kevin let him go.

'But we've given the kid a good home. Nuthin' but the best,' Liam croaked.

'So it was you killed my sister.' With that he grabbed Liam by the lapel, swung him round and belted him with a massive swing to the chin with his right fist. Liam fell over the table, sending the glasses flying and thumping his head against the mock fireplace. He then went and hurriedly picked him up.

'I'm sorry, Liam,' he said, 'or should I say Lee? I forgot to give you special regards from our Nellie.' And with that he belted him again. 'Tell your fancy woman I won't wait for dinner. It would make me sick.' With that he kicked over the table on top of the prostrate Liam and the glass top shattered in pieces. Kevin opened the study door to find Frankie there with the baseball bat upraised. He only managed to sidestep it in time as she brought it crashing down. He pulled the bat from her hand as he pushed her into the study in the direction of her Lee, who was now trying to rise from the debris.

'Oh, Lee, for God's sake,' she cried immediately and rushed to him. Kevin closed the door on them, and turned to find the two boys and the little girl staring up at him. He held the bat between the two boys.

'Here you are, kids. Fight it out amongst yourselves.' Then patting the girl on the head he turned towards the main door. He was just about to leave when he turned back. Lucky was holding the bat triumphantly, but Tito was staring at Kevin. Then he smiled – an impish smile. Just like Noreen's. Kevin gave him a little wave. 'See you, kid!' And left.

*

Kevin was late getting back to Hana's house in Brooklyn. He had been staying there since he arrived in New York. Hana's family were glad to have him as a lodger, and being very experienced in this role, Kevin knew how to keep that finely balanced line between the intimacy of family and the formality of the guest. The children worshipped him, because he was so obviously a younger version of their father and because he was good with them all in their different ways. To young Denny at fourteen, he was a welcome man about the house again. Fifteen-year-old Anna was a little more reserved. She told him pointedly the first night that she didn't like men. He said he quite understood. It was with Clara, however, that he had the strongest bond. She was nearly eighteen and a carbon copy of her mother, and all she wanted to do in life was to become Mrs Bradford Kominsky. As soon as she found out that Kevin's wife was just the same age, she never stopped pestering him about Teresa. Like any man in love with his wife, Kevin was only too happy to talk about her. Hana rather disapproved and was sure that if Teresa's father had been around, he wouldn't have given his permission, and anyway, was a marriage in a sitting-room a proper marriage in the eyes of God? Kevin laughed and said that he and God didn't see eye to eye all that well, but if God wanted us all to be happy, he and Teresa couldn't be happier, and therefore God must be pleased too. Hana wasn't convinced. Shouldn't he have talked to a priest first?

'I don't think so,' Kevin said dryly, 'but I'll tell you what, I'll talk it over with my brother.'

He was as good as his word. And much to the children's regret he left the next morning for Boston. Besides, he thought it advisable to get out of New York rather quickly. Just in case any of Lee Murphy's friends decided to pay him a visit in Brooklyn. He didn't think they would, but just to make sure, he decided to visit Paddy. He had no wish to bring any further trouble to the Brooklyn O'Neils. Anyway, he wanted to hear about Katya and Hana had forbidden her name to be mentioned in the house, so Paddy could do a lot towards bringing him up to date. And anyway, even if he were the newly appointed Auxiliary Bishop to the Diocese of Boston, he was still an O'Neil. He's still my brother, thought Kevin. Or was he? He would soon find out.

It was not Auxiliary Bishop O'Neil who welcomed Kevin into the interview room of the Bishop's House at Boston. It was his brother Paddy. No matter the better quality of clothing, the little touches of velvet, the pink refinement of his features, it was still two brothers who embraced as soon as they were left alone. It was a warm greeting indeed for a Bishop and a gunman.

'And is it business or pleasure brings my baby brother the other side of the water? Tea'll be along in a minute, or would you prefer coffee?'

'Tea'll do.'

'Quite so. Well, there we are,' said Paddy, leaning back. It was touching – the pleasure he had in seeing his young brother again.

'I would say it was more leisure than anything,' said Kevin.

'A chance to get round the family. See everybody again.' Paddy sighed. 'You mean those that are left? D'ye mind the boatload we made at Belfast? It seems a hundred years ago now. You were only a boy then seeing us off at Rosstrevor on the cart, and there's Noreen gone, and now poor Denis, God rest his soul.'

'Aye,' said Kevin. 'Who'll be next I wonder?'

'Now, don't let's be tempting fate, Kevin.' There was a pause as the brothers studied each other.

'How's my mother?' asked the Bishop. Kevin hesitated, uncertain how to answer.

'"In her dotage" is the phrase I think. She's senile.'

'Oh, God love her,' said Paddy. 'But she's a good age.'

'Ay,' said Kevin.

'Is she in care?'

'The best. Nellie's there of course, and my wife.' The phrase came strangely to his lips, but it caused Paddy to grin.

'Of course, you're a married man now. Hana was telling me when she rang to say you were coming. Just a minute.' He rose and went to the desk on the other side of the room and mumbled something on the telephone. He came back and sat down.

'To hell with the tea,' he said in a most unbishop-like way. 'I've ordered a bottle of Jamieson's. It's from the Bishop's own stock. I'm sure he wouldn't mind if I toasted my own brother's wedding. Even if it was without benefit of clergy. Do I know the girl?'

'You might not remember. She was a daughter of the house where I lodged.'

'Oh, yes, I do now – faintly. And her name again?'

'Teresa,' said Kevin, loving the lift the name gave to him.

'Teresa what?'

'O'Neil of course.'

Paddy laughed. 'Of course.'

Just then a nun entered with the bottle and two glasses. She came in so quietly that she might have entered under the door.

'Thank you, sister,' said Paddy in his other voice, and poured two stiff whiskies. 'To Kevin and Teresa O'Neil.'

'God Bless them,' said Kevin.

'Amen!' said the Bishop and they drank. 'And you're enjoying your stay with Hana and the family?'

'I am indeed.'

'Good, you couldn't be with better people. Hana is a saint, and those two girls are angels, though Denny can be a bit of a devil.'

'He just needs a man about the house,' said Kevin.

'True! Tell me, did they talk about Katya?' Paddy asked. 'Her name is not allowed to be mentioned, I understand.' He pursed his lips. 'Yes, it was a terrible business. She came to me, you know, right afterwards.'

'Where is she now?' asked Kevin. Paddy didn't answer, but took another sip of his drink. 'Well?'

'She's under instruction with the Carmelites.'

'She's going to be a nun?'

'God willing.' Kevin was a little taken aback. From one extreme to the other.

'That's Katya. But you didn't know her, did you?'

'No.'

'A lovely girl. Full of life. It was her own decision.'

'Does she know what she's doing?'

'God knows!' replied Paddy. 'And we'd best let them both work it out.'

'If there is a God,' added Kevin. Paddy looked down at his pectoral cross.

'I'll feel very silly if there's not!' He looked up at Kevin and his face was very serious. 'You know, Kevin, the Church may be God-made but it's man-managed, and in that lies both its strength and its weakness. God's given us His commandments and the Church has made its rules, and between them, Catholics can be caught in a pincer that can nip. You understand. But if we are secure in our faith, we can cope with all the little anomalies and contradictions and irritations that go to make Mother Church on earth. We can deal with them, Kevin, because they're man-size, but the things that are not of the earth are God-size, and that's why I say we can leave that to Him. You follow me?' Kevin wasn't sure and only gave the slightest shrug. He was slightly uneasy in recognising that his brother was a genuinely holy man. 'For instance,' Paddy went on, 'the Church in its wisdom will cast a person out for the terrible sin of divorce, if they marry again after taking the sacramental vows of matrimony. It will raise its holy hands in horror at such heinousness, and yet, you know, it will pardon a man for murder, if he makes a good confession.' At this Kevin rose and knelt at his brother's chair.

'Paddy, will you hear my confession?'

Kevin O'Neil limped along the board walk in Atlantic City wondering if he was still in America. He was only a couple of hours from New York, yet both places hardly seemed to be on the same planet. He was far from the concrete canyons now. Here, on one side was an ocean and on the other, row after row of garishly painted, two-storey wooden buildings from which came the new sounds of jazz played by every kind of combination along that two-mile frontage. He was glad to stretch his legs between the trumpets and the sea, and happy to have the chance to think things over. He had much to ponder. He had now been six weeks in the States and he had still no word from Sam, but he had collected his first money from the Chase Manhattan Bank and no questions had been asked. He felt the comfortable bulge of a full wallet in his breast pocket. Not that he really needed it. His family would easily have supported him till he found his feet, but Kevin preferred to be independent. That way he could keep moving.

He smiled when he remembered how he had left Paddy. Poor Paddy. That would give him something to think about. A real tussle of conscience under all that new red velvet. The dilemma was between Paddy, the Bishop, and Paddy, the brother, but underneath it all, he was still the old Paddy. Michael, however, was not the old Michael. He was the biggest shock of all, thought Kevin. Maybe he'd been away too long or something, but he hardly recognised the morose, middle-aged man he'd met last night as the twinkling, easy-going Michael of his youth. Perhaps living alone had changed him. For the first time in more than twenty years he and Sean were not living and working together.

'It's all that bitch Maxine's fault,' Michael had told him over many beers they'd had at his hotel. 'Things haven't been the same at all since that black whore came on the scene. I'm telling you Kevin, she's got Sean wasted so she has. Bewitched him so she has. I don't know why. I never thought sex was that important, but Sean can't get enough of it it seems.'

Michael looked around him dolefully. 'It was her idea to start all this up you know. She talked Sean into it, and you know me, I just go along with things. Although I wasn't too happy about it, I can tell you. We had a good thing going in New York. Sean and me. Yeah, I know they were cracking down on the speakeasies, but we had the linked cellars see, under the old Two by Two and when the raids came we just moved along one, get what I

mean, and the false walls would come down. Cost a lotta dough
to get the system right, but it was worth a lotta dough when it
was working. It was Liam Murphy's dollars did that. But he got
it all back – and some. You were saying you saw Lee Murphy?
I'm sorry you had to duff him up. He wasn't a bad guy. Since
he was living with that Italian woman he seems to have come real
good. Both of them have. Speaking of Italians, we ain't heard no
more from d'Agostino. The word was he'd quit Chicago and had
set up some swell place in Miami. That could mean drugs and that's
a hot game, but he's smart, he'll make sure that it's the other guy's
hands that get dirty. I hear he takes a box every time Maria sings
at the Met.' His tone changed. 'We don't see Maria in the family
these days. She's a big star now. I guess that's what she wanted.'
The wistful note in his voice was pronounced.

Kevin had to steel himself so as not to show any kind of reaction.
All he could remember was that night in the Dacre house in
Dublin. He was glad when Michael went on, 'We sold up at a
good time and I wanted to go legit – you know, straight – with
a restaurant or something – maybe out of town someplace and
Carmella – she was Uncle Mick's wife – could cook, and it would
give Joey, that was her son, he was a little bit slow, know what
I mean? – it would give Joey something to do. But old Auntie
Carmella died in her sleep. They lived out in New Jersey and she
was dead a day and a night it seems before her sister, Rosa, found
her. Poor Joey couldn't figure out why his mother was sleeping so
long, and once things in the icebox had gone down, he went to the
sister's house to get her to come and wake his mother up so she
could cook him a meal. The sister's husband, he was a doctor, I
think, wouldn't have anything to do with Joey and they put him in
a home. Poor Joey, he hasn't had much of a life. It seems the house
was full of gadgets he'd made with Meccano sets. You couldn't
move for the things. Yeah. Poor Joey.' He fell silent again.

Kevin left his older brother sitting, looking down on the
table full of beer bottles, and now he was on his way to the
Mayflower Hotel to meet Sean. It was also a gaming place like
Michael's. But gambling was legal in Atlantic City. It was only
a question of how much you could fiddle on the taxes, and
Michael had assured Kevin that Sean was up to every dodge
there was.

It was by now the middle of the afternoon, but Kevin found Sean
in bed. He was a little taken aback to be shown right in by the old
coloured fellow at the door. He was even more surprised to find
Maxine in bed with Sean. She was older than Kevin had expected,
but even so you could still see she was a siren. She was smoking a

cigarette and her teeth flashed in a broad smile when she saw him at the door.

'Why don't you join us, big man?' she said. 'Keep it all in the family!'

'Shut up!' said Sean as he sat up and threw the covers off. He was completely nude. Kevin turned back into the sitting-room. So this is living, Yankee style, he thought to himself. Sean came out in a few moments wrapped in a dressing gown. He too was smoking. Kevin had never seen Sean smoke. He was also flabbier and had lost that tautness Kevin had always associated with his older brother. But then of course that was a long time ago – now. Sean indicated a seat and offered him a cigarette.

'Drink?'

'No thanks.'

'You don't mind if I do?' Kevin watched as Sean poured himself a bourbon. I suppose it's inevitable, he thought. Heroes rarely last beyond middle age, and Kevin remembered how much Sean had been a hero of his when they were both boys. Sean, for his part, sat with his drink opposite his brother, and was similarly affected by the change he could see. Here was no pimply farm boy. Here was a lithe, well-set man in his mid-forties, with a steel in him that Sean could detect, for he had had it once himself. In this respect they were true brothers. Neither knew what to say at first. Almost thirty years had passed and it was a big jump to make in the middle of an afternoon.

'It's been a long time,' said Sean eventually.

'It has.' Kevin was quite happy to let Sean make the conversational running. He didn't feel as easy as he felt with Michael the night before. There was something he couldn't quite put his finger on.

'What line are you in yourself, Kevin?'

'Insurance.'

'Business good?'

'Good enough to give me a couple of months in America. See the family and that.'

'Business must be good.' They were eyeing each other warily, and not like brothers at all.

'And you?' said Kevin.

'We keep turning a dollar. Maybe insurance is something I could look into.' He laughed. 'We might be able to do some business.' They both laughed, but it was uneasy laughter. It was what was not being said that was disquieting.

'Would you like to try the tables tonight?' asked Sean.

'No thanks, I need all my luck.'

'In insurance?'

'It's a risk business.' The brothers now understood each other, more by inference and intuition, but each knew that the other played for the highest stakes, and they shared the same ruthlessness in achieving their different ends. Sean spoke next.

'And Paddy. You saw Paddy?'

'I did. The same old Paddy,' said Kevin. 'But then he's a Bishop now.'

'Sure, wouldn't that change anyone?' said Sean, suddenly sounding very Irish.

'Not our Paddy,' said Kevin firmly.

'You're staying with Michael?' Sean went on. Kevin nodded. 'Quiet man, Michael. Doesn't say much.' Kevin still didn't say anything. He wanted to shout. 'Come off it Sean. Come off your high horse. You're both kidding yourselves and you don't know it. You're both O'Neils. But you're both strangers to me now.' However, Kevin said nothing of this. Instead he rose up and offered his hand.

'Goodbye, Sean. I won't keep you from your bed.' And walked out quickly past the shuffling old serving man and into the bracing ozone of the boardwalk.

Sean sat for a long time in that armchair, smoking cigarette after cigarette, and staring into space, but only Sean knew what he saw. When Maxine called out from the bedroom, 'You OK, honey?' he never answered.

That night at Michael's place, he and Kevin had a meal together. Michael wanted to talk about the old days and as he did, some of his old sparkle came back. The spark itself had never gone. It had just been dimmed by recent events, and when he and Kevin started to reminisce about their old father and recount some of his exploits at Ingham's Bar, the laughter between the brothers was real and prolonged. But it was cut short by the clang of alarm bells on the street outside, and the wailing of sirens as a fire engine hurtled past. Michael jumped up to the window.

'A fire,' he yelled. 'That's the worst thing that could –' He lifted up the window and looked out. 'It's the risk of spreading,' he was saying as Kevin joined him. They peered along the front to where the smoke was coming from, and there they could see one of the hotels was ablaze. Strangely enough the jazz music was still coming from the night clubs on either side of it.

'Hell's teeth!' yelled Michael suddenly. 'That's Sean's place!'

They both tried to push their way through the crowd that had already gathered outside the Mayflower. The firemen were pouring all the water they could into the building, but it looked a pointless task. It was an inferno. They heard a fireman shout,

'There's a guy in there, but we can't reach him.'

'It must be Sean,' Kevin heard Michael say. 'I've got to get him.'

'Michael!' Kevin tried to grab him, but his brother elbowed him viciously back. The Fire Captain shouted, 'Stop that man!' but Michael had already disappeared through the wall of flame.

The fire raged all night. Just twenty-four hours after his long session with Michael, the smoke was cleared sufficiently to allow Kevin and the Fire Officers to splash their way through the soaking and charred debris. They found Michael with his arms around Sean, as if he had been trying to carry him clear.

'Poor bastards,' muttered a fireman. Kevin turned quickly away. There was no sign of Maxine.

It was more than a year later before Kevin met Liam Murphy again. He made his way as arranged to the twenty-eighth floor of the office block on Fifth Avenue, and there on the glazed door was the proud legend, 'Lee Murphy, INC.'

'What does the "INC " mean?' asked Kevin as he took his seat on the other side of the large desk.

'In the Name o' Christ!' answered Liam with a chortle. 'There's times I don't know what I'm doin', and that's the truth.' The Irishness was so put on that Kevin felt insulted, but guessed it was Liam's idea of a joke.

'You wanted to see me?' he said.

'Yes,' said Liam. 'It's about Sean and Michael. My attorney's finally got things straightened out and with everything and every-one paid off, there's a net total of three hundred and eighty-two grand.'

'Jesus!' said Kevin.

'Sure,' went on Liam. 'They were smart boys, and the insurance on the Mayflower paid up real good. Of course, that's your game too, isn't it?' he said, looking warily at Kevin.

'What?'

'Insurance.'

'Oh, yeah.'

'Yeah, and they still had some real estate here in New York, and I had put them on to some good bonds.' He looked over eagerly at Kevin, leaning forward in his best professional manner. 'And that's what I reckon you should do – for the sake of the family. All summer market prices have been rising, and take it from me, they'll go on rising. The Common Stock Price Index is over the 200 mark and we're now in the third year of a Boom market. You gotta get in on this, Kevin. Now you're a married man, you got responsibilities. You gotta make a dollar while you can. I keep telling all my clients the same. I'm doing the same thing myself. I've sold off all my real estate, and I'm into the market in a big way. If prices hold till Christmas, I'll be a billionaire.'

'And if not?' asked Kevin.

Liam spread his hands. 'It'll be Skid Row, I guess. But I don't even think about that. It's a gamble, but then so's life, and I just play the best odds I can like my old Pappy told me to.' True, Kevin thought, old Eugene Murphy would have been proud of his only son if he could have seen him now behind that big desk in front of that impressive window, skyscrapers rising even as Kevin watched, behind his shoulders. It was Boom time and Liam Murphy was booming. 'What do you say, Kevin?'

'I say I take my share and run. I've got to be out of the country by the end of June.'

'How come?'

'Your Immigration Act. Haven't you heard? National quotas are to be fixed to keep the country's ethnic composition balanced. You better watch it, Liam. They might kick you out next.'

'Never. I owe them too much in taxes.'

'Anyways, I've had my orders. I mean –' This was a slip and one which Liam noticed. His eyes narrowed.

'You mean from your wife?' he said. Kevin grinned.

'You could say that. I'm due in Dublin the last week of June. So I'll take for my mother, and for Nellie and me and leave you to see that Hana is squared up. And something for Joey – Uncle Mick's boy.'

Liam nodded. 'I know Joey.'

'And I guess you'd better give Paddy his share. He might want to build a new Church.'

'I'll see he gets it,' said Liam.

'And Michael, God rest him, would want something to go to Maria. Buy her a few new dresses, and I guess you'd want to put something by for Tito.'

'That's already in hand,' said Liam, almost prissily. Tito was a delicate subject between them and he had no wish to have his spectacles broken again.

'On second thoughts, Liam,' said Kevin, 'just you have your secretary out there –'

'Miss Jacobson.'

'– make out bank drafts for the appropriate shares to Mrs Agnes

O'Neil, Mrs Helen Cassidy, formerly Murphy –' Liam reacted, but said nothing '– Bishop Patrick O'Neil, Mrs Hana O'Neil, Mr Joseph O'Neil, Miss Maria d'Agostino, and last, but by no means least, Mr Kevin O'Neil of Dublin City in the Country of Eire.' Kevin finished the list triumphantly and straightened up. 'With your Tito that makes eight of us in all. That means half of a quarter share each, which means $47,750 each.'

'When did you work that out?'

'It's no big deal.'

'I think it's a very big deal, and I'm not sure I can square it with the banks just like that.'

'You mean, you've got it all out working for you already, don't you?'

'Well, it's my line of business.'

Kevin leaned in again. 'Well, Lee Murphy INC, this is my business. And I'm tellin' you, In the name of Christ, if you don't have those drafts made out exactly three days from now, I'll have you and that fancy desk of yours out of that window behind you.' And Liam knew he wasn't joking.

Kevin O'Neil came back to Dublin a very rich man. His mother of course didn't know him and kept calling him 'the American gentleman'. In his long time away, his urchin wife had developed into a beautifully rounded young woman. With the support she had received from Sam, she had converted her mother's house into a beautiful home all ready for his return. And it was in the new double bedroom there that Kevin and Teresa were happily reunited. Mrs Dacre could now afford to be in an almost continuous stupor, but nobody worried. Nessie was placed in one of the most exclusive homes for the elderly. Cassidy's was refurbished from top to bottom and the Georgian house next door bought as a home for Nellie and Sam, and a substantial contribution made to Dublin Cathedral for perpetual masses to be said for the repose of the souls of Sean and Michael O'Neil, late of Rosstrevor, County Down.

On 24th October, 1929, on a day that would be known thereafter as Black Thursday, thirteen million shares were traded on the New York Stock Exchange. Official trading stopped at three o'clock in the afternoon, but ticker tapes were still recording transactions well into the night. In the Lee Murphy INC office, the tape had gone mad, and Liam was a worried man. He had not been home for a few days and he knew he would have to stay at the desk tonight. It couldn't go on like this. Something had to break the fall. If not, he was ruined. A body flashed past the window. Miss Jacobson, who now had her desk in beside his to deal with the emergency, never even looked up from the typewriter. 'There goes another happy man,' she said.

'That's not funny, Miss Jacobson.'

'Sorry, Mr Murphy,' she answered in a monotone, quite unperturbed. That had been the fourth fall they had seen that day.

'I hope you won't do anything stupid like that, Mr Murphy,' she had said over her lunch sandwich and coffee.

'Don't worry, Miss Jacobson,' Liam had said as he helped himself to something stronger. 'I'll never throw myself out no window.' They had both been working all out to try and stem the awful tide that was sweeping all share values away. Liam suddenly remembered Kevin O'Neil's threat to throw him out of the window. That was only months ago and now his whole world seemed to have turned upside down.

The phone went on his desk. He grabbed at it. It was Frankie. 'No, I'm not coming home,' bellowed Liam into the receiver. 'Not till I'm sure I can pay for the gas in the car.'

'That ain't no way to talk to your wife, Mr Murphy.'

'Why don't you shut up?' he yelled at her.

'And that's no way to talk to your secretary,' answered Miss Jacobson, still in her New York monotone.

At five o'clock on the dot, she left. She always did. She gave her all to Murphy INC from nine till five, but by two minutes past that hour, she was already in her hat and coat and in the elevator. Miss Jacobson had a whole world outside that office building and nothing was going to prevent her getting to it. In their headier, lighter days, Liam had often teased little Miss Jacobson about her private life. She wasn't married. She wasn't pretty, but she was spirited, and he used to wonder how she used up all that vitality in her social life, but she gave him no hint at all, and the mystery remained.

Liam was forced to go home over the weekend, if only to change his suit and get a fresh shirt. He also needed to shave, but most of all, he needed to sleep. And did, all Sunday and most of Monday. He was furious with Frankie for not wakening him.

'I tried to, but you wouldn't waken, so I guess you needed it.' She had tried to question him about his difficulties, but he wouldn't tell her anything. All he would say was he had put the house in her name, and there was some money in Ruffiano's restaurant. Roberto would explain.

'Explain what?' asked Frankie.

'Don't bother me now, woman,' he shouted and went back into the bedroom.

He was at his office again before six o'clock on the Tuesday morning, and had a day's work done before Miss Jacobson came in at nine.

'What happened to you yesterday?' she said.

'I took a day off, do ya mind?'

'I don't mind. 'S your business.'

'You're too right, it is,' he said, looking gloomily at the reports in front of him.

Black Tuesday, 29th October, was to be the worst day in American market history. Sixteen million shares were sold and all at declining prices. Billions worth of stock were wiped out in hours, and more than one lifetime's fortune was lost. The skyscrapers around Wall Street rained bodies. The Great Depression had begun.

It hung particularly heavily over Liam Murphy, as he slumped behind his desk at one minute to five.

'Will there be anything else, Mr Murphy?' He looked up at her, his eyes red with fatigue and stress.

'You know, Miss Jacobson, I can't think of another thing.'

'Then I'll wish you good night, Mr Murphy.'

'Good night, Miss Jacobson.'

'See you in the morning, then,' she said as she pattered to the door. Liam didn't answer. The telephone rang on his desk, and he didn't answer that either. He had given up. After a few moments, it gave up too, and the office became silent. The ticker tape machine sat there with one shred of paper remaining as if it were its tongue hanging out, as if it had collapsed from exhaustion. He took the telephone off the hook and let it lie on the desk. It could sleep too for a while. He started to tidy things up and put things away. But then as he stood with two wire trays full of paper in his hands, he thought, what the hell, and let them drop to the floor. He moved to the window and looked out. He looked out at all the other lights in all the other offices and all the other men with a telephone at each ear, a pencil in each hand, adding up, subtracting, taking away the number they first thought of. What was it all about? What did it all matter? It wasn't even real money. It was paper. Bits of paper that passed from hand to hand, making a few cents here and there, as they went, building up into dollars, making the dollars into millions, while the balloon went up. But now the balloon had burst, and he wasn't worth a nickel.

He opened the window and the gust of air blew all the papers from his desk. He never even looked round. Faint noises could be heard from the street miles below. He looked down. Was he just one of those ants he saw crawling on the sidewalks? Any one of them was better off than him now. 'Are you there, Miss Jacobson?' he called out. He was getting dizzy looking down and he could hear the dance band playing on some wireless somewhere, 'Anything Goes'. Heaven knows, it goes alright, he thought. Now, it's gone. To hell with it, he said again. And closed the window.

He didn't know what time it was as he went down in the lift. All he knew was that he was alone. Even the lift boy had gone home. When he came out into the vestibule, everyone had gone and the main door was lying wide open. And Frankie was standing there.

'What are you doing?' he growled in surprise.

'I was worried about you. I came to take you home.'

'But I always go home on the subway,' he said.

'But I brought the car.'

'Why'd you do that?'

'I dunno. I just thought it would be nice if I take you home.'

They said nothing as they made their way round to the back of the building where Frankie had parked the car on the lot. She was driving. They were making their way along Roosevelt Drive, when Liam suddenly said very quickly, 'Stop the car.'

'What?'

'Stop the car!' They'd gone on a few blocks before she yielded to his insistence and brought the car to a halt at the kerb. 'Now, get out,' he said quietly. 'GET OUT!' he almost screamed.

'Lee, what's the matter with you?' She was crying by now. He reached across her and pushed the door open.

'Just get out of the goddamned car, will you?' He began to push her, the engine was still revving, and some passers-by were staring at them. He pushed her so hard that she fell on to the sidewalk. She could only pick herself up and stare after him as the car sped off at high speed along the dockside and straight into the East River.

INTERLUDE THREE

'Get your coat and get your hat,
Leave your worries on the doorstep
Just direct your feet
To the Sunny Side of the Street . . . .'

The hit song of 1930 might have been the theme song for the next seven years. It was an age when every man wore a soft hat, or at least a flat cap, and a very anxious expression beneath it. There were worries on nearly everybody's doorstep and millions of feet were directed to dole queues, soup kitchens and hunger marches. What had happened on Wall Street between Thursday and Tuesday of that black week in October 1929 reverberated around the world and brought the whole financial façade down like the pack of cards it really was. The credit veneer was found to be paper-thin, banks went bust, industries foundered, and, as always, when the top of the pyramid collapses, it gathered momentum and became an avalanche. Those at the bottom felt it most. The failure of the money market to manage its own affairs had repercussions greater than the collapse of mere usury. Not only corporations tottered in bankruptcy; whole regions, countries were stripped of their means to continue their traditional way of life, great cities virtually ground to a standstill; families were broken up because the father could no longer feed his children.

Yet such is the irony of the human situation, in whatever age, it was an undeniable fact that while millions starved there were many thousands on the sunny side of the street and they were making sure that they weren't going to be crowded off the sidewalk. These were the non-investors, the cash-in-hand transactors, the land grabbers and the money-lenders. Similarly, the aristocracies in Europe survived because their income was rent-based and when tenants couldn't pay in cash they could always pay in kind. This was the old way to get rich. The new way was to become a film star.

Which is exactly what Maria d'Agostino did. She had, in a sense,

523

become her father's hobby during the Depression years. Having been denied a son, he was making sure he would not lose a daughter and he resorted to any and every means to win her affection. Her love, he wasn't sure of yet and, in any case, Maria d'Agostino did not love easily. Except herself of course. She showered herself with affection and love. Her love affair with herself was one of the great amours of the age! Nobody really minded this self-centred pampering because her talent was vast and undeniable. She could sing, and for that she was forgiven much. Rico d'Agostino, as always, kept himself very much in the background, but he worked in his own way to make sure that Maria's way to the top was kept clear of any obstacles. And where he could help in terms of contacts, personal pressure, press publicity or plain cash – he helped. Maria really had no option but to succeed – and now Hollywood beckoned.

When Al Jolson had given voice to the silent film in 'The Jazz Singer' the year before, the noise he made was heard world-wide and everyone now wanted to 'hear' movies. The demand for voices was such that a whole generation of British actor-gentlemen became landed plutocrats in California because they could talk in the Talkies. Similarly, the musical film was the vogue and singers with looks and a waistline were at a premium. Maria d'Agostino had both. So, in the company of Vernon Drake, critic, musicologist and covert homosexual, she left New York after a spectacular 'Tosca' at the Met and took the famous Sunset Express to Los Angeles and the first year of a lucrative seven-year contract in Hollywood. It was more than three thousand miles across America, that train ride into riches and fame, and Rico saw that the story got nearly as much mileage in the State-wide press. She was twenty-eight years of age, not even near her prime, and this was why Maria sped through the dust-bowl of middle America without even noticing what was going on all around her. When you are in a luxury Pullman there's no need to look out.

Throughout 1930, with prices falling, unemployment rising and the national income collapsing, the United States of America took refuge in the United Artists of Hollywood. All may have been panic on the Stock Exchanges of the world but it was 'All Quiet On the Western Front' as far as the world of cinema was concerned. As if to counterbalance the effects of Depression the general public rushed headlong into the cheap, movie houses where they could escape their hunger for an hour and forget their joblessness. Uncle Oscar vied with Uncle Sam in his avuncular regard for the ordinary people, not only of America but of the whole English-speaking world. Especially that part of it that was still known in name, if not fact, as the British Empire. Mary Pickford was as popular in East Gore, New Zealand, as she was in East Northport, New York. Charlie Chaplain was as valid in Paddington, Sydney, as in Paddington, London. The entire globe was festooned in celluloid and up to its eyes in discarded banknotes. It kept its eyes on the film stars, and didn't look down to where its own feet were shuffling along in worn out shoes. Not everyone could ride in the Pullman. Most had to ride the rails under the freight car.

> 'Once I built a railroad,
> Made it run,
> Made it run against time,
> Once I built a railroad,
> Now it's done,
> Buddy, can you spare a dime?'

A few, however, had dimes to spare, and one such fortunate was Jim Keith in East Gore. Thanks to good soil, good man-management and good luck, Jim and Billy Keith had a splendid harvest that year and Billy chose to celebrate it by marrying Belinda Jackson. Annabel had been long resigned to losing her great passion to her young sister, and reluctantly agreed to be bridesmaid. The choice of best man aroused a great deal of curiosity in the district, for Billy had asked his cousin, Abel Keith, to come over from Sydney and bring his half-sister, Becky, with him. The twins, Kenny and Jamie, found this of great interest. Which half of her would he be bringing? Kenny had asked. Sudden stepsisters in any family are a problem to eleven-year olds. But this date was fixed and no world-wide depression was going to spoil it. Its impact, however, prevented Bobby coming. He had his hands full with so many hands idle. This particularly disappointed Gran Keith. But the great news was that Rachel had a sabbatical time from the university and would be chaperoning her son and new daughter to the festivities. Becky had delighted Bobby from the beginning. Her poise and independence even impressed Abel, and thanks to the good relationship she had already developed with Rachel, she now had a very good job with the Harbour Hotel, one of the best in Sydney. Her father was very proud of her indeed, and saw her as much as possible. Becky herself was looking forward to meeting the New Zealand Keiths. Preparations there were reaching a final stage. Only Gran Keith tried to remain aloof from it all.

'You'd think no one had ever been married before,' she grumbled. 'Spending all this money on a wedding, when there are folk haven't tuppence to make a meal.' As always with Gran Keith, there was a grain of truth in much of her chaff.

For in the Mackenzie household at Edendale, there was more anxiety than excitement on several counts. First of all, because Bruce and his boys had been as unlucky as Jim and Billy had been fortunate. Due to particularly heavy rains, they hadn't got their harvest in as early as they should have done, and by the time they did, prices had hit rock bottom, and they couldn't make a sale. Because they couldn't make a sale, they couldn't make the bank payments, and because they couldn't make the bank payments, the bank foreclosed on the property. Tina had begged Bruce to ring Jim and ask for help – even a loan on the year's mortgage, but Bruce had been too proud to make such a call, and besides he didn't want to tell Tina he was two years behind with the payments, not one. He had taken the risk of getting a good year in, but then the rains came. Bruce was a worried man. He was also worried for his wife, because he knew she worried for Sandy. He had wanted to marry his long-time sweetheart, Susan Reed. They'd had an understanding from their schooldays, but because of his father's critical financial position, Sandy hadn't the heart to saddle him with a wedding. Mr Reed, Susan's father, was in much the same position at his place, and Susan and Sandy were asked to wait a while. Like good kids, they said they would, but like good healthy young people in love, they couldn't avoid the inevitable and Susan had given birth to Sandy's child, Laura, just before Christmas 1929. She had to come to Edendale to have it, as old man Reed wouldn't have her in the house, and now Sandy was refusing to go up to the wedding as he didn't want to be part of 'them stuck-up Keiths'. Sandy's resentment was understandable, and despite all his mother's pleadings, he firmly held to his intention not to attend.

'Anyway, we can't leave Laura,' he said.

Young Chris was also adamant that she didn't want to go. At fourteen, she was ideal nursery-maid age and had already virtually adopted baby Laura as her own. Tina insisted that she couldn't go without her, so reluctantly young Chris had agreed. Bruce wondered how he'd find the money to get them there. The car had gone the way of all flesh some months before. Even the bikes had been sold, and during their last quarter on the farm, they had only a cart and two horses. Bruce had managed to get his three men unemployment relief, which they were most reluctant to take.

'We don't want their bloody charity, boss.'

'Listen, you jokers,' Bruce had said, 'you're only getting back what I pay in taxes, so take the money and get on with it.' They had.

What with one thing and another, Tina hadn't been really too well and sneaked in a visit to the doctor without letting Bruce know. Dr Rutherford didn't seem to be too worried. 'With what you've got on your plate at the moment, I'm not surprised you're feeling crook. You do too much. However, you are a bit peaky. Let me take some of your blood and I'll send it to the blokes in Invercargill for them to have a look. I'll let you know. Meantime, there's some iron pills if you can remember to take them.'

All sorts of things were happening around the world. And out of it. The planet Pluto had been discovered. The atomic cyclotron had been perfected. Frank Whittle, an aeronautical engineer, had invented the first jet-propelled engine, and William Beebe had made the first successful deep sea dive in a bathosphere. It was the year of T.S. Eliot's 'Ash Wednesday', Noel Coward's *Private Lives* and John Maynard Keynes' *Treatise on Money*. Le Corbusier had made his first house as 'a machine to be lived in', but as far as the Keiths and the Mackenzies were concerned, the big event was to be the wedding of William Keith to Belinda Jackson.

It was only a matter of weeks to go. All the plans had been made, the travel arrangements settled, the beds sorted, the presents wrapped, when Dr Rutherford called unexpectedly at the house. It was late in the afternoon and young Chris was practising the Chopin 'Impromptu' that was to be her showpiece for the wedding. The doctor was amazed at the young girl's talent, and insisted she play it through again for him. But then he asked to speak to Bruce and Tina alone. Chris was glad to jump up and go in search of Laura, who had just started crying.

'None of the boys about?' asked the doctor gravely. Bruce told him that Sandy had them out tightening up on the fencing and white painting some of the posts.

'Part of the sale agreement,' he said glumly. The doctor nodded.

'They're hard times, Dr Rutherford,' Bruce had said.

'And likely to get harder, Bruce.' Bruce remembered for the rest of his life how the doctor had looked at Tina.

'You're fifty-one, Tina,' he'd said. She nodded. 'Yes,' he went on. 'That's what I thought.'

'You've had news back from Invercargill, Doctor?' It was Tina herself who asked.

'What news?' Bruce had asked puzzled. Doctor Rutherford continued to look at Tina.

'Your wife has cancer, Bruce. Of the severest kind, and I'm afraid it is likely to be fatal.' Bruce had only stared at the doctor. But Tina herself had been remarkably calm.

'How long, doctor?'

'Three weeks.'

No one said anything for a long time, then Tina had whispered, 'Oh, I'm going to miss the wedding!'

So, while Billy Keith wed his wife, Bruce Mackenzie mourned his. The guests who had come early for the wedding also attended a funeral. Becky Friar did get to meet her other cousins, but it was a sombre first meeting. Rachel Keith did get to see her old friend Tina again, but when she did, it was in her coffin. However, as sometimes happens at an occasion like this, Tina at fifty-one years of age, looked young again in death. And Rachel had no difficulty in seeing again the eager young Scots girl she had known on the voyage. 'Sleep well, Tina,' she had whispered. 'Your long journey's over now.' Bruce sat in his big chair being comforted by Chris. Her journey was just beginning.

Throughout 1931 the depression deepened and spread throughout the world. Austria and Germany went bankrupt and Britain went off the Gold Standard resulting in another run on the banks. There were now nearly five million unemployed in the United States and unemployment led to rioting in the streets in Glasgow and London. American Hunger Marchers walked on the White House in Washington with a petition for President Hoover, but were turned away by Marine bullets. King Alfonso fled from Spain and a republic was established. Mao Tse-tung formed the first Chinese Soviet republic and the League of Nations condemned Japanese aggression in Manchuria. Ramsay Macdonald formed the first Coalition Government to cope with the worsening financial crisis and after many revisions, the Statute of Westminster was passed giving autonomy to the dominions within the British Commonwealth. This had little effect in Australia where they were going their own way in any case. The Scullin Labour Government, which had the vigorous support of Bobby Keith, fell to the United Australia Party which counted Abel Keith among its supporters. Once again, words flew and tempers rose across the dinner table and Abel had to take refuge with Becky in the Harbour Hotel until Rachel had cooled down his father again. To celebrate his degree, Becky gave Abel the gift of his first flying lesson.

In New Zealand, there was an earthquake in Hawke's Bay with the loss of 255 lives and massive destruction in Napier and Hastings. Big Bruce Mackenzie had been in that area only the week before working at Havelock North. He and the boys were working as 'sandbaggers' – men who had all their possessions in a sack or sandbag, hitch-hiking around New Zealand looking for work wherever they could find it. Any kind of work – shearers, rabbiters, wood-cutters, labouring on the railway or on the roads, or even as casual barmen on occasion. The boys liked that best. No money but as much beer as they could drink. That was at Blenheim before the landlord went bust and they got good work on the railways again, mending track all the way up the West Coast and this got them their passage across the Cook Strait to the North Island. Like many other New Zealand families, the Mackenzies operated as a team. In their case, three men. In this way, if one of them got something in the day, all three could eat. If all three worked, then they could even save for the bad days. In a good week, something could even be sent back to Edendale where Sandy and Susan were trying to hold on to a two-acre field of pumpkins while Susan was expecting a brother or sister for Laura. Chris had gone to live with Uncle Jim and Auntie Jean on Tina's death and she and her cousin Berta had struck up an instant friendship, despite the fact that there was an eight-year gap in their ages. Berta, because of her delicate health and tendency to asthma, had never worked and had employed herself as part-time bookkeeper to her father, and part-time companion to her querulous old grandmother. The impact of the effervescent Chris on this comparatively quiet household was enormous and on Berta in particular.

The tall, flaxen-haired sporting girl won all hearts, and all eyes. Even at fifteen, she was pleasingly shapely. But it was her remarkable piano playing that attracted all the attention. Her Uncle Jim's especially. He loved her to play the old songs, and he and his mother would sit on the verandah at night, listening in the dark as Chris played to them after dinner. She could play anything as far as they were concerned, except Irish songs.

'I don't like Irish songs,' Gran Keith told her. 'Your grandfather hated the Irish.'

'Why?' said Chris.

'Because they were all Catholics.' It seemed a strange reason to Chris for hating anybody. But then she thought for a minute and realised she had never met any Catholics. Her playing standard had now reached such a level that she had outgrown her old piano teacher, and went every Saturday to Invercargill, where she had a whole afternoon of special tuition from a nun who had once trained to be a concert pianist. She didn't dare tell her Gran. Berta always went with her, not only as a companion for the journey, but so that they could have tea out together and go to the cinema, which was their weekly treat. *Cimarron* with Richard Dix was their favourite that year. The year ended with the birth of Trevor to Belinda Keith (née Jackson), which in no way softened the disappointment Susan Reed felt at her own miscarriage and only added another little chip to Sandy's growing bitterness.

1932 opened with the marriage of Clara O'Neil and Brad Kominsky. Her patience had paid off and he had finally given in. Anna was a reluctant bridesmaid. She was still not sure of men, but when Brad produced his workmate, Scott Halliday, as his best man she changed her mind. Bishop O'Neil was not free to perform the ceremony, because of pressure of work, so Canon Donnelly obliged. Denny, now a lanky nineteen-year-old student at Fordham University, made his mark on the day by being booked for speeding when driving the bride to the church. He was so angry that he carelessly took a left at one intersection and rammed the side of a saloon car. An altercation followed from which Denny got a black eye. It was a tearful and relieved Clara who eventually arrived at St Bride's, where her brother gave her away at the altar with a closed left eye and a handkerchief held to his nose. The young wedding party, comprising Clara and Brad, Anna and Scott, plus Denny and his latest girlfriend, whom he didn't even bother to introduce, spent the afternoon of the wedding day visiting the Empire State Building, which had opened in the previous year. They went to the top of its 102 stories and looked down on the city from more than a thousand feet. At night they saw 'Grand Hotel' with Greta Garbo, before they all saw Brad and Clara off to Niagara Falls.

While they were away, US veterans began to arrive in Washington DC, where 17,000 of them set up camp to press their demand to be allowed to cash their bonus certificates from the First World War. They became known as the Bonus Army. Despite police attempts to remove them, they remained there until the end of July when troops, led by General McArthur, assisted by Major Dwight D. Eisenhower, forcibly evicted their former comrades-in-arms. This didn't do President Hoover's image much good, and at the end of the year he lost the Presidential election to Franklin Delano Roosevelt by a landslide. The National Socialists won the election in Germany, and Adolf Hitler emerged as the new German hope. The Lindbergh baby was kidnapped, and a ransom of $50,000 was demanded. The sum was paid, but the child was found dead.

Trevor Keith's little sister was born in 1933, and grandfather Jim celebrated the event by buying a new record for his gramaphone collection. It was of Maria d'Agostino singing her favourite operatic arias. Jim had always liked Maria d'Agostino since he first saw her films in Gore. Old Gran liked the new record as well, even though Jim pointed out that with a name like that she was bound to be Catholic. Most Italians were.

'But that's different,' Gran had insisted. 'They're foreigners!' Her chauvinistic attitudes were further appeased when a British film called *Cavalcade* won the 1933 Academy Award.

Civil War broke out in Spain, and Adolf Hitler became Chancellor of Germany. In the Dail, the Irish Government under Mr De Valera abolished the Loyalty Oath to the British Crown, and Kevin O'Neil, father of two, was re-commissioned in the IRA as a Major. Earlier that year a motion had come before the Oxford Union, 'that this house will in no circumstances fight for its King and country'. It was carried by 275 votes to 153. The year ended with the 21st Amendment to the Constitution of the United States, which repealed Prohibition, thus ending what its supporters still called 'the noble experiment'.

1934 saw the gradual build up of Fascist power in Italy and Spain and Nazi power in Germany. But all that was built up in the United States was dust, as a severe dust storm lifted an estimated 300,000,000 tons of top soil from Oklahoma and other middle states and blew it all the way to the Atlantic Ocean. In Yugoslavia, a Macedonian revolutionary assassinated King Alexander and the Act stirred the threat of war in Europe. People had not forgotten Sarajevo. But what startled the world out of its economic preoccupation was the discovery that Clark Gable didn't wear an undervest in *It Happened One Night*, the year's hit picture. When he stripped off his shirt to accommodate Claudette Colbert, audiences gasped at his hairy chest and sales of male underwear plummetted around the world. The Dionne quinns were born in Ontario, Canada, and were adopted by the entire world. And in New Zealand, Belinda Keith was expecting her third child, Sarah, born in February 1935.

This time grandfather Jim marked the event and his impending sixtieth birthday by giving Billy and the twins third shares in the farm, and with the endowment insurance, he made out a Christina Keith bequest, by which he and his mother made allowances over to each of Tina's four children. This allowed Bruce Mackenzie to keep his pride and accept funds on behalf of his children. This let Sandy extend the pumpkin farm, and brought Bruce back to Edendale to work on it with him. Stu and Ross elected to stay in the North Island as they liked their itinerant life in the sun and had eyes on Auckland. They had been made too restless by their lifestyle during the Depression, and anyway with Savage in as the first Labour Prime Minister they thought things could only get better now, and there might be a good life to be had in the Bay of

Islands. For her part, Chris used her bequest to move to Dunedin, where she enrolled at the University of Otago as a music student. Her prowess at games would also be well utilised. The only snag was Berta. She was devastated at losing her younger companion, and this brought on another bad asthma attack. Her father tried to propitiate her by promising her she could visit Chris in Dunedin whenever she liked. The fact was Roberta Keith was in love with her young cousin and didn't know what to do about it. She was a very young twenty-eight-year-old indeed. And this was her first emotional experience of any kind. Chris, of course, was completely unaware of this. Her sights were firmly set on university.

The Seven Year War on world recession was almost over, and another kind of war was being prepared for behind the scenes. Despite the famous Oxford motion and the continued agitation of the League of Nations and the overwhelming result of the Peace Ballot, nations were building up arms again, especially Germany. The Nazis had also begun their persecution of the Jews. Rachel Keith in Sydney had her first refugee family for a stay, the first of many. Italy invaded Ethiopia, and King George was ousted from Greece. An earthquake in India left 60,000 people dead, and President Roosevelt signed the Social Security Act. The Act established a system of Unemployment Insurance and Retirement Pensions, which would ensure that the hungry millions would not walk on Washington again. Benny Goodman and his Band opened at the Congress Hotel in Chicago and the Jazz Age gave way to the Age of Swing. Anna O'Neil married Scott Halliday in 1935 – 'to stop him from going on proposing to me', she said.

Denis O'Neil III graduated Master of Arts in Journalism from Fordham University in 1936.

The story continues . . .

THIRTY-THREE

'Gaudeamus igitur,
juvenes dum summus'

The strains of Brahms' 'Academic Overture' tentatively vocalised
by the Graduate class of 1936, none of whom could be described
honestly as a Latin scholar, filled the main hall and auditorium at
Fordham University, where Denny O'Neil received his Masters in
Journalism. Whatever he was going to do in his career, Denny had
been voted 'the boy most likely to' by his fellow students in his
Sophomore year. The trouble was Denny himself was not of this
opinion. He was well above average intelligence, but was careless
in his studies. A swimmer of national status, who had already won
many inter-collegiate and university titles, he found training a
bore. He was a replica of his father when young, with even an
extra ration of the O'Neil charm, yet was totally promiscuous
in his friendships, already notorious among the girls. He was the
despair of his Archbishop uncle in that he seldom went to church.
But all of these faults and all the exasperation and annoyance he
caused colleagues, mentors and close friends alike, all this was as
nothing when compared to the idolisation he received within his
own family.

Hana was convinced no finer son had ever been born, and
showered him not only with love, but with every conceivable
material assistance. What stopped him from being utterly spoiled
was the attitude of both his married sisters who constantly teased
him about being a 'Mama's boy', and the sensitive relationship he
had with his nun sister, Katya, whom he visited regularly. Denny
never spoke much of these visits, and no one ever asked him. His
mother still pretended that Katya had never existed.

Hana's gift to her son on his graduation was a gleaming new Ford
sports convertible with foldback sun roof and two-tone horn. It
was hard to see who was the more delighted, Denny on receiving
it, or Hana on giving it. Like any young boy growing up with
a loving mother, he took her entirely for granted, but was not

533

without the sudden gestures of love towards her that took her aback, and were ample rewards for her doting. Denny O'Neil even as an adolescent was not afraid to put his arms around his mother and give her a big hug and tell her that he loved her. For her part, she was happy to see her son develop as an animated version of her former Irish husband. The same black hair, the same green eyes, the same rogue's grin, the same propensity for all sports, but unlike his father, Denny had Hana's Bohemian depths. This was something he shared with his sister, Katya, and perhaps this underlay the reasons for his visits to her.

This particular Sunday, he had difficulty in getting away from the house. As usual, his mother was persuading him to go to Mass with her, and as usual, he was coming up with some kind of excuse for not doing so. It was always easy to talk his mother round, but this Sunday she was more than usually adamant.

'I think it's good that thanks you should give,' she said. 'You got the good education now, you got the new car, thanks to your uncles and the money they give for your poor Pops.' Hana had never touched the money when she received the cheque from the Lee Murphy office. It was such a huge amount, she was convinced there was something wrong and wouldn't touch a cent of it for months. It was only when her daughters persuaded her to use it for their father's sake that Hana relented. She had never been sure of Sean and Michael and their shadowy activities in New York and Atlantic City. She liked them well enough as men and as her husband's brothers, especially Michael. Sean was always too quiet for her liking, but she knew Denis had been worried about them and that made her uneasy. However, Clara and Anna worked on her until she agreed to spend it on them as her children, if not on herself. So two fine weddings had been paid for and two apartments had been bought and now Denis had his car. There was enough left to pay for a visit home to Czechoslovakia for her, but Hana wasn't so sure. Things were not so good there, she thought. 'And that man Hitler – I don't think he's up to no good,' she said. Denny was keen that she should go. That meant he could go as well.

Meantime, he had to go to Mass. As the parishioners spilled out of St Bride's that Sunday at noon, Denny's new car was the centre of admiration. He just wished they wouldn't admire it so much – all those hands touching the bodywork, feet kicking at the wheels, but he sat, pretending an air of indifference as his mother greeted this friend and that, finally finding her way to the passenger seat.

'Everybody says I should go lunch with them,' she panted between breaths as she climbed into the sleek roadster. 'But I say I make special lunch for my son because he's a Master now!'

'Oh, Mama!' groaned Denny. But his expostulation was drowned in the roar of the exhaust. This scattered the crowd around them, who all shouted in fright and glee as Denny sped off.

'Denny, you go too fast!' said his mother, as she clutched at the dashboard. But her son only laughed and put his foot on the accelerator.

Uncle Frantisek joined them with his Slavonic brood. Denny had never been very relaxed with his Czech uncle, who laughed and nodded at everything when he was sober, and only laughed when he was drunk. It was a horrible laugh and it embarrassed everybody. His wife was Polish and never said much, and one or other of the two children always seemed to be ill. As usual, Clara and Brad came round with little Harold who was only months old, and Anna and Scott came with their Kim, who was a few weeks younger. Denny always found it funny to see his two sisters sitting and swopping baby stories like two old mother hens. It was all that Clara had ever wanted, but it was the last thing Anna had wanted, and here she was, drooling like the rest of them over her Kim. Luckily Brad and Scott were nearly always there and he could have a beer with them in the den to talk about the ball game and chew the fat generally.

This Sunday lunch was a continuing family convention with the O'Neils, just as Nessie and Old Den had done the same thing in Ireland, so Uncle Mick and Auntie Carmella had done the same on 57th street, and Hana and Denis carried the tradition on. Even with Pops gone, Hana had kept it up and now here they were all round the table again on another Sunday. Denis was impatient. He wanted to get away. He had a date. But the talk had got round to his mother's taking in lodgers now that there was only Denis and her in the big house. But Hana wasn't keen on that either.

'Why should I all that work have?' she pointed out. 'It isn't dollars we need.'

'But it would be company for you, Mama,' said Clara.

'I got company. I got my records.' Hana had by now an extensive collection of gramaphone records, mainly classical, although at this very moment, Bing Crosby was singing 'Red Sails in the Sunset'. Anna suggested that Frantisek and his family should come and fill the empty rooms. He was still out of work and he could do all the jobs around the house that Denny was supposed to do.

'Could you imagine our Denny with a hammer in his hand?' asked Anna. Both sisters laughed. And so did Frantisek, making ludicrous banging noises on the table, repeating loudly as he did so.

'Denny and hammer! Denny and hammer! Ha, ha!'

Denny knew he had to leave before he got involved in all this.

He rose from his place, went to his Mama, gave her a quick peck on the cheek, 'See you later, Mama.' And before she could reply, he was off.

It hadn't been easy getting away. There was the usual crowd round the car,

'You gonna play for the Dodgers, Denny?' called one boy.

'Naw, he's gonna play for the Giants, ya mug!' called another.

'What about Joe Louis? Could you lick him?' cried a further.

'Denny O'Neil could lick anybody!' was the instant retort from someone. Everybody cheered. 'See ya, fellas!' Grinning and waving, he roared off down the middle of the street. He was soon over the bridges and speeding along the new freeway. The new car responded brilliantly to his slightest touch with Denny singing and laughing as he flew along with the wind in his face and the sun on his neck. This was the life. Studies over, his own car, the road ahead and dollars in his pocket. What more could a guy want? Nothing in the world, thought Denny. Except perhaps –? But that could wait for a bit yet. Today was today and it stretched as far as Orangeburg. All was well with Denny O'Neil's world as he purred in his new car through New York – through Ridgefield, where his Uncle Joey lived in a home for the mentally handicapped. Denny had never seen him for years. Nor frankly was he all that keen to see him now. Well, at least not today. He patted the dashboard of the car. 'You did great, baby!'

He grabbed the little bag from the jump seat behind him, and ran up the steps three at a time. The Convent of the Sisters of Mercy stood in its own grounds well off the main road. It was a large colonial type house that belonged in the days of eighteenth century Orangeburg and was still imposing, despite all its modern additions and extensions. A sister came to the door and let him in.

'Hi!' said Denny, but the young sister only smiled and lowered her eyes and motioned him to wait.

'Hi!' But this time the greeting was from his sister, Katya, now Sister Mary Josephine. She came as eagerly towards him as her robes would allow, and brother and sister embraced warmly.

'Always on time, Denny,' said Katya.

'That's right, Sister.' He always enjoyed the felicity of calling his sister, 'Sister'.

'I was late getting away but sure made up the time in my new car.'

'So you got it?'

'Sure did. You wanna come see it?' Sister Josephine smiled.

'No thanks. Why should I waste time admiring a piece of machinery when I could be admiring my kid brother?'

'What am I but a piece of biological machinery? Except that I don't run on gas.' He laughed.

'Don't you?' asked the nun slyly. And they both laughed again.

They had a very easy relationship, this brother and sister, and each looked forward – Denny, perhaps more than Katya – to this hour-long conversation on the first Sunday of every month. Denny had first come out of curiosity and then out of a sort of obligation, but now he came because he wanted to and because he needed to. Katya O'Neil in transforming herself to Sister Mary Josephine had made a happy transmutation which preserved the spirit and vitality of Katya, but over it she had veiled a serenity and calm, so the combination was potent to say the least. Denny found his older sister charming and responsive, intelligent and sympathetic, but best of all, she was still good fun.

'No, Denny,' Katya was saying, 'your particular machine runs on another kind of spirit, I think.'

'Now, don't give me all that holy stuff, Sister,' he said mockingly.

'I would never dream of it,' she said. 'I'll leave that to Saint Jude,' she said.

'Saint Jude?'

'He's the patron saint of Hopeless Cases.' By this time they had reached the end of the corridor which led out into the rose garden where they had their usual seat. It was quite secluded and was intended for quiet contemplation in the scented air of the garden, but for Denny and Katya it was their favourite talking spot. As soon as they had sat down, Denny lifted up his bag to his knee and produced a large bottle of Coca Cola. He swiftly unscrewed the cork and handed it to his sister, who took the first swig.

'Ah!' She licked her lips in satisfaction and handed it back to her brother. 'If Mother could see me now,' she said. She was of course meaning her Superior in the Convent, but it gave Denny an odd kind of feeling.

'You always say that,' he said.

'And you always say that I always say that,' she answered.

'This is hardly the conversation worthy of a Master of Arts,' continued Denny in his best academic tones. Katya nearly choked on her Coca Cola,

'Denny!' she spluttered. 'It was your graduation.'

'Certainly was,' he grinned. 'Hence the new car.'

'I see. Well, congratulations on both counts.'

'Thank you.' She handed back the bottle, almost empty.

'And thank you for my monthly gargle,' she said. 'It makes me feel so wicked.'

'Good,' said her brother, 'I'll have some.' And he drank the last of it in a gulp. 'That's better.' He put the bottle away in the bag and brought out his degree certificate all neatly rolled in its red ribbon. Proudly, he displayed it to his sister.

'Wow!' she exclaimed. She took it and examined it closely.

'It's more yours than mine,' said Denny.

'Nonsense.'

'Isn't nonsense. How many times was I gonna leave and you talked me into staying on. Remember, when the Giants were after me to play football.'

'I thought that was the Dodgers,' muttered Katya, still intent on the Latin of the Degree scroll.

'That was baseball, you silly Sis.'

'Was it? Well, they're all silly games, aren't they? I mean for grown men to be playing? It's not really important now, is it?'

'But it is!'

'Is it, Denny?' She handed him back his scroll. He took it. 'Oh come now.'

She was smiling as Denny went on, 'You bet it is!'

The World Series, the Rosebowl, the Masters in golf, the heavyweight championship of the world – wow! Denny was so flabbergasted he couldn't understand why she should even question it – the primacy of sport. Its gods were made in the shape of Man but that's as far as the resemblance went. The worship they demanded was their right. This is what he thought, but all he said was, 'Gee, Sis!' She was quite unperturbed.

'Don't worry, dear brother, keep your idols. Just remember though, that's all they are. They all have their five minutes in the sun and then it's the next man's turn. The ordinary man doesn't really mind who's at the top, as long as somebody is. As long as there is somebody for him to worship. He needs his heroes.'

'And who's your hero, Sis?'

'He's sitting here beside me.'

'No, seriously.' She suddenly looked serious.

'Yes, Denny. I have my heroes.'

'Who are they?' She didn't answer for a moment.

'My father. Our father. Whom I killed ten years ago.'

'Katya,' whispered Denny. It was the first time she had ever mentioned the matter. It was the first time he'd used her old name. He had been only thirteen then and asleep at the time but he had heard people whispering about it all his life.

'It was an accident,' he said. 'That's what the official report had said – "Superintendent Denis O'Neil died in pursuit of a burglar." But what had he stolen?' Sister Mary Josephine looked down.

'It said that so that Mama could get Pop's full Police pension.' There was an uncomfortable pause. Why were they talking about all this all of a sudden? thought Denny. This wasn't fun at all.

'My other hero is my other Father.' Sister Mary Josephine continued. 'Our Father. Who Art in Heaven. I suppose that embarrasses you?'

'No.' But it did. He tried not to let her see.

'He died for me, you see. It was that drew me here at first. That, and Paddy's encouragement. Dear Paddy. Imagine Denny, we have an uncle who's a Bishop, and he could even be an Archbishop yet.'

'Why not Pope? Why stick around at a crummy Archbishop?'

'Now Denny.' Her reproach was kindly, but it was a reproach.

'Sorry Sis.' This wasn't like their usual Sunday sessions.

'How is Mama?' she asked. This was more like it however. This was how Katya always ended the interview. He always said 'Fine' and she said 'Good', then as they got up she always said, 'Take care how you drive. God has plenty of saints in Heaven already,' and they would walk back along the corridor as the bell rang. But it wasn't like that this time.

'I have a message for her.' Denny was taken aback.

'Yeah?' he said hoarsely.

'I want you to tell her that she is to take that trip to Prague.' Denny was startled. How did Katya know about that?

'Tell her to see her own land again before –' She hesitated. 'Before it is changed forever –' Denny made to speak but she went on, 'Tell her I am still sorry about Pops.'

'Sis.'

'And tell her I still love her – very much, and I pray for her every day.' She reached for his hand. 'I pray for all my family.' They sat there in silence for quite a time and the silence was only broken by the sound of the visitor bell. They rose, and without a word between them they walked indoors and back along the long corridor to the front hall. There was only the slightest of hugs. 'Take care how you drive,' she smiled. 'God has plenty of saints in Heaven already'. They both said it together, and they both laughed a brother-and-sister laugh.

'Bye sis – see you.'

'God bless you, Denny.'

On the drive home he wondered about the change in her. He had never seen her so beautiful, so calm, so enigmatic, and he wondered how his mother would react when he gave her Katya's message. But then she wasn't Katya anymore. She was Sister Mary Josephine of the Order of the Sisters of Mercy and she was either a saint or she was mad. Denny was so agitated he put his foot down hard and took the sports car to its limit. He overtook an old Buick. It had a trailer attached but it could hardly be seen under the load it was carrying. There were a couple of mattresses, a roll of fence wire, various suitcases and bags and parcels tied on with rope and sitting on top a kitchen table upside down which made it look like a dead horse with its legs in the air. On top of the car itself were smaller mattresses, bedheads and two chairs interlocked. On the side, there was a scrawled message painted in red on a white sheet – 'OLD CAR – NEW BABY – CLEAN BROKE – ANY OFFERS?' Denny wondered if they were selling the baby. So engrossed was he in this extraordinary equipage that he didn't notice the big truck until it was almost on top of him. He stood on the brakes. There was a scream of tyres and the smell of burning rubber. 'MAMA!' yelled Denny O'Neil but it too sounded like a scream . . .

Chris Mackenzie's mouth opened wide in a yell and her hands rose high in the air. The screams and shouts all round her were deafening as she felt herself being lifted. She started to laugh, or was she crying? It didn't matter. They had won. And in the last minute too. And she had scored the winning goal! Now she was being carried to the pavilion by big Thelma, Rose Jones, and others she couldn't see. She could see her Dad, and Sandy and Uncle Jim standing among all the schoolgirls and parents along the sidelines. Dear old Berta was there too. She was crying. Chris hoped all the excitement wouldn't be too much for her. She had insisted on coming down to Dunedin even though she had had an awful cold. Berta had to be careful with colds. Chris was now beginning to find her high perch uncomfortable, however illustrious, and she was glad when the girls let her down again. Everyone was hugging and kissing her. All she'd done was shoot a goal in a game of basketball and yet you'd think they'd won a war. It was only a game. But was it when it created such total excitement, such complete elation, such a reaction? Admittedly, it was a representative game at a senior level. Otago versus Canterbury was only a provincial game, but the next step was the New Zealand team. Chris, typically, never thought much of her chances of playing for New Zealand, but most of her friends and most of her family did, especially Berta. She even wanted to write to the selectors and tell them so, but was forcibly prevented by Chris. She was happy enough to know she was good at games and to leave it at that. There was a move at Otago University to interest her in athletics in view of the forthcoming Olympics, but the time required for training cut too deeply into her piano practice, so she elected to stay with basketball. It was only a leisure pursuit after all, and a bit of relaxation after study. That's all sport should be at university, she thought. But some people, like big Thelma for instance, paid more attention to their sporting activity than to their university work. She was in Chris's year at Otago doing medicine, but at her present rate of progress, seemed likely to be the oldest woman doctor in New Zealand! For the moment, however, the game was the thing and celebrations were in order.

'Good on you, girl, you did great!' said her father giving her a huge bear hug. Big Bruce was less ebullient than before. He was a changed man since he no longer had his own place. But if he was bitter, he tried not to show it.

'I'll be getting one of these old age pensions,' he had said. 'Then it'll be pipe and slippers for me.' It was hardly imaginable, and it seemed a pity that such a fine big man should be reduced at sixty-five to counting pumpkins on his son's place. But such were the facts of the time and one just had to live with them. Uncle Jim was beaming. While he was infinitely prouder of her musical talents, he was delighted to see her do so well on the sporting field. But 'Well done, Chris,' and a handshake was his only expression of approval. Berta, on the other hand, was still jumping up and down with excitement and had to be restrained by Chris.

It was quite a family party that eventually repaired to the City Hotel for a celebration tea, and the five of them soon settled round the table, laughing and joking as they did so.

'Any news from Stu and Ross, Dad?' asked Chris, once things had settled down.

'Yeah, we'd a letter just last week. Apparently Stu's got a good number in the Bay of Islands, but he says that Ross has gone down to Auckland to chase up something there. He's always looking round the next corner is Ross.'

'Nice to hear that Stu's found something then,' said Jim.

'Or somebody, perhaps?' remarked Chris.

'Not Stu,' said Berta scornfully.

'You never know,' said Bruce. 'He's been a few years on the road now. It's about time he settled down. Not like your nippers, eh Jim?'

'Uncle Jim!' exclaimed Chris, 'you'll burst.' Jim was helping himself liberally to the potatoes.

'It doesn't matter,' he said amiably. 'I don't have to play any games, you know.'

'You don't have to do very much these days, you lucky blighter,' said Bruce. 'Not with a lad like Billy on the farm and the twins.'

'Yes, they're good boys,' said Jim. Sandy glanced at his father, but didn't say anything. Sandy had always resented that all the family luck seemed to have gone with the Keiths and not with the Mackenzies. But he was a better brother than he was a cousin, and this was Chris's night, so he said nothing. His sister was aware of his silence.

'How's our little Laura then?' she asked.

'Much as usual,' Sandy answered tersely. Sandy Mackenzie was not the happiest of men, but then nothing seemed to have worked out for poor Sandy. Even his athletic ambitions had to go by the board because of their money problems, and he was not just on the edge of being an embittered young man. This, after all, was an Olympic year, and only a few short years ago, Sandy had looked to have all the potential of a world class sprinter, but those dreams had been long since shattered, and he now kept himself mostly to himself and his pumpkins. Even his wedding had been a reticent affair. He and Sue had waited till Bruce had come back and they had gone with Mrs Reed, who was by then a widow, to Gore Registry Office. It was all over in half-an-hour. The only one who enjoyed it was Laura, because she got ice-cream afterwards. At seven, these things mattered. Sue had wanted another child as soon as possible after the miscarriage, but Sandy bluntly refused to feed another mouth and said he would walk out and go sandbagging himself if she ever got pregnant again. Just to make sure, they had sex as seldom as possible. If ever anyone had a right to be depressed in those Depression years it was Sue Mackenzie. Nonetheless, like so many wives of the time, she shrugged her shoulders, bent her back and got on with it. Anyway, Laura was a godsend and she brightened up her parents' lives much in the same way as Chris had done with Bruce after Tina's death. Sandy might have been saved from himself had he let his wife have her way, but Sandy didn't trust life any more.

The meal spread itself out for another hour of banalities, intimacies and family jokes – even Sandy laughed when Bruce got going. Jim was quiet as usual; Berta though, was in heaven. Her heroine was queen of the day and Berta rejoiced in the triumph like any dutiful vassal. She wasn't sorry when the rest of the family had to leave as that meant she could have Chris all to herself. Her father had driven her down to Edendale, where they had picked up Bruce and Sandy at their place. It was a poor-looking section. Their house was no more than a large hut, a corrugated iron shed that was no better than a batch. It had no telephone. When Jim had written saying he would come to pick them up for the game, a postcard had come back from Sandy at once saying they would get the bus up and not to bother. But Jim was determined to see

Sue and little Laura, so he sent a telegram saying they were coming anyway. Sandy was embarrassed to meet them. Even Bruce was quieter sensing his son's discomfort, but Sue was delighted, even if only for the cup of tea she was glad to offer. It was ironic to see the good teaset left over from better days still being used. Sue was delighted and Jim was glad to be able to leave her a supply of freshly spun wool, a big tin of biscuits and a leg of lamb for the meat safe. Berta had some sweets for Laura and a dress that Jean had made. They didn't spend long, or at least as long as Sue would have wished, for Berta was keen to get to Dunedin. Now it was time to make the return journey and before long Chris and Berta were waving them off from outside Chris's lodgings in George Street, where they had gone to leave off Berta's overnight bag.

The two cousins almost ran back to the Rotunda. The cinema there was showing *The Great Ziegfeld*. They got into their seats in time for the newsreel, which had one item of New Zealand interest in the international Pathé News: Jean Batten's intended flight from Great Britain to New Zealand. She would be the first woman to do so. There was a great cheer in the cinema. The two girls then settled back to watch the film and soon were lost in the action. At least Chris was. But was hurriedly startled by a hand on her knee. Berta's! For a moment, Chris was transfixed. She was aware of Berta's staring at her, eyes gleaming in the darkness. Chris tensed, her thigh like iron. She must do something. Then suddenly, Berta spoke.

'You OK, Chris?'

Chris shivered with relief, and whispered, 'I'm OK, thanks.' She shifted her position in the seat and the hand disappeared. Chris tried to get back into the film. 'A Pretty Girl is Like A Melody' flooded the cinema as the screen filled with girls, hundreds of them, till Chris was bored with wave after wave of smiling beauty. So much femininity. So much emphasis on breasts and legs. It was like a cattle market of curves and dimples. Chris kept longing for a really plain face to emerge or a squat, hirsute, ugly little man.

'Aren't they lovely?' breathed Berta through her nose.

'Yeah,' answered Chris, half-heartedly.

It was awkward in the lodgings that night. Berta prattled on about the film, and about William Powell and Myrna Loy. She undressed in her usual, carefree fashion displaying unfashionable lingerie in an unflattering fashion and being quite unperturbed in displaying an even more unflattering nudity in the bathroom. This sort of thing had never worried Chris before when her cousin had stayed over, but somehow tonight that hand on her thigh had left a searing imprint which was proving hard to efface.

'Did you like the film, Chris?'

'Yeah,' answered Chris, trying to sound enthusiastic.

'So did I.' There was a pause. 'Did you like the music?'

'Yeah.'

'So did I.' And so the catalogue went on in the dark and Chris tried not to feel uncomfortable in feeling her cousin's larger body growing warm beside hers. Stealthily, she tried to inch her body away.

'I like these weekends with you, Chris.'

'I like them with you, Berta.'

'That's good.' There was another pause, and Berta turned over. 'Good night Chris.'

'Good night, Berta.' It was a long time before Chris got to sleep that night.

In the morning, Chris was more embarrassed than contrite about her cinema suspicions and during the lazy Sunday that followed she tried her best to make up for her unfair thoughts. Berta was only too happy to accept any kind of notice from Chris that came her way. Chris, all-beautiful, all-talented, was all-things-nice, at least in Berta's eyes. The older woman still had the same crush on Chris that she'd had from her schooldays. She had never needed a man in her life.

During the lazy Sunday lunch the two talked of many things – the game, which was in all the papers, the film and what they might see next time, the family, especially Sandy and his situation, but most of all about Chris and what she might do in her musical career. Like her father, Berta had a great love of music through the Keiths' extensive gramophone record collection. And now that there was a National Broadcasting Service in New Zealand they had the chance of good music on the wireless as well. It was the recordings, however, they loved best and many of these heavy, cumbersome 78rpm discs were played over and over again. Chris, too, had her favourites and it was one of these that was playing now in the mid-afternoon languor of a Sunday in Dunedin. Rachmaninov's 'Rhapsody on the Theme of Paganini'. The Russian pianist-composer was Chris's great hero and as he played his own composition on record, Chris lay back on the bed and played it note for note on the wooden headboard of the bed. Berta watched from the easy chair by the tiny gas fire. She looked at her cousin, stretched out on the bed before her, her arms swept up above her head, her fingers tap-tapping rhythmically with the music, her eyes closed, her long legs spread under the flimsy housecoat. Berta thought that she had never seen anything more beautiful. Suddenly, she wanted to touch that body, to move her hands over those smooth lines and curves. Berta felt herself growing hot all over. Her face was red, she knew it. Her heart was thudding in her chest and she didn't know why. It was something to do with Chris, she knew that, but didn't know what. As the music reached its climax she felt her chest tightening, and she tried to take slow, deep breaths to offset an attack, but she could feel it getting worse. She sat up in the chair. The thudding was in her head now, beating with the music between her ears. She tried to shout to Chris but she was in her own world. Berta put her hand to her throat, then to her mouth as she felt her tongue rise to the roof of her mouth. She tried to pull her jaw down by pulling at her bottom teeth. With her eyes she appealed to Chris to open her eyes and see but now her grip was weakening, there were black and white spots before her eyes, she was beginning to stiffen, her legs shot out in front of her – Oh Chris! Chris! Help me! And still the music pounded. It seemed to be getting louder and louder. Her book? If she could reach her book! Get it in her mouth somehow. But where was it? Oh God, she was going blind! She couldn't see now. Oh Chris! CHRIS . . . !

It was the bump as Berta hit the floor that 'awakened' Chris. It coincided exactly with the last blazing arpeggio from Rachmaninov and Chris wasn't sure if it was that which brought her out of the reverie or the sudden noise. She glanced down –

'Berta!' She was beside her stricken cousin in a second. 'Berta! What is it?' Even as she asked she knew what it was. It had happened before, but that was long ago.

They had been at home on the farm and Auntie Jean had known what to do. Berta was now squirming on the carpet, her left hand beating against the bars of the gas fire, saliva bubbling from her mouth, her eyes staring. Her book was still in her right hand. It took all Chris's strength to pull her away from the fire and to prise open Berta's jaws and insert the poker from the fire-iron set.

It was fully five minutes before the writhings ceased and then there were only a few more kicking spasms before Berta was calm again. Chris took her in her arms and gently removed the steel poker. The jaw was now quite slack and the cheeks were wet with perspiration.

'Oh, my poor Berta,' crooned Chris, taking the older woman in her arms. 'Oh, my poor darling!' With a start, she realised that Berta wasn't breathing!

'Roberta!' she heard herself yelling, slapping the girl's cheeks as hard as she could. There was no response. Chris laid Berta flat on her back on the carpet. She found herself crying as she looked down on the pale face, the staring eyes, the inert body. 'Berta!' she moaned. Trying to keep calm she wondered what to do first.

Seconds could matter at a time like this. She started pummelling the heart with her closed fist, she remembered Berta's mother doing that. She listened for even the faintest heart-beat. Still nothing. 'Berta!' she screamed, and grabbing her cousin's wet cheeks in both hands, she made a roundel of her lips and pressed her own hard on them. All that time, she was saying inwardly 'Please God, Please God, Please God.' She put all her strength, all her breath, all her physical being, all her love into that frantic kiss, and then a miracle. She saw Berta's eyelids close over and blink, and putting her hand under Berta's breast she felt the beat of her heart. It was faint, then sluggish; Chris massaged the area gently and gradually, oh so gradually, life came back into Roberta Keith and she was breathing again. Chris pulled the covers from the bed and piled them over Berta. She put a pillow under her head, and Chris sat up on the edge of the bed looking down at her, remembering to say a quiet prayer of thanks. Silence fell in the little bed-sitting room, except for a clicking sound which Chris couldn't place at first, but looking up, she saw that it was the gramophone and poor old Rachmaninov was still going mutely round and round and round . . .

When Berta heard the next day that Chris had given her the kiss of life, she was aghast.

'Chris? How could you do such a thing?'

'I had to. It was the only thing I could do.'

'But you could've caught my cold!' exclaimed Berta nasally.

Berta stayed the whole of the next week with Chris, who looked after her like a baby. She telephoned Uncle Jim and said that Berta's cold had got worse and she was staying on till she was fit again to travel. Jim said he would come up for her again the following Sunday. Meantime, Chris was to make sure that Berta stayed warm and comfortable. She did, in the circle of the cinema! She and Chris went every night. Berta paid.

'Dad gave me the rail fare home and we may as well spend it, if he's coming to get me.' So they saw *The Broadway Melody of 1936* with Eleanor Powell, *Top Hat* with Ginger Rogers, H.G. Well's *Things to Come* which was boring and *East Meets West* with George Arliss as a turbanned Indian. Then it was Sunday again and Uncle Jim was at the door in his car.

'You'll be glad to get her off your hands, Chris,' he said.

'Not at all,' grinned Chris with her arm around Berta. 'What else are cousins for?' Jim took his daughter's bag and put it in the back.

'More like sisters you two.'

The girls exchanged smiles. 'So we are!' they both said together and laughed. Before she got into the car, Berta gave Chris a big kiss right on the mouth.

'What was that for?' cried the latter in surprise.

''Cos my cold's better!' replied Berta cheerfully before slamming the car door behind her. Chris waved till they were out of sight.

She was glad to get down to some real work the next morning. After such a week she had a lot to make up. It was the middle term and she wanted to make sure she got into the performing class next term under Professor Neinmann. He had only recently come to Otago from Vienna and had been a famous recitalist and accompanist in Europe, but he had been forced to leave because of the Brownshirts, which was the name he gave to the new Nazi party followers, who said they were going to wipe all the Jews off the face of the earth. 'How did they know you were a Jew, Professor?' one boy in the class had asked. 'Because I play the piano so well,' was the disarming answer. It was the Professor who would take her first professional appraisal and she worked hard on her programme. She wouldn't do the Chopin or the Debussy, the others would certainly do them. So she chose a short piece by Poulenc, another by Satie and a song by Chabrier. That'll keep him guessing she thought, and she practised hard for her Friday audition. She even stayed late at the Music Room and practised there. It was a lovely piano and it seemed to sound better when there was no one else around. She enjoyed losing hours out of the world with music. On the Wednesday afternoon she was suddenly summoned to Miss Simm's office. Students called her the Dreadnought and she was the administrative tyrant of the entire university.

She looked at Chris over her glasses. She was sitting at her desk and Professor Neinmann was also there.

'Miss Mackenzie,' intoned Miss Simms, in her lofty voice, 'we are of the opinion at this university, that you might go far in music.'

'Thank you.'

'It is a question of how far you want to go.'

'As far as possible I suppose,' said Chris, wondering what old Dreadnought was getting at. And why was the Professor smiling like that?

'As far as Berlin for instance?'

'What?'

'We have had a request from the New Zealand Olympic Committee to supply a pianist to accompany the Ladies Gymnastic Team in the Olympic Games in Berlin – that's in Germany, you know.'

'I know,' Chris wanted to say, but she could only nod.

'It would mean you'd be away for two months in all.' Chris glanced in a panic at the beaming Professor.

'But what about my appraisal?' she asked in a small voice. Professor Neinmann raised a hand.

'My dear Miss Mac,' – he always called her Miss Mac – 'I have had the pleasure of hearing you practise after the hours. I think we can take it that you will have your place in the Professional Performers Class when you return in September. Ja?' He referred the last enquiry to Miss Simms.

'Ja!' replied that lady without thinking, 'I mean, yes. It depends on whether you want to do it or not. But we thought, with your sporting interests . . . well?'

Chris was aware of four eyes gazing at her, waiting for her answer. The Olympics? Europe? Berlin?

The German director was in a terrible temper. He tore off his Tyrolean hat with the feather which was his trade-mark and jumped on it with both riding boots. Otto Minger was no von Stroheim, or a Fritz Lang or even a Billy Wilder, but at least he was German and he looked the part of the film director, with his jodhpurs and his monacle and his long cigarette-holder. But at this very moment, he was more angry than anything. His bald head was wet with exasperation as he let rip with a catalogue of Anglo-Saxon expletives that only gained in their ferocity from a heavy Teutonic intonation.

'Wo ist die bitch? Zwei times heute I bin vaiting fur diese opera bitch und Ich bin goink out of mein tree!' A laconic first assistant picked up the director's hat and handed it to him without a word. Monty Gumlach was a veteran of directorial outbursts and he knew the only way to ride them out was to say nothing. Herr Minger grabbed his hat and banged it on his head again. 'Wir waste time, time ist das kapital, wir waste das kapital! Keine kapital – keine film und Otto Minger is kaput!' With that he flopped in the canvas chair that bore his name in large letters on the back and let his head loll over it till Monty lit a little black cheroot, put it in the cigarette holder from the chair tray and, without a word, put it in the fat little German's mouth.

The scene was pure Hollywood in all its ridiculousness. Templar Studios were making yet another Maria d'Agostino musical and the star herself was late on the set again for the first shot after lunch. She had also been late that morning for the first shot after breakfast, hence Herr Direktor's burst of frenzy. He may not have been the best film director in the world but he knew what was expected of a director on the set and bursts of temper were a good bit of the props for the part. Another advantage at the time was a foreign accent and Otto was born with that. Not even his own mother could understand Otto when he really got going on his 'hoch horse' as he called it. However, placated by the cigar, he was now sulking and that meant he was at least quiet, so the playing cards came out behind the camera and the studio settled down once more for a long wait. Tony Marino, Maria's leading man, got up again from his chair and returned to his caravan where he and his stand-in played a never-ending game of chess. Between moves, Tony practised his English, and other parts, on the stream of young contract girls whose tutorial skills were not directed exclusively to the English language or chess. No, Tony didn't mind the frequent delays. Besides, he was on a generous daily rate if shooting ran over schedule, so he was hoping for the best. Mamma Marino, back in Naples, could look forward to another mink coat. Meantime, Tony was getting a lot of chess in.

At that moment, the cause of all this various perturbation was lying on the couch of her sumptuous caravan, which most ordinary families could never have bought on the longest mortgages, and complaining of a headache. She also said she had just started her period. She knew that would always shut Vernon up. The exquisite, though kindly, Vernon Drake couldn't bear to be confronted with the basic elements of Maria's woman-ness. He had fallen in love with her gorgeous voice and it was this faculty in her, and this alone, that he cosseted and protected. In any case, he was handsomely retained by Rico d'Agostino in Miami to do just that, although Maria didn't know this. She treated him on good days like a butler, and on bad days like an old faggot. This was one of Vernon's faggot days.

'But Maria,' he pleaded yet again. 'It's only the walk down the staircase with Tony. And all those poor extras. They've been under those lights all day –'

'That's what they're paid for, isn't it?' snapped Maria. 'They don't mind the overtime and Templar can afford it.'

There was reason behind Maria's apparent unreasonableness. She was in the last year of her original contract and during that time, Templar Studios had loaned her out to other companies at a huge profit, with no extra coming to her. Some of her biggest successes had been made this way, and thanks to them she had been big box office in her time. Now, however, she was beginning to slip and the studio was 'working her out' as they called it. She had no control over scripts or casting, so she had to do as she was told – or else. This infuriated Maria more than anything else. She knew that, even with her father's capital, she couldn't take a big studio through the courts. So she took it out on Vernon. He had never wanted her to go into films in the first place. He had it arranged that she should go to London after the Met and then to Italy – first Palermo, then Rome and then La Scala, Milan. He had it all worked out, but Maria wanted fame badly, so the Babylonian Hollywood won over the quality opera houses. The year before, Covent Garden had made another approach, but the first of the 'opera quickies' had also come out to disastrous reviews and the operatic feelers withdrew. Despite her treatment of him, or perhaps because of it, Vernon remained loyal to his idol. He knew, at thirty-four, she was still capable of great things, but there was no doubt the cheap movies had tarnished her classical image. This was why Maria d'Agostino was taking a studied revenge. And there was nothing Vernon or anyone could do about it. It was her last shot on her last day, and she was going to take her time about it.

Hollywood wondered about 'the Duck and the Drake' as they called the pair. Some thought he was her father. Others that he was her secret husband, but Maria insisted that she kept herself pure for her art, and would remain unmarried until the day she died. Hollywood of course winked and looked the other way, but couldn't fail to notice the long procession of husky masseurs who regularly attended her 'back trouble'. Vernon let it all go over his head, or beneath him, as he said. He realised, as she did, that he was the only friend she had. Her father had continued to be what might be called loosely a moral support. He had been hit by a stroke and was now confined largely to his Miami mansion, but he continued to take an abnormal interest in Maria's career. He screened her films every night in his private studio and bombarded Vernon with cables of instructions in the manner of Randolph Hearst a decade before. The only difference was Maria was indeed a great singer, who had only herself to blame for not reaching the heights of which she was capable, in the legitimate world at least. By the tinsel standards of Hollywood, she had more than done enough.

But there was something else other than her normal temperamental difficulties that was bothering Vernon that day. Instead of the normal cable, he had had a long telephone call from Rico that morning at the house. He had rung to tell Vernon to expect a very special visitor at the studio that afternoon. He was sending him from New York with Roberto Ruffiano, who was now retired from the restaurant, but still on the d'Agostino payroll. The restaurant, in fact, was now run by Francesca and her two children. Her other 'son', Tito, otherwise Guiglielmo Murphy, Noreen's child, was being sent as a gift to Maria!

'But Maria doesn't even know this child!' said Vernon.

'He's not a child,' said Rico's distorted voice from the other side of the continent. 'He's fifteen.'

'But what can she do with a fifteen-year-old boy?'

'She can love him like a brother, 'cos that's what he is.'

'But Rico –'

'Well, "fratellastro". Stepbrother, I think you say.'

'Oh, dear!' muttered Vernon, 'Why do families have to be so complicated?'

'That's what makes them families,' retorted Rico, and rang off.

The arrangements were that Ruffianio and the boy were to come to the main gate at 3.30p.m. to coincide with the normal tea break and Maria would meet them then in her caravan. But it was almost that time now. Vernon was in a quandary. Should he tell her, or should he get her on the set? The matter was decided by the telephone in the caravan, which rang in its tactful, muted way, so as not to disturb the star.

'Tell that dreadful little Kraut I'm still sick,' called out Maria with her hand over her eyes. She had hardly moved from the couch in the last hour. Vernon took up the receiver tentatively.

'Yes?' was his timid enquiry. The voice of the sergeant at the gate could clearly be heard as he bellowed into the mouthpiece.

'There's a guy at the gate here with a kid, and he says they've got an appointment with Miss d'Agostino.'

'That's right, Charlie. Would you be kind enough to send them along?'

'You sure? They don't look Hollywood to me.'

'That's alright. They're family.'

'You don't say.'

'Yes, send them along to Chalet 37.'

'I know where she is. Dat's what I'm paid for.' And for the second time that day a telephone was hung up on Vernon Drake.

'What was all that about?' asked Maria.

Vernon turned, took a breath and said quickly, 'Your brother is on his way to meet you.'

Maria sat bolt upright, staring at him.

Guiglielmo Murphy, or Tito, as everyone called him, was the handsomest young boy Vernon Drake had ever seen, and he had seen quite a few. He and Roberto Ruffiano, now looking very frail, tactfully left brother and sister alone after the first meeting. Maria had received him like a queen. At least she was all ready to put on the regal act, but the boy's steely simplicity had its own regality and she sat back on the couch, deflated.

'Oh, brother!' she said.

'Please call me Tito,' said the boy.

In the studio meantime, Otto Minger had fallen asleep in his chair and was snoring. 'Alright, Studio,' said Monty Gumlach quietly, taking the cigarette holder from the director's mouth. 'It's a wrap.' And one by one the lights went out on the sound stage, leaving Otto snoring in the dark.

I think I'm too old for this, thought Becky Friar as she buckled herself into the safety belt of the passenger seat. She was about to be taken up in an aeroplane for the first time and was doing her best to pretend to the pilot, her stepbrother, Abel Keith, that she wasn't absolutely terrified. Abel was at home again in Sydney from his latest job, crop-spraying in Queensland. He never seemed to have a job long, and when he was working it was always something to do with flying – mail deliveries in the outback, even baby deliveries when he was flying with the doctor, cargo trips up to Cairns, private hires, legitimate and illegitimate, all over the place. He was a flying freelance in every sense of the word. The only trouble was, he didn't have his own plane. He never could get enough money together, but that remained Abel Keith's big ambition – and his big problem.

Now he was taking Becky up. Ever since she had come so unexpectedly into the Keiths' Sydney life ten years before, she was very much part of the family. Indeed, had Abel had his way at one time, she would have been very much more. The fact that she was his half-sister didn't seem to deter him, and only the strong remonstrances of his father, and the gentle persuasions of his mother pulled him back from the impossible implications of a reckless infatuation with the striking Scottish girl who was his own father's daughter. Abel's obsession had been at its height at the time of Billy's wedding and Tina's funeral. He had been twenty-two, Becky was twenty-nine. The combination of both the tragic and the joyful did much to screen Abel's dilemma. He had tried to talk about it to Billy, but it so shocked the new bridegroom that an argument developed and they had even come to blows. Abel got very much the worst of it and spent the rest of the time in Otago trying to get drunk. If Becky herself was aware of Abel's futile passion she never showed any sign of it. Her cool and calm demeanour had made her a great favourite with all the New Zealanders, especially old Gran Keith, who virtually monopolised the girl. She insisted she stay with her as often as possible during that two-week period. Gran loved Becky's open Scottishness.

'She's the only one here I can understand,' Gran had said. Abel, on the few times he was sober, spent them with his mother to whom he would pour out his troubled heart – and his annoyance.

'Trust me,' he had said. 'Never even bothered with bloody Sheilas, and first time I do, Christ, she turns out to be my bloody sister!' Another time he was with her, he fulminated against all the Keith women, particularly Gran Keith. She had refused to interrupt her game of cards with Becky so that he could take her for a drink.

'Your sister's fine with me,' Gran had said pointedly. 'And anyway, you've had more than enough to drink already.' Abel had gone and tried to pass the time with Annabel Jackson and was rewarded for his social endeavours with a hefty smack on the face.

'I hate women,' Abel exclaimed vehemently to his mother.

'I'm a woman.'

'No, you're not. You're my mother.'

Those torrid days soon passed, however, and Abel came out of his temporary delirium and much to everybody's surprise, except perhaps Rachel's, Abel and Becky became really good friends, brother and sister in every sense. It was Becky who invited him to come as often as he liked to the Harbour Hotel, and got him his drink at a discount. She let him talk – about everything and anything so that he even talked away his fixation and came slowly to himself again. It was Becky who started him on flying, and Becky who suggested he should leave Sydney for a time. See a bit more of Australia. He did, and as a result, he had now seen most of it. Abel didn't tell Becky everything. He didn't, for instance, tell her about his dealing with an old guy, who was also a regular at the Harbour. A smart Englishman who maintained a suite there, and seemed to have all kinds of connections with all kinds of people. He always seemed to be well in funds. In fact, it was his plane that Abel was now revving up at the hanger; Abel had piloted it before for the old boy on another kind of flight. The kind where no questions were asked but where the money was good. Yes, he had plenty of money the old boy. His name was Dickenson – Captain Martin Dickenson, he called himself.

'OK?' yelled Abel with a grin.

'OK!' nodded Becky, trying to do the same. Then with a change of engine noise, the little plane started to taxi across the grass of the airfield towards the broad band of asphalt which was the only runway. It was a bumpy ride over the stubborn tufts and Becky felt herself being thrown from side to side in the tiny little cockpit seat she had behind Abel. She was glad of the safety belt. She only hoped it would hold once they were up in the air. At the thought, her fears swooped back again and her stomach turned.

'Ready?' Now wearing his leather helmet, with a silk scarf round his throat, Abel looked just like a little boy. A mischievous little boy at that. She nodded back, not trusting herself to speak and then they were off again. She hadn't realised that they would go so fast on the ground – and faster – and still faster till she was sure the engine must explode, then just when everything was screaming in the wind and she was fighting to catch her breath, there was a feeling as if someone had just kicked the legs from under her, and she was swinging in a hammock. But she wasn't in a hammock, she was in an aeroplane – and she was flying! Without thinking she looked over the side, and nearly died with fright. The ground was falling back as if retreating from her astonished eyes even as she watched. She didn't know whether she was enjoying it or not. The plane seemed such a puny thing to be flying so high. Strips of wood and canvas bound by wire and powered by a big car engine. Abel turned again and gave her the thumbs up sign with a gauntleted hand. She nodded again and found she was laughing. Laughing and flying. She was in her element. They both were. High above the ground, going at speed towards the clouds – free as air. Becky looked down again. The world was so far away from both of them.

'So you enjoyed your flight, Becky?'

'It was wonderful, Captain. Thank you very much.'

'Don't thank me, my dear. Thank your little brother Abel. And anyway, it's always a pleasure to give pleasure to a charming young lady like yourself – know what I mean?' Becky wasn't sure that she did, or rather, she hoped she didn't, but she just smiled her usual hotelier's professional smile.

'I'd better get back to work now,' she said. She and Captain Dickenson were in the Port Side Bar in the hotel and most of the lunchtime customers had gone. She was holding the fort behind the small bar after Mike, the barman, had finished the lunch shift. Often Abel would come in and cover for the quiet afternoon session till Mike resumed at five. It gave him some cash in his pocket between flying stints, and as Becky pointed out, there was nothing like working behind a bar to stop you from being an alcoholic. Becky herself was now Assistant-Manageress in the place. Tubby Weir, the actual Manager, was happy enough to leave the running of the hotel to her. This left him more time for the gaming tables at a place he knew up-town. Becky didn't object. It was good experience for her and it let her make her own decisions. Abel was one of these, and when he was broke, or in Sydney, which was always the same thing, he always did a few shifts for her behind the Port Side Bar.

Which is how he came to meet Captain Martin Dickenson. The dapper gentleman had his regular stool within an easy arm's reach of the whisky bottle and the telephone. The Englishman did a lot of business with each, for he was both alcoholic and workaholic. What his work was, no one could quite say, but it was obviously enough to keep the wolf well away from the door. In fact, down about the main road somewhere. There was a mystery about the man and Becky never knew whether it was deliberately created or not, but since he was a very good customer, she didn't enquire too closely.

'They keep you busy, my dear?'

'Yes, they do.'

'Still, busy hands keep the Devil at bay.'

'So they say.' Becky spoke with her mind more on Abel than on the old Captain's chatter. She didn't enjoy being alone with him. There were stories. He might be over sixty, but he had no wish to be pensioned off as far as women were concerned. Even though he always had one hand round a glass, the other one had a knack of wandering. Becky always made a point of staying well down wind of the bold old Captain.

'Wonder what's keeping Abe?' This was her pet name for him and she was the only one he would allow to call him that. 'I need to get on with a couple of things and I can't leave the bar untended.'

'I can always help myself,' offered the Captain.

'I doubt we could afford that, Captain.'

'Please call me Martin.'

'It's against company rules to first-person guests.'

'Rules are made to be bent, my dear. The original Command-ments were in stone and look what happened to them. They got broken. I suggest that, human nature being what it is, had they been made of rubber they would have lasted longer. Are you sure you won't join me?'

'No thanks.'

'Very well. Although it is not recommended in the best circles that one should drink alone.' Thereupon the former sailor poured his sixth generous tot of the day, and for the fourth time, Becky wiped the same non-existent water spill on the bar. The water jug was half full.

'Cheers,' she said.

'Bottoms up!' As the Captain drank, Abel entered in a hurry.

'Sorry I'm late, Becks! Got held up at Mum's.' Abel never referred to home, but only to 'Mum's'. He slid up on the stool facing his step-sister, glancing quickly at the Captain.

'Still in dry dock, I see, Captain?' he said wryly.

'Which is why I drink, dear boy – because I'm dry.' And he helped himself to number seven. Abel leaned into Becky.

'Listen Becks, you're not going to believe this.'

'Alright then, I won't. Now if you will just jump over –'

'No, wait, listen. Dad got a letter this morning from Uncle Jim. Mum showed it me.'

'Reading other people's mail?'

'Listen – Gran's coming over. Yeah, Gran Keith from New Zealand! Bloody ninety years old and she's coming to see us. She's coming to Sydney!'

'What's so wonderful about that?'

'At bloody ninety?' Becky glanced at the Captain, resenting that he should be party to personal and family news. But he seemed to be lost in his own thoughts.

'You're only as young as you feel. Isn't that right, Captain?'

'Quite right, my dear,' replied the said mariner. But he muttered under his breath, 'I feel every young thing I can!'

But Abel had heard – 'That's enough of that, Cap. Not in front of my sister.' The old man smiled and saluted the younger man silently. 'Well, what d'you think Becks?' went on Abel.

Becky didn't have the heart to tell her eager half-brother that she already knew that Gran Keith intended to visit Sydney. The old lady had written herself to tell her. Or rather, she had dictated a letter to Berta as usual. Berta was now virtually Gran Keith's constant companion. Ever since Becky's visit, Gran Keith and she had maintained a regular correspondence. At first, Gran had written her own letters, in a sprawling, unpractised hand going often into several pages all about her young days in Forres, and her early marriage and the first days in New Zealand. The only things she never wrote about were the voyage and her husband. She just said that was her 'sick time'. Everybody had a 'sick time' in their lives, she insisted, and that was hers, and that was that. Otherwise, the letters could be about everything and anything and everybody. Old Gran Keith might have been bed-ridden for years but her mind was mobile enough. Even though her eyes were failing she saw through most people and if she had become hard of hearing she heard enough to know what was going on. She knew all about the Abel/Becky situation and was the only one who was sympathetic to Abel.

'That's why I was always short with him when he was here,' she wrote afterwards. 'It was the best thing for him at the time.' Becky always thought Berta must have had a great time as Gran's amanuensis. Some of the letters were blunt to say the least. Now she was coming over with Berta and Uncle Jim. Aunt Jean thought that Berta needed a holiday and a bit of a change. So did she, so she wanted some time free of her mother-in-law. Now that Jim was semi-retired, he could go with them and anyway it was time he saw his brother again.

'How did your dad take it?'

'Mum said he laughed his head off.'

'Is he going to take that offer of the Labour seat?'

'I don't know. Mom says he might. Dad and I don't talk politics.'

'You mean Dad and you don't talk.'

'Suits me.'

'Abel Keith, you're –' She broke off, aware that the Captain was holding up the empty bottle. 'Another bottle for the Captain, Abel. It's the usual – Whyte and Mackay – back of the second cupboard. We'll talk later – I have some ordering to do in the office and a couple of letters. Try and get some sleep, Captain.' Dickenson made an heroic if futile move to rise from his stool as Becky swept efficiently past him. She went quickly because she was irritated. She always got irritated when she thought of Abel and their father. She loved them both. They loved her. Why couldn't they love each other? They did, of course, she knew that, but neither dared show it. How silly men are. But then, Becky Friar never thought very much about men. There was only one man for her and he was fading away as fast as he could in faraway Forres.

'Your sister works too hard,' said the Captain, struggling to get himself into a comfortable drinking position again.

'She gets her day off,' said Abel, unscrewing the next bottle.

'What does she do then, I wonder?' said Dickenson, proffering his glass.

'She goes and has a long lunch with Mum at the University Club every second Wednesday. They drink white wine and talk about my Dad.'

'And on the other week?' slurred the Captain.

'She goes to the Labour Club for lunch with Dad and they have red wine.'

'And they talk about your mother?'

'No. They talk about me.'

'Which is precisely what I wish to do at this moment.'

The Captain looked round to check that they were alone. Only Abel would not have been surprised at the immediate and total change in the Captain. He had seen this other person before. Here was no longer the slovenly drunk, the slumped solitary at the corner of the bar. His speech was no longer slurred. He had an air of authority that gave him at least a character right to the spurious rank of Captain. This was ex-Second Officer Dickenson to the life. A life that included several spells inside, a few near-misses of both death and good fortune, but still with the essential good luck that any freelance needs in whatever walk. And now here he was in Sydney, thirty-five years later, playing the harmless drunk and looking after Number One and out for the main chance.

'Will you join me in a drink, Abe?'

'The name's Abel.'

'Of course. Well?'

'No thanks. Never drink on duty.'

'Very wise. One never knows when duty calls. By the way, could I have more water?' He pushed the water jug towards Abel. 'That's one of my little secrets, you know. The further one goes down the whisky bottle, the more the water in the glass.'

'Every man to his trade,' quipped Abel. The Captain went on coldly.

'It's your trade that concerns me, young man. You still have your licence?'

'Yep.'

'Your pilot's licence, I mean?'

'I know that's what you mean.'

'And passport?'

'Yep.'

'And no criminal record?'

'Not as far as I know,' laughed Abel, but Dickenson didn't laugh. Instead, he looked round again, and motioned Abel to come nearer.

'How are you on night flying?'

'Instruments, you mean?' The Captain nodded.

'Oh, a real fly-by-night, me. A proper little owl. "Cat's Eyes" Keith, they called me at Sydney Flying School.'

'Please, I'm serious.'

'Alright, keep your bloody shirt on, Cap. Yeah, I've done night stuff. I had to do it sometimes on the Alice run.'

'Alice?'

'Alice Springs. They put down petrol flares.'

'There'll be no flares this time.'

'Crikey!'

'Could you do it?' Abel thought for a bit.

'I think it was 1929, just about the time of all that Stock Market stuff, a Yankee joker called Doolittle made an "all-blind" as its called in the trade, into Mitchell Field, New York, but he had a mate with him – just in case – keeping the old weather eye out. I'd need –'

'You'll be alone,' interrupted Dickenson tersely.
''Struth mate, you're being cautious.'
'I have to be.'
'Must be a big one.'
'It is.'
'What's the plane?'
'Mine. Or rather, the company's.'
'What?' expostulated Abel. 'The little kite I took Becks up in?'
'The same.'
'But the gas range –'
'You will have extra petrol tanks on both wings.'
'Like Lindbergh. It keeps you low.'
'I understand you can have an engine-booster.'
'All mod cons, eh?'
'No expense spared.'
'Except for my fee, of course?'
'One thousand pounds in used notes.'
'Australian?'
'British if you like.'
'You pay it up front?'
'Could be arranged.'
'You're taking a chance. I could scarper with that kind of loot on me.'
'Life is about taking chances, my dear Abel. Me, with my money, my contacts. You with your –'
'My life, yeah. Two thousand feet up with an over-loaded sewing-machine.'
'You're not doing anything here, are you?'
'Not much, as you can see. You're my only customer today.'
There was a pause.
'How much do you earn here, Abel?'
'You from the Revenue then?'
'Whatever it is, it's hardly a thousand a day.'
'You're forgetting the tips.'
'Even with tips. What do you say? Are you interested?'
'Tell me about it.'
When Captain Dickenson had finished telling Abel all about it, the young Australian said nothing but reached for the whisky bottle and poured himself a generous measure.
'Good health,' he said.
'Good luck,' replied the Captain. Abel took the first gulp.
'Too bloody true, mate,' he said. He declined the Captain's offer of the water jug.

THIRTY-FOUR

Denny O'Neil was a very lucky young man. You need luck to face an oncoming truck on the freeway, and on that particular Sunday afternoon, Denny had that quality in abundance. It was lucky too that the truck driver chose to swerve into the centre lane, rather than stand on his brakes and hope for the best. It was lucky as well that Denny's sports car was new and responded at once to the first touch of his own brake pressure, causing him to swerve right. And finally, it was lucky for both drivers that the rattling wreck of an old saloon, festooned with every possible kind of household appliance, was caught between both of them and emptied its high cargo of mattresses on to the road. For Denny was catapulted, not on to one, but two of these well-sprung dormitory appurtenances, and came out of a three-car collision with nothing worse than a dislocated right shoulder. On the other hand, the dusty little saloon taking the share-cropper's family north to better times, virtually collapsed of its own volition and miraculously with no hurt to its passengers – a young couple with their infant baby – but at considerable loss to their plethora of household effects, which, exploding from its bounds of rope, string and leather straps, covered at least a hundred yards of the freeway. The truck driver, a burly professional, suffered only the irritation of whiplash, and from the shock of incredulity in finding himself still alive. Denny was no less shocked, and more delighted than surprised, but this was as nothing compared to the elation of the ruined farmer, who after a temporary stay at a local hotel with wife and child, courtesy of two insurance companies, was paid sufficiently by them not only to buy a new car, but a positive cascade of new mattresses, which he and his wife no doubt put to good use in their new place outside Buffalo.

Thanks to still-recent memories of the late Superintendent Denis O'Neil of the Traffic Department, and even more, the folk legend that still attained to the larger-than-life, still-later person of Superintendent Michael O'Neil of the Manhattan precinct, the third Denis O'Neil was relieved of police action in respect of the New Jersey accident. This didn't prevent his being grilled at long length at the station by the new Traffic Superintendent, Charlie McGuinness, but fortunately Denis had the wit and good sense to bring his mother with him on each occasion and more out of deference to Hana than in strict accordance with driving regulations, Denis was let off with a severe reprimand.

'You're a lucky guy, Denny,' said Charlie. 'You had a father who was a cop, and even better he married a swell lady.' Denny gulped, muttered his thanks and slunk off. He was pleased though that some good had come from the incident, and now that he had their address, he promised he would look up the couple with the baby next time he was near Buffalo.

The injury and the shock put paid to Denny's Olympic ambitions. Nobody wanted a swimmer with a dislocated shoulder, but the enforced rest at home allowed Denny tentatively to broach the question of Katya, otherwise Sister Mary Josephine of the Sisters of Mercy. His sister's name had been taboo for so long in the family and he wasn't sure how to bring the matter up. One day, lying on top of his bed with his shoulder strapped and with only his mother and himself in the house, he decided that the only way to approach it was just to tell her straight out. So he did.

'Mama?' he said as she fussed around him.

'Yes, Denny?'

'Mama?'

'You just said that.'

'I know.' He felt himself floundering. The hell with it, he thought, why don't I just tell her? 'Mama, I saw Katya on Sunday.' There, it was out. His mother's face was an inch from his, her eyes boring into his. He gulped. 'I've seen her lotsa times. Lotsa Sundays.' What a stupid thing to say. Why was he so flustered? 'She says she loves you, Mama, and you gotta use Uncle Sean's money to visit home to Prague.' His mother's face moved sharply from his eye-line. Because of the way his shoulder was strapped, he had been unable to turn and see her as she moved out of his vision. But he knew she had walked to the window and had waited for her to speak. She was a long time in speaking. When she did speak, it was not what Denny had expected.

'I love my Katya,' she had said softly.

'She loves you too, Mama. I told you that,' Denny had replied.

'But my Katya is dead,' his mother continued.

'She's in a convent in New Jersey.'

'She's in hell.'

'Oh, Mama!'

'Well, she deserves to be who has killed her own father.'

'It was an accident. The railing –'

'It was an act of the devil.'

'It was an act of God. An accident.' His mother's voice rose.

'What God would kill my Denis?' she cried. The extent of her reaction took Denny by surprise. She had shown little emotion at the time of the awful incident and had quite coldly dealt with Katya according to what his sisters had told him in later years. The memory of their grief still hurt him and it told now in his voice.

'Mama!' he said. This was also a cry. A cry of remorse, as if he too were taking some of Katya's guilt. But he made it seem like a cry of pain from his shoulder and this brought his mother to him again.

'Oh, my poor boy! Your shoulder, does it hurt?'

'Yeah, Mama,' lied Denis, with his eyes closed. 'It sure does.'

And the subject of Katya, alias Sister Mary Josephine of the Order of the Sisters of Mercy, was closed once again among the O'Neils. She never spoke to him for the rest of the day, yet strangely enough when she brought his breakfast the next morning she said, 'I don't say definite, I just say maybe, but how find we a way to go home like you say?'

'Leave that to me, Mama,' he had said with a grin and rose up on one elbow to give her a big hug. This sent another spasm of acute pain shooting across his shoulder and caused him to cry out. His mother nearly dropped the tray.

'Denny? You OK?' she cried. He lay back on the bed, gasping, 'Couldn't be better, Mama,' he said.

Now that the decision had been made, plans went ahead very swiftly for the European trip. Denny wanted to travel on the airship Hindenburg, which had arrived from Frankfurt only a couple of months before and was now touring out of Lakehurst to the delight of the American public. But Hana was not so sure. She had decided that she didn't like anything German now that they had goose-stepped into the Rhineland.

'I can see what this Hitler is doing,' she said. 'He wants Prague, that's what he wants. And he is creeping up by the back door.'

'Why should he want Prague?' argued Denny.

'Why not?' retorted his mother. This was unanswerable and was about the extent in the O'Neil household of a political discussion. Considering that Mussolini had just walked into Abyssinia and that Palestine Arabs were involved against the Jews, that Civil War was simmering in Spain and Japanese had once again invaded Chinese territory, it was extraordinary that a newly-graduated Master in Journalism showed no interest whatsoever in contemporary world affairs. It was obvious to anyone looking at the situation globally that nationalist xenophobia in whatever country, plus the fear of the Communist hegemony, could only assist the rise of the Fascists and could only lead eventually to the end of the Depression, but at the cost of a second world war. Denny had no wish to dwell on such things. His interest, as with most young men of his age, in any country and in any class, was in the pleasureable and the transient. Around that time in Chicago, Benny Goodman and his Orchestra had begun to 'swing' and, thanks to radio, so had Denny – at least as far as his shoulder would allow. Not so long before the accident, he had gone to the band leader's Carnegie Hall concert. This was the first time a jazz band had played within those august portals and Goodman had supplemented his own line-up with the very best coloured players from Harlem. This was an innovation in itself and most of New York's population over eighteen and under twenty-five were determined to be there on the night. Tickets were scarce and expensive, but Denny had the contacts and his mother had the money, so Denny got his tickets. He then became without doubt the most popular guy on the block. He could have had his pick of the local belles who clamoured for the privilege of being his companion on the night. Not that Denny O'Neil lacked for night companions. This had often been a subject of much rancour between mother and son. Hana had been worried throughout his student days about Denny's cavalier attitude to girls, but he had promised her that he was too young to settle down yet. Once he had graduated . . .

But then he did graduate, and there seemed no change in what to her mind was a totally promiscuous attitude to women. Only Denny knew how harmless it really was. The truth was Denny O'Neil had never yet fallen in love. However, for the big Goodman concert, he had played safe and chosen Linda Bernardo, a quiet girl who at least had the legitimate excuse that she played the clarinet.

The idea of going to Prague that Fall took firmer root. The question now was not if Hana would go, but how and when. It was her other daughter, Clara, now a very happy and completely settled-down Mrs Kominsky, who first suggested that the two should make the trip on the Queen Mary. This very new Cunard liner, dubbed 'Britain's Masterpiece', was already advertising in New York for the return trip to Southampton – three thousand miles in less than four days. Even better, the cost was still under a hundred dollars and that included all meals and two nights hotel in England. Clara urged her mother to grab at the offer, and even offered to go uptown with her one day to ask about it, which she did. Though she would never admit it, Hana was getting quite excited about the idea of seeing her old homeland again. Thirty-seven years is a long time to be away. Denny was disappointed not to have the air trip. He had been building up hopes of the new sea plane possibility, since his mother was so set against the airship. But when he heard that there were no less than three dance bands aboard the Queen Mary, he was quick to change his mind and thanks to Clara, the travelling arrangements were duly made. Hana and Denny were to have a week in London before catching the boat train to Paris, to spend a few days there and then on by rail to Prague. The deposit was paid and a booking confirmed for Mrs Hana O'Neil and Master Denis O'Neil on the Queen Mary, departing New York on 27th August. His sisters laughed at the booking clerk's assumption when Hana had gone with Clara to make the booking, and Denny was 'Master' to all of them from that moment until the day he sailed.

The poster proclaiming the ninth Olympiad of the modern era depicted the silhouette of Berlin's Brandenberg Gate behind which, in a romantic red haze, towered a bronzed Aryan hero with arm upraised in triumph sporting the champion's laurel wreath under the famous five rings. This typified both the new nationalist aspirations of the non-Jewish, non-Catholic, Nordic-white Germany and expectations of the public at large. The Berlin Games of 1936 were little more than a propaganda exercise for the triumphant Nazi Party, which was now completely in power under its charismatic leader, Adolf Hitler. Now Chancellor of Germany, he saw the Games as an opportunity to glorify both himself and the Third Reich, but as always, it takes only the actions of one man to upset the best laid schemes.

In this case, the man was the all-American, all-black sprinter Jesse Owens. Of the 5,000 competing athletes from fifty-three nations, this modest man won four gold medals in track and field events, and thus single-handedly totally discredited the Nazi dogma of racial superiority over the coloured peoples. The irony was that he was nearly prevented from competing at all. The rich and persuasive Jewish lobby in the United States Congress had sought to boycott the games as a protest against Hitler's dictatorial anti-semitic policies, but the move failed and Owens sailed with the rest of the American team and into history. On the first Saturday Hitler opened the Games and when Hans Woellke won the shot putt for Germany he was personally congratulated by the Führer. Hitler came the second day, but when Owens won the 100 metres sprint he was ignored. Hitler came again on the third day and Owens won the long jump and was again ignored. On the fourth day Hitler saw Owens win the 200 metres and left the stadium in a fury. He never returned for the remainder of the Games. Consequently, he never saw Owens win his fourth gold medal in the Men's Relay. Nor did he see another All-Black triumph, that of Jack Lovelock in the All-Black vest of New Zealand in the 1,500 metres.

Chris Mackenzie and the rest of the New Zealand contingent were only a tiny part indeed of the 120,000 crowd that day but they cheered themselves hoarse as little Jack from Timaru Boys' High and Otago University glided past the favourite, the American and World record holder, Glenn Cunningham, and the Olympic record holder from Italy, Luigi Beccali, to win in a new record time of 3 mins 47.8 secs. The race was generally conceded to be the best track race ever run in the forty years of the modern Olympics and a masterpiece of tactics and pace on the part of the slim John Edward Lovelock. He had done medicine at Otago and had been one of big Thelma's heroes on the faculty, but he had left just as she and Chris arrived at the university so they never really knew him. Nevertheless, like everyone else in New Zealand, she was thrilled when he first broke the mile record in the University Games at Princeton in 1933 and again at the Empire Games in the following year, but this Olympic win was the biggest yet and the party that night in the gymnastic ladies boarding house was joyful and rowdy even though they only had a few beers, some Schnapps and a bottle of tepid white Riesling.

Breaking all the rules, some of the boys were there, but Miss Hacking, the chaperone, kept a wary eye on them. The male gymnasts found it difficult to leave the room to go to the bathroom. One boy suggested she should time them, but sensible discussion broke down as ripe vulgarity broke out. 'What's the present world record for a shit?' 'Is it a field or track event?' 'Does a piss require measurement for velocity or quantity?' And so on, till Miss Hacking was most confused, but for the most part it was all earthy, good fun and done with typical Kiwi candour until one of the girls called out, 'For God's sake, Chrissie, play something!' So Chris played.

The piano was off-key but so were most of the singers anyway so it didn't really matter. They sang all the usual songs. The songs they had sung after training sessions, on train journeys, during the eternity of the sea voyage. Chris more than earned her keep. She was not only the official accompanist to the gymnastics team but the unofficial accompanist to the whole New Zealand team in all their social hours. She didn't mind. She liked playing and she liked them – well, most of them anyway. Some of the officials were a bit pompous and snooty but then that's what most officials are.

They take a tiny bit of authority and tease it out to make a rope to hang you with. The New Zealanders hadn't a great deal of time for their officials. Tonight, however, all the recriminations, petty jealousies and animosities that arise in any group thrown tightly together for any length of time were forgotten as they celebrated the New Zealand gold and Jack Lovelock. He was their only medal and they were determined to make the most of him!

As in most New Zealand sing-songs, the songs they sang were mostly Irish and Scottish with a dash of the Negro to honour Jesse Owens:

> 'De Camptown ladies sing dis song, doo dah, doo dah,
> De Camptown racetrack five miles long, doo dah,
>   doo dah day . . .
> Gwine to run all night, gwine to run all day,
> I'll bet my money on de bobtail nag,
> Somebody bet on de bay.'

This song had almost become the New Zealand team's unofficial anthem and some of the athletes had added their own verses. They bawled it out raucously.

> 'We came over here with a lad named Jack,
>   doo dah, doo dah,
> For he's gonna bring a Gold Medal back, doo dah,
>   doo dah day . . .
> Glenn can run all night, Luigi run all day,
> But we'll put our money on Timaru Jack,
> He's gonna win all the way.'

And so on and so forth – 'When Irish Eyes are smiling', 'Annie Laurie', 'The Grandfather's Clock', 'John Brown's Body', and 'Oh, dear what can the matter be?', a parody on which the men had made their own, but which Chris staunchly refused to play. There were some things even she couldn't do to oblige them, and this lusty version was one of them. This surprised many in the party, for Chris Mackenzie, almost from the very beginning of the trip, had established herself as 'one of the boys'. She was without doubt one of the most popular young persons in the party, and was in as much demand for her witty company as for her playing.

What was noticed, however, was that she always kept in the crowd. Despite very strong advances from husky and handsome

566

young athletes during the long days and even longer nights on the voyage, Chris Mackenzie was still as much her own woman when she arrived in Europe as when she left Auckland. It wasn't as if she didn't enjoy the company of men, but as far as she was concerned there was safety in numbers. They were waiting only for a sign. But neither during that sing-song, nor during the trip, was any sign given. She never even made a close friend with any of the girls. They in their turn were so dedicated to their performances on the field or track or floor, that they had few thoughts for anything else. As a result, Chris was in a sense apart from the rest. This didn't worry her one iota. She was enjoying the whole life-changing experience and couldn't wait 'to do Europe' when the Games were over.

Her fingers played the old songs almost automatically, so she was free to let her mind wander. There would be a week free in London and that would mean seeing the Tower, the House of Commons, even Covent Garden if she could afford it. Pity there wasn't time to go to Scotland. It was so much a part of her, she had been told, more by Gran Keith than by her mother. But Scotland seemed very strange and foreign and distant when she was a child. She could only feel a New Zealander, for that's what she was. She had a Scottish mother, grandmother and uncle, but somehow they were different. They were family. They belonged in New Zealand. She remembered the sensation Becky Friar caused when she'd come with cousin, Abel, all those years ago. She thought at first she was Australian, because they'd come from Sydney, but her accent was just like Gran's, only softer, and Chris remembered being in awe of this tall, elegant Scots woman. She remembered too the nuisance Abel had made of himself and all the scandalous talk by the adults, but she had only been around fourteen at the time and hadn't paid much attention.

Now she was within a few days of London and her first real visit to England. Nearly every member of the team had a relative to meet them, but she had no one. Uncle Jim had written to his brother, John, in Forres, mentioning that Chris would be in London during the first week of September, but there had been no reply from him before she left and she didn't think it likely he would make the effort 'to come up', as they said, to the capital. She could never understand why they said 'up' to London, when it was so obviously 'down' from Forres. But that was just another quaint 'British-ism' she would have to live with. Anyway, Uncle John was now well over sixty, and according to Uncle Jim, didn't keep too well, whatever that meant, so she never gave her single remaining relative in Scotland another thought. There was so much else to think about. Other things to do. Other songs to sing . . .

*

Maria d'Agostino, for instance, was singing another kind of song. Her film career was now gladly over. After the meeting with her lost half-brother, she had returned the next morning and finished the last take in one. Seven years of saccharine celluloid were behind her. Now she must make up for that lost time. Vernon had called London that very morning. Could the opera offer be re-discussed?

'Who cares about the money, my dear fellow? She'll do it for nothing.' This would appeal to any management and Covent Garden was no less interested. A deal was quickly struck which meant she would do it for peanuts, if she could do it soon. Their first production was Mozart's *Don Giovanni*, already in rehearsal. As it happened, the soprano singing Donna Anna was proving difficult . . . Something might be worked out . . .

During these hectic days of negotiation by Vernon, Maria had eyes only for Tito. This reserved young man, already a generation beyond his fifteen years, eyed her with a regard that might politely be described as cool, but more accurately may be said to have been hostile. He had an adult disdain which was slightly less than endearing, but his exceptional good looks and Irish residual charm did much to offset this. In the first few days, the half-brother and sister were subtly trying to work out their respective positions. Each had a hauteur that indicated they were used to having their own way, and both knew one would have to yield in this situation if the two were to exist together.

Maria wondered why her father had sent him to her at this time. What did he expect her to do with him? Why had he not remained with the Italian woman? His Italian was impeccable, so it hadn't been entirely a waste of time. He could, in fact, prove very valuable to her if she was able to make the return to opera. Tito himself gave no clue as to his own feelings in the matter. He regarded Rico d'Agostino as his godfather, which in more senses than one, he was. Rico, for his part, was almost obsessed by the boy, because he was Noreen's son. When Liam Murphy had committed suicide, it seemed only natural that Rico should reclaim Tito for Noreen's sake and give him a better background and education than Francesca could give him in any of the New York schools. In his heart, Rico had never really forgiven Francesca, and bringing Tito first to Chicago and then to Miami was in a way part of his revenge. The upshot was that Tito Murphy was by this stage a thoroughly spoiled young man. Tall, good looking, intelligent, charming, but spoiled just the same. Maria recognised in him not only her half-brother, but nearly a whole replication of herself in terms of egotism and conceit. In effect, they virtually cancelled each other out, but their slight differences were sufficient to keep them interested in each other and antagonistic. All they had genuinely in common was their Irish mother, and neither ever mentioned her. This may have been because Tito had never known her, and because Maria wanted to forget her.

For his part, Vernon Drake was in heaven. In addition to his adorable Maria, he had now been sent this most beautiful young man. Vernon moved between the two of them like a shuttlecock, eager to be batted down by one and flipped aside by the other. Just as long as he was kept in the game, he was quite content. He was a precious vassal to two exquisites and, in Vernon's mind, that made for the perfect *modus vivendi*. In all practical aspects of their daily existence, they had to look to him and he revelled in their dependence on him. His eyes were only for their gilded gifts and he never looked down low enough to ever see their feet of clay.

His finest hour came when he brandished the cable from London.

'I've done it!' he preened. 'All conditions met, and first class travel and hotels if you will forfeit your usual percentage. I then asked that Tito here –' he beamed at the boy '– be included as your personal secretary and they've agreed. Which means that he travels First Class too.'

'Is there another way to travel?' said the boy unsmiling.

Maria laughed. 'When do we sail?' she said.

'Sunday.'

'As soon as that?'

'The sooner the better.'

'Why the hurry?'

'You might change your mind.' Kevin O'Neil laughed. 'You haven't changed much, Sam Cassidy.' Yet even as he said it he knew that old Sam had changed a great deal. His former commandant and now brother-in-law was dying and they both knew it. His liver had packed up and his saffron yellow face was proof of it if any were needed. He had come home from hospital only a few days before but no one was talking about the reasons why.

'You'll do it?' asked Sam feebly. His voice was drained of all vitality. Kevin had to bend over the bed to listen.

'How can I refuse if it's helping you out,' he said.

'It could be dangerous,' continued Sam weakly.

'So is crossing the road,' answered Kevin, trying to be cheerful.

'You could get yourself killed.'

'We've all got to die.' He had said it before he realised what he'd said. He reached for his old friend's hand on top of the covers. It was sticky with perspiration.

'I'm sorry, Sam.' Sam shook his head, then half-smiled.

'You couldn't have said a truer word,' he whispered, and closed his eyes. Kevin sat looking at him for a moment and a feeling of angry helplessness swept over him as he knew that Sam was slowly slipping away and there was nothing he could do about it. He rose and went back downstairs to the office where Nellie was bending over a large ledger. She looked up as her younger brother came in.

'Isn't it awful how the money goes? That's another two hundred for towels.' Kevin said nothing but took the seat at the other side of the small desk. 'See what I mean?' Her tone was sombre now.

Kevin nodded gravely. 'Worse than I thought,' he said.

'That's why he wanted to see you.' Nellie pursed her lips. She looked as if she might cry at any moment. 'Did he say –'

'We talked a bit.'

'What about?'

'This 'n that.' Nellie's head shot up, her eyes on fire.

'Now listen here, Kevin O'Neil,' she snapped, 'don't play your wee boys' games wi' me. Do ye think I've not lived with a man for this time and not guessed at what he does?' It was Kevin's turn to look angry. Nellie went on. 'Don't worry, he's never told me a thing. Sam wouldn't do that and you know it. But then there's the simple thing now – he talks in his sleep.' Kevin laughed. 'Oh you can laugh, but there it is.' She paused for a moment then went on. 'You're to take his place in Spain and you've to meet a man in London on Monday morning.' That wiped the laugh from Kevin's throat.

'How did you find out?' She shrugged.

'It wasn't clever or anything. You know me. But he was learning Spanish just before he went into hospital and the man in London kept ringing here to speak to him. Which was a very stupid thing to do.' Kevin couldn't agree more.

'What was the man's name?'

'O'Leary.' That was the contact right enough.

'What else did Sam say in his sleep?' Nellie managed a smile.

'Ah, that would be tellin',' she said. 'Tell me,' she went on, 'Teresa and the girls, are they well?'

'They're fine,' he replied. He couldn't even tell his own sister how it broke his heart to leave his wife and daughters, and their comfortable house. Especially not being able to tell Teresa when he might be back.

'Could be a month. Could be a year. Then again, I could be back tomorrow. You can never tell,' he had told her.

'No,' she had said to him, her big eyes welling with tears, 'and it's just as well is it not, for sure you might never be back at a' an' me an' the girls would be starved of you for all of our lives.' He had held her very close he remembered.

'Right enough, ye have a lovely family there, Kevin.'

'Ay so,' he said.

'I was sorry to hear about Mrs Dacre.' He nodded.

'She felt no pain.'

'No she wouldn't.' Kevin rose. He was impatient to be away.

'So you'll be going in the morning?'

'First thing. I'll be in London tomorrow night.'

'It's a fine place, London. A fine, big place. Not that I've been there mind. Here, I better get back to these accounts.' Her head bent over the ledger again and Kevin knew that no ostrich could have put its head further into the sand. As he looked down at her he thought how much like their mother she had become. My dear old Mother, he thought, God rest her soul. She had slipped away in her sleep as if she hadn't wanted to tell anyone she was going. She had never been to London either.

When the New Zealand Olympic team returned to London, Chris Mackenzie, much to her surprise, found a message waiting for her at the Victoria boarding house. It was addressed to Miss Christina Mackenzie, so Chris knew at once it was someone who didn't know her well. It was, in fact, someone who didn't know her at all: her Uncle John. He was in London at the Strand Palace Hotel with a friend, and would be glad to see her there if she could manage it. Would she please ring and ask for him in Room 125? She put in her two pennies in the public telephone box in the hall. Her heart was thumping as the coins fell into the empty coin box. It was a very strange voice which greeted her.

'Aye. This is John Keith,' it uttered sonorously. 'Who is that speaking?'

'It's Chris. Chris Mackenzie,' she answered breathily.

'I can't hear you very well. Will you speak up please?'

'Chris Mackenzie.' She almost shouted into the receiver.

'Oh, it's you, Tina's lass. Well, well . . .'

It was arranged that they meet at the hotel on the following night, Tuesday. They could then discuss what she wanted to do in the rest of the week. What she wanted to do most was to hear some music, particularly the Opera at Covent Garden or Sadler's Wells. There was also the New England Opera Company and the

Carl Rosa Touring Company. All of these names she knew from her studies in New Zealand, but she'd never actually seen a live opera. Or did she mean hear a live opera? This was perhaps her only chance. The point was, would Uncle John agree?

Uncle John beamed at her happily over the dinner table. 'If that's what ye want to do, lass, that's what we do. Isn't that so, Alec?'

'I couldn't have put it better, John,' grinned Alec Friar, still uncomfortable in his black suit, but mellowing by the minute under the influence of a steady succession of drams. It was his idea that they come to London. When John had received the letter from Jim, he had mentioned it to Alec only as being an impossibility.

'Why so?' Alec had asked. 'You've nothing else to do, and there's the lassie all alone in London for a week. She's your own flesh and blood, man. Your own sister's lassie. I think it's your duty to see her.'

'I can't afford it,' John had protested.

'Of course you can,' riposted Alec.

'How so?' went on John.

'Because I'm paying for both of us.' And that's how they had arrived at the Strand Palace Hotel in London, which was the only place John knew. And that's how Chris found herself sitting opposite two elderly Scottish gentlemen in the dining-room on the following night.

If she was overwhelmed by the sumptuousness of the hotel, the salutes of porters, the bowings of waiters, she was totally taken aback by the sight of her Uncle John. He was not at all like Uncle Jim. He was not even like Uncle Bobby. He was Uncle John, and that was that. Big, bluff as a bear, but gentle as a lamb, Chris took to him at once. She guessed he must be in his mid-sixties, but he looked older. The reason was never far from his right hand and yet he never seemed drunk. His speech was never slurred and he didn't stagger about. He was certainly no commonplace, maundering toper, but a soft-eyed giant with a mordant merriment in him and there was more than a hint of sadness. What was his sadness, she wondered?

'You're Tina ower the back,' he had said to her as soon as he saw her. It took several minutes for Chris to work out with both men's help that he meant she bore a more than usual resemblance to her mother.

'It's only natural, I suppose,' said Chris.

'No, it's not,' said Alec Friar with more than a called-for vehemence. John gave him a quick look. Alec looked down at his plate. What goes on here, wondered Chris, but she said nothing. John waved away a waiter with matches and lit his own pipe. Between puffs, he explained Alec to Chris.

'You see lass – this man here – is my friend. He is not only my friend – he is my host – and yours tonight too – so I'd better watch what I say – I don't want to offend him – or I might land a bill to pay! Anyway, Christina –' Uncle John insisted on calling her by her full Sunday name and he also insisted on being called 'Uncle' by her. 'They're titles that neither of us asked for you see, or worked for,' he had told her, 'so the only thing to do is use them!' She couldn't quite see the logic in this but she didn't demur. 'Anyway, as I was saying,' he went on, 'Alec here had a daughter who was, what ye might say, not all she might have been, but she in turn had a daughter, by my brother in fact, who was as fine a lass as I have ever met . . .' His voice drifted away at this point and both Alec and Chris waited for him to resume.

'What I mean is, things can skip a generation.'

'You mean like red hair?' asked Alec.

'That kinda thing. Ay,' replied John. Meantime, Chris had been thinking – and putting two and two together. She put down her knife and fork and waited until she had finished chewing.

'Uncle John?'

'Ay?'

'Do you mean Becky Friar?' John had been re-lighting his pipe again and the match was still in his hand. They watched as it went out.

Becky couldn't help laughing at the expression on her father's face. Bobby Keith had just come face to face with his mother for the first time in thirty-five years and her immediate response had not been flattering.

'Ye're awfy fat!' she'd said in a loud voice. Bobby had blustered something about just having the right figure for his age.

'Nonsense,' snapped his mother, peering at his middle. 'Ye've enough beer in that belly to float a dray!' Rachel joined in the general mirth but tried to save her husband's blushes by saying something about his being in a desk job these days, now that he was in Labour politics.

'All the more reason he should be out and about if he's in politics. The trouble with Labour is that it's not hard labour!' This was hardly the tender exchange that had been expected on the quayside on that September morning in Sydney. Bobby and Rachel had been preparing for her arrival for weeks and Bobby had even re-painted the guest-room for the old lady, but now they learned that she wasn't even going to be staying with them. She had decided to take a ground-floor room with bath in Becky's Harbour Hotel.

'It's all arranged,' she said with great finality. Bobby looked at his daughter keenly. Becky felt embarrassed and only shrugged.

'That's fine then,' said Bobby lamely.

'Well, let's get going then. We can't sit about here all day,' announced Gran Keith from her wheelchair. Bobby could still not take it in. This was hardly the sick woman he remembered from that long-ago emigration voyage. Or the pallid, domesticated drudge who had been his father's Scottish wife. She had suffered a considerable sea-change, although suffered was perhaps not the appropriate word for it. She had positively bloomed in her own sinewy kind of way. Life blazed in her frail frame as if she were determined to make every one of her ninety years count. He had always thought of her as a permanent invalid being shuttled from one New Zealand house to another throughout nearly four decades, but this doughty nonagenerian he was now pushing through the Customs Shed was almost a stranger to her own son.

Not, however, to her daughter-in-law. Rachel had perhaps seen Mrs Keith no more than three or four times on the ship all those years ago, and apart from those few weeks in New Zealand with Jim's family, she had not seen her since. The younger Mrs Keith was amazed by how much the old girl remembered about her and her work at the university.

'You're the one that's the professor at the university?' said Gran, squinting up at her as they moved through the sheds. Rachel smiled.

'Hardly a professor, Mrs Keith. A humble lecturer, I'm afraid.'

'If you're afraid, you'll never be a good lecturer. And if you're not a professor, that's only because you're a woman. How's Abel?' The sharpness of the old dear's speech and mind was something the Australian couple were finding it hard to get used to. Each waited for the other to speak. Eventually it was Rachel who spoke.

'You know Abel, Mrs Keith,' she began.

'No I don't. Not as well as I should.' They would have to get used to the literal quality of her language. She believed that words were valuable tools to be used sparingly and efficiently and not wasted in verbal effects or literary felicities. It was the Scot in her. Direct and to the point in hand – almost brutally so.

'Call me Gran,' she said. 'Everybody else does. We don't want two Mrs Keiths in the house. One's bad enough.'

'But you're not coming to the house, Mother.'

'You know what I mean,' was the testy retort. 'You never answered my question.'

'What was that, Mother?'

'Will I see Abel?' Again there was that slight hesitation between the parents. The old woman couldn't see it but she was aware of the looks between them.

'Well?' she said impatiently. This time it was Bobby who spoke.

'He's on some flying job, Mother. Somewhere out of the country I think.' He looked helplessly at Becky.

'He's expected back any day now, Gran,' she said. 'He's doing an errand for a man at the hotel. I'll speak to him tonight and see if I can get some news.'

'Good.' Becky looked at her father. He winked.

In quick time, the shore formalities and entry matters were dealt with. This was more Bobby's area of operations than dealing with a cranky old woman who just happened to be his mother. He had friends in most public places and he had no hesitation in using them when required. In the same way he expected to be used from time to time. It was called the 'favours' game and politics couldn't really operate without it. It was understood that if you were owed one you claimed it and if you owed one you paid it. It was as simple or as complicated as that. Even Gran was impressed by the large official car Bobby had waiting for her.

'It was to take the chair,' he explained sheepishly.

'Ay, so ye say,' snorted his mother. 'I just hope your hands are clean.'

'Harbour Hotel, please,' muttered Becky quickly to the official driver. During the drive, Bobby tried to explain to his mother what his job was.

'I began as a union man because there was a need for strong unions when I first came here. Gradually, as the unions got their shops in order, I found I was moving nearer and nearer the political platform. Being at heart a Socialist, although I'm just beginning to have my doubts about practical socialism, I naturally turned to the Labour party and began to help out where I could, first as an agent and then a lobbyist for my own union, until I was drawn into the back-room stuff and before I knew it they were offering me a seat. This was when the United Australia Party started coming through – that was Abel's crowd, at least when Abel showed any interest in politics. Or maybe he just chose them because they were opposed to me. You know what sons are. Anyway, Joe Lyons left us to lead them a few years ago and with Earle Page holding the middle for the Country Party, Joe offered to go into a coalition with us and he got the short straw as our Prime Minister and I got a safe seat as a back-bencher, which is what I do now. Joe's not so well these days but I don't think I'll be PM. The word has it that Bob Menzies has that one taped. He's got the degree, you see. What else would you expect of a bloody lawyer? Never mind, it does prove the value of a degree. Eh Rachel?' He turned round from the front seat to face his wife. She was pointing to Gran Keith who was squeezed between her and Becky. The old lady was asleep!

'Bloody hell!' muttered Bobby and turned again to the front.

Becky had things really well arranged at the hotel and even Bobby was impressed by the accommodation made available for his mother. There was even a ramp at the side door, which allowed her wheelchair to come out to the rear terrace and down on to street level if she wanted. Fortunately, this was not often, and during her Sydney stay, she would spend most of the time, either in her room, or on her own balcony. Meantime, the family get-together took the form of a meal served in her room by the best of Becky's staff. Even Mr Weir himself made a polite appearance to welcome Mrs Keith on his way to the Casino. Good old Tubby! He had remembered. Becky had chilled a couple of bottles of Rosemount Sauvignon Blanc, which she knew was a good Australian vintage. Gran, however, refused to drink it.

'I don't like table wine,' she said. They were all trying to persuade her with much jocularity and teasing, when there was a knock at the door and Tubby Weir reappeared, which was most surprising. Becky was on her feet at once.

'Is there something wrong, Mr Weir?'

'I'd like a word with you, Miss Friar.' He motioned her towards the door. Becky was puzzled as much by his formal behaviour as by his reappearance.

'Of course,' she said. 'Will you excuse me, Gran? Dad? Rachel?' The younger Keiths mumbled something polite and as Becky left the room, she heard Gran saying loudly, 'Where's the girl going?'

Tubby was waiting for her and motioned with his finger for her to follow him. They crossed the main foyer and into the office alcove where her own office adjoined his, and it was to the General Manager's office they went. He held the door open for her and as she went in, he followed quickly, closing the door behind him. Becky halted abruptly after only a step into the room, for there, seated on the couch staring straight at her was Abel.

'Abel!' Her instinct was to run forward and embrace him but there was something about the way his head jerked up at the sound of her voice that froze her on the spot. She could only stare at him as he continued to stare at her.

576

'Abel, what's –' Another voice spoke in the room. It was Captain Dickenson. He rose from a chair on the other side.

'I'm sorry to have to bring you from your family, Miss Friar –' (there was no sign of the familiar drunkard about him now, thought Becky) – 'but it was important that you should meet Abel again in what we might call controlled circumstances. So Mr Weir and I thought his office would be the best place in the circumstances.'

Becky glanced at Tubby who nodded, then looked quickly away towards Dickenson, whose eyes never left Becky. She in turn looked back to Abel. He was still staring at her with that same stare. There was something odd about that stare.

'I must explain,' she heard the Captain's voice continue, 'Abel is at present under strong sedation –' Becky wheeled round on him – 'He's quite capable of responding to you but you must understand his reactions might be a little – delayed.'

'What's the matter with him?' Becky almost shouted the query. Dickenson resumed his seat before answering.

'Abel is blind, my dear.' There was a stunned silence. Becky whirled round to look at her half-brother.

'I don't believe it,' she whispered.

'Is that you, Becky?' It was Abel. Rather, it was a voice coming from Abel. It didn't sound like him at all. More like a metallic recording of what he used to sound like. Was he drugged?

'Abel?' Becky heard herself say as if from miles away. 'You alright?' It sounded so banal, but what else could she say? Abel seemed to consider the question before he replied.

'Sure, I'm alright.' There was another pause in the tiny office. Tubby could be heard trying to stifle a cough. Becky turned to Dickenson.

'What happened?' She spoke in a low voice as if they were at a sick bed. Or a death bed. The Captain regarded her steadily.

'There was an accident,' he said.

'I'll tell you what happened.' She turned. It was Abel again.

The Captain quickly intervened. 'Abel, I don't think you can –'

'I'm not sure I can either, Captain, but I'll have a bloody good try.' He paused slightly as if making a supreme effort to concentrate, only it looked as if he were finding it hard to breathe. 'You still there, Becky?' His voice was weaker now, but oddly enough, more like himself. She went forward and knelt at his knees. His hand moved up. She grasped it and pressed it to her neck. His hand felt moist and clammy, and it was unnerving seeing the face she knew so well staring at something over her head. There was no sign of injury or damage, just this fixed stare.

'Yes, Abel?' Her own voice was no more than a whisper. She was sure that Abel's lips went into a grin before he spoke again.

'They put two extra tanks on, one on each wing. It was going to be a long flight, so they said. They put some kind of bag in the seat behind me, the seat you were in, remember?' She nodded, but then realised he couldn't see her. 'Then when we were all ready and I got myself strapped in and was all set to check the instruments, I switched on the engine, and the whole bloody thing went up.' He laughed again. This time it was louder and with a strange edge to it. 'I'm telling you, Becks, they blew their own plane up and with me in it.' He shook his head as if still not believing it. 'They must have got their wires crossed. And up went the tanks as soon as contact was made. I came to in a hospital somewhere. Couldn't tell you where. Couldn't see a thing. Thought it must be night time. It was eleven o'clock in the morning. Couldn't see a thing. Pitch black. I wasn't Cat's Eyes Keith any more. I was Abel Blind-as-a-Bat. And that's that.' There was a long silence. Becky continued to hold his hand, because she couldn't think of anything else to say. She heard the scrape of a chair behind her and the Captain's voice again.

'I've made arrangements with Mr Weir that Abel can remain in the hotel as a permanent guest. All costs of course will be met by me.'

'Should bloody well think so. Though that's a whole cargo up in smoke, eh Captain?'

'One of the hazards of the game, Abel.'

Becky wheeled round on him. 'And what sort of game is it, Captain, that costs my brother his sight?'

'It was a mere chance. Human error. One can never legislate for human error, my dear. At least your brother is alive.'

'What life is there for a blind pilot?' cried Becky. She found she was still holding Abel's hand in hers. Abel started to laugh again.

'I could always fly blind!' he said.

'You can come with me, that's what you can do,' said Becky firmly.

'Miss Friar, I don't –' began Tubby.

'And you can shut up for a start,' she hissed vehemently. Then, tenderly, she raised Abel to his feet. 'Come and meet Gran.'

She had to steel herself to open the door to Gran's suite, but, taking a breath, and keeping a firm hold on Abel's hand, she pushed the door open and pulled her half-brother in behind her. Affecting her brightest voice, she said, 'Gran, I've brought you a visitor.' The old lady immediately straightened up in her chair.

'Oh?' she said.

'It's Abel. Abel Keith. He's just got back.' She pushed Abel gently in front of her. Bobby and Rachel both rose slowly, staring at their son. Gran Keith peered around vaguely.

'Oh, these eyes o' mine! Where are you, son?'

'I'm here, Gran.'

'Oh, so you are. My, it's nice to see you, Abel.'

'It's nice to see you, Gran.'

The presidential campaign was in full swing throughout the United States. President Roosevelt was under heavy attack for his New Deal programme to fight the continuing Depression, and his National Recovery Administration was seen as an attempt by the Republican right to impose a centralised economy. During his campaign for a second term, the President was to say that one third of the American nation was ill-housed, ill-clad and ill-nourished. If this were so, Rico d'Agostino was well insulated from it in his Miami mansion. The stroke which he had suffered in the previous year had not only impeded his speech, but even worse, it had disfigured his once handsome face and wasted his left arm and leg. He spent most of his days now in his luxurious study looking on to the water at West Palm Beach with the telephone in his right hand. For some reason, his sibilant lisping into the receiver was more comprehensible to the listener at the other end than his direct speech to anyone in his presence. So he made more and more recourse to the telephone. He called everyone. Even the Republican aspirant, Alfred Landon, was called up and advised how to conduct his campaign. Alfred Landon was not disposed to take telephone calls from strangers, but the promise of one hundred thousand dollars from an Italian in Miami was sufficient to make him call back at once. Another call was to Il Duce in Rome. In this instance, Rico did not actually speak to Benito Mussolini himself, but spoke at length to Count Galeazzo Ciano, Mussolini's son-in-law, who was also his Foreign Minister. He professed interest in Rico's idea of an extension of the Axis in the Western Hemisphere in a vertical line from Canada to Cuba involving all Italian connections en route. Rico pointed out that he had all the connections and could find the money. All he needed from the Italian Government was the prestige. Prestige was important to Rico at this time. He had nothing else to live for. But his political aspirations came to nothing, and he contented himself with further screenings of Maria's movies and the playing of her records at full volume throughout the house.

This was partly why he suffered from a continuing changeover of staff, and why standards, domestically, were not of the quality he had hitherto applied. Given the old man's heightened obsessions, it was perhaps little wonder that he didn't notice he was being continually robbed by a succession of housekeepers and retainers. And it was when one of his cheques was marked 'Return to Drawer' that he realised something was terribly wrong. Hurried telephone conversations with accountants in New York, Chicago and Rome soon redressed his financial position, but it caused him to panic. All the staff were summarily dismissed, and only one old woman, Elvira Desti, who had been with the family for thirty years, remained. In fact, she had refused to go, and no amount of intimidation on his part, or Guiseppe's, could make her move from her kitchen. Guiseppe was Rico's only remaining brother – a dour, untypical Italian, he was content to be his older brother's valet and driver. Thus was the d'Agostino entourage shrunk and Rico's life shrunk with it. He had his bed placed in the studio/study and two large locked boxes of which only he knew the contents. As far as he was concerned, the rest of the house did not exist. The rest of the world did not exist. And before the year was out, Rico d'Agostino ceased to exist. Landon lost the election by a landslide to the Democratic Roosevelt and at least one third of America rejoiced.

So did Guiseppe d'Agostino. On his brother's death, he was seen to smile for the first time, and a most unexpected marriage of convenience took place between him and the matronly Elvira Desti. According to the will, everything went to Guiseppe. It was widely said that he had something of a hand in last minute codicils towards the end. The only exception was that the two boxes were to go to the two children, Maria and Tito, wherever they were. The keys were held by the lawyers, and the boxes could only be opened by them in the presence of the named parties. Both were in London while Maria rehearsed for her operatic comeback at Covent Garden, so a representative of the legal firm was empowered to accompany the boxes to London. The Customs insisted on opening both in New York. The lawyer insisted on being present and witnessed the fact that each box contained one million dollars in hundred dollar bills! So the money was kept in the family and the lucky one third remained fortunate.

The other third was best represented by Joey O'Neil. He was not ill-housed, ill-clad, or ill-nourished. But neither was he a dollar millionaire. In many ways, he was more fortunate. He was in the oblivious one third that lived in their own world, rather than the world's world. Despite the fact that he had inherited his mother's estate and his uncles' wealth, it was held in trust for him by the Police Association, who were responsible for paying his residential bills at the Ridgefield Park Nursing Home in New

Jersey. Since his mother's death, Joey had lived an idyllic life here. The only change as far as he was concerned since he was orphaned was that he had eschewed the Meccano Set in favour of Monopoly. He had taken up the game when it became all the rage only a few years before, and was by this time an undisputed master of it. What astounded the doctors was that in this game of chance there was an element of calculation and mental decision which might have been thought to have been beyond the genial and placid Joey. But so determined was he to master this parlour game, that he unwittingly exercised latent cerebral powers that were within him. That had always been within him. And this intrigued the medical authorities at Ridgefield Park and was the cause of much speculation and conjecture on their part. Joey, of course, was blissfully unaware of all this, due to the fact that for most of the time he was blissful. At fifty-four he was totally unmarked by life. Perhaps a thinning of the hair, an inch or two on his girth, but otherwise he loped around the wards and the grounds much as he had moved around the Brooklyn blocks. People who had pitied Joey O'Neil did not realise how wrong they had been. The only time he showed any human annoyance or manifested an approach to anger was when he lost a game of Monopoly – which wasn't often. He would ask everyone and anyone to play. The nursing home staff were constantly badgered into a game. Even visitors were not free from his demands. Few could refuse him, for Joey was ostensibly still the charming young man. No matter that he was blessed by default, he was blessed. He lived his own kind of charmed life and he lived it to the full. The world as it was then may have been unacceptable to the many, but Joey, like others in his kind of third world, lived in his own and happily ever after.

Only one incident looked to threaten this apparent idyll. The staff had decided to take the patients, most of whom were elderly, to the cinema in the town as a special treat. This was part of a new policy to see how their patients would function as a group in the outside world. As it happened, the film being shown on the afternoon of that first social experiment was *Mystery at the Opera*, starring Maria d'Agostino and Tony Marino. It was serendipity. A film with musical content would be a better choice for their group than one of the fashionable gangster dramas with violent action. They were therefore taken totally aback by the violent action that ensued, and Joey O'Neil was the reason.

Being less impaired than most of the others, he was often called on to assist the male nurses. On this occasion, he was in charge of one of the wheelchairs, and had happily seated himself beside it as the lights went down. The management had agreed to allow the chairs down one side aisle as long as hospital staff were seated in the adjacent seats. The matinee was crowded, perhaps because of the rain that they'd had that day. It could even have been because of Maria d'Agostino's popularity, but, for whatever reason, the auditorium gave a warm welcome to her name as it appeared on the screen in the way that cinema audiences welcome their favourite stars – not by applauding as in the theatre, but by a steady murmur of approbation and appreciation, which can be heard clearly in cinemas everywhere. The reaction of the patients in this case was not clear, as some of them were talking loudly to the nurses, and one was heard to say plainly, 'I don't like this dark!' However, everyone was eventually mollified and more or less quieted and the film began.

It was Maria's first appearance that did it. She was seen first at the top of a staircase as the music started, then as she descended, she started to sing. The effect on Joey O'Neil was astonishing. At first, he couldn't believe it. His eyes widened and his jaw dropped. He forgot completely where he was as he stared at the image on the screen of this beautiful young woman. He was entirely rapt. Maria was next seen in bed. It was morning and she was stretching her arms just before getting up. She looked particularly lovely and very young. Suddenly Joey's voice was heard calling, 'Hi, Noreena!' Everybody was so taken aback that they said nothing, until he called again. 'Gee, you look great, Noreena!' Maria didn't resemble her mother completely, but she was sufficiently like her to reawaken the memory of her in him. The usher was on him immediately with a torch, and the light flashed in his face.

'Hey, what are you doin'?' yelled Joey. Others in the audience made hushing sounds and various remarks like 'What's wrong with the guy?' And when the senior nurse, a woman, hurried down to him and said, 'You just be quiet now, Joey O'Neil.' Joey just shrugged.

'OK, OK.' he said. The film continued.

It was when Tony Marino appeared that the trouble started. When he tried to kiss Maria, Joey jumped up in his seat shouting,

'Hey, you leave her alone!' This time people shouted out loud for him to be quiet, but Joey had eyes only for the screen, and when Marino actually kissed Maria, that was too much for Joey. He pushed the wheelchair aside and ran down towards the screen. He stood in front of it, a pygmy silhouette, berating the images while they kissed. Two male ushers were on to him immediately, but he easily threw them off. They were joined by two of the male nurses, and a positive mêlée ensued in the narrow space between the screen and the front seats. Some cinema-goers rose up angrily and others screamed in fright. This caused the patients from the nursing home to become upset, particularly as Joey, their favourite, was involved and in fact was the victim in their eyes. Those who were ambulant started moving towards the scene of the live action, going underneath the duet being sung above their heads. The houselights now came on and the manager appeared on stage looking as if he'd just been wakened from sleep, which he had. Altogether it was mayhem and eventually the screen ran out in a series of diminishing numbers, and Joey was frogmarched out by no less than four men, who had a grip of each of his arms and legs. Joey was still protesting.

'Why does he do that to Noreena? It's not right. It's not right, I'm tellin' you.'

Joey was never allowed out in public again and the cinema excursion was discontinued as a social experiment. Joey himself forgot about the whole thing in a matter of days, and happily returned to his games of Monopoly.

THIRTY-FIVE

Patrick, Archbishop of Seattle, was playing chess with his secretary, Father John Conlan, in the quiet of the former's study.

'Come on now, John. I think you can take the Bishop.'

'Indeed, Your Grace,' replied the young priest, 'but it's the problem of taking the Archbishop more concerns me.' Paddy laughed. These games with his clever young secretary priest were the most enjoyable parts of the day for the new Archbishop. They were a brief respite from the onerous chores of administration which seemed to concern him more than any priestly duties. Clerical work for him had formerly meant pastoral work, but now it was largely a matter of bureaucracy, moving piles of paper from one end of the desk to another. These games after dinner were a necessary therapy as well as a pleasant and stimulating pastime. The long wait between the moves gave the Archbishop time to think. Some nights he remembered his first games of chess with Sven, the Swede, on the old Campania. Lord, that was a long time ago. Thirty-five years at least. And then how he'd broken the board over that fellow's head in Ellis Island. May God forgive me! It was a beautiful board too!

'What would you think, Father – oh, don't let me disturb your concentration –'

John Conlan smiled. 'Not at all, Your Grace.'

'Yes, what would you think if I told you that I once broke a beautiful chessboard over the head of a fellow.'

Father Conlan looked up. 'Were you being beaten then?'

'No, he was,' replied the Archbishop enigmatically. 'Your move.' He took another sip of his Bushmills Malt. Since he'd come to Seattle, he'd ordered this single malt especially. It was the only Irish single malt and the best.

'And why not the best for the Archbishop?' Father Conlan had remarked. But Paddy enjoyed it. It had a smoky taste to it and it gave him the same feeling in drinking it as in hearing John McCormack sing an Irish song. But almost as importantly, the Bushmills gave him a warm echo of his own father, who certainly

could never have afforded single malt. Sean and Michael in their
heyday might have done. Paddy sighed in remembering his lively
brothers. They that play with fire shall be consumed by fire, he
thought ruefully. He was glad his mother had slipped away as she
did. He would remember her as she had been when she was young.
When we were all young. Long ago in Ireland . . .

It was perhaps the good dinner, the good malt, the good
company, the comfort of the fireside, but that evening the good
Archbishop was wont to dwell thoughtfully on his family. There
had been so many of them and now so few. Maybe that was why
Irish families were so big. It improved the chances. As it was, there
had been untimely rippings-off. He wasn't thinking only of Sean
and Michael, but poor Noreen's going was a sad one. Still, she'd
left a daughter who'd made her mark. It's funny, he thought, that
she's become so famous and I've seen so little of her. My own
sister's girl, and she might be a stranger from another galaxy.
Well, she is a star, I suppose, he mused. In London, now, I see
from the newspapers. Covent Garden, no less. A long way from
twice-nightly at the South Broad Street Theatre in Philadelphia.

'Your move, Your Grace.'

'I'm sorry, John. I was far away.'

'In Rosstrevor, Your Grace?' asked the young secretary, gently.

'No, Philadelphia, actually.'

'Really, Your Grace.' There was a hint of surprise in his voice.

'Tell me, John,' said Paddy O'Neil, eyeing the board before
him.

'Yes, Your Grace?'

'Have we a gramophone recording of Maria d'Agostino?'

'Oh, yes, your niece?'

'That's right, John. My niece. I seem to remember –'

'Yes, I think I can put my hands on one of them over in the
cabinet there.'

'Is the gramophone still working?'

'Well, it was the last time you had Mr McCormack on. Remember there was talk of his singing at the Dublin Eucharistic
Congress?'

'Just so, John. Just so. Well, if you can separate the tenors from
the sopranos – they tell me by the way that it's a complicated
process – we'll have my niece on the turntable if you please.
And while you're up on your feet, I can get on with cheatin'
you here.'

'Yes, Your Grace,' grinned Father Conlan and rose up from
his armchair. Within minutes the voice of Maria d'Agostino was
flooding the room.

'Your move, John.'

'That was quick, Your Grace.'

'Sure I wanted to listen to the singing.' Father Conlan resumed his seat, and Archbishop Patrick O'Neil lay back in his. Maria's voice soared into the aria from *Don Giovanni*, – 'Batti, batti, o bel Masetto', as sung by Zerlina in the opera. As the aria began, Paddy gave in to the beautiful melody and the beautiful voice. This was the voice of the young Maria d'Agostino in the first bloom of her career, and on the wings of that gorgeous sound he was wafted in thought six thousand miles to London.

Outside Covent Garden Theatre in London, Denny felt his mother's fingers tighten on the muscles of his right arm.

'Not so tight, Mama!' he said, chidingly. 'That's my bad arm, remember?'

His mother didn't even seem to notice. Her eyes were on everyone and everything. The crowds in the street, the magnificent pillars of the theatre itself, the strange sounds and smells of a great city, another city, foreign to both of them. They were in Europe. They were in London. And they were about to see an opera. Denny wasn't so sure of the event. There were many places in London he would rather have been, like the Café de Paris, or those nice little places in Berkeley Square he had seen and the good jazz he'd heard coming from places up little narrow streets. He would love to have explored London for his kind of happening, but for now, this was his mother's trip and she was doing the choosing.

So far, in the first week, they had heard two orchestral concerts in the Albert Hall, a recital at the Wigmore Hall and now here they were at the Opera. His mother's Bohemian need for aesthetic sustenance was being well satisfied. Her happiness was his happiness, so patting her arm, he led her into the crowded foyer.

'To think, Denny,' said Hana, 'all these people just to see your cousin. Your Pops, he would have been proud man.'

'Sure, Mama. Come on. Gee, there's quite a crowd.'

At the same time and in the same street, a young New Zealander was no less enthusiastic. Chris Mackenzie had hardly been able to contain her excitement all that day, but the avuncular pressure shown by John and his crony, Alec, was not sufficient to stop her high anticipation, although it certainly slowed it down. Alec, particularly, was unenthusiastic.

'I don't think this operetta stuff is for me.'

'This isn't operetta, Mr Friar,' explained Chris. 'This is Mozart.'

'I don't care what kind of art it is.' Chris sighed, and appealed to her Uncle John.

'You tell him, Uncle John.'

'Alec, I'm sure in your time you've put into a few unlikely ports.'

'I have indeed.'

'Well, just look on this fruit market as a bad port of call.'

'You mean like Colombo or Port Said?'

'That's right.'

'What do you mean "fruit market", Uncle John?' asked Chris bemused.

'We're at Covent Garden, aren't we?'

'Yes.'

'It's a fruit market, isn't it?'

Chris couldn't tell from his expression whether he was kidding or not. So she just took the two men's arms and said in her best big sister voice, 'Oh, for goodness' sake you two, come on!'

As they came to the front of the theatre, there was a huge picture of Maria d'Agostino. She halted them and all three stared up at it.

'Uncle Jim's got a photo like that in his study,' said Chris. 'He keeps it with all her records.' There was a slight pause. 'Isn't she lovely?' she breathed.

Yes, she was, thought Kevin O'Neil, looking up at the same photograph at the same time. Lovely. He had just arrived at the Opera House fresh from another meeting with the O'Leary brothers in Kensal Green that afternoon and was standing beside John Keith looking at the same photograph. He could hardly believe that the assured woman pictured so superbly in a large frame at the front of a famous theatre was the same girl he knew that night thirteen years before in Dublin. Was it as long as that? Thirteen years? All the Teresa years. The years of love and marriage, the years of the children. And yet that night, feel as guilty as he might about it, it remained deep in his being. He rarely thought of it, but now, as he saw her face again smiling down at him up there on the wall, a tremor of memory went through him which he found rather disturbing, for as he looked at the operatic diva, the redoubtable d'Agostino, he was remembering a very young Maria. He was jolted from his reverie by being jostled by the man who had been standing beside him.

'I'm very sorry,' said John Keith.

'Not at all,' answered Kevin O'Neil. The man went past. A young girl followed with him leading an older man behind her. She gave Kevin a lovely smile as he let them pass. What a beautiful girl, he thought. Then, with a quick glance up to Maria again, he in turn went into the theatre.

He had just turned away into the crowd going into the foyer when his nephew and his sister-in-law came up to the very same portrait-still.

'Wow! Look at that!' Denny had hardly known Maria as part of the family, but he had grown up knowing of her as a distant cousin who kept her distance and as she became famous in the movies he had often been teased at school about her. Now here she was in person. Or at least as a photograph of that person they would actually be seeing in about ten minutes' time. Denny felt a thrill of excitement shiver through him, and mentioned as much to his mother. 'Isn't it exciting, Mama?'

'Ano,' she answered mechanically, staring up at the still as if it were a shrine. The Czech affirmative came spontaneously to her lips. A lump came to her throat as she looked at it, for she could only remember young Noreen as she had been in Carmella's time and how fond old Uncle Mick had been of her. It wasn't that Maria looked like her mother, but she immediately suggested Noreen to those who had known her young. Hana tried to remember when she'd last seen Maria in the family, but couldn't think. Maria had been away at school most of the time. Paddy was the one who kept in touch. Yes, Hana thought, she is lovely, but there's a hardness there. What a shame when she's so pretty.

'Come on, Mama.' It was Denny. He was beginning to get impatient and she let him lead her away from the photo-frame. 'I gotta get a programme.'

By the time he got it and they had found their way to the seats at the side of the second circle, it was almost time for the opera to begin. There was that exciting buzz that belongs to any theatre in the minutes before a performance is to begin and as he helped his mother to her seat, Denny could feel something of the same tension. This is great, he thought to himself, as he settled into the comfortable red velvet seat.

'You OK, Mama?'

'Sure, Denny.'

She began to look around. It was overwhelming. The interior of the Royal Opera House, Covent Garden, London, is an experience in itself and in seeing it for the first time Hana O'Neil had the oddest sensation of being back in the Smetana Hall in Prague. This was grander of course, and redder and brighter, but there was exactly the same feeling of being in a place that was built to house an art, being something of an art work itself. This was a monument to music, but in no way a memorial or something dead. Everything in the interior vibrated with the anticipation of the imminent performance and the excitement was like a contagion. Hana was infected at once. She felt like a young girl. She was sixteen-year-old Hana Karpiskova again and she was with her beloved father in Prague when it was called 'the conservatoire of Europe' and he took her to the Bertramka Villa, where Mozart had composed *Don Giovanni*, the very opera they were going to hear tonight. One aria from it, 'Deh, vieni alla finestra', she remembered, had virtually become the signature tune of Prague itself. But it was at the Smetana Hall that she'd heard all the music. Drahos Karpisek had loved music and took his only daughter to every concert he could. Dvorak, Janáček, Martinu and Josef Suk with his Czech String Quartet, but best of all for young Hana was Smetana, the womaniser and the madman, but the composer of genius. Everyone in her country grew up knowing 'Ma Vlast'. My Country, she thought, my beautiful Bohemia, soon I will be seeing you again. She almost hugged herself with happiness and glanced at her son. His eyes were popping out of his head. Hana laughed.

'Close your mouth, Denny. It don't look good.' Denny gulped.

'Sorry.' The fact was he felt himself just a little intimidated by the awesome dignity of it all. This was real class, he thought. To be this old it had to be class. It was almost on a par with the Paramount Theatre in New York, and in Denny's view that was really saying something. But here, it was heavier, denser somehow. This wasn't Roxy Cinema fool's gold – this was solid gold. This was the real thing. Yes, Denny was impressed. Even the audience was unreal. Tuxedos and tiaras. Men with monocles, ladies with lorgnettes, fancy furs and furbelows, white shirt fronts and the gleam of diamonds. If this were just the audience, what would the show itself be like? He looked around the circle slowly, taking it all in . . .

She was sitting between two old men, he thought. Almost directly opposite him on the other side of the circle. The most beautiful girl he had ever seen in his life. Her appearance as she chatted happily between the two older men was such that it sent a shock through him. And he could only stare. Who was she? Where had she come from? God, thought Denny, thank goodness I'm sitting down. My legs feel funny. My heart's thudding. I've got a tingling sensation in the back of my neck. What is this? Oh, God, she's looking this way. She's looking at me! He held her look, fascinated, as the houselights slowly faded down on her . . .

On the other side, even while she was talking to Uncle John and Mr Friar, Chris had found herself looking straight across at a young man whom she was sure was looking at her. He'd caught her eye and, try as she might, she couldn't look away. He was about her age, she thought, maybe a little older. Strikingly handsome, or maybe it was just the light. She was staring fascinated as the houselights slowly faded down on him . . .

Beside her, Uncle John was aware of her voice trailing away in the middle of her telling them what the opera was going to be about. He glanced to his side and saw that she was looking straight ahead of her. Following her look, he noticed the young man opposite who was staring at them. Well, well, John wondered. What have we here? And settled back in his seat as the lights went down . . .

On her other side, Alec Friar was feeling very uncomfortable, despite his plush seat. No amount of explanation about it all from Chris was going to satisfy him and he braced himself for what he was sure was going to be an ordeal. He took a deep breath as the lights went down . . .

Beside him, Kevin O'Neil suddenly realised that he was in the same row as the young girl he had seen outside. He noticed the two men beside her. One of them must be her father, he thought. As he settled himself in his seat, he glanced around the circle, and almost dropped his programme as he saw Hana O'Neil on the other side. I don't believe it, he thought to himself. It can't be. But it is. Glory to God, it is! What's she doing in London? That must be Denny with her! He's a grown man for heaven's sake! He moved restlessly in his seat. They mustn't see him! He needed time to think. Imagine, Hana O'Neil, his own brother's wife in London! Had she come all this way to see Maria, he wondered. But she didn't really know Maria. The lights slowly went down on his pondering. As the music from the overture resounded, and before the stage lights went up, he slipped quietly out of his seat.

'Is there anything wrong, sir?' whispered an elderly usher politely.

'Not a thing,' Kevin whispered back. 'I've forgotten something.'

'Will you be back, sir?' asked the usher in the same reverent hushed tones. But Kevin was already gone, and the usher closed the curtain again across the doorway and turned back to face the stage.

'Madamina, il catalogo e questo' . . .

Standing outside the door, Kevin could just hear the action and the female voices that indicated Maria's arrival on stage. An attendant approached him.

'Excuse me, sir, are you –'

'No, I'm not,' replied Kevin testily, and moved away towards the stair. Going down, he shook his head, annoyed that he was prevented from seeing her.

'Ah, well, it can't be helped,' he muttered to himself. Outside again, he stood once more in front of her picture.

'Good night, Maria, be seeing you,' he said to her image and moved away into the city lights. Maria's photo smiled down on to the empty street.

In Hana's eyes, she looked much older than she thought she might be, but she was astounded by her singing voice, which was very much richer and warmer than she remembered. John found it all mildly amusing, but Alec was totally mystified. Chris was fascinated, and watched and listened intently, but she was aware all the time of the look from across the circle. As far as Denny was concerned, there was nothing else happening in the theatre than a young, fair-haired girl, caught in the light from the stage.

'La ci darem la mano'. . .

The famous duet was so well performed that it was repeated. Chris was enchanted, and was almost beginning to lose herself in the performance, but not quite. While the singers were preparing to provide the encore, she gave a quick glance across. Yes, he was still there, and yes, he was still staring. She turned quickly away, wondering why she was feeling so pleased, so happy. So very happy. But then Donna Elvira came in again, breathing doom, and Maria as Donna Anna discovered the guilty lover with Zerlina. The plot thickened . . .

'Or sai chi l'onore'. . .

This was Donna Anna's main aria and it is one that Mozart did not make easy for the singer, but Maria coped with it effortlessly. She was loudly applauded, Hana and Chris being among the most vociferous. Denny thought she was even more attractive when animated. No encore was demanded, however. Perceptive members of the audience might have noticed a rather sulky expression on Donna Anna's face as she exited.

'Fin ch'han dal vino'. . .

The Don was among the girls again and even Alec Friar was beginning to take an interest. All this drinking was beginning to make him feel thirsty. He licked his lips and wondered when the first interval would be.

'Batti, batti, o bel Masetto'. . .

Zerlina's attempts to mollify her peasant lover carried the opera on its complicated way with no easing of the hectic pace.

'Are you enjoying it, Uncle John?' asked Chris in a stage whisper.

'Ay', replied the Scot, still looking at the stage. 'It's noisier than I thought it would be.' Chris smiled and sat back, aware that HE was still looking over in their direction. Then, with a great 'noise', the first act ended and it was the interval.

Denny applauded with the rest, although he had hardly seen a thing that had happened on stage. As the lights came up, he tried not to look over in the direction of the girl, and his pointed looking away was as obvious as his deliberate staring had been.

'Did you enjoy that, Denny?' asked his mother.

'Very much, Mama.' And he wasn't meaning the Mozart. 'Would you like a drink or something?' He was now eager to get out of the seat, but his mother was less keen.

'I don't think so, Denny. I guess I'll just sit here. See my programme. Think about it, you know.'

'Sure, I know. You don't mind if I –'

'No, you go ahead. Just make sure you come back.'

'Yeah,' he said laughing and, rising, made his way along the row to the steps that led to the door and to the bar outside.

When the lights went up, Chris was almost the last to finish applauding.

'Wasn't it wonderful?' she said.

'No' bad,' nodded Uncle John. This from him was high praise indeed. Chris turned to Mr Friar, but he was already gone. She turned back quickly to her uncle.

'Where's Mr –'

'Where's the bar?'

'I see,' said Chris. 'Would you like –'

'Why not?' He followed her as she led the way out and up the steps, just as Kevin had gone, and presumably where Alec Friar had also followed. The upper bar area was crowded and they had to push their way through, this time with Uncle John taking the lead. And this was how Chris and Denny came face to face again.

He was going vaguely forward, hoping that he could see her again, and yet at the same time not wanting to see her again. He wasn't sure if he wanted to keep the distance, as it were, and keep the spell intact. But he felt himself drawn on as if he couldn't help it, and almost upset several drinks in the process. He was quite oblivious to people's 'Tut-tuts' or haughty stares or 'I says' that he heard on all sides. She, for her part, found the congestion in her chest just as great as the congestion all round her. She was following Uncle John's broad back, but at the same time, looking and hoping and dreading and suddenly – there he was!

And there she was! The crowd was still moving and pushing and edging all around them, but they each held their ground with no more than four feet between them. Occasionally people with trays would intervene going this way and that, but Chris and Denny stood rock still in the middle of this sea of bar traffic, until Chris's hand was suddenly taken by Uncle John, and she was pulled away. Denny made as if to follow, but lost his nerve and then wasn't sure what to do, so he kept on moving with the surge of the crowd until he saw the sign, Gentlemen. Well, at least that would pass the interval.

In the bar, Alec Friar was already on his second as John approached with Chris. Alec indicated the dram for his friend and the large orange juice for Chris.

'It pays to be early, you see,' he said with a grin. They lifted their drinks, and, holding them high above the shoulders all around them, they jostled their way to the side where there was a bit of space against the wall and a convenient shelf for their drinks. They each gave a sigh of relief at finding room to breathe.

'It's worse than the Mason's Arms at Hogmanay,' quipped Alec.

'You haven't seen a pub in New Zealand just before six,' said Chris, taking a large gulp of the ice-cold orange. She was glad of the drink, glad of the chance to cool down and collect herself.

'I haven't seen a pub in New Zealand before or after six,' said Uncle John.

'You couldn't see one after six, Uncle John.'

'Why not?'

'Because they're closed.'

'At six o'clock!' John was incredulous.

Chris laughed. 'That's right.' John turned to his friend.

'D'ye hear that, Alec? Pubs in New Zealand close at six o'clock!'

'It's hardly worthwhile opening,' said Alec. The first bell sounded.

Denny heard the first bell in the washroom and hurried out again into the bar area. He felt relieved in more ways than one. He was beginning to think that the girl's face had been some kind of mirage. It would be better if he just forgot all about it. He began to make his way in the direction of his side of the circle when it happened again! The only difference this time was that he almost collided with her. He actually touched her before he drew back quickly.

'Sorry!' they both said together. He found he was breathing hard, and was aware that she smelled beautiful. She was so taken aback that she hadn't time to avert her eyes and found herself looking right into his. Pale green, they were. And soft. Black lashes. But then after a muttered apology he was gone again, and Chris, her hand still in her Uncle John's, was being pulled away in the opposite direction.

'You were a long time,' said Hana.

'It was quite a crowd.' He was glad to sit down and get his breath.

'You been running?'

'No, it's just a bit hot.' He wondered if his mother could see how he was feeling. Women were supposed to notice things like that. He wondered if SHE did. 'Can I see the programme, Mama?'

'Sure. I've read it all now.' He took it eagerly and was glad to concentrate on it. At least to try to concentrate on it. He must have read the first few lines half a dozen times – 'the inexorable journey of Don Giovanni to hell is not a tragedy in the classical meaning of the word. It has a grimly satisfying justice to it, that leaves the majority of the cast well pleased. The ambivalent quality of the plot is not so much tragedy made comic as comedy with a new element of melancholy.' What did all that mean? But by this time the lights were going down again, and four loud chords from the orchestra demanded the audience's attention, but just before the darkness fell again, he sneaked a quick look. Yes, she was looking over. He felt a great surge of happiness and pretended to give himself to the action on stage. This was the famous Canzonetta beneath the lighted window as the Don serenaded the maid servant.

'Dey, vieni alla finestra'. . .

Hana nudged her son in the darkness.

'This is our song from Prague,' she whispered.

'Yeah?' replied Denny. 'It's kinda cute.'

On the other side, Chris took the chance while Denny was watching the stage to watch Denny. He had a good profile, she thought. Then she remembered the collision and the way that it made her heart jump, the thrill she had got when they had collided and his hand had actually touched her breast. She'd better not think about that. And she turned away to the stage again. Zerlina was singing her song.

'Vedrai carino'. . . .

Various events then happened on stage, most of them in the dark, but the wonderful music continued and what couldn't be seen could be listened to. John Keith glanced along at his friend, Alec. He must have been listening because his eyes were closed. I hope he doesn't snore, thought John.

'Il mio tesoro intanto'. . .

Such is the beauty of this particular tenor aria, and so good was the voice quality of the tenor involved, that all eyes in the theatre went to him and to Maria as Donna Anna. Even she knew that this was the tenor's moment and everyone gave to him. The moment also drew Tito from the stalls bar, where he had spent most of the first act. This was the part of the opera he enjoyed most – where he watched his half-sister play second fiddle to a colleague. Tito had decided in the last few months that he did not like Maria, but she must never know that. At least not yet. Meantime, the tragedy was that Maria had come increasingly to like him – even to love him.

'O statua gentillissima'. . .

This duet between the two men always drew Vernon Drake from the dressing room. He always enjoyed the moment when the statue nodded and the drama when it spoke. It was also Maria's best acting scene, for unlike most opera singers, she could really act when she wanted to. But that was the key. Only when she wanted to. That's what hurt Vernon more than anything – how she herself so under-used her own gifts. He would almost have preferred that she abuse them. But as he stood in the darkened wings, he melted again at the appearance she had on stage, and regretted so much that young Tito had come into their lives and spoiled it all. It had promised so much, a beautiful woman and a beautiful young man to be with, but there was a cold streak in both of them, which could also be a cruel streak when they liked. She was getting too fond of him for Vernon's liking. She might even be in love with him. And this was a real tragedy from Vernon's point of view. For he loved Tito, too. Meantime, Don Giovanni was coming to his terrible end on stage. The dreadful moral was pronounced:

'All this you have earned and more.
Come there is worse in store.'

595

And the fires of Hell opened up to receive him.

'Quite so,' said Vernon to himself, and pursed his lips in satisfaction.

The audience rose almost as one to applaud the cast. As round after round went on and the singers expertly took their well-rehearsed bows – none more so than Maria – Denny turned to face Chris across the auditorium, and he unashamedly applauded her. To his great delight, she gleefully took up the idea and applauded him. This they did, quite oblivious to the rest of the audience and only Hana on Denny's part, and Uncle John on Chris's were suddenly aware of what was happening. Chris was the first to break it off, feeling highly embarrassed, but still palpitating inside from the excitement of it all – being in the famous Opera House, seeing a wonderful performance, hearing the glorious music and discovering HIM! Denny broke off as she did, but was less embarrassed. He felt almost triumphant.

'What you doing?' asked his mother.

'I'm applauding.'

'Yeah, but who you applauding?'

'Everybody, Mama,' replied Denny laughing.

In the street outside, Chris delayed as long as possible moving off in the direction of the Strand. They were to have supper before a cab would take her back to Victoria. Meantime, she looked at all the stills again, read all the notices for forthcoming productions, pointed out interesting people she could see in the crowd and generally did everything she could think of that would delay her two elderly knights and allow her the possibility of glimpsing again her Prince Charming. But there was no sign of him.

Denny, meantime, was furious. His mother had decided to go to the Ladies' washroom at the end, because she said, 'I'm so excited.' Then, ten minutes later, as they made their way slowly down the carpeted stairs, she had to look at just about every picture of every famous performer gracing the walls of that august palace of the performing arts. Nothing Denny could do would persuade her to hurry. They were among the last to leave the foyer and reach the street, and of course there was no one there. There were many people there. The whole of London might have been mingling around that market area, but as far as Denny O'Neil was concerned there was no one there.

'Oh, hell!' he expostulated.

'What's the matter?'

'I forgot my programme.'

'It's alright, Denny. I got it.'

She beamed at her tall son, who sighed and said, 'Have you,

Mama? I'm so glad. Come on, let's go see Maria.' He was glad to have a specific objective, as his mind was still full of that girl. He knew now it was a theatre phenomenon, a freak occasion that happens once in a blue moon. Well, the blue moon was out. And he felt freakish, for something had happened in that Opera House, and he knew it. He had fallen in love with a face at first sight and there was damn all he could do about it. 'Oh, hell!' he muttered again under his breath, and took his mother's arm as they moved up the street and round the corner to the stage door.

It was all such a stark contrast to the magnificent theatre they'd just left. This was the factory side of the dream world. It was the Tradesmen's Entrance for artists, and it was a very dismal waiting room for visitors. The stagedoor keeper wasn't very helpful, and insisted on finding out all about them before he would consent to send up their names. Hana at one point said to her son that it wasn't really worth all this, but Denny only got more determined.

'We're her relatives, Mama. She gotta see us.'

'I got my job to do, guv'ner. 'ow do I know that you are who you say you are?'

'Because I say so, goddamit. Just send in my mother's name, will ya?' Eventually, Vernon Drake came down. Denny and his mother were seated on a bench. He approached them tentatively.

'Mr and Mrs O'Neil?' Denny rose to his full height.

'The hell we are. This is my mother, mister. Mrs Denis O'Neil from Brooklyn, New York. She was married to the man whose sister is the mother of Maria d'Agostino. She would like to pay her respects to the same Maria d'Agostino on account of the fact that she is Maria d'Agostino's aunt. Does that make any sense to you?'

'Of course,' said Vernon taken slightly aback.

'Well, it sure didn't to that guy over there,' said Denis loudly pointing to the stagedoor keeper, who was by this time putting on his own coat.

'You must understand, Mr –er –'

'O'Neil, for Chrissake!'

'O'Neil. Yes, of course. But we get so many strange people.'

'Are you calling us strange people?'

'By no means. But it's my job –'

'Don't you start talking about jobs.'

'I am Vernon Drake. I am what you might call Miss d'Agostino's manager, and it's my pleasure to greet her friends – and relations – whenever they call at the stage door. If you will kindly come with me now, I'll – yes – thank you.' He dithered to the side a few paces, indicating vaguely with his hand.

'Mama,' said Denny, offering his to his mother. They followed Vernon along several corridors, trying not to stare at all the weird sights they saw on the way. Singers half-in and, in some of the men's cases, all-out of costume. Some with wigs, some without. Noise and banter. Loud shouts of greetings. Much kissing on both cheeks, and the smell of garlic and cigars. This was Opera backstage. There was a frequent popping of corks and clink of glass, and led by these sounds, Vernon eventually brought them to Dressing Room No. 3. It had been a great victory on his part to win this room for Maria. It was one of the few with a waiting room. As Denny and his mother entered, it was full of people and Denny felt the same nervous pressure on his arm from his mother as he had felt at the beginning of the evening when she first saw the theatre. He could tell she was very tense and he was on his guard to be extra protective.

Maria's appearance among her 'guests' was the best thing she had done all evening. It was some time before Vernon was able to extricate her from the tight knot of admirers, whom she played as skilfully as if they were keys on the piano, striking a different note from each of them and yet making that kind of personal harmony that makes everyone think they're making social music together. It's a very great skill and Maria had it in abundance. But like everything else that was done, it was done with the appearance of spontaneity, although with great calculation. Denny could only watch and admire. A very young man approached them and asked if they would like a drink. Hana shook her head.

'No, thanks,' said Denny with a smile.

'Please yourself,' said the boy.

He had an extraordinary poise for one so young and was not only beautifully dressed, but was beautiful himself. It was slightly unnerving, and Denny didn't quite know what to make of him. There was something familiar about him that he couldn't quite put his finger on. Hana was even more puzzled.

'Sorry I stare at you,' she said. 'I thought I knew you.'

'No problem,' smiled the boy and moved away among the crowd again.

'I see him before,' muttered Hana quietly to Denny. 'I don't know where, but I see him before, or someone much like him.'

It was then that Vernon brought Maria over. Hana rose, as if she were meeting royalty. Maria behaved as if she were.

'My, my,' she said. 'So you're my Aunt Hana.' She gave her a kiss on both cheeks without actually touching Hana's cheeks, then drew back and looked at the older woman. 'It's been a long time, Aunt Hana.' Hana nodded, not trusting herself to speak. 'And who is this?' went on Maria, looking at Denny.

'I'm Denny O'Neil,' said Denny, extending a hand. She barely touched it.

'Hi, Denny. I guess we're cousins.' He was relieved to hear how American she sounded. He was also amazed at how much better she looked off stage without all that make-up. Even better than she looked on the photo outside. And she knew it.

'Distant cousins, you might say,' said Denny.

'What a pity,' she replied, with a mock demureness, before turning to her aunt. 'Well, Aunt Hana –' There was just a perceptible pause before she used her aunt's name that was all the more insulting for being almost undiscernible. 'What brings you to quaint old London?'

'We are on our way to Prague.' At the mention of her own city, Hana's voice took on the added strength of pride and she spoke now with firmness. 'Denny and I are to have holiday in Czechoslovakia to see my homeland again, and –'

'Here, you haven't got a drink,' interrupted Maria.

'No thanks,' said Denny. 'Your son's already asked us,' he added.

'My son?' laughed Maria.

'Yeah, sure,' went on Denny, indicating Tito, who at the sound of the laughter, looked up in their direction.

'Tito, come here, will you?' called out Maria. 'Wait till he hears this,' she said to Hana while Tito approached. 'Tito, how would you like to be my son?' she said playfully.

'No thanks.'

'These people –' began Maria.

'These people?' exploded Denny.

'I'm sorry,' said Maria quickly, putting her fingers to her forehead, 'I wasn't thinking. Do forgive me. I mean my cousin here –' indicating Denny '– thought you were my son.' By this time, the joke had fallen rather flat and there was an uneasy silence. Maria quickly turned to Hana.

'Tito is my half-brother. We have the same mother.' Hana looked closely at the boy.

'Of course, Noreen.' Tito stepped closer to her.

'You knew my mother, Ma'am?'

'When she was very young,' answered Hana softly. 'It was a long time ago. She was very beautiful.' She looked into the young boy's eyes as they steadily regarded her.

'Thank you, Ma'am,' he said quietly.

'You said you were going home?' continued Maria in a loud party conversation voice.

'Ano. We are going to Prague the day after the next day.'

'But don't you live in New York? Vernon said –'

'Ano. We live in New York, but we are going home to Prague.' Hana was getting flustered again and didn't realise how contradicting she sounded.

'Mama and I are going on vacation to Prague on Saturday,' said Denny.

'No, Sunday, Denny,' said his mother.

'Yeah, Sunday,' he added.

'And then it's first to Paris,' continued Hana.

'And then it's first to Paris,' Denny repeated lamely. He wished now he had taken that drink.

'Oh, I see,' said Maria vaguely. She was getting bored. Vernon recognised the signs.

'I hope you will excuse Maria now,' he said to Hana. 'She is rather tired.' Before he could finish, Denny took his mother's arm again,

'Come on, Mama. Let's get outta here.' They started to go.

'Just a minute,' called Maria. 'I wanna talk to you.'

'Sorry, we've got an early start,' said Denny opening the door for his mother. 'Anyway, I'm sure you and your son have got lots to talk about. Bye, cousin.' He closed the door on Maria's astonished expression.

'You were very rude, Denny,' said his mother.

'Not as rude as she was, Mama. I don't think the Opera's our world. Let's get back to the hotel. I need a drink.' They moved down the corridor towards the stage door.

'You could have had a drink there,' said his mother, hurrying to keep up with him.

'Not that kind of drink, Mama.'

Alec Friar smacked his lips in appreciation. 'That's better,' he said. 'That right, John?'

'Aye,' said John. 'It was a good dram. I wish you would try one, Christina.'

'My name's Christine, Uncle John. I keep telling you. You can call me Chris, like everyone does.'

'No, you're Christina to me, lass. I canna help that, and I hope you won't mind. What's in a name anyway?' he added.

'A rose by any other name – who was it said that?' put in Alec.

'Well, it wisna Robert Burns anyway,' laughed John.

'It was Shakespeare, Mr Friar.'

'It nearly always is,' said Alec.

'"Romeo and Juliet",' added Chris.

'What page?' laughed Alec. They were having a very pleasant after-theatre supper in the Strand Palace smaller dining-room at the back. Chris was very much at ease with the two men now and their good company helped keep her mind off the young man at the theatre. But at the mention of *Romeo and Juliet* all kinds of reverberations started up in her again and she quickly looked down.

'You're tired, lass,' said her uncle, rising. 'It's time we got you that taxi.'

'Are you sure you don't want me to come and wave you off in the morning?'

'Quite sure, Christina,' replied Uncle John firmly, but kindly.

'Good-night, Mr Friar. Thank you again.'

'Don't mention it, lassie,' said Alec, 'the pleasure was ours.'

In the taxi heading for Victoria, she sat back against the warm leather of the seat and closed her eyes. She couldn't believe all that had happened to her in the last couple of days. Meeting a wonderful uncle, going to an opera at Covent Garden – seeing him, whoever he was. What was his name? 'What's in a name?' She smiled as she remembered the earlier quote, and tried to recollect its context. She had learned it at school. What was it again? 'Romeo, Romeo, wherefore art thou Romeo?' It was something about a name, she thought.

'A rose by any other name would smell as sweet,' and then it came to her,

> 'So Romeo would, were he not Romeo called,
> Retain that dear perfection which he owest
> Without that title . . .'

As Alec said, Shakespeare certainly had the words for it. Just the words for this great warm romantic feeling that surged through her when she thought of him that tingled in her toes and at her very fingertips. She folded her arms in frustration. But who was he? Where did he come from? Why hadn't he spoken? He'd only said one word to her, and it had to be 'sorry'. If there was one thing she wasn't, it was 'sorry' that she bumped into him. Could she ever forget those green eyes? Oh dear, this was getting terrible. She would either have to meet him soon or never see him again. The frustration was terrible. She stretched out her legs in front of her and tried to touch the small seats on the driver's panel. I wonder if he liked my legs, she found herself thinking.

Denny had been glad to get into bed. It had been a long, eventful day. So much had happened and yet he could only think of one thing. That girl. She must be the loveliest thing he'd ever seen. Yet who was she? He realised he didn't know a thing about her. Not even her name or where she came from. He had to see her again, but how? They were off to Paris at the end of the week, then Prague. Then back to America. When would he ever be in London again? He would never see her again. This feeling was awful. Was this what falling in love was like? Was this what all the fuss was about? All the movies, all the songs? If this was it he certainly wasn't going to make a song and dance about it. He wasn't enjoying it much. The frustration was murder. He sighed and turned over yet again. He'd been doing that all night. Hell, he'd better get some sleep. And he buried his head in the pillow.

In her suite at Claridges Hotel, Maria was pacing up and down in anger, while Vernon was sitting mournfully in the centre of the large couch, and Tito was sprawled carelessly over a large armchair.

'You let them just walk out like that. I still can't get over it. Walking out on me. Nobody's ever done that, but nobody. Least of all, a couple of schmucks from Brooklyn.'

'That's no way to speak of your relatives,' said Tito.

'They're your relatives, too,' she snapped at him.

'Well, that's no way to speak of my relatives.'

'Why didn't they let me know they were coming?'

'What's so important about an old aunt?' Vernon sounded tired and peevish. Maria rounded on him.

'It's not only my aunt, it's my cousin too.'

'Oh yes, it would be,' muttered Tito.

'I don't mean that.'

'Well, what do you mean?' asked Vernon.

'I mean, family,' she said.

'Aren't we your family?' said Vernon, looking archly at Tito.

'I mean, real family.'

'So we're not real then?' replied Vernon.

'You know what I mean.'

'No, I don't, and I don't see why we should all be out of our beds at this ungodly hour, while you fret about being walked out on by a couple of schmucks.'

'We're all here because I'm here. And because I want you here. Because I say so. You don't need any other reason other than that. Do you, Mr Vernon Drake?'

'Maria,' said her manager.

'Well do you?' Vernon rose and went to the door.

'Remember you have lunch with those people from Hamburg at twelve-thirty. And a costume session at three.'

'Are you running out on me as well?' Vernon never even looked back.

'Goodnight, Maria,' he said and closed the door. As he did so, her glass struck it and shattered on to the carpet.

'Now see what you've done,' Tito said wearily. With a great sigh he got up from his armchair and moved towards the door.

'And where are you going?' she yelled.

'I'm going to pick up what's left of the glass.'

'Oh, damn, damn, damn! I hate you all,' cried Maria and threw herself down on the couch.

'Ah, shit!' It was Tito's voice from the door. She sat up.

'What's the matter?'

'I cut my hand.'

'Let me see.' She got up and went to him. He had collected the main pieces of glass and put them on a small drinks tray, but somehow he'd cut the middle finger of his right hand and was prising a piece of glass from it as she approached.

'Oh, you're bleeding.'

'That normally happens when you cut yourself,' he said staring down at it.

'Here, let me.'

'No, it's alright.'

'No, come on.' She took his hand, where he was holding his thumb over the cut. She removed his thumb and the blood spurted.

'Hey!' he shouted.

Suddenly she put the finger in her mouth and sucked, all the time holding his eyes with hers. She withdrew it for a moment to say, 'That nice, Tito?' and put it back into her mouth. He felt his finger warm against her moist tongue, the knuckles just touching the edge of her teeth, her huge eyes holding his stare.

'You're mad,' he said.

THIRTY-SIX

Chris was more or less packed. Miss Hacking had told them to have their cases down in the front hall by 10.00a.m. A van would be taking them to the ship sometime in the late morning to meet up with the rest of the New Zealand team's effects from all the other boarding houses, and they themselves were free until 7.00p.m. when the boat train left for Victoria. That gave the young New Zealanders most of their last day in London to do with as they pleased. The breakfast room was shrill with girlish plans on what they were all going to do, but Chris had already made up her own mind. She had kept the programme from the *Don Giovanni* in her handbag and intended going to the theatre again to catch Maria d'Agostino after the matinee in the hope that she would sign it. That would really be a prize to take home – the signature of a world famous singer and film star. Berta would be thrilled, she knew. Even Uncle Jim might be pleased. So she couldn't wait to clear her room and, with only the hand luggage she could manage, she went out to find Miss Hacking so that she could sign out.

'Have you checked your room thoroughly?' said that lady, when Chris finally cornered her in the guests' lounge.

'Yes, Miss Hacking.'

'And you know that you've to be at Platform 14 before seven o'clock?'

'Yes, Miss Hacking.'

'What do you intend to do, Miss Mackenzie?'

'I'm just going to have a last look round London, Miss Hacking.'

'In an afternoon?'

'As much as I can manage.'

'And who are you going with?'

'No one, Miss Hacking.'

'Is that wise?'

'I don't know, Miss Hacking. I think I can cope.'

'I'm sure you can. It's just that we have to be extra careful on the last day. It wouldn't do to lose you now, would it?'

'No, Miss Hacking.'

'By the way, did you see your uncle?'

'Yes, I did, Miss Hacking.'

'Good. See you at Victoria, then? It's Saturday, remember, and the buses will be busy.'

'Yes, Miss Hacking.'

With only the small suitcase and her handbag, Chris set off jauntily up Buckingham Palace Road towards the West End. If this was to be her last day in London, then she was determined to make the most of it. The sun was shining and she felt happy at the thought of going home again, even though it would be a long time yet before she was back in Dunedin. Still, any journey can only begin with one step, and hers was light as she made her way up through the busy London street. The newspapers were full of Kind Edward VIII's romance with an American woman, and she noticed the placards as she passed them. Not that she gave much thought to world events. Neither the war in Spain, nor the war on want which would force those poor men to walk all the way from Jarrow in the next few weeks. If anything, she could relate more to the lovelorn King and Mrs Simpson. Their romance looked just as impossible as hers. I mean, she thought, it was a thousand to one chance that they met at all and a million to one that they would ever meet again. And she wasn't really thinking only of Mrs Simpson! Even as she thought about him again, she could feel the colour rise in her cheeks. I must be walking too fast, she thought, or else this case is getting heavier! Up till a few nights ago her mind had been full of sport and music and now it was full of a certain young man, whom she still couldn't get out of her head. It was crazy. Chris Mackenzie was intelligent enough to know that that would soon pass. She just wished it would hurry up. Dear old Uncle John had tried in his own shy way to quiz her about the young man on the other side of the circle. She didn't know that Uncle John had even noticed, but then, she hadn't known him long, only a night and day, yet she felt that she'd known him forever. She had, in fact, come to love this quiet big Scotsman who insisted on calling her Christina. That was her mother's name, of course, although it wasn't what he said or did, it was more what he didn't say. The way he just let her talk and let her be herself. He was a good man, she knew that. And he'd been hurt, she knew that too. He hadn't talked about that, so she wouldn't talk about the silly thing that had happened to her, because it was silly. How could she feel anything seriously for someone she had hardly seen and didn't know anything about? Nevertheless, they say that it happens that way, she thought to herself. But only in books. And books are silly. Well, some books anyway. She tried to put the whole thing out of her mind or that's what would happen – she'd go out of her mind!

She had her itinerary worked out. First, the National Gallery and then St Martin's-in-the-Fields for the organ recital and a sandwich in Trafalgar Square. Then a walk up Bond St to Oxford Circus, then into Regent's Park and a look at the Royal Academy of Music before going down through Shaftesbury Avenue to Covent Garden for the end of the matinee. Get that signature if possible, then a bus to Victoria. It should be possible. Yes, she said to herself, it's going to be a lovely last day.

At that very same time, Denny O'Neil lifted the receiver of the telephone in the hall of the hotel in Bayswater.

'Yeah. Denny O'Neil here.'

'Hello Denny. This is your cousin.' It was Maria.

'Hi,' he said tensely, immediately on guard.

'You sound like you gotta cold.' Her voice had a mock concern.

'Hope you don't catch it,' he said flippantly. He had to admit her laugh sounded delicious.

'I take care not to catch colds, Denny.'

'I'm sure you do.'

'Listen Denny, I'm sorry you had to rush away the other night –'

'How did you know where to find us?' Denny asked abruptly, unable to keep the peremptory note out of his voice.

'What? Oh, I had Vernon check around. That's what managers are for, you know.'

'Yeah?'

'Sure. I had him call Clara.'

'In New York?'

'Sure. She's Mrs Kominsky now. She gave us your hotel.' Denny was astonished.

'How'd you get her number. I mean, she's in Brooklyn.'

'Paddy gave me it.'

'Who?'

'Our Uncle Paddy, Denny. Remember, the one who's an Archbishop!' Denny could hardly believe what he was hearing. 'He's a sweetie, you know. We've always been pals since I was a little kid.'

'Yeah.'

'Yeah. So, I thought I'd call you see if you'd like to come and see me after the show today? We didn't get the chance to have a real talk –'

'I dunno.' Denny was on guard again. 'It's kinda late.'

'No, it's a matinee today. I've got the night off. We could have dinner at my hotel and catch up.'

'I'm not sure. I think Mama might –'

'Oh, I didn't mean Aunt Hana, Denny.'

'What?'

'No, I just meant us. What d'you think?'

'Well, I –' Denny didn't know what to think and he didn't like the kind of feeling that was being roused in him as she went on.

'I know we're cousins, but we don't need to be distant cousins you know.' She laughed again. That low laugh. 'We could even be kissing cousins, what about that?' He couldn't say anything. 'See you at five,' she said and rang off. He stood with the receiver in his hand for a long time before he put it back.

'Who was calling you?' asked his mother when he got back to their room.

'Aw, it was a wrong number. I guess somebody made a mistake.'

'Funny they should call you. Even by mistake. I thought it might be that girl.'

'What girl?'

'That girl you look at all the time in the Opera.' Denny stared at his mother.

Sam Cassidy's funeral in Dublin had been a quiet one. They were mostly men, men in raincoats and soft hats, who stood for a long time outside the hotel after the car had taken Sam to be cremated. It was the first cremation in the family and people weren't very sure what to do, but Sam had insisted 'no priests, no Masses, no prayers, no speeches, no expense. Just put me in a box, burn my body and drink my health when you get home.' Nellie had taken him quite literally, and that's how it was done. And so, on Saturday 12th September, 1936, the remains of Sam Cassidy were duly dispatched. Sam Cassidy would have been just as happy if the refuse department of Dublin Corporation had come along and taken him away in a sack. Sam had a great love of life and liberty, but no thought at all for the supernatural morrow and certainly none for the professional trappings of death in the family. He had seen too much of it outside the family.

His only regret, and Nellie's, was that they had no family of their own, which is why they looked upon Kevin's two daughters as much their own as his and Teresa's. As far as Nellie was concerned, little Siobhan and Roisin were O'Neils all the way, no matter the Dacre contribution. Sam had thought they had better keep quiet about the English connection. The little girls were six and four respectively, but Teresa treated them and dressed them as twins. She made most of their dresses, and it was cheaper to buy a large quantity of material every time. This made them a very pretty pair and they looked even more so on the grey day of Uncle Sam's funeral. Most of the men had had their whiskey, and the toast to Sam had been duly drunk. They left by the late afternoon, each one of them proferring a hand to Nellie.

'I'm sorry for your trouble, Mrs Cassidy.' They would then nod to Teresa and go silently.

Now Nellie and Teresa sat alone in the late afternoon, sharing a pot of tea. The little girls could be heard playing at the back.

'Will you have another cup, Teresa?'

'I will that. You make a lovely cup of tea.'

'There's not many does that these days. The secret is in the masking.'

'Is that what it is? I thought it was warming the pot.'

'You must do that too, of course.'

'I see.'

The ladies sipped their tea for a moment before Nellie asked, 'Any word yet about Kevin?'

'I had a postcard from London. He said he saw his niece in a show.'

'A show?'

'Yeah, the one that's the singer. She's on the films.' Teresa's tone had become noticeably chilly. She knew perfectly well who she was talking about, but had no wish to say Maria's name.

'You mean Maria? Noreen's girl?'

'Is that her?'

'Yes, she calls herself by an Italian name, but sure she's an O'Neil like the rest of us.'

Is she, wondered Teresa. She remembered that night at her mother's house and the hate she had felt for that shadowy figure on the landing thirteen years ago. She had never mentioned it to Kevin. She knew she never would. Some things are best kept secret, even between a couple as happily married as she and Kevin were. He had been the only man in her life, and even if something happened to him, wherever he was, he would still be the only man in her life.

'You're looking very solemn, Teresa.'

'It's a solemn day, Nellie.'

'Sure it's over now, and auld Sam would be the last one to grudge us a wee smile. In fact, if those men have left anything in any of the bottles at all, we could have a wee one ourselves while things are quiet.'

'Why not?' said Teresa. 'Here, I'll give you a hand.' She rose and joined her sister-in-law in a search amongst the dozen or so whiskey bottles, each with its own residue, sometimes as much as an inch or two of good Jamiesons in them still, so that an aggregate pouring gave them each a very generous glass.

'Here's to Sam,' said Teresa.

'Here's to Kevin,' said Nellie.

As she drank, why was it that Maria d'Agostino came into Teresa's mind?

Vernon had the drink ready for Maria as usual. It was always the same, brandy and American dry, and as she swept in allowing the applause to be heard for a moment before Tito closed the door again, she had the glass in her hand immediately. After the first sip, she put it down in disgust.

'On the rocks, Vernon! On the rocks!' and swept straight on towards the washroom. Vernon sighed and looked towards Tito.

'The lady wants more ice, Vernon.'

'I know what she wants,' retorted Vernon waspishly and muttered under his breath, 'She wants a good spanking, that's what she wants.'

'What was that, Vernon?'

'Nothing, Tito. Nothing.' Maria re-emerged again and took up the glass without a word of thanks.

'That's better,' she said as she sipped, then threw herself back on the comfortable armchair. 'I'm only expecting one visitor today,' she announced.

'But the Kents are coming, and they're bringing their daughter. You said –'

'The Kents can go to hell as far as I'm concerned. They can even go back to Kent if they like.' It must have been a good show. She was in a good humour, but it was a brittle humour and Vernon knew how dangerous it could be.

'Who's the lucky visitor, then?' said Tito.

'Ah, that would be telling.'

'What shall I tell the Kents?'

'Anything you like, my dear Vernon – I leave the lies to you. You're good at lies.' Vernon sighed again and helped himself to a large brandy.

'On the rocks, Vernon,' whispered Tito, sidling up to him. 'On the rocks!' Vernon turned to him angrily, but melted as soon as he saw again the beauty of the boy at such close quarters.

'Really, Tito,' he breathed.

'What time is it now?' called Maria, lying with her head back. Vernon had his own head back taking the drink and almost choked as he tried to reply.

'About ten before five,' said Tito.

'Good,' said Maria. 'You guys better think about going.'

'Where are we going?' said Tito, surprised.

'I know a place,' Vernon announced, looking at Tito over his glass. There was a knock at the door. Maria was up at once and into the washroom again, cursing under her breath. Tito swept up the drinks from the centre table and placed them on the dressing table, and Vernon buttoned his jacket and went to the door. It was a practised drill and all three were well used to it, and did it almost automatically whenever a knock on the door sounded.

'It'll be the Kents,' whispered Vernon with his hand on the door handle.

But it wasn't the Kents. It was the stagedoor keeper, with about half a dozen autograph books and programmes in his hand.

'This is the lot for today, Mr Drake. If you'll be kind enough to ring for me, I'll come and get them again when Miss Maria has put her monicker on 'em all. Alright?'

'It's alright, Bert. I'll bring them down myself.' Bert made as if to speak, as Vernon took the books. 'It's alright. I'll see she signs them.' He shut the door quickly on Bert's prowling eye. The stagedoor keeper was always trying to catch the artists unaware in the dressing rooms. But when the door shut in his face, he merely shrugged and turned away.

'Please yourself,' he said and shuffled off down the corridor again towards his cubby hole. 'She'll send 'em down in 'arf a mo',' he mumbled to the waiting theatre-goers.

Chris Mackenzie felt a little bit guilty sitting on the bench among the other members of that afternoon's audience. She hadn't been to the show, but she consoled herself by thinking she had seen it only three nights ago, and that surely entitled her to have her programme signed. She watched the scene all around her: the singers coming and going, musicians hurrying in and out and the rather grand couple with a young girl at the stagedoor keeper's window, who seemed to be making rather a fuss.

'But she's expecting us,' the tall man was saying.

'Your name ain't here,' Bert's voice could be heard wearily.

'Don't you know who I am?'

'That's beside the point, if you don't mind my saying so. It's whether she knows who you are.' And so the wrangle went on, while Chris listened fascinated.

Bert came off the telephone again.

'Sorry, sir, she ain't seeing nobody.' The tall man grew pink in the face. It looked all the pinker because of his silver white hair.

'Come, Dorothy,' he said to the woman. 'The Governors will

hear about this.' He swept out followed by Dorothy and the young girl, who caught Chris's eye as she passed, and gave her a little smile. Chris felt a little sorry for her.

'Yes, guv'ner,' Bert was saying into the telephone. 'I'll ring up as soon as he arrives. What was the name again? O'Neil. Got it.' It didn't matter that what Bert had written down was 'O-KNEEL'.

Meantime, Denny was standing outside the front of the theatre staring up at the large photo of Maria.

'Well, here I am,' he said to it rather grimly. He didn't know why he was here at all. He felt awful saying to his mother that he had to go out for a bit.

'Got some things to do,' he had said.

'What things?' she had asked.

'Just things, Mama, you wouldn't understand.'

'Who wants to understand things?' said his mother, quietly going on with her packing. 'You just be sure you're ready for the morning.' Hana was glad to be on the road again. After all, this was what she had come for. She didn't like London. She couldn't understand it. Therefore, she didn't mind staying on in the hotel while Denny went out. 'How long you be?' she had asked him.

'I dunno.' He felt really awful. Not being straight with his mother. It was just like with Katya. 'I'll give you a call if I'm gonna be late.'

Now here he was, standing outside the Opera House again. He had made up his mind he wouldn't go at all, and turned back several times, but somehow his feet seemed to turn round of their own volition and head for Covent Garden. It was as if he were fated to be here at this time, and he didn't enjoy the sensation it gave him. She is my cousin, after all. What am I worried about? I'll never see her again. I'll be in Paris tomorrow night. In Prague the week after. Who worries about a movie star? But he did, and he wondered why.

'Hell, let's get it over with,' he said aloud as he turned away towards the stage door. A distinguished couple passing him at the time, looked at him very oddly. Denny never even noticed and continued walking.

Two men came through the pass door from the artists' corridor. One was middle-aged and the other was very young, but both were very smartly dressed. Vernon and Tito. Vernon had in his hand all the books and programmes and there was a squeal of delight from the people waiting – mostly young women – as they saw the books being deposited at the stagedoor keeper's window. Chris didn't squeal. She rose as she saw the books arrive and waited until the bustle had diminished before she approached the window herself.

'My programme, please? It's got Mackenzie on it.'

'Here we are. 'S last one,' said Bert. 'Sorry it's all crumpled. Looks as if it's got a beer mark too.' There was a wet roundel as if made by a glass. But the signature was there – Maria d'Agostino – in a large, bold hand.

'That's alright,' said Chris. 'Thank you very much,' and taking it went to the door.

It was opened out for her as she approached it, and there on the threshold was – THAT MAN! He was as surprised as she was, and merely stood staring at her, then to her amazement, he let out a whoop like a Red Indian, and grabbed her round the waist. Before she could do anything, he had her outside and was looking down at her startled expression.

'It's you!' he yelled.

'Yes,' she gasped.

'It really is.' He was flushed with excitement, and to her eyes looked even better close up than he did across the other side of the theatre. 'Wow!' he said and gave her a bear hug.

'What are you doing?' she said, not entirely displeased. He pulled back and looked her straight in the face.

'I'm making sure I don't lose you again,' he said.

'But it's raining,' she said. Neither had noticed that it had started.

'So what?' he said.

'I haven't got an umbrella.'

'Who cares?' He was laughing loudly, but only Denny knew the element of relief that was in his laughter. This was more than fate. This was luck.

'Come on,' he said, grabbing her arm. The rain was glistening on her face and making her look all the prettier.

'Where to?' She was laughing as well.

'Anywhere as long as it's not here.' Chris felt a glorious surge of incomprehensible joy, and then her face fell.

'My case,' she said. 'I've left my case.' She disentangled herself and ran back through the stage door. He turned up the collar of his jacket and glanced fearfully up to the windows. She could be looking out. He stepped quickly into the wall, and was standing there against it as Chris re-emerged, holding a small suitcase in her hand.

'Let me take that,' he said. She gave it to him. 'Say, this is a big purse, isn't it?'

She laughed. 'It isn't my purse. It's my overnight bag.'

'Your what?'

'We leave tonight. For the boat.'

'Tonight!' He was aghast.

'Yes, with the team. We're going home to New Zealand.'

'Where?'

'New Zealand. You know, the one that's always off the map.'

'What?' he said, sounding and looking bewildered.

'Listen, I'm getting soaked. Come on,' she said. This time she took his hand and they ran towards the Strand.

'Where are we going?' he shouted as they ran along.

'Victoria Station,' she answered.

Chris had intended catching the appropriate bus, according to Miss Hacking's instructions, but Denny insisted that they take a cab.

'I don't want to share you with no goddam London bus,' he said. She sat back in the taxi hardly able to believe her luck, not only for being able to speed in comfort through the rain towards the boat train, but also for being in a taxi the second time in that week, and for being in it with HIM. Denny. It was a lovely name, she thought, although she really preferred Denis. Denis O'Neil. It sounded almost musical. The only snag was it was Irish. She wondered how old Gran would react. Mrs Denis O'Neil! What was she doing? She mustn't even think like that.

'Sorry,' she said, 'what were you saying? I was dreaming.'

'I was saying that you're the first person from New Zealand I've ever met. You're not what I expected.'

'What did you expect?'

'I dunno. South Seas, maybe.'

'Do you mean a grass skirt?' she asked, laughing.

'No,' he grinned. 'I was really thinking of a ring through your nose.' With that he leaned to the side and rubbed her nose with his, then stopped and stared at her, his face very serious.

She too looked grave, but only said in a whisper, 'That's what the Maoris do.'

'Well,' he said, in a low voice, 'let's all do what the Maoris do.' And with that, he kissed her. Tentatively at first. Gently. Oh, so gently. Then gradually applying a growing pressure, until he felt her hands come round his neck and then he took her in his arms. They were still locked together as the driver braked suddenly and they both fell to the floor in a heap.

'Victoria Station,' he said gruffly.

'Spoilsport,' said Denny laughing, helping Chris up. By the time he had paid the driver, she had found out where Platform 14 was, and took his arm as they walked towards it.

'We've got half an hour,' she said. 'We're early.'

'You mean just in time,' he said, putting his arm round her waist.

Other members of the team were around the platform area as

they approached and there were great cries of happy derision as they saw Chris draw near in tandem with such a handsome young man.

'Is this your uncle, then, Chris?' yelled one.

'He's too old to be her uncle,' shouted another.

'He's a beaut!' called another voice.

'A real corker!' cried a further. The sound of the girls' New Zealand voices echoed round the station and Denny was intrigued, not only by their accents, but by their smart, healthy appearance in contrast to the pallid Londoners.

'Who are these guys?' he said to Chris.

'They're the New Zealand Ladies Gymnastics Team, and we've just been to the Berlin Olympics!'

'Did you win anything?' he said to her.

She looked up to him. 'I think I might have.'

'Let's go find a coffee.'

They found a quiet corner in the tea-room and the words just tumbled from both of them as they sat opposite each other, their noses no more than an inch apart. Somewhere outside, a violinist was playing 'The Londonderry Air', and it only added to the extraordinary poignancy of the situation. They knew this was important, but couldn't understand why. They knew they were deeply in love, but they didn't know each other. There was so much they had to find out so quickly, but what they needed to find out about each other they knew they could only find out slowly. So, it was almost an impossible situation.

'I'll come to New Zealand,' he said, 'wherever it is.'

'Don't be silly,' she said, yet pleased all the same.

'You could take me as hand luggage,' he said. 'Keep me under your bed.'

'What a waste!' and she was amazed at her own boldness.

'Hey! Hey!' he said. 'I'll hold you to that someday.'

He told her about his trip, about his mother, about his sisters, about his dislocated shoulder that lost him a place in the swimming trials, about his Masters. He told her about everything, except his feelings. Somehow he couldn't put that into words. He didn't dare. She told him about her family and about her Uncle John and that she was a musician and might be a concert pianist one day.

'Gee!' he said. 'You could come to the Carnegie Hall. Just like Benny Goodman.'

'Who?' And he told her all about Benny Goodman. Then as the time approached for her train, the words stumbled and stuttered, hesitated and gradually came to a halt. They were sitting in silence when Miss Hacking appeared at the door.

'Miss Mackenzie,' she called.

'I better go,' she whispered.

'Oh, hell!' said Denny.

With a great banging of doors and blowing of whistles, the passengers were boarded. Denny stood among all the others who were seeing people off and stared at the girl who was letting down the window just above him. God, she was beautiful.

'Thank you very much for seeing me to the train.'

'Anything else?' he said looking up at her.

'And for the tea.'

'Anything else?' he insisted.

'Biscuits?'

'No. For this.' And he reached up and pulled her down to him. It was just then the whistles blew and the train started to move. He had to let her go as people shouted and more whistles blew. He walked alongside as the train inched forward. Then it suddenly occurred to him that he didn't have any address for her. At the same time, the thought came to Chris.

'Hey, what's your address?' he yelled.

'Where do I write to you?' Both queries cancelled each other out. By this time, the train's speed was increasing by the second and he was now running.

'Oh, hell, Chris. We gotta meet again. We can't – CHRIS!'

His voice was drowned in a great blast on the train hooter. And she was lost to him in a hiss of steam. He stood at the very edge of the platform watching the train disappear across the web of railway tracks, and towards Southampton. He was still breathing very heavily, and when he did get his breath, all he said was 'Oh, hell!' and turned back towards the main platform.

It was dark in Maria's dressing room, and she was drunk. She hadn't even bothered to get up to put on the main light, and the only illumination came from the light in the washroom and the alley light through the tiny little window above her dressing table. The make-up bulbs were at half. Like many ladies of the theatre, Maria preferred not to have them on full at any time. She was only thirty-four, but already she was taking no chances. Now she was not only thirty-four, she was well on the way to being truly intoxicated. Most of the brandy bottle was gone and there was still plenty of American dry left. Noticeably, she hadn't bothered about ice.

'The swine!' she kept muttering. 'The swine!' She'd gone to all that trouble to find him and he had stood her up as if she were a pimply girl. She, who could have any man she wanted and did. But she had liked him, even though he was her cousin. Perhaps because he was her cousin. She had had it all planned. The drinks, the meal, the talk . . .

'The swine!' she said again. 'The goddam swine!' She lurched forward to help herself to the remainder of the decanter, but she dropped it and it fell to the ground, where what was left of the brandy ran on to the white carpet. She watched it as if in a daze, and said drunkenly, 'It looks as if I peed myself.' She started to giggle at that, and move towards the dressing room, removing her wrap as she did so. Just then, Bert came down the corridor on his rounds, trying each door to check that they were locked. Maria's wasn't, and as it gave to his hand and opened, he was lucky enough for once to glimpse la d'Agostino *au naturel*. The torch in his hand instinctively rose up to capture her as she turned into it. She responded as if it were a spotlight.

'Why Bert, I thought you'd never come.' And Bert dropped his torch and ran!

It was very quiet at the old Athena Restaurant in Frith Street. It was always quiet at the Athena. That was part of its stock in trade. A quiet discretion, and a superb kitchen. If its customers were mainly of the demi-monde, there were no half measures about its standards. Authors, actresses, singers, and minor diplomats had to be doing rather well to afford its prices and it attracted the kind of clientèle that wasn't there to be seen. Latecomers, visitors and people whom Madame Helena didn't like, or whose accounts were overdue, were always seated at the centre tables. Vernon Drake, being in the visitor category, was centre, but not prominently so. He was glad of the pillar at his right shoulder. He could lean against this and show off the slim figure of Tito, who sat opposite him in a very flattering light. There was no music at the Athena. Only the quiet hum of voices. But there was no fear of being overheard. Everyone had the same secret. Vernon caught the waiter's eye and without a word the remainder of the very delicate Pouilly Fuisse was decanted into each of their glasses. A smile from the waiter, a nod from Vernon and both glasses were raised.

'To our survival, my dear,' said Vernon.

'I'll drink to that,' said Tito.

'A wonder you can drink to anything. You're just a boy. If Madame Helena knew you weren't even sixteen –'

'I'm sixteen in three weeks' time.'

'That we should live so long,' said Vernon.

'Just live it a day at a time. Isn't that what they say?' said Tito.

'It's not the days I worry about. It's the nights. I don't know how I get through them.'

'Can't you sleep?'

'I don't want to sleep. I want to live.'

'Isn't this living?'

'This isn't life.'

Tito looked round him. 'It looks pretty good to me,' he said.

'You're young, Tito. You don't understand. Things change. That's the tragedy.'

'Is change always a tragedy?'

'When it happens for the worse, yes.' He looked closely at the boy. 'You've changed, for instance.'

'Have I?'

'Yes, you have. When I first saw you, I thought you were an angel.' Tito giggled. 'No, I thought you were. You came into that dreadful caravan and lit it up, dear boy.'

'Did I switch on the light?'

'You carried a light. And it blinded me. Such repose. Such stillness in one so young. And now I think you're very old.'

'But it was only three months ago.'

'It might as well be centuries. My world has turned itself all upside down. La d'Agostino. I could manage. She has her funny ways, but then so have I. We understand each other. You I could manage.' Tito made as if to speak. 'No, please let me finish. There are many ways where we are alike and I could make you understand that, given time. But you and she together. It is impossible. And what is worse is knowing that it has not been I who has corrupted you, but she. Your own flesh and blood.' At the mention of blood, Tito started and began to look uncomfortable. Vernon immediately detected this and changed tone completely. 'My dear Tito, are you alright?'

'I think we should go home.'

'Why?'

'I don't think I want to be sixteen somehow.'

'"The two of them together are really funny, and we had lots of laughs when we had dinner together. Uncle John is quite serious and it's only when you get to know him you see that he sometimes means the very opposite of what he's saying, and when he and Mr Friar got talking together I found it difficult to understand, but I laughed anyway. I really like Uncle John and it was lovely to meet someone in the family so far away from home. We are going to the Opera tonight, believe it or not, and you wouldn't believe it, Uncle Jim, I will actually be seeing Maria d'Agostino in the flesh, if you see what I mean. Covent Garden is doing *Don Giovanni* and she is playing in it. I don't know what, but I don't care. It'll be lovely to see her for real. Remember all the times you and I and Berta" – that's me –' Everybody around the table laughed. Berta was reading aloud the latest letter from Chris. This was the last one they would probably receive before she started on the way home again and every time a letter came with a British stamp on it, Jim insisted that Berta read it to everyone around the table after tea.

'Go on, Berta,' said her mother. Berta was carrying on reading it herself.

'You must allow her at least a bit of rehearsal,' said her father.

'Get on with it,' said Billy. He was having his hands full trying to cope with his two children, Trevor and Gillian. The little girl wanted to sleep and the boy wanted to play railways round and round the table. Belinda couldn't do anything to help. She was breast-feeding little Sarah. It was a difficult audience altogether, because it was rather a large tableful. The twins, Kenny and Jamie, were trying to put up with it all as much as they could. They had no real interest in listening to Chris's news from England, but Jim had asked them to at least stay and hear Berta read it out. Then they could go to football practice if they liked. So they stretched their long seventeen-year-old legs under the table, put their hands behind their heads and were prepared to wait it all out.

'Let's hear you, girl,' said Kenny.

'Sure Berta, give it a go,' said Jamie. They always spoke with one laconic Kiwi voice, the Keith twins. Luckily they didn't speak that often. Berta was now ready to resume her performance.

'There's not much else really,' she said. 'She doesn't seem to have done anything exciting. Imagine being in Europe and not doing anything exciting.' Berta would be thirty on her next birthday but she certainly looked nearer thirteen as she read her cousin's letter to the family. Berta lived most of her emotional life vicariously through her effervescent cousin and she had followed Chris most of the way since the New Zealand party left two months before.

'"I expect I'll be going straight back to Dunedin as I will have so much work to catch up on, so tell Kenny and Jamie that they can have a room each for a while yet."' The twins raised their hands above their heads and gave a cheer.

'Quiet, you two,' said Jim. 'And you as well,' he called to little Trevor, who was going round the table with his hands above his head, cheering like his uncles. Berta turned over the letter again.

'That seems to be about all really.' She had hardly got the phrase out before the two boys were up and away with a great clatter of feet. Trevor went running after them.

'Not you, Trev!' called Billy, at which the little fellow immediately started to bawl. 'Oh, for Pete's sake,' went on Billy. 'Can you get him, Bel?'

'I've got my hands full here,' said his wife, rocking little Sarah in her arms.

'Come on, Trev,' said Jim rising. 'Come to your old grandad. Time enough yet for you to go to football practice, eh?'

'I think it's time we should be going too, Billy,' said Belinda.

'OK, any time you say,' said Billy.

'I wonder if you could hang on for a couple of ticks, Billy. Chris's letter wasn't the only one we got this morning. We heard from Uncle Bobby in Sydney.'

'Oh?' Billy was immediately interested. 'Is it about Abel?'

'Yes, it is. It's not too hot.'

Jean immediately rose. 'Berta, you give me a hand. Take in these things.'

Berta demurred, 'Oh, mum, I want to hold Sarah.'

'I'd be glad if you did,' said Belinda. 'I think your Dad's finding Trevor a handful. Come on, you little blighter.' She took her son from Jim. 'I think he's getting tired.'

When the women had gone, Jim sat down at the table again and re-lit his pipe.

'You remember Abel had an accident?'

'Yeah,' said Billy gravely.

'Well, he's not coming out of it too well, according to his Dad, although Becky at the hotel is just about doing everything for him, so he tells me.'

'She's a good girl.'

'She certainly is. But he's down, Billy. Way down.'

'Well, what can we do about it?'

'Well,' said his father, 'seeing as how you two were once mates, and how he was your best man, I wondered –' he stopped and looked at his son.

'You mean you want me to go to Sydney?'

Jim nodded. 'I was hoping you'd say that. Couple o' weeks would do it.'

'How will you manage on the farm?'

'I'll just work those two brothers of yours a bit harder. Might even do something myself. It's about time I did a decent day's work. If you like, your mother can go down and stay over with Belinda for a week or two. Berta can take care of me and the boys.'

'OK, Dad. When do I leave?'

'Good. Let's have a beer.' While he was pouring it, he added almost absently, 'Oh, by the way, while you're over, you could bring that old mother of mine back with you.'

Florence Keith was adamant. 'I'm a grown woman,' she said. 'I can manage fine on my own.'

'Gran, you're ninety years of age.'

'What's that?'

Becky sighed and said it louder. 'I said you're ninety!'

'There's no need to shout and let the whole world know.'

'Uncle Jim's letter said that Billy would be coming over on business to Sydney anyway. And he would take the chance of escorting you back, that's all.'

'I'm being treated like a wean.'

'You are a wean!' muttered Becky, untypically short. It had been a hard day. And to her surprise, Jim's letter suggesting it was time that Gran came back didn't please his mother at all. It certainly pleased Becky. Abel was proving more and more of a handful, and even with all the help she got from Rachel, it was still a lot of work on top of her day-to-day duties. Not that she grudged the constant attendance on the lad. It was just so draining. He knew everyone was sorry for him, but what made it worse was that he had become even sorrier for himself. Once the initial shock had worn off, he gradually realised that his blindness was permanent and he was finding it difficult to face up to. Becky had also reluctantly seen the effects of the original sedation given to him during the first hospitalisation. She had thought at first it was merely to kill the pain and ease the shock, but now it was obvious that whatever he'd been given was highly addictive, and Abel craved it more and more each day.

In the first months, she had relied on Dickenson to help her relieve Abel in this way. But only in the last week he had given up his suite and disappeared. The New South Wales police had been making enquiries after she had claimed for some sort of Security Benefit for Abel, and these enquiries extended into many unexpected areas, some of which involved the said Captain. And one morning she discovered he had made a moonlit flight from the hotel. He had left everything, which meant nothing of value. What was even stranger was that, following all these enquiries, Tubby Weir was arrested. Apparently his casino dealings were in some way connected with the Dickenson operations. She remembered how shifty he had seemed that awful morning in the office when they brought Abel back. All this meant that she was now Acting General Manager, so the last thing she needed was any extra stress. It was difficult enough being a woman in charge in Australia, without having to deal with a woman like Gran Keith. She was caught between her and Abel and was doing justice to neither. She loved them both, but that certainly didn't make it any easier.

Rachel had taken Abel home with her for a time, but because both she and Bobby had to be away so often, Abel was left alone too much, 'staring into space', he used to say sardonically. Rachel had been absolutely shattered by her son's accident and could do nothing but weep in his presence. It was difficult to see her with him and watch her trying to keep her sobbing quiet. Bobby, on the other hand, was rendered totally inarticulate by the event. When he first saw what had happened to his boy, he rose up and almost crushed him in an embrace, but never said a word then – nor had he since. He couldn't even speak to his son. He said he couldn't because it felt as if he were intruding into Abel's silence. When Becky tried to explain this to Abel in one of his more lucid moments, Abel gave a little smile, and said quietly, 'Yeah, that's my dad.'

But now the problem was Gran. How to get her quietened down and prepared for the return journey.

'I'll never survive it,' she said. 'I'm a sick woman.'

'Come on, Gran. First of all you object to being treated as a wean, and now you want to be treated as an invalid. Make up your mind.'

'I'll make it up in the morning,' said the old lady. 'I'm away to my bed.'

'Thank God!' said Becky to herself, but she felt bad about it and followed her Gran into the bedroom. She found her sitting on the edge of her bed and she thought she was crying. 'Gran, what's wrong? You know not to mind me.'

'It's not you, lassie.'

'What is it then?'

'I'm greetin' for Abel.' Becky put her arms round the frail old shoulders and they both sat there in silence for quite a time.

Abel was on the terrace in a deck chair when Becky came to him the next morning. She bent down and whispered in his ear.

'Abel.' Normally he always turned his head in the direction the voice had come from, but this time he just continued to face out. She bit her lip, but tried again. 'Abel, you're not going to believe this, but guess who's coming tomorrow?'

'Santa Claus,' he slurred.

'No, I'm serious, Abel. Who would you like to see above anyone else in the world?'

'My grandad.' Becky bent her head. Abel was often talking about his grandad these days, when he did talk.

'No, it's not your grandad,' she said. 'It's your best friend, Billy Keith.' This time the head did turn. Becky's heart leapt.

'That's right. Billy Keith, and he'll be here by tomorrow lunchtime.'

Next day Becky had arranged that Robert, her assistant, would take over all day, so she was able to give all her attention to both her patients, as she called them. Rachel, unfortunately, was at a conference in Melbourne, and Bobby was addressing a meeting that lunchtime in a Philip Street hotel. Becky wondered about this. Was Bobby still too shy to acknowledge his son's condition, even in front of his own nephew? But there was no time to persuade him to cancel his speaking engagement, so she would have to manage as best she could. She had Gran up early and in her best floral dress. She put her wheelchair beside Abel's deck chair and encouraged the old lady to talk to him. It was amazing the number of times her anecdotal meanderings had engaged Abel's attention. She would take his hand in her bony grasp and tell him all about some event at the Elgin Fair before the turn of the century and he would sit with his head inclined to her, showing that he was listening to every word. On other days, his head would just slump forward and the old lady would be just talking to herself and the other empty chairs in the terrace. Becky was in the foyer when the taxi drew up.

She'd forgotten what a big man Billy Keith was. He almost blocked out the sunlight in the doorway as he came forward to her, but then she remembered he'd been an All-Black at one time, – or almost an All-Black. Now, he extended a great hand towards her.

'Where is he?' he said at once, putting down his case. She motioned one of the porters.

'Room 14, Barry,' she said in her formal voice. 'He's on the terrace,' she added softly to Billy.

When Billy walked out on to the terrace, Mrs Keith was asleep and Becky watched as Billy turned to see his friend. The look of horror on the gentle giant's face was evident, even at the distance she was from him at the doorway. She saw his mouth form as if to say something, but no words came. Her knees felt weak as she watched and she couldn't trust herself to move. There was a slight forward movement of Abel's head, hardly perceptible, but it was there. Suddenly it seemed to her as if even the traffic had stopped. There was not a sound in the hotel, as if everything on the harbour front had held its breath to wait to hear what Abel was going to say.

'That you, you old bastard?' Billy was immediately on his knees before the deck chair, with his arms clumsily embracing both Abel and the deck chair. 'For Chris' sake, mate. For Chris' sake!'

622

'What's this Christ stuff?' Abel said. 'Remember you're talking to half a Jew.' Becky then saw that Billy was crying. There was no movement from Gran Keith at all. The moment belonged entirely to the two boys. Billy was totally inarticulate.

'Abel, Abel!' was all he was saying now, and to her joy, she saw Abel's hand come up and pat the big New Zealander's shoulder.

'She'll be right, mate!' said Abel quietly.

It was the first sign of the old Abel Becky had heard. Taking a deep breath, she came forward saying loudly and falsely, 'I see you two know each other.'

They didn't even bother to answer. Billy got up just as clumsily, but he was still holding Abel's hands. To her astonishment, the Kiwi pulled the Aussie up from the deck chair and, holding him under the armpits, lifted him up into the air. 'And who's an old bastard?' he shouted exultantly.

And Abel laughed. Gran Keith suddenly came to.

'What's so funny?' she said crossly. And everybody laughed.

THIRTY-SEVEN

Denny O'Neil sat with Sister Mary Josephine of the Sisters of Mercy in the usual secluded corner of the garden where they always sat on his visits to the New Jersey convent. Even though it was November and a rather chilly Sunday, they still preferred to sit here because it was their place.

'Sorry I didn't bring your Coke.'

Katya smiled. 'It might be rather cold for Coca-Cola,' she said.

'When did you get back?'

'Cupla' weeks ago. I couldn't get out before. Things to do.'

'I understand.'

He looked up at her. 'Do you?' She looked as calm and serene as she'd looked the last time he'd been with her. And look what had happened since then, he thought. 'It was your idea,' he said.

'Yes.' She bowed her head. 'Do you want to tell me about it?'

'No.' His voice had such an edge to it that she looked up quickly. 'But I will. It was Sunday, 13th September, and we left London for Paris . . . .' Sister Mary Josephine listened intently.

He had been rather subdued as he travelled through Europe in those autumn weeks, he told her. It wasn't because of the mounting political tension, although that was bad enough. The Axis powers, that is Germany and Italy, and to a certain extent, Hungary and Japan were already drawing up possible battle lines against the old alliance of Great Britain and France and to a lesser extent, Poland and Czechoslovakia. All the talk in Paris had been about the construction of the new Maginot Line, whose guns pointed east to the Rhur and the debatable miles of the Rhineland. Not all the talk but certainly some of it. Paris was more concerned about the fact that the King of England, as he was more commonly known, had given up his throne for a divorced commoner – and an American at that. This was the kind of sensational gossip Paris thrived on, for this was a love story to end all love stories. Denny though, had his own ideas about that. His brief London experience was still very much with him and the last thing he wanted to do at this time was to wander the romantic boulevards of Paris with his

624

mother. Certainly, he loved his mother, but when one is in love for the first time at the age of twenty-three, the city of Paris means more to a healthy young man than museum and gallery treks with his mother!

Denny was able to make his sister understand this easily enough and what was more important, his sister was more than able to understand him. Katya well appreciated her role as her younger brother's confidante and advisor, and he, for his part, was glad of the opportunity to talk to someone about Chris Mackenzie.

'Are you really in love with this girl,' she asked, 'or are you just in love, Denny?'

'I dunno what you mean, Kat.' Without thinking, he had slipped into her family name. She bowed her head for a moment, then looking up, asked him to go on with the story.

'Mama was in her element . . .'

She had discovered again her schoolgirl French and with it, a whole new energy. Denny could hardly keep up with her in those few days they spent seeing all the sights. She could have run up every single step of the Eiffel Tower, Denny thought, and still have had enough breath at the top to tell him all about the panorama below her. She soaked up every masterpiece in the Louvre and one would have thought that the Arc de Triomphe had been built especially for her! Denny was in the 'tristesse' stage of his infatuation with Chris Mackenzie. The sudden exhilaration had given way to a piquant sadness which had its own quiet, delicious pain and he preferred to spend his time alone, thinking of the girl and enjoying the luxurious misery such thoughts gave him. He knew it was unlikely they would ever meet again, but he couldn't wipe her out of his mind just like that. He could still see her face in the smoke and steam of Victoria Station.

She was his Kiwi Karenina. He only hoped she wouldn't take such drastic steps as Tolstoy's Anna did! No, his clean-cut, blue-eyed, fair-haired heroine wasn't like that. She was – and he realised that he didn't know what she was. Except that she had a lovely smile, came from New Zealand, played the piano and had been in London with a lot of girls from the Berlin Olympics. That was it! The Olympics! He would write to the New Zealand Athletes Association and ask them to forward his letter to her home address! Why hadn't he thought of that right away? Then he realised he had only been too happy to think of her all the time. His mother was off on yet another window-shopping spree. Now was his chance. Plundering all the writing paper from his hotel room, he hurried down to the street café where he and his mother normally had breakfast and set himself up with another cup of coffee and under the umbrella, and against all the noise of traffic and passers-by, he began his first love letter.

'Dear Chris –' No, that's the way you write to the bank!

'Darling Chris –' No, that's too much. Don't want to frighten her off. He knew he had to be careful how he approached this. Then suddenly, all caution was thrown into the Paris street. The hell with it. Tell the girl what you feel. All you have to do, he told himself, is to be honest and sincere about it and the letter will write itself. So he did. And tearing up his second attempt he started again and spoke directly from his heart on to the page:

'My dear Chris,' he wrote, 'I am writing from Paris to tell you that I love you . . .'

The O'Neils had left Paris the next day for Prague. The train journey took them through Berlin and Denny saw all around him all the signs of the New Germany. Young, blond men with armbands on their shirt-sleeves wandered the pavements four at a time, arms linked, defying anyone to break them up. If anyone did, they would beat the person up or measure his nose to see if he were a Jew. Given the chance, and if they had drunk enough, they would whip the poor victim's trousers down to see if he were circumcised. This emerging, swaggering, loud-mouthed, bully generation of Germans was obviously out to take revenge on someone for the humiliations piled on their country after the Great War. Hitler seemed to have touched a responsive chord in the people. They had only a day in the city, thank goodness, and this time, Denny kept close to his mother. Not to protect her, but so that she could protect him! He noticed that the brown-shirted louts never, or rarely, bothered women, and certainly not older women. So Denny clung on to the arm of his fifty-four-year-old mother and hoped for the best. He always spoke as loudly as he could in the street so that they would know he was American. As if they couldn't guess. If there is one species that is self-evident, it is the American tourist in Europe. The one little difficulty was that the revivification of Hana O'Neil begun in Paris was by no means diminished in Berlin. Hana did not like Germans and had no hesitation in showing it whenever the chance allowed. She was no ingenuous American tourist. She was a native-born Bohemian returning to her roots and was quick to realise that her homeland would soon be threatened by these thugs.

'What is the League of Nations doing to stop all this?' she asked her son on one occasion.

'I dunno, Mama.' Denny didn't know what good the League of Nations did anyway. Hana was pessimistic altogether. And said so.

'What's happening in Spain, you watch, it's just a rehearsal for the big thing. You'll see. War will come in Europe. They need it.'

Since when did my mother become a political pundit, Denny thought, but the fact was that Mrs O'Neil was an intelligent woman and was using her eyes. Others at the time were deliberately averting theirs. The possibilities were too horrible to contemplate. Denny, for the moment, was blind to everything except one thing. And in a café in the Unter der Linden, he wrote: 'My dear Chris – I am writing from Berlin to tell you that I love you . . .'

It had been wonderful for the son to see his mother's reaction to coming home to Czechoslovakia. She had never known Prague as part of this new country that had arisen after the war. To her it was still the old country, still essentially the old Bohemia, the old Praha. Her eyes swam in sentimental tears almost from the time she arrived and the old tongue tripped from her lips like music. Denny just had to stand apart and let her enjoy. He had no need to hold her arm here. It was all he could do to hang on to her coat-tails. Her energy was astonishing as she flew from place to place around the ancient city.

'Mama, you're doing too much!' Denny tried to tell her.

'Nonsense,' she replied, 'I am home again in Czechy. I cannot do enough.' Her own family had come from a place called Lidice, not many miles from Prague and Hana and Denis took the bus there one day. Denny watched as she visited old people in their houses and embraced them. He saw how moved they were and how affected she was as she tried to bridge thirty-six years. She was very quiet on the bus home to the hotel. When they got back, she said she didn't want to go out to the restaurant that night for dinner.

'You go Denny. You will meet young people.'

But Denny didn't want to go out on his own. He had met his 'young people' in London. He was just a bit worried about her.

'You OK?' he asked her, and for some reason she answered him in Czech. He ate in the hotel that night, while his mother had a tray in her room. After dinner, which he didn't really enjoy, he found writing paper once again and wrote: 'My dear Chris – I am writing from Prague to tell you that I love you . . .'

It had been five to five in the morning when he was wakened from his sleep by the telephone at his bedside. He was scared out of his wits by the sudden jangle in his right ear and sat up in the blackness wondering where the hell he was. His right hand found the telephone while his left searched for the bed-light. He lifted the receiver to his ear.

'Yes?' he muttered. A Czech voice mumbled in his ear.

'I can't understand a word you're saying,' he bellowed sleepily into the masterpiece. The voice continued. It was a woman's voice. It sounded strained, then he heard it say – 'Denny! Denny!' It was his mother!

'MAMA!' he shouted and was out of bed in a bound.

His mother was lying face down across the bed and she still had the bedside phone in her hand.

'Mama!' and he rushed to her from the doorway. He prised the instrument from her hand and pulled her up into a sitting position. Her eyes were opened but she didn't seem to be seeing him. He arranged the pillows to try and make her more comfortable but she fell away to one side like a limp sack.

'Mama!' What's wrong?' He grabbed at her again and pulled her up. He'd forgotten how small and slight she was. He tried patting her cheeks lightly but she still continued to stare. He patted her hands, but only felt foolish doing so. A hairpin had fallen out of her hair and the strand fell over one cheek, making her look drunk. She must've fainted, he thought. God, what do I do? He tried to reach the phone but it was just out of his reach. Steadying his mother with one hand, he managed to reach it and he heard it ring out.

'Oh come on!' he blurted out angrily. Then a man's voice answered gruffly in Czech. Denny didn't wait.

'Look, whoever you are, this is 106. Could you send somebody? My mama's fainted or something, and I can't get her to – it's my mama, sir, and I dunno what to do –' He broke off because he found he was crying like a baby.

The porter came up first, with his shirt over his trousers, then a woman, who seemed like his wife, came in in her housecoat and took Hana from Denny's arms and tried to make her more comfortable in the bed. The porter spoke on the phone to someone, then left the room. He came back in a moment with Denny's overcoat, which he made the young American put on having first pulled him away gently from the bottom of the bed where he'd been standing helplessly watching the prone figure of his mother who looked as if she were sleeping. The porter's wife, if that's who she was, brought him a cup of very strong, very sweet coffee then went to sit by the bed in a small chair she drew over from the writing table. Denny drank the coffee automatically, never taking his eyes from Hana. The porter came in again with a doctor who had a bristly moustache and looked extremely bad-tempered. He nodded to the porter and then to Denny but it was not in greeting. It was an order to leave. Denny let himself be led to his own room.

He was still sitting in his coat at the edge of the bed when the porter came back for him. The man was completely dressed by now and smelled of soap and hair oil.

'Please,' he said. His mother's room looked different. It was tidier and it was daylight. She was still lying in bed and still looked as if she were asleep but someone had combed her hair back. The woman was now standing at the window and the doctor was packing his bag. He spoke to Denny in Czech, then in German, then in French, but Denny could only stare at his mother. Was she dead? The doctor made an exasperated noise and said something to the porter, who came to Denny's side.

'Prosim. Lituji. Nemluvim anglicky. Mluvte pomalu. Doctor –tell-mother-sick – bad sick – nebezpeci – nouzovy –' He shook his head with impatience at his inability to explain to Denny. Then he turned Denny round to face him and pointed to his own heart. He mimed the beat and then made a cutting gesture towards Hana.

'She's dead!' yelled Denny and made an attempt to throw himself on the bed. The porter grabbed him and pushed his face into his,

'Ne, ne, ne,' he whispered fiercely and put a finger to his lips. The doctor then came to Denny and said something else in Czech and then shook his hand and left. The woman then came forward to the porter who was still staring at Denny. They both took him to the chair at the bedside and sat him down. He could feel their hands all about him and then the porter was putting his finger to his lips again. The woman tried to smile and the porter patted his shoulder. He heard them leave the room and close the door quietly, leaving the silence of the room to mother and son.

Denny kept his eyes on the still figure on the bed. He could see that she was breathing, but very gently. Her eyes were closed now and she looked so peaceful. Like a little girl. Outside, the city was stirring but there wasn't a move from Hana O'Neil. Then, with the tiniest of flickers, her eyes opened and she seemed to be looking at someone at the bottom of the bed. Denny leaned in.

'Here I am, Mama.' But Hana stared straight ahead. Then she smiled and spoke in a very small voice.

'Dobry den, Papa. Kde je Mama? Prosim, ukazte mne. . .ja bych chtel. . .ja studena. Je to dost.' Denny was bewildered.

'Mama,' he whimpered. When she spoke again it was in English. 'Hello Denis.'

'I'm Denny, Mama.'

'You are handsome in your uniform, yes?' She was smiling again.

'We will be happy, no?' Denny turned his head away, closing his eyes and clenching his teeth. Suddenly, his mother made a gasping noise and when he turned she was sitting bolt upright holding out her hands, her eyes wide open, looking radiant, but it was an unearthly radiance.

'Katya! My lovely Katya, it is you. You are come to your Mama again.' Then she leaned forward, her expression changing to one of entreaty, 'No Katya, wait – wait. I am coming. I am coming.' Denny couldn't watch any longer and buried his head in the bedcovers.

'Mama, Mama, Mama!' he wailed.

It had been very late that night. Denny sat at the writing table in Room 105 and slowly he pulled a piece of the hotel writing paper towards him. 'My dear sister Clara' – he wrote. 'I am writing from Prague to tell you that our beloved mother died here at five before ten this morning . . .'

'And you know the rest,' he said simply.

'Yes,' said Katya. 'Clara took it very badly. She came here and blamed me for suggesting that Mama go there.'

'Why did you do it?' he asked.

'It was right for Mama.'

'How do you know?' He felt himself getting angry again and he had promised himself he would try to control his temper, he loved his nun sister so, but like Clara and Anna he had blamed her too. She could see that he was agitated.

'Please be calm, dear brother. Only calm is constructive. "In quietness and confidence shall be your strength", as the book says. Our mother died in her own homeland, and you said yourself she was smiling.'

'She was.'

'She knew, you see. She had faith. She had trust. She had confidence. And now she is calm. For that is trust in action.'

'I don't understand.'

'Ah, that is faith.'

'Did she really see you, Katya?'

Katya smiled. 'Blessed are those who have not seen and yet still believe.' The visitors' bell sounded.

'That's the postie!'

'I'll get it, Mum!'

'Alright.'

'Coming.'

The brief exchange between mother in the kitchen and daughter in the study was a result of the doorbell's sounding which set voices going, dogs barking and the general household clamour that usually ensues on anyone calling at the front door. Normally the mail was left in a box at the road-end but lately, since the school bus stopped carrying it and it came now with the van from Gore, the postie came straight up the drive. He was a cheerful bloke and would always stop for a crack with whoever took in the letters.

'Lovely smell coming from somewhere!' he said chirpily, as he handed over a large bundle of letters. 'Your Mum baking?'

'Yes.' Berta was too impatient to chatter. 'Thank you.' She took the letters and hurried in again.

'Cheerio,' called the postman.

'Cheerio,' answered Berta flatly, closing the door.

'Anything interesting?' called her mother. That meant hand-written envelopes to Jean Keith. Anything typewritten meant bills or invoices. Berta was quickly flipping through them.

'No,' Berta called out, 'just the usual.' She carried them through to the back room which Jim Keith used as a study and office and left all the official-looking letters there and those envelopes with 'windows' in them. That left her with two in her hand – a larger envelope marked as from the New Zealand Olympic Committee and addressed to Chris Mackenzie and an ordinary letter in a blue envelope addressed to her. Berta knew that the big envelope would contain another one of 'those letters'. She hurried through to her bedroom.

'You alright, Berta?' called her mother from the kitchen.

'Yes, Mum. Won't be a minute. Got a letter from Chris.'

'That's nice.'

In her room, Berta went to her bedside cupboard and put the larger letter with the others. That made seven in all, she noted. What were they she wondered? Her Dad had wanted to send them on to Chris when the first one arrived a few weeks before but when she had phoned one time and Berta had told her there was an envelope from the Olympic Committee, Chris had said just to hang on to them until she got home. It would just be something official that she had to sign or something. So Berta had kept them all in her bedside cupboard. She thought it odd that there were so many letters from the Olympic Committee and had said so to her Mum one time, but she had said that's Chris's business not ours and Berta had more or less forgotten all about them till this one came today. She settled herself back on her bed and opened her letter from Chris. She was delighted to see there were lots of pages. She pulled them out and turning over to lie on her stomach, she started to read:

'Dear Berta, Hope this finds you as it leaves me – flat out. I've had to move flats from George Street as they let it to another girl while I was away in Europe. Good old Prof Neinmann has been very understanding since I came back and says I can have all the time I like to prepare for my end-of-term recital. If I can do well in this, I may have a chance of a scholarship next year to the Royal Academy in London. What about that? It's early yet but I'll let you know more about it when I come home at Christmas. I've promised Dad I'll go and see him and Sandy for a few days first before I get back to Gore. Poor old Dad. Sandy seems to get him down a bit, but you know Sandy. Anyway, I think they could do with a bit of cheering up before Christmas and I want to see wee Laura again. Although she's not so wee now.' Berta turned over the page. Good old Chris, she thought. 'However, why I'm writing now to you Berta, old girl, is to ask if any letters have arrived for me. I don't mean the Olympic thing you mentioned. No, I mean PERSONAL! Because, my dear old cousin, I want to let you into my great secret. I haven't told anyone yet and you must promise on your Guide's honour not to tell anyone either but, Berta, I can't keep it to myself any longer – I'm in love. Yes, IN LOVE WITH A MAN and I honestly do think this is the real thing.' At this, Berta looked up, flustered and bewildered. She turned over and sat up on the edge of the bed and read that particular page again. Chris in love? Berta didn't know how to react, how to cope with it. It was all so sudden. Her special Chris – and a man! Oh no! She knew it must happen sometime. It was only natural after all and Chris had always been attractive to boys but – A MAN? She looked at the letter again and turned over the next page – 'He's an American and his name is Denny O'Neil and he's gorgeous – honestly. I saw him first that night I went to the opera with Uncle John but I didn't speak to him. I thought that was that but then when I went back to get that programme for you I met him again quite by chance at the Covent Garden stage door and he took me in a taxi to catch the train. But Berta, he didn't give me his address or anything and I don't know how to get in touch with him, but I know I'm going to see him again, I just know it. I think he'll write to me. If he does –'

Berta looked up. A suspicion was growing in her mind. She put down the letter on the bed and hurriedly got the big envelopes from the bedside cupboard. She sat for a moment with them on her lap. I wonder, she thought. Should I? No, it's not my business remember. She was about to put them back but then she hesitated. But I'm her best friend aren't I? She said so herself. That decided her and she fell on the envelopes feverishly. As she quickly opened all seven trying hard not to tear them too much, the thoughts raced through her head. Like a green girl! Yet Chris was a grown woman with a great career ahead of her. If some awful man – Berta felt herself getting tight, and took a deep breath. Who would have thought that Chris, who could have had her pick in New Zealand, would go and fall for some crummy Yank! But I don't even know the man, insisted the more reasonable part of Berta Keith. It doesn't matter, answered the unreasonable part, Chris shouldn't be getting herself involved like this. She has better things to do. By this time Berta had all the envelopes opened and she saw that they each contained a letter addressed to Chris. This certainly was nothing official. 'For Miss Mackenzie' it said on the front of each one and PLEASE FORWARD was scrawled along the top.

They were all different kinds and colours of envelopes, and all with different stamps, British, French, German, and one she didn't recognise. Today made the third one from America. Yes, that's seven in all. She held the letters in her hand as if she were weighing them. She studied the writing. This was a man, without a doubt. Who was he? Some kind of traveller? All these different countries. Berta took up Chris's letter again – 'so if he does write by any chance will you let me know AT ONCE!' Was this my Chris? she thought? She didn't dare let herself think about it any more and hastily put the foreign letters back in their envelopes again and back in the cupboard. She finished reading the letter – 'So mum's the word, dear Berta, till I see you next.

Love to everyone. Are Billy and Gran back home yet?'

Berta took up her inhaler and took a few deep sniffs, still taken aback by what she'd just read. Chris hadn't mentioned anyone like that when she came back from Europe. Admittedly, she had to rush back to Dunedin right away to get back to her classes, but you would think she would have mentioned to her, Berta reasoned, if there had been anyone – well – special. She hadn't even said she was expecting any letters. Or asked Berta to send them on. A wave of guilt swept through her for having opened them. She knew she shouldn't have done that even if she were her best friend. Something made her. It was a sudden impulse she couldn't explain and now she wanted to tear the letters up – all of them. But they weren't my letters, they were Chris's. They should have been sent on to her right away. Berta knew now she wanted more than anything else in the world to read them. Dare she? Her mother was still in the kitchen. She couldn't go down now. But later perhaps? Tonight . . .

'Berta! What are you up to through there?' It was her mother.

'Coming, Mum!' she called back, and folding up Chris's letter she put it back in its envelope, put it in her drawer and hurried out.

It was well after midnight before she had the kitchen to herself and putting the kettle on the coal range, she steamed open all seven letters. All the time she was doing it she kept telling herself to stop.

She knew it was wrong but she couldn't help herself. When she had opened up the first one she found there were about three or four pages inside in the same writing that was on the envelope – 'My dear Chris, I am now back in London again and I am only writing to tell you that I love you –'

Berta felt the sweat of embarrassment on her brow. It was a terrible thing to do, but she was drawn on, fascinated –

'My dear Chris, I am now back in good old New York and I am writing to tell you that no matter all that's happened, I still love you . . .' All the letters were the same – saying the same thing – 'Chris I love you.' They were love letters – lovely letters, yet as soon as Berta read them she knew what she must do. She must destroy them and almost before she knew what she was doing she was pushing all of them into the stove – saying to herself, over and over again – vehemently and mechanically – 'Chris, I love you! Chris I love you! Chris, I love you . . . !'

Billy came home the next afternoon with Gran. Jean Keith had made a special cake for her mother-in-law to celebrate her homecoming. She brought it out with pride after tea that night and everybody cheered at the sight of it. Except Gran of course.

'I hope there are no nuts in it,' she said.

'No, Gran there are no nuts.'

'I hate nuts.'

'We know you do, Gran,' said Jean with a sigh, glad to see that the sojourn hadn't changed Florence Keith one little bit. Billy, though, looked a little bit sombre. His mother remarked on it.

'Just a bit tired, Mum, that's all,' he said. 'The trip was a bit rough.'

'Are ye talkin' about me?' said Gran.

'No Gran,' laughed Billy, 'I'm talking about Cook Strait.'

'How was everybody when you left them, Billy?' asked Jim.

'Alright 's'pose. Uncle Bobby is away most of the time. Rachel's busy with her courses and Becky with her hotel. She's the big chief there now, you know.'

'Isn't that nice?' said Jean, cutting the cake into slices. Everybody watched her.

'How's Abel?' asked Jim softly. Jean stopped her hand on the knife. Billy looked at his Gran.

'He's as blind as a bat!' she said matter-of-factly.

'Except that bats can fly, Gran,' said Billy ironically.

'What was that?' asked Gran.

'Nothing, Gran,' said Billy quickly before turning to his father, 'I was trying to persuade him to come over for Christmas, Dad.'

'Oh,' said his mother, resuming her cake-cutting, 'How would he manage? I mean –' Billy knew what his mother meant – how would they manage Abel?

'It's alright, Mum, he'd stay with us.'

'Good for you, son,' said Jim.

'What's a joker to do when his mate's crook?' said Billy simply.

'True,' said his father.

'Anyway,' went on Billy, 'it would depend on who could get away to bring him over. It's a busy time for Becks. The hotel and all that.'

'I could go,' said Berta suddenly.

'No you couldn't, Berta,' said her mother, 'Don't be silly.'

'What's so silly?' complained Berta, 'I'd love to go to Sydney.'

'You know you couldn't, Berta,' continued her mother.

'Why not?'

'You know why not and there's an end of it. More cake anybody?'

'Yes please!' This was shouted in unison by the twins, who each proffered their plates to their mother.

'Why don't we send these to Sydney?' said Jim with a grin.

'Why not?' said Kenny.

'Yeah,' said Jamie. 'Sydney'd be great!'

'We'll see,' said their mother, doling out two large portions.

'What about you, Billy?'

'No thanks Mum, let the peasants eat cake!' The twins made a derisory noise with their mouths full.

'Boys!' said their mother in mock-horror.

'I'd better be getting back,' said Billy, 'Bel'll be wondering.'

His father also rose from the table.

'I'll give you those papers I was telling you about. Just a tick, I'll get them from my desk.' He started towards the door and stopped. 'Oh by the way, Berta. There was another one of those letters for Chris.' Berta nearly dropped the cup she was holding.

'Letters, Dad?' she managed to say.

'Yeah,' he said, 'You know, those Olympic Association things. I'll get it and show you.' He went out. Berta heard Billy saying goodnight to Gran but she tried to keep her head down in case anyone would see.

'You alright, Berta?' asked her mother. Her father came in before she could answer. He was carrying one of the large envelopes in his hands – and it had been opened!

'I'm afraid I opened it. I thought it was for us.' Berta's heart was in her mouth. 'But I don't think it's all that important. Seems to be some kind of form or something. You'd better keep it for Chris just in case.' He handed it to his astonished daughter.

'That's what all those other ones must have been. They must have wondered why Chris hadn't replied,' he added. Berta took the envelope and pulled out its contents. It was a form with a covering letter from a Miss Hacking. Berta read –

'Now that final accounts are to be agreed with the Finance Committee for the team's participation in the recent Berlin Olympics, I would be grateful if you would complete the enclosed form . . .'

'Yes,' she said, 'It's just some kind of form or something.'

'I thought so,' said Jim. 'Might as well burn the others,' he added. The family wondered why Berta suddenly started to laugh.

Chris adjusted the piano stool yet again and flexed her fingers for the umpteenth time. She then wiped her palms on her dress and wished she'd worn the yellow one after all. It was her lucky dress. Never mind, it was too late now. Better make a start. She lifted her hands to the keyboard and both felt like lead. It's only nerves she said to herself. Everybody's like this before a recital. So they said. She just wished she weren't. Out of the corner of her eye, she caught the glimpse of Professor Neinmann's spectacles glinting in the panel light on his marking board. He would be alright she thought, but she wasn't so sure about some of the others – especially the female teachers. Even the old Dreadnought herself had come in to listen and some of the students were sitting at the back. She was never very happy about fellow students being allowed in on exam recitals. She could feel their 'evil eye' on her. No, that was just her silly imagination. They were just as nervous as she was and all of them had the same ambition – to get into the scholarship class next term. It could be worth a lot of money, not to mention the prestige. There was also a chance next year of a scholarship year in the London Royal Academy, so she had plenty to play for. Well here goes . . .

She had chosen an all-Chopin programme. After all, there was no better showcase for a piano performer and hackneyed as some of the pieces might be, they were tricky to play and needed all her skills of technique and interpretation. The thing was to get the balance right between these two essentials. Too great an emphasis on technique and the result was a cold performance. On the other hand, to give oneself over entirely to an emotional or sentimental interpretation and a sluggish, sloppy performance could result. Nobody minds the odd wrong note, old Neinmann had told her, if the overall, the total, the sum of the music is there. Trust the composer, he always said.

Her first piece was his Valse No 6 in D flat major – Opus 64 No 1, sometimes known as the Minute Waltz, a good 'finger-loosener' as they say in the business, and she felt all the better for it once she finished with not too many bum notes. She got the speed, the élan of the thing – the 'total' that the Professor talked about. Her second item was the old war-horse – the 'Revolutionary Study' or the Etude in C minor, Opus 10, No 12. This offered a good contrast and relaxed her completely. Uncle Jim had always liked to hear her play it on the old upright and she couldn't help thinking of him as she belted it out. And old Gran. And Berta. I wonder why she never replied to my letter? Whoops, better not think of that just yet, not with all these arpeggios coming up. She managed to finish with a flourish but still in control and was gratified to hear a kind of murmur from the back somewhere as she did so. It was a little unnerving, this absolute silence after each piece. Applause seemed needed somehow, to round the thing off. Still, there'd be plenty of time for applause when she started getting paid to play. The important thing was to get into that scholarship class. Her third and final Chopin was the big Ballade in G minor, Opus 23. This was the one that gave her most trouble for it had more twists and turns in it than an Otago creek. The thing was to take a step at a time and try not to show the joins. It was powerful stuff and always had a powerful effect on her. Not quite as overwhelming as her favourite Rachmaninov, but bad enough.

This morning, of all mornings, it got to her. Try as she might she could see Denny O'Neil's face in front of her all the time she played. Hear his voice, his laugh. Damn, she better be careful. Get to hell out of my mind, she told the apparition in her subconscious, I need to concentrate here! Try as she might, she couldn't clear it, so as the cadences rose and fell and the notes cascaded over the keyboard under her flying fingers she called out in her heart to this image of the young American and urged it to help her as the climaxes approached. She was lost too in the music, swimming in it. It was all or nothing now. This was not the way she'd been trained at all. This was hardly the classical approach required by her teachers. This was abandonment to Victorian Romanticism, more Liszt than Chopin, but there was little she seemed able to do about it, and the mighty opus moved inexorably to its conclusion.

When she finished, her hands felt limp. She could feel the damp of perspiration in her armpits and on her brow. Someone somewhere started to applaud. No more than three or four single handclaps, but they were there in the darkness and an involuntary response on somebody's part. She just hoped it was Professor Neinmann's. As she got up and bowed towards him, she could see his mane of white hair bent over his board, and some of the students were moving around at the back. She was glad to get off the stage and couldn't wait to get to the toilet.

She packed that night so that she could get away first thing in the morning. She was getting the train to Gore and then a bus to Edendale. She didn't want to trouble her father or Sandy, not knowing how they were placed to come and get her. She was looking forward to seeing her old Dad again and to telling them all about what had happened to her in Europe, but could she tell him everything? She would wait and see. She wondered how Sandy would be. If his moods had improved. Poor Sue. She has a hard time with my big brother, Chris thought, but she seems to love him and there's always little Laura. She'll be about seven, just the right age for Christmas. She remembered when she was seven, and her mother was alive. She rarely thought of her mother, and yet she remembered loving her so much. It was six years now since her death. At the time of Billy's wedding. Would she ever forget it? Trying to keep her father from going berserk in front of all those people who had come for a wedding and found instead they were attending a funeral. That helped her to forget her own grief at the time. Her own shock. Keeping an eye on the boys helped too. It was funny, but it might have been from that time that Sandy started getting sulky. He worshipped his mother. So did we all, she remembered.

Moving around the room, she suddenly caught sight of herself in the mirror which was on the centre panel of the big wardrobe. She put down the books she had in her hand and went over to study herself. Something that Chris Mackenzie didn't do often. She looked at the fair hair, the blue eyes, the straight nose, the thinnish lips, good chin. Was this her mother's face? Her mother as a young girl when she had come to New Zealand first? When she was starting out? She had only been twenty then, her mother, the same age as Chris was now. She was also starting out. Not, however, in a new country like Christina Keith did, but in a very ancient terrain – the whole universe of the arts, where many better travellers than her failed to survive. Today would tell. She would hear in the New Year. Meantime, she'd better get some sleep, if she had to catch that train in the morning.

At Archbishop Paddy's suggestion, Denny had invited everyone in the family to come to Brooklyn for Christmas. The whole thing started because Nellie had written to her Archbishop brother to say she was coming to America for a visit, and she wondered if she could come to him in Seattle. It was Paddy's idea that she should go instead to New York and he would come there, pastoral duties permitting. With a bit of luck he might be able to use his influence with the Mother Superior at the Orangeburg Convent to let Sister Mary Josephine have a few days vacation as well. He also suggested that Denny contact Joey in the hope that he too might be let out for the Christmas period. In this way, as Paddy saw it, all the remaining O'Neils would be together for the first time for years. Only Kevin was missing, and no one in the family had any idea how to contact him. Paddy understood from Nellie that their youngest brother was in Europe – 'on business'. At any rate, an O'Neil Christmas convention was on the cards, and appropriate arrangements were put in hand. Nellie had been the first to arrive and here she was meeting her nephew for the first time.

'You're the spittin' image of your father.'

'You think so?'

'Indeed I know so. I've only got to look at you.'

Denny didn't know what else to say to his Aunt Nellie. He had been a bit nervous about meeting her, and having her stay at the house. He heard she'd been a bit crazy at one time. He didn't quite know the whole story. And now here she was, coming to the house and he was the only one there to meet her. He stayed alone in the family house in Brooklyn while he made up his mind what he wanted to do on the work front. Jobs were still scarce, even for journalists with a Masters, so he spent most of his time at the house on his own.

Clara hoped to persuade Brad to move from Queen's into the big house as it was certainly too much for Denny on his own, but Anna also wanted to move in from the Bronx, and the two girls were having a kind of wrangle about that at the moment. It was the kind of thing that happens in every family after the parents die. There had been no will or clear instructions left by Hana, and the lawyer was just going on Denis's will, where the Superintendent had made it clear that Denny was to inherit the Brooklyn house as it was presumed the girls would have houses of their own. Hana had said that they could have any furniture they wanted from it, but no specific apportioning had ever been made and the two girls were even arguing about that. Apparently they each wanted the particular thing the other wanted, so for the moment, neither was having anything. Denny had called for a Christmas truce and though the sisters were still huffy towards each other, they were at least still speaking, and it was hoped they would forget their differences over Christmas and work something out in the New Year.

Aunt Nellie was having the time of her life. Organising a Brooklyn brownstone was kindergarten stuff after the demands

of Cassidy's Hotel in Dublin. She was in New York with a clear
conscience. First of all, it was what was left of her own brother's
money she was spending and second, her second husband's death
had made her the out-and-out owner of Cassidy's. She was now
a widow of property and didn't care who knew it. She had left
Teresa in charge and Teresa was capable. Nellie could now play
the widow, as merrily as she liked. There was only one time
Denny saw her solemn – one night during the evening meal,
which she had made, she suddenly asked him what he knew of
his uncle Liam.

'The one that killed himself?' Denny had asked.

'That's the one,' she said, looking into her tea cup.

'Not much. Except that he lived with an Italian woman.'

'It doesn't matter.' Then she resumed in her ordinary voice,
'Now then Denny boy, what is it we're doing tonight?'

Every night, Nellie wanted to do something, go somewhere.
Denny was finding it hard to keep up. She loved the Broadway
shows and would have seen one every night, if Denny would have
taken her. She refused to go anywhere unless he went with her,
but tonight he said, 'Let's stay home, Aunt Nellie, and listen to
the radio.' He was beginning to realise he was going to have to
pace himself if he was going to survive Christmas.

Joey was the first live-in guest to arrive. A car came from New
Jersey with a man and a woman in it, who had all the pleasant
demeanour of prison guards, but introduced themselves as nurses.
Joey was completely at ease, even though neither Denny nor Nellie
knew him at all. Once again, by one of those mental flukes or
aberrations, he was immediately aware of his environment and
recognised it at once as his boyhood home. The two nurses were
amazed at this and said they would report it to the doctors as soon
as they got back to Ridgefield Park. Joey went straight to his old
room at the back, carrying his large box of Monopoly under his
arm and, opening the door, announced triumphantly, 'Hey, this is
my room!'

Since it was empty anyway, Nellie said, 'Well, you might as well
have it.' She had cleaned out every inch of the place in the previous
week. The spring clean had also assisted towards Denny's fatigue.
'Sure, it's your room, Uncle Joey, help yourself.'

Joey walked in, put his box of Monopoly on the bed, took off
his coat and threw it over one chair, then, turning back to his two
relatives, said with a wide grin, 'Come on, I'll show you Noreen's
room.' He walked straight between them. They looked at each
other and followed.

'We'll call it Katya's room,' said Denny, 'if she comes.'

Paddy came later that day, also in a car and driven by two men, but two very different kinds of men. The younger one drove, and the older one sat in the front. Perhaps he was the reserve driver. At any rate, both were priests, and when Paddy O'Neil got out of the car to stand on the sidewalk at 59/57th street, and stood for a moment looking up at the old house, it was as if a Messiah had come to Brooklyn. The women in the street gasped and some of the men involuntarily made the sign of the cross. And they weren't even Catholics! He dismissed the sleek Cadillac and away it purred back towards St Patrick's. Paddy's shiny patent leather shoes carried him up the old familiar front steps, his smooth features pink under the mat of grey-white hair, his black eyebrows still sombre. He made a very imposing picture. When Nellie opened the door to him, all she could see was his cerise shirt under the white collar, the pectoral cross gleaming at her.

'In the name o' God, it's Paddy!' she said.

He smiled. 'That's as good a way of putting it as any, Nellie.' He gave her a hug that was more brotherly than bishop-like. She had to pull back in case the tears she felt coming would spoil that lovely cerise front. Arm in arm they came into the hall together and Denny thought what a lovely picture they made – two grey-topped black-eyed O'Neils. Paddy was delighted with Denny.

'By the good Lord, Denny, you're my own brother again, and I couldn't say better than that.'

'That's what Aunt Nellie said,' grinned Denny.

'And she's not telling a lie either,' said Paddy.

'Sure and when did I ever?' protested Nellie.

'The last time you were in confession,' joked Paddy.

'True enough,' said Nellie and laughingly they all went in to the sitting room to meet Joey. He had no memory of Paddy at all, but Paddy showed all his former pastoral gifts in the way that he greeted his cousin again and put him at ease. Paddy noticed the Monopoly board on the side table near the radiogram.

'Still playing games, Joey?'

'Yes sir,' beamed Joey. 'And still winning.'

'Ah, you haven't played me yet though,' said Paddy.

'Would you like a game now, er –'

'Just call me Paddy. That's my name when I'm at home. I'll give you a game after dinner.' And during dinner he had the three of them laughing with stories from the Diocese. Who could have believed an Archbishop's life could be so funny?

It was only after he had played a long game with Joey that Denny rose up and said, 'Right, that's it, Joey. It's past our bed time. Let's go and leave these old guys to reminisce.' So saying, he had taken his uncle off to bed. 'Say goodnight, Joey.'

'Goodnight.'

'Goodnight.' As soon as they were alone, Paddy looked serious. 'Tell me all about it, Nellie,' he said motioning her to sit down and pouring them each an ample Jamieson's.

'What do you mean, Paddy?'

'You know what I mean, Helen O'Neil – Murphy or Cassidy – or whatever you'd prefer your name to be.'

'You want to hear my confession, you mean?'

'What, and deny myself a good drink here? Not at all. I just feel you'd like to talk, that's all.' He was as easy and patient with her as he'd been with Joey, and Nellie marvelled that they had such a saint in the family. So she told him. She told him everything and left nothing out. Her time with Sam, their mother, and Kevin and his lovely young wife and daughters. She talked until her tongue was dry and the bottle of Jamieson's almost gone.

'Nellie?'

'Yes, Paddy?'

'Did Kevin tell you about the Italian woman?'

'He did.'

'And did he tell you about the children?'

'He did. A boy and a girl, as I remember. But they weren't Liam's, he said.'

'Indeed they weren't.' He reached for the bottle again. 'But there was another child there. Another boy.'

'Was he Liam's?'

'He was.'

'Who by?'

'By whom?' the Archbishop corrected jocularly, but Nellie never noticed. She was in no mood for jokes.

'Well?' she said.

'Our own sister Noreen,' he said in a low voice. To his surprise, Nellie burst out laughing.

'Paddy, isn't that the very thing now? Sure, wasn't Liam after Noreen from the very start, and didn't I confuse you all by running off with him? Well, they say the devil gets his own in the end. So I wish them the luck of it. It's not much either of them got, I'm thinking.'

'Liam had a small glimpse of it at the end and he took good care of the boy.'

'Where is he now?' Paddy hesitated again.

'In London last time I heard.'

'London?'

'Yes. His name is Guiglielmo.'

'What kind of name is that!'

'But they call him Tito,' said Paddy.

'I'm not sure but that's worse,' replied his sister.

The following day, Christmas Eve, Sister Mary Josephine arrived on foot and carrying a small suitcase. She had come in by bus and made her own way to the house. Denny was annoyed with her.

'Kat, I would have come and got you. You know that.'

'It's alright, Denny. I'm here, aren't I?' He watched her warily as she came in and looked about the old familiar rooms. He carried her case up to her old room and only the slightest hesitation at the door made him aware that she was suffering.

'You OK, Kat?' he said from behind her. She nodded her head and went in. He was about to follow when she immediately turned, her eyes wide.

'Could I stay in Anna's room, please?'

'Of course.' It took no time to settle her things in her room. She didn't have anything, so Denny brought her down to meet Joey in the front room.

'Not yet,' she whispered. 'There's something I need to do first.' And turning from him, she went through the back on to the old iron fire escape. It had now been long renewed and even looked good under a new coat of black paint. But she went straight to the fatal corner, and kneeling down and bending her head low, she began to pray.

Denny watched from the kitchen doorway. He heard a voice call out, 'Hey, would you come look at this, you guys? We got a praying nun on the balcony.' Neither Katya nor Denny paid any attention. Denny found himself bending his own head and saying in a whisper, 'Hail Mary, full of grace, the Lord is with thee . . .' It was a long time since he had prayed. He waited until Katya rose and when she came towards him again, her eyes were red, but she was smiling.

'Let's go meet Joey,' she said.

When Nellie and Paddy returned from shopping, Paddy greeted his sister in the cloth very warmly.

'You see, Nellie,' he explained to his sister, 'we're fellow professionals, you might say.' Nellie was rather in awe of Katya, and could only call her 'Sister'. And now they were five.

As planned, the family reunion took place at St Bride's, Brooklyn, after Midnight Mass. Canon Donnelly, now looking a little bit stooped, concelebrated the Mass, but the sensation at the service was not the three rows of O'Neils that suddenly appeared under their various marital designations, but the effect at Communion when the choir, instead of singing 'Silent Night' as everyone expected, suddenly hummed an introduction to 'Panis Angelicus' and a glorious soprano voice soared out above them all, singing the solo line. Maria d'Agostino had become an O'Neil again for the night and was singing for her family. When the good Archbishop turned with the communion cup in his hand, his smiling look up to the choir stalls said everything as that splendid voice filled the church.

> 'Panis Angelicus, fit panis hominum,
> Dat panis caelicus figuris terminum.
> Ores mirabilis . . .'

It was a miracle indeed! A miracle of organisation between Paddy's Diocescan wizard, Father Conlan, and the logistical expertise of Vernon Drake. Somehow they'd managed it, and managed it secretly and the church was buzzing with reaction, which was totally unbecoming to the solemnity of the occasion but was joyfully glorious for all that. Those who weren't laughing were crying, and for once, when the time came to sing 'Silent Night', it was sung as it was originally sung in Austria, simply and without accompaniment, by Maria's golden voice.

> 'Silent night, Holy night, all is calm, all is bright,
> Round yon virgin, mother and child, holy infant so tender
>   and mild
> Sleep in heavenly peace, sleep in heavenly peace . . .'

It was a merry Christmas in Brooklyn. Even Clara and Anna made it up with each other and Maria offered her hand to Denny in the street outside.

'Merry Christmas, cousin,' she said.

'Merry Christmas, Maria. Thank you for coming.'

'I couldn't refuse. I told you I was one of the family.'

'I always knew you were,' he said.

'I was sorry to hear about your mother.' And she almost sounded as if she meant it.

'Thank you,' said Denny.

A car came to the house for her within the hour. It had been a hard job smuggling her through the crowds and even now there were people on the pavement pointing in at the O'Neil lighted windows. It was another Cadillac, and the young man who stepped out of it caused the same buzz of reaction from the crowd on the sidewalk. Tito. He ran nimbly up the front steps and rang the bell. Denny answered the door. He had to make sure that there were no gatecrashers, even though a local policeman was trying to keep the crowd on the sidewalk, rather than on the front steps.

'Tito!' he said.

'I've called for Maria,' the young man said crisply. 'She has an airship to catch.'

'An airship? On Christmas Eve?'

'It's Christmas Day, and she has to be in Rome on Thursday.'

'I see. Come in.' Tito slipped in and Denny closed the door again. He had always wanted to go on an airship, he remembered.

When Tito entered the front room and stood at the door, Nellie saw him and rose slowly. She knew without being told that this was Tito. It wasn't that she could see Noreen in him. She could see Liam. She turned away. She was the only one in the family not introduced to Tito before he left with Maria. Nellie had not wanted to meet him. She had no desire to open an old wound. The family and the street gave Maria a royal farewell. Paddy took the chance in a quiet moment to thank her for what she had done.

'Don't mention it, Uncle Paddy,' she said. 'I would hate anybody to know I had done something decent for anybody. It would spoil my image!'

She gave him a hug.

'You'll get your reward in Heaven,' he jibed.

'But I'm in Heaven already. I'm a star, ain't I?' And with a laugh, she was gone. Tito looked back in his usual grave way and for a moment caught Nellie's eye.

'Merry Christmas,' he said quietly, 'everybody.' Then he too was gone. And the party resumed till dawn.

The party at East Gore was in full swing. They were not only celebrating Christmas in the sun, but the fact of Chris's scholarship win and the promise of direct entry to the Royal Academy in London as soon as she elected to go. The letter had come on the day after she had arrived from Edendale, and the celebrations had started almost at once, so Christmas was good for the New Zealand Keiths and Mackenzies. Even Sandy had cheered up sufficiently with the promise of a bigger place in the New Year. He and Bruce had had a good year, so they told Chris, and she was relieved to see her Dad something like his old self. She had wanted to talk to him about Denny, but there wasn't a chance, and anyway, he wasn't the kind of Dad for that sort of thing. She would talk to Berta when she got the chance. But up till now, there was hardly a chance to get a word in about anything, because the house was packed with relatives. In addition to the whole team of native Keiths and the five Mackenzies, Abel and Becky had arrived and even old Hilda, now very frail indeed, had travelled up with the Mackenzies and was sitting with Gran Keith on the couch. The twins were acting as waiters and making a happy mess of it.

Only Berta seemed out of the party mood and Chris got her aside at one point to ask what was the matter.

'Nothing,' replied her cousin. 'I just don't feel well.'

'What's upsetting you?'

'Nothing.'

'Come on, Berta. I know you better than that. You're hiding something.' Berta wheeled round on her.

'No, I'm not.'

'Yes you are. Now, what is it?'

'It's nothing, I'm telling you.'

'Come on, Berta.' Chris took her by the arm and led her to the bedroom. She sat her on the bed, and said quietly, 'Now you just tell me. This is Chris remember.'

Whether it was Chris's tone and manner or that fact of sitting in exactly the position she had been all those weeks before with the letters, or just that she was tired of feeling guilty, but Berta suddenly blurted out her whole secret. Chris listened quietly, and then at the end put her arm round her cousin again.

'Alright, Berta. Do you feel better now?'

'Oh, Chris,' said Berta looking at her soulfully. 'Will you ever forgive me? I mean, you've lost him now, haven't you, and it's all my fault.'

'Who knows, Berta?' said Chris, more calmly than she felt. 'As old Gran Keith says, "What's for you will no' go by you". If it has to be, it will be. So let's just leave it at that.'

'Are you sure, Chris?' Berta suddenly seemed much the younger of the two.

'No, I'm not, Berta, but what else can I say?' She rose.

'Where are you going?'

'I'm going to have a bloody good Christmas.' She went to the door, then turned and held out her hand to her cousin. 'And so are you, Berta. Come on!'

THIRTY-EIGHT

All through 1937, volunteers from the International Brigade were returning from the Spanish Civil War. They had marched off throughout the previous year from all over the world buoyed up by high ideals and comradeship to join in arms against a rebellious dictatorship and now the survivors returned, haggard, soured and bedraggled, victims of their own zeal and the military innocence of their Republican leaders. Some had fought for fun, like the aristocratic members of the English battalion, and lost an arm or a leg. Others, from the working classes, had gone merely to escape the boredom of pernicious unemployment, and came back with shattered minds, having seen places like Jarama and the Ebro. Americans, faced with the alternative of road-building with the WPA in their own country, enlisted in the Abraham Lincoln battalion of the International Brigade and died in the sun in defence of Madrid. There was the French Andre battalion and the Russian Dimitrov battalion, and nameless battalions from Romania, Czechoslovakia and Scandinavia – around 60,000 men in all, from every walk of life and of every known language. That was the problem. An order can't be obeyed if the soldiers can't understand what the orders are! So the great peoples' army gradually disintegrated, painfully dispersed and finally disappeared. The luckier ones came home again. Such a one was Major Kevin O'Neil of the Irish Republican Army. He had served in the Irish section so that he, as his own orders had put it – 'Might gain useful and important combat experience in modern war.' It made him laugh now. How useful and important were a couple of bullets in his knee? He was wounded in the left leg at Brunete. Fortunately, it was his bad leg anyway. Kevin was convinced that the wound had improved his limp!

As he carried his battered suitcase through the familiar Dublin streets again it gradually dawned on him that he'd been away for some time. The streets seemed dirtier than he remembered. There were more motor cars, more people in the streets, more advertising hoardings. Especially for the cinemas – Paul Muni in *The Life of*

647

Emile Zola for instance. He didn't know either of them! He found
it hard to stop from flinching as he turned every corner. It was a
habit he'd got into in Spain. Turning a corner could mean getting
a bullet. That's how he was wounded – the day one of the O'Leary
brothers was killed in that stupid attack. Eddie, the older one.
Kevin had saved Peter only the day before when they had been
ambushed coming out of that little café. Peter had run straight
out into the road, the fool. If he hadn't owed him fifty pesetas
for the drinks, Kevin told everyone afterwards, he would have left
him lying there! Afterwards, Peter never left Kevin's side.

'You never know,' he said, 'you might have to save my life again.'
They parted after a long night of drinking in London. The last
Kevin saw of Peter was seeing him stagger up Edgware Road in the
general direction of Kensal Green, determined to go home drunk.
It was the only way he could tell his mother about Eddie. Now it
was Kevin's turn to come home. Passing the Post Office again, he
remembered that November day when he had taken a man's life
for a cause. That mortal debt had been balanced by the life he'd
saved in that Spanish street. Another war and another cause, yet
what did it really amount to? Lives changed or lost. That's what
it all comes down to in the end. Nothing is ever gained by any
war – whether in Spain or China or Ethiopia or Palestine – except,
of course, a profit for the gun-makers. Everybody realises this, but
nothing is ever changed. Wars still happen. Probably always will
until the final apocalypse. But what will that change? Even as he
ruminated, Kevin knew that he had changed. He had seen Guernica
and knew that there was worse to come. Till then he would live at
peace, if not with himself, then with Teresa, Siobhan and Roisin.

At the very thought of the women in his life, his halting step
quickened and he found himself at the doors of Cassidy's Hotel.
My, he thought, as he looked at the old place, this had come up
in the world. The whole street façade had been changed and the
frontage looked as if it had been extended to the houses at either
side. Nellie must have done well since Sam passed away. He was
looking forward to seeing his sister again. He would also be glad
of a meal, a bath, a change of clothes and a decent shave before
going home to the girls. He would also need some money. He
had precisely eighteen shillings and eleven pence in his pocket.
That cheap London hotel the night before hadn't been as cheap
as he'd hoped. Thousands of visitors had flocked to London for
the summer coronation of the new King and Queen, and London
prices rose to greet them. They had remained high ever since and he
had to pay through the nose for a pretty mean room. To add insult
to injury, the red, white and blue bunting which had been put up

months before round the dull window had not been removed and it hung wetly and dismally on to the outside woodwork, a tatty remnant of monarchic rejoicing. No wonder he hadn't slept well! He hadn't enough cash left to buy himself a drink on the boat over. Which reminded him – he hadn't a present for anybody. Never mind, he had brought himself back in one piece and a whole head of new white hair to show them. That'll make them sit up, he thought as he mounted the three new marble steps and went in.

'DADDY! DADDY!' Two little flying female figures nearly knocked him over. Two little girls, Siobhan and Roisin, his own daughters, all frilly knickers, freckles and pigtails clambering all over him much to the amusement of some of the patrons in the vestibule – and there, in front of the new reception desk was Teresa, his lovely young wife, standing open-mouthed, staring at his hair.

It was a long time before he disentangled himself, and it took even longer to convince Teresa that he was indeed fit and well despite his white hair and was back with them for good. When little Roisin asked him if he'd brought her back a present, he looked helplessly at Teresa, who retrieved the situation by saying, 'Daddy got them, pet, but they'll be coming tomorrow.'

'Tomorrow's Sunday,' said Siobhan.

'Well?' said her mother.

'There's no postman on a Sunday,' said the seven-year-old. Her little sister began to cry and Kevin picked her up.

'Listen, darling,' he said, 'I've arranged a special messenger to bring them in the morning. Honestly.'

'Just like Santa Claus,' lisped Roisin.

'Just like Santa Claus,' and he gave her a big kiss.

It was only when the children were in bed that Teresa said they could have the new red dresses she was just finishing off. She was meaning them for little Roisin's birthday party, but they could have them now as presents from Spain. And Kevin gave his wife a big kiss. It took time that first day for both of them to get used to the sight and touch and feel of each other again, especially after the shock he had of seeing them there in the first place.

'Where's Nellie, then?' he asked. 'I haven't seen her about.'

'New York,' Teresa replied, as she unpacked his old case straight into the laundry sink.

'New York?'

'On holiday.'

'Since when?'

'Christmas.'

'Christmas?' He made a rapid calculation. 'That's some holiday!'

'She's enjoying herself.'

'And what about you here?'

'I'm enjoying myself as well. I told her she could stay as long as she liked. It seems she likes and she's stayed.'

'Eight months?'

'Is it that long already?' She looked disdainfully at a pair of old trousers. 'I think we'd be better to burn these rather than wash them.' Kevin took them from her fingers and let them drop into the sink. He then took his wife in his arms.

'I think we've better things to do than think about trousers,' he said. And he kissed her again. And again . . .

Nellie licked the envelope and pressed it down firmly with the heel of her hand on the kitchen table.

'That's it,' she said to Joey, who was making bread. It was something she had taught him to do and he loved it. He was kneading the dough at the other end of the table and he just smiled to her as he did no matter what she said. Unlike most people, Joey only responded to the tone in the voice, not the words it might utter. He was like a puppy in that respect. If he had had a tail, he would have wagged it! Nellie looked at the envelope in her hands. It hadn't taken her long to write the letter, but it had taken her a long time to make up her mind. Now it was made up and that was that. It was time now for a cup of tea. She rose to put the kettle on the stove, just as she heard the front door.

'That you, Denny?' she called out.

'Sure is,' came the answer. The door opened and a very tousled Denny looked in, red-eyed, unshaven, his tie undone, grinning from ear to ear. 'Morning all.' Joey waved a floury hand, but Nellie continued to watch the kettle.

'I don't recall you saying Goodnight.'

'It would have been hard for you to hear from Manhattan, Aunt Nellie.' His aunt turned round from the stove, trying to look angry.

'You were out all night, young man.'

'How time flies.'

'Who was it this time? The redhead or the blonde?'

Denny came in and moved straight to his aunt and started to waltz with her, as he sang, 'Casey would dance with the strawberry blonde and the band played on, He'd waltz 'cross the floor with the girl he adored, and the band . . .' He stumbled against a chair, and fell into it, pulling Nellie down with him. She shook herself clear, flustered, but as always won over by him.

'Agh, it's no use talking to you at all, at all.' Denny saw the letter.

'What's this?' he said. 'A letter to Ireland, I see.' He looked up at her, serious for once. 'You haven't –'

'I have. I made up my mind last night.'

'You said you would tell me before you –'

'Sure and where were you? Pickin' strawberries wi' some blonde?'

He laughed. 'Not quite, Auntie.' He looked at the letter in his hand again. 'So you gave her it, lock, stock and barrel?' he said. 'She might not want it.'

'That's up to her.'

'She's a lucky girl.'

'She will be if she gets her man back, and what's a hotel anyway, but a heap o' bricks and mortar and a whole lot o' worries? I'm better off here.'

'What have you got here?' Nellie looked around her.

'Another heap o' mortar, I suppose.' Then she looked pointedly at him. 'And one big worry.'

'Oh, come on, Auntie. You're not worried about me.'

'Am I not?' she said.

'Nellie.' It was Joey. He was standing beside her with the bread tin in his hand, motioning her to step aside so he could put the bread in the oven.

'Sorry, Joey,' she said and moved to the table. Denny rose up and opened the oven door, looking into Joey's face as he did so.

'You needing the dough again, Joey?'

'Yes, Denny,' replied Joey stoney-faced. Ever since Joey had started baking, Denny had been trying to get him to see that joke and failing every time.

'Never mind, Joey,' he said, and turning to his aunt asked, 'Is there a cup of tea for a thirsty man?'

'Help yourself,' she said. She looked at her nephew as he poured himself a cup. He had learned to enjoy her British tea. 'The sugar's by your hand.'

'Thanks.'

'What are you going to do today?' asked Nellie. 'Are you alright, Joey?' she went on.

'Sure am,' replied Joey, wiping his end of the table with a wet cloth.

'Sleep it off, to answer your question,' said Denny.

'How did you get on about the newspaper job?'

'No chance. "No experience," they said. How can I get experience if I can't get started?'

'How can you get started if you don't look?'

'But I do look, Aunt Nellie. The trouble is I can't see.'

'Oh, I don't understand you, Denny O'Neil.'

'That's something else we have in common, Auntie. But you do make a lovely cup of tea.' And he drank the last of it down, stood up, gave her a pat on the cheek and walked out saying, 'If Mr Rockerfeller rings, I'm in my room.'

She shook her head. He could be really annoying at times, but she knew she really loved him. It was common knowledge in the family that she spoiled him completely. And why not? He had been devastated by his mother's death. He was a changed boy when he came back from Europe. Something had happened. Anna had told her on one of her visits that Denny had met someone. He was always writing letters. Australia, she thought. Somewhere far away anyway. But then he stopped suddenly, just before Christmas, and he'd been running wild ever since. That was partly why Nellie stayed on. It had always been her intention to return to Dublin after the holidays, but somehow she got 'caught up' as she said. The truth was she got caught up in her nephew and, to the same extent, in her cousin, Joey.

It had appalled Nellie that such a friendly, easy-going, lovable man had to spend the rest of his days in a nursing home, when all he really needed was a home. She had decided to give him that and at the same time keep an eye on the wayward Denny. She was secretly delighted when Denny asked her to stay on for a couple of weeks longer to help him clear up after the marathon Christmas and New Year festivities. And then he asked her to stay on until he got a job. And then until he found a housekeeper. But what would happen to Joey? The nursing home kept ringing to see when they could have him back. Nellie told them bluntly that they were less interested in having Joey back than in resuming the fees. They weren't very pleased.

So, one way and another, Nellie had been constrained to remain and the months had flown past. Now she had made the big decision. She was giving Cassidy's Hotel to Teresa. She knew that Teresa, young as she was, was more than capable of managing it, especially with the good staff she had and the name the business had in Dublin. Besides, if anything happened to Kevin, it would be security for her and the girls. For herself, she would be sixty-five next birthday. Time enough to let someone else worry about bacon-and-egg breakfasts for thirty, or temperamental chefs walking out on her before dinner. Or any of the thousand and one little annoyances that attend to running a public hotel. It used to make her chuckle that Cassidy's was listed as a private hotel. Well, it would be Teresa's now and good luck to her.

Teresa's large eyes widened even wider in her elfin face. She put down the letter for a moment, shut her eyes, then opened them again and had another look at the page in front of her. Yes, that was Nellie's writing alright, and yes – she, Teresa O'Neil, twenty-seven, mother of two and spouse of Kevin O'Neil, retired – was now a hotel-owner! She looked across the kitchen table of the private flat at Cassidy's and found herself staring at a row of pots and pans. I own you, she thought, every single one of you, and you, and you, and you, she went on as her eyes made a giddy inventory of the room. She got up, put the letter in the pocket of her house-coat, and promised herself another read of it in the bath. She glanced at the clock. She'd better hurry – Kevin would be back any minute. He enjoyed taking the children to school, but he wasted no time coming back for a late breakfast with the papers while she started things off in the office. She turned the wireless on as loud as it could go and a man's voice was singing. She sang along with him while she splashed happily.

> 'The mere idea of you, the longing here for you,
> You'll never know how slow the moments go till I'm near
>   to you,
> I see your face in every flower, your eyes in stars above,
> It's just the thought of you, the very thought of you
>   I love.'

The water got cold as she thought of her handsome husband.
'I don't believe it!'
'I'm telling you, it's true.'
'Let me see the letter again.' She watched his face as he read it again, his breakfast forgotten as he digested its contents. His reaction had not been at all as she expected. In fact, she got the feeling he wasn't pleased at all. He put down the letter and looked at her.
'Of course you won't take it.'
'What?'
'The hotel. You don't mean to go ahead with it?'
'Why not? I thought –'
'Ach, that's it pet. You haven't.' She sat down at the table opposite him. She had a feeling she wasn't going to like this.
'Haven't what?' she said faintly. Kevin put his paper aside and leaned over to her.

'Thought about it. You see Teresa, I've had little else to do recently. Especially when they were picking bullets out of my knee.' Teresa didn't say anything, but just stared at him. He looked so solemn. 'Yes, my darlin',' he went on, 'I did a lot of thinkin', mostly about you and the wee ones. Sometimes about me and Ireland and the big, bad world, and I came to one simple conclusion. I want nothing more to do with it and I want everything there is to do with you and the girls. And why have I come to this conclusion? Because, you see, there are some people who think me a patriot, a hero for Ireland. But there are other people who think I'm nothing more than a common criminal, a murderer in fact.'

'And who's right?' she whispered.

'Ah, that's a difficult one. I suppose the only answer is that they both are. But for me now, having seen more than they maybe wanted me to see in Spain, I want to see no more.'

'What did you see?'

'I'll never tell you that, girl. I'll only ask you to respect my white hairs. They were won dearly, I can tell you that. So I tell you what I thought. I thought that we –' he pointed to her, '– you and I and the children of course, would go back home.'

'Home? I don't understand. We are home.'

'This is your home, Teresa. Not mine. It's a place I worked, once. Worked for Ireland, if you like. And what good has that done Ireland? And wasn't it an Irishman by the way, Oscar Wilde, I think, didn't he say, "Patriotism is the last refuge of the scoundrel"? He was a mad article, of course, but he might have been right there. I dreamed once of a United Ireland, and it'll happen. It might take a hundred years, but it'll happen. Not only a United Ireland, but even one day a United States of Europe, who knows? And who cares? Because I have other dreams now. I dream of home. Of going back to my roots. Back to the family. There's nothing left of it there now. Maybe I'm meant to put the last tendril back into the ground again and make another tree grow, where once there was a whole forest of O'Neils. That's my dream, Teresa, my darlin' wife, and I would love it dearly if I could share it with you.' She had never heard him talk like this, talk so much, or as softly and tenderly. Was his castle in Spain a little cot in Rosstrevor? 'Well,' he said huskily, 'what d'ye say girl?' There was only one thing she could say.

'She's not going to take it. Turned me down, she has.' Nellie was incredulous. 'She's saying here – do you hear what I'm sayin', Joey?'

'I hear you, Nellie.'

'– that her and Kevin are goin' back to Rosstrevor. And would you believe, they're goin' to buy Ingham's Bar, and call it Den's Bar after our old father! Would you credit it? What'll I do now?' As always, with any problem in the O'Neil family, Paddy was consulted. She phoned him up that night. He was very surprised to hear from his sister in New York, when she should have returned by now to Dublin. When she explained her dilemma to him, he didn't seem to be unduly perturbed.

'Of course,' he said, 'were I speaking to anyone else, Nellie, I would say we'll have to pray about it.'

'I haven't time for that, Paddy, you know that. Teresa wants to go north as soon as possible so the children won't miss too much of school and she can't leave Dublin with Cassidy's unsold.'

'What does Denny think?' came her brother's distant voice.

'I wouldn't know,' Nellie shouted back down the line. 'I haven't seen him for three days. I think he's on one of his binges.'

Paddy sounded immediately interested and concerned, but Nellie wasn't keen to talk about young Denny. She didn't want to be a tell-tale. But the wise Archbishop persisted, and soon the whole story of Denny's recent amorous activities came out. He still hadn't a job and Nellie was convinced now he wasn't even trying.

'He'll die of the drink or something worse if he goes on like this,' she told her brother, the whole hotel question being now forgotten. There was a pause at the other end. 'Paddy? Paddy, are you there?' called Nellie wildly.

'I'm here. I'm here,' responded Paddy. 'I was just thinking.'

'Well, don't do it so quietly. It gives me a start, that's all.'

She heard him laugh and then he said, 'Now this is what you must do, Nellie . . . .'

The operator's voice sounded very Scottish and very faraway.

'I'm sorry. The number's not answering. Are you there, caller?'

'Yes, thank you operator. I'll try again later.' Chris Mackenzie put the phone down. She couldn't understand that. Uncle Jim had said his brother rarely left the house these days. She looked at her watch. It was only five past seven. He surely couldn't be in bed already. She turned away and crossed the hallway to the landlady's room and knocked on the door.

'Come in,' came the voice. Chris opened the door and looked in at the landlady, who was sitting in her big armchair, surrounded by cats.

'There was no reply, Mrs Digby.'

'Was there not dear? Perhaps you can try again another time.' The landlady's voice was slow and a little slurred as if she were slightly drunk. Chris was to learn that she was most of the time!

'Thank you, Mrs Digby,' said Chris and closed the door quickly. She hated that cat smell.

She was sorry she hadn't got through to Forres. She wanted her Uncle John to know that she was in Britain again and a student for a year at the Royal Academy of Music in London. He would be as surprised as she was to hear that she was back so soon. She thought she would have taken up the scholarship next year, but she found she was very unsettled when she got back to Dunedin. Too much had happened to her – in Berlin and London – for her to settle back to provincial, student life in New Zealand. She had tried, goodness, she had tried. Professor Neinmann had seen how unsettled she was and was aware of the effect it had on her playing. She had been inspired on the day of the scholarship test, but since then she had hardly applied herself, so one day he called her in to his room to talk about it. In no time she had blurted out the whole story of London and Denny and the opera and Denny and Uncle John and Denny . . . Professor Neinmann understood. He came from Vienna after all.

'I think Miss Mackenzie,' he had said, 'you should take up the scholarship at once.'

'Why?' she remembered asking the old continental.

'Because it will take you back to England.' She could have kissed him.

Now here she was back in London and in the room the Academy had found for her. The landlady had given her permission to use the phone as long as she got the operator to tell her the cost. But Uncle John wasn't at home. She would try again tomorrow. Meantime, she put on her coat and hurried out. Catching a bus almost at once, she found herself in the West End in no time. She got off at Trafalgar Square, and since it was raining, she turned up her collar and hurried along the gleaming, lamp-lit Strand. Turning up Southampton Street she was soon standing in front of the Royal Opera House, Covent Garden. She wasn't sure why she had suddenly done this. All she knew was she had to see it again as soon as possible, and now here she was. She didn't know what she expected to see, but the bills were up for an English Opera production of *The Fair Maid of Perth*. She looked at the photographs and didn't know any of the singers, who were all British as far as she could see. Feeling very nostalgic, and a little bit silly, she went round the corner to the stage door. Unable to resist it, she opened the door and looked in. There was no one there. A Cockney voice called out, 'Can I help you, Miss?'

'That's alright,' she said hurriedly and closed the door again. What had she expected to see? Surely not – him? She almost ran back along the street. If she were really honest with herself, she thought, as the rain spattered on her face, had she come back to London to find him? No, she insisted to herself, she came back for the scholarship, for her music, her career. But a small voice wondered if a certain young New Zealand lady did protest too much? Turning the corner to return to the Strand, she glanced back to the magnificent porticos of the Opera House and she could have sworn she saw Maria d'Agostino's smiling face in the huge photo frame! She blinked, and it was gone again. Taking a deep breath, she hurried towards her bus stop and Mrs Digby's home for stray cats and music students.

Maria d'Agostino's face was still smiling from the immense photo frame as the front-of-house staff removed it from the front of the Sydney theatre. Even as the frame sagged lopsidedly as it was lowered to the ground, the gigantic and beautiful mouth still smiled and was still smiling as it was laid face-down on the pavement. She had caused a sensation on her first visit to Australia as part of her world tour in *Tosca*. Not so much for her looks or her singing or that of the excellent cast or the splendour of the production, but for the fact that she was murdered! Maria d'Agostino died in a Sydney hotel room from knife wounds. She had been viciously slashed across the throat and lay in a pool of her own blood beside her bed in her hotel suite. In the sitting room of the same suite, the body of a young man named as Guiglielmo Murphy was also found. He was referred to as Miss d'Agostino's secretary and had been stabbed several times in the chest. The police were now interviewing Miss d'Agostino's manager, Vernon Drake, in connection with the incident. It was he who had telephoned the police in the early hours of the previous morning.

'I think you'd better come round,' he had told them. 'Something's happened here.'

Something certainly had. As far as the police had been able to ascertain, Vernon Drake had simply had a brainstorm. He was sitting calmly in an armchair when the police and ambulance men and a doctor arrived with the hotel manager and the night porter. Drake still had the blood-covered knife in his red hands – an ordinary hotel knife, part of the supper-trolley which was still standing in the centre of the room, its plate of cold meats and bottle of white wine untouched and unopened. The waiter, a Portuguese, remembered bringing it into the suite late on the evening before. His English was not good, and he refused to go near the room again, but he told detectives that when he took it in, the lady and the boy were laughing at the old man he thought. The waiter asked

Mr Drake if he wanted the meat cut before he left but the American said he would do it himself. The frightened waiter remembered telling the old gentleman, 'Take care – knife very sharp – but good for carving!'

'Too bloody true, mate,' muttered the Sydney detective.

When he had tried to take the knife from Drake, the manager would not let it go. He pointed with it to the trolley, 'No, no! You see, I've got to carve the meat yet!' The detective exchanged a meaningful look with a colleague. It took the doctor and an ambulance man nearly an hour to get it from him and four policemen to drag him forcibly from the room.

'She needs me, she needs me,' he kept yelling, 'I mustn't leave her! I won't leave her!'

'Bloody little poof and he goes all Tarzan on us!' said one of the policeman, ruefully holding a bleeding nose. The press of course were there in force before daylight and they made their own story out of the tragedy – 'OPERA DIVA'S LOVE TRIANGLE'. 'SEX SADIST SLASHES SINGER', and headlines like, '"I KILLED FOR LOVE," SAYS SINGER'S MANAGER'. 'SOPRANO DIES IN SYDNEY HOTEL HORROR'.

'What a shame,' said Rachel Keith as the news came over the air next morning while they were having Sunday breakfast.

'Something funny there if you ask me,' said Bobby, who was only half listening in any case. Rachel took off her glasses.

'No, I mean I'd booked for us to go and see her next Wednesday. I was hoping Becky and Abel would join us.'

'Good,' said Bobby, immersed in the political pages of the *Morning Herald*. 'That'll be a few quid saved.' Rachel said nothing, but mused on the fact that the famous singer was just about Becky's age. Putting on her glasses again, she returned to her own reading – another student thesis to be assessed.

The tabloids had a field day. The murder had all the ingredients: a beautiful woman, a handsome secretary, a devoted manager, a star cut off in her prime – and they made the most of it. Yet the simple truth was that the delicate thread had snapped. What was extraordinary was that within twenty-four hours he professed not to remember a thing about it. At his trial he was pronounced insane.

In London, Chris Mackenzie was astonished to hear of Maria's death. She remembered the night she had gone to see Covent Garden and thought she had seen the singer's face in the frame. Was it a premonition, she wondered? Then she put it from her mind. She had work to do.

Of the O'Neil family, the tragic news hit Paddy in Seattle most of all. He had been nearest to Maria for most of her young life at least. To him she was still Noreen's girl, still an O'Neil. When he heard of her death on the radio, he immediately fell to his knees on the study carpet, 'Father, forgive them for they know not what they do . . .' And clenching his hands together on the desk top, he pondered on the fate of his young sister's children. Not one newspaper or radio report commented on the fact that Maria and Tito were brother and sister. And the good Archbishop wept for that fact.

Tears were also shed in Ruffiano's restaurant in New York. When she saw the headlines in the paper, Frankie Murphy, née Francesca Capaldi, hugged her two grown children to her as they cried for their 'brother', Tito.

Kevin O'Neil, still at Cassidy's Hotel, awaiting Nellie's return, showed no reaction at all when the news of Maria's violent end reached Dublin, but inside his heart was badly bruised for her. Teresa, on the other hand, only shrugged.

When Nellie O'Neil came back to Ireland she brought Denny with her. Part of Paddy's plan was that she should return to supervise the sale of Cassidy's and take their nephew with her. It would take him out of New York and break the reckless spiral of wine and women he had got into since his mother's death. Another inducement too, was that he should write a series of articles on 'The Irish At Home' for a newspaper group. If they liked the pieces they would be put out on a syndicated release across the United States. Archbishop Paddy had unashamedly used his Irish contacts in the US Press to secure Denny this commission in an attempt to get him started on a writing career.

Clara had agreed to move into the Brooklyn house for six months at least, so that Joey could continue to live there. Her former rivalry with her sister, Anna, about their mother's old house was neatly solved when Scott, Anna's husband, was offered a good job in Cleveland and he and Anna and their daughter, Kim, had already moved there. So the Kominskys moved into the old house. Clara was pregnant again, and Joey would be handy to have around the house for any heavy lifting.

Denny, for his part, wasn't so sure about the whole idea. As a bait, Nellie promised him a trip on the *Normandie*, which was the very latest Atlantic liner, and it featured, so she told him, French jazz. Denny was intrigued and let himself be carried along. So he had come to Ireland for the first time and was now resident in his aunt's Cassidy's Hotel. He had even made a start on the Irish articles. He let Nellie read the first two. She thought they were very good,

'Although I'm no judge,' she was quick to add.

'That's why I let you read it,' grinned Denny.

Denny was thrilled to meet Kevin again, but try as he might he couldn't get the older man to speak of his Spanish exploits. Significantly, the next article Denny wrote was entitled, 'The White-Headed Man'. The uncle and nephew talked several bottles of Jamieson's away in the O'Neil's private apartment. The former adventurer had much to say to one who was still desperately trying to make his own adventures. Kevin's new serenity intrigued the younger man and this was the basis of the essay he was to write on his favourite uncle. He was saddened by the thought that they would be going off to the north now that the sale had gone through.

'Why don't you come with us?' said Kevin.

'Great,' said Denny. However, Teresa was not so pleased.

'We won't be ready for visitors till Easter at least.'

'Denny's not a visitor,' protested her husband. 'He's family.'

'Well then, he'll not take offence if I tell him he can't come till Easter. Anyway, Nellie needs the time to get things sorted out here with the lawyers and everything. And haven't you got writing to do or something?'

'Alright, alright,' laughed Denny. 'We'll come at Easter.'

'And bring your own egg,' said Kevin.

Chris Mackenzie spent Christmas alone in London. She had never been so miserable. Her New Zealand Christmas was always a summer occasion. It was a time to go to the beach, down to the river, enjoy a swim and plum pudding in the sun. Her London Christmas of 1937, however, was a cold affair. Sleet, rain and snow and the smell of cats. She wanted to ring home, but Mrs Digby had been aghast.

'New Zealand, my dear! Goodness gracious,' she said, 'you can't do that. They haven't a wire would stretch all that way!' Chris couldn't persuade her that there was indeed a telephone connection to the other side of the world and had to be content with ringing Uncle John again.

He had been the first person she had rung when she arrived. She hadn't got through on that occasion because he wasn't at home that night. He was at Alec Friar's house. His old friend had been buried that day. After that occasion, however, she had got through to her uncle a few times. He was her one contact with family and whenever she got really depressed, she would go without her lunch one day and use the money to ring Forres. She had never told him she made this little sacrifice so that she could talk to him, but as always he guessed in his own way and to her delight and consternation, a money order for £5 arrived from him with a note on it – 'Buy yourself something for Christmas.' So she used some of it to buy another twelve minutes with him on the telephone. She spent at least half that time crying and both of them knew she was really crying for New Zealand. He invited her to come up to Scotland. He had asked her many times, but she could neither afford the fare nor the time. She promised she would try to make it before she returned home to New Zealand. Then the pips sounded. She had to finish.

'Merry Christmas, Uncle John!' she called into the receiver.

'And a Happy New Year to you, Christina.'

The first months of 1938 were busy for the Kevin O'Neils. Ingham's Bar was not what it once was and needed a lot of work. Tim, the barman, was now a very old man indeed and was desperate to retire to his sister's and spend the rest of his days on his allotment. He was intrigued by Kevin's return and embraced the younger man as if he were a hero returned triumphantly from the wars. Which in a way he was. Teresa, a city girl, was appalled at the primitive backwardness of Rosstrevor. She hadn't realised that a place only hundreds of miles from Dublin could be so far removed from it in time.

'It's not a new hotel they want here,' she told her husband. 'It's the missionaries!' Secretly though, she relished the challenge. She had her whole life before her, so there was plenty of time and she loved the new man her husband had become. It would be good here, she knew it. There was nothing that severe hard work and all their savings couldn't fix. Luckily money wasn't the problem. Rosstrevor itself was. Like most small villages, it resented any intrusion and closed its ranks against incomers. It wasn't, however, until Kevin sought out old Sergeant Davidson, now returned, and solemnly shook him by the hand that a sign was given to the village and Kevin O'Neil was welcomed home again.

By the time Nellie and Denny arrived, spring was in the air and things were beginning to look good at Den's Bar, which was now part of new premises called The Rosstrevor Arms Hotel. The Arms was a jocular intrusion by Kevin.

'What does it mean?' asked Siobhan.

'Whatever you like,' said her father.

'Well, it doesn't mean legs,' said Roisin.

Nellie took Denny to see Ballytreabhair Farm. He was astonished at how small the place was.

'You mean nine of you stayed in that little hut?'

'We did,' answered Nellie.

'Did you sleep standin' up?'

'We did not. We just took turns!'

'And where was the farm?'

'This was it. Just what you see before you.'

'No, I mean the land,' he said as he gazed around at the four little fields surrounding the house. 'Where's your land?' Nellie didn't answer at once. She just pointed to the trees at the back and the hedges at the side and the common ground beyond.

'That was our land,' she said softly.

For the first time, Denny saw a quieter Aunt Nellie and he had the tact not to say anything as she walked from the yard and looked up to the backfield. He knew she was seeing things he couldn't see. Handsome young brothers and a pretty young sister, a hard-pressed mother and an old devil of a father. All the ghosts huddled round her as she stood again looking at the old place. The house itself was totally derelict. No one had lived in it for years. She suddenly thought of the John McCormack song:

'Lonely I wander through scenes of my childhood,
They call back to memory the happy days of yore.
Gone are the old folks, the house stands deserted,
No light at the windows, no welcome at the door . . .
Lone is the house now and lonely the moorland,
The children are scattered, the old folks are gone,
Why stand I here like a ghost and a shadow,
'Tis time I were leaving, 'tis time I passed on.'

But family ghosts are hard to exorcise and they walked back to The Rosstrevor Arms in the shadows of their family silence.

Next morning Denny had a letter at the hotel forwarded from Cassidy's. It was from the newspaper chain. They liked his Irish articles and wanted more. In fact, they offered him a specific commission. They asked if he would cover the opening of the Empire Exhibition in Glasgow in May. It featured an Irish pavilion as one of its exhibits and they wanted 3,000 words on it. Denny was more than happy to oblige, especially when they promised a fee plus expenses. The money didn't mean a thing, but the professional confirmation was encouraging. There may be something in this writing business after all, he thought. Anyway he'd never seen Scotland. He had to ask Kevin for a map to see where Glasgow was.

Chris's scholarship year was coming to an end, and she had mixed feelings about it. The experience and the tuition now equipped her to consider a concert career as a pianist, but the fire seemed to have gone out of her somehow. She didn't get the same thing out of playing that she used to. These days she was tired, lonely, cold, hungry most of the time. Many great pianists had been all of these all of the time and won through to fame and fortune. She wasn't even all that worried about either of these.

'You need iron, my dear,' her landlady assured her. 'It's the blood you see. It's always the blood.' Yes, thought Chris, it's in the blood alright. The blood that was in her and calling her back to New Zealand. Something she forgot, however, was that it was Scots blood that was in her and this may have prompted her to look twice at the notice that appeared on the board at the Academy. Apparently there was to be a new Exhibition due to be held that summer in Glasgow. It was to be called the Empire Exhibition and would feature pavilions dedicated to each of the countries of the Commonwealth. The organisers now required artists and musicians for each of these colonial representations, and if any Commonwealth students were willing to be in Glasgow between May and October they should contact the Academy office. Applicants would require to audition and produce proof of residence.

Chris discovered that she was the only New Zealander to apply, so that she got the job without having to compete for it. She hadn't expected this and it meant delaying her return home. She hadn't time to write to New Zealand and get their reaction before giving her decision to the Exhibition people, so she rang Uncle John.

'Are you getting paid for it?' he said.

'Yes.'

'Well, take it,' he said.

THIRTY-NINE

The Empire Exhibition was the last of the great Durbars. It was a cheeky Glasgow gesture of defiance against the long grey years of the Depression, and it was a conception as brilliant as the sun which greeted its opening on Tuesday, 3rd May. It's not certain who got the bigger reception – the King and Queen as they drove through the festive streets in a landau, or Harry Lauder as he sang a welcome to the crowd at Ibrox Stadium. Bellahouston Park was a blaze of colour and light and an extraordinary winter of effort came to its happy and crowd-pleasing conclusion. Visitors flocked to the second city in the Empire in their thousands and even the locals paid it some attention, although they concentrated rather more on the amusement park and the open-air dance hall than on the pavilions devoted to industry, art and produce. It was on Dominion Avenue that the countries of the Empire had their sites. The Canadian pavilion had a tower a hundred feet high, but what interested the visitors more were the Canadian Mounties in their red coats and scout hats who paraded on their horses before it.

'Are they Mounties?' asked a wee Glasgow boy.

'Aye,' said his pal.

'Where are the Indians?'

'There's nae Indians.'

'Well, they canna be Mounties,' said the first, continuing to be unimpressed.

At Site Number 53 was the New Zealand pavilion. It was fronted by two Maori pillars and its most notable exhibit was a model of the longest railway tunnel within the Empire. Many Glaswegians could not be persuaded to go through it. They had a natural horror of dark, secluded places, but they loved the Maori singing, and the Polynesian harmonies. So did Chris Mackenzie. Coming from the South Island of New Zealand, she had a very limited Maori experience. She had only vague memories of Maori shearers singing on her father's farm when she was very young, and now here were the very best of them from her own country, singing every day in regular sessions. What the Glaswegians didn't know

664

was that they were even greater fun in the small hotel where they all stayed on the south side of the city. Some of the song sessions went on all night there, much to the delight of their Queen's Park neighbours and Chris's Berlin sing-song experience was put to good use. These happy leisure occasions did much to revivify her jaded feeling about music in general. Between the friendly Maoris on one hand and genial Glaswegians on the other, she was having the time of her life.

In her own field, performances were given in the vast concert hall. It was not an ideal venue for solo artists, and she was one of the few hundred who turned out one chilly evening to hear Frederic Lamond, a famous Scottish concert pianist, give his recital of Chopin and Liszt. There were less than fifty to hear the BBC Scottish Symphony Orchestra, and even the Glasgow Orpheus Choir could not draw a crowd, so Chris was not at all surprised when the authorities cancelled her recital. She did not feel at all humiliated. She was having too good a time. Her days and nights were full of every kind of music and she couldn't have been happier. In order to earn her wages, though, she was required to play in the New Zealand pavilion before and after the Maori song sessions. In this way, she was able to indulge her own musical tastes and happily draw a nice little crowd around her when she was on form. But most of all, she enjoyed hearing the great artists who attended. Names like Sir Thomas Beecham, Fritz Kreisler, Gracie Fields, but best of all, Paul Robeson. She saw all these great artists free because she was able to use her Exhibition Pass. However, perhaps her greatest enjoyment was at the Dance Hall. It was the most popular venue at the whole Exhibition, mainly because it was free! With orchestral concert seats as high as 10/6– and nothing less than 2/6–, crowds were easily attracted to something for nothing. Besides, all the big bands of the day were there – Ambrose, Giraldo, Henry Hall, Harry Roy and Roy Fox. The name didn't matter. It was the sound they made, the rhythm they engendered and the crowds they drew to the very modern open-air bandstand. At every opportunity she would be there – 'One-two-quick-quick- slow' to the strains of 'In the Mood' or 'Slow-slow-one-two-slow' to 'Begin the Beguine'. It was 'Music Maestro Please' and the musical Miss Mackenzie responded, with both feet, and thousands of Glaswegians, 'In the Still of the Night'.

With a typical lack of logic, the Irish Free State had a large pavilion at the Exhibition although, strictly speaking, Ireland was no longer a member of the British Empire. It was now very much a country of its own and this was a fact that Denny was to make much of in his article. There was no King's head on the stamps you could buy from the stall or on the Irish coins they gave as change, but Ireland was there for all that, and enjoying itself as much as the rest. Denny was also interested to see that just as typically, there was a Northern Ireland pavilion, sited miles away from the 'Free States'. In fact, had the Northern Ireland pavilion been any further away it would have been in Mosspark Boulevard! But on the day Denny arrived and showed his press card, both the Lord Mayors of Dublin and Belfast paid a visit to the Exhibition, and he joined both of them as they toured each pavilion amicably and agreeably.

Denny had come on his own. After much discussion at Rosstrevor, Nellie had decided to go back to New York rather than accompany him to Glasgow.

'It's not a good thing for a woman to go to a man's work with him,' she pointed out. She was constantly at pains to point out that Denny was a professional now with a job to do. 'Besides,' she added, 'they're not paying me to wander round a silly exhibition. With the feet I've got that would be no pleasure.'

'But, Auntie,' Denny had protested, 'it was your idea I should come to Europe.'

'And it was a good idea, wasn't it? And isn't Scotland in Europe?' No amount of argument could persuade her to accompany him. Her six months would be up at the end of May and she wanted to be back by then. Joey would expect her. Clara was expecting any week, and Nellie thought she should be there.

'It's great to be needed at sixty-five,' she had said.

It didn't take Denny long to tour the Irish pavilion and for Paddy's sake, he also took in the Roman Catholic pavilion. He enjoyed the Empire Tea pavilion, because you got free tea. He thought it wasn't nearly as good as Nellie's. He returned again to the South African pavilion for a second look, because it boasted the most attractive exposed female breasts in the whole exhibition. But what took his attention almost at once was the New Zealand pavilion. There it was at Site 53, just two doors away from the Ireland pavilion, and only the red-coated Mounties between them. As soon as he saw the Maori columns he was intrigued, and as soon as he entered, memories of Chris Mackenzie came flooding back. Only he knew that most of his excesses had been to forget her, rather than drown his grief for his mother, but the two occasions were inextricably bound, which was why he had found the whole emotional maelstrom almost too much to bear. And now, as he entered the New Zealand pavilion early on that June morning he looked around the interior with interest. So this is New Zealand, he thought.

A strange calm came down on him which he couldn't explain. There was no one in the place. There was a lovely peace somehow. Outside there were milling thousands, but for some reason in this green and brown place, there was hardly a sound. He wandered among the various exhibits, looked at the pictures of smiling faces, snow-capped peaks, dense forests, white sands. He could get to like New Zealand he thought, but most of all, he thought of Chris Mackenzie. She seemed to be in every frame he looked at as he slowly moved around. He heard footsteps as someone else came in, and he moved away to the far end.

It was the music that attracted his attention. He hadn't noticed a piano, but there was no way he could fail to notice the playing. It was Chopin. He knew that much. He felt himself irresistibly drawn to the sound. As he moved from behind one of the trees, he saw that it was a girl playing on an upright piano beside a small stage. The morning sun caught her fair hair delightfully. Even at the sight of her back, there was something that caught at his throat, as he gradually moved forward. It couldn't be! Could it? He came closer. The girl was completely engrossed, her hair bobbed on the shapely nape of her neck as her hands flicked at the notes of the Rainbow Prelude.

'Chris!' he whispered. She was totally absorbed, and paid no attention even as he came to her elbow. Yes, it was. It was Chris. He could hardly believe it, and very slowly, almost as if he were in the spell of the beautiful chords, he gradually edged to the side of the piano so that he was looking down on her. It was a moment before she was aware of him, and another before she looked up. When she did, her hands continued to play almost automatically, and when they did stop, they did so on a discord, which rather than detract from the moment, seemed to add to it.

'Denny!'
'Yes.'
'It's you?'
'Yes.'
'I don't believe it!'
'I don't believe it either.' They stared at each other in silence.
'I didn't realise you played so well,' he mumbled.
'Thank you.' Her heart was racing. So was his.
'What are you doing here?'
'I work here.'
'You mean – in New Zealand?' he said, looking around him. The silly remark was enough to break the tension. She laughed.
'Yes, in a way. In New Zealand.' He came round to stand over her.

'I knew I would like New Zealand.' She looked up at him, her eyes alight.

'It's the country that's always off the map, remember?'

'Not from where I'm looking.' She was suddenly aware of how American he sounded, just as he realised how un-English she was.

'Chris,' he said.

'Yes?' she answered, still looking up.

'Nothing,' he said and taking her hands gently, he lifted her up. Without a word, he put his hands on her shoulders and drew her to him. And at precisely half past ten in the morning, he kissed her fondly, tenderly, meaningfully and most of all, with relief. He had found her again. And she responded because she had found him.

'Oh, Denny!' she said as she came away from his lips and put her arms round his neck.

'Yes, Chris?' he said as he hugged her closely.

'Nothing,' she said, smiling.

It was Saturday 29th October 1938. Neither of them would forget that day. The Empire Exhibition was to close at 3.15p.m. At least the official closing ceremony was to take place then, but things would go on in the park till midnight – and still it rained. Not that Chris and Denny minded. All that day they had wandered among the crowds, wet and dazed and so very happy. Arms round each other's waist, they were only two among nearly 300,000 people in Bellahouston that afternoon, but as far as they were concerned they were the only two. Even when they joined the mêlée of the open-air dancing for the Lambeth Walk:

> 'Any evening, any day,
> Take a walk down Lambeth way,
> You'll find them all
> Doing the Lambeth Walk – OI!'

Joyously, they 'walked' over the pathways and avenues with all the others, mostly young people like themselves – but not all. One of the most energetic couples was a ferrety Glaswegian with his ample wife. He had his cloth cap down almost over his eyes and her wet headscarf framed a face almost as happy as Chris's. Glaswegians knew how to enjoy themselves even if it was raining, and Chris and Denny gladly joined in. The crowds thickened all around them as the dark-clouded dusk gradually gave way to the neon-lit darkness and the pipe bands began to assemble by the South Bandstand. This was better than the dreary old Empire Ball in the St Andrew's Hall, Chris thought. She should have gone there with the rest of the New Zealanders but instead here she was with her American. She looked up at him. He was watching the Hawker Hinds circling the Tower in a mock attack while the searchlights busied around them in the relentless drizzle and soldiers from the Territorial Army pretended to fire anti-aircraft guns. A raindrop sat on the edge of Denny's nose but to Chris he was still the handsomest man in the world. Why was he looking so serious? She gave his arm a squeeze.

'Wakey-wakey!' she shouted above the din.

He immediately glanced down and put his arm around her again, shouting into her ear, 'Sorry honey, it just seems a screwy idea to celebrate by showing us an air raid. Think they're trying to tell us something?'

'Who cares? Come on!'

The tramcars stood in a brightly-lit line forming a backdrop to the massed crowds, impervious to wet, who all joined hands and voices as a very limp Union Jack was struck on the Tower and a piper led them all into the whole world's anthem – Auld Lang Syne:

> 'Should auld acquaintance be forgot
> And never brought to mind
> Should auld acquaintance be forgot
> And auld lang syne –'

Neither Chris nor Denny knew a word of it but that didn't stop them joining in as best they could, especially when they had to cross hands with everyone and all these Glaswegians were roaring out in the rain:

> 'So here's a hand, my trusty freen
> And gie's a hand o' thine –'

They gladly joined because they both knew it was a special time for them as much as for Glasgow. This was not only the end of an Exhibition. It was the end of an era. The end of an old kind of world. Things would never be the same again somehow. Everyone seemed to sense this as the familiar strains rose up in the rain:

> 'For auld lang syne, my dear,
> For auld lang syne,
> We'll take a cup of kindness yet
> For auld lang syne.'

The bells rang out for midnight. It was all over. It was time to go home. Soaked to the skin, hair sticking to her cheeks, nose dripping just like Denny's, Chris knew that this wasn't the end for her. It was a beginning for both of them. Almost as if he had read her thoughts, Denny pulled her tightly to him and kissed her hard. And all round them the Glasgow crowd stood in the pouring rain and cheered.